Praise for

JOY FIELDING

"Joy Fielding has made the woman-in-jeopardy genre her own."
—*People*

"If you're in the mood to bury yourself in a good book . . . pick up Joy Fielding's latest novel . . . It's guaranteed to reduce you to tears, and once they've dried, will leave you feeling a little readier to tackle life's challenges."
—*The Gazette* (Montreal)

"Fielding masterfully manipulates our expectations."
—*The Washington Post*

"Fielding's specialty is stripping away the contemporary and trendy feminine masks to reveal the outrageous face of female rage. . . . But like any good mystery writer, she creates sympathy for the character."
—*The Globe and Mail*

"Joy Fielding handles her material with finesse; suspense is maintained at a high level, and the narrative is enriched by . . . sharply drawn, articulate characters."
—*Publishers Weekly*

"Fielding's writing is always strong and provocative."
—*Winnipeg Free Press*

Also by Joy Fielding

Shadow Creek

Now You See Her

The Wild Zone

Still Life

Charley's Web

Heartstopper

Mad River Road

Puppet

Lost

Whispers and Lies

Grand Avenue

The First Time

Missing Pieces

Don't Cry Now

Tell Me No Secrets

See Jane Run

Good Intentions

The Deep End

Life Penalty

The Other Woman

Kiss Mommy Goodbye

Trance

The Transformation

The Best of Friends

JOY

FIELDING

LOST

AND

WHISPERS AND LIES

ANCHOR CANADA

Anchor Canada omnibus edition published 2014

This edition contains the complete texts of the original works.

Library and Archives of Canada Cataloguing in Publication data is available upon request.

ISBN: 978-0-385-68322-7

Lost and *Whispers and Lies* are both works of fiction. Names, characters, places and incidents are products of the author's imagination or are used fictitiously. Any resemblance to actual events or locales or persons, living or dead, is entirely coincidental.

Cover images: (woman left) ajari/Getty Images; (woman right) Pixattitude/ Dreamstime.com
Printed and bound in the USA

Published in Canada by Anchor Canada,
a division of Random House of Canada Limited

www.penguinrandomhouse.ca

10 9 8 7 6 5 4 3 2 1

CONTENTS

Lost 1

Whispers and Lies 435

JOY

FIELDING

LOST

ANCHOR CANADA

To Annie, my sweet potato

ACKNOWLEDGMENTS

Once again, my thanks and gratitude to Owen Laster, Larry Mirkin, and Beverley Slopen for their continuing friendship, insight, advice, and unfailing generosity of spirit. Please know that your support means the world to me.

To my gorgeous editor, Emily Bestler, and her assistant Sarah Branham, for their smarts, hard work, and dedication. And to Owen's assistant, Jonathan Pecarsky, for always managing to sound pleased to hear from me.

To Judith Curr, Louise Burke, Laura Mullen, Estelle Laurence, and the wonderful people at Atria and Pocket, for their continuing efforts on my behalf—and for those wonderful chocolates at Christmas.

A special thank you to Michael Steeves from MacInfo, who responded to my frantic cries for help when my computer seemingly swallowed my disk. His efforts on my behalf were truly heroic.

To Maya Mavjee, John Neale, John Pearce, Stephanie Gowan, and the staff at Doubleday Canada, a division of Random House, who have never flagged in their support. Our association has spanned many years and several publishing upheavals, and I am both proud and happy we're still together.

Lost is the first of my novels to be set in my hometown of Toronto, and I realized as I was writing this book how much this beautiful city means to me. I am particularly indebted to Dr. Jim Cairns, the Deputy Chief Coroner for the province of Ontario, and to Gord Walker in the dispatch regional office for the time both so graciously took to answer my questions and share their expertise. My thanks also to the Toronto International Film Festival—the greatest film festival on earth—for providing both the backdrop for this book, and also some of my greatest film memories.

To my readers, again I thank you for your emails, your comments, and your enthusiasm. And a special thanks to those of you who show up at book signings. You make book tours worthwhile.

And lastly, to my family and friends, especially Warren, my amazing husband of almost thirty years, and our beautiful and talented daughters, Shannon and Annie. Without you, truly I would be lost.

LOST

ONE

The morning began, as did so many of their mornings, with an argument. Later, when it was important to recall the precise order of events, the way everything had spun so effortlessly out of control, Cindy would struggle to remember what exactly she and her older daughter had been fighting about. The dog, the shower, her niece's upcoming wedding—it would all seem so mundane, so trivial, so unworthy of raised voices and increased blood pressure. A blur of words that blew past their heads like a sudden storm, scattering debris but leaving the foundation intact. Nothing extraordinary to be sure. The start of an average day. Or so it had seemed at the time.

(Images: Cindy, in the ratty, green-and-navy terry-cloth bathrobe she'd bought just after Tom left, towel-drying her chin-length brown hair as she emerges from her bedroom; Julia at the opposite end of the wide upstairs hall, wrapped in a yellow-and-white-striped towel, pacing back and forth in front of the bathroom between her room and her sister's, impatience bubbling like lava from a volcano inside her reed-thin, six-foot frame; Elvis, the perpetually scruffy, apricot-colored Wheaten terrier Julia brought with her when she'd moved back home just under a year ago, barking and snapping at the air as he bounces along beside her.)

"Heather, what in God's name are you doing in there?" Julia banged on the bathroom door, then banged on it a second time when no answer was forthcoming.

"Sounds like she's taking a shower," Cindy offered, regretting her interference as soon as the words were out of her mouth.

Julia glared at her mother from underneath a mop of ash-blond hair, painstakingly straightened every morning to obliterate even a hint of its natural curl. "Obviously."

Cindy marveled that one word could contain so much venom, convey so much disdain. "I'm sure she'll be out in a minute."

"She's been in there for half an hour already. There'll be no hot water left for me."

"There'll be plenty of hot water."

Julia banged her fist a third time against the bathroom door.

"Stop that, Julia. You'll break it if you're not careful."

"Oh, yeah, right. Like I could break the door." As if to prove her point, she thumped it again.

"Julia. . . ."

"Mother. . . ."

Stalemate, Cindy thought. As usual. The way it had been between the two of them since Julia was two years old and had balked at wearing the frilly white dress Cindy had bought her for her birthday, the stubborn toddler refusing to attend her own party even after Cindy had conceded defeat, told her she could wear whatever she liked.

Nineteen years had passed. Julia was twenty-one. Nothing had changed.

"Did you walk the dog?" Cindy asked now.

"And just when would I have done that?"

Cindy pretended not to notice the sarcasm in her daughter's voice. "When you got up. Like you're supposed to."

Julia rolled large green eyes toward the ceiling.

"We had a deal," Cindy reminded her.

"I'll walk him later."

"He's been cooped up all night. He's probably desperate to go."

"He'll be fine."

"I don't want any more accidents."

"Then *you* take him out," Julia snapped. "I'm not exactly dressed for a walk."

"You're being obstinate."

"You're being anal."

"Julia. . . ."

"Mother. . . ."

Stalemate.

Julia slammed her open palm against the bathroom door. "Okay, time's up. Everybody out of the pool."

Cindy absorbed the reverberation from Julia's hand on the door like a slap on the face. She lifted her fingers to her cheek, felt the sting. "That's enough, Julia. She can't hear you."

"She's doing it on purpose. She knows I have a big audition today."

"You have an audition?"

"For Michael Kinsolving's new movie. He's in town for the film festival, and he's agreed to audition some local talent."

"That's great."

"Dad set it up."

Cindy forced a smile through tightly gritted teeth.

"You're doing it again." Julia mimicked her mother's strained expression. "If you're going to go catatonic every time I mention Dad. . . ."

"I'm not catatonic."

"The divorce was seven years ago, Mom. Get over it."

"I assure you, I'm well over your father."

Julia arched one thin eyebrow, plucked to within a hair of its life. "Anyway, they're looking for an unknown, which probably means every girl in North America will be up for the part. Heather, for God's sake," Julia shouted, as the shower shuddered to a halt. "You're not the only one who lives here, you know."

Cindy stared toward the thick cream-colored broadloom at her feet. It had been less than a year since Julia had decided to move back home with her mother and sister after seven years of living with her father, and only because her father's new wife had made it clear she considered their five-thousand-square-foot lakeside penthouse too cramped for the three of them. Julia had made it equally clear to her mother that her move home was temporary, one borne of financial necessity, and that she'd be moving into her own apartment as soon as her fledgling acting career took off. Cindy had been so eager to have her daughter back, to make up for the time missed, the years lost, that even the sight of Julia's unruly dog peeing on the living room carpet did little to dampen her initial enthusiasm. Cindy had welcomed Julia back with open arms and a grateful heart.

The door to Heather's bedroom opened, and a sleepy-eyed teenage girl in an oversized purple nightshirt spotted with tiny pink hearts squinted into the hall. Delicate long fingers pushed several tendrils of loose brown curls away from the slight oval of her Botticelli face, then rubbed at the freckles peppering the tip of her upturned nose. "What's all the racket?" she asked as Elvis jumped up to lick her chin.

"Oh, for God's sake," Julia muttered angrily when she saw her sister, then kicked at the bathroom door with her bare feet. "Duncan, get your bony ass out of there."

"Julia. . . ."

"Mother. . . ."

"Duncan's ass is not bony," Heather said.

"I can't believe I'm going to be late for my audition because my sister's moronic boyfriend is using my shower."

"It's not your shower; he's not a moron; and he's lived here longer than you have," Heather protested.

"A huge mistake," Julia said, looking accusingly at her mother.

"Says who?"

"Says Dad."

Cindy's lips formed the automatic smile that accompanied each mention of her ex-husband. "Let's not get into that right now."

"Fiona thinks so too," Julia persisted. "She says she can't understand whatever possessed you to let him move in here."

"Did you tell that pea-brained twit to mind her own goddamned business?" The angry words flew from Cindy's mouth. She couldn't have stopped them if she'd tried.

"Mom!" Heather's dark blue eyes widened in alarm.

"Mother, really," Julia said, green eyes rolling back toward the ceiling.

It was the "really" that did Cindy in. The word hit her like an arrow to the heart, and she had to lean against the nearest wall for support. As if eager to add his opinion, Elvis lifted his leg into the air and peed against the bathroom door.

"Oh no!" Cindy glared at her older daughter.

"Don't look at me. You're the one who swore and got him all upset."

"Just clean it up."

"I don't have time to clean it up. My audition's at eleven o'clock."

"It's eight-thirty!"

"You have an audition?" Heather asked her sister. "What for?"

"Michael Kinsolving's in town for the film festival, and he's decided to audition local talent for his new movie. Dad set it up."

"Cool," Heather said as Cindy's lips curled again into a frozen smile.

The bathroom door opened and a cloud of steam rushed into the hall, followed by tall, skinny Duncan Rossi, wet black hair falling across playful brown eyes, and wearing nothing but a small yellow-and-white bath towel and a large, lopsided grin. He quickly ducked into the bedroom he'd been sharing with Cindy's younger daughter for almost two years. Of course, the original deal had been that he occupy the spare room in the basement, an arrangement that lasted all of three months. Another three months were spent denying the obvious, that Duncan was creeping up to Heather's bedroom after Cindy was safely asleep, and then creeping back down before she got up, until everyone finally stopped pretending, although no one ever actually acknowledged the move out loud.

In truth Cindy had no problem with the fact Heather and Duncan were sleeping together. She genuinely liked Duncan, who was considerate and helpful around the house, and had somehow managed to maintain his equilibrium and good humor even after the maelstrom that was Julia moved in across the hall. Both Heather and Duncan were nice, responsible kids who'd started dating in their first year of high school, and had been talking about marriage ever since.

Which was the only thing that really worried Cindy.

Sometimes she'd look over at Duncan and her daughter as they were reading the morning paper at breakfast—Honey Nut Cheerios for him, Cinnamon Toast Crunch for her—and think they were almost too comfortable with each other, too settled. She marveled at Heather's eager embrace of such a safe, middle-aged lifestyle, and wondered if being the child of divorce had played any part in it. "Why is she in such a hurry to tie herself down? She's only nineteen. She's in college. She should be out sleeping around," Cindy had shocked her friends recently by confiding. "Well, when else is she going to do it?" she'd continued, painfully aware of her own reluctant celibacy.

Cindy could count on one hand the number of affairs she'd had since her divorce, two of those in the immediate aftermath of Tom's abrupt decision to leave her for another woman, a woman he'd left for yet another other woman as soon as his divorce from Cindy became final. Seven years of other women, Cindy thought now, each woman younger and tartier than the last. A dozen at least. A baker's dozen, she thought, feeling her jaw lock. And then along came little Fiona, the freshest tart of all. Hell, she was only eight years older than Julia. Not even a tart, for God's sake. A cookie!

"Mom?" Heather was asking.

"Hmm?"

"Is everything all right?"

"Mrs. Carver?" Duncan reappeared at Heather's side. The towel had been replaced by a pair of fashionably faded blue jeans. He slipped a navy T-shirt over his still-damp, utterly hairless chest. "Is something wrong? You have a very strange look on your face."

"She's thinking about my father," Julia announced wearily.

"What? I am not."

"Then why the rigor mortis smile?"

Cindy took a deep breath and tried to relax her mouth, feeling it wobble precariously from side to side. "I thought you were in such a hurry to get in the shower."

"It's only eight-thirty," Julia said as Elvis began barking.

"Would someone like to go for a walk?" Duncan asked the dog, whose response was to run around in increasingly frantic circles and bark even louder. "Let's go then, boy." Duncan bounded down the stairs, Elvis racing ahead of him, as the phone in Cindy's bedroom began to ring.

"If it's Sean, I'm not here," Julia told her mother.

"Why would Sean be calling on my line?"

"Because I won't speak to him on mine."

"Why won't you speak to him?"

"Because I broke up with him, and he won't take no for an answer. I'm not here," Julia insisted as the phone continued to ring.

"What about you?" Cindy asked her younger daughter playfully. "Are you here?"

"Why would I want to speak to Sean?"

"Be back in twenty minutes," Duncan called from the front door.

My best kid, Cindy thought, entering her room and reaching for the phone on the night table beside her bed.

"I'm not here," Julia repeated from the doorway.

"Hello."

"It's me," the voice announced as Cindy plopped down on the edge of her unmade bed, a headache slowly gnawing at the base of her neck.

"Is it Sean?" Julia whispered.

"It's Leigh," Cindy whispered back as Julia rolled disappointed eyes toward the window overlooking the backyard. Outside, the late-August sun created the illusion of peace and tranquility.

"Why are you whispering?" Cindy's sister asked. "You're not sick, are you?"

"I'm fine. How about you? You're calling awfully early."

"Early for you maybe. I've been up since six."

It was Cindy's turn to roll her eyes. Leigh had elevated sibling rivalry to a fine art. If Cindy had been up since seven o'clock, Leigh had been up since five; if Cindy had a sore throat, Leigh had a sore throat *and* a fever; if Cindy had a million things to do that day, Leigh had a million and *one*.

"This wedding is going to be the death of me," Leigh said. "You have no idea what planning a wedding this size is like. No idea."

"I thought everything was pretty much taken care of." Cindy knew that Leigh had been planning her daughter's wedding ever since Bianca was five years old. "Is there a problem?"

"Our mother is driving me absolutely nuts."

Cindy felt her headache spreading rapidly from the top of her spine to the bridge of her nose. She tried picturing her sister, who was three years younger, two inches shorter, and fifteen pounds heavier than she was, but she couldn't remember the color of her hair. Last week it had been a deep chestnut brown, the week before that an alarming carrot red.

"What's she done now?" Cindy asked reluctantly.

"She doesn't like her dress."

"So change it."

"It's too late to change it. The damn dress is already made. We have fittings this afternoon. I need you to be there."

"Me?"

"You have to convince her the dress looks fabulous. She'll believe *you*. Besides, don't you want to see Heather and Julia in their dresses?"

Cindy's head snapped toward Julia, still watching from the doorway. "Heather and Julia have fittings this afternoon?"

"No way!" Julia exclaimed. "I'm not going. I hate that stupid dress."

"Four o'clock. And they can't be late," Leigh continued, oblivious to Julia's rant.

"I'm not wearing that god-awful purple dress." Julia began pacing back and forth in the doorway. "I look like a giant grape."

"The girls will be there," Cindy said pointedly, watching her daughter throw her arms up into the air. "But I'm getting a really bad headache."

"A headache? Please, I've had a migraine for two days now. Look, I have a zillion things to do. I'll see you at four o'clock."

"I'm not going," Julia said as Cindy hung up the phone.

"You have to go. You're a bridesmaid."

"I'm busy."

"She's my sister."

"Then you wear the damn dress."

"Julia. . . ."

"Mother. . . ."

Julia spun around on her heels and disappeared into the bathroom at the end of the hall, slamming the door behind her.

(Flashback: Julia, a chubby toddler, her Shirley Temple curls framing dimpled, chipmunk cheeks, burrowing in against her mother's pregnant belly as Cindy reads her a bedtime story; Julia, age nine, proudly displaying the fiberglass casts she wore after breaking both arms in a fall off her bicycle; Julia at thirteen, already almost a head taller than her mother, defiantly refusing to apologize for swearing at her sister; Julia the following year, packing her clothes into the new Louis Vuitton suitcase her father had bought her, then carrying it outside to his waiting BMW, leaving her childhood—and her mother— behind.)

Later Cindy would wonder whether these images had been a premonition of disaster looming, of calamity about to strike, whether she'd somehow suspected that the glimpse she'd caught of Julia disappearing behind the slammed bathroom door was the last she would see of her difficult daughter.

Probably not. How could she, after all? *Why* would she? It was far too early in the day to be mindful of the fact that great calamity, like great evil, often springs from the womb of the hopelessly mundane, that defining moments rarely have meaning in the present and can be seen clearly only in retrospect. And so the morning of the day Julia went missing was rightly perceived by her mother as nothing more than one in a long string of such mornings, their argument only the latest installment of their ongoing debate. Cindy thought little of it beyond that which was obvious—her daughter was giving her a hard time, what else was new?

Julia. . . .

Mother. . . .

Checkmate.

TWO

I met this great guy."

Cindy stared across the picnic table at her friend. Trish Sinclair was all careless sophistication and ageless grace. She shouldn't have been beautiful, but she was, her face full of sharp, competing angles, her Modigliani-like features further exaggerated by the unnatural blackness of her hair, hair that hung in dramatic swirls past bony shoulders, toward the ample cleavage that peeked out over the top buttons of her bright yellow blouse. "You're married," Cindy reminded her.

"Not for me, silly. For you."

Cindy lowered the back of her head to the top of her spine, lifting her face to the sun and inhaling the faintest whiff of fall. A month from now it would probably be too cool to be sitting on a picnic bench in a friend's backyard in the middle of the day, choosing what movies to see at this year's festival, while eating open-faced tuna sandwiches and sipping glasses of chardonnay. "Not interested."

"Let me tell you about him before you make any hasty decisions."

"I thought we were here to discuss movies." Cindy looked to her friend, Meg, for help. Meg Taylor, looking closer to fifteen than forty, was as fair and flat-chested as Trish was dark and voluptuous. She sat on the other end of the long picnic bench, wearing cutoff jeans and a red-and-white-striped tank top, seemingly engrossed in the dauntingly thick catalog for this year's festival.

"The new Patricia Rozema film sounds good," she offered, her voice small and crinkly, like tin foil unraveling.

"What page?" Cindy asked gratefully, eager to move on. The last time Trish had fixed her up, just before Julia's move home, had been an unmitigated disaster. At the end of the relentlessly confrontational evening with the thrice-divorced divorce attorney, the man had leaned in for what Cindy assumed was a conciliatory peck on the cheek, then rammed his tongue so far down Cindy's throat, she'd had visions of having to call a plumber to get him out.

"*Special Presentation*," Meg told her. "Page 97."

Cindy quickly flipped through the pages of her festival catalog.

"'Elegantly shot and finely performed,'" Meg read from the notes, "'what is finally so impressive about Rozema's new work. . . .'"

"Isn't she the one who makes films about lesbians?" Trish interrupted.

"Is she?" Meg asked.

Cindy's eyes traveled back and forth between her two closest friends. Cindy and Meg had been inseparable since the eleventh grade; Cindy and Trish had bonded after

colliding at the Clinique counter at Holt's ten years ago.
"*Mansfield Park* wasn't about lesbians," Cindy said, thinking that neither woman had changed substantially over the years.

"It had lesbian overtones," Trish said.

"*Mansfield Park* is by Jane Austen," Meg reminded her.

"It had definite overtones."

"Your point being . . . ?"

"I don't want any lesbians this year."

"You don't want any lesbians?"

"I'm tired of lesbians. We saw enough films about lesbians last year."

Cindy laughed. "You have a quota on lesbians?"

"Does that include gays?" Meg grabbed a green apple from a nearby basket and took a loud bite.

"Yes." Trish pushed a thick layer of dark bangs away from her forehead, adjusted the heart-shaped diamond pendant at her throat. "I'm tired of them too."

"Well, there go half the movies." Cindy took a sip of wine, held it inside her mouth, feeling the late-August sun warm against her cheeks. Every year for the last six years, the three women had gathered in Meg's backyard to eat, drink, and select from the hundreds of movies being previewed at the annual Toronto International Film Festival. Another year had come and gone. Another festival was upon them. Not much had changed in the interim, except Julia had come home.

Which meant everything had changed.

"You'd really like him," Trish said, suddenly shifting gears, although it was obvious by the way she leaned into the table that she'd only been biding her time, waiting for her next opportunity to reintroduce the subject. "He's bright, funny, good-looking."

Cindy watched a parade of clouds float past her line of vision, several wisps breaking free to drape themselves across the sky, like cobwebs. "Not interested," she said again.

"His name is Neil Macfarlane, and he's Bill's new accountant. We had dinner with him last night, and he's to die for. I swear. You'll love him."

"What's he look like?" Meg asked.

"Tall, slim, really cute."

"How about *The Winds of Change*?" Cindy proposed, ignoring her two friends. "Page 257."

Trish groaned as the women flipped to the appropriate page.

"Yikes!" Meg said, almost choking on the apple she was chewing. "Are you kidding? An Iranian film? Have you forgotten *Caravan to Heaven*?"

"Was that the one where the camel got stuck in the sand and it took three hours to get him out?" Trish winced at the memory.

"That's the one."

"So much for Iran."

"What about France?" Cindy asked.

"All they do in French movies is talk and eat," Meg said.

"Sometimes they have sex," Trish told her.

"They talk during sex," Meg said.

"So France is out?" Cindy looked from Meg to Trish, then back again. "How about this one? *Night Crawlers*. Page 316. It's Swedish. Do we have a problem with Sweden?"

Meg lifted the thick, heavy catalog into her hands and read out loud, as if she'd been called on in class. "'The film has a gritty feel for the seedy side of suburban life. Uncompromising and . . .'"

"Hold it," Trish interrupted. "What did we decide 'uncompromising' means?"

"Well," Cindy said, "let's see if we can remember the code. Lyrical means . . ."

"Slow," Meg answered.

"Visually stunning means . . ."

"Boring as hell," Trish said.

"Uncompromising means . . ."

Trish and Meg exchanged knowing glances. "Handheld camera," they agreed.

"Good. Okay," Cindy said. "So, we don't want lyrical, visually stunning, or uncompromising."

"And we've eliminated gays, lesbians, and Iran."

"Don't forget France."

"Let's not be too hasty about France," Cindy pleaded.

"What about Germany?"

"No sense of humor."

"Hong Kong?"

"Too violent," Meg said.

"Canada?"

The women stared at each other blankly.

"How about the new movie by Michael Kinsolving?" Cindy asked. "Page 186."

"Isn't he a bit passé?"

"He could use a hit, that's for sure." Again Meg lifted the heavy tome into the air and read aloud. "'Fresh, stylish, contemporary, edgy.'" She lowered the catalog back to the picnic table, took another bite of her apple. "'Edgy' is a bit troublesome. It could be a code word for 'low-life.'"

"Julia had an audition with Michael Kinsolving this morning," Cindy said.

"Really? How'd it go?"

"I don't know." Cindy pulled her cell phone out of her leopard-print purse, pressed in Julia's home number, then listened as it rang once, twice, three times. She was about to hang up when she heard Julia's breathy whisper in her ear.

"This is Julia," the recorded message began with seductive grace. *"I'm so sorry I can't answer your call at the moment, but I wouldn't want to miss a thing you have to say, so please leave a message after the beep, and I'll get back to you as soon as I can. Or you can reach me on my cell at 416-555-4332. Thanks so much, and have a great day."*

Cindy hung up, quickly called Julia's cell phone. "It's your mother, sweetie," she said when confronted by the same message. "Just phoning to see how your audition went. Call me if you get the chance. Otherwise, I'll see you at four o'clock," she added, unable to stop herself.

"What's at four o'clock?" Meg asked as Cindy tucked her phone back inside her purse.

"Fittings for bridesmaids' dresses."

"Ugh," Trish said. "I remember being a bridesmaid at my sister's wedding. She had the ugliest dresses you've ever seen. Pink taffeta, of all things. Can you picture me in pink?"

"I love pink," Meg said.

"I was so embarrassed. I just wanted to crawl in a hole and die. And of course, the marriage didn't last, which, to this day, I blame on the dresses. Did you have bridesmaids when you married Gordon?" she asked Meg.

"Eight," Meg said flatly. "In pink taffeta."

Cindy laughed at both the memory and the look on Trish's face. "I was one of them."

"She looks fabulous in pink taffeta," Meg said, laughing now as well.

Strains of Beethoven's Ninth suddenly filled the air. "My phone," Cindy announced, reaching back into her purse. "Probably Julia." She lifted the phone to her ear.

"I gave him your number," Trish said quickly.

"What?"

"I gave Neil Macfarlane your number."

"Hello?" A large male voice pushed its way out of the small phone in Cindy's hand. "Hello? Is anybody there?"

"I can't believe you gave someone my number without asking me first," Cindy hissed, holding the phone tight against her chest.

"He's really cute," Trish said, by way of explanation.

"Hello?" the voice asked again.

"I'm sorry. Hello," Cindy said, fighting the urge to throw the phone at her friend's head.

"Cindy?"

"Neil?" Cindy asked in return.

He laughed. "Trish obviously told you I'd be calling."

Cindy glared at Trish, who was pouring herself another glass of wine. "What can I do for you, Neil? I'm afraid I already have an accountant."

"Be nice," Trish whispered.

"In that case," Neil said easily, "maybe you'd let me take you out to dinner one night."

"Dinner?"

"Just because you're mad at me, don't take it out on him," Trish said.

"When exactly did you have in mind?" Cindy heard herself ask.

"How about tonight?"

"Tonight?"

"He's really cute," Trish said, her voice a plea.

"Tonight is fine," Cindy said, giving in, as Trish squealed with delight and Meg jumped up and down with girlish excitement. "When and where?"

"The Pasta Bar? Seven o'clock?"

"I'll meet you there." Cindy flung the phone back into her purse, then confronted her friend, whose always broad smile now stretched from one side of her face to the other. "I can't believe you did that to me."

"Oh, relax. You'll have a wonderful time."

"I haven't had a date in over a year."

"Then it's about time, wouldn't you say?"

"I won't know what to talk about."

"Don't worry. You'll think of something."

"I haven't a clue what to wear."

"Something stylish," Trish said.

"Something sexy," Meg said.

"Oh sure, something stylish and sexy. I haven't had sex in, what . . . ?"

"Three years," Trish and Meg said in unison.

Cindy laughed. "You probably told him that, didn't you?"

"Are you kidding? I tell everyone." Trish poured Cindy a full glass of wine, raised her own glass in a toast. "To great movies, great wine, and great sex."

Meg took another bite of her apple. "This is so French, don't you think?"

"I can't believe she did that to me," Cindy muttered as she waited for the light at the corner of Balmoral and Avenue

Road to change. "I can't believe she gave him my number." She shook her head, growing impatient and running across the busy thoroughfare at the first break in the traffic. "I can't believe I said I'd go. What's the matter with me?"

She could hear Elvis barking as soon as her toe hit the sidewalk, even though her house was at the far end of the street. That meant no one was home, and the dog had probably peed on the hall rug, a favorite new protest spot for being left alone for more than thirty minutes. She'd tried locking him in the kitchen, but he always found a way out. He'd even figured out how to unlock the large wire crate Cindy had purchased, and that now sat empty in the garage. Cindy chuckled. He was Julia's dog all right.

A slight breeze whispered through the lush green leaves crowding the branches of the large maple trees lining the beautiful wide street in the heart of the city. Cindy and Tom had purchased the old, brown-brick home near the corner of Balmoral and Poplar Plains only months before Tom moved out, and she'd kept it as part of their divorce settlement. In return, Tom got to keep the oceanfront condo in Florida and the lakeside cottage in Muskoka, which was fine with Cindy, who'd always considered herself a city girl at heart.

It was one of the reasons she loved Toronto, and had loved it from the moment her father had relocated the family here from the suburbs of Detroit just after her thirteenth birthday. At first she'd been apprehensive about moving to a new city, a new country—*It's always snowing up there; the people only speak French; stand absolutely still if you see a bear!*—but within days all such fears had been dispelled by the pleasant reality that was Toronto. More than the interesting architecture, the diverse neighborhoods, the plethora of art galleries, trendy boutiques, and theaters, what Cindy loved most about the city was the fact that people actually lived there, that they didn't just work there during the day only to disappear into distant suburbs at night. The entire downtown core was residential. Stately old mansions with backyard swimming pools shared the same streets as towering new office buildings, and everything was only minutes away from a subway line—the subways clean, the streets safe, the people polite, if admittedly more reserved than their neighbors to the south. A city of over three million people—five million if you counted the surrounding areas—and there were rarely more than fifty murders a year. Amazing, Cindy thought now, stretching her arms into the air, hugging the city to her breast, forgiving even the summer humidity that sent spasms through her already curly hair.

After her father died, Cindy's mother had briefly considered moving back to Detroit, where her brother and sister still lived, but her daughters, by then both married and with families of their own, had talked her out of it. In truth, Norma Appleton hadn't needed much persuading. Within months, she'd sold the old family home on Wembley Avenue, and moved into a brand-new condominium on Prince Arthur, only a block north of the shopping mecca that was Bloor Street, and less than a five-minute drive from either of her children.

("We should have let her move back to Detroit," Leigh had lamented on more than one occasion. "She's driving me nuts."

"You take her too seriously. Don't let her get to you."

"Easy for you to say. You're the one who can do no wrong."

"I do plenty wrong."

"You don't have to tell me.")

A laugh escaped Cindy's mouth and skipped down the empty street. It always surprised Cindy that her mother and sister were so often at odds when, in fact, they were so much alike—a little of each went a long way.

Cindy checked her watch. It was almost three o'clock. She'd have just enough time to walk the dog and change out of her shorts before heading over to Marcel's for the fittings. Then she'd have to race back home and shower and change for her stupid date with Neil Macfarlane. And she still had no idea what she was going to wear. She didn't have any clothes that were both stylish and sexy. Whatever had possessed her to say yes? Did she need this kind of stress in her life? She crossed her fingers, said a silent prayer that Julia would be at the fitting promptly at four o'clock.

It was amazing, she thought, how much time and energy she expended fretting over her older daughter. When Julia was living with her father, Cindy had worried about her every minute of every day. Was she eating properly, getting to bed on time, doing her homework? Was she safe? Was she happy? Did the child cry herself to sleep every night, as Cindy often did, regretful of the choice she'd made? Did she wish she was home with her mother and sister where she knew in her heart she belonged? Was it misguided pride that kept her with her father year after stubborn year?

It seemed that even in her absence, Julia had taken up a disproportionate amount of space in the house on Balmoral Avenue. Missing Julia had become a steady part of Cindy's life, a persistent ache in the pit of her stomach, an ulcer that refused to heal even after Julia decided to move back home.

A slight movement caught Cindy's eye and she turned her head toward her next-door neighbor's house. Faith Sellick, a new mother at age thirty-one, was rocking back and forth on the top of her front steps, her long brown hair uncombed and all but covering her face.

"Faith?" Cindy cautiously approached her neighbor's front path, watched as the normally friendly and outgoing young woman slowly raised her head from her knees, tears streaking a face that was round and pretty and totally void of expression. "Faith, what's going on? Are you all right?"

Faith glanced over her shoulder toward the house, then back again at Cindy. Cindy saw that the front of the young woman's white blouse was stained with the milk leaking from her swollen breasts, creating quarter-sized circles in the thin fabric.

"What's the matter, Faith? Where's the baby?"

Faith stared at Cindy with sad, dull eyes.

Cindy looked past the young woman, straining to detect sounds of life from the interior of the house, but the only thing she heard was Elvis barking next door. A thousand thoughts rushed through Cindy's mind: that Faith and her husband had had a terrible fight; that he'd walked out on her and the baby; that something horrible had happened to Kyle, the couple's two-month-old son; that Faith had come outside to get a breath of fresh air and inadvertently locked herself out. Except none of that explained the blankness in Faith's eyes, and why she was staring at Cindy as if she'd never seen her before in her life. "Faith, what's the matter? Talk to me."

Faith said nothing.

"Faith, where's Kyle? Has something happened to Kyle?"

Faith stared at the house, fresh tears falling the length of her cheeks.

In the next instant, Cindy vaulted past the young woman and into her house. She took the stairs two at a time, racing toward the nursery and pushing open the door, her breath stabbing at her chest like a hunting knife. Tears stung her eyes as she threw herself toward the crib, terrified of what she might see.

The baby was lying on his back in the middle of crisp, blue-and-white gingham sheets. He was wearing a yellow sleeper and a matching yellow cap, his beautiful face as smooth and round as his mother's, his perfect lips settled into a perfect pout, red little fists curled into tight little balls, tiny knuckles white. Was he breathing?

Cindy edged closer to the crib, and leaned her body over the side bar, pressing her cheek to the baby's mouth and breathing in his wondrous infant scent. Gently she touched her cool lips to his warm chest, holding her breath until she felt his body shudder with the effort of a single deep breath. And then another. And another. "Thank God," Cindy whispered, feeling the infant's forehead with her lips to make sure he wasn't feverish, then straightening up and backing slowly out of the room, her legs wobbling as she closed the door behind her, having to remind herself to breathe. "Thank God, you're okay."

Faith was still sitting on the top of the outside landing, swaying rhythmically from side to side, as if mimicking the branches of the maple tree in the middle of her front lawn, when Cindy stepped back outside, sat down beside her. "Faith?"

Faith said nothing, continued rocking from side to side.

"Faith, what's wrong?"

"I'm sorry," Faith said, so quietly Cindy wasn't sure she'd heard her at all.

"Why are you sorry? Did something happen?"

Faith looked quizzical. "No."

"Then what's the matter? What are you doing out here?"

"Is the baby crying?"

"No. He's sound asleep."

Faith ran unsteady hands across her breasts. "He's probably hungry."

"He's asleep," Cindy repeated.

"I'm a terrible mother."

"No, you're not. You're a wonderful mother," Cindy assured her truthfully, recalling Faith's excitement when she'd knocked on Cindy's door to announce her pregnancy, how sweetly she'd asked for any advice Cindy could give her, how wonderfully gentle and patient she was with the baby. "I think we should go inside."

Faith offered no resistance as Cindy helped her to her feet, the top of her head in line with Cindy's chin. Cindy guided her through the large front foyer into the rectangular-shaped living room at the back of the house. A powder blue sweater lay on the hardwood floor next to the baby grand piano and Faith reached down to scoop it up, pushing her hands roughly through the sleeves, and quickly securing its three white buttons. Then she sank down into the green velvet sofa, and leaned her head against the pillows.

“What’s Ryan’s number at work?”

“Ryan’s at work,” Faith said.

“Yes, I know. I need his phone number.”

Faith stared blankly at the pale green wall ahead.

“It’s okay. I’ll find it. You stay here. Lie down.”

Faith smiled and obediently lifted her feet off the floor, bringing her knees to her chest.

Cindy quickly located Ryan’s work number from the bulletin board by the kitchen phone and punched in the correct numbers. It was answered on the first ring.

“Ryan Sellick,” the man said instead of hello.

“Ryan,” Cindy enunciated clearly, “this is Cindy Carver. I think you need to come home.”

THREE

You're late."

"I'm sorry. I got here as fast as I could."

"I said four o'clock," Leigh reminded her sister, square red nails tapping on the gold band of her watch for emphasis, then pushing newly streaked hair away from a face that was pinched with incipient hysteria. The impatience in her hazel eyes was underlined in heavy black pencil, and mascara sat like tiny lumps of coal on her lashes. Anxiety draped across her shoulders like a well-worn shawl. "It's almost four-thirty," she said. "Marcel has to leave at five."

"I'm really sorry." Cindy looked from her sister to the short, curly-haired man in tight brown leather pants who was conferring with his assistant in a far corner of the long, cluttered room. "There was a problem with my next-door neighbor. She's acting very strangely. I'm afraid things just kind of got away from me."

"They always do," Leigh said.

"What's that supposed to mean?"

"Look, you're here *now*. Let's not make a big deal out of it."

Cindy took a deep breath, silently counting to ten. If you hadn't picked a dressmaker whose shop is halfway out of the city, I might have been able to get here on time, she wanted to say. If you hadn't scheduled the damn fittings for the height of rush hour traffic, I might not have been so late. Besides, you're the one making the big deal out of it, not me. Instead she said, "So, how's it going so far?"

"As expected." Leigh lowered her voice to a whisper. "Mother is driving me nuts."

"What are you whispering about?" a woman's gravelly voice called from one of the dressing rooms at the back of the shop.

Cindy spun around, absorbing the details of the small dressmaking salon in a single glance: the wide front window, the bare white walls lined with racks of silk and satin gowns in varying stages of completion, bolts of bright fabric carpeting the floor and occupying the only two chairs in the room, a full-length mirror in one corner, three appropriately angled mirrors in another, another room at the back crowded with assorted tables, sewing machines, and ironing boards. Cindy sidled up to a rack of more casual suits and dresses that was pushed off to one side, wondering whether she might find something on it that was sufficiently stylish and sexy for her date with Neil Macfarlane.

"Cindy's here," Leigh called to her mother.

"Hi, dear," her mother's disembodied voice sang out.

"Hi, Mom. How's the dress?"

"You tell me." Cindy watched her normally vivacious, seventy-two-year-old mother push open the heavy white curtain that served as her dressing room door and frown uncertainly, her fingers pulling at the sides of the magenta satin gown.

"Tell her she looks beautiful," Leigh whispered behind cupped fingers, pretending to be scratching her nose.

"What did your sister say?"

"She said you look beautiful," Cindy told her.

"What do *you* think?"

"Naturally," Leigh said under her breath. "What *I* think doesn't count."

"What's your sister muttering about now?"

"I'm right here, Mother. You don't have to ask Cindy."

"I think you look beautiful," Cindy said, genuinely agreeing with her sister's assessment and reaching out to pat her mother's fashionable blond bob.

Norma Appleton made a dismissive gesture with her mouth. "Well, of course, you girls would stick together."

"What's the problem you're having with the dress, Mom?" Cindy asked, spotting a short red cocktail dress on the rack of more casual offerings, wondering if it was her size.

"I don't like the neckline." Her mother tugged at the offending area. "It's too plain."

The neckline might be too low-cut, Cindy thought, noting the daring bodice of the short red dress. She didn't want to give Neil Macfarlane the wrong idea. Did she?

He's really cute, Trish whispered in her ear.

"I've already explained to Mother a million times. . . ."

"I'm right here, you know," Norma Appleton said. "You can talk to *me*."

"I've already told *you* a zillion times that Marcel will be adding beading along the top."

Cindy mentally discarded the short red dress, her eyes moving down the rack to a long, shapeless, beige linen sack. Definitely not, she decided, picturing herself lost inside its voluminous folds. She didn't want Neil Macfarlane to think he was dating a nun. Did she?

You haven't had sex in three years.

"I hate beading," her mother was saying.

"Since when do you hate beading?"

"I've always hated beading."

"What about a jacket?" Cindy suggested, trying to still the voices in her head. "Maybe Marcel could make up something in lace. . . ." She glanced imploringly at Marcel, who promptly left his assistant's side to join them in the center of the room.

"A lace jacket is a lovely idea," her mother agreed.

"I thought you didn't like lace," Leigh said.

"I've always liked lace."

The last time she'd had sex, Cindy recalled, she'd been wearing a lace peignoir. The man's name was Alan and they'd met when he came into Meg's shop to buy a pair of crystal-and-turquoise earrings for his sister's birthday. Cindy found out that he didn't have a sister when his wife came by the following week to exchange the earrings for something subtler. By then, of course, it was too late. The peignoir had been purchased; the deed had been done.

"What do you think, Marcel?" Cindy asked now, her voice unnaturally loud. The poor man took a step back, glancing anxiously at Cindy's mother, trying not to fixate on the deep creases her fingers were inflicting on the delicate satin of his design.

Without hesitation, Marcel reached for the tape measure that circled his neck like a scarf. "Whatever you desire."

Whatever you desire, Cindy repeated silently, savoring the sound. How long had it been since anyone had offered her whatever she desired? Would Neil Macfarlane?

He's to die for. I swear. You'll love him.

"Did I hear you say something about problems with a neighbor?" her mother asked, lifting her arms to allow Marcel to measure their length.

"Yes," Cindy said, grateful for the chance to get her mind on something else. "You remember the Sellicks from next door? They had a baby a few months ago?" she asked, as if she weren't sure. "I think she might have postpartum depression."

"I had that," Leigh said.

"You had hemorrhoids," her mother said.

Marcel winced, wrapped the tape measure across Norma Appleton's expansive bosom.

"I had postpartum depression with both Jeffrey and Bianca."

"I don't remember that."

"Of course not. Now if I were Cindy. . . ."

"Cindy never had postpartum depression."

"And speaking of Bianca," Cindy interjected, "just where *is* the beautiful bride-to-be?" She looked around the salon, realizing for the first time that neither her niece nor her daughters were anywhere in sight.

"They got tired of waiting and went to Starbucks."

"Heather looks so beautiful in her dress," Norma Appleton said.

"And the bride, Mother?" Leigh asked pointedly. "How does Bianca look in her gown? Or doesn't she rate a mention?"

"What are you talking about? I said she looked beautiful."

"No, you didn't."

"I most certainly did."

"What about Julia?" Cindy interrupted.

"Julia?" Leigh scoffed. "Julia has yet to honor us with her presence."

"She isn't here yet?"

"I'm sure 'things just got away from her,'" Leigh said, forcing a smile.

"I said I was sorry." Cindy reached into her purse for her cell phone. "She had an audition. Maybe she had to wait. . . ."

"What kind of audition?" Her mother turned around so that Marcel could measure her back.

"For Michael Kinsolving, the director. He's in town for the film festival." Cindy pressed in her daughter's number, listened to the telephone ring.

"You and that stupid festival," Leigh said dismissively.

"Isn't Michael Kinsolving dating Cameron Diaz?" their mother asked. "Or maybe it's Drew Barrymore. Ever since *Charlie's Angels*, I can't keep the two of them straight. Anyway, I hear he has quite a reputation with the ladies."

"Oh, for heaven's sake, Mother," Leigh exclaimed impatiently. "How would you know anything about this Michael whoever-the hell-he-is?"

Her mother pulled her shoulders back with just enough righteous indignation to cause Marcel to lose his balance and drop his tape measure. "I read about him in *People* magazine."

"Michael Kinsolving is a very important director," Cindy said, as Julia's breathy voice caressed her ear.

"I'm so sorry I can't answer your call at the moment," the recording whispered seductively. Cindy immediately hung up, dialed Julia's cell phone, listened to the same breathy message.

"He hasn't had a hit in a long time," their mother said knowingly. "Apparently he's some sort of sex addict."

"I believe that's Michael Douglas," Marcel piped up enthusiastically, regaining his footing and retrieving the tape measure from the floor.

"Really?"

"Before he married Catherine Zeta-Jones."

"Are we actually having this conversation?" Leigh threw her hands into the air in frustration.

"What's your problem, dear?" her mother asked.

"My problem," Leigh began, as little beads of perspiration began breaking out across her forehead, causing her newly streaked bangs to curl in several awkward directions, "is that my daughter's wedding is less than two months away, and nobody seems to give a good goddamn that time is running out and there's still tons of stuff to do."

"It'll all work out, dear." Her mother tugged at the long taffeta skirt. "Doesn't there seem to be an awful lot of material here? It makes me look very hippy."

"She's not answering." Cindy returned the phone to her purse and stared at the front door, as if willing Julia to walk through.

"She's forty minutes late."

"Maybe she got lost."

"Lost?" Leigh asked incredulously. "She gets on the

subway at St. Clair; she gets off at Finch. How could she possibly get lost?"

"Maybe she missed her stop. You know Julia. Sometimes she gets distracted."

"Julia's never had a distracted moment in her life. She knows exactly what she's doing at all times."

"What's that supposed to mean?"

"Leigh, why don't you show us your dress?" their mother suggested.

"Yes," Cindy agreed wearily. "Mom says it's wonderful."

"Mom hasn't seen it."

"Good try," her mother whispered to Cindy as Leigh retreated to the dressing rooms at the back of the shop, shaking her head and muttering to herself. "You've got to say something to your sister, darling. She's driving me nuts."

Cindy caught her reflection in one panel of the three-sectioned full-length mirror, and advanced steadily toward it, horrified by what she saw but unable to turn away, as if she'd stumbled across the scene of an accident. When did I get so ugly? she wondered, hypnotized by the creases clustered around her large eyes and small mouth, staring at them until her still-delicate features blurred, then disappeared altogether, leaving only the telltale lines of middle age. She squinted, trying to find the young woman she'd once been, remembering that at one time, she'd been considered beautiful.

Like Julia.

When was the last time a man had told her she was beautiful? Cindy wondered now, backing away from the mirror, and pushing a bolt of fabric off one of the chairs. She sat down, her head heavy with conflicting emotions:

impatience with her sister, anger at her older daughter, curiosity about Neil Macfarlane. Was he really as smart, funny, and good-looking as Trish claimed? And if so, why would he be interested in a forty-two-year-old woman with less-than-perky breasts and a collapsing rear end? Undoubtedly such a prize catch could have his pick of any number of perfect young females eager to make his acquaintance. Certainly Tom had considered the choice a no-brainer.

Cindy checked her watch. Almost four forty-five already. By the time she finished up here and got home, assuming she wasn't a raving lunatic and was still capable of handling an automobile, she'd be lucky if there'd be enough time to shower and change, let alone make sure there was something in the house for the kids to eat. She sighed, thinking that Heather and Duncan could order in a pizza, and remembering that Julia had mentioned she might be having dinner with her father. Was that where she was?

"Ta dum!" Leigh announced, pulling back the dressing room curtain and appearing before her mother and startled sister in yards of pink taffeta.

This is not happening, Cindy thought. She opened her mouth to speak, but no words emerged.

"Of course, I'm planning to lose ten pounds before the wedding, so it'll be tighter here." Leigh pulled at the tucks at her waistline. "And here." She flattened the taffeta across her hips. It made a swishing sound. "So, what do you think?" She lifted her hands into the air above her head, did a slow turn around.

"I wouldn't do that, dear." Norma Appleton pointed to the underside of her daughter's arms.

"Do what?"

"Your 'Hi, Helens,'" her mother said, grimacing.

"My what?"

"Your 'Hi, Helens,'" her mother repeated with a point of her chin.

"What are you talking about? What is she talking about?" Leigh demanded of Cindy.

"Remember Auntie Molly?" Cindy asked reluctantly.

"Of course I remember Auntie Molly."

"Remember she had this friend Helen, who lived across the street?"

"I don't remember any Helen."

"Anyway," Cindy continued, bracing herself for the explosion she knew would follow, "whenever Auntie Molly saw Helen, she used to wave to her and say, 'Hi, Helen. Hi, Helen.' And the skin under her arms would jiggle, and so Mom started referring to that part of the arm as the 'Hi, Helens.'"

"What!"

"Hi, Helen," her mother said, waving to an invisible woman on the other side of the room. "Hi, Helen."

"You're saying my arms jiggle?!"

"Everybody's arms jiggle," Cindy offered.

"Yours don't," her mother said.

"No, Cindy's arms are perfect," Leigh agreed angrily, pacing back and forth in front of her mother and sister. "That's because Cindy has time to go to the gym five times a week."

"I don't go to the gym five times a week."

"Because Cindy only has to go to work when she feels like it . . ."

"That's not true. I work three afternoons a week."

". . . so she has lots of time to do things like go to the gym and the film festival and . . ."

"What's this problem you have with the film festival?"

"I don't have any problem with it. In fact, I'd dearly love to spend ten days doing nothing but running from one movie to the next. I love movies as much as you do, you know."

"Then why don't you go?"

"Because I have responsibilities. Because I have four kids and a husband to look after."

"Your daughter's getting married, your sons are in college, and your husband can take care of himself."

"As if you'd know anything about taking care of husbands," Leigh said, then blanched visibly. "I didn't mean that."

Cindy nodded, unable to find her voice.

"This is all your fault," Leigh accused her mother. "You and your damn 'Hi, Helens.'"

"You take things much too seriously," her mother said. "You always did. Besides, that's no excuse for being mean to your sister."

Leigh acknowledged her guilt with a bow of her head. "I'm really very sorry, Cindy. Please forgive me."

"You're under a lot of stress," Cindy acknowledged, trying to be generous.

"Trust me, you have no idea." Leigh hugged her arms to her sides, kept them absolutely still. "It's been one disaster after another. The hotel double-booked the ballroom, which took days to get straightened out; the florist says lilacs are out of the question for October. . . ."

"Who has lilacs in October?" their mother asked.

"My future in-laws haven't offered to pay for a thing, and now Jason has decided he wants a reggae band instead of the trio we hired."

"He's the groom," Cindy reminded her sister.

"He's an idiot," Leigh shot back as the front door opened.

"Who's an idiot?" Leigh's daughter, Bianca, marched into the store, followed by Cindy's daughter, Heather, two steps behind.

Cindy smiled at the two denim-clad young women standing before her. Like Leigh, twenty-two-year-old Bianca was slightly overweight, the extra weight concentrated mostly in her hips, which made her appear shorter than she actually was. Also like her mother, Bianca's eyes were hazel, her mouth full, her smile wide.

(Snapshots: Six-year-old Cindy, dressed in a Wonder Woman costume on Halloween, smiling shyly at the camera, while three-year-old Leigh, naked except for an awkward black mask, mugs outrageously in the background; thirteen-year-old Cindy and ten-year-old Leigh standing on either side of their mother in front of their new house on Wembley Avenue, Leigh's right hand stretched behind her mother, her fingers raised above Cindy's head like donkey ears; mother and teenage daughters sitting on a large rock at the edge of Lake Joseph, Cindy squinting into the sun, Leigh's face hidden in the shadows.)

"Hi, Aunt Cindy."

"Hi, sweetheart."

"Who's an idiot?" Bianca asked again.

Leigh shrugged off her daughter's question, pretended to be busy with the folds of her gown.

"Hi, Mom." Heather greeted Cindy with a kiss on the cheek.

"Hi, darling. I hear you're a knockout in your dress. Sorry I missed it."

"I'm sure there'll be other opportunities," Heather said with a wink. "Julia here yet?"

"Of course she isn't here," Leigh answered before Cindy had the chance.

"You look nice," Heather told her aunt.

Leigh raised one hand to her head, fiddled girlishly with her hair, before dropping her arm self-consciously back to her side, massaging the flesh above her elbow.

"Is your arm hurt?" Heather asked.

"Let me try Julia one more time." Again Cindy retrieved her phone from her purse, quickly punching in Julia's cell phone number. Again she heard the breathy voice, the fake regret. *I'm so sorry I can't answer your call at the moment.* Where are you, Julia? she wondered, feeling her sister's angry eyes burning holes in the back of her blue blouse. "Julia, it's almost five o'clock," Cindy said evenly. "Where the hell are you?"

FOUR

The first time Julia disappeared, she was four years old. Cindy had taken the girls to a nearby park and was busy pushing Heather on a swing when she realized that Julia was no longer among the children playing in the sandbox. She'd spent the next twenty minutes running around in increasingly frantic circles, accosting strangers, and shouting at hapless passersby: "I've lost my little girl. Please, has anyone seen my daughter?"

Cindy had run home to call the police, Heather slung across her shoulder like an old purse, only to find Julia sitting on the front steps. "What took you so long?" the child demanded. "I've been waiting for you."

Was Julia somewhere waiting for her now? Cindy wondered, entering her bedroom and walking past her younger daughter, who lay sprawled across Cindy's king-size bed, watching television, Elvis beside her. "What on earth are you watching?" Cindy asked, mesmerized by the sight of a staggeringly well-endowed young woman with big hair and a tiny white bikini rubbing great gobs of green fingerpaint over the expansive chest of a muscular young man. The young man was grinning so hard, his face looked as if it might explode. Cindy inched back, picturing white teeth spraying toward the pale blue walls of her bedroom, like confetti.

"It's called *Blind Date*."

How appropriate, Cindy thought, sitting down on the end of her bed, trying not to think of the night ahead. "What are they doing?"

"Getting to know each other," Heather deadpanned.

"I guess some people will do anything to get on TV." Cindy found herself thinking of Julia despite her best efforts not to. She was still angry that her older daughter hadn't shown up for her fitting, that she hadn't so much as called to offer an excuse. "Get down, Elvis," Cindy said sharply, transferring her anger at her daughter to her daughter's dog. Elvis looked at her with sleepy brown eyes, sighed deeply, and rolled over on his side.

The second time Julia had disappeared was less than a year after the first. This time Cindy had put Heather in bed for her afternoon nap and come downstairs to find the front door open and Julia gone. Cindy had torn the house apart looking for her, then raced up and down the block, screaming out her daughter's name. When she'd returned to the house, her phone was ringing. It was Tom. "Julia's here," he'd said simply, a smile lurking behind his words. Apparently, Julia had grown impatient with her mother, and walked the twelve blocks to her father's office. "You took too long with Heather," Julia scolded her mother when Tom brought her home.

Had Julia grown impatient with her mother yet again? Cindy wondered, pushing herself to her feet and walking toward her closet.

"You see, the premise of this show," Heather was explaining, "is that they fix two people up and then send them off to the beach, or rock climbing, or something like that, for the afternoon, and then later, they go out for an intimate dinner . . ."

Where *was* Julia? Why hadn't she phoned?

". . . and at the end of the date," Heather continued, "they each tell the camera whether or not they'd go out with that person a second time."

"Based on a deep spiritual connection, no doubt," Cindy said, snapping back into the present, her eyes scanning the line of wooden hangers in her closet for something that could conceivably pass for stylish and sexy. "There isn't a damn thing." Julia would be able to put together something, she thought.

"What?"

"I said I have nothing to wear."

"Me neither. Can we go shopping tomorrow?"

Cindy rifled through her pantsuits, dismissing one as too heavy, one as too lightweight, another as too formal for a first date, although it looked like something an accountant might like. She finally settled on a pair of gray linen slacks and a loose-fitting white blouse. At least they were clean.

"Oh, wow. You won't believe what they're doing now," Heather cried, her voice a mixture of shock and delight. "Mom, you've got to get out here and see this."

Cindy bolted from the closet in time to see the toothy muscleman aim a flowing waterhose down the bottom half of his companion's minuscule bikini, while the big-haired, big-breasted bimbo squealed with delight. "How can you watch this garbage?"

"Are you kidding? It's great." Then, noticing the clothes in her mother's hands, "What are you doing? Are you going out?" The latter question carried just a trace of indignation.

"I won't be late."

"Where are you going?"

"Just out for dinner. I won't be late."

"So you said. Who are you going to dinner with?"

"No one special."

"What does that mean?" Heather sat up on the bed, crossed her legs, balanced her chin in the palms of her hands, her radar on full alert.

"It doesn't mean anything."

"You're being very evasive."

"You're being very nosy."

You're being obstinate, she'd told Julia this morning.

You're being anal.

"I'm just curious," Heather was saying. "You always ask me where I'm going."

"That's because I'm your mother."

"Do you have a date?" Heather pressed. "You do, don't you? With who?"

"With *whom,*" Cindy corrected. "I thought you were majoring in English."

"With *whom* are you going out, Mother?" Heather asked in Julia's voice, the word "mother" snapping at Cindy like an elastic band.

Cindy shook her head in defeat. "His name is Neil Macfarlane. He's Trish's accountant."

"Is he cute?"

Cindy shrugged. "Trish says he is."

"You've never seen him?"

Cindy blushed.

"So this is like a . . . Blind Date?" Heather asked with exaggerated flourish, vocally capitalizing the last two words, and pointing toward the TV screen with both hands.

"You ever been part of a threesome?" the grinning Romeo was asking his giggling Juliet while hand-feeding her lobster, then licking at the butter that dripped from her chin.

"Oh my," Cindy said.

"Is that what you're going to wear?" Heather indicated the clothes in her mother's hands.

Cindy held the blouse up under her chin. "What do you think?"

"You might want to go with something a little more low-cut. You know, make more of an impression."

"I think this is exactly the impression I want to make. Where's Duncan?" Cindy asked, suddenly realizing she hadn't seen Duncan since they got home.

Heather feigned indifference, shrugged, leaned back on her elbows. "Don't know."

"You don't? That's unusual."

Heather shot her mother a look. "No, it's not. We're not joined at the hip, you know."

"You two have a fight?"

"It's no big deal."

Cindy could tell from her daughter's tone that it was a subject best not pursued. Besides, if Heather and Duncan were fighting, she really didn't want to know the details. In truth, she already knew way too much about their relationship. That was the problem with sleeping down the hall from your daughter and her live-in boyfriend. You heard every whisper, every playful sigh, every enthusiastic squeak of the bed. "Could you do me a favor?" Cindy said with a smile, waiting for her daughter to ask what, then continuing when she didn't. "Could you call your father for me?"

"Why?"

"Find out if Julia's having dinner over there."

"Why don't you call?"

"I don't want to," Cindy admitted.

"Why not?"

"Because I'm asking you to call."

Heather groaned. "What kind of answer is that?"

"Heather, please. . . ."

"I'll call when the show is over."

"When is that?"

"Another fifteen minutes."

"We connected on an intellectual level," the bimbo was telling the camera.

"Then you'll call your dad?"

"Julia's fine, you know. She told you she wasn't coming to the fitting. I don't know what you're so worried about."

"I'm not worried." Then, "You don't think she could have gotten lost, do you?"

"Lost?" Heather demanded in her aunt's voice.

The last time Julia disappeared, Cindy remembered, she was thirteen years old. Cindy was still reeling from her father's sudden death from a heart attack two months earlier, Tom was away on a "business trip" with his latest paramour, and Heather was singing a solo with her school choir that night. Julia was supposed to be home in time to accompany her mother to the concert, but by seven o'clock, she still wasn't back. Cindy spent the next hour calling all Julia's friends, checking with neighbors, driving up and down the rain-soaked streets. She'd tried reaching Tom in Montreal, but he wasn't at his hotel. Finally, at nine o'clock, distraught and unsure what to do next, she'd driven to the school to pick up Heather, only to find a defiant Julia comforting her sister. "I told you I'd meet you in the auditorium," Julia chastised her mother. "Don't you listen?"

Had Julia told her of her plans this morning? Cindy wondered now, throwing her clothes on the bed and walking into the bathroom. Was this mix-up all her fault? Had she not been listening?

"Look at me," she moaned. "I look awful."

"You don't look awful," Heather called from the bedroom.

"I'm short."

"Five six isn't short."

"My hair's a mess." Cindy pulled at her loose brown curls.

"Your hair is not a mess." Heather appeared in the bathroom doorway. "Mom, what's wrong?"

"Wrong?"

"Aren't I the one who's supposed to be whining about her appearance and you the one reassuring me with quaint, motherly platitudes?"

Cindy smiled. Heather was right. When had their roles suddenly reversed?

"You're probably just nervous about your date."

"It's not a date," Cindy corrected. "And I'm not nervous." She turned on the tap, began rigorously scrubbing her face.

"Shouldn't use soap," her daughter advised, stilling her mother's hand and reaching into the medicine cabinet for a jar of moisturizing cleanser. "I mean, you buy all this stuff. Why don't you use it?"

"It's too much work. I can't be bothered."

"Try this," Heather instructed. "Then this." She pulled an assortment of bottles off the shelf of the crowded cabinet and spread them across the cherrywood counter. "Then I'll do your makeup. And speaking of makeup, what's with Auntie Leigh and the Tammy Faye Bakker eyes?"

"I'm hoping it's a phase."

"Let's hope it's over by the wedding."

The phone rang.

"It's about time." Cindy marched back into her bedroom, grabbed for the phone. "Hello," she said eagerly, waiting for Julia's voice.

"Cindy, it's Leigh," her sister announced, as if she knew they'd been speaking about her. "I just want to apologize again for what I said earlier—about you spending all your time at the movies, and not knowing how to take care of a husband."

"Oh," Cindy said flatly. "That."

"I was out of line."

"Yeah," Cindy agreed. "You were."

"Anyway, I'm sorry."

"Apology accepted."

"It's just this wedding. And Mom, of course.",

"Of course."

"The pressure is nonstop. Sometimes I get a little overwhelmed."

Cindy nodded into the receiver.

Her sister sighed. "I wish I had your life," she said.

Cindy laughed as she hung up the phone.

"What's funny?" Heather asked.

"My sister's idea of an apology." Cindy stared at the TV. A second young woman, whose dark bikini matched her ebony skin, was climbing into a hot tub with a bald-headed, tattoo-covered man who looked like a black Mr. Clean.

"What's she sorry for?" Heather asked.

"That's just the point. She isn't." Cindy shook her head, trying to remember the last time she'd felt close to her younger sister.

(Memory: Eight-year-old Leigh shadowing Cindy's every move, following her from room to room, as if glued to her side. "Why does she have to do everything the same as me?" Cindy protests, pushing Leigh aside.

"The same as *I*," her mother corrects. "Besides, imitation is the sincerest form of flattery."

"I hate her."

"I hate her too," Leigh echoes.

"You'll love each other when you grow up," their mother promises.)

Did they? Cindy wondered now, watching as Mr. Clean explained his various tattoos to his curious companion. She and Leigh were so different. They had different interests, different styles, different tastes. In clothes, in politics, in men. Try as they might, and occasionally they really did try, they never quite seemed to connect. Their empathy was forced, their sympathy strained. They tolerated each other. Sometimes just barely.

Strangely enough, their relationship had been at its best just after Cindy got married and again just after she got divorced. When Cindy eloped with Tom to Niagara Falls without a word to anyone, it had been Leigh who'd convinced their parents to get over their anger and accept the young man Cindy had chosen. Leigh had been a regular guest at their tiny apartment, a co-conspirator after the fact.

After Tom walked out, taking Julia with him, Leigh had been equally supportive, dropping over dinners, going grocery shopping for her distraught sister, offering to baby-sit Heather. For months, she'd called first thing every morning and again before she went to bed. She'd made sure Cindy had the best divorce lawyer in the city. She'd literally clapped her hands when Cindy's settlement guaranteed her security for life.

Leigh's own marriage, to a high school principal, had always seemed happy enough. Warren was a kind man, patient to a fault, and he seemed to genuinely love his wife. "Warren would never cheat on me," Leigh had said on more than one occasion, and Cindy had nodded her agreement, confident in the rightness of her sister's assessment, pretending not to hear the silent addendum, "the way Tom cheated on you."

"Mom?" Heather was asking now. "What's the matter? Why are you smiling like that?"

Cindy unclenched her teeth. "Just this stupid TV show." She flicked off the remote control, watching Mr. Clean and his companion disappear into darkness.

"Hey . . ."

"Call your father for me. Please," Cindy added when her daughter failed to respond.

Heather slumped toward the phone. "I don't understand why you can't call him."

"I don't want to speak to the Cookie," Cindy muttered.

"What?"

"Just call him."

Heather punched in the numbers, shifting her weight from one foot to the other as she waited for someone to answer the phone. "Hey, Fiona," she said while Cindy scrunched up her nose, as if she'd just smelled something unpleasant. "It's Heather. I'm fine. How are you?"

Cindy walked back into the bathroom, stuck out her tongue at her reflection. "I'm just fine," she said in the Cookie's chirpy little voice. "Right as rain. Happy as a lark. Peachy perfect."

"Is my sister there?"

Cindy grabbed a brush, dragged it through her hair, listened for the answer.

"Is she expected there for dinner?"

So, Julia wasn't there. At least not yet. "Ask her if she's heard from her," Cindy instructed her daughter, returning to the bedroom, the brush dangling from her hair.

"Have you heard from her?" Heather asked dutifully, then shook her head in her mother's direction. "Okay, well, if you do," Heather continued over her mother's continued prompting, "have her call home. Okay? Yeah, everything's fine. I just want to speak to her. Okay, yeah. Bye." She hung up the phone.

"Julia's not there?"

Heather shrugged her indifference. "She's fine, Mom."

"It would be nice if she phoned, that's all."

"How come you call Fiona a cookie?"

Cindy shrugged, pulling roughly at the brush in her hair, feeling the handle break off in her hand. "Oh, that's just great."

"I'll do it." Slowly, gently, Heather extricated the head of the brush from her mother's hair. Then she slid it back into the handle and began tenderly manipulating Cindy's soft curls. "You'll see. I'm going to make you absolutely gorgeous for your date tonight."

"It's not a date."

"I know it's not."

"I probably shouldn't even be going."

"Don't be silly. I'll be fine here by myself."

"It's Julia I'm worried about."

Heather stopped her gentle ministrations.

"That's it? You're done?"

Heather nodded, returning the brush to her mother's hands. "You don't need me," she said.

FIVE

So, how do you know Trish?"

Cindy tucked her hair behind her right ear, less from necessity and more because it gave her something to do with her hands. She straightened the cutlery on the white tablecloth, although it was already perfectly straight, and refolded the burgundy-colored napkin in her lap. Then she tucked the hair behind her right ear a second time and stared out the long window behind Neil Macfarlane's head, watching the blue slowly leak from the sky, bathing the expansive panorama in muted gray. Soon it would be dark, she thought, mindful that the days were getting shorter. Hold that thought, she told herself. Save it for when the conversation runs dry, for when the small talk gets so tiny it threatens to disappear altogether. Isn't that why she stopped dating in the first place, why she vowed never to subject herself to the single scene's unpleasant vagaries again? Or was it because the men had simply stopped calling? "We met about ten years ago. At one of the makeup counters in Holt's. We actually walked right into one another, reaching for the same bottle of moisturizing cream," Cindy continued, unable to stop the unexpected torrent of words. "We were both in a hurry. It was during the film festival, and we didn't have much time between films."

The man across the table nodded. "I understand Trish is quite the movie fan."

"Yes. We both are." Of course, the most logical follow-up would be for her to ask, "And you? Do you like movies too?" But she didn't because such a question would imply she was interested in whether Neil Macfarlane liked movies or not. And she was determined not to be interested in anything about Neil Macfarlane at all. So instead, Cindy scratched at the back of her neck and reached for the bread basket, although she merely shifted it a little to the left before returning her hands to her lap. She didn't want to fill up on bread. She didn't want to get bread crumbs all over her white blouse and gray linen pants. She didn't want the waiter approaching with one of those frightening little gadgets they employed to clean the tables of assorted debris, each roll offering a silent rebuke for being such a sloppy eater. All she wanted was to finish her dinner, assuming the waiter ever came by to take their order, drink her wine, assuming the wine steward could locate the expensive Bordeaux Neil had ordered, and get the hell out of the restaurant and home to Julia, assuming her older daughter had finally decided to put in an appearance. Where was she anyway? At the very least, why hadn't she called? Cindy rifled through her purse and checked that her cell phone was on.

"Everything all right?" Neil asked.

"Fine." Cindy smiled, careful to avoid the intense scrutiny of his eyes, eyes she'd noticed immediately that were an amazing shade of blue. Somewhere between teal and turquoise. With a sparkle, no less, as if it had been dabbed on with silver paint. Trish hadn't been exaggerating. Neil Macfarlane was cute all right. More than cute. He was drop-dead gorgeous. Cindy had decided immediately that the less she looked at him the better off she'd be.

(First impressions: A man, tall and slender, wavy brown hair atop a boyish face, waits for her at the bottom of the elegant, open, red mahogany staircase, the city stretched out tantalizingly behind him in the long expanse of glass; he smiles, deep dimples creasing his cheeks as she warily approaches and the city blurs behind him; he is wearing a blue shirt that underlines the fierce blue of his eyes; his hands are warm as they reach for hers; his voice is soft as he speaks her name. "Cindy," he says with the quiet confidence of someone who is used to being right. "Neil?" she asks in return, feeling instantly foolish. Who else would he be? Already she feels inadequate.)

"So what kinds of movies do you like?" Neil was asking as the wine steward approached the table, proudly displaying the requested bottle for Neil's perusal. "Looks fine," Neil told him, although his eyes never strayed from Cindy.

Cindy, in turn, focused all her attention on the wine steward, watching as he slowly and expertly began the process of removing the cork from the bottle. "I like all movies," she said vaguely, disappointed when the cork put up no real resistance, sliding out of the bottle with ease.

The steward offered the cork to Neil, who dutifully sniffed at it and nodded his approval, then tasted the sampling the steward poured into his glass. "Fine," he said. "Excellent. It just needs a few minutes to breathe," Neil advised her.

I know how it feels, Cindy thought, but didn't say, watching as the steward filled her glass just short of halfway.

"So, you have no preferences at all?" Neil was asking.

What was the matter with him? Cindy wondered impatiently. Why did he insist on making conversation? He didn't really give a damn what kinds of movies she liked, or how she and Trish had met, or anything about her, for that matter. And if he did, it was only because he wanted to sleep with her, and he knew his chances would be greatly improved if he at least feigned an interest in her. Although why he would want to sleep with her was a total mystery. Look at him, for heaven's sake, Cindy thought, deliberately looking at the floor. On any given night, he undoubtedly had his choice of any number of much more attractive, much fitter, much *younger* women. Why would he want to sleep with her? That was easy, she decided. He wanted to sleep with her because she was here. It was as simple as that. It didn't mean anything.

It doesn't mean anything.

How many times had Tom told her exactly that?

Cindy raised her head, stared directly into Neil Macfarlane's brilliant blue eyes. "I like sex and violence," she stated honestly, the first time she'd admitted that to anyone.

"What?"

"You asked what kind of movies I like. I like sex and violence," she repeated, reaching for her wineglass, taking a long sip, feeling the wine slightly abrasive as it scratched against her throat. He was right. It needed a few more minutes to breathe. Cindy tossed her hair back, took another sip. "You look shocked."

Neil smiled, the dimples framing his mouth like quotation marks. "I understand liking sex. But blood and guts?"

"Not blood and guts so much," Cindy countered, feeling the wine curl into her stomach, like a contented cat in a wicker basket. "I don't like watching people get blown up ad nauseum. I guess what I like is more the threat of violence, the possibility that something terrible is about to happen."

"Women-in-jeopardy," Neil said matter-of-factly, nodding as if he understood, as if he already understood everything there was to know about her, as if there was nothing more to discover.

"I hate that term," Cindy said, stronger than she'd intended. "*Women-in-jeopardy,*" she repeated, taking another sip of wine, emboldened. "It's condescending. You never hear people say *men-in-jeopardy*. And, I mean, isn't that what drama is all about? *People* in jeopardy? Why is it somehow less valid when it concerns women? I'm really sick of that attitude." Whoa, she thought. Where had that come from?

Neil leaned back, lifted his hands in the air in a gesture of surrender. Cindy braced herself for his comeback, some smart remark that would put her in her place, reduce her to the role of angry, man-hating feminist. Instead he said, "You're right."

I'm right? she thought, relief washing over her, like an unexpected shower. She tapped her heart with her open palm. "I don't think anybody's ever said that to me before."

He laughed. "I guess I've just never really thought about it, but now that I do, I see your point—all drama is about people in peril, at a time in their lives when they're at risk, when they have to take a chance, make key decisions, get out of sticky situations, save themselves. The term 'women-in-jeopardy' *is* condescending. You're absolutely right."

Cindy smiled. He must really want to sleep with me, she thought. "Did Trish tell you I haven't had sex in three years?" The words were out of her mouth before she could stop them.

Neil's hand froze as he reached for his glass. "I don't think she mentioned that, no." Slowly, carefully, he brought the glass to his lips, then took a long sip of wine, holding it in his mouth, almost as if he were afraid to swallow.

"You think it's breathed long enough?" Cindy asked, enjoying his discomfort.

He gulped it down, exhaled deeply. "Definitely breathed long enough." The waiter approached, and asked if they'd reached a decision about their order. Neil grabbed for his menu. "Forgot what I wanted," he said sheepishly, blue eyes quickly scanning the night's offerings. "I guess I'll just have the special."

"The calves' liver sounds wonderful," Cindy said, thinking how nice it felt to be in control for a change. When was the last time she'd felt in control? Of anything? "And I'd like the endive and pear salad to start." Suddenly she felt ravenous.

"I'll start with the calamari," Neil said.

"Good choice," the waiter told him before departing with the menus.

What was the matter with my choice? Cindy wondered,

feeling oddly slighted, her power already deflating. What was the matter with her? What on earth had possessed her to tell a virtual stranger she hadn't had sex in three years? Trish's accountant, for God's sake. What he must think of her! "Have you noticed the days are getting shorter?" she asked, a bit desperately.

Neil looked toward the windows that embraced the east and south walls of the tony restaurant. "I guess they are." He looked back at Cindy, the look in his eyes a mixture of bemused curiosity and wary anticipation, as if he were slightly afraid of what she might say next, but was looking forward to it just the same.

"So tell me all about the joys of accounting. Are there any?"

"I like to think so," Neil answered, his voice a smile. "There's something very satisfying about numbers."

"How so?"

"Numbers are what they are. They're very straightforward. Unlike people."

Cindy nodded her agreement. "I can't imagine you have much trouble with people."

Neil shrugged, lifted his glass in a toast. "To people."

Cindy clicked her glass against his, avoided his eyes. "So, I guess you were always really good at math, right?"

"Right."

"I was horrible in math. It was my worst subject."

"English was my worst."

"My best," Cindy said.

There was a moment's silence. "Can we go back to talking about sex now?" Neil asked, and Cindy laughed in spite of her desire not to.

"Can we just forget I said anything about that?"

"That might be difficult."

"Can we try?"

"Absolutely."

Another moment of silence. "Look, I'm obviously not very good at this."

"At what?"

"This whole scene. Dating. You know."

"What makes you say that?"

"Well, I'm not exactly a sparkling conversationalist."

"On the contrary. You sure got my attention."

Again Cindy laughed. "Yeah, well, sex is a cheap way to get someone's attention."

"Not always so cheap."

Cindy quickly finished off the wine in her glass. "So, what *did* Trish tell you about me?"

Neil sat back in his chair, gave the question several seconds' thought. "She said that you were bright, beautiful, and extremely picky when it came to men."

"Which is a nice way of saying I haven't had sex in three years," Cindy heard herself say before throwing her hand over her mouth. "God, what's the matter with me?"

"You haven't had sex in three years," Neil answered with a sly smile.

A wave of heat spread across Cindy's face and neck, like a sunburn. She felt all eyes staring at her. "Maybe I should just make a general announcement. Hell, I think there are some people in the far corner over there who might not know."

"Why haven't you had sex in three years? Are you really that picky when it comes to men?"

"*Prickly* is probably a better word," Cindy admitted. "Men don't like angry women."

"And you're an angry woman?"

"Apparently."

I've always had trouble dealing with your anger, her ex-husband had told her.

"You okay?" Neil asked.

"Yes. Why?"

"I don't know. You just got this funny little look on your face."

"I'm fine," Cindy said. "I mean, other than the fact that I feel like a total idiot, I'm fine."

"I think you're charming. I'm having a great time."

"You are?"

"Aren't you?"

Cindy laughed. "Actually, yes. I am."

"Good. Have some more wine." He filled both their glasses, then clicked his glass against hers. "To angry women."

Cindy smiled. "To brave men."

(Memory: Tom's voice on the answering machine: *Hi, it's me. Look, there's no easy way to say this, so I'll just come right out with it. I'm leaving. Actually I've already left. Call me a coward, and a few other choice words I'm sure you'll think of, but I just thought it was better if we didn't speak in person. You know I've always had trouble dealing with your anger. Anyway, I'm at the Four Seasons Hotel. Call me when you stop swearing.*)

"So, Trish tells me you work in Hazelton Lanes," Neil was saying.

"Yes. A friend of mine owns this neat little jewelry store. I help her out three afternoons a week."

"How long have you been doing that?"

"About seven years."

"Since your divorce?"

"Trish told you about that?"

"She said you've been divorced seven years."

This was the part of dating Cindy liked least. The emotional résumé, where you were expected to trot out your dirty laundry and bare your soul, vent your frustrations, recount your pain, and hope for a sympathetic ear. But Cindy had no interest in trotting, baring, venting, and recounting. And she'd long since given up on hope. She took a deep breath. "Okay, I'm going to get this over with as quickly as possible, so listen carefully: My husband walked out on me seven years ago for another woman, which was no huge surprise since he'd been cheating on me for years. What was surprising was that my older daughter chose to go with him, although I probably shouldn't have been so surprised because she was always her father's little princess. Anyway," Cindy continued, glancing toward the phone in her purse, "my settlement ensured I didn't have to worry about finding a job, which was good because I only had a high school education, having eloped when I was eighteen. Still with me?"

"Hanging onto every word."

"After I got married, I worked at Eaton's for a couple of years, selling towels and bedding and exciting stuff like that, helping put my ex through law school, pretty standard stuff, and then I got pregnant and I quit work to stay home with Julia, and then two years later, Heather came along, something for which Julia never quite forgave me." Cindy strained to keep her voice light. "Witness her decision to go live with her father."

"But you saw her, didn't you? Weekends? Holidays?"

"She was a teenager. I saw her whenever she could fit me into her busy schedule. Which wasn't too often." Cindy felt her stomach cramp at the memory.

"That must have been very difficult for you."

"It was awful. I felt as if someone had ripped my guts out. I cried every day. Couldn't sleep, wondering what I'd done wrong. Sometimes I could barely get out of bed. I honestly thought I'd lose my mind. That's when Meg, my friend, offered me a job working at her little boutique. At first I said no, but eventually I decided I had to do something. And it's been great. I work three afternoons a week; I take off whenever I feel like it. And to top it off, my daughter's come back." Again Cindy glanced toward her purse.

"Do you keep her in there?" Neil asked.

Cindy smiled. "Sorry. It's just that she was supposed to call. Anyway, sorry about unloading on you like that. Can we do us both a favor and never mention my ex-husband or my divorce again?"

"I'll drink to that." They clicked glasses.

"Your turn." Cindy leaned back in her chair, sipped on her wine. "Family history in fifty words or less."

He laughed. "Well, I was married."

"For how long?"

"Fifteen years."

"And you've been divorced for how long?"

"I'm not divorced."

"Oh?"

"My wife died four years ago."

"Oh, I'm so sorry."

"She woke up one morning, said she wasn't feeling quite right, and six weeks later, she was dead. Ovarian cancer."

"How awful. Trish didn't tell me. . . ."

"I doubt she has any idea. I've only known her a short time, and all she asked me was whether I was married, and if I'd be interested in going out with her friend."

Cindy shook her head. "And you, poor man, said yes."

"I said yes."

"Do you have children?"

"A son. Max. He's seventeen. Great kid."

Cindy tried picturing Julia at seventeen, but the years between fourteen and twenty-one had pretty much melted together in Cindy's mind, like chocolates left too long in the sun. All those years lost. Years she could never get back.

The waiter was suddenly standing beside them. "Endive and pear salad for the lady," he announced, as if she might have forgotten. "Calamari for the gentleman." He put the dishes on the table. "Enjoy."

"Thank you." Cindy lifted her fork, stabbing it into her salad as she stole another glance at the phone in her purse. *Hi, Mom. Sorry about not calling earlier, but I've had the most incredible day.* But Cindy's phone remained stubbornly silent, and Julia remained, as ever, tantalizingly out of reach.

SIX

The phone rang at just after 2 A.M., cutting through Cindy's sleep like a dull blade. She flung her arm toward the sound, knocking the back of her hand against the night table beside her bed, and crying out in pain as she groped for the receiver. "Hello?" she said, barely recognizing the sound of her own voice.

"I understand you've lost your daughter," the caller said.

Instantly Cindy was wide awake, her body rigid, her feet on the floor, poised to run. "Who is this?"

"It doesn't matter who I am. What matters is, I found her."

Cindy's eyes shot through the darkness to the window, as if Julia might have been spirited through the slats of the California shutters and was now hidden among the leaves of the red maple trees in the backyard. Her heart pounded loudly against her ears, like a restless ocean surf. "Where is she? How is she?"

"You should take better care of your children," the caller scolded.

"Please, can you just tell me where she is?"

"You know what they say, don't you? Finders, keepers . . ."

"What?"

". . . losers, weepers."

"Who are you? What have you done with Julia?"

"I have to go now."

"Wait! Don't hang up. Please, don't hang up!" Cindy felt the line go dead in her hands, as if Julia herself had just died in her arms. "No! No!"

"Mom?" a frightened voice called from the doorway. "Mom, what's the matter?"

Cindy spun around, the blankets falling from her naked body as she jumped from the bed, her pupils dilating with disbelief as she absorbed the identity of the person walking toward her. "Julia! You're here. You're all right." She threw her arms around her daughter, wrapped her in a smothering embrace. "I was having the most awful nightmare. It was so real. But you're okay. You're okay." She kissed Julia's cheek and forehead, felt Julia's skin grow colder with each brush of her lips. "My poor baby. You're freezing. Come get into bed. What's the matter, darling? Are you sick?" Cindy maneuvered her daughter into her bed, Julia's body going limp as she lay back against the pillow, her blond hair floating around her face, like seaweed in a shallow lake. "Everything's okay now, sweetheart. Mommy's here. I'll take care of you."

Julia stared at her mother through cold, dead eyes. She spoke without moving her lips. "This is all your fault," she said.

Cindy screamed.

And then suddenly someone was at her side, touching her shoulder, stroking her arm. "Mom! Mom! What's the matter? Mom, wake up. Wake up." And then something wet on her cheek, a rhythmic thumping at the side of the bed.

Cindy opened her eyes, saw Heather trembling beside her, the moonlight through the bedroom shutters drawing a series of broad horizontal stripes across her face. Elvis was on his hind legs at the side of the bed, his eager tongue extending toward her face, his tail slapping enthusiastically at the sideboard. "What's happening?"

"You tell me. Are you all right?" Somewhere behind Heather, something stirred.

Cindy arched forward, strained through the darkness past her younger child. "Is someone there? Julia? Is that you?"

"It's me, Mrs. Carver," Duncan replied, joining Heather and Elvis at Cindy's side. He was wearing only the bottom half of a pair of blue-and-white-striped pajamas; Heather was wearing its matching top.

"Oh." Cindy quickly pulled the covers up around her chin. "My robe," she said, motioning vaguely toward the foot of the bed.

Heather reached for the green-and-navy terry-cloth robe, draped it across her mother's shoulders. "You must have been having a nightmare."

Cindy stared blankly toward the foot of the bed, the details of her dream already receding, bursting like bubbles against the night air, evaporating, taking Julia away. "A nightmare. Yes. It was awful."

"You want some warm milk or something?" Heather asked. "I can make you a cup."

Cindy shook her head. "Is Julia home?"

Even in the dark, Cindy could see the frown on her younger daughter's face.

"Her door's closed," Duncan volunteered.

"It's always closed," Heather reminded him. "You want me to check?"

"I'll do it." Cindy secured her robe around her and climbed out of bed. "You two go back to bed. Get some sleep. It's late." She followed them out of the room and into the wide hall, stopping with them in front of Julia's door, Elvis licking at her bare toes. Her fingers stretched toward the doorknob.

"She's gonna be real mad if you wake her up," Heather warned.

She's going to be really angry, Cindy corrected silently, too tired to say the words out loud. She felt the doorknob twist in her palm, heard the loud creak as she pushed open Julia's door. Cindy poked her head inside the room, her eyes straining through the darkness toward the bed.

It was empty.

Cindy knew it instantly, even before Elvis went charging past her and began wrestling with the stuffed animals propped against Julia's pillows. Heather ran after him, stubbing her toes on several of the CDs scattered across the blue carpet, and swearing loudly.

"Shit," she cried as Cindy flipped on the overhead light.

"Good thing Julia's not here," Duncan observed wryly as Elvis began barking.

"Where the hell is she?" Cindy surveyed the mess that was

her daughter's room. Discarded clothes lay scattered across the floor, on the bookshelves lining one wall, on the walnut desk propped against another, and over the back of the black leather chair in front of it. A hot pink mini-dress was draped across the top of the white shutters; a pair of outrageously high-heeled sandals hung from their straps on a bedpost.

"She's probably at Dad's," Heather said, shooing Elvis off Julia's bed.

"Then why hasn't she called?"

"Because she's Julia," Heather reminded her mother. Then, "Maybe she's with Sean."

"I thought they broke up."

"So?" Heather asked.

Cindy nodded, wondering whether she could call Sean at this hour of the morning.

"Don't even think about it," Heather warned, as if reading her mother's mind. "She's fine, Mom. Stop worrying. You can bet she's not worrying about you."

"You're right," Cindy said, trying not to picture Julia lying bleeding and alone in some ditch at the side of a dark road. Or worse.

"You never said how your date went tonight." Heather stared at her mother expectantly.

"It wasn't a date."

"Yeah, okay, so, the question is, did you connect on a deep intellectual and spiritual level?"

Cindy pictured Neil's wondrous dimples when he laughed, felt the touch of his skin as his hand repeatedly brushed up against her arm as he walked her home, tasted his sweet breath as he leaned in to kiss her cheek good night. "We connected."

"So there'll be a second nondate?"

"We'll see." Cindy kissed Heather's forehead, patted Duncan's bare arm. "Get some sleep."

"You too," Heather said. "Come on, Elvis."

Elvis immediately spread himself across Cindy's feet, refused to move.

"Looks like he's sleeping with you tonight," Heather said, following Duncan into their bedroom and closing the door.

"Great." Elvis rolled over onto his back, offered his stomach to be rubbed. "Come on, you nut. Let's go to bed." Elvis flipped back onto his feet, took two steps, then stopped, sat down, and stared back at Julia's room, as if he, too, were confused by her absence. "She's fine," Cindy told him, as Elvis cocked his head to one side attentively. "Except that I'm going to kill her when she gets home." She shuffled toward her room, plopped down on her bed, then lay down on top of her covers. Elvis immediately jumped on the bed and burrowed in against the inside of her knees. Cindy turned on one side; Elvis snuggled closer. "I don't think this is going to work," Cindy told the dog after several minutes spent in a futile effort to get comfortable. "I guess I'm just not used to sharing my space anymore. Sorry about that." She sat up, flipped on the light beside her bed, reached for the phone.

Don't even think about it, she heard Heather say.

But it was too late. Already Cindy's fingers were punching in the numbers she hadn't realized she knew by heart.

The voice that answered the phone on its fourth ring was wary and weighted with sleep. "Hello?"

Cindy pictured the young woman sitting up in bed,

pushing lush red ringlets away from her Kewpie-doll face, the strap of an expensive pink silk peignoir slipping down one milk-white shoulder, full bosom heaving fetchingly in the soft moonlight. A book cover, Cindy thought, picturing it in her mind: *Romance for Cookies.*

"Fiona," Cindy said, imagining Tom sitting up beside his young wife, playful fingers sliding the errant strap back over her shoulder. "It's Cindy."

"It's two o'clock in the morning, Cindy."

"I know what time it is."

"Is something wrong?"

"Is Julia there?"

"Julia? No."

"What's going on?" Cindy heard Tom grumble.

"She's your ex-wife. You ask her," the Cookie said, as Cindy pictured her flopping back on her pillow and covering her eyes with a disinterested hand.

"Cindy, what the hell's going on? It's after two o'clock."

Cindy felt her throat constrict, as it always did when she was forced to actually speak to her former husband. "Fiona has already told me the time. And I'm sorry to bother you at this hour, I really am, but Julia's not home, and I haven't heard from her all day, and I just wondered if you'd spoken to her."

There was a long pause. "Not since around ten-thirty this morning."

"She didn't call you after her audition?"

"No."

"And you're not worried?" Cindy heard the growing panic in her voice.

"Why would I be worried?" Cindy recognized the once-familiar tone. His lawyer's voice. I don't have time for your petty insecurities, it said. "I don't demand that my daughter check in with me every minute of the day and night."

"Neither do I."

"You have to let go, Cindy . . ." Tom said.

Tears stung Cindy's eyes. How can I let go of something I never had? she thought.

". . . or you'll drive her away again."

I didn't drive her away, Cindy thought bitterly. *You* drove her away. In your goddamn BMW.

"She's probably with Sean."

Cindy nodded.

"Don't even think of calling him now," Tom said.

Cindy hung up without saying good night. "Bastard," she whispered, as if afraid he could still hear her. She remained motionless in her bed for several seconds, Elvis pressing against her side. "What about you?" she asked the dog. "You think I'm overly protective? You think I've driven her away again?"

In response, Elvis jumped off the bed and ran to the bedroom door, then stopped and looked back, as if expecting her to follow.

"I don't think you understand."

The dog began pacing restlessly back and forth in the doorway.

"What? You have to go out?"

Elvis barked.

"Ssh! Okay, okay. I'll take you out." Cindy tightened the sash of her terry-cloth bathrobe and slid her feet into a pair of well-worn white slippers, stomping down the stairs to the front door. "I can't believe I'm doing this. You better have to pee, that's all I can say." She opened the door to the cool night air and stepped onto the front landing. Elvis immediately took off down the front steps and disappeared. "Elvis, wait! Where are you going?" A sudden blur raced across her front lawn, cutting through the bushes that separated her property from her next-door neighbor's. "Elvis! Get back here. I can't believe this." Her slippers flopping noisily around her feet like rubber flippers, Cindy inched her way down the front steps. "Elvis, get back here. You're a very bad dog." Oh, sure, she thought, that'll get him back here in a hurry. "You're a really good dog, Elvis," she said, trying again. "Come to Mommy." Except she wasn't his mommy. Julia was his mommy. Which made her Elvis's grandmother. "Dear God," she wailed.

"It's okay, Cindy. He's over here," a voice announced from somewhere beside her.

Cindy gasped, her head snapping toward the sound.

"Sorry. I didn't mean to scare you." The voice was coming from beyond the bushes. "It's me. Ryan."

Cindy kicked off her slippers and pushed herself through the bushes, several branches slapping against her face as she stepped onto Ryan Sellick's front lawn, the damp grass creeping between her bare toes. Ryan was sitting on his top step, in much the same position his wife, Faith, had occupied earlier in the day. Light from two brass lanterns hanging to either side of the front door illuminated his fine features: the long, straight nose; the thin lips; the sculpted cheekbones; the slight cleft in his chin. Dark hair fell across his forehead and over the back collar of his shirt, a shirt that was either black or brown, as were his eyes. Julia had always considered him terribly handsome, Cindy remembered as she approached, seeing Elvis with his head resting comfortably in Ryan's lap, contentedly licking at the crisp denim of Ryan's jeans. She noticed Ryan's feet were as bare as her own, and that there was a long, fresh scratch beneath his right eye that hadn't been there earlier in the day. "I'm sorry to bother you." Cindy remained at the foot of the outside steps, not wanting to intrude any further into his privacy. "Elvis, get down here."

"He's fine." Ryan stroked behind the dog's ears. "Actually, I'm grateful for the company."

"Are you okay?"

"Couldn't sleep."

Cindy nodded. "How's Faith?"

He shrugged, as if he weren't sure how to answer the question.

"My sister had postpartum depression," Cindy offered. "With two of her children."

"Really? And what happened?"

Cindy struggled to remember, but like her mother, she actually had no recollection of Leigh having suffered from any such affliction. "I guess it just went away with time."

"That's pretty much what her doctor says will happen. Apparently it's not all that uncommon."

"So I've heard."

"You never had it?"

"No. I was lucky, I guess." Cindy had sailed through both her pregnancies and their aftermath, relishing the time when her daughters were infants, despite the fact that Julia had been colicky and demanding from the moment of her birth. Heather, on the other hand, had slept through the night at ten weeks, settled into a three-feedings-a-day schedule the week after that, and potty-trained herself at thirteen months. Cindy sat down on the bottom step and stared down the quiet street, half expecting to see her older daughter emerge from the shadows of the streetlamps. "Has the doctor recommended any medication?"

"He prescribed Valium, but it doesn't seem to be doing much good. Maybe she needs something stronger."

"Maybe she needs to talk to a psychiatrist."

"Maybe." Ryan Sellick massaged the bridge of his nose, as if trying to keep a budding headache at bay.

"What about Faith's mother? Any chance she could help out for a few weeks?"

"Her mother's been back and forth from Vancouver several times already. I can't expect her to keep flying over every time there's a problem. And my parents are both dead, so . . ."

"What about hiring a nanny?"

"Faith won't hear of it. 'What kind of mother can't take care of her own child?' she says whenever I so much as mention the idea." Ryan shook his head, gingerly patting the deep scratch beneath his eye. "I don't know what to do. I can't keep taking time off work, that's for sure. I didn't get to the office today till almost noon, and then I had to leave again when you called."

"Maybe I could drop by a few times a week," Cindy suggested.

"No. I couldn't put you to that much trouble."

"It's no trouble," Cindy assured him. "And I'll talk to Heather and Julia, see if they'd be willing to baby-sit occasionally."

Ryan laughed, an unexpectedly hearty sound.

"What's funny?"

He shook his head. "Julia just doesn't strike me as the baby-sitting type."

Cindy had to agree. "I didn't realize you knew my daughter so well."

"It's all in the way she walks. Nobody struts a street quite like Julia."

Cindy watched Julia's image step out of the shadows and walk toward them, head high, shoulders rotating in time with her hips, arms swinging at her sides. She moves as if a camera is following her, Cindy thought, recording her every move.

"Everything all right at home?" Ryan asked.

What was he talking about? "What do you mean?"

"Well, Julia and Heather's boyfriend, I've forgotten his name. . . ."

"Duncan."

"Yeah, Duncan. They were going at it pretty good this morning."

"They were fighting?"

"In the driveway. I heard the yelling from inside my house." He motioned toward the dining room to the left of the front door.

It must have been when I was out shopping for chardonnay, Cindy thought, recalling today's lunch with genuine nostalgia. Already it seemed so long ago. Why would Julia have been fighting with Duncan? And why hadn't he mentioned their argument to her earlier? Why hadn't Heather?

"What time was that?"

"A little before eleven, I think."

So Julia had been fighting with Duncan just before she'd had to leave for her appointment. Maybe the argument had upset her, caused her to blow the most important audition of her career. Maybe that's why she hadn't come home—because she was too angry and embarrassed and upset. Damn that Duncan anyway, Cindy thought, pushing herself to her feet. She should never have allowed him to move into her house. "I should get home. Let you get some sleep," she said. "Come on, Elvis. Party's over." Surprisingly, the dog immediately jumped to his feet and followed after her.

"Thanks for being such a good neighbor," Ryan called as Cindy reached the sidewalk in front of the house.

Cindy waited while Elvis relieved himself against the side of a tall maple tree. "Everything's going to work out fine. You'll see." Confidence radiated from her voice, and it was only later, when she was lying in her bed, wide awake at nearly 4 A.M., Julia still not home, that Cindy wondered who it was she'd been trying so hard to convince.

SEVEN

At precisely seven-thirty the next morning Cindy phoned Sean Banack. "Sean, this is Julia's mother," she said instead of hello. "Is Julia there?"

"What?" The sleepy voice was raspy with cigarettes and alcohol. "I'm sorry, what?" he said again.

"It's Cindy Carver. Julia's mother," Cindy repeated, picturing Sean Banack slowly propping himself up on one elbow in the middle of rumpled white sheets, his free hand pushing long blond hair away from his forehead, then rubbing at tired brown eyes. She wondered if Julia was stretched out beside him. *I'm not here,* she could almost hear her daughter whisper before flipping onto her other side and covering her head with a pillow.

"Mrs. Carver?" Sean asked, as if he still wasn't sure who she was.

"I'm sorry to be calling so early, but I need to speak to Julia."

"Julia's not here."

"Please, Sean. This is really important."

"She's not here," he repeated stubbornly.

"Do you know where she is?"

Sean made a sound halfway between a laugh and a cry. "I'm very sorry, Mrs. Carver, but Julia is no longer my problem."

"What does that mean?"

"It means we broke up. It means I don't have a clue where she is. It means it's seven-thirty in the morning and I didn't get to bed till after three. Which means I'm still a little drunk and I've got to get some sleep."

"Sean," Cindy cried before he could disconnect. "Please. Julia didn't come home last night and I'm very worried. If you have any idea at all where she might be. . . ."

"Sorry, Mrs. Carver," Sean said before hanging up the phone. "I'm not the one you should be speaking to."

"What do you mean? Who should I . . . ?" Cindy stared at the dead phone in her hands for several long seconds before dropping it back into its carriage. "Great. Just great." Elvis stirred beside her, then jumped from the bed, stared at her expectantly. "What does that mean, 'I'm not the one you should be speaking to?'" she asked the dog, who cocked his head from side to side, as if carefully considering his response. Then he ran to the bedroom door and barked. "That's all you have to say?" Elvis barked again, and began digging at the carpet. "I know. I know. You have to go out. Give me a minute, okay?" Elvis promptly sat down, patiently waiting as Cindy showered and slipped into a pair of jeans and an old orange T-shirt. "Did Julia come home while I was in the shower?" she asked the dog as he dutifully followed her into Julia's empty room.

Cindy glanced toward the closed door of the bedroom Heather shared with Duncan. It bothered her that neither of them had said anything about Duncan's fight with Julia, a fight so acrimonious it had spilled from the house to the street, so loud it had attracted the attention of their next-door neighbor. She thought of storming into their room and demanding an explanation, but decided such confrontations were better left till she got back from walking the dog. Perhaps by that time, Julia would be home.

"Come on, boy." Cindy attached Elvis's leash to his collar and grabbed a plastic bag from the kitchen. It was only after she'd stepped outside and closed the front door behind her that she realized she'd forgotten her key. At least now she had an excuse for having to wake everyone up early.

"Where are you, Julia?" Cindy asked the sun-dappled street, listening to the whir of cars already clogging Avenue Road. Avenue Road, she repeated silently, turning in the opposite direction and waiting as Elvis relieved himself on a neighbor's front lawn. What a strange thing to call a street. Almost as if the city council had run out of names. "Where are you, Julia?" she repeated, stopping again while Elvis left his mark on a newly planted strip of grass.

She turned left on Poplar Plains and proceeded south, letting Elvis lead the way. It was going to be a beautiful day, she thought, feeling the sun warm on her arms, the slightest of breezes teasing the leaves on the trees. A week from now, the University of Toronto's fall semester would be getting under way, and Heather and Duncan would be back in class, Cindy would be sitting in a crowded movie theater with hundreds of other avid film devotees, and Julia . . . Julia would be where?

Where was she now?

"Where are you, Julia?" Cindy asked again, tugging on Elvis's leash when he stopped too long at the corner of Poplar Plains and Clarendon, picking up the pace as they turned the corner onto Edmund. "Hurry up and do your stuff," Cindy instructed, amazed when the dog immediately squatted, leaving a large, steaming deposit in the middle of the sidewalk. Cindy held her breath as she scooped the dog poop into the clear plastic bag. "Good boy," she said. All my children should listen so well, she thought.

What had Sean meant when he said Julia was no longer his problem? Clearly he was upset about their breakup, but he'd sounded so bitter. *I'm not the one you should be speaking to.* What did that mean exactly? *Whom* should she be speaking to?

"Damn it, Julia. Where are you?" Cindy nodded hello to a heavyset man who was skipping rope in front of a mustard-yellow apartment building on the other side of the street. Even from this distance she could see he was sweating profusely, and she wondered if such intense exercise was good for him. She checked her watch. It was a little past eight o'clock. Maybe that's where Julia was—at an early-morning exercise class. Yes, that was it. She'd probably met up with a group of friends after her audition and they'd spent the afternoon together, gone out for a dinner of sushi and wine, then partied until it was too late to call home. When she woke up, she'd gone directly to her yoga class. There was nothing to worry about; nothing awful had happened. Julia hadn't been hurt, molested, kidnapped, murdered, dismembered, her body parts hurled into the middle of Lake Ontario. She was perfectly fine, and she'd be back within the hour to shower and blow-dry her hair razor-straight for the undoubtedly busy day ahead. She hadn't called because she simply wasn't used to reporting her whereabouts to her mother. Her father had never demanded that she—how was it he so sensitively put it?—check in with him every minute of the day and night.

"I hope you're picking up after your dog," a woman called from a nearby apartment window.

Cindy waved the plastic bag full of poop above her head. "What do you think this is?" she snapped. "A purse?"

The woman quickly retreated, lowering her window with a loud bang.

So many angry people, Cindy thought, proceeding up Avenue Road, dropping the plastic bag into a garbage bin already overflowing with them. She turned west on Balmoral, heading for home. *I've always had trouble dealing with your anger,* she heard Tom say, as she ran up the steps and banged on her front door.

"I don't understand how you could leave the house without your keys," Heather scolded her mother, yawning as she poured herself a large bowl of Cinnamon Toast Crunch and plopped down at the kitchen table, burying her face in the morning paper.

"You didn't tell me Duncan and Julia had a fight yesterday," Cindy said in return.

"It was no big deal."

"Big enough to concern several of the neighbors," Cindy embellished.

"Really? Who?"

"That's not the issue."

"There is no issue."

"What was the fight about?"

"Nothing." Heather shrugged, tossed the front section of the *Globe and Mail* onto the round pine table. "You know Julia."

"And you know what Julia and Duncan were fighting about. Tell me."

Heather lowered the paper and released a deep breath of air, looking imploringly toward the doorway, as if hoping Duncan would miraculously appear. But the shower was still running and it was unlikely Duncan would be down for a while. "It was nothing. Really. Her Highness was running late, as usual, and she wanted a ride to her audition. When Duncan said he was going in the opposite direction and didn't have time to chauffeur her around, she got angry and started yelling. She even followed him to his car."

Cindy silently berated herself for not having been home to drive her daughter to her audition. "Would it have killed him to give her a lift?"

"Would it kill her to get her driver's license? How can anyone fail that stupid test three times?"

Cindy had occasionally wondered the same thing. But not even the sight of Julia's mesmerizingly long legs had been enough to influence the instructor's decision. "That's not the point."

"The point is that not everyone's life revolves around Julia. Stop worrying, Mom. She's fine."

"Then where is she? Why hasn't she called?" Cindy braced herself for her daughter's careless shrug, but surprisingly, none came.

"Did you check with Dad?"

Cindy nodded.

"And Sean?"

"He says Julia is no longer his problem. He hinted she might be seeing someone else."

"Really?"

"You have no idea who that might be?"

"No, but then I'm not exactly Julia's main confidante. You could ask Lindsey."

"Lindsey?"

"Lindsey—Julia's latest, greatest, best friend ever. She met her last month. The one with the enormous implants."

A huge bosom balancing precariously atop a skinny torso flashed before Cindy's eyes. The implants wafted into the air like two helium-filled balloons, blocking the young woman's face. "Do you know her number?"

"It's probably in Julia's address book."

Several minutes later, Cindy was in Julia's bedroom, guiltily rummaging through her things. But if Julia had an address book, she'd taken it with her. Cindy looked under every piece of clothing, searched through every drawer. Amid a sea of debris, she found a crumpled five-dollar bill, a sweater she'd been looking for all winter, and several packets of condoms, but no address book. Did it matter? She couldn't remember Lindsey's last name. Cindy slapped angrily at her thighs. What kind of mother doesn't know the names of her daughter's friends?

"I'm absolutely positive she's okay," Heather said when Cindy returned to the kitchen. "But maybe you should call the hospitals," she added quietly. "Just in case."

———

Cindy spent the next hour calling every hospital in the city. She started with the downtown hospitals—Mount Sinai, the Toronto Hospital, Women's College, the Western, St. Mike's, even the Hospital for Sick Children, and then she branched out, calling Sunnybrook, North York General, Humber Memorial, and even Scarborough. They all told her the same thing. No one named Julia Carver was registered as a patient; no one fitting her description had been brought into the emergency department in the last twenty-four hours.

She called the police, asked whether there'd been any accidents or incidents that might have involved her daughter, but the answer was no, and she hung up, feeling relieved, grateful, and alarmed all at the same time.

She noted the time on the microwave oven. It was ten o'clock. A full day had elapsed since she'd seen Julia.

Cindy looked around the now-empty kitchen. Heather and Duncan were upstairs, engaged in a quiet but unmistakable argument. They'd tried to pretend nothing was amiss, but Cindy could feel the tension between them. Was Julia in any way responsible for that tension? She found herself remembering how often she and Tom had put on similar fronts, smiling pleasantly for the children before retreating to their bedroom to unleash angry words between tightly gritted teeth, their hostility all the more intense for being so zealously suppressed. Cindy reached for the phone, punched in Tom's office number, smiling tightly as she waited for his secretary to answer.

"Thomas Carver's office," the secretary chirped in her little-girl voice, although the woman was almost Cindy's age.

"Mr. Carver, please."

"Cindy?" the secretary asked. "Is that you?"

"Irena," Cindy acknowledged, amazed her voice was still recognizable after all this time. "How are you?"

"Great. Run off my feet, as usual. Haven't heard from you in forever. How are you doing?"

"I'm doing very well, thank you," Cindy lied. "Is he in?" she asked, not sure exactly what to call her ex-husband. Couldn't very well ask to speak to "the shithead."

"He's not. He's in meetings most of the day, and I don't think he's planning on coming back to the office. Being Friday and the long weekend and everything. You know."

Cindy nodded, although she didn't know. When she and Tom had been married, one day was pretty much the same as the next. There'd been no such thing as a weekend, let alone a long one. He was always at the office. As was Irena. "Will he be checking in this morning?"

"I'm sure he will."

"Could you please tell him to call me as soon as possible? It's very important."

"Is it anything I can help you with?" Irena asked.

"I don't think so." Cindy pictured the attractive, middle-aged woman leaning forward in her chair, crossing one dimpled knee over the other, and tucking her short blond hair behind her right ear. She'd known about Irena's long-standing affair with her husband almost from its inception. It wove in and around his other affairs like threads in a large tapestry. Cindy wondered if it was still going on, or whether it had ended with the Cookie's arrival. That's the way the cookie crumbles, she found herself thinking as she hung up the phone.

It rang immediately.

"Julia?" Cindy felt her heart pounding against her chest, the blood rushing to her ears.

"No, it's Trish. Just calling to see how last night went."

"Last night?"

"Your date with Neil Macfarlane?"

"My date with Neil," Cindy repeated, trying to calm herself down.

"It didn't go well?"

"No, it went great."

"Details," Trish pressed with a girlish giggle. "I need details. Tell me everything."

"Trish, can I call you later?" Cindy implored. "I'm expecting an important call."

"Everything all right?"

"Everything's fine."

There was a brief pause. "Okay. Call me later."

Cindy replaced the receiver, glared at the phone. Why hadn't she told Trish about Julia? "Damn it, Julia. Call me." As if on cue, the phone rang. "Julia?"

"No. Me," her sister said.

Cindy felt her shoulders slump toward the floor. "Leigh, can I call you back later?"

"Are you kidding? Your line's been busy all morning. I'm not waiting around for you to fit me into your busy schedule."

"It's just that I'm expecting Julia to call. . . ."

"Yeah, and when she does, would you tell her that I rescheduled her fitting for next Wednesday at two o'clock, and that if she doesn't show up then, there's no way Marcel can have her dress ready on time, which would mean she won't be in the wedding party."

"I'll tell her." What was the point in saying anything else?

"Tell her Bianca's counting on her," Leigh said instead of good-bye.

As soon as Cindy hung up, the phone rang yet again. "Hello? Julia?"

"It's Meg. How'd your date go last night?"

Cindy felt her knees go weak. She grabbed onto the side of a chair for support. "It was fine."

"Just fine?"

"Great. It was great."

"Was he as cute as Trish claimed?"

"He's very cute," Cindy said.

"Are you okay? You don't sound like yourself."

"Actually, I'm not feeling so hot."

"Oh no. You can't get sick now. The festival starts next week."

"I'm sure I'll be fine."

"Well, we're not taking any chances. Don't come in this afternoon. I can manage the store by myself."

"Would you mind terribly?"

"Of course not. Just feel better."

Cindy hung up the phone, wondering why she hadn't told her two closest friends that Julia hadn't come home last night, that she hadn't seen or heard from her since yesterday morning? She'd been desperate to tell them, but something had held her back. What? Embarrassment? Shame? Fear? Fear of what exactly? That if she spoke the words out loud, they might come true, and Julia might be lost forever?

She thought of Lindsey, Julia's *latest, greatest, best friend ever.*

Who was she anyway? Unlike both Cindy and Heather, Julia was always forming attachments that were as short-lived as they were intense. Men and women flitted around the circumference of Julia's life, drifting in and out, occasionally penetrating the inner circle, but more likely succumbing to the force of gravity and falling, unheralded, off the ever-rolling curve. Some emerged unscathed, grateful for the ride, however brief. Some left resentful and angry, nursing ugly wounds that refused to heal.

Why hadn't she kept a closer vigil? What kind of mother was she?

Cindy crossed to the counter on the other side of the room, holding her hands beneath her arms to keep them from shaking. Luckily, there was still some coffee in the coffeemaker, and she poured herself a cup. It tasted bitter, but she drank it anyway, repeatedly glancing back at the phone, silently begging Julia to call, assure her she was alive and well. "This is silly. You're making yourself nuts," Cindy said out loud. "Just calm down. Breathe deeply. Repeat after me: there is nothing to worry about, there is nothing to worry about."

The phone rang.

Cindy lunged at it as if she'd been shot from a cannon. "Hello? Julia?"

"Neil Macfarlane," the voice announced. "Cindy, is that you?"

Cindy swallowed the threat of tears. "Yes. Neil. Hello."

"Is this a bad time?"

"My daughter didn't come home last night," she heard herself whimper. "I'm so scared."

"I'll be right over," he said.

EIGHT

Has she ever done anything like this before?"

"You mean, stayed out all night?"

Neil nodded. He was sitting beside Cindy on one of two tan leather sofas in her living room. Behind them a wall of windows overlooked the spacious backyard. Facing them were three paintings of pears in varying degrees of ripeness. Cindy couldn't remember the name of the artist who'd painted these pictures. Tom had bought them without asking either her opinion or approval, *I make the money; I make the decisions,* being pretty much the theme of their marriage. Along with the never-ending parade of other women, Cindy thought, smiling sadly at the good-looking man perched on the opposite end of the couch and wondering if he'd ever cheated on his wife. She ran her hand across the sofa's buttery surface. Fine Italian leather. Guaranteed to last a lifetime. Unlike her marriage, she thought. The sofas had also been Tom's decision, as was the checkered print of the two wing chairs sitting in front of the black marble fireplace. Why had she never bothered to change anything after he left? Had she been subconsciously waiting for him to return? She shook her head, trying to excise her former husband from her brain.

"Cindy?" Neil was asking, leaning forward, extending his hands toward hers. "Are you all right? You have this very strange look on your face."

"Yes, she's stayed out all night before," Cindy said, answering his question, wondering how long ago he'd asked it. "But she always calls. She's never not called." Except once just after she moved back home, Cindy recalled, when she was making a point about being an adult and no longer answerable to her mother. Her *father,* she'd argued pointedly, had never placed any such restrictions on her. Her *mother,* Cindy had countered, needed to be assured of her safety. It was a matter of consideration, not constraint. In reply, Julia had rolled her eyes and flounced out of the room, but she'd never stayed out all night again without first phoning home.

Except one other time when she forgot, Cindy remembered, but then she'd called first thing the next morning and apologized profusely.

"Shouldn't you be at work?" she asked Neil, trying to prevent another example from springing to mind.

"I take Fridays off in the summer."

Cindy vaguely recalled him having told her that last night. "Look, you don't have to stay. I mean, it was very thoughtful of you to come over and everything. I really appreciate it, but I'm sure you have plans for the long weekend. . . ."

"I have no plans."

". . . and Julia should be home any minute now," Cindy continued, ignoring the implications of his remark, "at which point I'm going to strangle her, and everything will be back to normal." She tried to laugh, cried out instead. "Oh God, what if something terrible has happened to her?"

"Nothing terrible has happened to her."

Cindy stared at Neil imploringly. "You promise?"

"I promise," he said simply.

Amazingly, Cindy felt better. "Thank you."

Neil reached over, took her hands in his.

There was a sudden avalanche of footsteps on the stairs, and Heather bounded into view. "I heard the door. Is Julia home?"

Cindy quickly extricated her hands from Neil's, returned them primly to her lap.

"Who are you?"

"Heather, this is Neil Macfarlane."

"The accountant." Heather advanced warily, quick eyes absorbing Neil's black jeans and denim shirt.

"Neil, this is my younger daughter, Heather."

Neil stood up, shook Heather's hand. "Nice to meet you, Heather."

Heather nodded. "I thought maybe Julia was back."

"No," Cindy said.

Heather swayed from one foot to the other. "Duncan and I were just going to head down to Queen Street. Unless you need me for anything."

"No, honey. I'm fine."

"You're sure? 'Cause I can stay if you want."

"No, sweetheart. You go. I'll be fine."

"You'll call me as soon as Julia gets home?"

Cindy nodded, looked anxiously toward the front door.

"You know my cell number?"

"Of course." Cindy pictured a series of numbers, realized they were Julia's. "Maybe you'd better write it down."

Heather walked into the kitchen. "I'm leaving it by the phone," she called back as Duncan came barreling down the stairs.

"Julia home?" he asked.

"Not yet."

He stared blankly at Neil, crossed one arm protectively over the other. "Are you a cop?"

Cindy blanched. Why would he ask that?

"He's an accountant," Heather said, reentering the room. "We should go." She guided Duncan toward the front door. "Remember to call me when Julia gets home."

Cindy nodded, watching them leave. "Do you think I should call the police?"

"If you're worried, yes," Neil said.

"It's only been twenty-four hours."

"That's long enough."

She thought of Tom. Probably she should wait for him to return her call, discuss the matter with him before she did anything rash. "I should probably wait a little longer."

"Have you checked with the place where Julia had her audition, to make sure she showed up?"

"I don't know who to contact," Cindy admitted. "I mean, I know the audition was for Michael Kinsolving, but he's probably just renting some space, and I don't know the address or the phone number." I don't know anything, she wailed silently. What kind of mother am I, who doesn't know anything? "Tom will know," she said. "My ex-husband. Julia's father. He arranged the audition. He'll know." All the more reason to wait until she spoke to him before calling the police, she acknowledged to herself.

Neil walked to the fireplace, lifted a Plexiglas frame from the mantel. "Is this Julia?"

Cindy stared at the picture of Julia that had been taken several days after her eighteenth birthday. She was smiling, showing a mouthful of perfect, professionally straightened and whitened teeth, elegant shoulders thrust proudly back in her new cream-colored Gucci leather jacket, a present from her father. Diamond studs sparkled from each ear, another present from Daddy. The night this picture was taken, Cindy had presented her daughter with a delicate necklace with her name spelled out in gold. Less than a month later, Julia had broken it while trying to pull a turtleneck sweater over her head. *I forgot I had it on,* she'd announced nonchalantly, returning the necklace to her mother to be fixed. Cindy dutifully had the necklace repaired, only to have Julia lose it a few weeks later. "That's an old picture," Cindy said now, taking the photograph from Neil's hands and returning it to the mantel, one finger lingering, caressing her daughter's cheek through the small square of glass.

"She's a very beautiful girl."

"Yes, she is."

"Like her mother."

The phone rang. Cindy raced to the kitchen, tripping on the large sisal rug in the front hall, banging her hip against the side of the kitchen door. "Damn it," she swore, lifting the phone to her ear. "Hello?"

"Well, damn it yourself," her mother replied. "What's the matter, darling? Forgot to put on your makeup?"

Cindy raised a hand to her bare cheek, realized she had indeed forgotten to put on any makeup. Still Neil had said she was beautiful, she thought gratefully, shaking her head as he approached, signaling the caller wasn't Julia. "I'm fine, Mom. Just a little busy at the moment. Can I call you back?"

"You don't have to bother. I'm just checking in. Everything all right? Your sister said you sounded pissy, and I'm afraid I have to agree with her."

Cindy closed her eyes, ran her free hand through her hair. "Everything's fine, Mom. I'll call you later. Okay?"

"Fine, darling. Take care."

"My mother," Cindy said, hanging up the phone and immediately checking her voice-mail to make sure no one else had called. "My sister told her I sounded pissy when she called earlier."

"I'm sure she meant pithy," Neil offered.

Cindy laughed. "Thanks for coming over. I really appreciate it."

"I just wish there was something more I could do."

Something clicked in Cindy's mind. "You can take me to see Sean Banack," she announced suddenly.

"Who?"

"I'll explain on the way." Cindy grabbed a piece of paper and scribbled a note for Julia, leaving it in the middle of the kitchen table, in case her daughter should return while she was gone. On the way out the door, she called Julia's cell phone again and left another message. There'd been something in Sean's voice when she'd talked to him earlier,

Cindy thought, replaying their conversation in her mind, word for word. Something more than cigarettes and alcohol. Something more than fatigue and impatience and hurt feelings.

Anger, she realized.

He'd sounded pissy.

"Is Sean here?"

"He isn't," the young man said, standing in the doorway, blocking Cindy's entrance to the small, second-floor apartment that was situated over an old variety store on the south side of Dupont Street near Christie. The man was tall and black, with an athletic build and a shiny, bald head. A silver loop dangled from his left ear. A set of earphones wrapped around his neck, like a noose. He was wearing a sleeveless white T-shirt and black sweatpants, and his left hand clutched a large plastic bottle of Evian.

"You must be Paul," Cindy said, pulling the name of Sean's roommate from the recesses of her subconscious. She extended her hand, gently pushing her way inside the stuffy, non-airconditioned apartment, Neil following right behind.

The young man smiled warily. "And you are?"

"This is Neil Macfarlane, and I'm Cindy Carver. Julia's mother."

The expression on the young man's face altered ever so slightly. "Nice to meet you, Mrs. Carver, Mr. Macfarlane. Excuse the mess." He looked sheepishly toward the cluttered L of the living-dining room behind him.

Cindy's eyes followed his. Books and papers covered the light hardwood floor and brown corduroy sofa in the middle of the room. A deeply scratched wooden door balancing on four short stacks of red bricks served as a coffee table. Several old copies of the *Toronto Star* lay stretched across the small dining room table, like a linen tablecloth. HUSBAND PHONED WIFE AFTER BEHEADING HER screamed an inside headline. MAN STALKED VICTIM FOR THREE DAYS BEFORE FATAL ATTACK announced another.

"Sean's doing research on aberrant behavior," Paul explained, following her eyes. "For a script he's writing."

Cindy nodded, remembering Julia had once boasted that Sean was writing a script especially for her. As far as Cindy knew, Sean had yet to find a producer for any of his efforts. He supported himself by bartending at Fluid, a popular downtown club. "Has Julia been around lately?" she asked, straining to sound casual.

"Haven't seen her since . . ." There was an uncomfortable pause. "You should probably talk to Sean."

"Do you have any idea when he's coming back?"

"No. I wasn't here when he went out."

"Do you mind if we wait?" Cindy immediately plopped herself down on the sofa, moving a well-thumbed copy of a paperback book to the cushion beside her. The book was called *Mortal Prey*.

Paul hesitated. "The thing is . . . I have to be somewhere by noon, and I was just gonna hop in the shower. . . ."

"Oh, you go right ahead," Cindy instructed. "We'll be fine."

"Sean could be a while."

"If he's not back by the time you're ready to leave, we'll go."

"All right. I guess it's all right," the young man muttered under his breath, perhaps sensing Cindy's determination, and not wanting to make a scene. "I won't be long."

"Take your time."

As soon as Cindy heard the shower running, she was on her feet.

"What are you doing?" Neil asked. "Where are you going?"

The second question was by far the easier of the two to answer. "To Sean's room," she said, trying to decide which of the two rooms at the back of the apartment was his, opening the first door she came to, grateful when she saw a row of high school football trophies bearing Sean's name lined up in front of the open window.

Posters from popular movies covered the walls: *Spider-Man; Invasion of the Body Snatchers; From Hell; The Texas Chainsaw Massacre.* Cindy winced at the image of a horrifying, leather-faced figure brandishing a chainsaw in front of him like a giant phallus, a helpless young woman secured to the wall behind him. She remembered that movie, hated herself now for enjoying it. What was the matter with her that she liked such things?

"I don't think this is such a good idea," Neil said, his voice a strained whisper as he followed her inside the tiny bedroom.

"Probably not," Cindy admitted, looking from the unmade bed to the water-stained desk on the opposite wall. An empty picture frame sat to one side of a bright blue iMac in the middle of the desk; a neat stack of blank paper was piled on the other.

"What is it you're looking for?"

"I don't know." Cindy took a step back, her ankle brushing up against the wastepaper basket on the floor. Her attention was immediately captured by the torn and crumpled remains of an eight-by-ten glossy. She bent down and scooped the battered picture of her daughter into her shaking hands. "It's Julia's most recent head shot. She just had it taken a few weeks ago." Cindy tried vainly to iron out the creases of the black-and-white photograph, piece together the smile on her daughter's face. Obviously Sean had torn it from its frame in a fit of fury. Was it possible he'd attacked her daughter in a similar rage?

"Maybe you should just leave it," Neil advised, removing the picture from her trembling hands.

"What else is in here?" Cindy asked, ignoring Neil's warning, turning the wastepaper basket upside down, and watching as scrap pieces of paper, used tissues, pencil shavings, and a browning apple core tumbled toward the floor. "Garbage, garbage, garbage," she muttered, her fingers loosening their grip on the white plastic container, allowing it to slip from her hand. She began pulling open the desk drawers, poking around inside them. There was nothing of consequence in the first drawer, and she was just about to close the second when her fingers located something at the very back. An envelope, she realized, pulling it out, and opening it, a small gasp escaping her lips.

"What is it?"

Cindy's mouth opened, but no words emerged, as her fingers flipped through a succession of small color photographs, all of Julia, all in various stages of undress: Julia in a see-through lavender bra and thong set; Julia wearing only the bottom half of a black string bikini, her hands playfully covering obviously bare breasts; Julia in profile, the curve of one naked breast visible beneath the crook of her elbow, the top of her bare bottom rounding out of the frame; Julia wrapped provocatively in a bedsheet; Julia wearing high heels and a man's unbuttoned shirt and crooked tie.

"Why would she do this?" Cindy wondered out loud, showing the pictures to Neil before tucking them into the pocket of her khaki cotton pants. What was the matter with Julia? Had she no common sense whatsoever?

Cindy rifled through a few more items, and was about to close the drawer when her eyes fell across a sheet of densely typed paper.

The Dead Girl, she read.

By Sean Banack.

Cindy pulled the piece of paper from the drawer and carried it over to the bed, where she sank down, her lips moving silently across the page as she read.

The Dead Girl
by Sean Banack

Chapter One

She stares up at him defiantly, despite the fact her hands and feet are bound behind her naked body and she knows beyond any shadow of a doubt that he is going to kill her. He should have taped her eyes shut as well as her mouth, he thinks; then he wouldn't have to see the look of contempt he knows so well. But he wants her to see him. He wants her to know what's coming, to see the knives and other medieval instruments of torture spread out across the floor, and understand what hell he has prepared for her. He lifts the smallest, yet sharpest of the knives into his hands, cradles it delicately between his fingers, fingers she claims are hopelessly inept. Fairy fingers, she calls them to his face. A faggot's hands.

He draws a fine line down the taut flesh of her inner arm. Her eyes widen as she watches a thin red streak wind its way across the whiteness of her skin. Slowly he lifts a second knife into the air in a graceful arc, then plunges it into her side, careful to keep the blade a safe distance from her vital organs, making sure the thrust isn't hard enough to kill her, because what would be the fun in that? Over so soon, so quick, before he's had a chance to really enjoy himself, before she's had a chance to fully suffer for her sins. And she must suffer. As he has suffered for so long.

What are you doing? Let go of me, she'd yelled when he pulled up beside her, then bundled her into the trunk of his car. She, this spoiled child of privilege, who claimed nosebleeds anywhere north of Highway 401, is about to bleed to death in an abandoned shed just south of the King Sideroad, in the middle of bloody nowhere. Serves you right, bitch, he says, slicing at her legs before throwing her on her back, pushing the largest of the knives between her thighs.

Green eyes widen in alarm as the knife slides higher, cuts deeper. Not laughing now, are you, bitch? Where's all that defiance now? With his free hand he grabs another knife, slashes at her breasts.

> Her blood is everywhere: on her, on him, on the floor, on his clothes, in his eyes, beneath his fingernails. His faggot fingernails, he thinks, rejoicing as he plunges the knife deep inside her, then savagely rips the duct tape away from her mouth so that he can hear her final screams.

"Oh, dear God," Cindy cried, rocking back and forth.

Neil extricated the paper from Cindy's hands. "What is it?"

"No, please no."

It was then she heard the noise from somewhere beside them. "What's going on in here?" Paul asked from the doorway. "Mrs. Carver? What are you doing in here?"

Cindy scrambled to her feet, lunged at the startled young man, naked except for the white towel wrapped around his waist. "Where's my daughter? What have you done with her?"

Paul took a step back, clutching the towel at his hips. "I don't know. Honestly, I have no idea where she is."

"You're lying."

"I really think you should leave."

"I'm not going anywhere until I speak to Sean."

"I already told you I don't know when he'll be back."

"Is he with Julia?"

"No way. Julia ripped his guts out, man. Look, I'm gonna have to call the police if you don't clear out of here right now."

Neil looked up from the pages he was reading and yanked the phone from the small table beside Sean's bed, thrust it toward Paul. "Call them," he said.

NINE

A dark green Jaguar was parked in Cindy's driveway when she got home.

"Oh no," Cindy said, panicking as Neil pulled his black Nissan alongside it. "It's my ex-husband. Why is he here?"

"Maybe he brought Julia home," Neil offered hopefully.

Cindy bolted from the car and was halfway up the steps when her front door opened. Tom stood in the doorway to her house, one well-toned arm crossed over the other, a look of bemused impatience creasing his tanned face. He was dressed head to toe in beige linen, a color that complemented the recent blond streaks in his still shockingly full head of hair. His feet were bare inside brown tasseled loafers. As smugly handsome at forty-five as he'd been at twenty-five, Cindy thought, disappointed that middle-age hadn't damaged him in any obvious way, that he hadn't grown fat or bald, that his wrinkles actually added to his appeal. Elvis was sitting at his feet, as if he were used to having Tom there, Cindy groused silently, when behind him, something moved. A young woman, Cindy realized, relief pulsing through her veins. "Julia!" she cried out.

A shape emerged from the inside shadows, took its place in the doorway, snaked a proprietary hand through Tom Carver's arm. "Hello, Cindy," the Cookie said, pushing the dog away with her feet. She was wearing a tight cream-colored jersey over tight cream-colored pants, which at first glance, made her seem nude. A most disconcerting thought, Cindy decided, thinking of the pictures of Julia in her pocket, and watching the Cookie lean her head on Tom's shoulder, as if to say, "He's mine now."

I get the point, Cindy said to herself. You don't have to work so hard. Aloud she said, "Is Julia inside?"

Tom shook his head.

"We don't know where Julia is," the Cookie informed her. Then, noticing Neil standing in the driveway, "Who's this?"

Cindy spun around as Neil came up behind her. "This is Neil Macfarlane. My accountant," she added, stumbling over the lie. "Neil, this is my ex-husband, Tom Carver, and the . . . Fiona, his current wife." She stressed the word current, as if the condition were temporary.

"I didn't realize accountants made house calls," Tom said slyly, extending his hand.

"Special circumstances," Neil said genially. Then quietly, to Cindy, "Would you like me to leave?"

"No. Please stay. The police might want to ask you some more questions."

"The police? What's going on here?" Tom stood back to let them enter.

As if the house is still his, Cindy thought, feeling herself bristle as she sidestepped around her ex-husband's young wife, Elvis licking at her legs. "Julia didn't come home last night," she reminded him, looking around for Heather. "Heather?"

"Heather's not here," the Cookie said.

"What do you mean, she's not here? Who let you in?"

Tom smiled sheepishly. "I have a key," he said, having the grace to look at least moderately embarrassed. "Look, let's not make this into a big deal, okay?"

"What do you mean, you have a key?"

"I said, let's not make this . . ."

"And I said, what do you mean, you have a key? I changed the locks seven years ago. What do you mean, you have a key?"

"Julia thought I should have one."

"Julia gave you a key to the house?"

"The key *and* the alarm code," the Cookie said, possible payback for Cindy's earlier use of the word *current*. "She thought her father and me should have a key in case she ever needed something or . . ."

"Her father and *I,*" Cindy corrected impatiently. "And with all due respect, this really isn't any of your business."

"It certainly *is* my business."

"Okay, okay," Tom said, arms outstretched, as if trying to placate both women. He glanced over at Neil. Women, his eyes said, clearly enjoying the fuss, knowing it was about him.

"I can't believe you came into my house when I wasn't here."

"Here's your key." Tom dropped the key into Cindy's outstretched hand.

"I don't understand what you're so worked up about," the Cookie said. "We're the ones who should be upset. We were halfway to the cottage when Irena called, and we had to come racing back."

"I thought you were in a meeting," Cindy said to her ex-husband, pointedly ignoring his young wife. "Secretary's still lying for you, I see."

Tom shrugged.

(Scenes from a marriage: Cindy cleans up the kitchen after getting both children ready for bed. She wraps Tom's dinner in plastic wrap and puts it in the fridge for him to eat when he gets home, then recorks the bottle of wine. "When's Daddy coming home?" Julia calls out from the top of the stairs.

"Soon," Cindy assures her.

"He promised to read me a story," Julia says an hour later, sitting up in her bed, stubbornly refusing to fall asleep.

"I'll read to you," Cindy offers, but Julia turns from her, covering her face with her pillow, as if she senses her father's absence is somehow her mother's fault.

Cindy retreats to her own room, thumbs through the latest issue of *Vanity Fair,* and watches TV until her eyes are so heavy with fatigue she can no longer focus. It's ten o'clock. She reaches for the phone, her arm stopping in midair, falling to her side. Irena has already told her Tom is stuck in meetings and can't be disturbed. At eleven o'clock, Cindy turns off the lights and gives in to sleep. At twenty minutes after midnight, she awakens to the sound of a key turning in the front door, and hears her husband's guilty footsteps on the stairs.

"Daddy!" she hears Julia cry with sleepy delight as he visits her room to kiss her good night.

Cindy feigns sleep as he creeps into their room and takes off his clothes, crawling in beside her without washing up. Even though he has undoubtedly showered before coming home, she can smell another woman on his skin. She moves to the far side of the bed, hugs her knees to her chest till morning.)

"Earth to Cindy." A voice snapped at the silence.

Cindy turned toward the grating sound.

"My husband asked you a question," the Cookie said.

"You called the police?" Tom asked a second time.

"Yes, I did. They should be here any minute."

"Julia's going to be so pissed," the Cookie said.

"I don't understand why you felt it necessary to involve the police."

"What exactly is it you don't understand?" Cindy asked her ex-husband, checking her watch. "It's almost one o'clock. Nobody has seen or heard from Julia since yesterday morning."

"She's going to be so pissed."

"Do you know where she is?"

"No," Tom admitted. "But . . ."

"But what?"

"You don't think it's a little early to be sending in the cavalry?"

"Did you know she broke up with her boyfriend?"

"Yes, I knew that. So what? Kid's a loser."

"A very angry loser," Cindy said. "So angry he wrote a really scary story about a man who kidnaps his former girlfriend and tortures her to death."

Tom waved a dismissive hand in front of his face, as if swatting away a fly. "I think you're overreacting."

"Really? Well, the police don't think so. They've asked me for a recent photograph of Julia." She patted the pocket of her khaki pants, tried not to see the pictures inside it.

"I still don't understand when exactly you spoke to the police."

"I'll explain," Neil said, motioning Tom and Fiona toward the living room. "You go find the photograph," he directed Cindy.

"And what exactly is your part in all this?" Tom was asking Neil as Cindy left the room, running up the stairs, Elvis at her heels.

Cindy stood motionless outside Julia's bedroom for several seconds, as if waiting to be invited in, Elvis's tail slapping happily against the door. Her daughter wouldn't like her snooping around in her room any more than Cindy had appreciated seeing Tom on the wrong side of her front door. How dare he come inside the house, make himself at home, bring that silly twit he married into her space, rub her nose in his new life—what was the matter with him? Did he think that just because he'd once lived here that gave him some kind of residual rights?

I make the money. I make the decisions.

Cindy took a deep breath, trying to calm herself down. What exactly was she so angry about? The fact that Tom seemed so unconcerned about their daughter's whereabouts, or the fact that he still looked so damned good, that despite the years and everything that had happened, he still had the power to make her go weak in the knees? "It's not fair," she muttered, turning around in helpless circles, trying to think where Julia might have stored her most recent head shots. Probably in the same place she keeps her address book, she thought, shaking her head, aware this was the second time today she'd invaded her daughter's privacy.

"She's going to be so pissed," she told the dog in the Cookie's voice, as once more, she rifled through the drawers of Julia's desk. Getting pretty good at this, Cindy thought, counting three boxes of unused stationery, at least thirty black pens, several scraps of paper with nameless phone numbers scribbled across them, four unused key chains, two empty picture frames, a leopard-print chiffon scarf, a dozen matchbooks, and three unopened packages of Juicy Fruit gum.

No head shots.

She opened the closet, slapped at the size-two clothing dangling precariously from the wooden hangers, again rummaging through the stacks of sweaters piled carelessly on the built-in shelves, and straightening the shoes lined up across the closet floor.

No head shots.

She ransacked each drawer of her daughter's dresser, suppressing a shudder when she came across Julia's collection of sexy push-up bras and thong panties. Doesn't she have any normal underwear? Cindy wondered, recalling the days of her own youth, how she hadn't even owned a bra when she married Tom. Her sister, Leigh, who was several cup sizes larger than Cindy, used to tease her about her lack of endowment. "My breasts might be small," Cindy had countered, "but they're perfect."

Now they're just small, she thought dryly, closing the last of Julia's dresser drawers, and looking out the front window in time to see a police cruiser pull up in front of the house.

The police had arrived at Sean's apartment within twenty minutes of his roommate's call. They'd listened with interest as Paul apprised them of the situation, told them that he'd asked Cindy and Neil to leave repeatedly, and that they'd refused. Cindy, in turn, patiently explained that her daughter had recently broken up with her boyfriend, Paul's roommate, and that she was now missing. She and Neil had come by to talk to Sean, only to find Julia's torn picture in his wastepaper basket and this alarmingly odious little story, she said, her voice cracking, her patience evaporating, as she thrust the offending piece of paper at the two police officers, and suggested they start combing the area immediately south of the King Sideroad for any abandoned shacks. "Hey, hey, hold on a moment," they'd said, trying to slow her down.

"Slow down," Cindy repeated now, falling to her knees and peeking under her daughter's bed, the dog's nose wet against her cheek. She saw an old electric keyboard and a new acoustic guitar, both covered in dust, which wasn't surprising since Cindy couldn't remember the last time she'd heard Julia play either. She was about to give up in defeat, go downstairs and tell the police that Julia must have taken the head shots with her when she went to her audition, when she saw the large manila envelope peeking out from under the shaft of the guitar. "Perfectly logical place to keep them," Cindy said, stretching to retrieve the envelope and opening it as the front doorbell rang. Elvis barked loudly in her ear, then ran from the room. "I'll be right down," she called over the dog's repeated yapping.

"Hello, Officers. Please come in," she heard Tom say, as if this were still his house.

Cindy pulled a handful of photographs out of the envelope, smiled sadly at her daughter's beautiful face. She looks so radiant, Cindy thought, admiring the determination in her daughter's eyes. As if nothing can stop her, as if nothing can get in her way. "Julia gives good attitude," Tom had once remarked, and as much as Cindy hated to admit her ex-husband was right about anything, he was right about that. Julia stared back at her mother from the black-and-white glossy, her head tilted provocatively to one side, straight blond hair cascading toward her right shoulder, her skin flawless, with just the hint of a smile on her enviably full lips.

And yet Cindy knew that beneath all the bravado lay a bundle of insecurities, wriggling like snakes inside a canvas bag. Unlike Heather, who had the confidence but not the attitude, Julia had the attitude without the confidence. It was an interesting contradiction, Cindy thought, removing several of the head shots from the top of the pile to give to the police. She thought of the pictures in her pocket. Can't very well show these to the police, she thought, removing them from her pocket and glancing through them.

"Cindy?" Tom appeared in the doorway, as if he'd been lurking there all along, just waiting for the right moment to pop into view. Clearly a man who understood the value of good timing, who knew how to make an entrance. "What's taking you so long? The police are waiting."

Cindy jumped to her feet, only to stand frozen to the spot, unable to move.

"What's going on?" Tom said. "What are you doing?" He walked to her side and removed the pictures from Cindy's hand.

"I found them in Sean's apartment."

"She looks pretty good," Tom remarked casually.

Cindy shook her head in dismay. "You're unbelievable."

"Come on, Cindy. Lighten up. You can't see anything."

"You can see she's naked."

"You can also see she's enjoying herself thoroughly."

"Which makes it all right?"

"Which makes it none of our business."

"She's your daughter!"

"She's a consenting adult."

"Do you think I should show these pictures to the police?"

"Only if you want to cloud the issue," he warned her.

"What do you mean?"

"I mean the police are easily distracted. One look at these and they aren't going to take your concerns too seriously. I thought the objective here was to find our daughter."

"So suddenly I'm not overreacting?"

"Of course you're overreacting. It's part of your charm."

"Don't patronize me."

"Don't punish me for something that happened seven years ago."

Cindy's eyes widened in disbelief. "You think this is about you? About our divorce?"

"Isn't it?"

"It's about our daughter."

"Our daughter who's missing," he reminded her, as if she didn't know.

The air rushed from Cindy's lungs. "You don't think something's happened to her, do you?"

"No, I don't," Tom said evenly. "I think she just decided to get away for a few days."

"Without telling anyone?"

Tom shrugged. "It wouldn't be the first time."

"She's done this before?"

"Once," he admitted. "She was upset about my getting married, so she took off, came back a couple of days later, apologized, said she'd just needed some time to get her head clear."

"And you didn't tell me?"

"I didn't want to worry you unnecessarily." He reached over, touched her arm. "I know our daughter. She likes to stir things up a little. Like her mother," he added with a smile.

Cindy looked toward the window. "You're so full of shit," she said.

"Maybe," he conceded. "But I still think we should wait until Tuesday before dispatching the troops, or we're going to be awfully embarrassed when Julia comes waltzing home."

"I don't give a rat's ass about being embarrassed."

"Really, Cindy, your language. . . ."

"Fuck you," Cindy told her ex-husband, watched him wince.

"Well, I guess there's a certain comfort in knowing that some things never change." He shook his head. "Look. Your *accountant* suggested I call Michael Kinsolving to see if Julia showed up for her audition. Who knows? Maybe she mentioned something to him about her plans for the weekend."

"Do you think that's possible?"

"Anything's possible. Come on, the police are waiting." They were halfway down the stairs before Cindy realized that Tom hadn't returned the photographs of Julia. She was about to ask for them back when one of the police officers appeared at the bottom of the stairs, staring toward them expectantly.

Cindy watched her former husband smile as he slipped the provocative photographs of Julia into the pocket of his linen pants.

TEN

Maybe she eloped," the Cookie was suggesting to the second police officer as Cindy and her ex-husband re-entered the living room beside Detective Andy Bartolli. Detective Bartolli was the elder of the two men, and the stockier; his partner, Detective Tyrone Gill, was younger by a decade and taller by several inches. Both had necks the size of tree stumps.

"What did you say?" Cindy felt the sudden constraint of Tom's hand on her arm, as if he feared she was about to throw herself at his wife's head.

The Cookie tossed long red hair from one shoulder to the other. "Maybe she eloped," she repeated, as if she really thought Cindy might not have heard her the first time.

Cindy stole a glance at the two detectives, sensing their interest already starting to wane.

There's no urgency here, the looks they exchanged suggested.

"What makes you think she might have eloped?" Detective Bartolli asked.

"Julia would never elope," Cindy interjected.

"Oh, please," the Cookie said. "How many times have I had to listen to that stupid story about you and Tom running off to Niagara Falls without telling anyone? She thought it was so romantic."

She did? Cindy fought back tears. Julia had never said anything of the sort to her.

The police waited as Tom called Michael Kinsolving, whose assistant said the famous director had left town until Tuesday and couldn't be reached, although the assistant confirmed that Julia had indeed shown up for her fifteen-minute audition promptly at eleven o'clock.

After asking several pointed questions about Julia's recent state of mind—*Has she been depressed lately? How upset was she about the breakup with her boyfriend?*—the policemen left with several copies of her head shots, promising to phone as soon as they spoke to Sean Banack. With Tom's approval, and over Cindy's objections, they decided to wait until after the long weekend before launching a more formal investigation.

"What now?" Cindy asked when they were gone.

"Try to relax," her ex-husband advised. "Call me in Muskoka if you hear anything."

"You're going to the cottage?" Cindy asked incredulously.

"I can't do anything here."

"Julia's fine," the Cookie said with a yawn. "She's a big girl. She probably just needed some time away from her mother."

"Would somebody please get this moron out of my house?" Cindy pleaded, looking from Tom to Neil.

The Cookie turned a sickly shade of beige that perfectly matched her outfit. The dog started barking. "I think it's time we left," Tom said.

"Yes. You're very good at that," Cindy agreed, only half under her breath.

The phone rang. Both Tom and Cindy strode purposefully into the kitchen, colliding in the doorway as they reached for the phone. "Hello," Cindy said, pressing the phone to her ear, her eyes warning Tom to back off.

"What's wrong?" her mother asked.

Cindy's shoulders slumped with disappointment. "What makes you think something's wrong, Mom?"

Tom rolled his eyes toward the ceiling. So that's where Julia gets it, Cindy thought.

"A mother always knows when something's wrong," her mother said, and Cindy felt her heart sink, thinking of Julia.

"We'll go," Tom whispered.

"Who's that?" her mother asked. "Was that Tom?"

"You're amazing, Mother." Cindy watched Tom usher the Cookie out the front door.

"What's he doing there? Now I know something's wrong."

"It's nothing."

"I'll be right there."

"No. Mom! Mother! Damn it!" She dropped the phone into its carriage. "Shit!"

"What's up?" Neil asked good-naturedly, coming into the kitchen.

"My mother's coming over. Sorry for the language," she said, still smarting from Tom's earlier admonition.

"What language?"

Cindy fought the urge to kiss him full on the mouth. "You should probably go."

"I'm happy to stay."

And I would dearly love you to stay, Cindy thought. "I think you've met enough of my family for one day," she said instead, walking him to the door, thinking how his body contrasted with Tom's. While both men were approximately the same height and weight, Tom had a way of overwhelming everything in his path, rather like Julia. Neil was more like Heather, an easier, more accommodating fit. "Thank you," Cindy told him, both eager and reluctant to say good-bye. Talk about bad timing. "I don't think I could have managed without you."

He smiled. "I bet you say that to all your accountants."

Cindy reached out, touched his cheek. Beside her, Elvis growled. "Got a little more than you bargained for, didn't you?"

"I'll call you later," he said, patting Elvis on the head.

She watched him back his car out of the driveway. "I won't hold my breath," she said wistfully, as his car disappeared down the street.

It was only then that Cindy became aware that she herself was being watched. She swiveled toward her neighbor's house. "Faith," she said, returning the other woman's wan smile. "I didn't see you there. How are you feeling?"

"Fine." Faith Sellick was wearing a sloppy red-and-black-checkered shirt over a pair of black capris. A red ribbon dangled from her hair. "Lots of activity at your house today."

"Yes."

"I saw the police car."

"It was nothing."

Faith nodded, stared at the street.

"Where's the baby?"

"Ryan took him to the office this morning."

"That was nice of him. It gives you a chance to relax."

"I guess."

"It's such a beautiful day," Cindy remarked when she could think of nothing else to say. "Would you like a cup of tea?" she heard herself ask, realizing she was reluctant to go back inside the house, that she was afraid to be alone. Time alone meant time to think. Time to think meant time to worry. Time to worry meant time to imagine the worst.

"That would be nice," Faith said, carefully measuring out each word. "Tea would be very nice."

"Good. Come on over."

She walks as if she's asleep, Cindy observed, her eyes following Faith Sellick as the young woman floated down her front steps and along the sidewalk. Elvis ran forward to nip at her heels.

"Hello, boy," Faith said absently.

"Come inside." Cindy stood back to let Faith enter.

"This is really very sweet of you."

"My pleasure." Cindy led Faith into the kitchen, motioned toward the four pine chairs at the rectangular pine table. Faith sank into the closest one, stared at Cindy expectantly. "Regular or herbal?" Cindy asked as Elvis spread himself across the top of Faith's feet.

Faith said nothing, and for a moment, Cindy wondered if she'd understood the question. She was about to ask it again when Faith finally answered. "Herbal," she said, her sudden smile at odds with the sadness in her eyes.

"Ginger peach or spearmint?"

"Spearmint." Faith laughed, a delicate tinkle that danced in the air like wind chimes.

Cindy filled the kettle with water, turned on the burner, turned back to Faith, thinking that the young woman looked much older than her years, closer to forty than thirty, Cindy thought, noting the dark circles rimming Faith's eyes, the sallowness of her complexion. "Did you get any sleep at all last night?"

Faith nodded. "A bit."

"It's not easy being a new mother." Cindy pictured Julia as a baby. "It's not easy being a mother, period," she added, picturing her now.

"Seems easy enough for most people."

"Don't kid yourself."

"Your girls are so beautiful. They've turned out so well."

"Thank you." Cindy crossed her fingers, said a silent prayer.

"Did you worry about them a lot when they were babies?"

"Of course."

"I worry about Kyle all the time."

"That's perfectly normal."

"I worry about everything," Faith continued as if Cindy hadn't spoken. "His safety, his health, whether he'll be happy when he grows up."

"I don't think you ever really stop worrying about those things." Again Cindy thought of Julia.

"I mean, look at what's going on in the world today. Terrorists, suicide bombers, AIDS, poverty, child abuse . . ."

"Faith," Cindy advised gently, interrupting the seamless flow of catastrophes, "you'll make yourself nuts if you worry about all those things."

"How can you not worry? All you have to do is pick up the morning paper."

"Don't pick it up."

"You have to know what's happening. You can't just bury your head in the sand."

"Why can't you?"

"Because things won't get any better that way."

"And you think worrying yourself sick is going to make things better?"

"No, but you should be aware."

"You can be aware again when Kyle starts sleeping through the night."

"It just doesn't seem right to bring a child into a world where so many bad things are happening, where there are so many evil people."

"There are good people too," Cindy said, trying to reassure them both.

"I try to be a good person."

"You *are* a good person."

Faith grimaced, as if she'd had a sudden spasm. "I'm not a very good mother."

"Why would you think that?"

"Kyle cries all the time."

"He has colic. It has nothing to do with you."

"I try to comfort him. I feed him. I hold him. I even sing to him. But he still cries."

"Julia was the same when she was a baby. The only one who could get her to stop crying was Tom."

"Tom's your ex-husband?"

"Yes."

"Was that him before? With the redhead?"

"That was him."

"Is she his new girlfriend?"

"Wife."

"I think Ryan has a girlfriend," Faith said matter-of-factly as the kettle began whistling.

"No," Cindy started, then stopped. How would she know whether or not Ryan had a girlfriend? "What makes you say that?" she asked, busying herself with making the tea.

"I can see it in his eyes."

"What do you see?"

"It's more what I don't see."

Cindy understood without asking exactly what Faith meant. She'd seen the same lack of substance in Tom's eyes before he walked out, as if he were already gone. Still she said, "He's probably just tired."

"No. It's more than that. Less," she corrected. "I don't think he loves me anymore."

"I'm sure Ryan loves you, Faith." Cindy pictured Ryan's troubled face as he sat on his front steps, Elvis's head in his lap. The subtle scent of spearmint filled the air as Cindy deposited the steaming mug of herbal tea on the table in front of Faith. "He's just worried about you, that's all."

"Worry isn't love." Faith lifted the mug to her lips, quickly laid it back down. "It's hot."

"Better give it a few minutes to cool off."

"My grandmother used to say that." Faith smiled at the memory. "'Give it a few minutes to cool off,'" she repeated in a voice not her own. "She died last year. Cancer."

"I'm sorry."

"She'd had this really hard life. Her oldest son committed suicide, you know."

"How awful."

"Yeah. My uncle Barry. He was schizophrenic. I don't really remember him. He died when I was still a kid. He hanged himself in the bathroom. My grandmother found him." Faith raised the mug to her lips a second time, breathed in the aromatic steam still rising from its surface. "Suicide kind of runs in my family."

"What?" Cindy recalled Detective Bartolli's questions about her daughter's recent state of mind. *Has she been depressed lately? How upset was she about the breakup with her boyfriend?*

"I had a great-aunt who threw herself off a tall building," Faith was saying, "and two cousins who slashed their wrists. And my mom took too many pills once, but then she called all the neighbors and told them what she'd done, so they rushed her to the hospital and she had to have her stomach pumped."

"That's terrible." Cindy gingerly sipped at her tea, not quite sure what to say next. "You would never . . ."

Julia would never . . .

"What? Oh. Oh no! No, of course not. I would never do anything like that."

"Because things are never as black as they seem," Cindy said earnestly, the cliché filling her mouth like a wad of cottonballs. "Things always get better." Unless they get worse, she added silently.

"I don't have the courage to kill myself," Faith was saying.

"You think it's a question of courage?"

Has she been depressed lately?

"I know some people consider suicide the coward's way out, but I never thought of it that way. I mean, to do something as drastic as taking your own life, I think that requires tremendous guts. More guts than I have, that's for sure."

"Good." Cindy suppressed a shudder as she settled into the chair across from Faith, vaguely recalling an article she'd read about the ripple effect of suicide, how the suicide of one family member often served to validate another's, that such action came to be seen as an acceptable alternative, a viable option for solving one's problems. She shook her head. The women in her family might be emotional, headstrong, and impulsive, but they were definitely not suicidal. And they were far too interested in having the last word to take themselves out of the argument early. "Because you have everything to live for," Cindy heard herself continue. "I mean, it's hard now. You're going through a very difficult time. You're exhausted. Your hormones are raging. But it'll get better. Trust me. A year from now, you'll feel so much better about everything."

"Do you think Ryan will leave me?"

"Ryan's not going anywhere, Faith."

"He says he wants three more children."

"What do you want?"

"I don't know."

"What about your job?"

"I'm on maternity leave till the new year. But I don't think I should go back."

"Why not? I thought you loved teaching."

"How can I possibly handle twenty-five kids when I can't take care of one?"

Cindy watched ominous clouds gather in Faith's eyes

as she sipped steadily at her tea. "Well, you don't have to make any major decisions right now."

"I guess that's right."

"You have plenty of time."

Faith's eyes filled with tears. "Ryan's so busy these days. I hardly see him anymore." She lifted her shoulders to her ears in a prolonged shrug. "When he first started working at Granger, McAllister, it was just this tiny firm. Now there are seven architects, secretaries, assistants, so many people, and they're busy all the time. He's always having to rush off somewhere. This tea is really good," she said, finishing what remained in her mug.

"Would you like some more?"

"Oh no, thank you. I should be getting home. I promised Ryan I'd try to straighten things up a bit. He says the house is a pigsty."

"Why don't you take a nap first?" Cindy suggested, hearing a car pull into the driveway. Julia! she thought, running to the door, opening it in time to see a cab backing into the street and her mother walking up the front steps as Elvis ran down to greet her.

"What's the matter?" her mother said, ignoring the dog. "And don't tell me nothing. I can see it in your face. Who's this?" Cindy followed her mother's eyes to the woman standing behind her.

"Mom, this is Faith Sellick, my neighbor. Faith, this is my mother."

"Pleased to meet you." Faith stepped outside, shielding her eyes from the sun. "Thanks again for the tea."

"You don't have to leave on my account," Cindy's mother said.

"No, I have to go. I have so much to do."

"First, you have to take a nap."

"Right." Faith ambled down the steps.

"There's something not quite right about that one," her mother remarked as soon as Faith was out of earshot.

"She's the one I was talking about yesterday. With the postpartum depression."

Her mother nodded. "So, are you going to invite me in, tell me what Tom was doing here?"

Cindy led her mother into the kitchen, motioned toward the recently vacated chair. "I think you better sit down."

ELEVEN

At exactly 2:29 A.M. Cindy bolted upright in her bed and cried, "Oh no, I forgot!" She jumped out of bed and rushed into the bathroom, Elvis jumping excitedly into the air beside her, as if this were some great new game they were playing. Almost tripping over him as she lunged toward the medicine cabinet, Cindy tried to focus on the assorted bottles of headache remedies, half-empty boxes of Band-Aids, partially squeezed tubes of ointments, abandoned spools of dental floss, and discarded brands of hair gel that met her half-closed eyes. The detritus of everyday life, she thought, reaching into the cabinet, hoping she wasn't too late. The doctor had warned her that if she didn't take her pills at the same time every day, she would die. How long ago was that? Weeks, months, years? How long had it been since she'd last remembered to take her pills? Oh no. Oh no.

"What the hell am I doing?" Cindy suddenly asked herself, coming wide awake and staring at her reflection, regarding the woman in the glass as if she were some alien being. "What is the matter with you? What pills?"

Slowly, Cindy took stock of the situation, her panic gradually subsiding, her heartbeat returning to normal. She was standing naked in her bathroom in the middle of the night searching for pills that didn't exist on the advice of a doctor who also didn't exist. Obviously she'd been having another nightmare, although she couldn't remember a single detail. "It's that damn herbal tea," she told the woman in the glass. "That stuff'll kill you."

Her reflection nodded.

Cindy watched the woman run a tired hand through her lifeless hair, her eyes filling with tears. "Would somebody please just shoot me now. Put me out of my misery."

In response, her reflection dropped her chin toward her chest, the silence buzzing around their respective heads like determined mosquitoes.

"You've got to get some sleep," Cindy muttered on her way back to bed, but even as she was climbing back under the covers, she knew sleep was lost to her, that the hours between now and seven o'clock would be spent in restless tossing and turning, that if she slept at all, it would be in fits and starts, and that she would wake up feeling even less refreshed and more tired than before. She closed her eyes, trying not to picture her daughter hog-tied and bleeding on the dirt floor of some abandoned shack in the middle of nowhere. "Please, no," she whispered into the pillow, feeling it wet against her skin. "Please let Julia be all right. Please let this whole thing be nothing but a bad dream." A terribly long, bad dream, Cindy thought, flipping onto her other side, hearing Elvis groan beside her, knowing that this nightmare was horribly real, and that if her daughter didn't come home soon, she would most assuredly die, as the imaginary doctor of her dreams had warned.

"Oh God." Cindy sat up only to flop back down. She rolled onto her other side, sat up, turned on the light, reached for the paperback novel on the nightstand beside her bed, and glared at the phone. Undoubtedly Tom and the Cookie were having no such trouble sleeping. She pictured the cottage on Lake Joseph, the large, rustic bedroom she'd once shared with Tom, the long, side window open to allow the cool Muskoka breezes entry. The image of her former husband in bed with his young wife pasted itself across the pages of her book. Cindy brushed it aside with a disdainful swipe of her hand, accidentally ripping off the top corner of the page. She read, then reread the first few paragraphs of the chapter before tossing the novel to the foot of the bed in defeat. How could she read when she couldn't concentrate? "Where are you, Julia?"

Had she really considered her parents' elopement so romantic? Was it possible she might have pulled the same stunt herself? With whom?

Just come home, Cindy prayed. Please. Come home.

When she comes home, Cindy vowed silently, I'm going to buy her those brown suede boots she was admiring in David's, the ones I told her were way too expensive.

When she comes home, I'm going to take her to her favorite sushi restaurant for dinner. And lunch. And even breakfast, if that's what she wants.

When she comes home, I won't yell or complain or get on her case about inconsequentials. I'll be more understanding of her problems, less judgmental, more patient, less critical. I'll be the perfect mother, the perfect friend. Our lives will be perfect when she comes home.

When she comes home, Cindy repeated hopefully in her head, as she'd been repeating for so much of Julia's life.

She'd already lost her daughter once. She wasn't about to lose her again.

Cindy pushed herself out of bed, slipped a pink cotton nightshirt over her head, and tiptoed down the hall to Julia's room, Elvis at her heels. She stood in the doorway, and peered toward Julia's bed.

"Is someone there?" a voice asked, cutting through the darkness like a laser.

Cindy gasped as a figure sat up in the bed, reaching for the lamp on the night table just as Cindy flipped on the overhead light. "Julia!" she cried, arms extending into the room, then dropping heavily to her sides, her feet coming to an abrupt halt, as if she'd just waded into cement.

"Sweetheart," her mother said softly, getting out of Julia's bed and walking slowly toward her. "Are you all right?"

Cindy shook her head, dislodging a steady flow of tears. "I'm sorry. I forgot you were here." Her mother had insisted on spending the night after Cindy confided that Julia was missing. "Did I wake you up?"

Her mother led her to the side of Julia's bed, sat down next to her. "Not really. I heard some kind of noise a few minutes ago. I thought it might be Julia coming home."

"That was probably me. I woke up in a sweat because I'd forgotten to take my pills."

"What pills?"

"There are no pills." Cindy raised her hands helplessly in the air. "I must be losing my mind."

Her mother laughed.

"Something funny about that?"

Norma Appleton took Cindy's hands in hers. "Only that I remember going through a very similar experience years ago, constantly waking up in the middle of the night, convinced I'd forgotten something terribly important. I think it has to do with menopause."

"Menopause? I'm not in menopause."

"Close."

"No way. I'm only forty-two."

"All right, dear."

"That's all I need to worry about right now."

"You're missing the point here, darling."

"The point being?"

"The point being that I think this is pretty common in women of a certain age."

"Mother. . . ."

"I used to call it the OFIFs."

"The what?"

"The OFIFs—'Oh, fuck—I forgot!'"

"Excuse me?"

"What—you think you're the only one who knows words like that? Close your mouth, dear. A bug will fly in."

Cindy stared at her mother in disbelief. So that's where I get it, she thought.

Here comes the mouth, Tom used to say at the start of any argument. *You and that mouth,* he used to say.

Sorry for the language, she'd apologized to Neil earlier.

What language? he'd asked.

"What are you thinking?" her mother asked now.

"What?"

"You're smiling."

"I am?" God, her mother didn't miss a thing. "Must be gas."

"She'll come home," her mother said, her eyes on the distant past, her voice heavy with experience. "You'll see. Tomorrow morning she'll come waltzing through the front door as if nothing's happened, amazed at all the fuss, angry you were worried, furious you called the police."

A flush of shame bowed Cindy's head. "I put you through hell when I ran off with Tom," she acknowledged.

"You were young and in love," her mother said generously.

"I was willful and self-absorbed."

"That too."

Cindy shook her head. "What was I thinking?"

"I don't think you were."

"I was actually angry at you for having worried?"

"You were livid. How dare I call your friends! How dare I embarrass you like that! How could I involve the police? You were gone less than forty-eight hours! You're a grown woman! A married woman, no less! What was the matter with me? Oh, you went on and on."

"Is it too late for me to apologize?"

Her mother draped a protective arm around Cindy's shoulder, hugged her to her side. "It's never too late," she whispered, kissing her daughter's wet cheek.

"You think this is payback time? God's idea of poetic justice?"

"I like to think that God has better things to do with His time."

"Do you think Julia could have eloped with some guy?"

"Do you?"

Cindy shook her head. When Julia spoke about getting married, she talked about Vera Wang dresses and a photo spread in *People* magazine. "It's not her style. Besides, she broke up with her boyfriend." She thought of Sean Banack. "You don't think she was overly upset about that, do you? I mean, upset enough to do something stupid."

"Julia hurt herself over a man?"

Her mother's question was answer enough. "Then what's happened to her? Where is she?"

"I don't know, sweetheart. I *do* know you need to get some sleep or you're not going to be in any shape to yell at her when she comes home. Come on," her mother urged, pulling down the covers on the other side of Julia's queen-size bed. "Why don't you sleep with me tonight? I could use the company."

Wordlessly, Cindy climbed into Julia's bed, burrowing in against her mother's side, her mother's arm falling across her hip, as Elvis flopped down between their feet. The lingering aroma of Julia's Angel perfume on her pillow filled Cindy's nostrils. She closed her eyes, sucked at the scent as if she were a baby at her mother's breast. When Julia comes home, Cindy recited silently, I'll buy her the biggest bottle of Angel perfume they sell. When she comes home, I'll get her a Gold Pass to the film festival, so she can attend all the galas. When she comes home, I'll hold my tongue, hold my temper, hold my baby in my arms again.

When she comes home, Cindy repeated over and over again in her mind, until she fell asleep.

When she comes home. When she comes home.

———

"Mom? Grandma?" Heather asked from somewhere above their heads. "What's going on?"

Cindy opened her eyes, saw Heather looming above her, the pull of gravity distorting her sweet features. Cindy pushed herself up against the headboard, rubbing her eyes as Elvis bounded over to lick her face.

"My heavens, what's that?" Cindy's mother asked, as the dog poked his nose under the covers. "Get out of here," she groused as Elvis's long tongue flicked toward her lips. "He stuck his tongue in my mouth! Get away from me, you silly dog."

Heather shooed Elvis off the bed. "I didn't know you were here, Grandma."

"I was in bed before you came home."

"I thought Julia was back."

Cindy felt her heart cramp. "No. I take it you haven't heard anything. . . ."

Heather shook her head. "Why are you sleeping in here?"

Cindy and her mother shrugged in unison. "What time is it?" Cindy asked.

"Almost nine o'clock."

"Nine o'clock?" When was the last time she'd slept till nine o'clock, even on a weekend?

"What's the matter?" Heather asked. "Do you have to be somewhere?"

"No," both women answered.

"But I have a lot to do," Cindy added quickly.

"Like what?"

Cindy brushed the question aside with an impatient wave of her hand. "Is Duncan still asleep? I need to talk to him."

"He's not here."

"Where is he?"

Heather shrugged. "Not here."

"Heather. . . ."

"Look, Mom, I'm real sorry, but I don't know where Duncan is every minute of the day."

"*Really* sorry," Cindy and her mother corrected together.

"What?"

"It's an adverb," Heather's grandmother explained.

Heather nodded, backing slowly out of the room. "I think I'll take Elvis out for his walk now, if that's all right with the grammar police."

Cindy smiled. "Thank you, darling."

"I made coffee," Heather said.

"Thank you," Cindy said again, marveling at her daughter's easy grace. Even dressed in tight, low-fitting jeans and a navel-baring, candy-apple-red tank top, she somehow managed to look elegant.

"She's a very sweet thing," her mother said after Heather had left the room.

"Yes, she is."

"Like her mother." She kissed Cindy's forehead.

Cindy felt her eyes fill with tears. "Thanks for being here, Mom," she said.

By ten o'clock, Cindy had showered and dressed and was on her fourth cup of coffee.

"You should eat something," her mother advised.

"I'm not hungry."

"You should eat something anyway. You have to keep up your strength."

Cindy nodded, irritation beginning to mingle with gratitude. While it was nice to have her mother here, to feel her love and support in this difficult time, Norma Appleton had an annoying tendency of taking up more than her fair share of oxygen. Prolonged exposure to her company rendered breathing increasingly difficult. Grown women had been known to run screaming from the room, overcome by intense feelings of suffocation. Was that how Cindy made Julia feel? As if there weren't enough air in the room? "Don't feel you have to stay here with me, Mom," she said delicately. "I'm sure you have a million other things to do."

"What things?"

"I don't know."

"What's more important than this?"

Cindy shook her head in defeat, finished the coffee in her cup, poured herself another.

"You should eat something," her mother said.

Cindy pulled several crumpled pieces of paper out of the pocket of her gray sweatpants, glanced at the phone.

"What's that?" her mother asked.

"Just some phone numbers I found in Julia's room."

"Whose are they?"

Cindy studied the numbers on the scraps of paper, tried willing them into familiarity. "I don't know."

Her mother reached across the kitchen table, turned the pieces of paper in Cindy's hand toward her so that she could read them, then repeated the numbers out loud. "Are you going to call them?"

"Should I?"

"Might as well."

"What'll I say?" Cindy crossed the room in three quick

strides, then lifted the phone to her ear, her fingers already pressing in the first of the numbers.

"Start with hello."

"Thanks, Mom," Cindy said as the phone was answered on its first ring.

"Esthetics by Noelise," a woman's voice announced.

"I'm sorry. What?"

"Esthetics by Noelise?" the woman repeated, as if she were no longer sure.

"Oh. Oh, I'm sorry. I must have the wrong number."

"No problem."

"Esthetics by Noelise," Cindy told her mother, hanging up the phone.

"What's that?"

"Where Julia gets her legs waxed."

"Try the next one."

The second number belonged to Sushi Supreme, the third to a local talent agency Julia was hoping to sign with. "Last one," Cindy said, punching in the final set of numbers, listening as the phone rang four times before being picked up by voice-mail.

"You have reached the offices of Granger, McAllister," the taped message began. "Our normal hours of operation are from nine to five, Monday through Friday. If you know the extension of the person you wish to speak to, you may enter it now. If you would like to access our company directory . . ."

Cindy hung up the phone.

"What's the matter?" her mother asked, already at her side.

"Granger, McAllister," Cindy repeated. "Why do I know that name?"

"A law firm?"

"No, I don't think so." Cindy pictured the name written in broad strokes across the beige tile floor.

When he first started working at Granger, McAllister, it was just this tiny firm.

"They're architects," Cindy said flatly, hearing Faith's voice.

"What would Julia want with an architect?"

"I have no idea." *I think Ryan has a girlfriend.* Was it possible Julia and Ryan were involved? "But I'm damn sure going to find out."

The phone rang just as she was reaching for it.

"It's Julia's line," Cindy said, her finger hesitating over the key for line two.

"Answer it," her mother urged.

Cindy took a deep breath, pressed the appropriate key, picked up the phone. "Hello."

"Julia, it's Lindsey. I'm at The Yoga Studio. What's taking you so long?"

"I'll be right there," Cindy replied in Julia's breathy whisper, then hung up the phone, her heart racing. "I've got to go."

"What do you mean, you've got to go? Where are you going all of a sudden? What are you doing?"

Cindy didn't answer. The truth was she had no idea what she was doing, or what she would do when she got to The Yoga Studio. She grabbed her purse from the front closet and was already at the door when the phone rang again. Her line. She turned toward the sound, Julia's name freezing on her lips, as her mother picked up the phone.

"It's Leigh," her mother said. "She's calling to see if you know where I am."

Cindy opened the front door, swallowed a deep gulp of air. “Don’t tell her anything.”

Her mother nodded understanding. “I’m sorry you were worried,” Cindy heard her say as she was closing the front door. “But something’s happened here. Julia’s missing.”

TWELVE

The Yoga Studio was located in an old six-story building on the north side of Bloor Street just west of Spadina, across the street from a large grocery store and the central branch of the JCC. For some reason, in the last several years, this nondescript studio in an unfashionable part of town had become a favorite spot for visiting celebrities to unwind and work out, which was the main reason Cindy knew her daughter frequented the place. Occasionally Julia had regaled her mother with tales of stretching out beside the likes of Gwyneth Paltrow and Elisabeth Shue. One day, she'd vowed, other girls would be telling their mothers they'd worked out beside Julia Carver.

There was nowhere out front to park, so Cindy spent almost fifteen minutes navigating the area's frustrating arrangement of one-way streets before ending up back on the main road. Spotting someone pulling out of a space on the south side of Bloor, Cindy promptly executed an illegal

U-turn, causing the driver in the car behind her to jam on her brakes, and eliciting a raised middle finger from the driver in the oncoming lane, a middle-aged man who pulled up beside Cindy's tan-colored Camry as she was backing into the freshly vacated spot and sat on his horn until she turned off her engine. Cindy sat staring out her front window, refusing to look at the man in the car beside her, knowing he hadn't left her enough room to open her door, and that if she wanted to leave her car, she'd have to climb across the front seat and use the passenger door. She checked her watch, feeling the man's eyes burning acid-powered holes through the car window.

"What's the hurry, lady?" she heard him shout through two layers of glass. "You have a bladder problem?"

Oh dear, she thought, not sure what to do. So many angry people in this world. So many crazy people. She shuddered. What if Julia had encountered such a man? Suppose she'd inadvertently said or done the wrong thing, offended someone in some innocent, unforeseen way?

"You almost got us both killed back there," the man raged.

Cindy saw his arms waving with much agitation around his head, as if he'd stumbled into a nest of bees. She pictured a knife in those hands, heard Julia's distant screams. Her eyes filled with tears. Behind the man's car, horns began beeping, urging him forward. Still he didn't move. Was he planning to sit there all day?

Cindy pushed the tears from her cheeks and rechecked the time. It was getting late. The yoga class would be half over by now. Lindsey might have already given up on her tardy friend and gone home. She couldn't just sit here all morning waiting for this lunatic to leave. "I'm sorry," she said sincerely, turning in the man's direction, noting that fury had reddened his complexion and distorted his features, like a clumsy finger through clay. "I didn't mean to cut you off."

"Lady, you should be shot," came the man's instant retort. Then he pulled away, extending his middle finger high out the window in a final blistering farewell.

Cindy pushed open her door, hearing the blast of another horn, and feeling a hot gust of exhaust on her legs as a red Porsche barely missed running over her toes. Another middle finger waved back in her direction. She fought back the renewed threat of tears as she waited for a break in the traffic. A man begging for change in front of a nearby convenience store shook his head in dismay as she scurried across the street, then turned away as she approached, as if repelled by her carelessness. "Fine, then," she muttered, returning a fistful of coins to her pocket. "Don't take my money."

Cindy pulled open the outside door to The Yoga Studio and approached the ancient elevators, pressing, then repressing the call button at least four times before she heard the old wires groan somewhere above her head, signaling the elevator's excruciatingly slow and shaky descent. She pushed her way through the elevator's heavy metal doors before they were fully open, then realized she didn't know what floor the studio was on. "What's the matter with you? How could you be so stupid?" she asked out loud, exiting the elevator just as a sloppily dressed young woman chewing an enormous wad of gum shuffled in. "Excuse me, do you know what floor The Yoga Studio is on?" she asked the girl, who stared at her blankly and continued chewing her gum. "Could you hold the elevator a minute, please?"

Cindy raced to the directory on the wall to the left of the building's entrance. She quickly scanned the list, noted the correct floor, and ran back just as the elevator doors were drawing to a close. "Could you hold the door . . . ?" she began, but the girl chewed her gum and stared right through her, as if Cindy didn't exist.

"I don't believe this! Would it have killed you to wait two goddamn seconds?" Cindy's voice followed the elevator's ascent as her fist slammed repeatedly against the call button. "Oh God, I'm losing it." She looked around for the stairs, taking them two at a time. So many angry people in this world, she was thinking again. So many crazy people. "And I'm definitely one of them," she acknowledged, reaching the fourth-floor landing, her thighs quivering, her knees about to give way, the tips of her fingers brushing against the concrete floor as she collapsed from the waist, gasping for breath.

What was the matter with her? Where was she going in such a hurry? And what was she going to do when she got there?

Cindy pushed damp hair away from her face, straightened her shoulders, and waited until her breathing had returned to normal before stepping into the hall, and winding her way past the offices of several small companies, until she found the door to The Yoga Studio. She pressed her forehead against it, listening to the silence.

Suddenly the door opened and Cindy fell into the room.

"I'm so sorry. Are you all right?" A middle-aged woman in an unflattering black leotard reached out to block

Cindy's fall. "I had no idea anyone was there." Wild gray hair shot out at right angles from the woman's worried face, as if she'd been struck by lightning.

I did that to her, Cindy thought. "Forgive me," she said. "It was my fault."

"Can I help you?" a voice asked from somewhere behind the shock of gray hair.

Cindy's eyes swept from one end of the long, rectangular room to the other. An old brown sofa and a couple of shabby beige chairs were hunched around a low coffee table in one corner, a high glass cabinet containing yoga-related books and merchandise stood in another, and a cluttered reception desk sat in the middle. Several styles of white, gray, and black T-shirts imprinted with The Yoga Studio logo were pinned to one wall, like artwork, and the scent of oranges, courtesy of several plates of freshly cut orange quarters, filled the air, like cologne. Two women were sipping bottled water and eating oranges on the sofa; another woman was straightening a bunch of yoga mats that were stacked beside the doors to the inner rooms.

"Can I help you?" the receptionist asked again. She was a pale young woman approximately Julia's age, with fine reddish-blond hair and a smattering of oversized freckles that was smeared across her nose like peanut butter.

"I'm looking for Lindsey."

"Lindsey . . . ?"

"Lindsey," Cindy repeated, as if the simple repetition of the name was enough. "I was supposed to meet her here at ten o'clock. She may already be in class. I'm very late," Cindy added unnecessarily.

The receptionist nodded. "We have several classes going

on at the moment. Do you know who her class was with?"

"No. But how many Lindseys can there be?"

"Actually, we have several Lindseys, and I believe two of them are here this morning." The girl checked the register. "Yes. Lindsey Josephson and Lindsey Krauss."

Lindsey Josephson and Lindsey Krauss, Cindy repeated silently. Neither name was the least bit familiar. "She was waiting for my daughter, Julia. Julia Carver."

A smile danced across the receptionist's face. "Julia's your daughter?"

Cindy nodded, feeling a surge of motherly pride so strong it brought tears back to her eyes.

"She's so gorgeous."

"Yes, she is."

"Julia's going to be famous. Then I'll get to say 'I knew her when.'"

Again Cindy nodded. Please, God, she was thinking, just let Julia be all right.

"It's Lindsey Krauss."

"What?"

"Her friend. It's Lindsey Krauss. She's in Peter's class." She pointed toward one of the closed doors beyond the cabinet at the far end of the room.

"Can I go in?"

"Well, it's eighteen dollars and the class is almost over. Why don't you just wait until it finishes." She indicated the sofa and chairs with her chin.

Cindy dropped a twenty-dollar bill onto the desk, and headed toward the studio.

"Wait. Your change . . ." the receptionist called after her. Then, when Cindy failed to respond, "You'll need a mat."

Cindy grabbed a bright blue mat from the shelf as she opened the door and peeked inside the room. Ten people, eight women and two men, all with their eyes closed, stood beside their mats, balancing on the hardwood floor on one foot, like human flamingos. Their other legs were crossed over the knees of their standing legs, their hands brought together in front of them, as if in prayer, their elbows extended at their sides. Several of the women wobbled precariously on the balls of their feet, fighting to stay upright, and the face of one man was pinched in such concentration he looked in danger of imploding. There were no movie stars that Cindy could identify, but she did recognize Lindsey Krauss, a tall, willowy brunette whose surgically enhanced bosom overwhelmed her otherwise boyish frame. Cindy made her way over slowly to where Lindsey was standing in the center of the room, setting her mat down behind her and wondering how best to approach her. She isn't wobbling at all, Cindy thought, marveling at the young woman's effortless mastery of the exercise. She's perfect, Cindy thought.

Like Julia.

The teacher, a supple young man with light brown hair and clear blue eyes, nodded almost imperceptibly at Cindy as she tried to assume the proper position. What the hell am I doing? she wondered, struggling to balance on one foot. Why hadn't she just relaxed in the comfortable waiting area, sipping bottled water and eating fresh orange quarters until the class was over? What did she possibly hope to accomplish in here?

"Focus on your breath," the instructor advised gently, his voice a whisper. "If your mind starts to wander, just bring it back to the breath. It will help you stay balanced."

Not when you're as seriously *un*balanced as I am, Cindy thought, sliding her left foot up along her right thigh, her right foot cramping in protest.

"Now, slowly lower your leg," Peter instructed, as Cindy's foot hit the floor with a resounding thud. A slight grimace creased Peter's unlined brow. "Very good. Now, let's take a final Vinyasa before we move into relaxation."

A final what? Cindy wondered, as the instructor lifted his hands into the air above his head. The class immediately followed suit, lifting their own arms into the air, then bending from the waist and rapidly extending one leg forward, the other one back.

Lindsey's right leg shot back, kicked at Cindy's shin. She swiveled around guiltily. "I'm sorry," she whispered.

"Lindsey," Cindy said, seizing the opportunity.

Lindsey glanced over her shoulder as she brought her other leg back to meet the first. "Mrs. Carver?"

"And now slide gently into the Cobra," Peter directed.

"I need to talk to you."

Lindsey, along with the rest of the class, slid forward on her belly, then raised herself up on her arms, before pushing herself into something the instructor referred to as the Downward Dog. She stared at Cindy upside down from between legs spread shoulder-distance apart. "I don't understand. What are you doing here? Where's Julia?"

"That's what I need to talk to you about."

"Allow your shoulders to relax," the instructor intoned, a slight edge creeping into his voice.

"I don't understand," Lindsey said again, pushing herself into an upright position.

"Ladies, please. Can we save the conversation until after class?"

"Sorry," Lindsey said.

"Can we talk later?" Cindy whispered. "It won't take long."

"All right."

"Thank you."

"Ladies, please."

"Sorry," Cindy said.

"Very good. Now slowly, lie down on your back and concentrate all your energy on your breathing."

Cindy lay down, feeling the muscles in her back melt into the rubber of the mat. She took a deep breath, the air filling her nostrils and traveling to her lungs, her abdomen gradually expanding. Like when I was pregnant with Julia, she thought, remembering the pride she'd felt as her stomach filled with life.

"Very good," Peter was saying. "Now release that breath, ridding all toxins and stress from your pores. Blow the worries of the world gently from your lips. Feel them leave your body."

Cindy had loved being pregnant despite the morning sickness and overwhelming fatigue of the first few months. She'd loved that her breasts were so voluptuous, her skin so glowing. She'd even loved the ugly, loose-fitting clothes. And she'd loved that Tom was so solicitous, so caring, so eager to be a father. Looking back, their marriage was probably its happiest during her first pregnancy.

"Now take another deep breath and open your heart, feel it fill with positive energy."

Her second pregnancy had been a completely different story. This time the morning sickness lasted all day and water retention caused her to swell from head to toe. The constant nausea meant Cindy was unable to devote much time or energy to Julia, who'd grown used to both, and it was during those nine months that Julia's allegiance had subtly shifted from her mother to her father. It was also during this time that Cindy first discovered Tom was cheating on her.

"If your mind starts to wander," Peter was saying somewhere above her head, "bring it back to the breath."

Cindy had blamed herself for Tom's affair. The fact that she was always sick, always tired. Sick and tired of feeling sick and tired. As special as she'd felt during her pregnancy with Julia was how superfluous she felt during her pregnancy with Heather, almost like an afterthought in her own home. Tom had taken over Cindy's role with relish, playing Barbie with Julia for hours on end, reading her story after story, taking her to the park on weekend afternoons. After he'd tucked Julia into bed at night, he'd lock himself in the den, or go back to the office to catch up on his work. Or he'd go for a drive. To relax, he said.

"Relax," the voice continued now, floating across the room. "Relax. Let go."

The pattern had continued after Heather's birth. The fact that Heather had proved as easy an infant as Julia had been difficult strangely only made things worse. Julia blamed Cindy for bringing this unwanted intruder into their lives, turned increasingly to her father, shut her mother out almost completely. "She's never forgiven me for Heather," Cindy told her mother, who said that Cindy had once felt the same way about Leigh.

"Let go," Peter was saying, soft hands on Cindy's, trying to manipulate her fingers. "Let go. Let go."

"I'm sorry," Cindy whispered, realizing how tightly her fists were clenched at her sides.

"Feel your breath seep into your fingertips. Allow your hands to relax."

Cindy felt her fists gradually open under Peter's expert and gentle touch. Tom used to touch her with that same kind of tender strength, she thought. The best lover she'd ever had, his caress as addictive as the most powerful narcotic. They'd made love through all his infidelities, made love that awful night he'd told her he was leaving, and for several months after he'd moved out, when she thought there was still a chance he might come home, and for several months after that, while they were hammering out a settlement, and even after their divorce was final, when she knew there was no hope at all. The lovemaking had finally stopped the afternoon Julia packed her new suitcase and left her mother's house to go live with her father.

"That's it," Peter said, his voice filled with quiet pride as he patted Cindy's fingers. "You're smiling."

"What's going on?" Lindsey asked as Cindy followed her into the main reception area. "Is Julia sick?" She grabbed an orange quarter from the bowl on the desk.

"Here's your change," the receptionist offered Cindy, holding out a two-dollar coin.

Cindy ignored the money, watching Lindsey suck the juice from the sliver of orange. "When was the last time you spoke to Julia?"

"This morning."

"This morning?" Cindy's heart began to race.

"Yeah, I called and asked her what she was doing. We were supposed to meet for coffee at nine-thirty."

Cindy felt her heart sink. "That was me."

"What?"

"That was me you spoke to."

"I don't understand. Why would you . . . ?"

"Julia's missing."

"What?"

"Since Thursday." Cindy saw the movement in Lindsey's brown eyes as the girl retraced the last two days in her mind. "Have you heard from her since then?"

"No. No, I haven't. I left her a message yesterday, but she didn't get back to me."

"Is that unusual?"

"Not really. Julia's not great about returning calls."

"Do you have any idea where she might be?"

Lindsey shook her head, discarded the orange peel.

"Please, Lindsey," Cindy urged, sensing that Lindsey knew something she wasn't telling. "If you know anything at all. . . ."

"Excuse me." A woman from Lindsey's class reached between them to grab a piece of orange.

"I know she had an audition with that big-shot Hollywood director, Michael something . . ."

"Kinsolving. Yes, we know that."

"We?"

"The police have been notified," Cindy said, hoping to shock Lindsey into revealing whatever it was she knew. Around her, several women lingered, pretending not to listen.

"The police? You really think something's happened to Julia?"

"I don't know what to think."

"I'm sure she's all right, Mrs. Carver."

"How are you sure?"

Lindsey grabbed another orange slice, stuffed it inside her mouth. "I just can't imagine. . . . Look, I really have to go. My boyfriend's waiting downstairs."

"Let him wait, damn it."

"Excuse me," the receptionist asked meekly. "Is there a problem here?"

"My daughter is missing," Cindy announced to a chorus of Oh, my's. "And I think this girl might know something about it."

"I don't," Lindsey protested to the gathering crowd. "Honestly, I don't."

"But?" Cindy demanded. "I know there's a 'but' there. What aren't you telling me?"

Lindsey lowered her head, spoke out of the side of her mouth, her voice no more than a whisper. "There was this guy. Maybe she's with him."

"What guy?"

"I don't know his name. Really, I don't," Lindsey insisted as Cindy was about to interrupt. "She was very secretive about him. She wouldn't tell me anything except . . ."

"Except what?"

"Except that she was crazy about him."

"She told you she was crazy about him but she wouldn't tell you his name?"

"She said she couldn't."

"What do you mean, she couldn't?"

"She said it was a very complicated situation."

"Complicated in what way? Is he married?" Ryan Sellick

winked at her from the dark corners of her imagination. "What exactly did she tell you about him?"

"Nothing. Honestly. I've told you everything I know. I really have to go now. I'm sure there's nothing to worry about."

Lindsey fled the room as a woman from her class approached. "Can I get you a glass of water?" the woman asked Cindy.

Tears filled Cindy's eyes, causing the woman's face to blur, her features to overlap, like a cubist painting.

"Do you need a ride home?" another woman offered.

"Thank you. I have my car," Cindy said, her voice a monotone.

"Is there anything we can do?"

Cindy nodded. "You can find my daughter."

THIRTEEN

As soon as she left The Yoga Studio, Cindy drove north on Spadina to Dupont, fully intending to go home. But instead of turning right toward Poplar Plains, she turned left, continuing west to Christie, where she pulled to a stop across the street from an old convenience store on the corner, then turned the engine off and sat staring up at Sean Banack's apartment. What am I doing here? she thought now, pressing her forehead against the leather of the steering wheel. Hadn't the police told her to let them handle things?

Except that the police were waiting until Tuesday.

And Tuesday might be too late.

Cindy lifted her head, looked across the street. Sean Banack was standing in front of the convenience store, staring at her.

In the next instant Cindy was out of the car and running across the road. "Sean, Sean, wait," she shouted at him over the tops of the passing cars. "I need to talk to you."

Sean Banack took several steps back as Cindy drew near, muscular arms raised, as if warning her to keep her distance. He was of medium height and build, handsome in a careless sort of way, his normally long blond hair cut very short, his blue jeans worn very tight, light brown eyes challenging hers. "I don't think we have anything to talk about, Mrs. Carver."

"I do."

"So . . . what I want doesn't count?" Sean lifted his palms into the air, as if already conceding defeat. "Now I see where Julia gets it."

"Gets what?"

"Her—how can I put this politely?—her single-minded determination."

Cindy smiled at the thought that her daughter might resemble her in any way at all. "Where's Julia?"

"Not here."

"Where then?"

"I have absolutely no idea."

"I don't believe you."

Sean Banack took another step back, until he was literally up against the redbrick wall of the convenience store. "Mrs. Carver, what's going on here?"

"My daughter is missing, Sean. She hasn't been home in two days."

"And that gives you the right to show up at my apartment and hassle my roommate? To go through my things? To tell the police I had something to do with Julia's disappearance?"

"You're saying you didn't?"

"Of course I didn't."

"I read your story."

Sean looked at the sidewalk, swayed from one foot to the other, scratched the side of his head. "It was just a story. I'm a writer. It's what I do."

"It was a vile, horrible story."

"I didn't say I was a good writer." He looked sheepishly at his feet, as if ashamed of his meager stab at humor. "Look, Mrs. Carver, I can see that you're really upset, and I understand why reading that story would freak you out in light of what's happened. . . ."

"What's happened?" Cindy repeated. "What did you do to her?"

"I didn't do anything."

"Please, just tell me where she is."

"I don't *know* where she is."

"You wrote that you had her tied up in an abandoned shack. . . ."

"What I wrote was a goddamn story! A story that has nothing whatsoever to do with Julia. For God's sake, Mrs. Carver, I loved your daughter. I could never hurt her."

Two young boys suddenly bounded from the convenience store, laughing and punching one another in the arm.

"What happened between the two of you?" Cindy persisted, stepping aside to let an elderly couple pass by. "Why did you break up?"

"That's really none of your business."

"Please, Sean. Just tell me."

Sean laughed, but the laugh was hollow, joyless. "You want to know why your daughter and I broke up, Mrs. Carver? All right, I'll tell you. Julia and I broke up because she was cheating on me. I found out she'd been seeing someone behind my back for months."

"Who was it?"

"I don't know."

Cindy felt her knees wobble, then give way. She crumpled to the sidewalk like a balled piece of paper tossed from someone's fist.

Sean Banack was instantly on his knees beside her. "Mrs. Carver? Mrs. Carver, are you all right?"

"My little girl is missing," Cindy cried helplessly.

"I'll get you some water," Sean offered. "Stay where you are. I'll be right back." He disappeared into the convenience store.

But when he returned, Cindy was already gone.

"Where have you been?" her sister asked as Cindy walked through the front door, Elvis immediately at her feet. "Your phone's been ringing all morning."

"Julia . . . ?" Cindy asked, staring at her sister, afraid to say more.

"No," Leigh said, following Cindy into the kitchen. "Nobody's heard from her. I can't believe she's been missing for two days and you didn't tell me. I had to hear it from Mom."

Norma Appleton shrugged from her seat at the kitchen table as Leigh crossed the room. "I made some fresh coffee," Leigh said. "You want some?"

"Thank you." Cindy sank into the chair beside her mother, feeling displaced, like an unwelcome guest in her own home, admiring the effortless way her sister had assumed control. Elvis stretched himself heavily across her feet. "When did you get here?"

"Couple of hours ago." Leigh deposited the cup of black coffee on the table in front of Cindy. "Where have you been? It's almost one."

"I talked to a friend of Julia's."

"And?"

"Nothing."

"I'll have another cup of coffee," her mother said.

"You've had enough coffee today."

"Leigh. . . ."

"Mom, don't argue with me, okay? It's lunchtime. I'll make you some soup."

"I don't want soup. What kind of soup?"

Leigh crossed to the cupboards, her eyes scanning the shelves. "Cream of mushroom, cream of asparagus, split pea."

"Split pea."

"Where's the can opener?"

Cindy pointed to a corner of the crowded counter, next to a spice rack that had fallen off the wall, and behind a stack of unopened mail and old fashion magazines Julia had been saving.

"You've been gone all morning. Where else did you go?" Leigh opened the soup tin and poured its contents into a waiting pot.

Cindy retraced in her mind all the streets she'd traveled since leaving Sean. North on Poplar Plains, east along St. Clair, north on Yonge, east on Eglinton, south on Mount Pleasant, east on Elm, circling blindly through the expensive, old-money labyrinth that was Rosedale, escaping to the blossoming seediness of Sherbourne, heading south to the downtown core, then west, then north again, up and down, back and forth, eyes scanning each pedestrian on both sides of the streets, peering into parked cars, squinting into the sun, hoping the shadow on the opposite corner might be Julia's. "Who phoned?" she asked, not bothering to answer Leigh's question, and thinking how much softer her sister looked without her normal layers of makeup, how much prettier she looked with her hair brushed away from her face.

"Meg. Wondered how you were feeling. Said she'd call you later. And Trish. Said to tell you she picked up the tickets for the film festival. I take it they don't know about Julia."

Cindy nodded, feeling both guilty and relieved. Guilty she hadn't yet confided in her two best friends, relieved her sister knew that.

"And your neighbor. Faith? Is that her name? It was hard to make out what she was saying with that baby screaming in the background."

Again Cindy pictured Ryan, saw his phone number scribbled across the scrap of paper she'd found in Julia's room. What would Julia be doing with Ryan's phone number at work? Was it possible he was the mystery man her daughter was involved with? Or was it someone else at Granger, McAllister? "What did she want?"

"Just to tell you she's feeling a hundred percent better, she and her husband are off to Lake Simcoe for the day, she'll call you tomorrow, she didn't want you to worry."

So Ryan would have to wait till tomorrow.

"Oh, and Heather called to see if Julia was back yet."

Cindy looked toward the hall. "What about Duncan? Is he here?"

"Haven't seen him. You want some soup?"

"No."

"You should eat," Leigh said. "It's important to keep up your strength. Mom says you didn't get much sleep last night."

"She had a bad dream," their mother explained. "Thought she forgot to take her pills."

"What pills?"

"It was just a dream," Cindy said.

"Wish bad dreams were all I had." Leigh carefully measured out two bowls of soup. "Me, I have something called benign positional vertigo."

"What's that?" her mother asked.

"Apparently the calcium stones in my inner ear have come loose, and they send a signal to my brain that I'm moving when I'm not. So the minute I lie down on my back or turn over on my side—only my right side, mind you, good thing I sleep on my left—the next thing I know, the room is spinning around like I'm on one of those crazy rides at the Exhibition. The doctor says it's benign positional vertigo." She put the bowls of soup on the table. "Don't let it get cold."

"Aren't you having any?" Cindy asked.

"Nah. I hate canned soups. If I have time tomorrow, I'll make you some real soup."

Tomorrow, Cindy thought, desperately hoping that by this time tomorrow, Julia would be standing where her sister was now.

Tomorrow, she thought, silently repeating the word as if it were a prayer.

Tomorrow.

When Cindy woke up the next morning, Leigh was already in the kitchen preparing breakfast.

"Bacon and eggs," Heather marveled, smiling at her mother from her seat at the kitchen table. She was wearing an old pair of pink pajamas Cindy hadn't seen in years. Elvis was sitting beside her expectantly, clearly hoping a few errant scraps might come his way.

"You're up early." Cindy kissed her daughter's cheek, patted the top of Elvis's head.

"I smelled the bacon."

"You didn't have to do this," Cindy said as her sister handed her a plate of crispy bacon slices and two depressingly perfect sunny-side up eggs.

Leigh popped two pieces of raisin bread into the toaster. "How'd you sleep?"

"Okay," Cindy lied, sitting down and cutting into the eggs. "You?"

"Not great. That mattress downstairs is a killer. But what can you expect from a sofabed? Mom still asleep?"

Cindy nodded. "What about Duncan?" she asked Heather.

The familiar shrug. "Don't know."

"You don't know?"

"He slept at Mac's last night."

"Mac?" Leigh repeated, turning the name over on her tongue. "Why does that name . . . ? Oh, my God." She turned to Cindy. "You had a call yesterday from a Neil Mac-something. I'm so sorry. I didn't recognize the name and I couldn't find a piece of paper to write on, so I forgot all about him. You really should keep a pad and pencil by the phone. Then this sort of thing wouldn't happen."

"It's okay, Leigh," Cindy said, Neil's face appearing before her eyes, only to smudge, fade, be blinked to the periphery of her line of sight. Bad timing, she thought again, banishing the image altogether. She had enough on her plate at the moment. When Julia came home, maybe. . . . "Why is Duncan sleeping over at Mac's?"

"Why shouldn't he sleep at Mac's?" came Heather's too-quick reply.

"Well, it's the long weekend. I assumed you'd have plans."

"Trouble in Paradise?" asked Leigh, grabbing the pieces of raisin bread as they popped from the toaster.

"Everything's fine," Heather said. "No toast for me, thanks." She swallowed the last of her bacon, and carried her plate to the sink. "I have to get dressed."

"It's not even eight o'clock," Leigh said. "Where are you going?"

"Thanks for the breakfast," Heather said sweetly. "It was a real treat."

"Is she always so forthcoming?" Leigh asked after Heather left the room.

"She's not used to getting the third degree."

"You're not curious where she's off to? Coffee?" Leigh asked in the same breath.

"Yes, and no," Cindy said. "Yes to the coffee."

"You were always way too lenient with them."

"I beg your pardon?"

"I'm just saying that it doesn't hurt to ask a few simple questions." Leigh poured her sister a cup of coffee, and put it on the table along with the raisin toast. "Honestly, Cindy, I just don't understand you. I mean, it's one thing to respect your kids' privacy, but you always go too far."

"I go too far?" Cindy repeated numbly.

"You're almost pathologically fair."

"*Pathologically* fair? What does that mean?"

"It means you can't be both their mother *and* their friend."

"What are you talking about?"

"Please don't take that tone with me."

"Then stop talking to me like I'm one of your kids."

"I'm just trying to help."

"Well, news flash—this isn't helping."

"Look, I know you're upset, but don't try to make me feel badly because I made some polite inquiries."

"*Bad*," Cindy snapped.

"What?"

"Don't try to make me feel *bad*," Cindy continued, feeling the anger rise in her throat. "You don't say, 'I feel sadly,' do you? No. You say, 'I feel sad.' In the same way, you shouldn't say, 'I feel badly.' You should say, 'I feel bad.' You feel *what*, not *how*. It's an emotion, not an adverb."

Leigh's mouth fell open. "You're correcting my grammar?"

Cindy lowered her head. Not even eight o'clock in the morning and already she was exhausted. Maybe she'd spend the day in bed. Maybe she'd go to church and pray. Maybe she'd badger the police, even though she knew they were waiting until the end of the long weekend, confident Julia would turn up on her own.

Would she?

There had to be something she could do. Something to keep her from going out of her mind. She just couldn't sit idly by and wait until Tuesday, especially with Supermom hovering, telegraphing her disapproval with every look and utterance. "Look. I can manage here," she told her sister. "You don't have to stay."

"Don't be silly. Of course I'll stay."

"You have your own family to look after."

"You're my family."

Tears filled Cindy's eyes. "Where is she, Leigh?" she asked, burying her face in her hands.

"Have you checked her voicemail for messages?"

Cindy was immediately on her feet and at the telephone. Why hadn't she thought to check her daughter's voicemail? What was the matter with her? "I don't know her code," she whispered, suspecting that Leigh knew all her children's voicemail codes by heart.

Cindy heard Heather's footsteps on the stairs. "Everything okay?" Heather asked, freshly changed into jeans and a light blue jersey.

"Heather," Leigh said, "do you know your sister's voicemail code?"

Heather quickly rattled off the four digits. "I've got to go." She kissed her mother's cheek. "I'll call you later. Try not to worry."

Even before the front door closed, Cindy was entering the code to Julia's voicemail, feeling guilty for snooping into her daughter's personal life. When Julia got home, she'd apologize, Cindy decided, hearing her sister's earlier pronouncement ringing in her ear. Almost pathologically fair, she'd said.

"You have seven new messages," a recorded voice chirped in Cindy's ear.

"Seven new messages," Cindy repeated, looking around in vain for a pencil and a piece of paper.

Her sister lifted her hands in the air. *Told you so*, said the expression on her face.

In the end there was no need for paper and pencil. Five of the messages were from Cindy, forwarded from Julia's cell phone, one was from Lindsey, the last one was a hang-up. Cindy replaced the receiver, desperation gnawing at her insides, like a dull hunger.

"Are you all right?" Cindy heard Leigh asking through the ringing in her ears. "You don't look so hot."

Cindy watched the room sway precariously from side to side, as if she were riding on a high swing, the earth pulling away from her feet. Benign positional vertigo, she thought, watching the ceiling swoop toward her, like a giant bird. It plucked her into the air, shaking her this way and that, leaving her limp and helpless, before abuptly letting go. Cindy felt herself plummeting to the ground. Just before she landed, she heard Elvis yelp, saw her sister's eyes widen in alarm. "What are you doing?" Leigh demanded, hands on her hips.

Cindy's last thought before the darkness overtook her was that she hoped Leigh could move fast enough to catch her before her head hit the floor.

FOURTEEN

When Cindy opened her eyes, she saw Neil Macfarlane's handsome face. I'm in heaven, she thought, watching her mother and sister insert themselves into the frame. I'm in hell, she thought, quickly amending her earlier assessment.

The tan leather of the living room sofa groaned as Cindy pushed herself into a sitting position. "What's going on?"

"Apparently you fainted," Neil said from the seat beside her. He was casually dressed in jeans and a yellow golf shirt. His amazingly blue eyes were flecked with worry.

"Scared the hell out of me," Leigh said, backing away from the sofa and rubbing her right hand with her left. "I think I may have done something to my wrist when I blocked your fall."

Cindy tried shaking the heavy fog from inside her head, but it hung on, like a dead weight. "I don't understand. How long was I out?"

"Not more than a couple of minutes," her mother

answered. "I was in the bathroom when I heard your sister screaming."

"Well, she scared the hell out of me," Leigh repeated.

"And then the doorbell was ringing."

"That was me," Neil said with a smile.

"He brought bagels," Cindy's mother said.

"He helped me lift you onto the sofa," Leigh told her.

"And so concludes our up-to-the-minute report," Neil said.

Cindy shook her head. "I don't think I've ever fainted before."

"It's because you don't eat enough," her sister pronounced.

"Which is why I brought bagels," Neil said.

"Maybe later." Cindy smiled, so grateful for his presence she almost cried. "You've obviously met my mother and sister."

"The necessary introductions have all been made."

"Can I get you a cup of coffee, Mr. Macfarlane?" Leigh asked, hovering like a waiting helicopter.

"No, thank you."

Cindy pushed herself to her feet. "I could use some fresh air."

"How about a walk?" Neil asked.

Elvis barked his enthusiastic approval, headed for the door.

Cindy laughed. "You said the magic word. Actually, a walk sounds great." Elvis began circling the hall, barking even louder. "Okay, okay, you can come." She walked slowly into the kitchen, retrieved Elvis's leash, and attached it to his collar.

"You're sure you're all right to go out?" her mother asked.

"I'm fine, Mom."

"Don't go too far," she advised as Cindy and Neil headed down the outside stairs, Neil's hand guiding Cindy's elbow. "Don't let her do too much," her mother called after them.

"For heaven's sake, Mom," Cindy heard Leigh hiss from the doorway. "She's not a child. Stop fussing over her. Ouch, my arm. . . ."

"You're sure you're okay?" Neil asked Cindy as they continued down the street.

Cindy felt her legs grow stronger, her footing more secure, with each step away from her house. "I'll be fine as soon as we get around the corner." The dog yanked on Cindy's arm, demanding that she pick up the pace.

Neil took the leash from Cindy's hand. "Let me do this."

"Thank you." Cindy marveled at the way the dog immediately slowed down, fell into step beside Neil. "How did you do that?"

"It's all in the pressure."

"I'm not very good with pressure," Cindy said.

"Well, there's only so much anyone can take." They turned south on Poplar Plains. "I assume no one's heard from Julia."

Cindy nodded, pointed to her right. "Let's go to the park." They walked in silence for several seconds along Clarendon. "What made you drop by?"

"I wanted to see how everything was. I called yesterday. . . ."

"I didn't get your message until today."

"Yes, your sister mentioned something about there being no pad and pencil by the phone."

"She doesn't waste any time."

"That's the impression I got."

Cindy smiled. "She's really a very nice person."

"I'm sure she is."

"I shouldn't sound so ungrateful."

"You don't." They stopped for Elvis to pee against a line of scraggly red and yellow rosebushes. "Anyway, when I didn't hear back from you, I thought I'd take a chance and drop by, see for myself how you were doing."

"And you found me sprawled across the kitchen floor."

He nodded. "What happened to make you faint?"

Cindy shook her head. "Damned if I know. One minute I was looking at my sister; next minute, I was looking at you."

"Maybe you should call your doctor."

"I'm sure my mother is doing exactly that as we speak."

They crossed Russell Hill Road and headed up the side entrance to Winston Churchill Park, where Cindy bent down and unhooked the leash from Elvis's collar, letting the dog run free. He bounded up the slight incline to the foot of a steep hill. DANGER, a sign proclaimed in big, bold letters at its base. SLOPE & FENCE HAZARD, SLEIGHING, TOBOGGANING PROHIBITED. A collapsing orange wire fence looped casually along the ground; a flight of wooden steps ran diagonally up the right side of the hill. Elvis was already halfway to the top by the time Cindy and Neil began their climb.

"You sure you're up for this?" Neil asked.

"Lead on."

The top of the hill plateaued into a small field of dry, yellow grass. Cindy and Neil arrived at the top step in time to see Elvis bound between a father and his young son, who were struggling with a large, blue-and-gold kite, then pounce on a young couple sunbathing near the row of tennis courts at the far end of the park. "Elvis, stop that. Come back here," Cindy called as the dog chased after a jogger in a pair of lime green shorts who was puffing along the well-worn perimeter of the park. An elderly Chinese woman, who was exercising with meticulous deliberation near a set of concrete stairs that led to a nearby ravine, stopped to give Elvis a pat on the head. "I'm sorry if he bothered you," Cindy said just as she was hit in the leg by a well-chewed, misaimed rubber ball. Immediately, a large white poodle was at her feet, grabbing the ball in his teeth, then taking off for the middle of the park, Elvis in quick pursuit, to where a group of pet owners were clustered together.

"Quite the scene," Neil remarked as Elvis raced circles around the other dogs.

"Elvis!" a woman shouted warmly in greeting. "How are you, boy?"

"Sorry about that ball," a middle-aged man apologized as Cindy approached the group. "Didn't realize I could throw that far. How you doin', Elvis?"

"You know my dog?"

"Oh, sure," another woman answered easily. "We all know Elvis. You want a treat, boy?" The woman, her short pixie hair peeking out from under a Blue Jays baseball cap, reached into the side pocket of her baggy olive green pants and pulled out a biscuit. "Sit," she instructed.

Elvis promptly did as he was told.

"Amazing," Cindy said.

Immediately, six other dogs rushed the woman, begging for treats. Along with the white poodle, there was a smaller red one, a big German shepherd, a bigger Golden Lab, and two medium-sized black dogs whose breeds Cindy couldn't identify.

"Where's Julia?" a young girl asked as Elvis chewed on his treat. The girl was about twelve years old, with thin yellow hair and a mouthful of braces. She stood beside a younger girl with the exact same face, minus the hardware.

Cindy hadn't expected to hear her daughter's name. It stabbed at her heart like a sharp stick. Instinctively, her hand reached for Neil's. She felt his fingers fold over her own. "You know Julia?"

"She's so pretty," the younger of the two sisters answered with a laugh.

"Haven't seen her around in a while," the woman with the treats said, pushing gray-streaked black hair away from her narrow face. "Did she take off for Hollywood?"

Did she? Cindy wondered. "When was the last time you saw her?" she asked, trying to make the question sound as casual as possible.

"I'm not sure. About two weeks ago, I guess."

"Was she with anyone?"

The woman looked puzzled by the question.

"She was with her new boyfriend," the younger of the two sisters offered with a giggle.

"Her new boyfriend?" Cindy felt her throat constricting, as if a stranger's hands were around her neck, strangling further attempts at conversation. "Do you know his name?" she whispered hoarsely, kneeling down on the grass in front of the younger, yellow-haired girl.

The child shook her head, looked anxiously toward her sister.

"Can you tell me what Julia's boyfriend looked like? Please, it's very important."

The little girl shrugged, backed against her older sister's side.

"Is there a problem?" someone asked from above her head.

"Julia's been missing since Thursday," Cindy said, eyes focused on the two girls.

"Oh, dear."

"I saw her yesterday," a man said.

Instantly, Cindy was on her feet, advancing toward him. "You saw her yesterday?"

The man, who was fortyish, heavyset, and balding, took a step back. "She was sitting right ovcr there." IIe pointed toward a lone bench at the far end of the park. "She was crying."

"Crying?"

"That wasn't Julia," the man's wife corrected. "It was the other one. Heather. Is that her name? Such a nice girl."

"Heather was here yesterday?"

"About four o'clock. Sitting right over there," the man repeated. "Crying her heart out. You're sure that wasn't Julia?" he asked his wife.

Was she?

"It was the other one," his wife insisted.

What would Heather be doing in the park, crying?

"I wanted to ask her if there was anything we could do to help, but . . ." The woman shook her head in her husband's direction, as if her failure to take action was his fault.

"We decided it was none of our business," her husband replied defensively.

"Have you called the police?" someone asked, the voices beginning to blend together in Cindy's ears, becoming indistinguishable one from the other.

"The police have been contacted," Neil answered for her. "But if any of you can think of anything that might be of help. . . ."

"Can't think of a thing," someone said.

"I'm sure she'll turn up."

"I'm so sorry," said someone else.

"Good luck."

Their voices receded as their footsteps pulled away. Cindy stared at the trampled grass until it grew quiet. When she looked up again, she and Neil were alone in the center of the park.

"Are you all right?" Neil asked.

Cindy shrugged, realized she was still holding tightly onto Neil's hand. "Sorry," she said, releasing his fingers from her vise-like grip.

"Any time."

Cindy's eyes swept across the dry field. The father and his young son were still struggling with their uncooperative kite; the sunbathers were still stretched out on their blanket by the tennis courts; the jogger in the lime green shorts was still running in hapless circles around the track; the elderly Chinese woman was still doing her exercises. "Where's Elvis?" Cindy asked, spinning around. "Elvis!" She ran to the edge of the hill, looked down, saw a bunch of other dogs playing at the bottom. No Elvis. "Oh no." She raced to the other side of the park. "Elvis! Where is he? Elvis! Where are you?"

Neil was right beside her. "Take it easy, Cindy. We'll find him."

"I can't believe it. I can't believe I lost Julia's dog."

"We'll find him," Neil repeated.

She was crying now. "Julia will never forgive me. She'll never forgive me."

Neil took her arm, deliberately slowed her pace, led her toward the tennis courts. "Elvis!" he called out, his voice racing ahead of them as they walked around the side of the double row of courts to the front part of the park. They passed a group of young men playing soccer, dodged between two teenage boys tossing a bright orange Frisbee back and forth.

"He's not here," Cindy said, eyes scanning the crowded children's playground by the front row of tennis courts. She approached a group of young mothers pushing their children on the swings. "Excuse me, have you seen a Wheaten terrier, about this big?" She held her hand about two feet off the ground. "He's apricot-colored," she continued, even as the women were shaking their heads no. Cindy ran toward the tiny brick building that was the headquarters of the Winston Churchill Tennis Association. "I can't believe it. First I lose Julia; now I lose her dog."

"You haven't lost anyone." Neil poked his head inside the men's washroom to the left of the small structure. "We'll find him," he said. "Elvis! Elvis!"

"Elvis!" Cindy echoed.

"Is this your dog?" someone called from inside the main room.

Cindy poked her head into the open door of the tennis association's headquarters. The single room was long and casually furnished, with a large desk to one side, a soft drink machine at the back, and several rows of blue chairs positioned around a small TV that was tuned to the U.S. Open. Two young men in tennis whites were lounging across a dark blue couch propped against one wall, a large pizza box open between them. Elvis was sitting on the floor in front of them, his eyes glued to what remained of the pizza.

"Elvis!" Cindy cried, falling to her knees and hugging the dog to her chest, feeling his wet tongue on the underside of her chin. "You scared me half to death."

"Your dog sure loves pizza," one of the boys said as Elvis barked his desire for more.

"I'm very sorry he bothered you." Cindy quickly attached Elvis's leash to his collar and pulled at the stubborn dog. "Come on, you."

"Elvis has left the building," she heard one of the young men say as they stepped outside.

The sun smacked Cindy full in the face, so she didn't see the two young sisters in her path until she was almost on top of them. "I'm so sorry," she apologized. How many times had she said that in the last several days?

"Does Julia have a baby?" the younger of the two girls asked.

"What?"

"Come on," the older girl urged, pulling on her sister's arm.

"Wait," Cindy said. "Please. What makes you think Julia has a baby?"

"'Cause I saw her with one."

"Come on, Anne-Marie. We have to go home."

"You saw Julia with a baby?" Cindy pressed.

"She was pushing it in a carriage. I asked her if it was her baby, and she laughed."

Cindy took a long, deep breath, tried to digest this latest piece of information. What did it mean? Did it mean anything at all? "Damn it," she muttered, as once again Ryan's face imposed itself on her consciousness. "That miserable son of a bitch."

Anne-Marie gasped. "You said a bad word."

"I'm sorry. I didn't mean . . ." Cindy began, but the two girls were already fleeing the park.

"What is it?" Neil asked.

Cindy stared blankly at the horizon. Somewhere above her head, the old children's rhyme kept circling: *First comes love, then comes marriage. Then comes Julia with a baby carriage.*

"Cindy, hi," Faith Sellick said, pulling open her front door, seemingly oblivious to the streak of green bile staining the front of her white shirt.

"Can I speak to Ryan for a minute?"

"He's not home."

"Where is he?"

"Golfing. Somewhere up north."

"Could you have him call me as soon as he gets back?"

"Sure. Is something wrong?"

"I just need to talk to him."

"He might be pretty late."

"That doesn't matter."

From upstairs, a baby's cry pierced the air. Faith's eyes closed as her shoulders slumped. "We had such a nice day yesterday," she said wistfully.

"Do you need some help?" Cindy asked, glancing down the front steps to where Neil stood waiting.

"No. You go. I'll be fine."

But when Cindy reached her own front door, she saw that Faith was still standing in her doorway, not moving, eyes tightly closed.

"Maybe it's better to wait until Tuesday, let the police talk to Ryan," Neil advised later that night.

They were sitting at Cindy's kitchen table, finishing off the last of a bottle of red Zinfandel. It was almost midnight. Heather and Duncan were out; her mother was upstairs asleep; her sister had gone home.

Ryan still hadn't phoned.

"Bastard," Cindy said. "Where is he?" She checked her watch. "Do you think I'm overreacting?" Tom would have said she was overreacting.

"No."

"I mean, the kid could be mistaken. It might not have been Julia she saw with the baby. And the baby doesn't have to be Ryan's. Even if it was, that doesn't necessarily mean that Ryan is Julia's mystery boyfriend. Do you think I'm jumping to conclusions?" Tom would have said she was jumping to conclusions.

"I think you have good instincts. You should trust them."

Cindy smiled across the table at a tired-looking Neil Macfarlane. I think I could love this man, she thought. Out loud she said, "It's late. You should probably go."

At eight o'clock the next morning, Cindy was knocking on Ryan Sellick's front door.

"Hold your horses," Ryan called groggily from inside.

Cindy heard him shuffling toward the door, braced herself for the encounter to follow. "Easy does it. You catch more flies with honey than with vinegar," she could almost hear her mother advise.

She'd been up most of the night preparing what she was going to say, rehearsing exactly how she was going to say it. She'd even spent twenty minutes doing deep-breathing exercises to help her relax, and she was determined to stay calm. But the minute she saw Ryan standing in the doorway, black shirt unbuttoned, light khaki pants hanging low on his hips, a line of short, black hairs twisting down from his belly button and disappearing under his waistband, feet bare, long hair falling into sleepy eyes, the scratch beneath his right eye still prominent, it took all her resolve to keep from hurling herself at his throat. *You lying, motherfucking, son of a bitch,* she wanted to shout. "I need to talk to you," she said instead.

Ryan wiped some sleep from the corner of his right eye. "Is something wrong?"

"I'm not sure."

"Is this about Faith?" He glanced warily over his shoulder toward the stairs.

"No."

He looked confused.

"It's about Julia."

"Julia?"

"She's been missing since Thursday."

"Missing?"

"Have you seen her?"

"Not since I saw her arguing with Duncan in the driveway. Was that Thursday?"

"You haven't seen her since then?"

Ryan shook his head. He was wide awake now.

"She didn't say anything to you about maybe going away for the long weekend?"

The same stubborn shake of his head. "Nothing."

"Has she confided in you lately about being depressed or upset?"

"Why would she confide in me?"

"I don't know," Cindy answered simply. "Maybe because the two of you were sleeping together?" The words tumbled from her mouth before she could stop them. *Trust your instincts,* she heard Neil say, remembering he had also suggested waiting until Tuesday, letting the police question Ryan. Why hadn't she listened? she thought now, watching the summer tan drain from Ryan's complexion. Why was she always barreling off half-cocked?

Ryan raised the fingers of his left hand to his lips, his eyes shooting toward his upstairs bedroom. "Look, maybe we should take this outside. I don't want to wake Faith. She was up half the night with the baby." They stepped onto the front landing. "What the hell are you talking about?"

"Where were you yesterday?"

"Where was I?" he repeated, as if trying to make sense of the question.

"Where were you?" Cindy repeated.

"I was golfing up at Rocky Crest. Why? What . . . ?"

"Was Julia with you?"

"Of course not."

"Where did you get that scratch under your eye?"

"What?"

"Did Julia do that to you?"

"No. Of course not. I walked into a branch in the backyard." Ryan pressed down on the scratch, as if trying to make it disappear. "Look, I think you better tell me what's going on." He lowered his voice to a whisper. "Why would you think I'm involved with Julia?"

"Julia recently broke up with her boyfriend. He says she was seeing someone else."

"What would make you think that someone is me?"

"You were seen together. In the park. With the baby."

Ryan's face was a road map of confusing wrinkles. "I don't know . . . wait . . . okay. Yes, I did run into Julia in the park. A few weeks ago, I think it was. I was there with Kyle. Julia was walking the dog. We talked for a few minutes. Is that what this is about?"

Cindy quickly digested this new information. Could she be mistaken? Had Ryan and Julia simply bumped into each other in the park? Was that all there was to it? "I found the phone number for Granger, McAllister among Julia's things," she said with renewed determination.

"So?"

"So . . . what would Julia be doing with the number for Granger, McAllister?"

"I have no idea."

Hadn't Tom once told her that innocent people rarely embellish, that only the guilty feel compelled to provide answers or excuses? Was she wrong about Ryan being the new mystery man in Julia's life? Was he as innocent as he appeared to be?

The door swung open, as if by itself, and a ghostly apparition suddenly materialized in the front hall. "That's probably my fault," Faith said, her voice seeming to emanate from somewhere outside her body. "I'm so sorry, Cindy. I forgot to tell Ryan you wanted him to call."

Ryan rushed toward his wife, who was looking pale and glassy-eyed in her long white cotton nightgown. He snaked his arm protectively around her waist. "What do you mean? What's your fault?"

"About a month ago," Faith recited without emotion, "I locked myself out of the house. I didn't know what to do—the baby was inside—and then I saw Julia coming down the street, so I asked her to please call Ryan at work. But then I remembered we keep a spare set of keys under the mat, so there was no need to call him after all. I'm so sorry."

Cindy shook her head, feeling both foolish and dejected. "There's nothing for you to be sorry about. If anything, I'm the one who should be apologizing to both of you."

"Is something wrong?" Faith asked.

"Julia's missing," her husband told her.

"Missing?"

"Since Thursday morning," Cindy said. "I was hoping Ryan might know something. Anything."

"I wish I could help you," Ryan said.

"We haven't seen her," Faith added.

"Okay, well, if you think of anything, anything at all. . . ."

"We'll call you," the Sellicks said together.

Cindy walked down the outside steps, hearing their front door close behind her.

FIFTEEN

The police arrived at just after ten o'clock Tuesday morning.

Cindy had been up since three, when she'd jumped out of bed in a sweat, certain she'd forgotten to take the pills that were keeping her alive. She'd let out a long chain of expletives and climbed back under the covers. But, of course, sleep was now impossible. Too many thoughts, too much fear. Too many possibilities, too much anger.

How could she have confronted Ryan that way? What was the matter with her?

At five, she'd given up on sleep and turned on the TV, hoping for something suitably mind-numbing to lull her back into unconsciousness. Something like *Blind Date,* she'd hoped, thoughts drifting to Neil.

She doubted she'd hear from him again. Despite his promises to call later, she recognized there was only so much unsolicited drama a man could take. There was a point when intrigue degenerated into irritant. Cindy suspected she'd already passed that point.

At seven she was walking Elvis around the block. At seven-thirty, Tom called to say he'd just driven back from Muskoka, had she heard from their daughter?

She told him Julia was still missing and he should get his ass over to her house as soon as possible. He told her he didn't appreciate the profanity. She told him to fuck off.

An hour and a half later, resplendent in a dark blue suit, a lighter blue shirt, and a blue-and-gold-striped tie, Tom arrived with the Cookie, who was wearing black pants and a pink silk shirt. She took one look at Cindy in her baggy jeans and old mauve T-shirt and shook her head, as if she couldn't quite believe her husband had once actually shared a bed with this woman, let alone produced a child as beautiful and fashion-savvy as Julia.

At nine-thirty, Cindy called the police. A few minutes after ten o'clock, Detectives Bartolli and Gill were at her door.

Cindy ushered them into the living room, introducing the policemen to her mother and her younger daughter, as Elvis ran around in excited circles, convinced they were all there to see him. Cindy remained in the entranceway, as everyone arranged themselves around the room, the two policemen pulling out their notepads and perching on the ends of their chairs.

"What was your daughter wearing when you saw her last?" Detective Gill asked, his voice carrying traces of a soft Jamaican lilt.

A towel, Cindy realized, looking to Heather for help.

Heather was sitting on the sofa between her father and

her grandmother. Norma Appleton had insisted she wasn't going anywhere until Julia was found. ("What? I'm going to leave with you fainting all over the place?" she'd asked.) Thank God Leigh had gone home, although she was threatening to come back later.

"She was wearing her red leather pants and that white top she has with the V-neck and short sleeves," Heather said.

Detective Bartolli jotted that down, then held up the photograph Cindy had given him Friday. "And this is the most recent picture you have of her?"

Cindy looked from her husband to the Cookie, who was standing in front of the fireplace, as if afraid she might crease her pants were she to sit down. "Yes." Cindy tried not to picture the other photographs of her daughter in varying stages of undress.

"Can you describe Julia's mood on Thursday morning?" Detective Bartolli asked, as he had asked last Friday.

She was screaming at everyone, banging on doors, being totally unreasonable, Cindy thought. What she said was, "She was excited, a little nervous. She had a big audition coming up." She was being Julia, Cindy thought, listening as Tom explained the nature of Julia's audition.

"I'll need an address for this Michael Kinsolver," Detective Gill said.

"Kinsolving," Tom corrected, spelling the name slowly. "Three-two-zero Yorkville. Suite two-zero-four. I can get you his phone number. . . ."

"That won't be necessary, thank you."

"So, you last saw Julia at what time, Mrs. Carver?"

"I haven't seen her since last Tuesday," the Cookie replied.

"He was talking to me," Cindy said icily.

The Cookie raised her eyebrows, arranged her lips in a stubborn pout.

"It was a little after ten," Cindy said. "I was going out, so I went to her room to say good-bye and wish her good luck on her audition." And she yelled at me not to come in because she was naked, said I was slowing her down. "I just peeked my head in the door. Wished her good luck," she repeated.

"And then you went out?" the Cookie asked accusingly.

"Yes, I'm allowed out every now and then."

"I was here," Heather volunteered.

"You were here when Julia left?"

"Yes. It was around eleven o'clock."

"Apparently Julia had a fight with Heather's boyfriend just before she went out," Cindy interjected.

"It was nothing." Heather glared at her mother. "She was yelling at me too."

Detective Gill looked up from his notepad, exchanged looks with his partner. "Your boyfriend's name is . . . ?"

"Duncan. Duncan Rossi."

"Address?"

"He lives here."

Again the partners exchanged glances, while Cindy's mother shifted uncomfortably in her seat and the Cookie rolled her eyes.

Tom gave a look that said, It wasn't my idea.

"Where is Duncan now?"

"Out," Heather said. "I don't know where," she added when the look on everyone's faces made it clear more information was expected.

"We'll have to talk to him," Detective Bartolli said.

Heather nodded, turned away.

"We'll need a list of all Julia's friends," Detective Gill said.

Cindy felt a wave of guilt so strong it nearly knocked her off her feet. What kind of mother was she that she didn't know her daughter's friends?

"I can probably be of help to you in that regard," Tom said, as if reading Cindy's mind. "Until quite recently, Julia lived with me."

The officers nodded, as if this was something they heard every day. But Cindy knew what they were thinking. They were questioning what kind of mother she was that her daughter had chosen to live with her father. She couldn't blame them. How many times had she asked herself that same question?

"But she was living with you now?"

"Yes," Cindy said. "For almost a year."

"Do you mind my asking why she was no longer living with you, Mr. Carver?" Detective Bartolli asked.

Tom smiled, although Cindy could tell from the tight set of his jaw that he most certainly did mind. He was uncomfortable with being questioned, unused to being put on the spot. That was *his* job, after all.

"Tom and I moved into a new condo after we got married," the Cookie answered for him. "There's only so much room."

"Five thousand square feet," Cindy said, just loud enough to be heard.

"How did Julia feel about your remarriage?" Detective Gill asked Tom. "Was she upset about it?"

"The marriage was almost two years ago, and no, Julia wasn't the least bit upset. She loves Fiona."

The Cookie smiled and tossed her hair proudly from one shoulder to the other.

"And where were you on Thursday, Mr. Carver?"

"I beg your pardon!"

"We have to ask," Detective Gill apologized.

"Are you insinuating I had anything to do with my daughter's disappearance?"

"My husband is a very important attorney," the Cookie said.

Cindy rolled her eyes, amazed that people actually said things like, "My husband is a very important attorney," except on television.

"I was at my office," Tom replied testily. "You can check with my colleagues, if you honestly think that's necessary."

Detective Bartolli nodded, jotted this information in his notepad, and turned toward Cindy, who'd been discreetly enjoying her ex-husband's discomfort. How often, after all, did she get to see Tom squirm? "Was your daughter on any kind of medication?" he asked.

"Medication?"

"Painkillers, antidepressants . . ."

"Julia wasn't depressed," Cindy told the two officers, as she had told them at least half a dozen times already. "Why do you keep insisting she was depressed?"

"Mrs. Carver," Detective Bartolli explained patiently, "you have to understand that we get missing persons reports like this every day, and half the time, the person in question turns out to be someone who was feeling a little down and just decided to take off for a few days."

"And the other half?"

Detective Bartolli looked toward his partner. Detective Gill closed his notepad, leaned forward sympathetically. "To be frank, with people your daughter's age, suicide is our biggest worry."

"Suicide," Cindy repeated numbly.

"Julia would never commit suicide," Heather protested.

"Suicide is not an option," Cindy said, recalling her conversation with Faith Sellick. "What else do you worry about?"

"Well, of course, there exists the possibility of foul play. . . ."

Cindy put her hand across her mouth, stifled the cry pushing against her lips.

"But we're getting way ahead of ourselves here, Mrs. Carver. There's nothing to suggest any harm has come to your daughter."

"Except that nobody's heard from her for five days," Cindy reminded him.

"And that's unusual?"

"Of course it's unusual."

"Cindy," Tom said, in the voice he used whenever he sensed she was about to lose control. She'd heard that voice often during their marriage. There was something perversely comforting in hearing it now.

"Does she have any friends who live out-of-town?"

"She has several acquaintances in New York," Tom said.

Cindy stared blankly out the back window. This whole conversation was ridiculous. "Don't you think she would have told me if she were planning a trip to New York?"

"Maybe she told you and you forgot," the Cookie said.

"Is it possible she told you and you forgot?" Tom repeated, as if the Cookie had never spoken.

(Flashback: Julia, at thirteen, gets up from the kitchen table after dinner and walks out of the room. Her mother calls her back, reminds her to put her dishes in the dishwasher. Her father immediately echoes that request. "Julia, put your dishes in the dishwasher," he repeats. Julia reluctantly saunters back to the table, does as her father says.

"Why do you always do that?" Cindy demands after Julia has retreated to her room.

"Do what?"

"I tell her to do something, then you repeat it, as if my word doesn't carry enough weight."

"I'm supporting you, damn it."

"No. You're undermining me.")

Nice to see some things never change, even if wives do, Cindy thought now, smiling in spite of herself. "She didn't tell me," she told her ex-husband. "I didn't forget."

"You're sure?"

"She didn't," Cindy repeated, biting off each word. "I didn't."

"Fine. No need to get upset."

"No need to get upset?" Cindy countered. "Nobody has seen or heard from Julia since Thursday morning. I'd say there's plenty of reason to get upset."

Tom glanced at the detectives, as if to say, You see what I have to deal with? You understand now why I left?

"So you were of the understanding that Julia was coming home directly after her audition?" Detective Bartolli asked.

"I wasn't sure what her plans were, but she was supposed to be at a dress fitting at four o'clock."

"My granddaughter, Bianca, is getting married," Norma Appleton interjected. "Julia and Heather are bridesmaids."

"So, she didn't show up for her fitting." Detective Gill scribbled this fact in his notepad. "Was it common for Julia not to show up for appointments?"

"No," Cindy said.

"Yes," Tom corrected. "Julia can be very willful."

"In what way?"

"In the way of most twenty-one-year-old women." Tom smiled knowingly at the two detectives.

"But you can't think of any reason your daughter might take off for a few days without telling anyone?"

"No," Cindy said.

"Yes," the Cookie disagreed.

"Excuse me?"

"Why is that, Mrs. Carver?"

"Because she's a moron," Cindy answered.

"I believe Detective Gill was talking to *me,*" the Cookie said pointedly.

"You think Julia might have taken off without telling anyone?"

"I think it's possible."

"Why is that?"

"Because she was always complaining that she didn't have any privacy, that her mother was always on her case. . . ."

"You are so full of shit," Cindy said.

"Cindy, please," Tom warned.

"What exactly is this birdbrain trying to do here, Tom?"

"What did you call me?"

"Is she trying to sabotage this investigation? Is she trying to make it seem less urgent than it is?"

"Excuse me, but I'm right here," the Cookie said, waving her hand in the air, the huge diamond sparkler on her ring finger flashing like a strobe light in Cindy's eyes.

"Maybe it *is* less urgent than it *seems*," Tom said.

"Very clever," Cindy admitted, despising his easy glibness. "Our daughter has been missing for five days."

"I know that."

"Then what's the matter with you? Why aren't you more concerned? Why aren't you tearing your hair out?"

"Because you won't let me." Tom jumped to his feet, began pacing back and forth, Elvis barking beside him. "Because you're frantic enough for everybody. Somebody has to stay calm. Somebody has to behave like a rational human being. Shut up, Elvis."

"Oh God."

"Are you going to faint again?" Cindy's mother demanded, rushing to her daughter's side.

"You fainted?" Heather asked. "When?"

"The other day," her grandmother said. "Good thing her sister was here to catch her."

"I'm fine," Cindy assured everyone. "I'm not going to faint."

"I'll make some coffee," Norma Appleton offered, heading for the kitchen. "You sit down."

"I don't want to sit down."

"Don't be so stubborn," Tom said.

"Don't tell me what to do."

Again Tom looked at the detectives, as if to say, You see what I have put up with? You see why I had to leave?

"Mrs. Carver," Detective Bartolli said.

"Yes?" said Cindy.

"Yes?" said the Cookie.

Cindy gritted her teeth, took a deep breath, grabbed one hand with the other to keep from wrapping them around the Cookie's neck.

"Can we go over the events of last Thursday morning one more time?" Detective Bartolli asked.

"There's nothing to go over," Cindy insisted. "Julia was getting ready for her audition. She was excited, nervous. I went out about ten-fifteen to buy some wine. Apparently she was running late, so she asked Duncan to give her a lift. They had a fight," Cindy said. A fight so intense it spilled out into the street, so loud it attracted the attention of the neighbors.

"What was the fight about?"

"Julia got angry when Duncan said he didn't have time to take her to her audition," Heather explained patiently, "and she threw her usual tantrum. She was fighting with every one that morning." She looked guiltily toward her mother.

"You had a fight with your daughter, Mrs. Carver?" Detective Gill asked.

"It was hardly a fight."

"What were you fighting about?" Tom asked.

"It was nothing." Cindy motioned toward the dog. "I wanted her to take Elvis for a walk. She said she had to take a shower. She was banging on the bathroom door, trying to get Duncan to hurry up. I told her to stop. Stuff like that. Nothing important."

"Nothing else?"

"She didn't want to go to the fitting," Heather said.

"She would have gone," Cindy insisted. "She wouldn't just not show up. She wouldn't not come home for five days. She wouldn't not call."

"Take it easy," Tom cautioned.

"I don't want to take it easy. I want these policemen to stop asking questions and go out and find my daughter. Have you talked to Sean Banack?"

"What's Sean got to do with this?" Norma Appleton asked, coming back into the living room. "Coffee'll be ready in just a minute."

"We talked to him briefly on Friday. And we'll be talking to him again this morning."

"What about?" Cindy's mother asked.

"Mom, please. I'll tell you later."

"I understand this is a very difficult time for you, Mrs. Carver," Detective Gill said, staring directly at Cindy, leaving no doubt whom he was talking to, "but the more we know about Julia, the better our chances are of finding her. Can you tell me anything else about her? Her hobbies, what she likes to do, places she frequents . . . ."

"She likes the Rivoli," the Cookie answered before Cindy had a chance to formulate a response.

"The Rivoli?"

"Comedy club on Queen Street," Heather said.

I didn't know that, Cindy thought. Why didn't I know that?

"What about the dance clubs?"

Tom smiled. "She gave that scene up years ago."

"Does your daughter drink?"

"No," Cindy said.

"Occasionally," Tom corrected.

"What about drugs?"

"What about them?" Cindy asked.

"She went through the usual phase all young people do," Tom said.

She did? Cindy wondered. Why wasn't I told? Why didn't I know?

"But I sat her down," Tom continued, "had a long talk with her, told her that if she wanted to be a successful actress, she had to get serious, that I'd help her as much as I could, but only if she stopped goofing around and started focusing. Luckily, she listened."

You sat her down, Cindy thought. *You* talked to her. *You* told her she had to get serious, that *you'd* help her as much as *you* could. *You* pompous ass. Cindy rubbed her forehead. "What happens now?" she asked.

"We go back to the station, file a missing person's report."

"The reporters'll be all over this one." Detective Gill held up Julia's picture. "A pretty girl like this. Actress. Daughter of a prominent attorney. It'll be front page news."

"Is that good or bad?" Cindy asked.

"A bit of both. The public can be very helpful, but don't be surprised if once this news gets out, you start getting a lot of crank calls. If necessary, we'll put a tap on your phone, try weeding out the crazies."

"Try not to worry, Mrs. Carver," Detective Bartolli said. "She'll turn up."

Cindy stared at the detectives through eyes rapidly filling with tears. "Thank you," she said.

"In the meantime, if you think of anything else . . ."

"There is something," Cindy said, seeing Ryan's face in the blur of her tears, wondering again if he was really as innocent as he claimed.

"What's that?"

"My neighbor, Ryan Sellick. You might want to have a talk with him."

SIXTEEN

Okay, Cindy, what's going on? Why haven't you returned any of our messages?" Meg was asking. "Cindy? Cindy, are you there?"

Cindy brushed her lips against the receiver, pictured Meg and Trish huddled together on the other end of the line. "Julia's missing," she whispered.

"What? I didn't hear you."

"Julia's missing," Cindy repeated, louder this time.

"What do you mean, she's missing?"

Cindy said nothing. What more was there to say?

"We'll be right over."

Cindy replaced the receiver, shifted her gaze to the floor. She didn't look up. If she did, she knew she'd see her mother and daughter watching her from their seats at the kitchen table, and she'd have to contend with the worry in their eyes, and she didn't want to have to deal with their worry, she didn't want to have to deal with their fears, she didn't want to have to deal with anybody else's problems, damn it, she just wanted Julia to come home.

Wasn't that all she'd ever wanted?

"Who was that?" her mother asked.

"Meg. She and Trish are coming over." Cindy's voice wobbled, like a tire running out of air.

"I better make some more coffee."

Cindy continued staring at the floor.

"Mom?" Heather asked. "Are you okay?"

I can't move, Cindy thought. I can't think. I can't breathe. "I'm okay," she said.

"You're not going to faint again, are you?" her mother asked.

"I'm not going to faint."

"Is there anything you want me to do?" Heather asked.

"You can take the dog for a walk."

"Sure. Come on, Elvis. Let's go to the park."

Elvis was immediately up and at the front door, his tail wagging in blissful abandon.

I saw her yesterday, Cindy heard a man say. *She was sitting right over there.* He pointed at the park bench. *She was crying her heart out.*

"Heather, wait."

"What?"

Cindy watched her daughter's feet cut across her line of vision. She needs new sneakers, Cindy thought idly. And some new clothes for school. Didn't classes start this week? Cindy shook her head. She couldn't remember. "Why were you crying in the park?"

"What?"

"A man saw you there last week. Crying your eyes out, he said."

Heather shrugged, shook her head. "Wasn't me."

"Heather. . . ."

"Be back soon." She headed for the front door.

"Why don't you sit down," Cindy's mother advised after Heather was gone.

"I don't want to sit down."

"You'll make yourself sick."

"By standing?"

Her mother approached, put gentle arms around Cindy's shoulders, led her to the nearest chair, sat her down. "You've done everything you can, sweetheart. Now you have to let the police handle things."

"What if they can't? What if they never find her?"

"They'll find her."

"Young women disappear all the time. Sometimes they never come home."

"She'll come home," her mother insisted as Cindy sucked the words into her lungs, as if she were running out of air.

Suddenly she was back on her feet. "I can't just sit here and do nothing."

"You have to stay calm. You have to stay hopeful. The police will call as soon as they have any information."

"I can't wait. I have to do something." Cindy ran to the front door and opened it.

"Wait! Cindy! What are you doing? Where are you going?"

"I have to get out of here." Cindy ran down the steps to her driveway, climbed inside her car.

"Darling, please. Your friends will be here any minute. Where are you . . . ?"

Cindy backed her car onto the street, shot toward Avenue Road.

Less than five minutes later, she was running along Yorkville, almost colliding with several camera-toting tourists on the popular, boutique-lined street. "I'm sorry," she shouted as she ran, her eyes scanning the numbers of the tony, two-story buildings until she found Number 320. She pulled open the front door, took a deep breath, then waited until she was confident she'd regained her composure before slowly walking up the stairs to Suite 204. Seconds later, she was standing in a small waiting area, in front of a pencil-thin young man with pointy black hair. "I'm here to see Michael Kinsolving," she told him with a confidence that surprised her.

The young man raised his fingers to his face, the back of his left hand resting against the tip of his long nose, then leaned across his desk to check his datebook. "And you are?"

"Cindy Appleton," she replied, her maiden name feeling clumsy on her tongue, like a once-stylish suit that no longer fit. "I'm with the film festival."

"Do you have an appointment?"

"Of course." Cindy checked her watch. "Eleven-thirty. Right on time."

The young man rifled through the pages of his appointment calendar. "I'm sorry. There's obviously been some mistake. I don't seem to have you down. . . ."

"It's very important. I'm afraid there's a scheduling problem with regard to Mr. Kinsolving's new film . . ."

"A scheduling problem? Oh dear. Well, hold on. I'll see if Mr. Kinsolving can spare a few minutes. Your name again?"

"Cindy Appleton," Cindy repeated, the name a more comfortable fit the second time. Why had she never thought to reclaim it?

The skinny young man disappeared into the inner office, popped his head out seconds later. "Mr. Kinsolving will see you now."

"Thank you." Cindy slowly crossed the sparsely furnished waiting room, its walls lined with posters from past Toronto film festivals, thinking, What now?

At first she saw no one, just the back of a tall black leather chair, a large desk, and the grainy image of a beautiful young woman filling a large-screen TV on the opposite wall of the small room. "Well, well, look who's here," the young woman said, as if speaking directly to Cindy. Cindy froze, her eyes glued to the young woman's face, a face that was similar to Julia's in certain respects, but fuller, slightly coarser. "What happened? Forget your cigarettes?"

A click of a button and the image suddenly halted, reversed, stopped, started up again. "Well, well, look who's here," the woman repeated. "What happened? Forget your cigarettes?"

Another click. This time the image froze, vibrating slightly in its enforced stillness.

"Well, what do you think?" a deep voice asked from behind the high-backed leather chair. "Would you like to fuck her?"

"What?" Cindy took a step back, felt the crunch of the assistant's toes beneath her feet as he tried in vain to get out of her way.

The chair swiveled around abruptly, revealing a gnome-like man with a handsomely craggy face. Cindy recognized the famous director immediately from his rumpled hair and trademark black T-shirt. "I'm sorry," he said, not bothering to get to his feet, a slow smile spreading across his cherubic face. Magazine profiles always mentioned his roguish green eyes and acne-scarred skin. Both were more pronounced in person than in photographs. "I thought you were a man. I should have realized 'Sydney' could be a woman's name as well."

"Cindy," she corrected.

"Cindy," Michael Kinsolving repeated slyly, and Cindy understood in that moment that no mistake had been made, that this was a man who knew what he was doing at all times, that he'd said what he did to throw her off-guard, a subtly sadistic way of controlling the situation and putting her in her place. Clearly this was a man who was used to directing his reality. He motioned toward the TV screen. "Fucking her aside, what do you think of her?"

Cindy struggled to maintain her composure. "I'm not sure what you want me to say."

"Do you think she's beautiful?"

"Yes."

"Sexy?"

"I suppose."

"Her eyes aren't too small?"

"I don't think. . . ."

"Her lips aren't too thin?"

Cindy straightened her shoulders, took a deep breath. "Mr. Kinsolving. . . ."

"I'm going for a very specific look here. I want women to look at this girl and think 'lost soul.' I want men to look at her and think 'blow-job.' That's why I think her lips might be too thin," he said, as if they were discussing the weather.

Cindy tried not to give him the satisfaction of looking shocked. Was this how all directors talked about the young women who auditioned for them? Young women who bared their souls, and often a good deal more, for a chance to make their dreams come true? Women examined and dissected and ultimately reduced to a series of body parts that never quite measured up? Eyes that were too small; lips that were too thin. Souls that were lost. "What about talent?"

"Talent?" Michael Kinsolving looked amused.

"Is she a good actress?"

Michael Kinsolving laughed out loud. "Who cares? They're all good. That's the least of it."

"The least of it?"

"You have to want to fuck them," the gnomish director declared, leaning back in his chair. "That's what makes a star. They're bankable if they're fuckable."

"Mr. Kinsolving . . ."

"Who are you?" he asked, studying his manicured fingernails. "I know you're not who you say you are. You're certainly not from the film festival."

Cindy released a deep breath of air, eyes flitting across the bare white walls. "My name is Cindy Carver."

"Carver," Michael repeated, still not looking at her. "Why is that name familiar?"

"My husband, my *ex*-husband, is Tom Carver." A smile forced its way onto her lips.

Still no sign the Hollywood director had any idea who she was.

"My daughter is Julia Carver. She had an audition with you last Thursday morning at eleven o'clock."

Michael Kinsolving glanced questioningly at the skinny, spiky-haired young man hovering in the doorway.

"Yes," the young man replied, drawing out the word into several syllables. "I believe someone from Mr. Carver's office called to ask whether she'd kept that appointment."

"And had she?" Michael Kinsolving's voice was strong and clear, the voice of a man used to giving orders.

"Yes."

"So, what's the problem?" the director asked.

"She's missing," Cindy told him, watching his brow crease, his green eyes narrow. The same color eyes as Julia, she thought.

"Missing?"

"Nobody has seen or heard from her since she left this office."

"What are you saying? That she walked out of here and vanished into thin air?"

"We don't know what's happened to her," Cindy admitted, her voice filling with tears. "I guess I was hoping you might be able to shed some light on the situation. If you know anything at all that might help us find her. . . ."

Michael Kinsolving stood up slowly and walked to Cindy's side, the top of his head in line with the tip of her nose. "And what would I know exactly?"

"I guess I was hoping that she might have said something to you about her plans."

"Why would she do that?"

"I don't know." Already Cindy regretted her decision to come here. Had she really thought Michael Kinsolving might be able to help her?

"She probably took off with some guy she knew you

wouldn't approve of," he offered with a smirk. "Trust me, I know whereof I speak. I have three daughters myself."

Cindy vaguely recalled having read that Michael Kinsolving had five children from four different marriages.

"Of course they live with their mothers."

Of course, Cindy acknowledged with a nod. Didn't all daughters choose to live with their mothers after their parents divorced?

All except Julia.

"I'm sorry, but I don't see how I can help you." The director pulled a tissue from his jeans pocket and offered it to Cindy.

Cindy noted how muscular his arms were despite his diminutive size. "Did she give a good audition?" *Talent is the least of it.* "Did you say anything to her that might have upset her?" *Your eyes are too small; your lips are too thin.* "Did she seem depressed to you when she left?" *Did women look at her and think 'lost soul'? Did men look at her and think . . .* Dear God.

"I wish there was something I could tell you to put your mind at ease," Michael Kinsolving was saying. "But to be perfectly frank, I don't even remember the girl."

"Oh, you'd remember Julia. She's twenty-one, very beautiful, slim, blond . . ." Cindy stopped, looked at the television screen, understanding that for the past week, Michael Kinsolving's office had been inundated with slim, blond, beautiful women.

The director looked to his assistant for help. "Do we have a tape on her?"

The assistant nodded. "I'll get it." He backed out of the room.

Michael Kinsolving guided Cindy around his desk to his chair. "Would you like some bottled water or maybe an espresso?"

"Water would be great."

"With gas or without?"

Cindy shook her head, unable to choose.

"Philip," Michael Kinsolving called toward the next room, "some Perrier for Mrs. Carver. Can I call you Cindy?"

"Of course."

"Cindy." The director smiled, extended his hand. "Michael."

She took his hand, felt the strength in his fingers, suddenly understood why women found him so attractive. "My hands are cold," she apologized.

"Cold hands, warm heart," he said with a smile.

Was he flirting with her? Cindy wondered, quickly returning her hand to her lap, disconcerted by the thought. Was it possible he'd come on to Julia?

Philip reentered the room carrying a glass of sparkling water and a tape cassette. He handed the glass to Cindy, then crossed to the television against the far wall. "I believe she's on this tape. Shall I put it on?"

"Please," Michael directed as his assistant removed the existing tape and replaced it with another.

Cindy took a small sip of water, felt the bubbles bursting against her nose, like smelling salts. She watched the tape flicker on, held her breath as a young woman's face filled the screen. Like the woman before her, this woman was blond and beautiful. Cindy found herself focusing on her lips. Were they too thin? she wondered.

"I believe she's number eight." Philip fast-forwarded the tape.

A parade of lovely young women flew across the large-screen TV, their arms jerking up and down like marionettes, their heads turning this way and that, as if controlled by invisible strings, their blond hair shaking from one shoulder to the other, as the tape raced to find her daughter.

"So many women, so little time," Michael mused out loud. "Sorry. Didn't mean to sound glib."

Cindy shook her head. In truth, she'd barely heard him, and it was only his apology that gave the words weight, allowed them to sink in. She winced as the tape came to an abrupt halt, Julia's face filling the screen. Philip pressed another button and the image froze. Julia sat across the room, staring at her mother from inside a large, rectangular box, her bright smile frozen on her face.

"Oh yes," Michael said. "I remember her now. Her father's a lawyer. He does some work for our company."

"That's the one," Philip confirmed, once more receding into the background.

"Yes, she gave a very nice reading," Michael continued absently, leaning back against the front of his desk. "Are you sure you want to see this?"

"Please."

He signaled to his assistant, who pressed the appropriate button, unfreezing the frame and bringing Julia to life.

(Julia's Audition: A beautiful young woman sits on a small wooden chair, crosses one spectacular leg over the other. She is wearing red leather pants and a white blouse, which glares slightly under the harsh light. The camera slowly moves in on her face as she states her name. "Julia Carver," she pronounces clearly, then gives the name of her agent. She lowers her head, her hair falling across her face. Several seconds pass before she raises her head again, and when she does, it is almost as if Julia has disappeared and another girl has taken her place. This girl is tougher, angrier, sexier. And there is something else, something her defiant posture tries to hide. Behind the anger, the toughness, the undeniable sexuality, there is a sadness, a hunger, a raw need. Julia leans back, throws one elbow over the back of her chair, her eyes moving up and down an invisible visitor. The eyes of a lost soul. "Well, well, look who's here," she says. "What happened? Forget your cigarettes?"

"I came back to see you," an off-camera voice replies.

Julia's eyebrows arch in a gesture that is achingly familiar. "Is that supposed to make me go all weak in the knees?" she asks. "Is it? Because if it is, it's not working. See? My knees aren't weak at all." She recrosses her legs with provocative slowness, then leans forward, speaks directly into the camera lens. "What's the matter, baby? Disappointed? Surprised? Thought you could just waltz back into my life and everything would be the same as it was before you ran off with my best friend? How is Amy, by the way? No, don't tell me. The fact you're back is all the answer I need."

"Caroline . . ." the off-camera voice interrupts.

"I could have told you she was a lousy lay." The words roll off Julia's tongue like a stray caress. "I could have spared you the time and trouble. I was her roommate for . . . how many years? I saw the men come and go. I heard the phony groans, the fake orgasms she thought were fooling them. But none of them were the fool you turned out to be." Julia throws her head back, laughs unpleasantly. "What's the matter, baby? You come back for a real woman? Someone who doesn't have to fake it when you touch her? Someone who loves the feel of you pounding away inside her? Night and day. Day and night." Julia begins fidgeting in her seat, moving her hips in time to some distant, obscene rhythm. "Any time. All the time. Is that what you miss, baby? Is that why you've come home?"

"Caroline," the voice says flatly. "Amy and I got married last night."

The hard mask covering Julia's face melts away as tears overwhelm her eyes. "You got married?"

"Last night."

Julia says nothing. She simply stares into the camera, her tears spilling down her cheeks, washing away all traces of pride, her face an open wound.)

The push of a button. The scene ended. Julia's anguished face stared at her mother from inside her fifty-two-inch prison.

"I had no idea . . ." Cindy began.

"How good she is?" Michael asked quietly.

"Yes."

"Yes, she's very good," Michael agreed. "Would you like to see it again?"

Cindy shook her head. Another viewing of the tape and they'd have to scrape her off the floor.

"I could have a copy made, if you'd like."

"Thank you."

There was the sound of footsteps on the stairs. Philip stepped into the waiting room, returned seconds later, his pale face ashen. "It's the police."

"You called the police?" Michael asked, clearly more amused than annoyed.

Cindy shook her head as the two detectives strode purposefully into the room.

"Michael Kinsolving?" Detective Bartolli asked, his partner right behind. Both men stopped abruptly when they saw Julia's face on the large TV screen. Slowly, they pivoted in Cindy's direction. "Mrs. Carver?"

"What are you doing here?" Detective Gill asked accusingly.

Michael Kinsolving shook the officers' hands. "Mrs. Carver was hoping I might be able to be of some help in finding her daughter."

"And were you?"

"I'm afraid I have no idea where her daughter might be."

"We were just showing Mrs. Carver a tape of Julia's audition," Philip volunteered from the doorway. "Can I get anyone some bottled water or an espresso, perhaps?"

Detective Bartolli shook his head. "Detective Gill will drive you home, Mrs. Carver," he said, his voice bristling with annoyance at her unexpected presence.

"That's all right. I have my car."

"I'll walk you to it," Detective Gill said, leaving no room for discussion.

"I'll get a copy of the audition tape over to you as soon as possible," Michael said.

"Thank you." Cindy rose slowly from the chair, depositing her barely touched glass of Perrier on the director's desk, then shuffling toward the door, her feet numb, unable to feel the floor. She paused in the doorway. "Good luck at the festival."

"Thank you. Good luck finding your daughter."

Cindy nodded, aware of Detective Gill's firm grasp on her elbow.

"I'd like to have a look at that tape," she heard Detective Bartolli say as the door to the inner office closed and Detective Gill led her toward the stairs.

SEVENTEEN

Dark clouds were gathering overhead as Cindy pulled into her driveway. She recognized Meg's red Mercedes on the street as she ran up the front stairs to her house, fumbling in her purse for her key.

The front door opened just as she was reaching for it. "Where have you been?" Trish asked, pulling her inside, Elvis leaping toward her thighs. "Your mother's been frantic."

"Just like old times," Meg said, joining Trish in the hallway and taking Cindy into her arms. "Are you all right?"

Cindy nodded against her friend's shoulder. "I'm okay."

"Where have you been?" Trish asked again.

"Where did you go?" Norma Appleton demanded, joining the women in the front hall.

"I went to see Michael Kinsolving."

"Michael Kinsolving, the director?" Trish asked.

"Why'd you go see him?" Meg asked.

"Does he know where Julia is?" Cindy's mother asked at the same time.

Cindy shook her head. "He says he doesn't."

"You don't believe him?"

"I don't know." *Would you like to fuck her?* she heard the director ask, wondering if he'd posed the same question to others regarding Julia. "He claimed he didn't even remember her, that he's seen so many girls . . ." Her voice faded, disappeared. But then he acknowledged how very good she was. And how could anyone forget Julia?

"Have some lunch," Norma Appleton urged, ushering the women into the kitchen.

"I'm not hungry."

"Your mother's been filling us in," Meg said. "I can't imagine what you're going through."

"What do the police think?" Trish asked.

Cindy shrugged. "That it's too early to panic."

"They're right."

"I know."

"Doesn't help, does it?"

"No."

Trish hugged her, sat down beside her, as Meg pulled up another chair, wrapped her arms around Cindy.

"Where's Heather?" Cindy asked.

"Out. Said she'd be back later." Norma Appleton swayed from one foot to the other, as if weighing her options. "I think I'll go upstairs and watch TV," she announced finally. "Come on, Elvis, you can keep me company. Meg," she called from the top of the stairs, "make sure she eats something."

"Will do," Meg called back. Then, "Is she driving you nuts?"

"Only a little."

"I remember when my mother came to help out after Jeremy was born," Trish began. "What a time that was!"

"Trish," Meg said, "that was twenty years ago."

"Trust me, I'm still reeling."

Cindy laughed, a tentative trickle that wobbled through the still air.

"She flew in from Florida, arrived in the middle of a giant snowstorm, the plane was like three hours late arriving, and she was angry because no one could get to the airport to pick her up, and God forbid, she had to take a limo, and she marched into the apartment complaining about all things Canadian, especially her oldest daughter, who was inconsiderate enough to have given birth in February, of all months. I can still hear her say that—*February, of all months!* Anyway, she proceeded to wreak havoc for the next several weeks. I couldn't do anything right. Why had I allowed myself to gain so much weight during my pregnancy? Why was I nursing when I probably didn't have enough milk? I was going to have one awfully spoiled baby on my hands if I insisted on feeding him each time he cried. I could literally hear her gasp with horror every time I picked him up. *His head! Watch his head!* Like I was this total moron. Of course, I couldn't yell at her, so I took it out on Bill. Almost ended the marriage right then and there. No wonder Jeremy's an only child."

"Families." Meg shook her head. "You gotta love 'em."

"Do you?" Trish asked.

"In the end, what else is there?"

"Friends," Cindy said, reaching for their hands, entwining her fingers with theirs, trying to ignore the echo of

Tom's distant voice in her ear. *Friends,* he'd said dismissively. *Friends come and go.* Which probably accounted for Julia's revolving door approach to friendship.

"So, tell your friends exactly what's going on," Trish said.

Cindy immediately recounted the details of last Thursday morning, the chaos surrounding her final moments with Julia.

"So, you'd been arguing," Trish said in summation.

"We weren't arguing."

"All right. You weren't arguing. You were upset. . . ."

"I wasn't upset. . . ."

"Okay. You weren't upset."

"Maybe her audition didn't go well," Meg offered, as others had offered before. "Maybe she just needed some space."

"Could there be a new guy?" Trish asked.

"It's been five days," Cindy interrupted her friends, verbally italicizing each word.

"Yes, but . . ."

"But what?"

"This is Julia we're talking about," Trish reminded her.

"You know how she can be," Meg said.

"Do you honestly think she's that inconsiderate, that she'd disappear for this long without a word to anyone?" Had Trish always been this obtuse? Cindy found herself wondering.

"Tom hasn't heard from her either?" Meg asked.

"Tom hasn't heard from her either," Cindy repeated, sliding her hands into her lap as a tight smile froze on her lips. She imagined her body melting into liquid and spilling off her chair, forming an unwieldy puddle on the floor, much like the Wicked Witch of the West, who dissolved when Dorothy threw water at her head.

Meg's question was like that water, Cindy thought. Seemingly innocent on the surface, but capable of great damage, like acid. It seeped painfully between Cindy's ears, burning the words into delicate tissue.

Tom hasn't heard from her either?

Cindy felt strangely insubstantial, a feeling she'd often experienced during her marriage, and then again immediately after her divorce, as if she were somehow less solid without Tom at her side, as if his presence was necessary to give hers relevance, as if her opinions, her worries, her observations, weren't enough without his acknowledgment and approval.

Tom hasn't heard from her either?

Cindy knew that Meg would be both alarmed and horrified to think her words had been interpreted in such a manner, so Cindy tried hard to give the question context, assign it its proper perspective. Still, the words lingered, small thorns tearing at her already bruised flesh. She smiled at her oldest and closest friend, understanding that despite Meg's obvious sympathy for her plight, she had absolutely no idea of the turmoil raging inside her brain.

How little we know of what really goes on in people's minds, Cindy was thinking, her eyes traveling back and forth between the two women, the smile slowly sliding from her lips. How little we know one another at all.

"Are you all right?" Meg asked, her hand reaching over to smooth some fine hairs from Cindy's forehead.

Cindy shrugged, stared toward the backyard.

"So, tell us about Michael Kinsolving," Trish said. "Is he as sexy as people say?"

Cindy recognized Trish's question for the diversionary tactic it was. Still, it felt strange to be talking about Michael Kinsolving's sexuality under the circumstances. *Bankable is fuckable,* she heard him say. "His face is all pockmarked," she answered, deciding to go with the flow. "And he's short."

"How short?"

"Tom Cruise-short."

"Why are all the men in Hollywood so little?" Trish asked.

"And he didn't remember Julia?" Meg asked incredulously.

Cindy's heartbeat quickened at the mention of her daughter's name. "Not at first. But after we watched the tape . . ."

"What tape?"

"Julia's audition. You should see it. She's amazing."

"I'm not surprised," Meg said.

"She's so talented," Trish concurred, although neither woman had ever seen Julia act.

Cindy recalled the director's face at the conclusion of the viewing. "I think he was impressed. I think he'd forgotten how good she was." *Talent? Talent is the least of it. Do you want to fuck her?*

"Well, that's great then," Meg enthused. "It means he'll remember her. When she comes home," she added, her voice trailing away, disappearing into the air, like smoke from a cigarette.

When she comes home, Cindy repeated, clinging to the words, as if they were life buoys in a choppy sea. When she comes home, I'll buy her those Miss Sixty jeans she's been coveting. I'll take her to New York for a holiday weekend. Just the two of us.

"She's okay, Cindy," Trish was saying. "She'll turn up. Safe and sound. You'll see."

"How can that be?" Cindy demanded, hearing her voice rise. "How can someone disappear for almost a week and then just show up, safe and sound? How is that possible? Julia's not a child. She didn't wander off and get lost. And she didn't run away from home because she had a fight with her mother."

Had she?

"She's not a silly romantic like I was. She didn't elope with some guy to Niagara Falls."

Had she?

"She's not flighty or naïve. She's had disappointing auditions before. She knows the odds of getting cast in a major Hollywood movie."

Did she?

"I know you both think she's selfish and self-absorbed. . . ."

"No. We don't think that."

"It's okay, sweetie," Meg said soothingly. "It's okay."

"It's not okay," Cindy shot back angrily. "Julia wouldn't just take off without telling me. She certainly wouldn't take off without telling her father."

"I didn't mean . . ." Trish began.

"I was just trying . . ." Meg continued.

"She knows her actions have consequences. She knows I'd be worried sick. She wouldn't put me through this."

"Of course she wouldn't," the two friends agreed.

"So, where is she?" Cindy wailed, the sound of her voice bringing Elvis galloping back down the stairs, his barking mixing with her cries, underlining and surrounding her anguish. "Where is she?"

Cindy was lying in her bed, watching a peppy young woman named Ricki Lake interviewing a bunch of alternately sullen and giggly teenage girls. "Why do you think your friend dresses like a slut?" Ricki asked sprightly, pushing the phallic-shaped microphone into a girl's face.

Her lips aren't too thin?

Cindy flipped the channel before the girl could reply, watched as a handsome man named Montel Williams cast overly earnest eyes toward a trembling young woman in the seat beside him. "How old were you when your father first molested you?" he asked.

I want women to look at this girl and think, "lost soul." I want men to look at her and think, "blow-job."

Another press of the button and Montel was replaced by Oprah, then Jenny, then Maury, then someone named Judge Judy, a thoroughly unpleasant woman who seemed to think that justice could best be served by insulting all those who stood before her. "Did she ask for your advice?" Judge Judy demanded angrily of the hapless middle-aged woman in front of her. "Just because she's your daughter doesn't mean you can tell her how to run her life."

My daughter is Julia Carver.

Cindy flipped to Comedy Central, hoping for a laugh. "My mother's from another planet," a young female comic was espousing. She paused. "Actually, she's from Hell."

Cindy turned off the TV, tossing the remote to the end of the bed, just missing Elvis, who glanced at her with accusing eyes before jumping to the floor and skulking from the room. Downstairs, she could hear her mother in the kitchen, preparing dinner. Probably she should get out of bed, go down, and help out, but she was too tired to move, too drained to offer even token assistance.

The phone rang.

"Hello?" Cindy prayed for the sound of her daughter's voice, braced herself for the inevitable disappointment.

"Are you okay?" Meg asked on the other end of the line.

"I'm fine."

"I felt terrible after we left," Meg continued. "Like we failed you somehow."

"You didn't."

"I just wish there was something we could say or do. . . ."

"There isn't."

"I could come over later. . . ."

"No, that's all right. I'm pretty tired."

"You need your rest."

"I need Julia."

Awkward silence.

"Try to think positive."

Sure. Why not? Why didn't I think of that? "I'm trying."

"I love you," Meg said.

"I know," Cindy told her. "I love you too."

Cindy replaced the receiver, buried her face in her hands. "Think positively," she corrected, feeling her breath warm inside her cupped palms. She lifted her head, glared at the phone. "Did I ask for your advice?" she demanded in Judge Judy's strident voice.

She knew she was being unfair, that Meg was only saying what she herself would probably say if their situations were reversed. She knew her friend's concern was genuine, her love and support unwavering. She understood that both Meg and Trish wanted to be there for her, to comfort and protect her, but she also recognized that despite their best intentions, they could never really understand what she was going through. Just as they'd never wholly comprehended the sorrow she'd lived with all those years Julia spent living with her dad. Trish, with her husband and perfect son, Meg with two wonderful boys of her own. "Mothers of just sons," her own mother had once told her. "They're a different breed. They have no idea."

It wasn't that her friends were insensitive, Cindy thought. In fact, they were kind and considerate and thoughtful and everything true friends should be. They just didn't get it. How could they? They had no idea.

This is Julia we're talking about.

You know how she can be.

(Defining Moment: Tom across from her at the breakfast table, fingers digging into the morning paper he holds high in front of his face. "Nothing's ever enough for you," he says between tightly gritted teeth.

They've been fighting since last night. Cindy can barely remember what the argument is about. "That's not true," she counters weakly, lifting her glass of orange juice to her lips, wishing he would put the paper down so that she could see his face.

"Of course it's true. Face it, Cindy. I just don't measure up to your lofty standards."

"What are you talking about? I never said that."

"You said I stabbed Leo Marshall in the back."

"I said I was surprised you bad-mouthed the man in front of his client."

"His client is worth four hundred million dollars. He wasn't getting his money's worth with Leo. He will with me."

"I thought Leo Marshall was your friend."

"Friends." Tom sniffs. "Friends come and go."

Cindy feels the glass of orange juice tremble in her hands. "So the end justifies the means?"

"In most cases, yes. Can you get off your high horse now?"

"Can you put the paper down?"

"I don't know what more you want from me."

"I want you to put the paper down. Please."

He lowers the paper, glowers at her from across the table. "There. You happy? Paper's down. You got your way."

"This isn't about getting my way."

"Paper's down, isn't it?"

"That's not the issue."

Tom glances impatiently at his watch. "Look, it's eight-thirty. Much as I'd love to sit here arguing issues with you all morning, some of us have to go to work." He pushes back his chair. "I have a meeting tonight. Don't count on me for dinner."

"Who is she this time?" Cindy asks.

Tom gets to his feet, says nothing.

"Tom?" she says, her grip on her glass tightening.

He looks at her, shakes his head. "What now?" he says.

Probably it is the *now*, and not the fact of another woman that gets her. "This," she says simply, then hurls the contents of the glass at his face.)

That moment was the end of her marriage.

Although she and Tom remained together for several more years, the minute that orange juice left her glass, divorce was inevitable. It became strictly a matter of time, a gathering of energy.

It was the same with Meg and Trish, Cindy realized now, an ineffable sadness seeping through her pores, settling into her bones.

This is Julia we're talking about.

You know how she can be.

Maybe it hadn't been as dramatic as a tossed glass of juice, but another defining moment had quietly, yet inexorably, slipped by. Yes, Meg and Trish were her dearest friends. Yes, she loved them and they loved her. But unforeseen circumstance had intervened, and their friendship had been subtly and forever altered. Try as the three friends might to pretend otherwise, Cindy understood that their relationship would never quite be the same again.

Another woman had come between them.

Her name was Julia.

EIGHTEEN

Cindy opened her eyes to find Julia staring at her from across the room.

She pushed herself away from her pillow, holding her breath, watching as the familiar photo of her daughter enlarged to fill the entire TV screen. Cindy lunged toward it, straining to hear the announcer's voice, but the words failed to register. She reached for the remote control to raise the volume, but it wasn't beside her. "Where are you, damn it?" she said, frantic hands pawing at the folds of the blue-and-white-flowered comforter. She vaguely remembered having tossed it toward the end of the bed earlier in the day. How long ago? she wondered, glancing at the clock, noting that it was just minutes after six P.M., that despite the bleakness of the sky, darkness was still several hours away.

She must have fallen asleep, she realized, as the back of her hand slapped against the remote, knocking it from the bed. It shot into the air and plummeted to the floor, landing with a dull thud on the carpet, before bouncing out of sight.

Instantly, Cindy was off the bed and on her hands and knees, the carpet's stale scent pushing into her nostrils as she pressed her cheek against its soft pile. She lifted the white dust ruffle and poked her head under the bed, her hands fumbling around in the dark until they connected with the stubborn object. "Damn it," she said, bumping her head as she struggled to her feet, aiming the remote at the television screen, as if it were a gun, increasing the volume until the announcer's voice was all but shouting in her ear. Except that he was no longer talking about Julia. Her daughter's picture had been replaced by an aerial view of Canada's Wonderland, where the announcer intoned solemnly, a little boy of eight had been sexually molested only hours before.

Cindy changed the channel. A farmer's field popped into view. It took Cindy several seconds to realize she was looking at an old, dilapidated barn in a sea of swaying cornstalks. "Oh no." Cindy clasped her hand across her mouth to still the screams building in her throat. They'd found Julia's body in an abandoned barn off the King Sideroad. Sean's story had led them to her torn and battered remains. "No. No. No."

"Cindy!" her mother was yelling as Elvis began barking from somewhere beside her. "Cindy, what's wrong?"

Her mother was suddenly beside her, sliding the remote control unit from her daughter's hands, returning the TV's volume to a normal level. It was only then that Cindy was able to digest the announcer's words, to understand that the cornfield in question wasn't anywhere near the King Sideroad, but rather somewhere outside Midland, that the story concerned bumper crops of corn and had absolutely nothing to do with Julia.

"I thought. . . ."

"What, darling?"

"Julia. . . ."

"Was there something about Julia?" Her mother began flipping through the channels.

"I saw her picture. They were talking about her." Were they? Or had she just dreamed it?

And then there she was again: the tilted head, the dazzling eyes, the straight blond hair falling toward her shoulder, the knowing smile.

"Turn it up, turn it up."

"Police are searching for clues in the disappearance of twenty-one-year-old Julia Carver, daughter of prominent entertainment lawyer, Tom Carver. The aspiring actress was last seen Thursday morning, August twenty-ninth, after leaving an audition with noted Hollywood director Michael Kinsolving."

Julia's photo was instantly replaced by one of Michael Kinsolving, his arms around two voluptuous blond starlets.

"Police have questioned the famed director, in town to preview his latest film at the Toronto International Film Festival, and to scout locations for his next movie, but insist he is not a suspect in the young woman's disappearance."

The newscaster's bland face replaced Michael Kinsolving's, while Julia's picture reappeared in a small square at the right top of the screen. *"Anyone with any information regarding Julia Carver's whereabouts is urged to contact local police."*

"I guess that makes it official," Norma Appleton said, collapsing on the end of the bed, her face ashen, her eyes wide and blank.

Immediately Cindy was at her mother's side. "Oh, Mom," she said. "I'm so sorry. I've been so consumed with my own worry. I haven't even thought about how this might be affecting you."

"The last thing I want is for you to start worrying about me."

"You're her grandmother."

Her mother lowered her head. "My first grandchild," she whispered.

"Oh, Mom. What if she doesn't come home? What if we never find out what happened to her?"

"She'll come home," her mother said, her voice strong, as if the sheer force of her will could keep her granddaughter safe, bring her back home.

Cindy nodded, afraid to question her further. The two women sat at the foot of the bed, holding tightly onto one another, waiting for more news of Julia.

It was almost ten o'clock when Cindy heard the front door open and close. She leaned forward in her bed, pressed the mute button on the TV, and waited as footsteps filled the upstairs hall. "Heather?" she called. Heather had phoned to say she wouldn't be home for dinner, that she was meeting up with friends but wouldn't be late.

Elvis jumped from the bed, ran out of the room. "Heather?" Cindy called again.

"It's me," Duncan answered, his face appearing in the doorway, Elvis leaping against his legs with such enthusiasm he almost knocked him over.

"Duncan," Cindy acknowledged. "Is Heather with you?"

Duncan shook his head. Dark hair fell across his

forehead. He looked tired, as if he hadn't slept in days. His normally smooth skin was splotchy and pale. The stale odor of too many cigarettes wafted from his clothes. "I'm sure she'll be back soon," he said, swaying. He leaned his shoulder against the wall, as if to steady himself.

"Are you okay?" Then, "Are you drunk?"

Duncan's eyebrows drew together at the bridge of his nose, as if he were giving the question serious consideration. "No. Well, maybe. Just a bit."

"Why?"

"Why?" he repeated.

"Why were you drinking?"

He laughed, an annoyingly girlish giggle Cindy hadn't heard before. "Does there have to be a reason?"

"I don't think I've ever seen you drunk before."

"Yeah, well . . ."

"When did you start smoking?" Cindy pressed.

"What?"

"Smoking and drinking—it's just not you."

"I don't do it very often," Duncan said defensively. "Just every now and then. You know."

"I don't know."

"Mrs. Carver, you're making me a little nervous here."

"What are you nervous about?"

"Are you upset with me about something?"

"Why would I be upset with you?"

"I don't know. You just seem . . ."

"Upset?"

"Yeah."

"You don't think I have good reason to be upset?"

Duncan glanced down the hall toward the bedroom he shared with Heather. "I didn't say that." He paused, pushed himself away from the wall, wobbled on his heels. He took two steps, then stopped, stared hard at Cindy. "Has there been any news?" he asked, carefully. "About Julia?"

"No. Duncan . . ." Cindy called as he was about to turn away.

"Yes?"

"What's going on with you and Heather?"

Duncan swallowed, rubbed the side of his nose. "I don't know what you mean."

"Something's obviously not right between the two of you. . . ."

"We're just going through a bit of a rough patch, Mrs. Carver. That's all. I really don't feel comfortable talking about it."

"You'd tell me, wouldn't you, if there was anything I should know?"

"I don't understand."

"You know something, don't you?"

"I know I'm drunker than I thought I was." He tried to laugh, coughed instead.

"You know something about Julia," Cindy said over the sound of his hacking.

Blood drained from the young man's already pale face. He seemed to sober up on the spot. "About Julia? No. Of course not."

"You were fighting with her . . ."

"Yeah, but . . ."

"And then she disappeared."

"Mrs. Carver, you can't think I had anything to do with Julia's disappearance."

"Did you?"

"No!"

Cindy fell back against her pillow. Did she really think the boy she'd welcomed into her home, this young man who was her younger daughter's lover, was in any way responsible for her older daughter's disappearance? Could she really think that? She shook her head. She didn't know what to think anymore.

Duncan stood silently in the doorway, his arms hanging limply at his sides. "Maybe I should spend the night at Mac's," he said finally. "You'd probably feel more comfortable if I weren't around."

Cindy said nothing.

"I'll just get a few of my things."

Cindy listened as he shuffled down the hall. She thought of running after him, wrestling him to the ground, beating a confession out of him. Then she thought of her mother asleep in Julia's bed. What was the point in waking her up by creating a scene? Duncan wasn't about to confess to anything. Did she really think he had anything to confess?

Cindy heard him rummaging around in the closet. A few seconds later, she caught sight of his shadow as it hurried by her room. He left without saying good-bye.

"How have you been holding out, Mrs. Carver?" the doctor was asking, his face drifting in and out of focus. He was a big man with a full beard, bushy eyebrows, and thinning gray hair.

"I've been better," Cindy said, adjusting the white sheet tucked around her breasts.

"Remembering to take your pills?"

Cindy rubbed her eyes, watching the doctor's features flatten and slide across his face. "What pills?"

"It's very important that you take your pills, Mrs. Carver," he was saying. "If you don't take your pills, you'll die."

"Oh no!" Cindy shot up in bed. "I forgot. I forgot." She was halfway to the bathroom, her heart pounding against her chest when she stopped. "What pills?" she asked out loud, glancing toward the television set, realizing it was still on, that she'd fallen asleep sometime before midnight during a rerun of *Law & Order,* and that she was standing naked in the middle of her room in the middle of the night in the middle of the recurring nightmare that was her life. "What pills?" she asked again, collapsing on the floor, and staring at a handsome man in an orange jumpsuit walking glumly across her TV screen. The camera lowered to reveal the man's hands in shackles as his head of curly brown hair was pushed roughly inside a waiting police car.

It took Cindy a minute to realize that the man she was watching was Ted Bundy, notorious killer of dozens, possibly even hundreds, of young women. She shuddered, unable to turn away, transfixed by the announcer's deep voice and the killer's bottomless stare. *"Stay tuned as Ted Bundy makes a daring escape,"* the announcer intoned solemnly. *"*American Justice *continues after these messages."*

Was that what happened to Julia? Cindy couldn't stop herself from wondering. Had she run into a man whose boyishly handsome exterior belied the heart and soul of a deranged killer? Had he tricked her into getting into his car, charmed her into going back to his place? Had she tried to fight him off? Had he used drugs or chains to subdue her? Was he keeping her prisoner in some dank underground cave?

So many madmen out there, Cindy was thinking. So many *mad men*. Had one of them taken out his rage on her little girl?

She pushed herself to her feet just as Ted Bundy's smiling face once again filled the screen, his crazed eyes quickly settling on her own, daring her to confront him.

"The boy next door," the announcer proclaimed as Cindy groped for the remote control. For a station that was ostensibly about art and entertainment, it seemed to spend an awful lot of time detailing grisly murders. She clicked it off, watching the room go instantly dark, as if the TV itself had swallowed the light. Eating its young, she thought, walking to the window, pushing aside the curtains to stare at the backyard. There was only a sliver of moon, and it was pretty much hidden by the tall maple tree that sat in the center of the Sellicks' unruly and overgrown lawn. She should really do something about the cedar fence that divided their property, she thought absently. It was starting to cave in at the far end, buckling under the extended pressure of a nearby sumac tree. All it would take was one good snowfall and that fence would collapse altogether.

And "Good fences make good neighbors," she thought, recalling the lines by Robert Frost, projecting ahead to the coming winter, trying to imagine herself in three months time. Would she still be standing by her bedroom window, staring into the darkness, waiting for her daughter to come home?

It was then she saw her.

She was sitting on the bottom step leading from the patio off the kitchen to the backyard, and while Cindy couldn't see her face, she knew immediately it was Julia. "Julia. My God—Julia!" She pulled on her terry-cloth robe and raced down the stairs, Elvis at her heels. She ran into the kitchen, unlocked and opened the sliding glass door in one fluid gesture, and vaulted outside, the cool night air whipping against her face like a wet towel. "Julia!" she cried, as the girl on the bottom step jumped to her feet and backed into the night.

"Mom, no. It's me."

"Heather?!"

"You scared me. What are you doing?"

"What am *I* doing? What are *you* doing?" Cindy demanded. "It's after three in the morning."

"I couldn't sleep."

"I saw you from my bedroom window. I thought you were Julia."

"Sorry," Heather said. "It's only me." There was a strange, gargled quality to Heather's voice.

"Are you crying?" Cindy inched her way down the steps, as if her daughter were a stray kitten who might run away if she moved too fast.

Heather shook her head, the sliver of moonlight catching her cheek, revealing a path of still-wet tears.

"What is it, sweetheart? And please don't tell me, nothing," she added just as the word was leaving Heather's lips. "Does it have something to do with Duncan?"

Heather turned away. "We split up," she acknowledged, after a long pause.

"You split up? When?"

"Tonight."

"Why?" Cindy asked, her voice low.

"I don't know." Heather released a deep breath of air, lifted her palms into the air. "We've been fighting a lot lately."

"About Julia?"

Heather looked confused. "About Julia? No. What's Julia got to do with this?"

"What were you fighting about, sweetheart?" Cindy asked, ignoring the question.

Heather shook her head. "I don't know. Everything. Nothing. It's just so stupid."

"What is?"

"We were at this party a few weeks ago," Heather began slowly, "and I was talking to this guy. I was just talking to him. It was perfectly innocent, but Duncan said I was flirting, and we had this whole big argument. I thought we'd patched it up, but then it started up again last week. I'd gone to this club with Sheri and Jessica, and Duncan was really upset about it. He said I shouldn't be going places like that without him, and I said, Why shouldn't I? I'm not doing anything wrong. Why can't I just hang out with my girlfriends and have a good time? And he said, if that's what I wanted, I could hang out with my girlfriends every night. Then tonight we had another big fight, and Duncan got pretty drunk, and I got mad and left with Jessica, and when I got home, I saw his stuff wasn't here, so I called him at Mac's, and he said he wasn't coming back, that it was over between us."

"Oh, sweetie, he doesn't mean that."

"Yes, he does. He said he doesn't want anything more to do with any of us, that we're all crazy. Why would he say that?"

"I don't know," Cindy lied, thinking of their earlier confrontation.

"Did you see him when he came home?"

"Yes," Cindy admitted.

"And?"

"He was pretty drunk."

"What did you say to him?"

"Nothing. I just asked him a few questions."

"What sort of questions?"

"I just asked him . . . if there was anything he thought I should know."

"About what?"

"About Julia."

"About Julia? Why would you ask him about her?"

"I don't know."

"Why does everything always have to be about Julia?" Heather demanded suddenly. "I am so sick and tired of everything always being about Julia. This isn't about her. It's about me. Heather. Your other daughter. Remember me?"

"Heather, please. Your sister is missing. . . ."

"Julia's not missing."

"What?"

Heather looked toward the ground.

"What are you talking about? Are you saying you know where she is?"

"No."

"What *are* you saying?"

Heather reluctantly met her mother's gaze. "I didn't think she was serious. I didn't think she'd actually do it."

"What are you saying?" Cindy repeated, her voice a low growl. "Tell me."

"The whole thing is just so stupid," Heather began. "Julia was mad at Duncan because he wouldn't give her a lift. She was calling him names, accusing him of being selfish and ungrateful. She said if he was going to live here free of charge, the least he could do was make himself useful. He told her he wasn't her chauffeur; she told him to get the hell out of the house. I told *her* to get the hell out, that everyone was sick and tired of her stupid tantrums, and she said she couldn't wait to get out, that she hated me, that I was 'the bane of her existence.' And then she said that maybe she wouldn't wait until she'd saved up enough money to get her own place, maybe she'd move out right away. Today, she said. Maybe she wouldn't even bother coming home after her audition."

The words pounded against Cindy's consciousness like a boxer's fists. "What?"

"I didn't think she really meant it."

"Why didn't you tell me this before?"

"When? When the police were here? You got so angry when Fiona suggested Julia might want some time to herself. You said she was trying to sabotage the investigation. I didn't want . . . I mean, just in case . . . I didn't know . . ."

Cindy fought to make sense of her daughter's words. Was it possible Julia had simply taken off in a fit of pique? That she could be so vengeful, so thoughtless, so cruel? That she could disappear as a way of making a point?

No. It wasn't possible. No matter how angry Julia was at her sister, no matter how selfish and self-absorbed she might be, she would never put her family through this kind of prolonged torture. She might have stayed away a few hours to teach her sister a lesson, possibly even overnight. But not this long. Not this long. "No," Cindy said out loud. "Julia would never pull a stunt like this. She knows how worried we'd all be."

"Mom, wake up," Heather said forcefully. "The only person Julia has ever worried about is Julia. She . . ."

Whatever else Heather was about to say was lost as the palm of Cindy's hand came crashing down against the side of her daughter's face. Heather gasped, fell back, staggered to the ground.

"Oh, my baby, I'm so sorry," Cindy cried immediately, reaching for her daughter in the darkness, the sliver of moon spotlighting the trickle of blood slowly spreading across Heather's mouth like lipstick carelessly applied.

Heather recoiled from her mother's touch. "No, you're not." She pushed herself to her feet and ran up the back steps to the patio. "Face it, Mom," she said, clinging to the sliding glass door, "the only thing you're sorry about is that I'm standing here and Julia isn't." The simple sentence tumbled down the steps, then ricocheted off the damp grass to hit Cindy right between the eyes.

Cindy stood at the bottom of the outside steps, too weak to move, too numb to fall. This must be what it feels like to be shot, she thought, as Heather disappeared inside the house. The moment right before you collapse.

Cindy looked up at the moon's thin arc, searching for stars in the cloud-carpeted sky. But if there were stars, they were hiding, she thought, her eyes drifting toward the house next door.

Faith was at her bedroom window, staring down at her. It was too dark to read the expression on her face.

NINETEEN

The phone rang at seven o'clock the next morning, abruptly pulling Cindy out of a boxing ring in the middle of a close match with a faceless opponent. Blood seeped from her bandaged fingers as she stretched her hand toward the phone, the dream receding as she opened her eyes, disappearing altogether at the sound of her voice. "Hello," she said, trying to sound as if she'd been up for hours, and not, as was the case, as if she'd just fallen asleep.

"Cindy Carver?"

Cindy pushed herself into a sitting position as Elvis adjusted his position at her feet. "Who is this?"

"It's Elizabeth Kapiza from the *National Post*. First, let me say how very sorry I am about your daughter."

"What's happened?" Cindy grabbed for the remote control and turned on the television, rapidly flipping through the channels, her heart pounding wildly against her chest, as if trying to escape before the dreadful news descended.

"Nothing," Elizabeth Kapiza assured her quickly. "There's nothing new."

Cindy fell back against her pillows, fighting the urge to throw up, her forehead clammy and bathed in sweat.

"I don't know if you're familiar with my work," Elizabeth Kapiza was saying.

Cindy pictured the thirty-five-year-old woman with the pixie haircut and gold loop earrings that were her trademark smiling at her from the side of newspaper boxes across the city. "I know who you are." Everyone knew Elizabeth Kapiza, Cindy thought, even if they didn't read her columns. Her increasingly high profile was the result of a canny mixture of talent and self-promotion, achieved by carefully injecting herself into the middle of every tragedy she covered, be it a local case of child abuse or a case of international terrorism. In theory, she wrote human interest stories. In actual fact, she wrote about herself.

"I was wondering if I could come by and talk to you."

"It's seven o'clock in the morning," Cindy reminded her, glancing at the clock.

"Whenever it's convenient for you."

"What is it you want to talk about?"

"About Julia, of course," Elizabeth answered, the name sliding easily off her tongue, as if she'd known Julia all her life. "And you."

"Me?"

"What you're going through."

"You have no idea what I'm going through." Cindy brushed an unwanted tear away from her cheek, felt another one rush to take its place.

"That's what I need you to tell me," the woman urged gently.

Cindy shook her head, as if Elizabeth Kapiza could see her. "I don't think so."

"Please," the reporter said softly. "I can help you."

"By exploiting my daughter?"

"Cindy," Elizabeth Kapiza said, the name wrapping itself around Cindy's shoulder like a lover's arm, "the more publicity there is in cases like this, the more chance there is of a happy ending."

A happy ending, Cindy repeated silently. How long had it been since she'd believed in happy endings? "I'm sorry. I don't think there's anything I can tell you that would help."

"You're her mother," Elizabeth said simply.

"Yes," Cindy agreed, unable to find the strength to say more.

"Would you at least think about it, and call me if you change your mind?" Elizabeth Kapiza relayed her office telephone number, her home number, and the number of her cell phone, then repeated them all again as Cindy obligingly scribbled them across the bottom of a Kleenex box, although she had no intention of calling the woman back.

She barely had one foot out of bed when the phone rang again. This time it was a reporter from the *Globe and Mail*, calling for a quote. Cindy mumbled something about just wanting her daughter back home safe and sound, then mumbled roughly the same sentiments to the reporters from the *Star* and the *Sun*, both of whom phoned just after she'd emerged from the shower. *How long has your daughter been acting?* they asked. *What are some of her credits?*

Cindy combed her wet hair away from her face, then pulled on a pair of blue jeans and a white T-shirt, and went downstairs, Elvis running along ahead of her, impatiently pacing back and forth in front of the door as she opened it.

Julia's face stared up at her from the front pages of both the *Globe* and the *Star*. ACTRESS, 21, MISSING 6 DAYS, read the copy beneath the familiar black-and-white photograph. From the kitchen, the phone started ringing. Cindy ignored it as she walked into the room, and spread the papers across the table.

Police are investigating the disappearance of beautiful aspiring actress, Julia Carver, 21, missing since last Thursday. Ms. Carver, daughter of prominent entertainment lawyer Tom Carver, vanished without a trace after a meeting with renowned Hollywood director Michael Kinsolving.

Cindy read the paragraph once, then read it again out loud as the phone continued its stubborn ringing.

"'Police are investigating the disappearance of beautiful aspiring actress, Julia Carver, 21, missing since last Thursday. Ms. Carver, daughter of prominent entertainment lawyer Tom Carver. . . .'"

Cindy smiled, pushing the *Globe* out of the way, and reaching for the *Star*. The phone stopped ringing, started up again almost immediately.

ACTRESS GOES MISSING AFTER AUDITION WITH HOLLYWOOD DIRECTOR, read the caption underneath Julia's picture. *Julia Carver, 21, the beautiful actress-daughter of entertainment lawyer Tom Carver, has been missing from her Toronto home since Thursday, August 29.*

"No," Cindy said, reading it again, and then again.

Beautiful actress-daughter of entertainment lawyer Tom Carver.

Daughter of prominent entertainment lawyer Tom Carver.

As if Julia has only one parent, Cindy thought, a feeling of outrage growing inside her stomach, like a malignant tumor. When had she become nonexistent? When had she ceased to matter? It was almost as if, like her daughter, Cindy Carver had suddenly and without notice vanished from the face of the earth. The newspapers, with a couple of careless phrases, had erased her from the landscape, swept her from her daughter's life.

Once again, Tom had stolen Julia from her. This time, without even trying.

The press had made it official: Julia was Tom Carver's daughter.

Her mother was nowhere in sight.

The phone stopped ringing.

"I don't exist," Cindy told Elvis, whose response was to lift his leg and pee against the side of her chair. Cindy stared at her daughter's scruffy terrier, torn between crying and laughing out loud. "It's okay," she said, grabbing some paper towels from the counter and soaking up the mess, quietly accepting the blame for the dog's errant behavior. It was her fault, after all. She should have taken him out. *Everything* was her fault. She was as lousy a mother to Elvis as she'd been to Julia. "Julia Carver," she whispered, staring at her daughter's picture on the front pages of the papers, "daughter of Cindy. Daughter of *Cindy*, damn it." And I will not be brushed aside again, she added silently. I will not just disappear.

I don't think there's anything I can tell you that would help, she'd told Elizabeth Kapiza.

You're her mother.

"Yes, I am," Cindy said, pushing herself to her feet and walking to the phone, quickly punching in the last of the numbers she'd scribbled on the bottom of the Kleenex box earlier, and had no trouble recalling now. "Elizabeth Kapiza?" she asked the woman who answered on the first ring, as if she'd been waiting for Cindy to call. "This is Cindy Carver."

"When can I see you?" the reporter asked.

"How's nine o'clock?"

By eight-thirty, Cindy had changed her clothes three times and was on her fourth cup of coffee.

"You look nice," her mother told her, coming into the kitchen, neatly dressed in varying shades of blue. "Is that a new blouse?"

Cindy smoothed the front of a pink silk shirt she'd bought on impulse at Andrew's the previous summer, but had never worn because it wasn't really *her*. Was it her now that she was no longer a person of substance? she wondered, securing the button at the top. "You want some breakfast?"

"Coffee's fine for now," her mother said, helping herself. "Who's been phoning so early in the morning?"

"Who hasn't?"

Her mother shrugged. "I take it nothing's new."

Cindy pushed the morning papers toward her. "See for yourself."

Norma Appleton scanned the front pages of both papers. "Oh, my," she said, sinking into one of the kitchen chairs.

"Elizabeth Kapiza's coming to the house in half an hour to interview me."

"You think that's wise?"

"I phoned the police," Cindy told her mother. "They

said they don't have a problem with it as long as I don't talk about the investigation. They said it might even help."

Her mother sipped her coffee slowly, ran shaking fingers along her granddaughter's grainy cheek. "Where's Heather off to so early?"

Cindy regarded her mother quizzically. What was she talking about?

"Where's Heather going?" Norma Appleton asked again.

"I don't understand."

It was her mother's turn to look confused. "When I got up, she was packing."

"Packing? What are you talking about?" Cindy ran into the front hall just as Heather appeared at the top of the stairs, an overnight bag in her hands. "What are you doing?"

"I thought I'd stay over at Daddy's for a few days," Heather said, proceeding slowly down the steps, dropping the black leather overnight bag to the floor as she reached the bottom. "Hi, Grandma." She waved to the woman watching from the kitchen doorway.

"Hi, sweetheart."

"Why are you doing this?" Cindy asked.

"What's going on?" Norma Appleton's eyes darted back and forth between her daughter and her grandchild.

"Things are pretty intense around here. I thought Mom could use a little space," Heather explained. "And it's been a while since I spent any serious time at Dad's. It's just for a few days," she said again.

"Heather, please, if this is about last night. . . ."

"What happened last night?" her mother asked.

"I've already called Dad," Heather said. "He's picking me up in a few minutes."

"You know how sorry I am. You know I didn't mean to slap you."

"You slapped her?" her mother said.

"It's not that," Heather said.

"Then why are you going?"

Heather hesitated, her eyes filling with tears. "I just think it'll be better for everyone if we take a small break."

Cindy shook her head. "Not for me."

Heather hesitated, her body swaying toward her mother. "I've already called Dad."

"Call him back."

The doorbell rang.

"Please, darling," Cindy continued, following Heather to the front door. "Tell him you changed your mind. He'll understand."

Heather took a deep breath, opened the door.

"I take it you've seen the morning papers," Leigh said, her hair a war zone of conflicting curls. She dropped a small suitcase to the floor at Heather's feet.

"What's this?" Cindy eyed the beat-up, brown leather suitcase suspiciously.

"I've been calling you for over an hour. Either the phone is busy or nobody answers. I finally got fed up and told Warren that's it. I can't stand not knowing what's going on. He'll have to manage without me for a while. I'm moving in with you guys until we know what's what."

"No," Cindy said quickly. Then, "That's really not necessary."

"Heather and Duncan can sleep downstairs. I'm sure they won't mind. My back's too fragile for sofa beds."

"Actually, I'll be staying at my father's for a few days."

"Well, then, that worked out perfectly, didn't it?" Leigh said.

"No," Cindy protested again, as outside a car horn honked twice.

"That'll be Dad." Heather glanced out the open door as Tom's dark green Jaguar pulled into view.

"Please, Heather," Cindy tried one last time.

"Don't worry, Mom. It'll be okay. I'll call you later." Heather's lips brushed against her mother's cheek. Then she ran down the front steps, throwing her overnight bag into the backseat of her father's car, and climbing into the front seat beside him.

(Flashback: Julia carries her new Louis Vuitton luggage to Tom's waiting BMW, waits while he puts it inside the trunk, then slides into the front seat next to him.)

Cindy watched as Tom's car pulled away from the curb.

She was still standing at the front door staring down the empty street when Elizabeth Kapiza showed up at precisely nine o'clock, tape recorder in hand, photographer in tow.

THE NATIONAL POST
THURSDAY, SEPTEMBER 5, 2002
A MOTHER'S ANGUISH
BY ELIZABETH KAPIZA

Toronto, September 5—She sits in the living room of her spacious, art-filled home in midtown Toronto, a woman whose pale face is ravaged by uncertainty and fear. Tears are never far from her expressive blue eyes; they stain the front of her stylish, pink silk blouse. "I'm sorry," she apologizes repeatedly, twisting an already shredded tissue in her lap. She offers me coffee and a bagel, inquires after my health, asks if I'm comfortable. A typical mother, I find myself thinking. Except sadly, Cindy Carver is anything but typical.

Because Cindy Carver is the mother of Julia Carver, the stunning twenty-one-year-old actress who went missing a week ago, and whose father is well-known entertainment lawyer Tom Carver, from whom Cindy has been divorced for seven years. Cindy smiles at the mention of her ex-husband's name, and it is obvious that whatever their past differences, their daughter's disappearance has brought them closer together.

It is also obvious that beauty runs in the family, for Cindy Carver, despite the anguish of her situation, is still, at forty-two, a very beautiful woman. As she perches on the end of one of two exquisitely appointed tan leather sofas, one can see traces of Julia in her face, in the tilt of her head, in the soft fullness of her lips, in the determination of her gaze. "My daughter will be coming home," she says, and I ache to believe her.

The odds, of course, aren't good. Young women who go missing rarely come home. Once lost, they are rarely found. And if they are, it is usually in shallow graves, after weeks, months, even years of soul-destroying searching. One has only to think of the grisly discoveries on that infamous pig farm in British Columbia, or the recent rash of kidnappings south of the border. One has only to mention the names Amber and Chandra. One has to pray that the name Julia will not be added to the list.

"What do you think has happened to your

daughter?" I ask gently, thinking of my own daughter, age five, safe at home.

Cindy shakes her head, dislodging several fresh tears, unable to formulate a response, to say out loud what must surely be going through her mind, that her beloved firstborn child has fallen victim to the kind of senseless violence that is so much a part of big-city life, that her daughter's sweet smile might have been misinterpreted by a mind unhinged by alcohol and drugs, that her natural exuberance might have acted as a red flag waving in the face of insanity.

"Julia is so full of life," her mother says lovingly. "She's got all this energy, all this drive. You take one look at Julia and you know she's going to be a success at whatever she decides to do."

What she's decided to do, of course, is act. Julia, according to the woman who is her biggest fan, is an extremely gifted actress whose talent and beauty are matched only by her determination to succeed. Indeed, according to famed Hollywood director Michael Kinsolving, no stranger to beautiful, talented women, and the man for whom Julia not only auditioned on the morning of her disappearance, but who may have been the last person to have seen her, Julia had stardom written all over her. "An extraordinary talent," he confides later over cocktails. "Gorgeous, of course. But more than that. She has that extra something that defines a star."

What does Julia's mother think of the rumors swirling around the well-known ladies' man, rumors that hint at a possible romantic involvement between the aging Lothario and the young starlet? "Ridiculous," Cindy Carver scoffs succinctly. "They just met that morning." Does she give any credence to the speculation that Michael Kinsolving might somehow be involved in her daughter's disappearance? "I can't imagine . . ." she begins, her voice breaking.

Immediately, her mother and sister, both of whom are staying with Cindy until Julia comes home, rush to her side, smoothing several wayward hairs away from her face, wrapping her in their protective embrace. Families, I marvel, as I show myself to the door, anxious to get home to my daughter and her three-year-old brother. Already I picture their wondrous smiles as I walk through the door, their eager arms extended to welcome me home. How lucky I am, I think, aching to hold my babies in my arms. Tonight, when I tuck them into their beds, I will ask them to say a little prayer for Julia.

And one for her mother as well.

TWENTY

On Saturday morning, another girl was reported missing.

Like Julia, she was described as tall, blond, and beautiful, although the photograph that ran on the front page of all four major Toronto papers revealed a slight cast in her left eye that made her appear slightly cross-eyed. Her name was Sally Hanson, and she was three years older than Julia, and maybe ten pounds heavier. Since her graduation from Queen's University two years earlier, she'd been working in the editorial department of *Toronto Life* magazine, and according to the hastily assembled remarks from a number of her coworkers, she was outgoing and popular.

Like Julia, Sally Hanson had recently broken up with her boyfriend, whom police were reportedly most anxious to contact. Apparently he'd taken off on his motorcycle around the same time Sally's worried parents were letting themselves into their daughter's empty apartment.

Like Julia, Sally had disappeared on a Thursday, and like Julia, Sally was a movie buff, having planned her vacation to coincide with the film festival. She'd bought thirty coupons and, according to her mother, she'd been looking forward to seeing three films a day, every day, for the ten days of the festival's duration. Among those films for which she had tickets was Michael Kinsolving's highly anticipated new movie, *Lost*.

And yet, police were downplaying the speculation that there was any connection between the two disappearances. *"We have no reason at all to suspect these two cases are related,"* someone named Lieutenant Petersen was quoted as saying. The *Globe* and the *Post* largely echoed that sentiment, while the *Star* printed a lengthy article comparing and contrasting the lives of the two young women and the events leading up to their disappearances. Only the *Sun* asked the obvious question: SERIAL KILLER STALKING TORONTO FILM FESTIVAL? it queried in headline type.

"Don't read that garbage," Leigh said, wresting the tabloid from Cindy's hands.

"Hey, give that back." Cindy jumped up from her seat at the kitchen table and reclaimed the paper before her sister could stuff it into the trash container under the sink.

"Really, Cindy. What's the point?" Leigh assumed their mother's once-familiar stance, legs spread shoulder-length apart, hands on her hips, chin lowered, eyes raised, as if she were peering up over the top of a pair of reading glasses. She was wearing an unflattering, sky blue track suit that flattened her bosom and widened her hips, and a matching blue headband that pulled her eyebrows into her forehead and made her look vaguely deranged.

"The point is I want to read it," Cindy said.

"What for? It'll only upset you."

Cindy shrugged. What else is new? the shrug said.

"It's all just speculation anyway," Leigh told her.

"I know that."

"I'm sure that if the police thought there was any connection between the two cases, they'd say so."

Cindy stared at her sister, trying to digest Leigh's latest pronouncement. When had Julia lost her humanity, become merely a "case"?

The phone rang.

"I'll get it." Leigh was instantly at the phone. "Hello?" Immediately her face darkened. "Who is this?"

"Who is it?" Cindy echoed.

"You sick fuck!" Leigh slammed the phone into its carriage.

"Who was that?" Cindy asked, more amused than alarmed by her sister's outburst. "Who was that?" she asked again, although she already knew the answer.

"What difference does it make? They're all the same."

"What'd this one say?"

"The usual crap."

"Such as?"

"*I have your daughter. I'm going to cut her up into little pieces.* Yada, yada."

Cindy shook her head, amazed, though no longer surprised, by the cruelty of others. The police had warned her about all the twisted minds out there, the perverts who feasted on other people's suffering, who wallowed in their misery. *Hang up,* they'd told her. *Better still, don't answer your phone.* Sometimes Cindy heeded their advice. Other times, she didn't.

Ten minutes later, the phone rang again.

"I'll get it," Cindy said, this time beating her sister to the phone.

"Honestly, Cindy, you almost knocked me down."

"Hello," Cindy said.

"Hi, yourself," the voice answered.

The voice was both husky and light, soothing and creepy, alien and familiar. An obvious attempt at disguise. Why? Was it someone she knew?

"Who is this?"

"Have you seen the morning papers?"

"Who is this?" Cindy repeated.

"They think Julia might be the victim of a serial killer."

"Who is it?" Leigh asked impatiently. "What's he saying?"

"It would serve her right," the voice continued. "Your daughter's a slut, Cindy. She's nothing but a cheap whore."

A sharp cry suddenly stabbed at the air, tore through the phone wires, pierced Cindy's ear.

"My God," Cindy said, feeling her face drain of blood as she identified the sound.

"For heaven's sake, Cindy," Leigh said, "hang up the damn phone."

Cindy held her breath, listened for the sound again. It didn't come, but it didn't matter. Cindy knew exactly what it was.

The sound of a baby crying.

"Faith?" Cindy whispered.

The phone went dead.

In the next second, Cindy was out of the kitchen and at her front door, Leigh following right behind.

"Where are you going? What are you doing?" her sister

shouted after her, as Cindy ran down the steps and cut through the bushes into her neighbor's front yard.

Cindy felt Leigh's hand on her arm, tried shaking it away, but Leigh's fingers were like stubborn vines, refusing to be severed with a simple shrug. "Let go," Cindy hissed between tightly gritted teeth as she yanked her arm away.

"Cindy!" she heard Leigh shout as she raced up the front steps of the Sellick home, not looking back.

The door opened just as Cindy reached the top step. "Cindy!" Faith exclaimed, clearly surprised to see her. She closed the door behind her and adjusted the green corduroy Snuggly at her breasts. Inside it, Kyle was sleeping soundly, his eyes tightly closed, his lips sucking contentedly at his pacifier. "What's happened? Has there been any news?"

"Did you just call me?" Cindy asked.

"What?"

"Did you just call me?"

"Call you? No. Why?"

"You didn't just phone me?"

"What's going on?" Faith glanced past Cindy to Leigh, who was now standing at the bottom of the stairs.

Leigh lifted her hands into the air, as if to say, You tell me.

"Somebody just phoned my house. I heard a baby crying in the background."

"Well, no wonder you thought it was me." Faith smiled, tenderly stroking the top of her baby's head. "It wasn't Kyle. Believe it or not, he's been sleeping like an angel all morning. I really think we've turned a corner. Are you okay? You don't look so hot."

"Come on, Cindy," Leigh was saying. "We'll let the police handle it."

"The police?" Faith asked.

"They're tapping the phone."

"The police are tapping your phone? Why?"

"We've been getting a lot of crank calls," Leigh explained. "Which wouldn't happen so often," she continued, reaching for Cindy's hand, "if my sister would get Caller ID." She guided Cindy down the stairs toward the sidewalk. "We'll take the long way home, if you don't mind."

"I'm sorry I yanked your arm like that," Cindy said.

"Don't give it another thought."

"She almost broke my arm, she yanked it so hard," Leigh told her mother as soon as she returned from walking the dog.

"You yanked your sister's arm?" their mother asked Cindy incredulously, following the dog into the kitchen. "Hmm, what smells so good?"

"I'm making a lemon cake," Leigh said.

"You shouldn't fight with your sister," her mother said with a shake of her head. "Honestly, I can't leave you girls alone for a minute."

The phone rang.

"Don't answer it," Leigh instructed.

"Maybe it's Julia," Cindy said hopefully.

"This wouldn't happen if you had Caller ID," her mother said.

Cindy picked up the phone, braced herself for the worst.

It was Meg. "How're you doing?" Her voice sounded rushed, as if she were talking while running. Which, of course, was exactly what she was doing, Cindy realized, picturing Meg racing along Bloor Street, trying to get from one movie to the next as quickly as she could, desperate not to miss anything. The festival had been up and running for two days now, and although neither Meg nor Trish had so much as mentioned the festival, Cindy knew they were going without her.

Life goes on, she understood, wishing she could press a button, freeze time as easily as she could freeze an image on her television screen.

She knew she shouldn't judge Meg and Trish harshly. Her friends couldn't be expected to drop everything, abandon all their plans, put their lives on hold, because of something that didn't directly concern them. She shouldn't resent them for enjoying themselves, for laughing, for forgetting about her for hours at a stretch. She shouldn't, she thought. But she did.

"I read in the paper about that other missing girl," Meg said, as a car honked in the background. "What do the police really think?"

Cindy shook her head, said nothing.

"Look, you must be going stir-crazy over there. Why don't you come to a movie with us?"

"A movie?"

"I know it sounds frivolous, and I don't mean to sound insensitive. I just think it might be a good idea for you to get out of the house for a while, get some fresh air, get away from your mother, take your mind off everything."

"You think it's that easy?"

Meg sighed the sigh of the deliberately misunderstood. "Of course it's not that easy. I didn't mean to imply. . . ."

"I know. I'm sorry."

"Will you think about it?"

"Sure," Cindy said, although she had no intention of doing so.

"Call me on my cell. I'll keep it on all day."

Cindy smiled, recalling how enraged festival patrons got whenever anyone's cell phone rang during a screening.

"I love you," Meg said.

"I love you too."

Her mother and sister were staring at her from across the room, their bodies tensed to take action at the first sign of distress. Ever since Cindy had fainted, their eyes were on constant vigil, never allowing her far out of their reach. She wondered whether anyone would ever look at her the way they used to—without pity, without sadness, without fear.

Cindy shook her head, trying to rid her brain of such depressing thoughts. Meg was right—she was going stir-crazy. She needed air.

"I'm going upstairs to shower," her mother said. "Why don't you lie down for a while?"

"Because I'm not tired," Cindy said.

"You're sure?" Leigh asked as their mother left the room.

Cindy sank into one of the kitchen chairs, watched as her sister began preparing the icing for the cake. "You don't have to do this, you know."

"I know."

"Have you spoken to Warren today?"

"Of course."

"I'm sure he's wondering when you're coming home."

"He's fine. He'll be over later."

Cindy nodded. "Is everything all right?"

"What do you mean?"

"Between the two of you?"

"Of course it's all right," Leigh said. "Why wouldn't it be all right?"

"I don't know. I'm just asking."

"Everything's fine."

"Good."

"Warren's a good man. Not the most exciting man in the world, maybe. Not like Tom. . . ."

"Thank goodness."

"But he's sweet and he's decent, and he'd never cheat on me."

"I didn't mean to imply. . . ."

"I don't understand why you'd ask me something like that."

"I'm sorry. I honestly didn't mean. . . ."

"It's just this damn wedding. You know. People get tense."

"I'm sure."

"It's a huge expense, and we're not getting any help from the groom's parents. I've told you."

"Yes."

"So there's bound to be tension. Especially now, with Julia missing, and everything so up in the air."

"I'm sorry."

"There's nothing to be sorry for. We're fine."

"Good."

The doorbell rang.

"I'll get it," Cindy said, walking briskly to the front door, trying to sort out in her mind what had just happened.

"Check who it is before you open the door," Leigh called after her.

It was the police. Cindy held her breath as she tried reading the expressions on their faces.

"Can we come in?" Detective Bartolli asked.

"Oh God." Cindy fell back into the house, covered her mouth with her hand, as Leigh rushed to her side.

"What's happened?" Leigh asked, as Cindy struggled to stay upright.

"It's all right," Detective Gill assured the two women quickly. "We've just come to fill you in on what's been happening."

"Julia . . . ?"

"There's nothing new."

"Can we come in?" Detective Bartolli asked again as Elvis bounded down the stairs to jump against his thighs.

Cindy led the two men into the living room, motioned for them to sit down. Above her head, Cindy could hear the water from the shower running through the pipes.

"I assume you've heard about the Hanson girl," Detective Gill stated as he lowered himself onto one of the tan leather sofas.

"Do you think there's any connection?" Cindy asked.

"We have no reason at this time to assume the two incidents are related," came the automatic response from Detective Bartolli.

"But you think there's a chance?"

"It's a possibility," Detective Gill admitted. "We're looking into it."

"How exactly are you doing that?" Leigh asked.

The detectives exchanged glances, ignored the question. "We've had several conversations with Sean Banack," Detective Bartolli said.

"And?"

"We're still checking out his alibi for last Thursday. Unfortunately, because we don't know the exact time your daughter disappeared . . ."

"We know it was between eleven-fifteen and four-thirty," Cindy said.

"Yes, but that's a lot of time to account for. Sean can account for his whereabouts for part of the day, but not all."

"Then arrest him."

"We need evidence to arrest him, Mrs. Carver."

"That story he wrote. . . ."

"Not enough."

"We've had someone watching him," Detective Gill said.

"And?"

"So far, nothing."

"Have you talked to Lindsey Krauss?"

Detective Bartolli checked his notes. "Yes. And to the other names on the list your husband gave us."

"Ex-husband," Cindy said.

"Ex-husband, yes. Sorry about that." The detective smiled sheepishly, scratched at his ear. "The consensus among several of Julia's friends is that she was involved with a married man."

"That's ridiculous," Leigh said.

Cindy said nothing.

"Cindy?" her sister said.

"Have you talked to Ryan Sellick?" Cindy asked.

"He denies any romantic involvement with your daughter."

"Do you believe him?"

"Is there some reason we shouldn't?"

Cindy shrugged, filling the policemen in on everything that had taken place in the last week between herself and the Sellicks. She watched Detective Gill dutifully jot this information down, and wondered whether she really believed Ryan and Julia were having an affair, whether Faith had phoned her earlier, whether either one could have played a part in her daughter's disappearance. "What about Michael Kinsolving?" she asked.

"We have no evidence to suggest he was in any way involved."

"He left town right after he saw Julia," Cindy reminded them.

"He claims he was in the country, scouting locations."

"And? Was he?"

"We're still checking into that."

Cindy lowered her head. "So, basically what you're telling me is that we're no farther ahead than we were last week. Except now, another girl has disappeared."

"Mrs. Carver . . ."

"I know. There's no reason to assume the two cases are connected."

An hour later, Cindy was lying on her bed, looking through her festival catalog. In the section marked *Masters*, she found a photograph of what appeared to be an ambulance or a police car racing along a dark, metropolitan street, the deliberately blurred image bathed in an eerie orange-red light, a woman's darkened silhouette in the foreground. The notes underneath it read: *Lost, Michael Kinsolving's sensational new film deals with the underside of contemporary society, with disaffected youth and the appalling generation who created and raised them. We meet Catherine, age twenty-two and already a seasoned con artist, and her sister, Sarah, five years her junior, addicted to cocaine and men old enough to be her father.*

Cindy closed the book, rifled through the envelope of movie coupons Meg had left for her, then scanned the *Volkswagen Guide to the Festival Official Film Schedule* booklet, locating the listing for *Lost.* Tonight at seven-fifteen at the Uptown 1, she read, reaching for the phone.

"Hello?" Meg answered, her voice a hoarse whisper. "Cindy?"

Cindy pictured Meg crouching down in her seat in the darkened theater, felt the angry glares of the people sitting around her.

"I'll meet you inside the theater at seven," Cindy said, then hung up before she had a chance to change her mind.

TWENTY-ONE

The Uptown 1 was already filled to capacity by the time Cindy arrived at just after seven o'clock that evening. She searched through the dim light of the large, old-fashioned auditorium for her friends, praying she wouldn't run into anyone else she knew. She could only imagine what they might say. *Can you believe it? Her daughter's been missing for over a week, God only knows what's happened to her, and she's out galavanting around. She's going to the movies!*

And they'd be right, Cindy thought, wondering what the hell she was doing here. Did she seriously think she'd glean anything of significance from Michael Kinsolving's new film? That there'd be hidden clues pointing to her daughter's whereabouts? That she'd gain insight into the director's tortured psyche? Or had she merely been desperate to get out of the house? Away from her mother, her sister, the dog? *What is my objective?* she asked herself, twisting sharply around, fleeing the crowded auditorium for the equally crowded lobby, coming to an abrupt halt in front of a long table covered with sushi and exotic sandwiches.

"Can I help you?" A young woman stared at her expectantly from behind the food-laden table.

Cindy suddenly realized she was ravenously hungry, not having eaten anything since breakfast, despite Leigh's constant efforts to stuff food down her throat. She'd pleaded exhaustion when Warren invited them all out for dinner, insisting her mother and sister go without her, then vaulted from the house the minute they were gone. She'd left them a note—*Needed some air. Back by ten,* she'd scribbled—so they wouldn't worry. Although they'd worry anyway, she knew, guilt sitting heavy in her chest, like heartburn. She'd grab a sandwich and head straight for home, she decided now. Coming here had been a mistake. What had she been thinking? "What kind of sandwich is that?" she asked the pale-faced young woman whose name tag identified her as a festival volunteer.

"Tomato, Havarti cheese, and avocado on whole wheat."

Cindy nodded her approval, her mouth watering as she reached inside her purse for some money.

"I'll get that," a man said from somewhere behind her, and Cindy turned to see Neil Macfarlane.

"Where did you come from?" Cindy said, startled by his unexpected presence. What was he doing here?

Neil motioned toward the inside auditorium. "We're sitting near the back. Meg was just about to call you when you went running out."

"I didn't realize you'd be here."

"Trish had an extra ticket." Dimples creased the skin around Neil's mouth as his lips flirted with a smile. "She called me, told me you were coming. I hope you don't mind. If it makes you at all uncomfortable. . . ."

"It doesn't."

"Good." He took her elbow, led her toward a relatively quiet corner of the old lobby, whose walls were the color of dark blood. "I've called a few times. . . ."

"Yes, I know. I'm really sorry I haven't returned your messages." I wanted to call you, she thought. So many times. "It's been so crazy," she said.

"You don't have to explain."

"Thank you." Cindy smiled, fought the urge to caress his cheek. Had his eyes always been so blue? she wondered, before deliberately looking away.

"Are you ready to go back inside?"

Cindy straightened her shoulders, took a deep breath. "Ready or not."

It was completely dark in the auditorium as Neil led Cindy up the steep rows of stairs to where Meg and Trish were sitting near the back of the theater. The two friends greeted her with prolonged hugs and kisses.

"You okay?" Meg grabbed Cindy's hand and held it tightly in her lap. "I'm so glad you came."

"We were afraid you'd bolted," Trish said.

"I thought about it."

"You don't mind . . . about Neil?" she whispered.

"I don't mind."

"Ssh," said several nearby voices as a large spotlight jumped across the stage, ultimately coming to rest on a solitary figure standing to the left of the giant screen.

"Hello, I'm Richard Pearlman, and I'm one of the

organizers of this year's festival," the casually dressed young man announced to a smattering of light applause. "First, I want to thank our sponsors," he said, gamely naming each one in turn. "Tonight, we are extremely privileged to be hosting the North American premiere of Michael Kinsolving's amazing new movie, *Lost*, a film of astonishing power and resonance. We are also honored to have Michael Kinsolving here with us this evening."

A pleased gasp trickled through the audience, like a breeze through a wheatfield.

"Ladies and gentlemen . . . Michael Kinsolving."

The applause was heartfelt and enthusiastic as the famed Hollywood director, in his trademark black T-shirt and tight jeans, hopped onto the stage and waved. Then he cupped his right hand over his eyes, and stared out at the audience.

Can he see me? Cindy wondered, torn between leaning forward and sinking low in her seat.

"I hope you still feel like clapping after you see the film," Michael said to much laughter. "Anyway, what can I say? I love this festival. I love this city. As you may know, I'm planning to film my next movie here." Another burst of applause. "We tried to do something a little different with *Lost*, so I hope you don't mind. Anyway, I'll be available for a Q&A after the film." More applause. "Enjoy."

He jumped from the stage and the spotlight promptly evaporated. Enjoy, Cindy repeated silently as a haunting musical refrain began swirling about her head, and the screen filled with a group of ghostly, seminude dancers, whose arms and legs were painted in the black-and-white stripes of a movie clapboard, an arresting series of images that were part of this year's festival's logo. After several more promos, the movie began.

Cindy sank back in her chair as Meg squeezed her hand. What am I doing here? she wondered again, as the credits rolled across a deserted inner-city street. What do I hope to achieve? *What is my objective?*

(Documentary Footage: Cindy, in the bedroom of the house on Balmoral Avenue, the month before Tom packs his bags and moves out. It's a few minutes after 10 P.M. and he's just come home. Cindy has been waiting for him all night, intent on putting their marriage back on track, ready to accept at least part of the blame for its derailment. It's possible she's been too demanding, too critical, too angry all the time, as Tom is always saying. They've been married for seventeen years, nearly half her life. They were children when they eloped. Her entire adult life has been interlocked with his. Could she survive without him? And what of their two beautiful daughters, daughters who would be devastated should she fail to make things right between them? While she finally recognizes that she can't change her husband's behavior, she can certainly change her own. She can show Tom the love and respect he needs, even if he is not always deserving of either. To that end, she is wearing a new, short, red satin nightgown and pointy-toed shoes with skinny stiletto heels, the kind he's always admired on other women.

He pleads exhaustion as she burrows into his arms and tugs at his tie. She can smell another woman's perfume on his skin. Stubbornly, even recklessly, Cindy closes her eyes, covers her husband's lips with her own. She tastes another woman's lipstick, and fights the urge to gag, determined to ignore the bile rising in her throat, as Tom's body slowly, reluctantly, begins to respond to her ministrations. Soon, they are on the bed and he is unzipping his pants, lifting up her nightgown, although he doesn't look at her, has barely looked at her since he walked into the room, as if she no longer exists for him, as if she no longer exists at all. Can you see me? Cindy wonders, feeling herself shrink beneath his weight, become less visible, less viable, with each mindless thrust of his hips. "Look at me," she demands suddenly, grabbing his chin in her hands, forcing his eyes to hers, the fierceness in her voice catching them both by surprise. Immediately she feels him grow soft. He pulls away from her in disgust.

She tries to apologize, to explain, but apologies and explanations lead only to recriminations, recriminations to accusations, accusations to more accusations. They end up fighting, the same fight they've been having for weeks, months, years. "What do you hope to achieve when you say things like that?" he asks. "I mean, really, Cindy. *What is your objective?*")

I don't know, Cindy acknowledged now, watching as a young woman's face overtook the screen, light bouncing off her long black hair, so that it sparkled like diamonds against the night sky. Her full lips were open and trembling. Huge, coffee-colored eyes scanned the desolate street.

I don't know anything anymore, Cindy thought, following the young woman on the screen into a run-down diner, noticing the hungry looks from the men and boys already inside.

"Has anyone here seen Julia?" the girl asked the decidedly motley crew.

Cindy gasped, clutched her stomach, the sandwich in her lap dropping to the floor.

"What's wrong?" Neil leaned forward as Meg's hand tightened its grip on Cindy's fingers.

"Jimmy doesn't come around much these days," someone answered.

Jimmy, Cindy realized, collapsing forward in her seat, the air rushing from her lungs as if she'd been sucker-punched. Jimmy. Not Julia.

"Are you okay?" Trish asked.

Cindy nodded, unable to find her voice.

"I'll get you another sandwich," Neil offered.

"No," Cindy whispered hoarsely, her appetite gone. "It's all right."

"Ssh," someone said from the row behind.

The rest of the movie passed in a merciful blur. Cindy saw a succession of faces, a panorama of flesh. Raised voices, loud sighs, long silences. Sex, drugs, and rock 'n' roll. Love and pain, and the whole damn thing. When it was over, the entire audience jumped to its feet, hooting and hollering its prolonged approval. "I think he finally has another hit," Meg exclaimed, sitting back down, clapping wildly.

Cindy realized that, although her eyes had never left the screen, she hadn't absorbed a single frame. Although she'd heard each word, she couldn't recall a single one. If there'd been anything of value to be gleaned by being here, she'd missed it. She'd missed everything. As usual.

The lights came up. Richard Pearlman vaulted back to the stage. "Ladies and gentlemen, once again I give you Michael Kinsolving."

The director acknowledged the deafening ovation with a modest bow. "Does that mean you approve?"

The audience roared. Loud whistles pierced the air.

"Thank you," Michael said, clearly reveling in the sound. "You're very kind."

The applause abated as Richard Pearlman leaned his lanky torso into the microphone. "Michael's generously agreed to answer some questions." He peered into the audience.

Can he see me? Cindy thought. Can anybody see me?

"Yes," Richard Pearlman said. "You, there, in the middle."

A heavyset woman in stretch leopard-print pants scrambled to her feet. "First, I want to congratulate you on a brilliant film. And I couldn't help but be struck by the parallels to Dante . . ."

"Show-off," Trish muttered.

"What parallels to Dante?" Meg asked.

"And I wondered whether you were consciously going after something more literary with this film?" the woman continued.

"More literary?" the director repeated, obviously tickled by the question. "First time I've ever been accused of that."

The audience laughed.

Richard Pearlman pointed to a man in the second row. "Yes?"

"How long did it take you to shoot the film?"

"A little over three months."

"Where did you find the lead actress?" a woman shouted, not bothering to wait her turn.

"Monica Mason, yes. She was great, wasn't she?"

More applause.

"I wish I could say that I discovered her sitting at the soda fountain at Schwab's, or tell you one of those apocryphal

Hollywood stories you always hear about, but the truth is that she was just one of dozens of very talented young actresses who auditioned for the part. Her agent sent her over one afternoon, she read for us, and that was that. Nothing very dramatic, I'm afraid."

Richard Pearlman pointed to a middle-aged woman in the upper right corner of the theater. "Yes?"

"Speaking of dramatic stories," the woman began, "do you know anything about what's happening with the police investigation into the two missing girls?"

"Oh, my God," Cindy whispered. Was this what she'd been waiting for? Was this the reason she was here?

"No," Michael answered curtly. "I don't know any more than you do."

"I understand one of the girls is an actress," the woman continued.

"Yes, I believe that's true."

"Didn't she audition for you the morning she disappeared?"

"I believe she did, yes." Michael scratched uncomfortably at the tip of his nose, looked to Richard Pearlman for help.

"Could we confine your questions to the wonderful movie we've just seen?" Richard asked. "Thank you." He pointed to another woman on his left.

"How does it feel to be the subject of a police investigation? Do you feel like you're in the middle of one of your own movies?"

Michael laughed, but the laugh was strained. "A bit, yes. Any more questions about *Lost*?"

"If they find her, you should give her the part," a man

shouted out from the last row. "Then you'd have that apocryphal Hollywood story to tell us next time."

"That's true," Michael conceded as the audience laughed.

An apocryphal Hollywood story, Cindy thought, feeling sick to her stomach. Her daughter's disappearance reduced to an amusing anecdote for the film cognoscenti. "I have to get out of here," she said, jumping to her feet, Neil right beside her.

"Are you all right?" Meg asked.

"I have to go."

"We'll come too," Trish offered.

"No."

"I'll take her home," Neil said.

"We'll come with you," Meg insisted, following after them down the stairs.

"No," Cindy said forcefully, spinning around. "Please."

Meg stopped, tears filling her eyes. "You're sure?"

Cindy nodded. "I'll call you tomorrow."

"The gentleman in the third row," Richard Pearlman was saying as Cindy and Neil clambered down the steps and into the lobby.

The man's voice trailed after her. "Has being questioned by the police changed your opinion about Toronto?"

An hour later, Cindy was quietly ushering Neil inside her front hall. "I think everyone's asleep," she whispered. "Can I get you anything? Something to drink?"

"I'm fine," he whispered back.

"Follow me." Cindy tiptoed down the stairs leading to the bottom floor, cringing at each creak of the floor beneath her feet, feeling like a teenager sneaking home after curfew.

"Can you see okay?" she asked, relying on the half-moon peeking through the windows to guide them, reluctant to turn on any lights.

"I'm fine," he said again, settling in beside her on the family room sofa.

"Thanks for dinner." Cindy was glad it was too dark to make out the stains on the old brown corduroy couch, a couch that pulled out into a queen-size bed, Cindy thought, and felt her face flush. "I was hungrier than I realized."

And suddenly she was moving toward him, taking his face in her hands and drawing his lips toward hers, then kissing him full on the mouth, her tongue seeking his, her arms wrapping around him, crushing him tightly against her, her hands burying themselves in his hair, pulling him closer, as if there were still too much space between them, her legs curling around his hips, as if she could somehow manage to climb out of her own body and escape into his, as if she needed the air in his lungs to breathe.

"Oh God," she cried, abruptly pulling away and pushing herself toward the far end of the sofa. "What am I doing? What's the matter with me?"

"It's all right, Cindy. It's all right."

"It's not all right. I was all over you."

"Cindy," Neil said, trying to calm her, "you didn't do anything wrong."

"What you must think of me."

Neil stared at her through the semidarkness. "I think you're the most beautiful, most courageous woman I know," he said softly.

"Courageous?" Cindy swiped at the tears now falling the

length of her cheeks. "Courage implies choice. I didn't choose any of this."

"Which makes you all the more courageous in my book."

Cindy stared wistfully at the man beside her. Where had he come from? Were there really men like this in the world? "Make love to me," she said. Then more forcefully, "I really need for you to make love to me."

Neil said nothing. He simply reached for her, strong arms surrounding her like a cape. He kissed her once, then again and again, tender kisses, like the gentle flutter of a butterfly's wings against her skin, then deeper, his touch sure, unhurried, deliberate, as he began to caress and undress her. She felt the warmth of his fingers, the cool wetness of his tongue, and cried out with joy when he entered her, urgency replacing delicacy as he rocked inside her. Gradually, almost reluctantly, she felt her body building to a climax and tried hard to fight it, to prolong the moment as long as humanly possible, until it was no longer something she could control, and she cried out again, her nails digging into the flesh of his back, her fingers clinging to him as if he were a life preserver in a treacherous ocean. Seconds later, they collapsed against one another, their bodies bathed in a thin coating of sweat.

"Are you all right?" Neil asked after a silence of several seconds.

"Are you kidding?" Cindy asked in return, then laughed out loud.

Neil laughed with her, kissed her forehead, gathered her inside his arms.

"Thank you," Cindy said.

"Now who's kidding?"

He kissed her again, drawing her back against the well-stuffed pillows, their bodies folding comfortably together, their breathing steady and rhythmic.

And then there were footsteps shuffling above their heads, and upstairs' lights being turned on, and familiar voices sliding down the banister. "I told you there's no one here," Cindy's mother was saying as Elvis began barking beside her.

"And I'm telling you I heard something," Leigh argued. "Hello? Hello?"

"Hello?" Norma Appleton echoed. "Is someone there?"

The dog raced down the steps, bounded into the family room.

"Oh, for Pete's sake," Cindy said, fending off Elvis's eager paws as she scrambled into her clothes.

"Cindy? Cindy, is that you?"

"It's me, Mom," Cindy called out, pulling her T-shirt over her head as Elvis jumped against Neil's thighs. "It's all right. You don't have to come down."

"What are you doing downstairs?" Two sets of footsteps headed for the stairs.

"Please don't come down," Cindy urged, pulling her slacks over her hips, knowing such exhortations were futile, that it was only a matter of seconds before her mother and sister peeked their heads into the room. "I can't believe this," she whispered to Neil, who was hurriedly tucking his shirt inside his pants. "It's like when I was fifteen and she caught me making out with Martin Crawley."

"What do you mean, don't come down?" Leigh was asking, her voice edging closer. "What are you doing down here in the dark?" Her hand reached into the room, flipped on the switch for the overhead light, her eyes taking a second to adjust to the sudden brightness, another second to adjust to the fact that Cindy wasn't alone. "Oh."

"What's going on down here?" Norma Appleton asked.

"I think maybe we should go back upstairs," Leigh ventured, trying to back out of the room.

But her mother was already blocking her exit. "Don't be silly. What's . . . ? Oh." She stared at Neil Macfarlane. "I'm sorry, Cindy. I didn't realize you had company."

"You remember Neil," Cindy ventured meekly.

"Yes, of course," her mother said. "How are you, Neil?"

"I'm fine, thank you, Mrs. Appleton."

"Hi," Leigh offered weakly.

"Nice to see you again," Neil said.

Nobody moved.

"I guess I should probably go," Neil said finally.

"Please don't leave on our account," Norma Appleton said.

"It's late. I really should get going."

"I'll walk you to the door." Cindy followed him up the stairs. She, in turn, was trailed by her mother, her sister, and the dog.

Cindy closed the front door behind her as she walked Neil to his car. "I don't suppose I'll hear from you again," she said, smiling as he leaned over to kiss her good night.

"Was Martin Crawley so easily deterred?"

Cindy smiled, waited until his car disappeared down the street before turning back to the house. The front door opened just as she was reaching for it, her mother and sister waiting on the other side, Elvis between them.

"Sort of like old times," her mother said with a smile.

"I'll make us some tea," said Leigh.

TWENTY-TWO

Have you seen a copy of this morning's *Sun*?" Meg asked Cindy, at barely seven o'clock Monday morning.

It had been eleven days since Julia went missing.

Cindy lowered the phone in her hand and stared at Elvis, who was waiting for her by the front door. "No. I haven't been out yet. I was just about to take the dog for a walk when you called."

"Maybe you should let someone else take him," Meg suggested.

"Why? What are you getting at? What's in the *Sun* that you don't think I should see?"

"I just think you should be prepared."

"For what? Has another girl disappeared?" There'd been nothing in the other papers about any more disappearances.

"There's a picture of Julia on the front page," Meg said.

"Again?"

"It's a different picture. She's . . . well, it's pretty suggestive.

And there are more pictures inside. I don't know where they got them. . . ."

Cindy dropped the receiver, ran for the door.

"Cindy?" she heard Meg's voice call after her. "Cindy, are you there?"

Elvis barked in angry protest as Cindy slammed the door behind her and ran down the street. What was Meg talking about? What picture? She'd only given the police that one head shot of Julia. Where could they have gotten more? "What pictures, damn it?" she asked out loud, hurling herself at the newspaper box on the corner, recoiling in horror at the full-page photograph of her daughter that stared back at her with almost deliberate provocation.

Julia was staring directly into the camera lens, her eyes challenging the viewer. She was wearing only the bottom half of a black string bikini, her hands cupped coyly over high, bare breasts. JULIA'S LOST JEWELS, the caption beside the picture read.

Cindy stumbled back on her heels as if she'd been struck. It was one of the photographs she'd found in Sean's apartment, photographs Tom had stuffed inside the pocket of his beige linen pants. How had the paper gotten its hands on it? And what of the other pictures inside? Were they part of the same collection?

She reached into her pocket for some change, realized she'd forgotten to bring any, and slammed her fist on the top of the red metal box in frustration. She cast a wary glance over each shoulder to make sure no one was watching, then kicked at the side of the box, and jiggled its handle, trying to force it open. The damn thing refused to budge. "Shit!" she yelled, spinning around in helpless circles.

A woman walking a small white dog rounded the corner at Lynwood. "Excuse me," Cindy called to her. "I don't suppose you have some spare change for the paper? I could pay. you back later."

The woman's eyes narrowed, as if she'd just been approached by a foul-smelling panhandler, and she promptly picked up her dog and crossed to the other side of the street.

"Great," Cindy muttered, racing back down Balmoral toward her house, hearing Elvis barking all the way down the street. "Okay, okay," she said, opening her door and trying to keep the dog from knocking her down as she rifled through her purse for some change. "Okay, you can come," she told the dog, grabbing his leash, heading back out the door.

"What's all the commotion?" her mother called from the top of the stairs.

"I'm just getting the paper," Cindy said. "Go back to sleep."

She hurried down the steps and along Balmoral to Avenue Road. But Elvis refused to be rushed, stopping repeatedly to sniff at the grass and lift his leg. "Come on. Come on. We haven't got all day."

Cindy stopped abruptly, the absurdity of what she'd just said hitting her square in the forehead, as if she'd just walked into a brick wall. *We haven't got all day?* All day was exactly what she had. And the day after that. And the day after that. How many days? she wondered, importuning the cloudless sky. How many more awful, blank days waiting to be filled? How many more endless days spent in aimless, if frantic, pursuit of her daughter? How many more useless meetings with police, well-meaning conversations with friends, sadistic phone calls from strangers? How many more such days could she tolerate? How many more could she survive?

As many as it takes, Cindy understood, continuing toward the corner. What choice did she have? "No choice, no control," she told the dog as he lifted his rump into the air and dropped several steaming turds into the middle of the sidewalk. "That's just great," she said, realizing she'd forgotten to bring a plastic bag. She looked helplessly up and down the street, wondering what to do. What *could* she do? She wasn't about to pick it up with her hands. "I'll come back later," she apologized to the empty street, stepping around the unsightly pile, pulling Elvis after her before he could do more damage.

She reached the newspaper box at the same time as an immaculately dressed, middle-aged man, who nodded hello as he dropped the appropriate coinage into the slot and pulled out a paper, his fingers unconsciously folding across her daughter's partially exposed breasts. Cindy felt a scream rising in her throat, and turned away. "Have a nice day," the man said in parting.

Cindy's eyes trailed after him. Did he know anything about her daughter's disappearance? He obviously lived in the area, had probably seen Julia around. He was neatly dressed to the point of fastidiousness, nattily bland, unnecessarily polite. Middle-aged. Repressed. Probably lived alone, or with his mother. Exactly the type you always read about, the quiet ones, the ones with smiles on their lips and mayhem in their hearts.

Men like him were everywhere, Cindy thought as she dropped her money in the slot and reached inside the box for the paper. She couldn't look at a man anymore without wondering whether he knew something about Julia, whether he'd seen her, or talked to her, or plotted her harm. Every stranger was a possible fiend; every friend a possible foe. How well do we really know anybody?

How well do we know ourselves?

Cindy's thoughts drifted to Neil, to the events of last Saturday night. Again she felt his arms around her, his lips on hers, his hands in her hair, on her breasts, between her legs. She felt him moving inside her, and even now, it felt wonderful. To lose herself so completely in the moment, to forget for a brief spasm of time what else she might have lost. Followed by the dog's paws on her bare thighs, the priceless looks on the faces of her mother and sister, the reassuring smile in Neil's eyes as he kissed her good night. The Lord giveth, she found herself thinking, as she stared at the picture of her daughter in the morning paper, trying to make sense of what she was seeing.

And the Lord taketh away.

More pictures, page 3.

Cindy flipped the page over, gasped when she saw two more familiar photos—one of Julia wearing a push-up bra and matching thong, the other of Julia in profile, her elbow pressing against the curve of her naked breast, the bare cheeks of her round bottom playing peekaboo with the camera.

How did the *Sun* get these pictures? Was it possible Sean had duplicates, that he'd sold the negatives to the tabloid? She stuffed more coins into the box, pulling out the last remaining copies of the paper, and running with them along the street, feeling one of her sandals suddenly connect with something squishy. "Oh, shit!" she yelled, sliding to a stop, knowing exactly what she'd stepped in. "Serves me right," she shouted. "Serves me goddamn right." She ripped off her sandal, the bottom of which was covered in dog poop, and hurled it into the middle of the road.

"Where's your sandal?" her mother asked as Cindy limped into the kitchen several minutes later on only one shoe.

Cindy waved the question aside as she spread the papers across the kitchen table, then walked to the phone, asked information for the number of the *Toronto Sun*.

"Oh, my," her mother whispered, staring at the pictures. Then again, "Oh, my."

"I need to speak to Frank Landau," Cindy said, checking the name under the article that accompanied the racy pictures of her daughter.

"This is Frank Landau," a man answered seconds later.

"Where did you get those pictures of my daughter?"

"Excuse me?"

"The pictures of Julia Carver. Where did you get them?"

"Mrs. Carver?"

"I will sue your goddamn paper. I will sue you personally. . . ."

"Mrs. Carver, wait. Wait. Calm down. Please."

"Don't tell me to calm down. Tell me how you got those pictures."

There was a long pause. By the time the reporter answered, Cindy knew what he was going to say. "I got them from your ex-husband," he told her evenly. "Tom Carver hand-delivered them to me in person yesterday afternoon."

———

"Where is he?" Cindy demanded as she pushed through the door to Tom's office at just after one o'clock that afternoon.

Irena Ruskin jumped to her feet behind her appropriately cluttered desk. "He's not here. Wait," she called, scrambling after Cindy into Tom's inner office. "Mrs. Carver! Cindy!"

Cindy spun around, absorbing the faithful secretary in a single glance. Her hair was still the same unsubtle shade of blond, although a few inches longer than Cindy last remembered it, possibly to hide the scars of her most recent plastic surgery, Cindy thought unkindly, wondering whether the woman chose her wardrobe to coordinate with the dark blue of the two chairs in front of the massive oak desk. "Where is he?"

"He's in a meeting."

"He's been in that meeting since nine o'clock this morning."

"I gave him all your messages."

"I need to speak to him, Irena. It's pretty urgent or I wouldn't be here."

"Cindy. . . ."

"Could you get him for me? Please?"

"Was that Cindy Carver I just saw walk by?" a man's voice asked from the doorway.

Cindy took a deep breath, forced herself to smile as she extended her hand to one of her ex-husband's law partners. "Hello, Alan. How are you?"

"I'm well. How are you holding up?"

"Today isn't a great day." Cindy marveled at her use of understatement. She might even have laughed had Alan Reynolds not looked quite so earnest. "I'm sure you saw the pictures in the *Sun*."

Alan Reynolds nodded. "You're waiting for Tom, I take it."

"Apparently he's stuck in one of those all-day meetings." Cindy glanced at Irena, who nodded uncomfortably.

"Really? Well, they must be taking a break. I just saw him talking to Mitchell Pritchard. Let me see if I can get him for you."

"I'd appreciate that."

"Can I get you anything in the meantime? A cup of coffee? Some water, perhaps?"

"Nothing, thank you."

"Has there been any news about Julia?" Irena asked when he was gone.

"You didn't see the spread in the *Sun*?"

"I saw it."

"Quite impressive, don't you think?"

Irena shuffled from one foot to the other, looked as if she were seriously considering jumping out the twenty-fifth-floor window. "If there's anything I can do for you during this difficult time. . . ."

You're the first person I'll call, Cindy thought. Aloud she said, "Thank you." She turned toward the floor-to-ceiling window with its magnificent view of the waterfront, saw her own pathetic image reflected back. She was wearing her standard uniform of blue jeans and faded T-shirt, and her hair was greasy from constantly tugging at it. *Take your hands away from your hair,* she could hear Tom scold. "How many partners are there in the firm now?" she asked Irena, in an effort to silence him.

"Sixteen partners. Forty-eight associates."

"Wow," Cindy said without enthusiasm.

"Half a dozen students," Irena continued.

Cindy wondered if Irena was still sleeping with Tom. She folded her arms across her chest, as if to keep her heart from falling out.

"Are you sure you wouldn't like a cup of coffee?"

"Quite sure, thank you."

"Well, I could certainly use one," Tom said, sweeping into the room, resplendent in a gray suit and red print tie. "If you wouldn't mind."

"No problem." Irena obediently slipped from the room, drawing the door closed behind her, then leaving it open a small crack.

"So, what brings you all the way down here?" Tom asked, examining his ex-wife as if she were an unpleasant document.

Cindy walked to the door, pushed it shut all the way, then turned back to her ex-husband. "You miserable son of a bitch," she began.

"Okay, ground rules," Tom stated, retreating behind his heavy oak desk. "No swearing. No name calling. No yelling."

"No shit," Cindy said.

Tom shook his head. "You look like crap."

Tears stung Cindy's eyes. Seven years after he'd left, and still, his words had the power to wound. "What the hell is wrong with you?"

"What's wrong with *me*?" he countered.

"How could you do it?"

"Do what?"

"Don't play games with me."

"I take it you're upset about the pictures in the *Sun*."

"Pictures you hand-delivered yourself, you son of a bitch. Don't try to deny it."

"Why would I deny it?"

"Why would you *do* it?"

"Think about it a minute."

"Think about what? What's to think about?"

"Think about the best way to keep Julia front and center on everyone's minds," Tom said evenly, sitting down and leaning forward, elbows on his desk. "She's been missing for eleven days."

"I know exactly how long she's been missing."

"Then you also know her disappearance is old news. Another girl's already taken her place. Not to mention, the city is filled with visiting celebrities and movie stars, eager for a good photo-op. I had to do something to make sure Julia wouldn't be forgotten. Those pictures will more than accomplish that."

"So the end still justifies the means," Cindy said, aware there was a grain of truth to what Tom was saying, not wanting to acknowledge it.

"Cindy, be reasonable. How long do you think the police are going to keep Julia's case a priority?"

"How seriously do *you* think they're going to treat her disappearance after seeing these pictures? They'll dismiss her as flighty and foolish, maybe even flighty and foolish enough to take off without telling anyone. Or worse—they'll think she's a little tramp who got what she deserved."

"They'll think they better get off their asses and solve this case before it gets international exposure," Tom snapped. "I'm already fielding calls from Associated Press and *People* magazine."

"Oh God." Cindy felt her body crumpling like tissue paper, and collapsed into one of the two blue chairs in front of Tom's desk.

Tom stood up, warily approached his former wife. "Cindy, you have to calm down. You can't keep flying off half-cocked. It's not good for you."

"You mean it's not good for *you*," she said, refusing to look at him.

"Look at you." He smoothed some hairs away from her face.

Cindy slapped his hand aside. "I know. I look like crap. You already told me."

"I'm just worried about you."

Cindy pushed herself out of the chair, and walked to the window, stared toward Lake Ontario. "If you're so damn worried about me, why didn't you tell me what you were planning to do with the pictures? Why didn't you warn me?"

"Because I knew you wouldn't approve. And I didn't feel like going through . . ."

"This?"

"Exactly."

"Coward."

Tom shook his head. "Okay, look. I think we've said all we have to say."

"I haven't."

"Of course," he said with an audible sigh. "Okay, I'm ready. Give it your best shot."

Cindy looked at her former husband, his feet spread shoulder-distance apart, his arms hanging limply at his sides, handsome face void of all expression. She'd once loved this man, she found herself thinking. Loved him from the time she was seventeen. Loved him so much she'd eloped with him at eighteen, had two children with him. *Two* children, she reminded herself, her lower lip quivering as once again, tears clouded her eyes. "How's Heather?" she asked, realizing she'd barely thought about Heather since she left.

"She's fine."

"Did she tell you what happened?"

"Just that the house was getting a little crowded." Tom paused. "You know I'm right about the pictures, don't you?"

Cindy pushed her hair impatiently behind her ears. "I hate it when you're right."

"You hate everything about me," he said softly, going to her side.

"Pretty much," Cindy acknowledged, allowing him to gather her into his arms and pull her toward him. She cried softly against his chest, his silk tie serving as a blotter for her tears. How had she ever allowed herself to fall in love with someone she'd never really liked?

"Cindy . . ."

"What?"

"Everything will be all right," he said, as the door to his office opened, and Irena stepped inside, a coffee mug shaking in her hands, the color drained from her face. "Something the matter?" Tom asked as Detectives Bartolli and Gill strode into the room. "What is it? Has something happened?"

Detective Bartolli stepped forward, his gaze shifting uneasily from Tom to Cindy. "We've found a body," he said slowly. "We'd like you to come with us."

TWENTY-THREE

The regional office of the Chief Coroner for the Province of Ontario is located at 26 Grenville Street, at the corner of Yonge, next to the large Credit Union Bank, in the heart of downtown Toronto. It is a squat, two-story structure fashioned in brown stucco and glass that manages to be both bland and ominous. A giant, government-operated funeral parlor, Cindy found herself thinking as the police car pulled to a stop in the adjacent parking lot. Which is exactly what the damn thing is, she thought, suppressing the panic that was bubbling inside her body, like water boiling in a pot.

You have to stay calm, she admonished herself, scratching painfully at her arms, her skin on fire, as if she'd just slipped into a burning sweater. She wanted to jump from the car, strip off all her clothes, accost total strangers, laugh hysterically in their faces, scream at them until she was hoarse, but she couldn't do any of those things because Tom would tell her she was behaving inappropriately. And he'd be right, of course. He was always right. She did behave inappropriately. She yelled when whispers would suffice, laughed when others might cry, lashed out when what she wanted most was the comfort of someone's arms.

How was it that Tom managed to stay so focused, so in control? Cindy wondered, glancing over at her ex-husband, who was sitting beside her in the backseat of the police car, staring out the side window. How was it that his feathers never seemed to ruffle? That even faced with the loss of his daughter, he remained stoic and cool?

Was it possible such composure was all an act? That underneath the deceptively placid surface, a smoldering geyser was waiting to erupt? That behind the pat phrases, the condescending nods, the maddening reserve, he was every bit as panicky as she was?

"Do you remember how much Julia used to talk when she was a little girl?" Cindy asked Tom, who either didn't hear her question or chose to ignore it. "You couldn't shut her up," Cindy continued, undeterred. "She'd start talking the minute she opened her eyes in the morning, and she didn't stop until she closed them again at night. And sometimes she'd even talk in her sleep. It was so cute. Remember, Tom?"

Tom's shoulders stiffened. "Cindy. . . ."

"You'd keep waiting for her to take a breath, so you could get a word in, but it would never come. You'd think, surely she has to come up for air at some point, but she just breezed from one topic into the next. Isn't that right, Tom?"

Tom's head turned slowly toward her. "Cindy. . . ."

"And you didn't dare interrupt her," Cindy continued, chuckling at the memory. "If you did, she'd just start all over again from the beginning. And you'd have to listen to the whole thing again until she got to the part where you'd cut her off, and then she'd give you this little look. Remember that look, Tom? You used to say it could cut glass."

"Cindy. . . ."

"*What?*" Cindy snapped, understanding now how Julia must have felt at being interrupted. Why had she always interrupted her? Why couldn't she just have let her speak?

"I think we should go inside now," Tom said quietly.

"Why? What's the rush? Is she going anywhere?" Cindy caught the look of horror on her ex-husband's face. "Oh, I'm sorry. Was that inappropriate?"

"Mrs. Carver, are you all right?" Detective Gill asked from the front seat.

"I'm fine," Cindy told him. "I mean, why wouldn't I be fine? We're just here to identify my daughter's body, right? Nothing to get upset about."

"Mrs. Carver . . ." Detective Bartolli said.

"She always wanted to be an actress, you know," Cindy told the two detectives, trying to prolong her time in the car, to postpone the inevitable. "She used to prance around the house in my high heels and nightgowns, like a fairy princess—you should have seen her—and she'd make up these cute little plays, and act out all the parts. She'd sing and dance. She was really very good. Wasn't she, Tom?"

"Cindy. . . ."

"I remember one afternoon when Julia was maybe four years old. I was busy with Heather, and Julia was playing with her Barbies—she had at least fifty of them—and I suddenly realized it was awfully quiet in Julia's room. So I put Heather in her crib and went to see what was going on. And there was Julia standing naked in the middle of her bedroom, in front of all her Barbies, whom she'd arranged in this kind of free-floating semicircle, and she was holding up this pencil, and she was saying, 'And now, audience, we're going to operate on my vagina.'" Cindy laughed out loud.

"Cindy, for God's sake," Tom said.

The smile slid from Cindy's face, as if rubbed off by a harsh abrasive. "What? Not appropriate?"

"Mrs. Carver," Detective Bartolli said gently. "Maybe Detective Gill should take you home. Mr. Carver can make the identification."

"No!" Cindy said quickly. "I'm fine."

"You're not fine," Tom said.

"There is no way you're going to go into that room without me."

"Cindy. . . ."

"She's my daughter too."

"Nobody disputes that."

"We recognize how difficult this is for you," Detective Gill said.

"Then you also recognize there's no way you're keeping me from her."

"Mrs. Carver," Detective Bartolli continued, "it's very important that if you go inside, you stay calm."

"Why?" Cindy asked, genuinely curious. "Are you afraid I'll upset the other corpses?"

"Okay, that's enough," Tom said. "Clearly my wife is hysterical."

"I'm not your wife," Cindy reminded him curtly.

"But you *are* hysterical."

"I'm fine," Cindy assured the two detectives. "I'll be okay. I promise." I'll be a good girl, the child in her protested, pulling back her shoulders, and taking a deep breath, determined to prove she could be as rational, as grown-up, as they were. I'll be as cool as a cucumber, she decided, puzzling over the origin of that expression. Why a cucumber? Why not "cool as a carrot" or "cool as a cabbage"? How about "cool as a corpse"?

Now *that's* appropriate, she thought, almost laughing as she pushed open the car door and stepped onto the pavement, the unseasonably hot September air descending on her head like a collapsing parachute. Better to keep such musings to herself, she decided. Any more outbursts and they wouldn't let her into the building, let alone into the viewing room. They wouldn't let her see her daughter. Or what was left of her. "Oh God," she said, trying not to picture Julia lying battered and lifeless on a cold, steel slab.

She felt her knees buckle, her legs give way, as if someone had kicked at them from behind, the reality she'd worked so hard to keep at bay pushing itself on top of her, holding her down, tearing through her body, like a rapist.

"Cindy," Tom said, catching her by the elbow before she could collapse.

"I'm all right," she told him, regaining her composure, putting one tenuous foot in front of the other.

"Mrs. Carver?"

"I'm fine."

They walked slowly around to the front of the building, Detective Gill rushing ahead to open the heavy glass door, then stepping back to allow them entry. Cindy crossed into the main lobby, a cold but efficient use of space that was typical of most government buildings. Detective Bartolli checked in with the dispatcher, a middle-aged man whose lush black beard was in stark contrast to his shiny bald head, then quickly ushered the small group toward a room to the right of the lobby.

"What's in here?" Cindy asked, pulling back as they reached the door.

"It's just a room," Detective Gill assured her as they stepped over the threshold.

"This is Mark Evert." Detective Bartolli introduced the surprisingly robust-looking morgue attendant, who was waiting for them inside.

"Mr. Evert," Tom said, shaking the man's hand.

"What is this, some sort of bereavement room?" Cindy asked.

"We call it the comfort room," Mark Evert replied.

"Really? What kind of comfort are you offering exactly?"

Mark Evert smiled sadly, as if he understood her pain. "If you'd like to sit down . . . ." He pointed toward a grouping of recently refurbished sofa and chairs. "And there's a bathroom, if you'd like. . . ."

"To freshen up?" Cindy asked.

"Cindy. . . ." Tom's voice warned from somewhere beside her.

She looked around the small room, its dim lights meant to be soothing, the smell of new carpeting permeating the cool air. "I think I *would* like to use the bathroom," she said, disappearing into the tiny room, and locking the door after her. She turned on the tap, splashed several handfuls of cold water at her face. "Stay calm," she whispered at her reflection in the mirror over the sink. The face in the glass stared back at her through hopelessly dazed eyes. Cindy noted the greenish-yellow of the woman's cheeks, the dark circles under her eyes, the circles spreading out in ripples, like a still lake disturbed by a stone. You can do this, her reflection admonished silently. You can do this.

"No, I can't," Cindy said out loud. "I can't."

There was a gentle knock on the bathroom door. "Cindy?" Tom called. "Are you all right in there?"

I'm fine in here, she wanted to answer. It's out there I have a problem. Instead she said, "I'll just be half a minute." She took a deep breath, then reached for the door, stopped, walked back to the toilet and flushed it, watching as the water swirled aimlessly around the bowl before being sucked down the drain. Gone. Just like that. "Okay," she said, coming back into the so-called comfort room, noting how quiet it was. This is what they mean by the term "deathly quiet," she thought, knowing it would be *inappropriate* to voice such an observation out loud. "What happens now?"

"We go inside." Mark Evert indicated the door directly behind him. "We'll show you the body of a young woman. She's been strangled."

Cindy drew in a sharp intake of air, automatically reached for Tom's hand, felt his fingers close around hers.

"I thought you had closed-circuit TVs for this," Tom said, his body stiffening along with his voice.

The morgue attendant nodded. "We do, and generally speaking, we prefer to make identifications that way, especially in cases where's there's been significant trauma to the face. . . ."

"There's been trauma to her face?" Cindy repeated, struggling to understand the man's words.

"There are a few bruises, along with some swelling and discoloration."

"Oh no."

"You can't just show us a photograph?" Tom pressed.

"Unfortunately, in cases of homicide, this isn't an option. We require a direct identification."

"But on TV, people usually stand behind a window or something."

"Procedures vary in every jurisdiction," Mark Evert explained patiently. "If you need a few more minutes, Mr. Carver. . . ."

"Are you all right?" Cindy asked her ex-husband, surprised to find their roles suddenly reversed.

"Just tell us what to expect," Tom said tersely.

"The young woman you're going to see was strangled some time in the last forty-eight hours. We haven't done an autopsy yet to determine the exact time of death, but decomposition has started. . . ."

"Decomposition?" The terrible word assaulted Cindy's ears like an icepick to the brain.

"We'll try to spare you as much as we can. I'm afraid we aren't allowed to clean up the body in any way."

"Is there a lot of blood?" Tom asked.

"No."

A prolonged sigh leaked from Cindy's lungs.

"You'll be asked to make a formal identification in the presence of these detectives, myself, and the pathologist."

"What if we're not sure?" Tom asked.

Cindy moaned, the prospect of not being able to recognize her own child almost too much to bear.

"Then we'll ask you to supply us with Julia's dental records, or her hairbrush. . . ."

"Can we go in now?" Cindy interrupted, knowing that if they waited any longer, if she had to listen to any more malignant words like decomposition and discoloration, or even to formerly benign words like dental records and hairbrush, she would go mad.

Mark Evert's hand hesitated on the doorknob. "You're sure you're ready?"

Cindy marveled at the question. How could anyone ever be ready for something like this? "I'm ready," she said, feeling Tom's fingers digging into her own as the door opened, and they stepped into the morgue.

It was like a huge operating room. Cindy's eyes bounced from the cream-colored tiles on the walls to the darker tiles at her feet. In the center of the room, and running its entire width was a big, stainless steel refrigerator at least ten feet high, containing three rows of compartments. There must be room for a hundred bodies in there, Cindy thought with a shudder, wondering how the attendants removed those bodies from the lockers without straining their backs, becoming only slowly aware of the narrow table directly in front of her, of the white vinyl body bag stretched out across its smooth surface.

"This is Dr. Jong, the pathologist," Mark Evert said of the disconcertingly young-looking man doing his best to look invisible, the doctor responding with an almost imperceptible nod of his head.

He's here to cut her up, Cindy realized, a sudden, loud buzzing filling her ears, as if a thousand bees were trapped there.

"Remember," Mark Evert was saying, "you have to be one hundred percent sure."

Cindy turned to Tom. "Do you remember when Julia was a little girl, and she was showing off on that new bicycle you bought her, and she fell off and broke both her arms?"

"I remember," Tom said, clutching tightly to her hands.

"And I rushed her to the hospital, and of course, we had to wait about four hours till somebody saw us, and she kept saying, 'Why doesn't God like me, Mommy? Why doesn't He like me?' And I told her, 'Don't be silly. Of course God likes you. He loves you.' But she was adamant. 'No, He doesn't love me, or He wouldn't have broken my arms.' And we laughed about that later. Do you remember how we laughed about that later?"

"I remember," Tom said again.

"And then the poor thing couldn't feed herself or go to the bathroom with both her arms in casts."

"It didn't take her long to get the knack."

"And she was embarrassed to go to school."

"The teachers probably thought she was an abused child."

"And then you got that rock 'n' roll band you represented—who were they again?"

"Rush."

"Yeah, Rush. I remember. Such nice guys. They all signed her casts. Then she couldn't wait to get to school to show everybody. And when it came time to take the casts off, she cried and carried on."

"We had to keep those damn, smelly things for years."

"I remember that just after the doctor removed them, Julia fainted, and the doctor, who was standing on the other side of the room, came flying back and caught her before she fell off the table. She might have cracked her head open on the floor. And there I was, standing right beside her, and I didn't realize what was happening."

"Cindy," Tom said softly, "don't do this."

"If I'd watched her more closely, she would never have fallen off her bicycle."

"Kids fall off their bicycles every day."

"If I'd paid closer attention. . . ."

"Mrs. Carver," the morgue attendant said gently. "Do you think you're ready now?"

"Do you think she had any idea how much I love her?" Cindy asked her former husband, tears filling her eyes and spilling down her cheeks.

"She knows," Tom said.

"I yelled at her. The morning of her audition. I yelled at her about the dog, I yelled at her for banging on the bathroom door, I insisted she come to the bridal fitting that afternoon when I knew she didn't want to come."

"This didn't happen because you yelled at her."

"What if she was kidnapped on her way to the fitting? What if whoever did this to her saw her as she was getting on the subway and followed her?"

"Cindy. . . ."

"I should have been paying more attention."

"You're a great mother, Cindy," Tom told her.

"She must have been so scared."

"Mrs. Carver," Detective Bartolli ventured, then stopped.

Cindy confronted the young-looking pathologist. "How long does it take to strangle someone?"

"Cindy. . . ."

"Please, Dr. Jong. Tell me how long it takes to strangle someone?"

"Approximately two minutes," the doctor answered.

"Two minutes," Cindy repeated. "Such a long time." The buzzing in her ears grew louder.

"We'll get through this," she thought she heard Tom say.

Words jumped out at her only to retreat.

"Are . . . ready . . . Mrs. . . ?"

Cindy noticed the police shield on the front of the body bag as a man's hand reached for the zipper, the sound of the zipper cutting through the buzzing in her ears, like a chainsaw through a chunk of wood, one sound magnifying the other, until Cindy felt her head about to burst.

Hands parted the zipper. A head emerged, as if from the womb. Cindy saw the straight blond hair plastered against the ghostly white skin, tried not to absorb the unsightly blotches of purple, blue, and red that stained the colorless cheeks like paint on canvas.

Oh God, she thought, recognizing the once-lovely face.

And then the room filled with the sound of angry bees, and Cindy fell unconscious to the floor.

TWENTY-FOUR

Are you all right?" Tom was asking.

Cindy opened her eyes, lifted her head from the soft beige-and-ivory-print silk of the sofa, stared at the man looming over her. "I don't know."

"Maybe this will help." He pushed a tall glass of something cold into her hands.

"What is it?"

"Vodka and cranberry juice."

Cindy pushed herself into a sitting position, took a long sip. "It's good."

Tom sank down beside her. He stretched his long legs across the wood-and-glass coffee table in front of him, laid his head back against one of the pillows. "That was quite the ordeal." He leaned sideways toward her, clicked his glass against hers. "To better days." He promptly downed half his glass in a single gulp.

"Better days," Cindy agreed, taking another sip of her

drink, the presence of the vodka both flattening and emphasizing the tartness of the cranberries. She looked around the large, expensively appointed room, with its muted furniture and bright needlepoint rugs, its bold splashes of modern art against pale ecru walls, its south wall of floor-to-ceiling windows providing a magnificent view of Lake Ontario. "This is some place you've got here."

"You've seen it before, haven't you?"

"First time," she reminded him. "It's beautiful. I didn't realize the Cookie had such good taste."

"The Cookie?" Tom looked genuinely perplexed.

Cindy turned her head to hide an unexpected blush. "Sorry. Fiona."

A slow smile crept across Tom's handsome face. "You call my wife 'the Cookie'?"

"Term of endearment." Cindy took another sip of her drink. "What am I doing here?"

"You fainted. Remember?"

"Yes. I seem to be doing that a lot lately. But then I woke up."

"And said you couldn't face going home, that your mother and sister were driving you nuts."

"They mean well."

"Yes," he said cryptically. "I remember."

"So you brought me to your condominium," Cindy stated, choosing not to explore his last remark, marveling at everything that had transpired in the last hour. "Where's the . . . Fiona?" she asked, listening for the click of the woman's high-heeled shoes on the marble floors.

"Muskoka."

"She's at the cottage?"

"We decided it was probably a good idea for her to stay up there this week, what with everything that's going on, and Heather being here."

Cindy glanced toward the long hall that ran the length of the huge apartment. "Is Heather at school?"

"I think she said she has classes till six."

Cindy checked her watch. It was barely four.

Tom brought his feet to the floor, leaned forward, rested his elbows on his knees. "She's planning to go back home this weekend."

Cindy nodded gratefully. "And Julia?" she asked, speaking the name that had gone unvoiced since that awful moment in the morgue when the attendant had unzipped the white vinyl bag.

It's not her, she heard Tom whisper. *It's not Julia.*

"We wait," he said now. "What else can we do?"

Cindy jumped to her feet, her drink sloshing around in her glass, spilling onto her hand. "I feel so guilty," she said, wiping the back of her hand on her jeans.

"Guilty? Why on earth would you feel guilty?"

"Because when I saw that poor girl's face and realized it wasn't Julia, I was so relieved, so grateful, so happy."

"Of course you'd feel that way."

"I think it's Sally Hanson," Cindy said.

"Who?"

"The girl who disappeared the week after Julia. Her poor parents. . . ."

"At least they'll know." Tom swallowed the last of his drink, then deposited his glass on the coffee table with an authority that was missing from his voice.

Cindy nodded. Would it be better to know? she wondered.

"At least there wasn't any blood," Tom said, his eyes returning to the morgue, still clearly haunted by what he'd seen.

"As we were leaving, I heard the dispatcher talking to Detective Gill about some couple who were killed in a car accident this morning," Cindy said, remembering. "He said the car exploded, and the people were badly burned. He called them 'crispy critters.'" Cindy stared at her former husband in disbelief. "Did he really say that or did I just imagine it?"

Tom shook his head. "I heard the same thing."

"I can't believe they talk that way."

"I guess you'd have to develop a pretty thick skin in order to survive in that kind of environment."

"Still . . ." Cindy shuddered. *"Crispy critters?"*

"Think they're anything like Krispy Kremes?" Tom asked.

A bubble of laughter suddenly burst inside Cindy's throat, then tumbled into the air, like a child tossed from a toboggan. Immediately, Tom's laughter somersaulted after hers, the disparate sounds becoming hopelessly enmeshed, impossible to separate one from the other. "I can't believe we're laughing," Cindy said, laughing harder.

"I'll have an order of Crispy Critters, please," Tom said.

"Hold the mayo," Cindy embellished.

"Oh, that hurts," Tom said, doubling over from the waist, holding his sides.

"What's wrong with us?"

"We could use another drink." Tom took Cindy's almost empty glass from her outstretched hand, retrieved his own glass from the coffee table, and marched out of the room.

Cindy followed after him, as if afraid to be left alone, even for an instant. She ran her hand along the dark oak finish of the long dining room table as she walked purposefully toward the kitchen, stopping to stare at the impressive wine cabinet built into the wall between the two rooms, each bottle of wine neatly labeled behind the thick layer of glass, the bottles secured in metal berths, stacked one on top of the other. Like bodies in a morgue, Cindy thought, fresh giggles gathering in her throat. "That's quite a collection," she said, coming into the gleaming marble-and-tile kitchen, watching as Tom refilled their glasses. "How many bodies are there?"

"What?"

"Bottles," she corrected. "I meant to say bottles."

Tom smiled. "There's room for four hundred."

"You always wanted a wine cellar."

"I always wanted a wine cellar," he agreed.

It was Cindy's turn to smile. "So, what shall we toast this time?"

"How about no more visits to the morgue?" Tom offered.

"Sounds good to me." Cindy took a long swallow. This time the vodka overwhelmed the subtle hint of cranberries. She noticed that a pleasant tingle was beginning to settle around the back of her neck. Any minute, her head would separate from the rest of her body and float into the air, like a helium-filled balloon. "So, how many bodies *do* you think that thing at the morgue holds?"

Tom laughed, once again finishing half his drink in a single swallow. "You asked that question on the drive home."

"I did? What was the answer?"

"Detective Bartolli said ninety. Apparently, it's at three

quarters of its capacity right now, and most bodies are in and out within forty-eight hours."

"And they use a forklift to take the bodies from the top row. I remember now."

"You were very concerned about their backs."

Cindy laughed, shook her head, grabbed the side of the island in the middle of the room to steady herself.

"You all right?"

"Feeling better every minute." Cindy took another swallow. "So, are you going to show me around this dump?"

"My pleasure." Tom made a sweeping gesture with his hands. "This is the kitchen."

"We can skip the kitchen."

"Still don't like to cook?"

"Hate it."

"Which is a real shame, because if memory serves me correctly, you were a very good cook."

"Really? How would you know? You were never home. What's down this way?" she asked before he could protest. She let go of the island, skipped from the kitchen, turned left at the hall.

"This is the library," Tom said of the wood-paneled room they came to first. Except for the southern expanse of window overlooking the waterfront, the room was essentially wallpapered with hardcover books.

"Very impressive."

"The view helps."

"And I didn't even realize the Cookie could read."

"Fiona is a very prolific reader," Tom said curtly, although there was laughter in his eyes.

"A woman of many talents."

"Yes, indeed." Tom led Cindy into the next room, its east wall completely taken up by an enormous flat-screen TV. "This is the media room."

"Still like leather, I see." Cindy gave the dark red leather sofa a seductive squeeze. "Where are the bedrooms?"

"Down this way." Tom led her back down the hall, past the marble powder room to the right of the marble entrance. "You're sure you're okay?"

"I'm fine." Cindy followed after him. Like a puppy at his heels, she thought, recognizing she was way beyond fine and teetering into plastered. It didn't take much, she thought. A dead body, a couple of vodkas—pretty soon she was sailing.

"This is the guest room."

Cindy peeked inside the green-and-white bedroom, saw a pair of Heather's jeans draped over a small, flowered-print chair, several of her blouses strewn across the white bedspread covering the queen-size bed. "It's lovely."

"It has its own bathroom, of course."

"Just like the comfort room." Cindy giggled. "Amazing how they think of everything, isn't it?"

"Amazing," Tom agreed.

"You think Granger, McAllister designed it?"

"Who's Granger, McAllister?"

"Our neighbors, the Sellicks. *My* neighbors," she corrected, leaning against a wall to keep from lying down on the floor. "He's an architect with Granger, McAllister."

"You think he designed the morgue?" Tom asked, one word sliding into the next as he directed her toward the master bedroom suite.

"No." Cindy giggled. "You're so silly."

"You're so drunk."

"I certainly hope so." Cindy kicked off her shoes, burying her toes in the plush white carpeting. "Wow," she said, her eyes sweeping across the enormous room, taking in the full-length sofa and chairs that were grouped in front of the southern wall of windows, the ornate credenza that sat against the wall opposite the bed, the bed itself a king-size extravaganza complete with tall pillars swathed in yards of cream-colored satin. "Looks like something out of the *Arabian Nights*. Spend much time in it?" she asked pointedly.

"Cindy, Cindy," Tom said, coming up behind her, his hands falling heavily on her shoulders, his slender hips pressing into her backside. "What am I going to do with you?"

Cindy felt his breath on the back of her neck, recognized the once-familiar tingle creeping between her legs. "What's in here?" she asked, extricating herself from his grasp and diving toward a small area off the main bedroom. "Wow. Do you actually use all this equipment?"

Tom moved easily between the treadmill, the StairMaster, and the stationary bicycle. There was also a large, red, exercise ball in one corner, and an impressive selection of free weights stacked against one wall. A medium-sized TV sat on a high shelf across from the treadmill. "I work out most days for about an hour. What about you?"

"I do yoga," Cindy told him, recalling her one visit to The Yoga Studio.

"Really? I wouldn't have pegged you for the yoga type."

"Why is that?"

"I wouldn't have thought you had the patience." He laughed. "I can just see you lying there, thinking, Can we please speed this up a bit?" He shook his head. "What do I know? Anyway, it obviously agrees with you."

"You told me before that I look like crap."

"I did? When?"

"In your office."

"Ah, yes. But that was before our little trip to the morgue."

"You're saying I look great in comparison to that girl on the table?"

"I'm saying you look great. Period."

"So you lied before, when you said I looked like crap."

"I lied."

"You're a liar?" she pressed giddily.

"I'm a lawyer," he agreed, and they both laughed.

"And the bathroom?" Cindy asked as he leaned toward her. "This way?" She ducked out of his reach, tripped past the two walk-in closets toward the en suite master bathroom.

It was a big room, its walls the same beige marble as the floor, with a double Jacuzzi, a large open shower stall, his-and-hers counters and sinks, and enough mirrors to satisfy even the most dedicated narcissist.

"Oh, jeez," Cindy said, seeing her reflection bounce from one mirror to the next: the old T-shirt, the sloppy jeans, the stringy hair, the zombie-like eyes. "I do look like crap."

"You look beautiful," Tom said, leaving his glass on the counter and coming up behind her.

"Lawyer," Cindy said, falling back against his chest, his arms wrapping around hers, and the side of his cheek pressing against her own as he removed the glass from her hand and placed it on the other counter. Was he really going to kiss her? she wondered, as he slowly spun her around. Was she really going to let him?

(Flashback: Cindy stands in front of her bathroom mirror, removing the makeup she painstakingly applied only an hour earlier, replaying Tom's phone call in her mind. "Sorry, babe. I can't make the movie. We've got something of an emergency going on here, and I'm going to be tied up for at least a few more hours. Give the sitter an extra couple of bucks, and see if you can line her up for next week.")

He tasted of vodka and cranberries, Cindy thought now, luxuriating in the softness of his lips, feeling his tongue slide gently across hers. Not too much, not too little. Just the right amount. Just like old times, she thought, recalling her mother's words.

What about Neil? she thought, seeing his reflection in the mirror behind Tom's head.

You're the most courageous woman I know, she heard him say.

"It was always so good with you," Tom was whispering, his hands tugging at her T-shirt, expert fingers disappearing beneath it, unhooking her bra. "God, real breasts. I'd almost forgotten how good they feel."

(Flashback: Cindy lying in bed, her pillow moist with her tears, as Tom crawls in beside her, reaches under her nightgown, cups her breasts in his hands. "Sorry I'm so late," he says, kissing her neck. She smells the wine on his breath, as his fingers reach between her legs. "Client wouldn't stop talking. I thought dinner would never end." He buries his face in the side of her neck. Cindy inhales another woman's perfume as he enters her from behind.)

"Come here," Tom said now, guiding her between the treadmill and the stationary bicycle toward the bedroom, pulling her T-shirt over her head as he pushed the layers of satin aside, her bra falling from her shoulders, disappearing into the white carpet, like a child's mitten into snow. "You always had such beautiful breasts," he marveled, pushing her back on the bed, and unbuttoning his shirt.

What am I doing? Cindy wondered, again thinking of Neil. Three years of being a nun and suddenly I'm the town slut? I don't feel so great, she thought as Tom's tongue found her nipples, and his fingers struggled with the button of her jeans.

(Flashback: Cindy in bed, chilled and nauseous, sipping herbal tea and fighting the urge to throw up, when she hears the front door open and the sound of a woman's laugh. She crawls out of bed and staggers to the top of the stairs.

"Can I get you a drink?" she hears Tom ask from the kitchen.

"Hello? Tom?" she calls, watching as Tom emerges at the bottom of the steps, clearly surprised to see her.

"What are you doing home? Isn't this your day to help out at Heather's school?"

"I wasn't feeling well. I had to cancel. What's going on?"

"Forgot my briefcase," Tom says breezily. "Look who I ran into coming down the street," he adds, almost as an afterthought.

A woman's head pops into view. Cindy recognizes her as the mother of one of Heather's friends.)

What on earth was she doing? Cindy wondered now, shaking her head in an effort to clear it, the motion making her dizzy and nauseous.

"We had some pretty good times together," Tom was saying, clearly oblivious to her discomfort.

As always, Cindy thought. "When you weren't cheating on me," she said flatly.

A nervous chuckle. "You took all that much too seriously. You know it meant nothing to me."

Was that supposed to make her feel better? "It meant something to me."

Silence. His hand froze on her bare skin. "You're killing the mood here, babe."

"You'd really make love to me in this apartment? In this bed?"

"Jesus," Tom said, sitting up and lifting his hands into the air, as if there were a gun pointing at his head. "You can't just relax and let things happen, can you? Damn it, Cindy. You haven't changed at all."

"Damn it, Tom. Neither have you." Cindy pushed herself off the bed, rezipped her jeans, her eyes searching through the white carpet for her bra. Probably not a good idea to move so fast, she decided, falling to her knees and locating the bra with her fingers, already back on her feet when she heard the voice from the doorway.

"Dad? What are you doing home so early?"

It was too late to do anything but turn around.

"Oh, wow!" Heather's eyes opened wide with disbelief, moving from her bare-chested father to her half-crouching, half-naked mother.

"It's not what you think," Tom said lamely, fiddling with the buttons of his shirt.

"Nothing happened," Cindy said, pulling her bra into position, securing the clasp at the back. First her mother and sister walk in on her and Neil; now her daughter finds her with Tom. That's what I get for not having sex in three years, Cindy thought.

"Sure. Okay. Wow."

"It was a momentary lapse in judgment," Cindy explained.

"I thought you had classes till six."

"Does this mean you're getting back together?"

"Absolutely not," Tom said forcefully.

"God, no," Cindy echoed.

"Okay, well, wow. Okay," Heather said, backing out of the room. "I think I should probably get going."

"Sweetie . . ." Cindy called.

"I'm fine. Don't worry about me. I'll phone you later." The front door closed after her.

Tom looked at Cindy. "I hope you're proud of yourself," he said.

TWENTY-FIVE

Wednesday, September 11, Cindy stayed in bed watching TV as the country relived the agony of the previous year's terrorist attacks on the World Trade Center.

Like everyone else she knew, Cindy could recall the exact time and the place she'd been when she'd learned the devastating news. It was during the film festival, and she and Meg had just emerged from the Uptown after a screening of the British film, *Last Orders*, starring Michael Caine and Bob Hoskins. It was around 11 A.M. and they were heading up Yonge Street to meet Trish and grab a sandwich before their next movie. "Where is everyone?" Cindy asked, wondering at the lack of a lineup for the next movie.

"Something's happening at the corner," Meg said.

When they reached the intersection of Yonge and Bloor, they joined a crowd of several hundred people standing in stunned silence, watching the gigantic TV screen on top of the low-rise building on the southeast corner, as the two hijacked planes flew repeatedly, and from a multitude of sickening angles, into the giant twin towers. She and Meg had watched in openmouthed horror as the buildings collapsed, peeling downward from top to bottom, like the skin of a banana, the resultant debris spilling over onto the streets of New York, covering everything in its path in a sickening gray dust.

At the time, Cindy thought nothing could be worse.

Leigh walked into the bedroom. "You've got to talk to Mom," she was saying, dimpled knees peeking out from under light khaki shorts, her white sleeveless blouse in sharp contrast to her deeply tanned arms. "She canceled the fitting with Marcel. What are you watching?" She reached toward the bed and pressed the OFF button on the remote.

"What are you doing?" Cindy grabbed the remote, flipped the TV back on.

Leigh wrestled the unit from Cindy's hands, switched the TV off. "You shouldn't be watching this."

"What do you mean, I shouldn't be watching it? What are you talking about?"

"It'll only upset you."

"Give me that," Cindy told her younger sister, whose response was to hide the remote behind her back. Cindy jumped off the bed, tried reaching around her sister. "Leigh, I'm warning you. Give it back."

"No."

"Leigh . . ."

"I won't."

"Oh, for Pete's sake." Cindy marched back to the television and triumphantly pressed the manual ON switch.

Her sister was right behind her, pressing it off.

"What the hell do you think you're doing?"

"I'm protecting you."

"Protecting me? From what?"

"From yourself."

"From myself," Cindy repeated, incredulously.

"Your judgment isn't the best lately."

"My judgment isn't the best." Cindy shook her head. "What are you talking about?"

"I'm talking about the fact that first you slept with your accountant, then you went to bed with your ex-husband. . . ."

Cindy rolled her eyes. "Neil is not my accountant, and I didn't go to bed with Tom."

"Only because Heather walked in on you."

"It was over by the time she walked in."

"What was over? You said nothing happened."

"Nothing *did* happen."

"But it almost did. Which is my point exactly."

Cindy sank down on the bed. "This conversation makes no sense whatsoever."

"You need to get dressed," Leigh said.

Cindy glanced down at her yellow cotton nightshirt. "I'm fine."

"It's almost noon, and you're still in your pajamas."

Cindy gave her sister a look that said, So?

Leigh marched into Cindy's closet.

"Where are you going? What are you doing?"

Leigh returned seconds later carrying a pair of black capri pants and a green-and-white-striped jersey. She threw them on the bed, along with some freshly washed underwear. "Here. Wear this."

"I don't want to wear that."

"I'm not leaving this room till you get dressed."

"Well, then you might as well make yourself comfortable because I'm not wearing that."

"For Pete's sake, Cindy. You're worse than my kids."

"For Pete's sake, Leigh. You're worse than our mother."

"Cindy. . . ."

"Leigh. . . ."

Stalemate, Cindy thought.

"So, what's it going to be?" Leigh asked, the remote seemingly attached to the palm of her right hand, both hands on her hips.

Cindy shook her head. "Okay. Okay. You win."

"You'll get dressed?"

"I'll need some help with this." Cindy pulled at the front of her nightgown.

Leigh approached warily. "What kind of help?"

In the next second, Cindy lunged at her sister, knocking her to the floor as she grabbed for the remote.

"What are you doing?" Leigh gasped as Cindy collapsed on top of her. "What's wrong with you?"

"Give me that thing."

"No!"

"Give it to me."

"Mom!"

"Give me the goddamn remote."

"Mom!"

"Coming," their mother called from downstairs. "Is something wrong?"

"You're such a baby," Cindy told her sister, scratching at her arm.

"You're such a brat."

Norma Appleton ran into the room, took one look at her daughters rolling around on the floor, and threw her hands up into the air. "What on earth is going on in here?"

"She scratched my arm."

"She took my remote."

"Stop this. The two of you. Right now."

The girls stopped struggling, sat on the floor glaring at one another.

"It's my remote," Cindy said petulantly.

"Give her back her remote," their mother instructed.

Leigh tossed the unit to the floor. Cindy promptly scooped it up.

"Look what she did to my arm." Leigh extended her forearm, displaying a thin red scratch running above her elbow.

"Apologize to your sister," Norma Appleton said.

Cindy shook her head, looked the other way.

"Apologize to your sister," her mother repeated.

"Sorry," Cindy mumbled under her breath.

"What did you say?" Leigh asked. "I didn't hear you."

"Mother," Cindy warned.

"Don't press your luck," their mother said, helping her younger daughter to her feet.

"Oh, sure. Take her side."

"I'm not taking sides."

"*Don't press your luck?* What would you call that?" Leigh practically shook with indignation.

"Oh, darling, your 'Hi, Helens.'" Norma Appleton pointed with her chin toward the underside of Leigh's arms. "Maybe a different blouse. . . ."

Cindy started laughing.

"You're both nuttier than fruitcakes. You know that?" Leigh said.

Cindy scrambled to her feet, laughed harder.

"What's so funny?"

"You are. You're being ridiculous."

"*I'm* being ridiculous? *I'm* being ridiculous?"

"*You're* being ridiculous."

"Girls, please."

"Am I the one who's refusing to get dressed? Am I the one whose daughter walked in on her half-naked with her former husband?"

"Heather was not half-naked," Cindy said.

"Sure. Make jokes. Correct my grammar. It's easier than facing the truth."

"The truth being?"

"Girls . . ." their mother warned.

"The truth being that you're behaving irresponsibly."

"What!"

"You're always flying out of this house without telling anyone where you're going or what time you'll be back."

"It's my house. I'm an adult. I didn't realize I had to report to anyone."

"It's not a matter of reporting. It's a matter of consideration."

"What if I don't know where I'm going or when I'll be back?"

"That's exactly what I'm saying. You go off half-cocked."

"You're starting to sound like Tom, you know that?"

"Well, maybe he's right."

"Sorry if I'm not behaving completely rationally these days."

"Since when has it ever been any different?" Leigh scoffed. "Cindy does exactly what Cindy wants to do, just as she always has. Where do you think Julia gets it from?"

"Whoa," Cindy warned.

"If Cindy wants to get married when she's eighteen and her parents are dead-set against it, no problem," Leigh continued, undeterred. "She'll just elope to Niagara Falls. Doesn't matter if her parents go crazy with worry for two days, wondering where the hell she is. Doesn't matter that they miss their younger daughter's performance in *Our Town*. So what if she's the lead and she's been rehearsing for months? Hell, it's only a school play. There'll be plenty of other opportunities. Isn't that what you said, Mom?"

"Sweetheart," their mother demurred, "where is all this coming from?"

"*Our Town*?" Cindy marveled. "You've got to be kidding."

"Why? Because it was important to *me*?"

"Leigh, darling, please. . . ."

"Please what, Mother? Please don't make a fuss? Please don't be upset because you still can't find any time for me?"

"If this is about the fitting I had to cancel this afternoon. . . ."

"You didn't *have* to cancel the fitting, Mother. You *chose* to cancel the fitting."

"It just seemed like there were other things that were more important. . . ."

"More important than your granddaughter's wedding?"

"I didn't say that."

"Why is Cindy's daughter any more important than mine?"

"In case you hadn't noticed," Cindy interrupted, "*my* daughter is missing." She burst into a flood of angry, confused tears.

"Cindy," her mother said, rushing to her side.

"Leave her alone, will you. Stop babying her."

"What's the matter with you?" Norma Appleton demanded of her younger daughter. "Why are you acting this way?"

"Because I am sick and tired of being ignored."

"Who's ignoring you?"

"I all but abandon my family to come over here, I cook for you, I clean up after you. . . ."

"Nobody asked you to do any of that."

"I've been doing it all your life," Leigh snapped. "After you got married, who was there for you? Who made sure things got patched up between you and Mom and Dad? Who was there after that wonderful husband of yours walked out? Who sat beside you and listened to that damn message he left on the answering machine, over and over again? Who rushed over after Julia decided she wanted to live with her father? Who sat up all night with you while you cried your heart out?"

"*You!*" Cindy shouted, punching her fists into the air, like a boxer flailing at an invincible opponent. "*You. You. You.* Always the first one at the scene of an accident. Always available in times of crisis. Tell me, when else do you ever come around?"

Silence.

"When else do you ever let me in?"

The two sisters stared at one another. The doorbell rang.

"Shit," Cindy said.

"Shit," echoed Leigh.

"Shit," said their mother.

Nobody moved.

The doorbell rang again.

"I'll get it," Norma Appleton said finally, walking slowly toward the hall. "Can I leave you two alone?" she asked, turning back.

The doorbell rang a third time.

"Coming." Norma Appleton hurried down the stairs. "I'm coming. Hold your horses."

"Are you expecting anyone?" Leigh asked.

Cindy shook her head, listening for the sound of voices. "I know it's stupid," she said, "but every time it rings, I think it might be Julia."

"Me too," Leigh said.

In the next instant, Cindy was in her sister's arms, crying on her shoulder.

"Oh, Cindy," Leigh whispered, crying too. "I'm so sorry. You know I didn't mean any of those things I said."

"No. You're right. I've treated you very badly."

"No, you haven't."

"I haven't thanked you for any of the things you've done."

"I don't need thanks."

"Yes, you do," Cindy told her. "You need to be thanked. You deserve to be valued."

Leigh smiled sadly, hugged her sister tighter to her chest. "It probably wasn't the best time to bring up *Our Town*."

"I'm sure you were terrific."

"I love you."

"I love you too." Cindy brushed an errant curl away from her sister's face. "Did I tell you how much I like your hair this color?"

"Really? 'Cause I was thinking of maybe adding a couple of darker streaks."

"That would be nice too."

"Cindy," her mother called from the front hall. "Come look at what just arrived for you."

"What is it?"

"Looks like a plant of some kind." Norma Appleton was already tearing at the cellophane by the time Cindy and Leigh reached the bottom of the stairs.

Cindy unpinned the small white envelope from the side of the wrapping as her mother extricated a lovely arrangement of African violets.

Thinking of you, the card read. *Martin Crawley.*

Cindy laughed, tucked the card into the pocket of her nightshirt, felt it warm against her breast.

"Who's it from?"

Cindy smiled. "My accountant," she said.

"He seems like a very nice man," Leigh acknowledged, lifting the plant from her mother's hands and carrying it into the kitchen. "So, I was thinking of making my famous lemon chicken that Julia loves so much, maybe freezing it," she called back, "so that she can have some when she comes home. What do you think?"

"I think she'd like that very much," Cindy said, following her sister into the kitchen.

"Good. Then that's what I'll do."

"Leigh?"

"Hmm?"

Cindy paused, took a deep breath. "Thank you," she said.

TWENTY-SIX

What did you say to get them to leave?" Neil was asking.

"I said 'please,'" Cindy answered. "Something I haven't been saying nearly enough these days." It was almost midnight and she and Neil were sitting naked in her bed, having finished making love for the third time since his arrival some two hours earlier. Elvis lay on the floor beside them, as if he'd sensed their need for privacy. Or maybe he'd just gotten tired of the constant motion, of having to adjust his position to accommodate their fevered acrobatics. "Actually, I think they were quite happy for the break. My brother-in-law's been pretty patient, but I'm sure he's glad to have his wife back, even if it's only for a day or two. And my mother's been here since . . ." Cindy stopped, reluctant to say Julia's name out loud, to bring the continuing agony of her daughter's disappearance into bed with them, when being in bed with Neil was the only respite she'd had since Julia went missing.

But it was already too late. Her pain, which had gradually morphed from constant, daggerlike thrusts to her chest and abdomen into a steadier, duller, though no less constant, ache that infused every fiber in her body—a chronic illness as opposed to a surprise attack—had already wormed its way under the sheets to insinuate itself between them.

"What say we watch some TV." Cindy flipped on the television set, began restlessly surfing through the channels.

"What's that?" Neil asked as Cindy's fingers froze on the remote. The screen filled with the distorted image of Edvard Munch's masterpiece, *The Scream,* now reborn as a hideous mask, hiding the face of a merciless killer as he stalked a group of nubile teenagers.

"*Scream,*" Cindy said with authority, shaking her head at the irony that such a breathtaking work of art had achieved its greatest fame via a series of teenage slasher movies, then shaking her head again with the realization that she'd seen the entire *Scream* franchise.

No, I won't see Scream 3 *with you,* Julia had protested when the film was first released. *It's supposed to be terrible. I can't believe you're going. How can you like that garbage?*

Before Julia went missing, Cindy had an easy answer, similar to the one she'd given Neil on their first date. She enjoyed such vicarious torment, she'd told Julia, precisely because it *was* vicarious. She could relish the thrill of danger without experiencing its real threat. The danger was entirely illusory. She was perfectly safe.

Except no one was safe, she understood now. It was the notion of safety, not the threat of danger, that was the real illusion.

The monsters were very real.

Cindy flipped to another channel, then another and another. "Stop me if you see anything interesting."

Neil gently removed the remote control unit from her hand, turned the TV off. "It's late. Why don't we just get some sleep?"

"Did you ever cheat on your wife?" Cindy asked suddenly, carefully monitoring Neil's reaction.

"No," he said. "Not my style."

"Tom cheated on me all the time."

"Tom's an ass."

"Yes, he is, isn't he?" Cindy smiled, although this time the smile was genuine and not the stiff, automatic reflex that normally accompanied each reference to her ex-husband.

The divorce was seven years ago, she heard Julia say. *Get over it.*

Amazing, Cindy thought, her smile widening. I *am* over it.

"You hungry?" she asked Neil, suddenly energized. "Thirsty?"

"Just sleepy."

Cindy felt her body tense. *To sleep,* she thought uneasily. *Perchance to dream.* "Quick," she said. "Name all the seven dwarfs."

"What?"

"From *Snow White*. You know Sleepy, Bashful, Grumpy, Doc, Happy. . . ."

"Cindy, what's wrong?"

"Wrong? Why do you think something's wrong?"

"Because it's midnight and we're talking about *Snow White and the Seven Dwarfs*. What is it? Don't you want me to stay?"

"No, of course I want you to stay."

"You're sure? Because if you're not comfortable. . . ."

"It's not that." Cindy reached for her robe and climbed out of bed, crossing to the window and opening the shutters, staring past the backyard toward the roofs of the large homes along Clarendon, wondering absently what secrets were hidden beneath those roofs.

"What is it?" Neil asked, coming up behind her, surrounding her with his arms.

"It's just that I'm a bit of a restless sleeper these days."

"That's understandable."

"I'm not so sure how understanding you'll be when my screaming wakes you up a couple of hours from now."

"You've been having nightmares?"

"I don't know what you'd call them. They're so stupid." Cindy told Neil of waking up in a sweat night after night, convinced she was dying because she'd forgotten to take some nonexistent pills. "My mother says it's hormonal. My sister says it's a natural by-product of my anxiety. Either way, it's making me crazy."

"I think I might be able to help you," Neil offered.

"Really? How?"

"Come here." Neil led her back to bed and sat her down, then disappeared into the en suite bathroom.

Seconds later Cindy heard him rummaging around in her medicine cabinet, heard the sound of water running from the taps.

"I don't want any sleeping pills," she said as he reentered the room, a glass of water in his right hand.

"You need to sleep, Cindy."

"Not everything can be cured by taking a pill."

"Try these." Neil perched on the side of the bed and opened the fist of his free hand.

Cindy stared into his empty palm. "What's this—the emperor's new pills?"

"Take as many as you need."

Cindy smiled, stared into the deep blue of his eyes. "You really think this is going to work?"

"Can't hurt. Go on. Doctor's orders."

Cindy's fingers hesitated over the invisible pills. She took one, raised it to her mouth, then dropped it onto the tip of her tongue, and swallowed it down with some water. Then she reached over, took another one.

"Why don't you have one more, for good luck."

"For good luck," Cindy agreed, swallowing the third invisible pill and returning the glass of water to Neil's waiting hand. "Now what?"

Neil deposited the empty glass on the night table beside the bed, then climbed into bed beside Cindy, sliding down under the covers and taking her in his arms. "Good night, Cindy," he said, kissing her softly. "Sleep well."

When Cindy woke up at seven-thirty the next morning, Neil was already in the shower. "Well, what do you know? The damn pills actually worked." She laughed out loud, was considering joining Neil in the shower when the phone rang.

"Cindy, it's Ryan Sellick," the voice boomed across the phone wires. "I know it's early, and I'm probably the last person in the world you want to be hearing from under the circumstances, but . . ."

Neil emerged from the bathroom, towel-drying his hair.

"Is something wrong?" Cindy asked, the expression on Neil's face asking the same thing. "My neighbor," she whispered, her hand over the mouthpiece.

"Believe me, I wouldn't be calling you if I weren't absolutely desperate."

"What is it, Ryan?"

Neil crossed the room, kissed Cindy's forehead, began gathering up his clothes.

"It's just that you've always been so kind to Faith, and I don't know who else to turn to."

"Is Faith all right?"

"She's had a really rough couple of days. She was up most of the night, and she just fell asleep about fifteen minutes ago. Unfortunately, I have to be in Hamilton all day."

"You want me to look in on her?"

"I was wondering if you could take care of Kyle until Faith wakes up. I know it's a hell of a thing for me to be asking. Especially when you think I might have. . . ." He paused. "It's just that I'm being picked up in less than half an hour, and. . . ."

"Okay," Cindy told him, watching Neil get dressed.

"Okay?"

"I'll be over in fifteen minutes," Cindy said.

"Thank you. Cindy. . . ."

"What?"

Silence. Then, "Please believe I had nothing to do with Julia's disappearance."

"I'll be over soon." Cindy hung up the phone.

"You're sure that's a good idea?" Neil asked.

Cindy shrugged. She wasn't sure of anything anymore. "Maybe immersing myself in someone else's problems for a few hours will take my mind off my own."

"You're amazing," Neil said.

"I had a good night's sleep."

Neil kissed her gently on the lips. His hair smelled of green apple shampoo. "I better go home, get changed for work."

"Thank Max for me for letting his father stay out all night," Cindy said as she was walking him to the front door minutes later.

"I'll call you later."

Cindy watched Neil drive off, then hurried upstairs to get dressed, realizing she was feeling better—more positive—than she had in days. Was it because she'd actually slept through the night for the first time in weeks? Because she was having sex for the first time in years? Because she thought she might be falling in love? "How can I even be thinking about falling in love at a time like this?" she asked the silent house, discarding her terry-cloth robe and standing naked in the upstairs hall, knowing that she was completely alone, that her mother wasn't here to warn her of the dangers of catching a draft, her sister wasn't waiting to point out that she too could have a flat stomach if she had the time Cindy had to work out, that Heather wasn't gasping in embarrassment and dismay at what the future held in store, that Julia wasn't here to tell her to *please* put something on. . . .

That Julia wasn't here.

"I'm all alone," Cindy said as the dog rushed over to lick at her toes. "Well, maybe not *all* alone," she amended, surprisingly grateful for the animal's presence. She knelt to stroke his side, watched him roll over to offer his belly. "Thank you for being here," she told him, obliging him with a few heartfelt scratches. Elvis groaned his pleasure, stretched himself out to his full length, pawed at the air for more.

Don't stop, he seemed to be saying. *Don't stop.*

Don't stop, she heard herself cry out in joyous abandon as Neil buried his head between her thighs.

"I'm doing it again," she said out loud. How can I be happy? How can I be hopeful for the future when the present is so unsettled?

And yet hope was exactly what she was experiencing. Was it some kind of premonition? Cindy wondered as she showered and dressed. Was her intuition telling her that things were about to change, that all was not lost, that there was indeed reason to be optimistic?

Maybe at this very instant, Julia was being rescued, Cindy projected, racing down the stairs to the kitchen. Maybe any minute now, the police would be turning up at her front door with the good news. "And I won't be here," she said, deciding to call Detective Bartolli, tell him where she'd be. Just in case. She left the Sellicks' phone number with the officer who answered the phone, then shut Elvis in the kitchen, and quickly exited the house.

She arrived at the Sellicks' door at the same time a black Caprice was pulling into the driveway.

"Would you tell Ryan his lift is here?" an attractive young woman called, leaning out the window of the driver's seat.

Cindy smiled at the woman, whose long coral-colored ringlets hung past the shoulders of her low-cut, floral-print blouse, acknowledging the young woman's request with a nod of her head as she rang the bell.

"Cindy, thank God," Ryan said as he opened the door.

"Your lift is here." Cindy motioned toward the driveway, stepped into the hall.

Ryan signaled with his index finger to the young woman,

then closed the door. "The baby's asleep," he said, straightening his dark blue tie, speaking quickly. "Faith's been expressing her milk, so there are a few bottles in the fridge. All you have to do is heat one up for a minute in the microwave. . . ."

"Ryan," Cindy interrupted gently. "It's okay. I know what to do."

"Of course you do." His eyes swept across the floor, like a broom. "Damn it. Where'd I put my briefcase?"

"Is that it?" Cindy pointed to a black leather briefcase propped against the wall next to the kitchen.

"That's it." He took two giant steps toward it, scooped it into his hands, held it tight against his gray suit, his eyes shooting from the kitchen to the living room. "I'm sorry the place is such a mess."

"I'll try to straighten up a little."

"Oh no, please. You don't have to do that."

"It's fine. Gives me something to do."

Outside, a car horn honked.

"I've got to go."

"Go."

"I look okay?"

"You look great."

"Very important potential client or I'd send somebody else."

"Knock 'em dead."

"You're a godsend, Cindy. I don't know how to thank you."

You can find my little girl, she thought. "Your ride's waiting," she said.

Ryan opened the door. "I've left my cell phone number on the kitchen counter, in case there are any problems."

"There won't be."

"I'll call you as soon as I get two minutes."

"Try not to worry."

Ryan ran down the front steps to the car, then stopped, his hand on the door handle. "Has there been any news?" he called back, an obvious afterthought.

Cindy shook her head. "Drive carefully," she advised the impatient young woman behind the wheel of the car.

"I'll phone you later."

Cindy waved as the woman backed her car onto the street and turned west toward Poplar Plains, not envying them the traffic they faced. Hamilton was almost close enough to be considered a suburb, but rush hour traffic would add at least twenty minutes to the normally hour-long drive. And that was providing there were no accidents along the way.

(Typical Altercation: "It was an accident, for God's sake." Julia, age thirteen and already towering over her mother, stares unapologetically at the broken Lalique vase her careless hand has swept off the mantel above the fireplace.

"I know it was an accident," Cindy says evenly. "I just said you should be more careful."

"It's just a damn vase. I don't know what you're getting so bent out of shape about."

"It was a birthday gift from Meg. And please watch your language."

"What'd I say? Damn? You call that language?"

"Julia. . . ."

"I hear you say much worse."

"That doesn't mean. . . ."

"It means you're a hyprocrite."

"Julia. . . ."

"Mother. . . ."

Stalemate.)

Cindy closed the front door, leaned her head against it, trying not to hear the echo of Julia's recriminations clawing at her through the years. I have to stop doing this, she thought. I have to stop projecting Julia into every scenario, stop putting her inflection into every casual utterance.

How do I do that? she asked, pushing herself away from the door. How do I stop thinking about my daughter? How do I get used to living without her?

She walked into the living room, the hope she'd felt only moments earlier rapidly dissipating as she surveyed the chaos. Pillows from the living room sofa lay scattered on the hardwood floor. There were used coffee cups everywhere. Something sticky grabbed at the soles of her shoes. A plate of leftover pieces of Kentucky Fried Chicken sat largely untouched on the water-stained coffee table in the middle of the room. Cindy carried the plate into the kitchen, swept the food into the garbage disposal under the sink, the sink full of dirty dishes. "What a mess." She stacked the dishes in the dishwasher, then rinsed out by hand the half dozen wine glasses on the counter.

Was Faith drinking? Or was it Ryan?

Does your daughter drink? Detective Gill had asked.

No, Cindy said.

Occasionally, Tom corrected.

"Stop it," Cindy said out loud. Not everything is about Julia.

Julia's reflection winked at her from the large window overlooking the backyard. "Of course it is," she said, as upstairs, a baby started to cry.

TWENTY-SEVEN

Cindy hurried up the stairs to the nursery, glancing toward the closed doors of the master bedroom as she tiptoed past, hoping the baby's cries wouldn't disturb Faith. "It's okay. It's okay," she cooed at the screaming infant, his face scrunched into a tight, wrinkled ball, like a roll of bright pink yarn. She reached into the crib and drew the baby gingerly to her chest, kissing his soft, sweet-smelling forehead as she rocked him gently back and forth. "It's okay, baby. Don't cry. Don't cry."

Amazingly, the infant stopped howling almost immediately.

That was easy, Cindy thought, standing by the side of the crib, continuing her rhythmic rocking. Too easy, she realized, as seconds later, the baby stiffened in her arms, his hands and feet shooting from his body like the limbs of a leaping frog. A fresh round of screams pierced the air. "My goodness," Cindy muttered, tapping the door to the nursery closed with her foot. Had Julia ever screamed this loudly? "Do you need changing? Is that the problem?"

Cindy looked around the nursery, noticing for the first time what a lovely room it was. Pale blue walls, bleached wood crib and hand-painted dresser, a high shelf filled with soft, colorful, stuffed animals that ran along three of the walls, a bentwood rocking chair by the small side window, its curtains the same delicate blue-and-white gingham as the crib sheets. A mobile of dancing elephants hung from the overhead light fixture; another mobile, this one of pastel-colored butterflies, dangled over the crib. "Everything you could ask for," Cindy told the crying infant, lying him across the changing table against one wall and reaching for the giant box of disposable diapers at her feet. "We'll get you all cleaned up and then you'll be happy. You'll see." She unsnapped the baby's clean white sleeper and removed his diaper with a sure and steady hand. "Just like riding a bicycle," she told the baby, whose response was to scream even louder. "Not too impressed, I see." And not wet either, she realized, replacing the dry diaper with another, then leaning forward to secure the tabs just as a sudden arch of urine sprayed into the air, narrowly missing her eye. Cindy pulled back, startled. "Oh, my," she said with her mother's voice. "Well, I only had girls. They didn't do things like that." She wiped off the top of the changing table and replaced the now-wet diaper with another clean one, then gently maneuvered the baby's wriggling feet back into the legs of his sleeper, before carrying him out of the room. "Ssh," she cautioned, hurrying past the master bedroom and down the stairs. "We don't want to wake Mommy. Mommy needs her sleep." Mommy needs a psychiatrist, Cindy thought, proceeding past the messy living room into the now-tidy kitchen. Or, at the very least, a housekeeper. She reached into the fridge, located one of the baby's bottles, and popped it into the microwave, the baby screaming steadily in her ear. "It's okay, sweetheart. We'll have you all fixed up in no time."

Or not, Cindy thought when the infant refused to take the bottle. "Come on, sweetheart. You can do it. Mmmm. Warm milk. Yummy delicious. Try some."

Cindy carried the baby into the living room, and sank down on the pillowless green velvet sofa, cradling Kyle the way she remembered cradling Julia. She'd nursed Julia for almost a year, she remembered fondly, as Kyle's lips bounced across her white T-shirt, searching for her breast. "Oh, sweetheart, I'm so sorry. I don't have any milk. But I have this yummy bottle." She slid the rubber nipple into his mouth, even as Kyle tried turning his head away in protest. "Come on, sweetheart. Give it a chance."

Kyle's lips suddenly locked around the rubber nipple, his crying shuddering to a halt as he devoted all his energy to draining the liquid from the bottle.

"That's a good boy. Yes, that's it. Now you've got it."

Julia used to suckle with that same ferocious determination, Cindy found herself thinking, recalling the hard tug at her breast each time Julia would settle in against her to be fed. She kissed the top of Kyle's down-covered head, tried remembering the same scene with Heather. But Cindy had few memories of nursing Heather, and those few she did have revolved more around Julia, who'd sit screaming at Cindy's feet, her arms wrapped tightly around her mother's knees, every time Cindy tried breast-feeding her younger child. Ultimately, everyone involved was a nervous wreck, and Cindy switched Heather over to a bottle when she was barely two months old.

"Well, well. Look at you go." Cindy watched the milk rapidly disappear from the bottle. When the bottle was empty, Cindy lifted Kyle over her shoulder and gently patted his back until she heard him burp. "What a guy," Cindy murmured, rocking him back and forth in her arms until he drifted off to sleep.

She'd always loved this part. The baby part. She knew a lot of women didn't, that they had trouble relating to their children until their children started relating to them. Maybe Faith was one of those women. Maybe once Kyle started responding to her, she'd stop viewing his outbursts as evidence of her own failure. Maybe as the year progressed, and Kyle started sitting up, trying to stand, to walk, to talk, she'd realize what a miracle she and her husband had created together, the tremendous gift they'd been given, and she'd be happy.

Except it wasn't as easy as that, and Cindy knew it. Postpartum depression, if indeed that's what Faith was suffering from, couldn't be cured with simple platitudes or even common sense. Another case of hormones running amok, Cindy thought, wondering if Ryan had taken her earlier advice, talked to Faith's doctor about prescribing stronger medication.

I certainly can't keep running over here every time there's a problem, she thought, carrying Kyle up the stairs to the nursery.

Why not? she wondered. What else do I have to do?

Cindy felt an unexpected tear wend its way down her cheek, then drop onto the top of Kyle's head. He stirred, his little fist shooting instinctively into the air, as if preparing to defend himself. Cindy pressed him tighter to her breast, hunkered down in the chair, began rocking back and forth.

Within minutes, she was fast asleep.

(Dream: Cindy is walking down the empty corridor of Forest Hill Collegiate, where she attended high school, trying to locate the principal's office. *It's over there,* Ryan tells her, appearing out of nowhere to pass her in the hall. Suddenly Cindy is standing in front of the long reception desk in the middle of the main office. *I'm looking for Julia Carver,* Cindy tells Irena, who is too busy ironing a pair of men's slacks to look up. *Room 113,* Irena says curtly. Cindy races down the hall, past a drinking fountain that is shooting water blindly into the air, then bursts through the door to Room 113, her eyes sweeping across the rows of curious student faces. *Where's Julia?* she demands of the dwarflike man at the head of the class. Michael Kinsolving lowers the script he is holding to his sides and walks menacingly toward her. *Who's Julia?* he asks.)

Cindy woke with a start, causing the infant in her arms to stiffen and cry out. "It's okay," she reassured him softly, coming fully awake, grateful when the baby's body drifted back into sleep. She took a deep breath, carefully adjusted Kyle's position, and checked her watch. Eleven o'clock! She'd been asleep almost two hours. She checked the time again to make sure, then pushed herself out of the rocking chair, her legs wobbly, her shoulders and arms stiff. "Those pills of Neil's were really something."

Slowly, with meticulous care, Cindy deposited Kyle on

his back in the crib, then crept from the room, closing the door after her. She proceeded down the hall to the master bedroom, each step a deliberate exaggeration, then cocked her ear against the closed door, wondering if Faith was still asleep. After several seconds, she pushed open the door, and stepped inside.

The room was dark and stuffy, an etherlike pall filtering through the air, like a miasmal mist. Cindy inched her way across the clothes-strewn broadloom toward the huge cast-iron bed that sat against the far wall. Faith lay on her back in the middle of the bed, one arm tossed carelessly above her head, one foot peeking out from underneath a pile of heavy blankets, her uncombed hair matted against her forehead, her mouth open, a series of snores emanating from between parched lips. Cindy smoothed the damp hair away from Faith's face, then replaced her foot beneath the covers. How many times had she done the same thing for Julia? How many times had she tucked in errant toes and smoothed away stray hairs?

Don't do that, Julia would protest, slapping at her mother's hand, even in her sleep.

Cindy was halfway down the stairs when she heard the steady sound of barking and realized it was coming from next door. Elvis! She'd forgotten all about him. Had he been barking the whole time she'd been away?

"I should run home and let him out," Cindy said to an imaginary panel of judges. "It'll just take two minutes." Except it wouldn't. You just didn't let Elvis out. You escorted him around the block and waited while he sniffed each blade of grass until he found just the right one on which to do his business, and then you went through the whole ritual again. And again. And again. There was no such thing as two minutes with Elvis. Twenty minutes was closer to the truth. And she couldn't leave Kyle alone for twenty minutes, even with his mother sleeping in the next room. Faith was practically comatose. She couldn't just take off. Who knew what might happen? How many times had she read articles about children dying in fires while their caregivers were out of the house? *I only left him alone for two minutes!*

"Okay, so what do I do?" Cindy asked the empty hall.

Shouldn't have been so quick to get rid of me, she heard her mother say.

Please, her sister added. *You think this is a problem? You should spend a day at my house.*

The baby started crying.

"Well, that settles that." Cindy scribbled a note for Faith telling her she was taking Kyle for a walk, then left it on the floor outside her bedroom door. "We'll change you later," she told the baby, carrying him down the stairs and grabbing the house key hanging from a nail near the front door.

She located the large English-style carriage hidden along the side of the house, and laid Kyle inside it, the baby's fierce screams bracketing Elvis's angry barks. Leaving the carriage in her driveway, she bounded up the outside steps and unlocked her front door. Elvis shot out at her, as if from a cannon, almost knocking her over. "How did you get out of the kitchen?" Cindy asked in amazement, watching as Elvis ran down the front steps, and peed against the wheel of the carriage. "Great. Oh, that's great. Okay, wait. Let me get your leash." Cindy opened the hall closet, her hand whipping across the floor in search of the dog's leash.

"Where is it? Damn it, where are you?" Where had she put the silly thing? "Okay, stay there," she directed the dog, whose response was to bark loudly four times, then run toward the sidewalk. "Where's the leash?" Cindy yelled at the empty house, racing into the kitchen, checking the countertops, trying not to look too closely at the floor.

She finally located the leash in one of the drawers she reserved for old birthday cards and unsolicited stationery that had been sent by various charities trying to pressure her into making a donation. "Elvis," Cindy called out, carrying the leash outside, seeing the dog disappear around the corner. "Come back here." Cindy pushed the carriage to the sidewalk, then stopped dead, her heartbeat freezing in her chest.

The baby was gone.

She knew it even before she looked down.

She'd left him alone for no more than sixty seconds, and in those sixty seconds some lunatic had jumped out from behind a nearby maple tree and absconded with her neighbor's child. Already the abductor was in his car, speeding toward parts unknown. She'd lost another child. The Sellicks would never see their baby again.

"No," Cindy pleaded, fearfully lowering her eyes to the carriage, her knees buckling as she saw Kyle's huge blue eyes staring up at her, his tongue poking out between his lips, a cascading bouquet of tiny bubbles balanced on its tip.

He was there. He was safe.

Cindy crumpled to the sidewalk, as if her legs were made of paper, her heart all but exploding in her chest. "You're going to give yourself a heart attack if you keep this up," she whispered into the sweaty palm of her hand. And suddenly Elvis was at her side, licking her face and poking his head toward his leash, his tail pounding eagerly against the side of the carriage.

What are you doing goofing off down here? he seemed to be asking.

Cindy attached the leash to the dog's collar, then pulled herself to her feet. Kyle lay on his back, kicking his legs into the air and gurgling happily. "Thank you, God," Cindy whispered, pushing the pram toward Poplar Plains, then continuing south toward Edmund. So much construction going on, she thought absently, noting the new fence going up around a sprawling Tudor-style home on the corner of Clarendon and a concrete porch being erected in front of a modern town house just across the street. Large trucks were everywhere. Workers in hard hats and tight jeans toted heavy rocks and tall ladders, nodding as she walked by. How long had they been in the neighborhood? Long enough to notice Julia?

Nobody struts a street quite like Julia, Ryan had remarked.

On Edmund Street, Cindy turned left, her eyes flitting warily between the large duplexes on the north side of the street and the single-family homes and large apartment buildings on the south. Was Julia somewhere inside one of these structures?

Cindy had always considered the area around Avenue Road and St. Clair to be so safe.

Was it?

Hadn't Julia stepped onto these very streets—soon after eleven o'clock in the morning, almost the same time as now—and disappeared without a trace?

Cindy shivered, feeling cold despite the unseasonable

heat, and picked up her pace, all but colliding with a frizzy-haired woman juggling an empty stroller while trying to maintain a grip on her squirming toddler's hand. That's right, Cindy urged the woman silently. Hold on tight. It's not as safe as you think.

It's not safe anywhere.

Elvis balked when they rounded the corner back onto Balmoral, obviously sensing his brief walk was about to end. "Sorry, boy," Cindy told him, dragging him up the outside steps of her home and pushing him through the front door. Clearly there was no point in trying to lock him in the kitchen. "I'll take you for a really long walk when Ryan gets home. I promise. Please don't pee on the floor."

The baby started crying almost the second they were back inside the Sellick house. Cindy carried him into the kitchen and retrieved another bottle of Faith's breast milk from the fridge, then popped it into the microwave oven. She fed the baby, took him back upstairs, retrieved the untouched note she'd left for Faith, and changed Kyle's diaper, careful this time to stand well out of the line of fire. After swaddling him tightly in a soft blue cotton receiving blanket, she laid him on his back in the crib and stood over him, gently rubbing his tummy until he fell asleep.

Her own stomach started rumbling, and she realized she'd forgotten to have breakfast. How many times in the last several weeks had she forgotten to eat, despite the constant prodding of her mother and sister? Her face was starting to look thinner, more drawn. Her bra was feeling a little roomy. *Women gain weight from the bottom up and lose it from the top down,* Julia had once remarked.

And Julia would know. Julia knew about such things.

Cindy checked on Faith to see if she was awake and interested in lunch, but she was still fast asleep, her bare toes once again protruding outside their covers. Cindy closed the door, found herself staring down the narrow upstairs hallway toward the bedroom at the front of the house. What was in that room? she wondered. Why was the door closed?

What if Julia is inside? she suddenly thought, marching down the hall and reaching for the doorknob, knowing she was being ridiculous, but unable to keep such thoughts out of her head. What if the Sellicks were a couple of deranged perverts who'd kidnapped Julia and were deriving sadistic satisfaction from having both mother and daughter under the same roof at the same time?

(Image: Julia, bound and gagged, struggling against her restraints, unable to give voice to her desperate cries, while her mother, oblivious to her daughter's presence, changes diapers in the next room.)

Was it possible?

She'd read that murderers often attended their victims' funerals, prolonging their sick pleasure by luxuriating in the family's suffering.

Was it possible such monsters lived right next door?

The door fell open and Cindy stepped over the threshold, both relieved and disappointed by the thoroughly ordinary room that greeted her eyes, its furnishings utilitarian and undistinguished. Obviously Ryan's home office, Cindy realized, noting the cluttered desk, the stacks of books, the architectural drawings spread across the large drafting table in front of the window. Black-and-white photographs of local buildings adorned the walls. Cindy's eyes swooped into each corner of the room, seeing no trace of her daughter anywhere. Had she really expected to find anything?

The phone rang, poking her in the back like an accusing finger.

Cindy gasped, grabbed for the phone on the desk before it could ring a second time. "Hello?"

"Cindy, it's Ryan," the voice said evenly. "I'm so sorry, but this is the first chance I've had to call you all morning. How's it going?"

"Everything's fine." Cindy noticed a closet in the far corner of the room. What did they keep in there? "Faith and the baby are both asleep."

"That's good. Look, we're almost finished here. Shouldn't take too much longer, and then we'll head home. Think you can hold out another couple of hours?"

Cindy checked her watch. A few more hours and it would be almost two o'clock. Her eyes returned to the closet door. "No problem."

"I can't tell you how much I appreciate this."

"I'll see you soon." Cindy hung up the phone, walked to the closet, pulled open the door.

(Image: Julia, her mouth covered by duct tape, her hands bound behind her back, her feet tied at the ankles, sits naked and shivering in a corner of the closet.)

The closet was filled with winter clothes, each item freshly cleaned and hanging inside a long plastic bag. Cindy examined each article of clothing—a man's heavy brown coat, a woman's purple fleece jacket, men's wool suits in brown, gray, and navy, a woman's black dress, a long teal skirt. She rifled through the built-in shelf full of sweaters, extricating a strong-smelling bar of soap from inside the layers of soft wool. By the time she realized someone was watching her, it was too late. Cindy spun around, the bar of soap flying from her hand and landing at Faith Sellick's feet.

Faith looked from Cindy to the closet, then back to Cindy, her eyes as cold as steel. "What the hell are you doing?" she asked.

TWENTY-EIGHT

Faith. I didn't hear you."

"What are you doing here? Where's Ryan?" Faith shifted from one foot to the other, her toes disappearing into the soft pile of the beige broadloom. She was wearing a pair of red tartan flannel pajamas that were too big for her body and too warm for the weather, although she didn't seem to notice either. Several hairs drooped lazily into her eyes and she made no effort to push them aside.

"He had to go to Hamilton. You were sleeping. He didn't want to wake you."

"So he asked you to come over and baby-sit his incompetent wife."

"No, of course not. He just wanted you to catch up on your sleep."

"What time was this?"

"Around eight. Apparently he had an important meeting. . . ."

"They're always important." Faith looked toward the window. "What time is it now?"

Cindy glanced at her watch. "Almost noon."

"So I've been unconscious all morning," Faith noted dully.

"Obviously you were exhausted."

"Kyle . . . ?"

"Sleeping like a baby," Cindy said, hoping to elicit a smile. Failing. "I've fed him twice, taken him for a walk around the block. . . ."

"You've been very busy."

Cindy cleared her throat, coughed into her hand. "Are you hungry? I could make us some lunch."

"You can tell me what you were doing snooping around in my closet."

"I'm really sorry about that," Cindy said, stalling, trying desperately to come up with a believable excuse. "It's just that I was feeling a little cold, and I thought you might have a sweater I could throw on."

Faith's shoulders relaxed as she rushed to embrace the lie. "It *is* cold in this house. I keep telling Ryan that, but he insists the temperature's just right. If it were up to me, I'd do away with air-conditioning altogether." She pointed to a long yellow sweater hanging from a thick wooden hanger toward the back of the closet. "Try that one."

Cindy slipped the luxurious cashmere sweater from its hanger. "That's better," she said, the warm wool lying like a sunburn across her back.

"Color looks good on you."

"Thank you."

"You should keep it."

"What?"

"It looks better on you than it does on me. You might as well have it."

"Oh no. I couldn't do that."

"Why not?"

"Because it's yours."

Faith shrugged. "Ryan's in Hamilton, you said?"

"Actually, he just called, said he should be home in a few hours."

"Is Marcy with him?"

"Marcy?"

"Orange hair, big boobs, lots of teeth."

"Sounds like the woman who picked him up."

Faith nodded knowingly. "Marcy Granger. The senior partner's daughter and Ryan's close associate." She verbally underlined the word "close." "I'm pretty sure they're having an affair." She bent down and scooped up the bar of soap. "You think soap really keeps moths away?"

"I don't know. I've never tried it."

"Your husband used to cheat on you all the time, right?" Faith asked.

Cindy tried not to look too shocked by the question. Had she heard Faith correctly?

"Sorry. I guess it's none of my business."

"Who told you my husband cheated on me?"

"You did."

"I did?"

It was Faith's turn to look flustered. "Last week. When I had tea over at your place."

Cindy fought to remember the conversation over tea. She vaguely recalled talk of children, of Faith's concerns for the future, her calm recitation of family suicides, her concern that Ryan no longer loved her. She remembered clarifying that the Cookie was Tom's wife, but she had no memory of having mentioned anything about Tom's assorted infidelities.

"I'm hungry," Faith announced. "Did you say something about lunch?"

Cindy took the soap from Faith's hands, returned it to the middle of the pile of sweaters, and closed the closet door, her mind racing. If she hadn't said anything to Faith about Tom's affairs, who had?

Julia?

Questions began racing around Cindy's brain, like a dog chasing its tail. Was it possible Julia had told Faith about Tom's indiscretions, even though the two women barely knew one another? Or was it more likely that Julia had confided the information to Ryan during a romantic encounter? Had Ryan then carelessly passed the juicy tidbit along to his wife?

"I think there's some leftover tuna in the fridge," Faith was saying, already halfway down the hall. She stopped in front of the nursery door. "I guess I should check on Kyle," she said with obvious reluctance, making no attempt to go inside.

"Why don't we just let him sleep?" Cindy led Faith down the stairs, hoping for more time alone with her. There was no telling what she might say.

Relief washed across Faith's face. "Did he give you a hard time?" she asked, making herself comfortable at the kitchen table while Cindy rifled through her fridge, looking for the tuna.

"No. He was great. Although he *did* almost pee in my eye."

"I think he does that on purpose."

Cindy was about to laugh when it occurred to her that Faith was actually serious. There was a strange flatness to her voice that belied any attempt at humor. Disconcerted, Cindy did a final survey of the contents of the fridge, ultimately abandoning the search for tuna, and emerging with a handful of eggs she hoped were reasonably fresh. "How about I make us an omelet?"

"With cheese?"

"Do you have any?"

"I love cheese," Faith said, as if this were answer enough.

"One cheese omelet coming up." Cindy located a large chunk of old Cheddar at the very back of the fridge, as well as several loose sticks of butter and a container of milk that had never been opened and was one day short of its expiration date. The salt and pepper were in plain sight on the counter, but she had to search through several cupboards for a medium-sized bowl and a frypan. "I think that's everything," she told Faith, who said nothing. Nor did she say anything as Cindy cracked open the eggs, mixed them with the milk, and stirred them in the frypan. Only when Cindy was adding the Cheddar did Faith show any interest in what she was doing.

"I love cheese," she said again.

They ate in silence, Faith cutting her omelet into neat little bits, then slowly chewing and swallowing each piece. Cindy watched her as she ate, wishing she could pick the young woman up by her heels and shake her, as if she were a branch on one of the outside maple trees. How many loose acorns would fall out? Cindy wondered, thinking,

Does she know something? Something she's not telling me?

Something about Julia?

"Is there anything new with the investigation?" Faith asked suddenly, as if reading Cindy's mind. She laid her fork down, pushed her plate into the middle of the table, sat back in her chair, her knife in her right hand.

"No," Cindy said. "Nothing new."

"It must be horrible for you."

"It is."

"So many horrible things in this world." Faith lifted the knife toward her face, checked her reflection in the narrow sliver of stainless steel. "I look like shit," she said.

"No, you don't."

"Do you ever wish you could just crawl into bed and never wake up?"

"Faith . . ." Cindy began, not sure what to say next.

"I'm tired." Faith pushed her chair away from the table, struggled to her feet. "I think I should lie down for a while." Without another word, she turned and walked purposefully from the room. It was only when Cindy heard her opening the door to the nursery that she realized Faith still had the knife.

Cindy raced up the stairs, the omelet sitting heavy in her stomach, like a large stone, impeding the flow of oxygen to her lungs. Why hadn't she been paying closer attention? What if she was already too late?

Too late for what?

"Faith!" Cindy ran down the hall, Faith's sweater slipping from her shoulders and sliding off her back. "Faith, wait!"

A baby's screams filled the air, followed by the sound of Faith's tortured cries. Together they shook the floor beneath Cindy's feet, like a powerful earthquake.

"No!" Cindy threw herself into the nursery, stopping dead in her tracks at the horrifying sight that greeted her eyes.

Faith Sellick was standing over her son's crib, one hand pulling at her hair, her face a twisted mask of grief and fury, the other hand on her baby's chest, his tiny body convulsing with outrage.

"Faith, no! What have you done?" Cindy pushed Faith out of the way with such force that Faith lost her footing and fell back against the rocking chair before collapsing to the floor. Cindy scooped the baby from the crib, her eyes frantically searching his white sleeper for blood. But there was no blood on the baby's sleeper. Just as there was no blood on the sheets. No blood anywhere, Cindy realized with audible relief, seeing the knife lying innocently at the foot of the crib. "What happened in here?" she demanded over Kyle's continuing howls. "What did you do to him? Tell me!"

"I didn't do anything," Faith cried helplessly. "I was just looking at him, and he opened his eyes and started screaming."

"Did you poke him with the knife?"

"What knife?" Faith asked, her confusion palpable.

"You didn't touch him?"

Faith shook her head, covering her ears with her hands, trying to block out the baby's cries. "He hates me," she whimpered. "He hates the sight of me."

"He doesn't hate you." Cindy returned the screaming baby to his crib, lowered herself to the floor beside Faith.

"Listen to him."

"Babies cry, Faith. It's what they do."

"I can't stand it when he cries."

"I know." Cindy took Faith in her arms, rocked her back and forth, as earlier she had rocked the woman's infant son. "I know."

"Sometimes when he cries, it feels like my head is going to explode."

"I know," Cindy said again. What else could she say? It was the truth. She *did* know. There was nothing worse, nothing more heartbreaking, than the sound of your child's unhappiness. "You need to see a doctor," she told Faith gently. "I'll talk to my friends. Find out the name of a good psychiatrist."

"You think I'm crazy?"

"No. I just think you need more help than I can give you."

Faith shook her head. "You think I'm crazy," she said.

Ryan walked in the house at just after four o'clock, his arms full of blood-orange roses. "For you," he told Cindy, laying them across her arms. "Along with my heartfelt apologies for being so late."

"Your meeting went on longer than you thought," Cindy stated rather than asked. This was familiar territory after all. Tom had long ago given her a tour of its terrain.

"I'm really so sorry. When I phoned you, I honestly thought we had everything all worked out."

Cindy did her best at a sympathetic smile.

"We resolved everything eventually," he said, as if seeking to reassure her.

"You got the commission?"

"Just in time for the start of rush hour traffic. It was brutal."

"You must be exhausted."

"I'm more than a little drained, to tell you the truth. I could use a drink. How about you?"

Cindy thought she already detected a faint odor of booze on Ryan's breath. "I really should be getting home, get these flowers in water."

"One little drink. To celebrate my success." Ryan disappeared into the dining room, returned minutes later with a bottle of red wine and two glasses. "Red okay with you?"

"Fine."

He uncorked the bottle as Cindy lowered the roses to the coffee table. "To you," he said, clicking his glass against hers. "With my undying gratitude."

"To Julia's safe return." Cindy lifted the glass to her mouth, took a long sip, the taste of blackberries lingering on her tongue.

Ryan winced. "How are you holding up?"

"Just barely."

"I wish there was something I could do."

"Me too."

"Honestly, Cindy, I told the police everything I know." Ryan took another sip of his wine, glanced toward the ceiling. "It's so quiet."

"Everyone's asleep."

"Amazing. You obviously have the magic touch."

"Your wife thinks you're having an affair," Cindy said matter-of-factly.

"What?"

"Your wife . . ."

"My wife's imagination is working overtime these days," Ryan said testily, cutting Cindy off before she could say it again.

"Women are usually right about this sort of thing." Cindy watched the color drain from Ryan's face as effortlessly as he drained the wine from his glass.

"My wife is depressed . . ."

"That doesn't mean she's delusional."

"You know as well as I do how strange she's been acting lately."

Cindy had to admit he was right. "What does her doctor say?"

Ryan shook his head. "I've been meaning to call him. It's just that I've been so damn busy."

"Your wife needs help, Ryan."

"Agreed," Ryan said briskly, finishing the wine in his glass, looking sorry he'd ever suggested she stay for a drink. "I'll call him first thing in the morning."

As if on cue, the telephone rang.

Cindy carried her glass to the kitchen and left it in the sink, wondering how long it would be before someone got around to washing it. "I should get going," she said, waving good-bye as Ryan picked up the phone.

"Don't forget your flowers," he whispered, hand over the mouthpiece.

"Oh, right." Cindy returned to the living room, scooped the two dozen roses off the coffee table, pricking her finger on an unseen thorn. She brought her injured finger to her mouth, sucked at the blood, thought it sweeter than the wine.

"Just a minute," she heard Ryan say. Then, walking toward her, extending the portable phone in his hand, "It's for you."

"For me?" Cindy suddenly remembered she'd left the Sellicks' phone number with the police in case they needed to reach her. Had something happened? Had her earlier premonition been correct? Had they found Julia? Cindy lifted the phone to her ear as Ryan moved a discreet distance away. "Hello?"

"Mrs. Carver, it's Detective Bartolli."

"Has something happened?"

"Are you all right?"

"Yes. Of course. Have you found Julia?"

"No." A pause. Then, "Is Ryan Sellick in the room with you?"

Cindy felt her pulse quicken. She stole a glance at Ryan, who was standing at the window, pretending to be engrossed in the late afternoon sky. "Yes."

"Okay, I want you to listen to me, and not do anything stupid. Do you understand?"

"Yes, but . . ."

"No buts. I want you to make whatever excuses are necessary and get out of that house as quickly as possible. We're on our way."

"What are you talking about?"

"Just do what I tell you."

"I don't understand."

"We did a check on those crank calls you've been receiving. Several of them came from the Sellick house."

"What?"

"You heard me."

"What does it mean?"

"We don't know what it means, but we intend to find out. Now get the hell out of that house, and let us handle it."

Cindy clicked off the phone as Ryan turned around.

"Problems?" he asked.

"I have to go."

"Was that the police?"

Don't say anything, Cindy cautioned herself. Don't do anything stupid. Just listen to Detective Bartolli, and get the hell out. Let the police handle things.

"Cindy?"

Cindy dropped the roses to the floor. "What have you done with my daughter?" she demanded, hurling the portable phone at Ryan's head. "What have you done with Julia?"

TWENTY-NINE

The phone whizzed by Ryan's head like a bullet, missing the side of his skull by mere centimeters, and slamming into the piano, taking a crescent-shaped nick out of its ebony side. It crashed to the floor, then lay on its back, its underside exposed and vulnerable, like a dead turtle.

"Cindy—Jesus!—what the hell are you doing?" Ryan swayed from one foot to the other, as if not sure whether to bolt for the door or wrestle her to the ground.

Cindy made the decision for him, throwing herself at his chest and grabbing hold of his dark blue tie, weaving it between her fingers, and pulling it up and out, like a noose. "Where is she? What have you done with her?"

Ryan tried wriggling out of her grasp, but Cindy's grip on his tie was unyielding. His complexion went from soft pink to angry red, as his right hand reached for his throat, and his left tried in vain to ward off the blows of her open palm.

A sudden jolt of pain shot through Cindy's arm, like an electric shock, as Ryan succeeded in grabbing her wrist and twisting it back. Cindy responded with a sharp kick to his shin.

"Cindy, what the hell . . . ?"

"Where's Julia? Where is she?"

"I don't know."

Cindy hauled back and slapped Ryan, hard, across the face.

"Shit!" he yelled, his cheek whitening with the imprint of her hand. The slap seemed to knock him into action, for suddenly he was all masculine strength and rage, his arms extending and corralling and subduing. In seconds, he overpowered Cindy's intemperate flailings, reducing them to an ineffectual montage of arms and legs, hands and feet, fingers and toes.

Cindy cried out as she felt the point of his shoe crack against the back of her knees, then watched helplessly as her body was propelled into the air, before falling—ass over teakettle, as her mother might say—to the floor. Her elbow smacked against the top of the piano stool, and she swore, the word *fuck* flying from her mouth in a sudden rush of air, as Ryan fell on top of her, pinning her arms to the floor above her head. Roses scattered in all directions as Cindy tried to sit up, to push him away, to roll out from under him, but she couldn't move. "Shit! Fuck!" she sputtered, sounding increasingly weak, her words having lost their power to shield and protect. After several more minutes of aimless showboating, she gave up, stopped struggling, lay still.

"Okay, now," Ryan began, his voice that of the conqueror, despite his shortness of breath.

Cindy stared up at the man lying on top of her, gravity pulling on his handsome face, distorting his delicate features, like a silk sweater that's been left too long on a hanger. Ryan was bruised and sweaty, and his dark hair fell across his forehead like loosely shredded bits of carbon paper. Anger intensified the black of his eyes; confusion softened it. But something else was present in those eyes, Cindy recognized. Mingled with the anger and confusion was an unmistakable glint of excitement. Ryan Sellick was enjoying himself.

"Tell me what the hell is going on," he said.

In response, Cindy expelled a wad of saliva from her mouth, aiming it directly at Ryan's face. Unfortunately, the gesture proved more symbolic than successful, with only a tiny fraction of the spittle reaching its intended target, and the rest raining back across her lips.

"Are you crazy?" Ryan was shouting now. "Have you completely lost your mind?"

"Let go of me."

Ryan tightened his grip on her wrists. "Not until you promise to calm down."

"You're only making things worse for yourself."

"What are you talking about?"

"The police will be here any minute."

Ryan suddenly let go of her arms, sank back on his hips. "The police?"

"They know all about your affair with Julia," Cindy improvised.

Ryan fell away from her then, leaning back against the stubby front leg of the piano, the color draining from his face in uneven bursts, leaving jagged splotches of red on his cheeks, like too much makeup haphazardly applied. "That's ridiculous," he said, but his words lacked the moral outrage necessary to sustain them, and they burst upon contact with the air, like soap bubbles.

Cindy scooted along the floor on her rear end until she felt the sofa at her back. She was too tired to stand up, too spent to launch another attack. "Just tell me where Julia is," she said softly, when what she really wanted to say was, Just tell me Julia's alive.

"I don't *know* where she is."

"The police think you do."

"The police are wrong."

"Just like they're wrong about the crank calls I've been getting?"

"What crank calls?"

"The ones telling me my daughter is a tramp, that she got what she deserved."

"I don't understand."

"The calls coming from this house."

"What!"

"Are the police wrong about that too, Ryan?"

A shadow fell across Ryan's face. Like in the movies, Cindy thought, when the screen slowly fades to black. His eyes registered disbelief, acceptance, and alarm almost simultaneously, and he shook his head, muttering, "No, it's impossible. It can't be."

"What can't be?" Cindy asked, distracted by the sound of footsteps on the stairs. She turned, saw Faith standing in the doorway. She was wearing the same red tartan pajamas she'd been wearing all day, and the smell of sour milk emanated from her body like an unpleasant perfume.

"What's going on in here?" Faith asked, her eyes flitting between Cindy and her husband.

Cindy remained on the floor as Ryan struggled to his feet, limped toward his wife.

"What happened to your face?" Faith touched her husband's cheek. "What's going on?" she asked again, her voice flat and faraway, as if she were talking in her sleep.

"Faith," Ryan began, then stopped, smoothed the hair away from his wife's forehead with a solicitous hand.

"The police are on their way over," Cindy informed her.

"The police? Why?"

"They think we know something about Julia," her husband explained.

"But you already talked to them."

"Apparently some calls were made from this house . . ."

"What are you talking about?"

"The police have a tap on my phone," Cindy said, her voice cold, her sympathy spent. "Apparently it's not unusual in cases like this for the victim's family to receive crank calls," she continued, bracing herself for Faith's heated denials.

Instead she heard, "You think Julia's the victim here?"

"What?" asked Cindy, rising quickly to her feet.

"What?" echoed Ryan, his hands dropping to his sides.

"Trust me," Faith continued, tugging at the bottom of her pajama top, pulling it up and away from her leaking breasts. "Julia's no sweet, innocent little victim."

"Faith," Ryan began warily. "I don't think you should say anything else."

"Yes, you'd like that, wouldn't you? You'd like me to be the good little girl, the quiet little mouse, the perfect little wifey who stays home and cooks and cleans and looks after your demon seed, all the while smiling and looking happy, never saying a word about the fact that her husband is busy screwing everything that moves."

"Faith, please. . . ."

"What? You think I don't know? You think I don't know about Brooke, about Ellen, about Marcy?" She paused briefly. "About Julia?"

"What about Julia?" Cindy asked quietly, almost reluctant to interrupt, to interfere with the violent flow of words.

Faith abruptly shifted her focus from Ryan to Cindy. "Well, I hate to be the bearer of bad tidings, knowing how special you think your precious Julia is, but your little girl was just one of the crowd. Wasn't she, Ryan? Pick a number—the line forms to the right."

"Faith," her husband warned. "Enough."

"Enough? Are you kidding? What's ever been enough for you?"

"Look. You're upset. You're exhausted. You don't know what you're saying."

"I'm saying you're a lying, cheating piece of shit who sleeps with his clients' wives, his partner's daughter, and his neighbor's pride and joy. Except there's not a whole lot to be proud of, is there, Cindy? Trust me on this: Julia's no innocent little victim. She wasn't lured into the backseat of a stranger's car by a piece of candy. She was sleeping with a married man, and in my book, she deserves whatever happened to her."

"Faith," Cindy urged, trying desperately to maintain control, "if you know where Julia is . . ."

"Have you checked the Yellow Pages under 'Whores'?"

Ryan's hand suddenly sliced through the air, came down hard across his wife's cheek. "Shut up, Faith! Just shut up!"

Faith staggered back, grabbed the side of her face. "I will not shut up," she screamed. "I am not a silent partner in this relationship, and I will not be quiet any longer."

"If you have any idea, any idea at all, what happened to Julia . . ." Cindy pleaded.

Faith squinted at Cindy as if she were staring directly into the sun. "You think I had something to do with your daughter's disappearance?"

"Did you?"

Faith emitted a low, guttural sound, halfway between a scoff and a snarl, then sank to the living room sofa. Above their heads, a baby began to cry. "Well, what do you know? Another quarter heard from. What took you so long?" she hollered at the ceiling.

"Did you have anything to do with Julia's disappearance?" Cindy pressed, aware that Ryan was staring at his wife with equal intensity.

Faith caught the question in her husband's eyes and made another sound, this one more moan than defiance. "You think I actually did something to your golden girl?" she asked, ignoring Cindy, directing the question at Ryan. "Tell me, when was I supposed to have done this? In between breast-feeding and changing diapers? Between putting your son down to sleep and trying to get some sleep myself? How about between blow-jobs?"

"Faith, for God's sake. . . ."

"I didn't touch your precious Julia," Faith told Cindy. "I have absolutely no idea where she is or what happened to her." She lowered her head into her hands, spoke through slightly parted fingers. "Yes, I made those calls. Don't ask me why. You've always been so nice to me. My friend. My *only* friend." She lifted her legs off the floor and curled into a fetal position on the couch, her arms wrapping around her head, as if seeking to protect herself from further blows. "Oh God, would somebody please get that damn baby to stop screaming."

"How long were you involved with my daughter?" Cindy asked Ryan, her voice low, her eyes locked on his wife.

"Cindy. . . ."

"Please don't insult me by continuing to deny it." She turned slowly in his direction.

Ryan nodded. "Two months. Maybe a bit more."

"Why did you lie?"

"What else was I supposed to do? Tell me, Cindy. What was I supposed to do?"

"You were supposed to tell the truth."

"And what good would that have done? What good does knowing about my relationship with Julia do anyone? Is it going to help find her?"

"I don't know. Is it?"

"Honestly, Cindy. If I thought for one minute that telling the police about my affair with Julia would have helped find her, I would have done it. I was just trying to protect her."

"Protect her? The only person you've been trying to protect in this whole mess is yourself."

"I don't know where Julia is," Ryan said again. "Yes, I lied about my involvement with her, and yes, I'm a no-good piece of shit who cheats on his wife. But do you have any idea what it's like being married to someone who's constantly depressed, who acts as if she's the only woman in the world who ever gave birth, who looks at her own son as if he's some infectious disease? So yes, I tend to respond favorably when a beautiful woman looks at me with adoration instead of contempt. But that only means I'm human. It doesn't mean I had anything to do with Julia's disappearance. Please, Cindy, you have to believe me. I would never hurt Julia."

"Do you love my daughter?" Cindy asked, hearing the police car pull into the driveway, the sound of car doors slamming.

Ryan looked away, said nothing.

Of all times not to lie, Cindy thought. "You really are a jerk," she told him, listening as heavy footsteps bounded up the outside steps, and impatient hands pounded on the front door.

It was almost nine o'clock that night when the police finally phoned Cindy to say they'd concluded their questioning of the Sellicks, first at their home, then at the police station, and ultimately decided to release them.

"What do you mean, you released them?"

"We have nothing to hold them on," Detective Gill explained.

"What do you mean, you have nothing?" How many times did she start sentences these days with the phrase, What do you mean? "Ryan Sellick admitted he lied about his affair with Julia. His wife admitted calling my house."

"Yes, and we questioned them for more than four hours. That's *all* they admitted."

"Four hours? My daughter's been missing for two weeks!"

"Mrs. Carver," Detective Gill interrupted gently. "Of course we will continue to investigate all angles here, but Ryan Sellick's alibi checks out, and it's highly unlikely that Faith Sellick could have been involved in Julia's disappearance. Think of it logically. It means she would have had to follow Julia to her audition, wait for her, ambush her. . . ."

"She wouldn't have had to ambush her," Cindy protested, knowing she was grasping at straws. "All she'd have to do was pretend to be in the area shopping, and then casually offer Julia a lift. . . ."

"And the baby?"

"Maybe she left him at home. Maybe he was in the backseat. Maybe she used him to lure Julia into the car." Like offering a child a piece of candy, Cindy thought, recalling Faith's own words. There was a second's silence. Cindy could almost feel Detective Gill shrug. "Are you going to get a search warrant?"

"That won't be necessary."

"What do you mean, it won't be necessary? Why not?"

"The Sellicks have already given us their permission to search their cars and premises."

"They have? What does that mean?"

"It means we're unlikely to find anything."

"And that's what you think?" Why was she asking him that? It was obviously what he thought.

"I think we have to wait and see if forensics can come up with any real evidence linking the Sellicks to your daughter."

"And if they can't? Can't you arrest them anyway?"

"We need evidence to arrest people, Mrs. Carver,"

Detective Gill reminded her patiently. "We could charge Mrs. Sellick with making those crank calls, but I'm not sure there's any point to that, given her delicate emotional state."

Cindy took a deep breath, swallowed the scream that was building in her throat. Elvis, lying on the kitchen floor, rolled to his feet and ambled over to where she was sitting, then laid his chin in her lap. Cindy found herself smiling in spite of her distress, and patted the top of his head appreciatively. "What about Sean Banack?"

"His alibis have pretty much checked out."

"Pretty much?"

"It seems unlikely he was involved in Julia's disappearance."

"What about Michael Kinsolving? Duncan Rossi? Any of Julia's friends?"

"So far, nothing."

"So you're no farther ahead than you were two weeks ago. In fact, if anything, you're farther behind." Hadn't she read somewhere that the longer a case dragged on, the colder its trail became? "What exactly are you people doing to find my daughter, Detective?"

"Our job, Mrs. Carver," the detective said simply. "And you're not making things any easier for us by barging into people's homes and interfering with our investigation."

"I didn't barge into the Sellicks' house. I was asked to come over."

"You know what I mean."

"So I'm just supposed to sit back and do nothing?"

"That's exactly what you're supposed to do."

"I don't think I can do that."

"You have no choice here, Mrs. Carver."

Cindy clenched her fists in her lap, swallowed another scream. Elvis immediately poked his wet nose into the palm of her hand, demanding to be stroked. Cindy absently obliged, replaying Detective Gill's words in her mind—*You have no choice here*—and wondering how many major events in her life had been decided without her approval. There was no such thing as choice, she was thinking. It was an illusion, a comforting yet basically specious concept that human beings had developed in order to fool themselves into believing they had some control over their lives.

Control—another illusion.

"Mrs. Carver," Detective Gill was saying. "Did you understand what I just said?"

"I understand, Detective Gill. I'm not an idiot."

"Then please stop acting like one," he said, a sudden sharpness cutting through his soft Jamaican lilt. "You could end up sabotaging this whole investigation," he continued, softening. "Or worse. You could get hurt. And what good would that do anyone?"

"You're right." Cindy looked around the kitchen, thinking that if she didn't get off this phone, get out of this house, she would go insane. "I'm sorry, Detective. It won't happen again."

"We'll keep in touch."

"Thank you." Cindy hung up the phone and jumped to her feet, Elvis leaping to attention beside her. "We have to get out of here," Cindy told the dog, who promptly dragged his leash to the front door, understanding her intent, if not her words.

Seconds later, the two were running down the street toward Avenue Road.

They ran down the steep slope between Edmund and Cottingham. Even after nine o'clock at night, Avenue Road was still busy. Three lanes of traffic moved steadily in each direction, and pedestrians ambled along both sides of the street—joggers, people walking their dogs, couples out for an evening stroll. Such a nice night after all. Still warm. Summer hanging on, more stubborn than usual.

A few more months and this hill would be as treacherous as a mountain of ice. Cindy remembered winters when this stretch of road became almost unnavigable, when cars on the ascent stalled and faltered, their wheels spinning aimlessly before succumbing to the pull of gravity and sliding back down the hill, colliding with other automobiles powerless to get out of the way, causing traffic tie-ups all the way to Queen's Park.

Cindy passed an elderly couple strolling hand in hand, the wife using the handrail that ran along the side of the street to help her manage the incline, then scooted past a jogger in bright orange shorts and the latest in running shoes. What was she doing? she asked herself. She wasn't a jogger, let alone a long-distance runner, yet here she was running much too fast down a steep hill, wearing jeans that were way too tight and sandals that offered no support at all, a rambunctious and unpredictable terrier at her feet. She'd be stiff as a board in the morning, she thought, and laughed out loud, the sound scraping at the darkness, like a pick through ice. Oh well. At least that would keep her from barging into people's homes and offices, from interfering with the police investigation. Hah, she thought, and laughed again.

At the bottom of the hill, she turned right, running along Cottingham, glancing at the semidetached brownstones that lined both sides of the wide street, wondering what mayhem was being unleashed behind thin venetian blinds and antique lace curtains. She slowed her pace as she drew near two young women who were talking beside a low, white picket fence. Both were blond. Neither was Julia.

"What's your favorite film so far?" one was asking the other.

"It's between *The Magdelene Sisters* and *L'Homme du Train.* They were awesome."

"Am I wrong, but is the quality of films better this year?"

Cindy resumed her former pace, passing the two young women, then turning left, then left again, and running briskly down Rathnelly, a quirky little avenue whose even quirkier inhabitants had once declared their street a republic. She turned left again, Elvis beside her, somehow knowing not to stop, to keep running, to keep turning left, then right, then left again, then right, watching one familiar street blur into another. Cindy kept on going, hoping to disappear, to lose herself in the welcoming darkness.

She ran beside the railway tracks along Dupont, past the tiny Tarragon Theater on Bridgeman, where she'd once had a subscription, past majestic old Casa Loma, where Meg had held her wedding reception, then across the bridge at Spadina, back up to St. Clair, and finally back down Poplar Plains to Balmoral.

She reached the corner in time to see Ryan and Faith Sellick pulling into their driveway, climbing out of their car, and carrying their infant son up the front steps, before disappearing inside their home.

Home, she thought, coming to an abrupt halt.

All her running, and where had it gotten her? Back where she started.

She couldn't get lost if she tried.

At just after two o'clock in the morning, Cindy's phone rang.

"Is this Cindy Carver?" a voice asked, jolting her awake.

"Who is this?"

"It's Officer Medavoy from Fifty-third Division. We have your daughter, Mrs. Carver," the officer began.

He was still speaking as Cindy threw down the phone and raced for the door.

THIRTY

The Fifty-third Division of the Metropolitan Police Department is a vine-covered, redbrick building with a dramatic glass atrium over its entranceway, located on the southwest corner of Eglinton and Duplex, across from the Eglinton subway station. Cindy pulled her car into the narrow lot at the rear of the building, parking it between two black-and-white police cars, and running along Duplex to the front of the three-story structure. Her legs were cramping as she reached the glass double doors, and she stopped to rub behind one knee, taking several deep breaths in an effort to calm herself down.

They'd found Julia. She was alive.

"I'm Cindy Carver," she announced as she burst through the front door and threw herself at the long counter that cut across the middle of the large, high-ceilinged room. "Where's my daughter?"

A dark-haired woman with a wide forehead and a long,

pinched nose was sitting at one of four desks behind the counter. She immediately jumped to her feet, glancing anxiously over one shoulder, before returning wary eyes to Cindy. "I'm sorry?" she began, absently smoothing the creases of her police uniform.

"My daughter, Julia Carver. Someone called me. . . . Officer Medavak. . . ."

"Medavoy," the policewoman corrected.

"Where is he?"

"I'll see if I can find him."

Cindy nodded, her eyes quickly scanning the bulletin board to her left, crowded with pictures of missing children, as the policewoman shuffled slowly toward a door at the back of the room. Cindy had to bite down on her tongue to keep from yelling, Move!

The officer suddenly stopped, turned back to Cindy. "I'm sorry. Your name again?"

"Cindy Carver." What's the matter with her? Cindy thought. Doesn't she know who I am? Doesn't she read the papers? Hasn't she seen Julia's photograph plastered across the front pages for weeks now? Although there'd been no pictures of her for several days, not since the police arrested Sally Hanson's boyfriend for her murder and eliminated the likelihood of a serial killer on the loose. Was it possible Julia had already been forgotten? That Tom had been right—out of sight, out of mind?

"Tom," she thought, saying his name out loud. Was he here? Had anyone thought to phone him?

Certainly she hadn't, she realized guiltily, although she hadn't been thinking too clearly when the police officer called. It had been all she could do to remember to put on some clothes before tearing out the door. She looked down at her black V-neck sweatshirt, hoped it was clean, that she didn't smell. She couldn't remember the last time she'd done any laundry. Not since her sister left, she thought, thinking she should call Leigh, tell her the good news. And her mother. She should phone her. And Tom. Somebody should phone Tom.

She reached for the cell phone in her purse, felt her fist close around it, then released it, brought her hand back to her side. She wanted some time alone with Julia first, time before Tom arrived. It was horribly selfish of her, Cindy knew, but she also knew that once Tom swept onto the scene, she might as well disappear. There was no question where Julia's first allegiance lay. Cindy wanted—needed—at least a few minutes alone with her daughter before Tom effortlessly assumed control. She needed those precious minutes alone with Julia to touch her, hold her, tell her how much she loved her. Time to stake her claim.

Unless it was already too late.

Unless Tom was already here. Unless they'd called him first—of course they'd called him first—and he'd arrived before her. A five-minute drive, for heaven's sake, especially at two in the morning with only a few cars on the road, and it had taken her almost three times that long to get here. Imagine taking the wrong turn, heading west on Chaplin when she knew to go east, getting stuck behind some joker doing five miles an hour. Where was the idiot going anyway? Why wasn't he home in bed? What was he doing out at two in the morning, this middle-aged man with thinning hair and watery eyes, who scowled when she passed him on the inside lane? And then forgetting what side street was quickest, getting lost *now*, now when her daughter had finally been found.

Tom had undoubtedly proceeded with appropriate calm, had announced himself with the proper politeness to the officer behind the desk, who, of course, had been totally charmed, and who'd immediately ushered him into the backroom without unnecessary prompting. He'd probably asked for a few minutes alone with his daughter, and that's what was taking so long now.

Or maybe he'd already taken Julia home with him, and that was why it was taking forever to find Officer Madavak or Medicare or whatever his name was. Why wasn't he here? And where were Detectives Bartolli and Gill? Why hadn't they been the ones to phone her with the good news?

Unless the news wasn't good, Cindy realized, her stomach suddenly doing flip-flops, her already sore knees buckling. Unless there was something they weren't telling her.

The front door opened and Cindy spun toward the sound. A uniformed policeman—surprisingly short, beefy, standard-issue bull neck, crossed the room, smiled, and said hello.

"Officer Medavoy?" Cindy asked hopefully.

"No, sorry. Are you looking for him?"

"I'm Cindy Carver. Officer Medavoy called my house to say you have my daughter." Had he? Cindy wondered. Or had it been just another crank call? Why hadn't she thought of that possibility before? Maybe there was no Officer Medavoy.

"Let me see if I can find him for you," the policeman was saying, his voice cheerily noncommittal, his demeanor friendly and nonjudgmental, as if she looked like a normal human being, and not like some escapee from the Clarke Institute, as if her skin wasn't ghostly white and her eyes weren't swollen with worry and fatigue, as if her hair wasn't sticking out in a variety of weird angles, as if she didn't smell fetid and stale, her breath heavy with sleep, as if talking to half-crazed mothers at two o'clock in the morning was something he did every day.

And maybe he did, Cindy thought, understanding there was a whole other world that operated between the hours of midnight and 7 A.M., an inverse world where people lived and worked and carried on relatively normal lives. Except what was normal? Cindy wondered, watching the officer disappear into the station's inner sanctum.

Almost immediately, the policewoman reentered the main room from another door. "Officer Medavoy will be with you in a moment," she told Cindy, before returning to her desk and pretending to busy herself with paperwork.

"Can I go in? Can I see my daughter?" It was taking all of Cindy's self-control to keep from leaping over the counter.

"Officer Medavoy would like to talk to you first."

"Why? Is something wrong? Is my daughter all right?"

"She's been throwing up."

"Throwing up?"

"They're getting her cleaned up now."

"I can do that. Please—just let me see her."

"I'm sorry. You'll have to wait for Officer Medavoy," the policewoman cautioned as the other officer reappeared.

"Officer Medavoy will be right with you," he said, stooping to search for something behind the counter.

Cindy watched in growing amazement as the two

officers went about their business. What's the matter with everybody? she wondered again. Why are they so calm, so blasé, so indifferent? Why won't they let me see my baby?

Something isn't right here, she decided. Why such a lack of concern, especially if Julia was sick and throwing up? Didn't they realize who she was? Where were Detectives Bartolli and Gill? Why weren't they here?

"Are Detectives Bartolli and Gill here?" Cindy asked, louder than she'd intended.

The two officers exchanged glances, although neither head turned. "I don't believe so," the woman officer responded. "No."

"Why not? Why hasn't anybody called them? What's going on here?"

Both officers approached cautiously. "Mrs. Carver, are you all right?"

"No, of course I'm not all right. I want to see my daughter."

"You have to calm down."

"Calm down? You expect me to calm down? What's the matter with you people?" Had she dreamed the phone call after all? Was this whole episode nothing but a cruel hoax?

Another door opened at the back of the room, and a tall, heavyset man stepped inside. He was about forty, with brown hair, a square jaw, and a nose that had been broken several times. "Mrs. Carver?"

"Where's my daughter?"

"I'm Officer Medavoy," the man answered, coming around the counter, extending his hand.

Cindy shook his hand because it was obviously expected. What she really wanted to do was swat it aside and push the imposing figure out of her way. Why all the formalities? Why couldn't they just take her to Julia? Why the need to talk to her first? What grim reality were they preparing her for? "Please, Officer Medavoy. I need to see my daughter."

He nodded. "You understand she's not in the best of shape."

"No, I don't understand. I don't understand anything. Where did you find her? *When* did you find her?"

"We picked her up about an hour ago in an underground parking garage off Queen Street."

"An underground parking garage?"

"She'd been in a fight with some other girls. They smacked her around a bit."

"A fight?"

"Apparently over some guy."

"I don't understand."

"Well, she was pretty drunk."

"Drunk?"

"She's been throwing up for the last ten minutes," Officer Medavoy said matter-of-factly, leading Cindy around the counter toward one of the backrooms. "Maybe you should go easy on her. At least until morning." He opened the door.

"Julia!" Cindy cried, rushing toward the young girl who sat, battered and wan, on a gray plastic chair in front of a dull brown desk.

Tear-soaked blue eyes stared back at Cindy. "Sorry, Mom," Heather replied, her voice breaking as she wiped a thin line of spittle away from her bruised chin. "It's only me. Sorry," she said again.

"Heather! My God—Heather!" Cindy didn't know

whether to laugh or cry, so she did both. Heather, not Julia. She hadn't even considered the possibility it might be Heather. "Oh, my poor baby," she said, falling to her knees in front of her younger child. "What happened? What did they do to you?" Her fingers fluttered nervously in front of Heather's trembling chin.

Heather turned her head away, revealing a large scratch on her left cheek. "It's nothing. I'm okay."

"The police said you were in a fight with some girls. . . ."

"It was so stupid. I was at this club. There were these girls—I thought we were getting along great. They offered me a lift home. We got to the garage, and next thing I knew they were all over me, saying I was flirting with one of their boyfriends. It was so ridiculous. He wasn't even cute."

"Did you arrest the girls?" Cindy asked the officer.

"They took off before we arrived. Your daughter claims she can't identify anyone."

"Heather. . . ."

"It was dark. It's no big deal."

"Of course it's a big deal. Look at you."

"I'm okay, Mom. It's not important. Please, can we just go home?"

Cindy looked to Officer Medavoy for help, but he only shrugged. "Maybe you should take her home, let her sleep on it. Her memory might improve after a good night's sleep."

Cindy put her arms around her daughter, helped her to her feet. "Are you okay to walk?"

"I'm fine," Heather insisted, clinging to Cindy's side as mother and daughter staggered out into the night.

They drove home in silence. Several times Cindy turned toward her younger child and tried to speak, but the words froze on her tongue, like pieces of dry ice.

(Flashback: Heather, at eight months, her cherubic little face aglow as she sits on her bedroom carpet watching her big sister dance around the room; Heather, at thirteen months, a proud smile filling her cheeks as she sits on the potty, happily chanting, "Pee pee, pee pee"; Heather, three years old, listening intently as Cindy reads her a bedtime story, the second and fourth fingers of her right hand stuffed inside her mouth, her index finger rubbing a disintegrating pink blanket against the tip of her upturned nose; Heather, at six, dressed as an angel for Halloween; Heather, age twelve, tears filling her eyes as she watches her mother watch Julia drive away in her father's car.)

"Can I get you anything?" Cindy asked as they walked through the front door, Elvis jumping all over them. "Some hot chocolate? Tea?"

"It's three o'clock in the morning," Heather reminded her mother, as she bent down to let Elvis lick the scratches on her cheek.

"Maybe you shouldn't let him do that," Cindy cautioned.

Heather straightened her back, headed for the stairs, stopped. "Is Leigh still sleeping in my room?"

"She went home for a few days," Cindy told her. "Grandma too."

Heather looked relieved. "Then I think I'll take a bath, if that's all right."

"Do you want me to get it started?"

"I can do it." Heather was already half out of her clothes by the time she reached the top of the stairs.

"Why don't you use my tub?" Cindy offered.

Normally Heather jumped at the chance to use Cindy's bathtub, with its extra leg room and high-powered Jacuzzi. Tonight she just said, "Okay."

"Maybe tomorrow you should see the doctor," Cindy said over the sound of running water. "Make sure nothing's broken."

"Nothing's broken, Mom."

Cindy watched her daughter shed the last of her clothing, then climb into the still-filling tub. "Don't make it too hot."

"I won't."

"You want some privacy?"

Heather shook her head. "You can stay."

Cindy lowered the lid on the toilet seat, sat down, gazed at her daughter's wondrously slim body through her reflection in the mirror, a million questions free-floating around in her brain: What were you doing at that club alone? What were you drinking? How *much* were you drinking? *Why* were you drinking? Instead she asked, "Still feeling sick?"

"No. I'm okay now."

"You're sure?"

"I don't usually get drunk, you know."

"I know."

"I don't usually drink at all."

"That's good."

"Are you going to tell Dad?"

"I don't know."

"Have you seen him since . . . ?" Heather's voice evaporated along with the steam rising from the tub.

"No."

Heather turned off the taps, then pressed the button on the side of the tub to start the Jacuzzi. Instantly, water began flooding into the tub from several strategically placed openings.

"What about your blind date? Have you seen him again?"

Cindy pictured Neil's handsome face, tried not to picture it between her legs. "He was here last night."

"Yeah?"

"Does that upset you?"

"Why would it upset me?"

"Because I know that children of divorce are always kind of hoping their parents will get back together one day."

"I'm not a child, Mom."

"I know that."

"I just want you to be happy," Heather said.

"Isn't that supposed to be my line?"

"You can use it too."

Cindy smiled. "Have you heard from Duncan?"

"We had a long talk. You were right. We're too young to be so settled. We should be out sleeping around. Like you said."

Dear God, Cindy thought. Of all times to start listening to me. "How about sleeping with me tonight?"

It was Heather's turn to smile. "About you and Neil . . ."

"What about him?"

"Just that I have a good feeling about the two of you." Heather closed her eyes, didn't open them again until the automatic timer turned the Jacuzzi off.

Elvis was already asleep on Cindy's bed when Cindy guided Heather between the covers. Grudgingly, the dog moved over to accommodate them, eyeing them warily, as if remembering the acrobatics of the other night. Cindy threw her arm across her daughter's hip, and hugged her close, Heather's round little bottom snug against the inverse curve of her mother. They lay together in silence for several minutes, like spoons in a drawer, one breathing out as the other breathed in, two parts of the same whole. My baby, Cindy thought. My beautiful, beautiful little girl. "I love you," she whispered.

And suddenly Heather was sitting up and sobbing in her arms, her slender body convulsing in unexpected anguish. "Oh, Mom, I'm so sorry. Please forgive me. I'm so sorry."

"What are you talking about? Sweetheart, there's nothing to forgive."

"I've been such a brat."

"No, you haven't."

"I wasn't thinking clearly when I gave the police your phone number. I didn't realize you'd assume it was Julia they had in custody. Of course you'd assume it was Julia. What else would you think? And that awful look on your face when you saw it was only me, how disappointed you were. . . ."

"No, sweetheart, no. You just caught me off-guard."

"I said such awful things to her that day, Mom. I told her I never wanted to talk to her again, that the sight of her made me sick."

Cindy thought of her recent altercation with Leigh. "We all say things in anger that we regret. Julia knows you didn't really mean them."

"Does she? I told her I was sorry she'd ever come home, that I wanted her to get out and never come back. Mom," Heather wailed, "I told her I wished she was dead."

Cindy slowly pushed Heather away from her side, held her at arm's length, stared deep into her eyes. "Heather, listen to me. This is very important. No matter what happens, no matter where Julia is or what's keeping her from us, it has nothing to do with you. Do you understand? You do not have that kind of power. You are not to blame. Do you hear me? You are not to blame."

Once again, Cindy folded her daughter into her arms, rocking her gently until eventually, Heather drifted into a restless sleep. Through a steady stream of tears, Cindy watched the minutes tick away on the digital clock radio on the nightstand beside the bed. Occasionally Heather muttered something in her sleep, and Cindy strained to make out the words.

"I'm not to blame," she was saying. "I'm not to blame."

THIRTY-ONE

At exactly seven o'clock the next morning, Cindy got out of bed, sliding up and out from between her daughter and the dog, and tiptoeing into the bathroom, where she showered, brushed her teeth and hair, put on a little makeup, then headed for the closet, where she dressed in a pair of coffee-colored chinos and a crisp white blouse. It had been a long time since she looked crisp, she knew, and it was important that she start keeping up appearances. For Heather's sake, as well as her own, she decided. She had *two* daughters after all. Not just one.

Heather was still sound asleep when Cindy returned to the bedroom. Elvis had shifted his position, and was now curled up on Cindy's pillow. He lifted his head as Cindy approached, as if to question what she was doing up after so few hours, sleep, then lowered it again as she walked out of the room.

Cindy also questioned what she was doing up so early, but the truth was that she'd never really fallen asleep, and she was getting stiff just lying there in bed. It was better to be up and moving, to try behaving like a functioning adult, to make a pretense at normalcy. When Heather woke up, she would find her mother dressed and presentable, fixing her pancakes, and eager to hear her plans for the upcoming weekend.

But for now, she would let her daughter sleep.

Cindy walked down the stairs and into the kitchen, prepared a pot of coffee, then sank down at the kitchen table and stared out the sliding glass door. Outside was another perfect day. Leaning back in her chair, Cindy studied the early-morning sky. A large pink cloud, backlit with just a hint of yellow, hung heavy over the Sellicks' backyard, its lilac underbelly exposed and friendly, like a puppy sleeping on its back. Several wisps had broken free and were drifting to her right. The drifts were purple and in the shape of a woman's mouth, imprinted on the air like a blot of lipstick on a tissue. Cindy watched the stray fragments gradually fade, then get lost in the deepening blue of day.

Everything disappears, she was thinking. Clouds, people, entire civilizations. Human beings were as fragile, as fleeting, as cool wisps of air.

She stretched her legs out in front of her, hearing her joints groan, like hinges needing to be oiled. Yesterday's impromptu run had been a foolish venture, especially since she hadn't worked out in weeks. This is how the body slips into middle age, she thought, patting the slight rounding of her belly as she pushed off her chair, feeling her thigh muscles cramp as she headed for the front door. She needed to start exercising again, she decided, thinking she'd ask Leigh to join her at the gym one afternoon.

The *Globe* and the *Star* lay at her feet when she opened the door, and Cindy scanned the headlines, noting that the unflattering picture of the Prime Minister was the same on both front pages. "Well, what do you know?" she asked him, bending down to scoop up the papers. "It's Friday the thirteenth." Cradling both papers in her arms, she backed into the house, about to close the door when she heard another door opening beside her.

Cindy froze as Faith Sellick emerged from her house and hurried down her front steps, clutching Kyle tightly to her chest, and disappearing around the side of the house. Like Cindy, Faith was neatly dressed for the first time in weeks, the slovenly tartan pajamas replaced by a calf-length, blue cotton dress, her hair pulled into a neat ponytail that pointed, like an arrow, down the center of her back. Seconds later, Faith reentered her line of vision, pushing Kyle's carriage toward the street, the baby crying loudly inside it.

Where would they be headed this early in the morning? Cindy wondered, straining to see where Faith was going, then abruptly pulling her head back inside her door, like a startled turtle returning to its shell, when Faith suddenly spun around, as if aware of Cindy's watchful eye.

Cindy waited half a second, then peeked back outside, her eyes following Faith's swift departure. Ryan's car was still in the driveway, and Cindy wondered if he knew where his wife was going, if he was even aware she was gone. She thought of phoning him, alerting him to his wife's absence, then thought better of it, knowing she was the last person in the world he would appreciate hearing from under the circumstances.

Whatever had possessed Julia to get involved with a married man? She could have her pick of any man she wanted. Why choose this one?

Cindy knew the answer even before she'd finished asking herself the question. Julia had been attracted to Ryan Sellick because he was a younger version of the man she loved best in the world. Deliberately or subconsciously, Julia had picked a man just like dear old dad.

"And so it goes," Cindy muttered, watching Faith push the carriage into the middle of the road from between two parked cars. Where is she going in such a hurry? Cindy asked herself, dropping the newspapers to the floor and stepping onto her front landing, watching Faith turn left onto Avenue Road, heading north.

Almost without thinking, Cindy grabbed her purse from the hall closet and chased after her, careful to stay in the shadows, to keep a comfortable distance between them. Faith was moving quickly, and Cindy's legs were stiff and hurting from last night's ill-conceived marathon. They rebelled each time Cindy tried to widen her stride, pick up her pace. She almost lost Faith at the corner of Avenue Road and St. Clair when Faith caught the traffic light and she didn't, but she spotted her again several blocks later in front of Granite Place, two large apartment complexes that sat well back from the main street.

Faith stopped at the corner of St. Clair and Yonge, despite the green light that indicated she had the right of way. Once more she spun around, as if suspicious she was being followed, and Cindy had to duck into the doorway of Black's One-Hour Photo to keep from being spotted. Her breath was labored and audible. A thin trickle of perspiration ran down the open V of her blouse, and she flicked it away with her finger before it could reach inside her bra. Seven-thirty in the morning and already the outside temperature was creeping toward eighty degrees. Already she was hot and sweaty, the humidity twisting her hair into tight little curls that crept around her head like vines. So much for keeping up appearances, she thought, hearing wary footsteps approach. Cindy took a deep breath, braced herself for yet another unpleasant confrontation with her neighbor.

But the woman who hurried by cast only a furtive glance in her direction, careful to keep a wide berth between them, as if afraid Cindy was one of those crazy ladies who wandered the streets, asking for money and talking to themselves. And maybe she's right, Cindy thought. Maybe I *am* crazy. How else to explain what she was doing, trailing after her neighbor, like some middle-aged Nancy Drew, only a day after the police had ordered her to back off. What was the matter with her? Why couldn't she just mind her own business? So much for acting like a functioning adult.

"Go home," Cindy told herself. "Go home now."

But even as she was saying the words, she was running across the already busy intersection at Yonge and St. Clair, trying to locate Faith. "Where is she?" Cindy muttered underneath her breath, her eyes shooting back and forth across the four corners, seeing no trace of her neighbor. Maybe she went into McDonald's, Cindy thought, glancing toward the tiny takeout restaurant that was squeezed between the Bank of Nova Scotia and the St. Clair subway station.

It was then Cindy saw the baby carriage. It was standing outside the subway's glass doors, blocking the entranceway, until a man in a hurry shoved it rudely to one side. "Kyle?" Cindy called, rushing toward the carriage. But the carriage was empty. The baby was gone.

Why would Faith abandon an expensive carriage in the middle of the street? Had she spotted Cindy, decided it was faster and easier to proceed without it? And where was she taking Kyle so early in the morning? Did she have a plan, or had she impulsively opted for an early-morning subway ride, much as Cindy had opted for a late-night run?

"Did a woman with a baby just go through here?" she asked the bored-looking attendant who sat in a large glass booth inside the subway entrance. "It couldn't have been more than a few minutes ago," Cindy continued when the attendant failed to respond.

"Wasn't paying attention," the man answered finally. Then, "You're holding up the line."

Cindy tried to push through the turnstile, but it refused to move.

"You need a token," the attendant reminded her.

"I don't have a token."

"Then it's two dollars and twenty-five cents."

Cindy fished in her purse for the correct change, as several disgruntled commuters wove past her impatiently, while those forced to wait in line behind her groaned as one. "Sorry," she said, the apology floating toward the ceiling, like steam from a kettle, as she offered the money to the attendant, who rolled his eyes and pointed at the proper container.

Cindy ran down the stairs on the other side of the turnstile, trying to guess if Faith had headed north or south. She opted for south, running down a second set of stairs to the subway platform, her eyes panning the yellow tiles that lined the walls for any sign of Faith and her baby. Had she missed them? Had the southbound train already come and gone?

It was then she heard a baby's loud wail and saw Faith standing at the other end of the platform on the opposite side of the station. She was rocking Kyle in her arms and smiling calmly. She looks okay, Cindy thought, and waved, a broad gesture that caught Faith's attention. Faith smiled, as if seeing Cindy in the subway at this hour of the morning was not unexpected, then turned her attention back to the baby squirming in her arms.

Something's not right, Cindy thought, walking briskly back toward the stairs, pushing against the crowd surging in the other direction, vaulting up one set of stairs and down the other. Seconds later, she reached the north platform, the tunnel stretched out before her, like a long, dark pipe.

"Careful," a man cautioned as she ran beside the wide yellow stripe that ran along the edge of the platform. "Shouldn't get so close to the edge."

Cindy heeded his advice, moving closer to the wall and proceeding quickly to the far end of the platform.

"No need to run," she heard someone say. "A train just left." Was he talking to her?

"Damn, I'm going to be late," another man replied. "How long till the next one?"

"Couple of minutes."

Cindy continued walking toward the far end of the platform, watching Faith's smile broaden as she approached, as if she were genuinely pleased to see her.

"Cindy. What are you doing here?"

"I was just about to ask you the same thing."

"Kyle has a doctor's appointment."

"So early?"

"It was the only time she could fit me in."

"Is the baby all right?"

"He has this rash."

"Rash?" Cindy hadn't noticed any rash yesterday.

"I called Dr. Pitfield as soon as I saw it. She said to bring Kyle in first thing this morning, and she'd have a look at him."

"Isn't Dr. Pitfield's office on Wellesley?" Cindy had recommended Dr. Pitfield to Faith when Faith first found out she was pregnant. Dr. Pitfield had been both Julia's and Heather's pediatrician.

"She moved."

"Really? She was on Wellesley forever. Where is she now?"

"Lawrence."

"Well, that's great. We can go together."

"You're going to Lawrence?"

"Yoga class," Cindy said quickly, wondering why Dr. Pitfield had suddenly uprooted her practice after more than thirty years in the same location. And why wouldn't Ryan have driven his wife to the doctor's instead of letting her struggle with public transportation? Why was Faith being so nice to her after what had happened yesterday? "Was that Kyle's carriage I saw in front of the station?"

Faith shrugged. "Never liked the stupid thing," she said. Then, "You look nice." As if this was the most natural of follow-ups.

"Thank you. You too. New dress?"

Faith glanced briefly down, as if she couldn't remember what she was wearing. "No. It's old."

"It's very pretty. The color looks great on you."

"You think so?"

"I do."

Faith smiled. "Another beautiful day," she said.

"Yes, it is."

"They get kind of boring, after a while. All that sunshine."

"I guess we could use some rain."

"That would be nice. I like the rain, don't you?"

"Sometimes," Cindy agreed. "There's nothing like a good thunderstorm." Were they actually talking about the weather?

"Lightning scares me," Faith confided.

"Me too."

"Have you ever seen a tornado?"

"A tornado? No, not a real one, anyway. I saw that movie though, *Twister*, I think it was called."

"I saw that," Faith said, nodding. "It wasn't very good."

"No. The story was pretty lame."

"The special effects were great though."

"Yes, they were. What's your favorite movie?" Cindy asked.

Faith raised her eyes, pursed her lips, as if giving the question serious consideration. "I don't think I have one."

"Really? What about *Titanic?* Did you see that? Or *The Godfather*?"

"I saw that on television. On Bravo, I think. They were showing it over and over again. You couldn't miss it."

"Did you see the sequel? People say Part Two was even better than Part One, which is really rare in a sequel, although Part Three was lousy."

"I didn't see Part Three."

"You're lucky."

The baby renewed his squirming. Faith began rocking him absently, looking over her shoulder for the train.

"My favorite movie is *Invasion of the Body Snatchers*," Cindy continued, a growing unease spreading through her joints, although she wasn't sure why. "The original, with Kevin McCarthy and Dana Wynter, not the remake."

"I don't know that one."

"I have a tape of it at home. I could show it to you."

"I don't know. It sounds kind of scary."

"I guess it is, a little. I could watch it with you, if you'd like."

Faith shook her head, began rocking back and forth on her heels. "I don't think so. Thanks anyway."

"Have you ever been to the film festival? I go every year with a couple of friends. Lots and lots of fabulous films. Maybe next year, you'd like to go with us."

Faith smiled, said nothing. The baby in her arms began whimpering. "Ssh," Faith told him, as several sharp cries pierced the air. "Come on, Kyle. Be a good boy. Please don't cry."

"Would you like me to hold him for a few minutes? He must be getting pretty heavy."

Faith shook her head, took a few steps back. "He's okay."

"He sounds hungry."

"No. I just fed him."

"Maybe he needs changing."

"He's fine." Faith began turning around in small circles, each spin bringing her a little bit closer to the edge of the platform.

"Be careful," Cindy warned. "You're getting too close to the edge."

Faith smiled, said nothing.

In the distance, Cindy heard the rumble of an approaching train. "I have an idea," she said. "Why don't we go somewhere and have breakfast?"

"I'm not hungry."

"Coffee, then. There's a million places we could go for coffee."

"I don't want coffee."

"Faith, you're not thinking about doing anything foolish, are you?"

"Foolish?"

"You know what I'm talking about." Cindy felt the rush of air from a southbound train as it pulled into the station on the opposite track, knew she didn't have much time before a northbound train came barreling along.

"I think you should go now," Faith said.

"I'm not leaving here without you."

Faith looked confused. "Why are you doing this?"

"Because you're my friend. Because I'm worried about you."

"There's nothing to worry about. Everything's all right now."

"It is?"

"Yes. I've worked everything out."

"Worked what out?"

"What I have to do."

"You have to move away from the edge of the platform," Cindy told her evenly. "Please, Faith. I know that whatever you think you have to do, you wouldn't want to hurt Kyle."

"I'd never do anything to hurt Kyle."

"Then move away from the edge of the platform."

"I'm not the one who'd hurt him," Faith said. "It's you."

"Me?"

Faith glanced past Cindy to the other people standing idly by. "All of you."

Cindy's eyes also scanned the waiting crowd, trying to transmit her concern. But no one was watching them. "Nobody here would do anything to hurt Kyle," she said loudly, trying to attract someone's attention.

"The world isn't a very nice place, Cindy. You know that better than anyone."

"Yes, I do," Cindy said, wondering whether she should scream for help, afraid such action might only make things worse. "I do know that. But I also know that no matter how grim things may seem, they always get better."

"You really believe that?"

"I have to believe it."

"And if things don't get better? What then?"

Cindy's eyes filled with tears. "Then we have to go on."

"Really? Why?"

Cindy pictured Heather asleep in her bed. "Because there are other people who need us, who would be devastated if we did something so final, so irreversible." She heard a low roar, and realized with horror that it was the sound of an approaching train. "Please, Faith. Listen to me. Things will get better. Honestly, they will."

"You promise?" Faith whispered, her eyes aching to believe.

"I do. I promise," Cindy repeated, crossing her fingers for both of them, balancing on the balls of her feet, preparing to throw herself at the other woman, to wrestle her to the ground, if need be.

And then Faith took a long, deep breath, and smiled, her shoulders relaxing. "Okay," she said simply, allowing Cindy to wrap her in her arms.

Thank God, Cindy said silently, clinging tightly to the other woman, slowly leading Faith away from the edge of the platform toward the stairs.

"Oh," Faith said, stopping suddenly.

"What is it?"

"Could you hold Kyle a minute?" Faith pushed the crying infant into Cindy's arms before Cindy realized what was happening. Then she wriggled away from Cindy's grasp, ran toward the end of the platform, and threw herself in front of the oncoming train.

THIRTY-TWO

Instant Replay: Cindy hears a noise, like distant thunder, and realizes it is the sound of an approaching train. She pleads with her neighbor. "Please, Faith. Don't do anything foolish. Things will get better. Honestly, they will."

"You promise?" Faith asks imploringly.

"I promise."

Faith takes a long, deep breath, her shoulders relaxing. "Okay," she says, collapsing into Cindy's arms.

"Thank God." Cindy clings tightly to the other woman, begins maneuvering her through the crowd toward the exit. They are almost at the stairs.

"Oh," Faith says, stopping abruptly, as if she's forgotten something.

"What is it?"

"Could you hold Kyle a minute?")

Cindy sat on one of the sofas in her living room, staring at the far wall, trying to keep her gaze from drifting to the window, to keep the awful events of the morning from reflecting across the dark panes of glass. But all it took was one flicker of the midnight moon peeking through the clouds, and suddenly she was back on the northbound platform of the St. Clair subway station at the beginning of the early-morning rush hour, her arms gripping the shoulders of her seemingly acquiescent neighbor, and one second they were walking peacefully toward the exit, the crisis miraculously averted, and the next second, Faith was pushing her baby into Cindy's arms, then bolting from her side and throwing herself in front of the speeding train. Cindy heard the awful thud of flesh against metal, the sickening squeal of brakes, the horrified screams of onlookers.

And then chaos.

(Chaos: People running in all directions. Passengers locked inside the subway cars, banging on the doors to be let out. The smell of vomit. The ashen-faced conductor, his forehead pressed against the glass of a side window, yelling into his radio transmitter. Sirens wailing somewhere above their heads. Paramedics and police arriving. The police demanding information. Someone pointing at Cindy, sitting on the dirty floor, her back against the dull yellow tiles, her feet stretched out in front of her, like a lifeless rag doll, cradling the now-sleeping baby in her arms and staring blankly into space.

"Can you tell us what happened?" a policeman asks, kneeling down in front of Cindy, forcing his massive shoulders into her line of vision. "You knew this woman?"

Cindy stares at the young man, whose face refuses to register beyond the deep brown of his eyes. "She's my neighbor," an unfamiliar voice responds from what seems like a great distance away.

"Can you tell us her name?"

"Faith Sellick. Faith," Cindy repeats, the irony of the name imploding against her lungs, the strange voice floating to the ceiling, like a moth to light. "Is she dead?"

Silence.

Silly question, Cindy thinks, as the officer's eyes close in confirmation.

"Is there someone we can notify?"

"Her husband." The voice supplies the officer with the necessary information. Cindy watches him jot it down in his notepad. How many times has she seen that lately? Too many times. Way too many. "This is Kyle," the voice continues. "Faith's baby."

"We'll need you to tell us exactly what happened here." The officer signals to a colleague for help. "Can you do that?"

The two uniformed officers take hold of Cindy's elbows, help her up, although the ground feels less than steady beneath her feet, as if she is standing on a moving sidewalk. Cindy clings tightly to Kyle, resisting attempts to take him from her.

"Are you going to be all right?" the policeman with the brown eyes asks, although his words are garbled, as if someone is playing them at the wrong speed.

Cindy nods, walking slowly between the two officers as they guide her toward the exit.

"We'll need your name," the police officer is saying as Cindy's attention is diverted by a sudden movement on the subway track.

"Cindy," the unfamiliar voice answers, and for an instant

Cindy wishes this person would stop talking, let her answer for herself. "Cindy Carver."

"Cindy Carver?" the second officer repeats, stopping in almost the exact spot as Faith stopped only moments before. "The mother of that missing girl?"

And then Cindy sees the paramedics carefully lifting Faith's hopelessly twisted body onto a stretcher, and notices a torn fragment of Faith's blue cotton dress lying across the tracks. She turns back, sees bits of human flesh dripping from the blood-soaked front window of the train.

"Are you Julia Carver's mother?" the first officer is asking, staring at Cindy with his puppy dog brown eyes.

A persistent buzz fills Cindy's ears, almost blocking out his words. *Are . . . Julia Carver's mother? Are you . . . Carver's mother? Are you Julia . . .'s mother?*

And then the unfamiliar voice once again assumes control. "Excuse me," it says calmly as Cindy hands Kyle to the policeman with the puppy dog eyes, in much the same way Faith earlier handed him over to her. "I think I'm going to faint." And then Cindy feels her knees bend, her hips sway, her eyes roll back in her head, everything happening in slow motion, as her body begins folding in on itself, like a collapsible chair. I'm getting rather good at this, she thinks as she falls toward the hard tile.

"She saved that baby, you know," someone says, as strange arms reach out to block her fall. "She should get a medal. She's a hero."

I'm a hero, Cindy thinks, and might have laughed but for the darkness that envelops her.)

"So, according to the eleven o'clock news, I'm a hero," Cindy said now, watching Neil walk toward her with a freshly brewed cup of tea. He was wearing khaki pants and a beige shirt, and Cindy thought he was the most welcome sight she'd ever seen. On either side of her sat her mother and sister. Leigh stood up as Neil approached, moved to the other sofa, scooted in beside Heather, Meg, and Trish.

"Not feeling very heroic?" Neil sat down beside her, stroked the back of Cindy's neck as she gingerly sipped her tea, Elvis keeping close watch on everyone from the floor.

Cindy smiled at the handsome man who'd rushed to her side when she'd regained consciousness and phoned him from the subway station. "I feel like such a fraud."

"How are you a fraud?" Meg asked.

"Because I didn't do anything."

"You saved a baby's life," Trish reminded her.

"*Faith* saved him, not me."

"It's only because of you that they're not both dead," Cindy's mother said.

Cindy shook her head. "This whole thing is my fault."

"How can it possibly be your fault?"

"Because I'm the one who drove her over the edge," Cindy said, the words she'd been trying to swallow all day spilling from her mouth in a sudden rush. "Literally. I did everything but push her over the side of that platform myself."

"Cindy . . ."

"I'm the one who rubbed her nose in her husband's affair with Julia. I'm the one who called the police, who had her hauled off to the station for questioning when she was so tired she could barely stand up. I knew how fragile she was, I *knew*, but that didn't stop me from flinging all sorts of ridiculous accusations in her face, even after the police warned me to back off, even after they ordered me to stop interfering with their investigation. And now look what's happened. . . ."

"Cindy . . ." her mother said.

"Please don't tell me it's not my fault."

"Do you really think you have that kind of power?" Heather asked, using the same words her mother had used the night before.

Cindy smiled sadly, holding open her arms as her daughter slid into them.

"Thanks for being here," she said, kissing the top of Heather's head. "All of you."

"Where else would we be?" everyone answered, almost in unison.

Heather had been waiting for her when Neil brought her home from the subway. Her mother and sister, who'd been at the dressmaker's, rushed over as soon as they heard the news, as had Meg and Trish several hours ago. Only Tom hadn't bothered to call. Probably halfway to Muskoka when the reports were first broadcast.

Normally, subway suicides went unreported in the media, lest it encourage others to take similar action. But Cindy's presence at the scene had changed everything. The fact that Julia Carver's mother had been instrumental in saving another woman's child from certain death had been the lead story on every newscast on every radio and television station in the city, and the fact that the victim was Cindy's next-door neighbor had only added to the intrigue. Reporters had been calling or knocking on her door since early this afternoon, theorizing about a possible connection between Julia's disappearance and her neighbor's suicide. The story was sure to make tomorrow's headlines, Cindy understood, sighing audibly, especially once the press got wind of Ryan's affair with her daughter, as surely they would.

"Are you okay?" Neil asked.

"I should have realized what was happening sooner."

"Then she might have jumped sooner, taken Kyle with her."

Cindy looked toward the front door. "Is the house still surrounded?"

"I thought I saw someone from CITY-TV lurking in the bushes about an hour ago, but I think he finally gave up and went home."

"What about you?" Cindy asked reluctantly. "Shouldn't you be heading home? It's almost midnight. Your son . . ."

"I can stay a little longer."

The phone rang. Everyone looked toward the sound. No one made a move to get up.

"You want me to answer that?" Meg asked.

Cindy shook her head. "Let voice-mail take it."

After four rings, the phone went silent. Two minutes later, it rang again. And again, two minutes after that.

"Persistent little devil," Trish said.

"Maybe it's important," Leigh added.

"It isn't." How many crank calls had she received already today? Between the reporters and the kooks, her phone had been ringing almost constantly, although it had tapered off in the last several hours. At one point, things had gotten so disruptive—the phone ringing, cameramen banging their equipment against the windows, the dog barking each time someone came to the door—Cindy had briefly considered grabbing Neil and taking refuge in a hotel. But she knew her mother and sister would insist on coming along, as would Heather, Meg, and Trish, and the thought of all of them crowded into a small hotel room had been enough to put the kibosh on that idea.

Cindy pushed herself off the sofa and shuffled into the kitchen, where she checked her voice-mail for messages. "Nothing," she informed their eager faces upon her return. "Whoever it was didn't leave a message."

"Next time it rings, I'll answer it," her mother said.

"Why don't you go upstairs to bed?" Neil suggested.

"I don't think I could sleep. Every time I close my eyes, I see. . . ." Even when I don't close them, she thought, as once again, Faith materialized to hurl herself in front of an oncoming train. Cindy heard the helpless squeal of brakes, the gut-wrenching thud of cold steel against warm flesh, saw the torn sliver of baby-blue cotton clinging to the coal-black of the subway tracks, Faith's blood splattered across the front window of the car, like mud, burning its way into the glass, like acid rain, branding itself into her soul.

"I may have a few of those pills left," Neil whispered underneath his breath.

"Really? What kind of pills are those?" Leigh asked. "Because I haven't had a good night's sleep in months."

"Have you heard anything from Detective Bartolli?" Trish asked.

Cindy grimaced, remembering how angry Detectives Bartolli and Gill had been upon hearing the news of Faith's suicide and Cindy's presence at the scene, how Detective Bartolli had gone so far as to threaten to arrest her if there were any further incidents. "Listen, you guys, you don't have to stay. Really."

"Do you want us to leave?" Meg asked.

"No," Cindy admitted. "I want you to stay forever."

"Okay," they all said, and Cindy smiled.

They sat together for another hour, exchanging idle chatter, hugs, and sighs, until Norma Appleton announced she could no longer keep her eyes open, and she and Leigh went upstairs to bed, as did Heather ten minutes after that. Meg and Trish reluctantly said goodbye several minutes later, both promising to call the next day.

"Your turn," Cindy told Neil, standing by the open front door.

"You're sure?"

"Only if you promise to come back tomorrow."

"How's breakfast? I'll bring bagels."

"If memory serves, my family loves your bagels."

Neil smiled. "Maybe I'll bring Max. He likes bagels too."

"I'd like that."

Neil leaned over, kissed Cindy tenderly on the lips. "See you in the morning."

Cindy watched him drive off before retreating back inside the house. She was about to close the door when she stopped, stepped back onto the landing, her eyes staring through the darkness toward several cars parked at the far end of the street. How long had they been there? And were they empty or was someone sitting inside them? Cindy squinted, trying to differentiate between flesh and shadow. More reporters? she wondered. The police?

Probably no one.

Cindy locked the door and headed upstairs for bed, trying to shake the uncomfortable feeling she was being watched.

THIRTY-THREE

She was almost asleep when she heard something outside her bedroom window. Cindy sat up in bed, careful not to disturb Heather, who was curled up beside her, Elvis at their feet. She waited, the silence of the night swirling around her head like a potent perfume. And then she heard it again, a tap on the glass, quick and sharp. And then another.

Cindy's first thought was that it was a bird, pecking on the glass to be let in. But birds didn't fly at night, she knew, climbing out of bed and going to the window, peeking through the shutters. Almost immediately, something slapped against the windowpane, and Cindy gasped, pulled away from the glass, her heart pounding wildly, convinced someone had fired a bullet at her head. But the glass hadn't shattered. It hadn't even cracked. Cindy inched back toward the window as once again, something ricocheted off the glass. A pebble, she realized.

Someone was throwing stones at her window.

Cindy reached for her robe and raced down the stairs to the kitchen, flipping on the light over the back patio.

A man, dressed entirely in black, was standing in the middle of her backyard. Cindy stifled a scream as he turned his head toward the light, the scream freezing in her throat when she recognized the familiar look of consternation on his handsome face.

"Tom?!" Cindy unlocked the sliding glass door, watched her ex-husband toss a fistful of pebbles to the ground, then bound up the stairs. Immediately, the Cookie, also entirely in black, stepped out of the darkness to follow after him. "What on earth are you doing here? What are you *doing*?"

"Trying to get your attention, damn it. Why didn't you answer your goddamn phone?"

"What?"

They stepped into the kitchen, the Cookie closing the door as Tom flipped off the patio light, the full moon falling into the space between them, like an errant spotlight. "What was going on here tonight? A party?"

"You were watching the house?"

"I need to talk to you. I couldn't do it when everyone was here."

"I don't understand. Has something happened?" A feeling of dread trickled into Cindy's veins, like a transfusion of tainted blood. She felt her body grow cold, as if a hand had reached out to her from beyond the grave. "Does this have something to do with Julia?"

Tom pushed his fingers roughly through his hair. "Okay, listen. I recognize this is going to be a shock, but it's very important that you stay calm. I understand it's already been one hell of a day for you, but I need your assurances you aren't going to freak out."

"I think you'd better tell me what's going on."

"I came here to prepare you."

"Prepare me for what?"

Tom said nothing for several long seconds, then he reached back to the sliding glass door and pulled it open. "Okay," he said to the surrounding darkness. "You can come in now."

The night air stirred as a shape began forming inside it, gradually separating from it. Cindy held her breath as the shape assumed human form, began its slow ascent up the patio steps, its face hidden by the hood of a black sweatshirt.

And then there she was, standing in the doorway, the hood falling from her head to reveal the straight blond hair beneath, looking as impossibly beautiful as she had the last time Cindy saw her over two weeks ago.

Julia.

"Julia!" Cindy threw herself at the apparition, casting an invisible net over its head, and trapping it in her arms before it could fly away, as if she'd stumbled across a rare butterfly. She knew her mind was playing tricks, that the awful events of the day combined with her fatigue had disrupted the normal patterns of her brain, so that not only was she seeing lost young women jumping from her side, she was seeing other lost young women miraculously appearing to take their place. "Julia," she uttered, staring at the vision in the black velour jumpsuit, touching her face, her shoulders, her hair. "Julia," she said again, as if the repetition of the name would be enough to give the ghost weight, provide it with the substance needed to sustain it. "Julia," Cindy cried, bracing herself for her daughter's sudden absence.

And then the mirage that was Julia was folding herself inside Cindy's arms. And Cindy was hugging her and kissing her, and her skinny frame felt solid and real, and her soft, smooth skin smelled of Angel perfume. Cindy tasted her daughter on her tongue, like tiny bubbles of champagne. "Are you really here?" Cindy cried, squeezing Julia's broad shoulders, her toned arms, her slender hips. "Are you really here?"

"I'm really here," the apparition said, sounding just like Julia.

"It *is* you. You're here. You're real."

Julia laughed. "I'm real. I'm here."

And now Cindy was sobbing, her whole body shaking as she pulled her daughter to her chest, as if trying to solder them both together, all the while smothering the side of Julia's face with kisses, as if she couldn't get enough of her, as if she intended to devour her.

Julia was back. She was in her mother's arms. She was alive and well. And she looked wonderful. She looked rested and beautiful, more beautiful than ever. No bruises stained her flawless complexion; no nameless terrors clouded her eyes. "You're here," Cindy kept repeating. "You're all right."

"I'm here. I'm all right."

Despite the assurances, Cindy refused to relinquish her daughter's hands. If she did, the dream would surely end. She'd wake up. It would be over. Her daughter would be gone. "You're not hurt?"

"I'm fine," Julia said again.

"You're fine," Cindy repeated, unable to staunch the flood of tears streaming down her cheeks. Her daughter was alive and well and back home where she belonged. She wasn't a ghost. She was really here. And no harm had befallen her. How was that possible? "I don't understand. Where have you been?"

Julia looked from her mother to her father, who nodded his silent encouragement. "You have to promise you won't be angry."

"Angry?" What was Julia talking about? "Why would I be angry?"

"Promise me you'll at least try to understand."

"Understand what? What's going on? Tom," Cindy implored, her eyes veering reluctantly from her daughter to her ex-husband. "Tom, what is she talking about? Where did you find her?"

"Don't you get it yet?" he asked, looking at Cindy with a mixture of pity and scorn.

"Get what?"

A second's hesitation before Julia's simple response. "I was never lost."

The words ripped through Cindy as if fired from a gun. She staggered back, dropped her daughter's hand. "What are you talking about? Where have you been?"

There was a long pause, a second exchange of glances between father and daughter before Julia answered. "At the cottage."

"What?"

"She insisted on coming back as soon as we heard the news about Faith Sellick," the Cookie interjected quickly.

"Is Ryan okay?" Julia asked. "The news reports barely mentioned him."

"You've been in Muskoka all this time?" Cindy's head was spinning. Her daughter was back. She wasn't injured. She hadn't been kidnapped, or raped and murdered, then buried in a shallow grave. She was alive and well. Wasn't that all that mattered? What difference did it make where she'd been, that it appeared she'd been relaxing in the country while her mother was going crazy in the city, that instead of being concerned about her sister, her grandmother, her aunt, she was asking after Ryan, that even more astounding, she seemed oblivious to the hell she'd put her family through these awful last two weeks?

Cindy turned toward Tom, another horrifying thought slowly crystallizing. "Did you know about this? Did you know where Julia was all along?"

"You promised you wouldn't get angry," Julia reminded her.

"Maybe you should sit down," Tom said.

Without protest, Cindy lowered herself into a kitchen chair, braced herself for whatever staggering revelations might follow.

"This doesn't leave this room," Tom warned, closing, then locking, the sliding glass door.

Julia took a deep breath, blew it out slowly, as if she were savoring a forbidden cigarette. "As you know, two weeks ago, I had an audition with Michael Kinsolving for a part in his next movie. Dad said you saw the tape."

"Yes," Cindy acknowledged quietly. "You were wonderful."

Julia smiled proudly. "Thank you."

"Unfortunately, wonderful auditions aren't enough these days," Tom continued, assuming control. "There are too many beautiful, talented actresses out there, and Julia needed something that would give her an edge over the competition, something that would get her the attention she deserves." He paused dramatically. "And what better way to get noticed than to disappear?"

The room went in and out of focus as Cindy shook her head in disbelief. Surely she'd misunderstood. Surely she'd misinterpreted what her daughter and ex-husband were trying to tell her. "You're saying this was a publicity stunt?"

"I just wanted a chance, Mom. Michael was auditioning so many girls. He hasn't had a hit in a while, and Dad said the studio was pressuring him to give the part to a name Hollywood actress. We knew we had to do something to level the playing field."

"So you concocted this scheme . . ."

"To make Julia as recognizable as any of the famous actresses in town for the festival," Tom continued, unable to disguise his enthusiasm. "Cindy, I'm an entertainment lawyer. I know how this business works. I knew we had to do something pretty drastic to get the results we needed. And it worked. Hell, Julia's practically a household name. *Entertainment Tonight* did two whole minutes on Michael's possible involvement in her disappearance the other night. Do you have any idea what that kind of exposure is worth? Michael would be a fool not to give her the part now, and trust me, Michael Kinsolving is nobody's fool. He knows a good story. So does the studio. And they also know everybody likes a happy ending."

"Good story?" Cindy repeated incredulously. "Happy ending?"

"Okay, Cindy. It's obvious you're upset. But can you at least try to keep an open mind?"

"Why didn't you tell me?" Cindy looked at her daughter through wide, disbelieving eyes. Could her daughter really be so unfeeling, so monstrously self-absorbed? "Do you have any idea what I've been going through? What we've *all* been going through? Why didn't you tell me?"

"We thought about it," Julia began.

"You *thought* about it?"

"We couldn't tell you," Tom said curtly. "We knew that, at the very least, you'd feel compelled to tell your mother and Heather. And then Heather would tell Duncan, and your mother would tell Leigh, and then where would we be? Don't you see? It wouldn't have worked if you didn't honestly believe that Julia was missing. Your daughter's the actress in the family, Cindy. Not you. The police would have seen through you in a heartbeat."

"Besides," the Cookie added matter-of-factly, "we knew you'd never agree to it."

Cindy felt suddenly sick to her stomach. "That afternoon at the morgue . . ."

"Not my idea, believe me." Tom waved his hands in front of his face, as if to rid himself of the memory. "I wouldn't want to go through that again."

"And what happened afterward in your apartment . . ."

"What happened in our apartment?" the Cookie asked.

"All the people the police questioned—Sean, Duncan, Ryan—people whose lives have been turned upside down as a result of this little charade. And Faith. My God, poor

Faith!" Again, Cindy saw the hapless young woman hurl herself in front of the speeding train, heard the sickening thud of metal against flesh.

"Faith didn't kill herself because of me," Julia protested.

"She was suffering from postpartum depression." Cindy struggled to stay calm, to keep her voice down. "Do you think it helped her to be hauled into the police station for questioning? To find out you'd been sleeping with her husband?"

"And exactly whose fault was it she found that out?" Tom asked, narrowing his eyes accusingly.

"I'm really very sorry about what happened to Faith," Julia said. "But she was Loony Tunes to begin with. You can't blame me for what she did. We had no way of knowing she'd pull something like this."

"You had no way of knowing that *she'd pull something like this*?" Cindy repeated incredulously.

"Kindly lower your voice," Tom instructed.

"Kindly go fuck yourself," Cindy shot back.

"I told you it was a mistake coming here," the Cookie said, throwing her hands into the air in defeat.

"You didn't consider that there might be consequences to your actions?" Cindy asked her daughter. "It never occurred to you that not everything works out exactly as planned? That sometimes the things we set in motion have a way of spiraling out of control?"

"I just want to be famous," Julia said evenly, as if this made everything understandable, as if it made everything all right.

"So the end justifies the means?" Cindy stared at her daughter, the young woman who only moments before she would have given her life just to hold in her arms. Julia was her father's daughter, she realized in that instant. She always had been.

(Flashback: Julia, four years old, Shirley Temple curls tamed into two long braids, holding tightly to her father's hand as they walk down the street; Julia, age eight, proudly sitting on the shiny red bicycle her father bought her for her birthday; Julia, at thirteen, wearing a fancy brown-and-blue-striped taffeta dress, posing beside her father, so handsome in his tuxedo, before they leave for the annual Havergal father-daughter dinner-dance; Julia the following year, packing her clothes into the new Louis Vuitton suitcase her father bought her, then carrying it outside to his waiting BMW, leaving her childhood—and her mother—behind.)

"So what happens now?" Cindy asked, her energy sapped. "What exactly are you planning on telling people? That Julia was a victim of amnesia?"

"It's simple," Tom said. "We tell them that Julia was feeling down because she thought she'd blown her audition, so she wandered the countryside for a couple of weeks, trying to clear her head, didn't even look at a paper until today. . . ."

"The police will never buy it."

"Are you kidding?" Tom reminded her. "It was their idea."

"And I'm just supposed to go along with this charade?"

"Do you have any other choice?"

Did she?

"I could tell them the truth."

"You could, yes," Tom agreed. "But then, in all likelihood, Julia will be arrested, a promising career will be nipped in the bud, and I'll be disbarred. Is that what you really want?" Tom paused, allowed his words the necessary time to sink in before continuing. "Look, Cindy. Right now you're hurt and you're angry, and that's completely understandable. You've been through hell these last few weeks. Nobody knows that better than I do. But I urge you to think this through, and consider our daughter's best interests."

"Our daughter's best interests," Cindy repeated numbly.

"Please, Mom. I'm so close to getting everything I've ever wanted."

"You can't really want to see your daughter go to jail," the Cookie said.

"I thought all you ever wanted was for Julia to come home," Tom reminded Cindy.

"I thought so too," she said.

There was a noise in the hallway and Elvis suddenly galloped into the room.

"Elvis!" Julia fell to her knees, hugged her dog to her chest. "How are you, boy?"

Heather appeared in the kitchen doorway. "I heard voices," she said, falling silent when she saw her sister.

"What's going on?" Norma Appleton called from the top of the stairs.

"Julia's home," Heather shouted back at her.

"Julia?! Leigh, wake up! Julia's home."

In the next instant, Cindy's mother and sister came flying into the room, crying happily, and gathered Julia inside their arms, smothering her face with kisses.

Moments later, the women sat huddled together at the kitchen table, their bewildered faces heavy with anger, relief, and pain, as they tried to recover from the shock of the early-morning revelations.

"I'm really sorry," Julia told them, standing next to her father on the other side of the room. "I honestly didn't think everybody would be so upset."

"You didn't think we'd be upset?" Her grandmother's head shook from side to side in disbelief.

"You didn't think, period," Leigh said bitterly.

"How could you do this to Mom?" Heather asked.

"I said I was sorry," Julia said testily.

"Okay," the Cookie chirped into the silence that followed. "I think we've said everything that needs to be said. There's nothing to be gained from going over the whole thing ad nauseam."

"I'll call the newspapers first thing in the morning," Tom said. "Tell them Julia's come home." He squeezed Julia's hand. "That she's ready for her close-up."

Julia smiled, her free hand automatically reaching up to smooth the side of her hair.

Cindy stared at her older daughter. Still just a child really, despite her twenty-one years. Maybe there was still hope. Maybe time would bring some measure of maturity. Or maybe not. Maybe Julia would always be a bit of a monster. Maybe her single-minded self-absorption was the very quality that would make her a star, her obvious contempt for the feelings of others resulting in her being adored by millions.

Her father's daughter all right.

But her daughter too.

Cindy walked to the phone and punched in the number for the Fifty-third Division. "I'd like to speak to the officer in charge, please."

"What do you think you're doing?" Tom demanded.

"If you tell the police the truth, I'll deny it," Julia said quickly. "I'll say you were in on the whole thing from the beginning."

"This is ridiculous," the Cookie snapped. "You're just doing this to get back at Tom and I."

"Tom and *me*," Heather said from her seat at the kitchen table.

"What?"

"Object of the preposition," Heather said.

"I don't believe this! Tom, do something."

"Mom, please," Julia pleaded. "I just want to come home."

The words tugged at Cindy's heart.

"Officer Medavoy," a familiar voice announced in Cindy's ear.

"Officer Medavoy, it's Cindy Carver. We met the other night. My daughter Heather . . ."

"Yes, of course. How is she?"

"She's wonderful. Wonderful," Cindy repeated, her eyes absorbing the miracle that was her younger child. All these years she'd overlooked Heather's quiet light because she'd been so blinded by the raging fire that was Julia. All those years Cindy had given short shrift to one daughter because she was so busy mourning the loss of the other. And now Julia was back, and she was saying exactly what Cindy had been waiting a lifetime to hear: *Please, Mom. I just want to come home.*

And it was too late.

"It's my other daughter I'm calling about. Julia."

A collective intake of breath.

"She's home," Cindy told the officer. She closed her

eyes, shook her head, a cry escaping her mouth as she tried to continue. Could she really tell the police the truth, knowing that her daughter might go to jail, her dreams of stardom over? Hadn't the last two weeks seen enough misery and shattered dreams to last a lifetime? "She waltzed in about an hour ago," Cindy announced, "totally unaware of everything that's been happening."

"Thank God," she heard the Cookie whisper, as Julia burst into a flood of grateful tears against her father's chest.

Cindy continued reading from the invisible script her ex-husband and daughter had prepared, surprised by how convincing she managed to sound. Tom was right. When all was said and done, what other choice did she have? "Thank you," she told the officer before hanging up the phone and facing the others. "He said he'll let Detectives Bartolli and Gill know what's happened, that they'll probably contact us first thing in the morning."

"Thank you so much, Mom," Julia whispered.

"You did the right thing," Tom said.

Cindy glanced toward the kitchen table, expecting to see at least a hint of recrimination in her mother's eyes, a scowl of disapproval on her sister's lips, a look of disappointment on Heather's face. But all three women were nodding their tearful support. There were no judgments here, Cindy realized. Only love.

Tom kissed Julia's forehead. "Try to get some sleep, sweetie. You want to look good for the reporters in the morning." He touched the Cookie's elbow, began leading her toward the hall.

"Wait," Cindy called out. What was she doing now?

"Cindy, we're all beat. Can't this wait until tomorrow?"

"Julia can't stay here." The words were out of Cindy's mouth almost before she realized they were in her head.

"What?" Tom stopped abruptly.

"What?" Julia echoed.

"You can't stay here," Cindy said again, the words sounding no less strange for having repeated them.

"I don't understand."

Cindy took a deep breath, releasing the air slowly from her lungs, feeling her heart about to burst. "I love you, darling. I always will. You know that. And I'm so sorry." She glanced from Julia to Tom, then back again. "It's just that I can't spend any more time living with someone I don't really like."

Julia's eyes filled with unexpected tears. She quickly lowered her head, her hair falling across her face as it had during her audition for Michael Kinsolving.

(Fantasy: Julia raises her head, tears falling the length of her cheeks. "I'm so sorry," she says. "Please forgive me. I never meant to hurt you. I love you more than anything in the world. I promise I'll change. I promise things will be so different from now on.")

Julia remained in that posture for several seconds, then a toss of her hair, a shrug of her shoulders, brought her head back up. When her eyes next met her mother's, the tears were gone. "Whatever. I'll stay at Dad's."

The Cookie's eyes widened in alarm.

Could she really do this? Cindy wondered. Could she really send her daughter away? Was she prepared to lose her again, possibly forever? Cindy felt her body shudder, as if finally absorbing the fact that Julia had been lost to her a long time ago.

Julia stood in the middle of the kitchen, not moving, as if giving her mother a few extra seconds to change her mind. "Okay, then. If that's the way you want it. Come on, Elvis. We're going back to Dad's."

"Oh no," the Cookie wailed. "I will not have that mangy mutt peeing on my good carpets again."

"Come on, Elvis," Julia repeated, as if the Cookie hadn't spoken.

Elvis slowly raised himself up from his position underneath the kitchen table and lumbered over to the middle of the room to where Cindy was standing. Then he barked loudly three times, and stretched himself across the top of Cindy's feet.

"Fine." Julia rolled her eyes in exasperation. "Stay here, if that's what you want."

"Thank God," the Cookie muttered.

"Shut up," Julia snapped.

"You shut up."

"Ladies, please," Tom implored, ushering the two young women toward the front door without so much as a backward glance.

Cindy followed, her eyes trailing after them as they walked down the street. She saw Julia climb into her father's car, watched that car pull away from the curb, then turn the corner onto Avenue Road.

And then she was gone.

(Flashback: Julia, age fourteen, her ponytail waving behind her, carries her suitcase into her father's waiting BMW, leaving her childhood—and her mother—behind.)

"Are you all right?" Heather asked, coming up behind her.

Cindy nodded. "I'm okay," she said, realizing that she was.

Maybe nothing would ever completely heal the wound in her heart, maybe there would always be a part of her that wanted to run down the street after her older daughter and beg her to come home. But it was too late for that. Julia wasn't fourteen anymore. She was all grown up now. An adult, with a mind and a will of her own. And, thank God, she was healthy and strong and safe. Hell, she was indestructible.

They were the ones who'd been battered and bruised and beaten these last few weeks, Cindy realized. For fourteen days they'd been treading water and holding their breath, struggling to keep their heads above the cruel current. Their lives had been turned upside down and inside out. And now, suddenly, it was over. Just like that. Two weeks of slow torture resolved in mere seconds.

And yet those seconds would resonate with all of them for the rest of their lives.

"How are you guys?"

"Tired," said her mother.

"Exhausted," said Leigh.

"We should get to bed."

"What do you think will happen tomorrow?" her mother asked.

"I don't know."

"Neil's coming over with bagels," Heather reminded them.

Cindy smiled at the three women. "I love you," she said simply.

"We love you too," they said in unison.

Elvis lifted himself off Cindy's feet and stared at her expectantly.

"Don't worry," Cindy told the dog. "We love you too."

(Final images: Cindy drapes one arm across her daughter's shoulder as the other arm stretches to accommodate both her mother and sister; the dog's tail snaps hopefully against her leg as she guides everyone toward the stairs.)

JOY

FIELDING

WHISPERS AND LIES

ANCHOR CANADA

For Shannon,
my daughter, my helper, my friend.

ACKNOWLEDGMENTS

As always, a special thank you to Owen Laster, Beverley Slopen, and Larry Mirkin, good friends as well as trusted advisors. Thank you also to Emily Bestler, the editor of my dreams, and her assistant Sarah Branham, for their assistance and good humor in the creation of this novel. I also count myself very lucky to have the support of Judith Curr, Louise Burke, Cathy Gruhn, Stephen Boldt, and all the other terrific people at Atria and Pocket who work so hard to make my books a success.

Writing this novel would have been very difficult without the help of Donna and Jack Frysinger, who gave generously of their time and energy to provide me with all the information I needed to bring the charming, oceanside city of Delray to life. I look forward to seeing you there soon.

My love to Warren, Shannon, Annie, Renee, Aurora and Rosie, and all my friends in Toronto and Palm Beach. Thank you for being patient, loyal, and always interesting (especially important for a writer). Note to Annie: You could be a little less interesting for a while.

And lastly, a special thank you to those readers who have sent such wonderful messages to me via my Web site. While there's not enough time to thank you each in person, please know that your letters have meant more to me than I can ever adequately express. Your kind thoughts and good wishes buoy my spirits and make my day. Thank you.

WHISPERS AND LIES

ONE

She said her name was Alison Simms.

The name tumbled slowly, almost languorously, from her lips, the way honey slides from the blade of a knife. Her voice was soft, tentative, slightly girlish, although her handshake was firm and she looked me straight in the eye. I liked that. I liked *her*, I decided, almost on the spot, although I'm the first to admit that I'm not always the best judge of character. Still, my first impression of the amazingly tall young woman with the shoulder-length, strawberry-blond curls who stood tightly clasping my hand in the living room of my small two-bedroom home was positive. And first impressions are lasting impressions, as my mother used to say.

"This is a real pretty house," Alison said, her head nodding up and down, as if agreeing with her own assessment, her eyes darting appreciatively between the overstuffed sofa and the two delicate Queen Anne chairs, the cushioned valances framing the windows and the sculpted area rug lying across the light hardwood floor. "I love pink and mauve together. It's my favorite color combination." Then she smiled, this enormous, wide, slightly goofy smile that made me want to smile right back. "I always wanted a pink and mauve wedding."

I had to laugh. It seemed such a wonderfully strange thing to say to someone you'd just met. She laughed with me, and I motioned toward the sofa for her to sit down. She immediately sank into the deep, down-filled cushions, her blue sundress all but disappearing inside the swirl of pink and mauve fabric flowers, and crossed one long, skinny leg over the other, the rest of her body folding itself artfully around her knees as she leaned toward me. I perched on the edge of the striped Queen Anne chair directly across from her, thinking that she reminded me of a pretty pink flamingo, a real one, not one of those awful plastic things you see stabbed into people's front lawns. "You're very tall," I commented lamely, thinking she'd probably heard that remark all her life.

"Five feet ten inches," she acknowledged graciously. "I look taller."

"Yes, you do," I agreed, although at barely five feet four inches, everyone looks tall to me. "Do you mind my asking how old you are?"

"Twenty-eight." A slight blush suddenly scraped her cheeks. "I look younger."

"Yes, you do," I said again. "You're lucky. I've always looked my age."

"How old are you? That is, if you don't mind . . ."

"Take a guess."

The sudden intensity of her gaze caught me off-guard. She scrutinized me as if I were an exotic specimen in a lab, trapped between two tiny pieces of glass, under an invisible microscope. Her clear green eyes burrowed into my tired brown ones, then moved across my face, examining each telltale line, weighing the evidence of my years. I have few illusions. I saw myself exactly the way I knew she must: a reasonably attractive woman with good cheekbones, large breasts, and a bad haircut.

"I don't know," she said. "Forty?"

"Exactly." I laughed. "Told you."

We fell silent, frozen in the warmth of the afternoon sun that surrounded us like a spotlight, highlighting small flecks of dust that danced in the air between us, like hundreds of tiny insects. She smiled, folded her hands together in her lap, the fingers of one hand playing carelessly with the fingers of the other. She wore no rings of any kind, and no polish, although her nails were long and cared-for. I could tell she was nervous. She wanted me to like her.

"Did you have any trouble finding the house?" I asked.

"No. Your directions were great: east on Atlantic, south on Seventh Avenue, past the white church, between Second and Third Street. No problem at all. Except for the traffic. I didn't realize that Delray was such a busy place."

"Well, it's November," I reminded her. "The snowbirds are starting to arrive."

"Snowbirds?"

"Tourists," I explained. "You're obviously new to Florida."

She looked toward her sandaled feet. "I like this rug. You're very brave to have a white carpet in the living room."

"Not really. I don't do much entertaining."

"I guess your job keeps you pretty busy. I always thought it would be so great to be a nurse," she offered. "It must be very rewarding."

I laughed. "*Rewarding* is not exactly the word I would use."

"What word would you use?"

She seemed genuinely curious, something I found both refreshing and endearing. It had been so long since anyone had expressed any real interest in me that I guess I was flattered. But there was also something so touchingly naive about the question that I wanted to cross over to where she sat and hug her, as a mother hugs her child, and tell her that it was all right, she didn't have to work so hard, that the tiny cottage behind my house was hers to occupy, that the decision had been made the minute she walked through my front door.

"What word would I use to describe the nursing profession?" I repeated, mulling over several possibilities. "Exhausting," I said finally. "Exacting. Infuriating."

"Good words."

I laughed again, as I seemed to have done often in the short amount of time she'd been in my home. It would be nice having someone around who made me laugh, I remember thinking. "What sort of work do you do?" I asked.

Alison stood up, walked to the window, and stared out at the wide street, lined with several varieties of shady palms. Bettye McCoy, third wife of Richard McCoy, and some thirty years his junior, not an unusual occurrence in South Florida, was being pulled along the sidewalk by her two small white dogs. She was dressed from head to toe in beige Armani, and in her free hand she carried a small white plastic bag full of dog poop, a fashion irony seemingly lost on the third Mrs. McCoy. "Oh, would you just look at that. Aren't they just the sweetest things? What are they, poodles?"

"Bichons," I said, coming up beside her, the top of my head in line with the bottom of her chin. "The bimbos of the canine world."

It was Alison's turn to laugh. The sound filled the room, danced between us, like the flecks of dust in the afternoon sun. "They sure are cute though. Don't you think?"

"*Cute* is not exactly the word I would use," I told her, consciously echoing my earlier remark.

She smiled conspiratorially. "What word would you use?"

"Let me see," I said, warming to the game. "Yappy. Pesky. Destructive."

"Destructive? How could anything that sweet be destructive?"

"One of her dogs got into my garden a few months back, dug up all my hibiscus. Trust me, it was neither sweet nor cute." I backed away from the window, catching sight, as I did so, of a man's silhouette among the many outside shadows on the opposite corner of the street. "Is someone waiting for you?"

"For me? No. Why?"

I edged forward to have a better look, but the man, if he'd existed at all, had taken his shadow and disappeared. I looked down the street, but there was no one there.

"I thought I saw someone standing under that tree over there." I pointed with my chin.

"I don't see anyone."

"Well, I'm sure it was nothing. Would you like some coffee?"

"I'd love some." She followed me through the small dining area that stood perpendicular to the living room, and into the predominantly white kitchen at the back of the house. "Oh, would you just look at these," she exclaimed with obvious delight, gliding toward the rows of shelves that lined the wall beside the small breakfast nook, her arms extended, fingers fluttering eagerly in the air. "What are these? Where did you get them?"

My eyes quickly scanned the sixty-five china heads that gazed at us from five rows of wooden shelves. "They're called 'ladies' head vases,'" I explained. "My mother used to collect them. They're from the fifties, mostly made in Japan. They have holes in the tops of their heads, for flowers, I guess, although they don't hold a lot. When they first came out, they were worth maybe a couple of dollars."

"And now?"

"Apparently they're quite valuable. *Collectibles*, I believe, is the word they use."

"And what word would you use?" She waited eagerly, a mischievous smile twisting her full lips this way and that.

I didn't have to think very hard. "Junk," I said concisely.

"I think they're great," she protested. "Just look at the eyelashes on this one. Oh, and the earrings on this one. And the tiny string of pearls. Oh, and look at this one. Don't you just love the expression on her face?" She lifted one of the heads gingerly into her hands. The china figurine was about six inches tall, with arched painted eyebrows and pursed red lips, her light brown curls peeking out from under a pink and white turban, a pink rose at her throat. "She's not as ornate as some of the others, but she has such a superior look about her, you know, like some snooty society matron, looking down her nose at the rest of us."

"Actually, she looks like my mother," I said.

The china head almost slipped through Alison's fingers. "Oh my God, I'm so sorry." She quickly returned the head vase to its original position on the shelf, between two doe-eyed girls with ribbons in their hair. "I didn't mean . . ."

I laughed. "It's interesting you picked that one. It was her favorite. What do you take in your coffee?"

"Cream, three sugars?" she asked, as if she weren't sure, her eyes still on the china heads.

I poured us each a mug of the coffee I'd been brewing since she'd phoned from the hospital, said she'd seen my notice posted to the bulletin board at one of the nurses' stations, and could she come over as soon as possible.

"Does your mother still collect?"

"She died five years ago."

"I'm so sorry."

"Me too. I miss her. It's why I haven't been able to sell off any of her friends. How about a piece of cranberry-and-pumpkin cake?" I asked, changing the subject for fear of getting maudlin. "I just made it this morning."

"You can bake? Now I'm really impressed. I'm absolutely hopeless in the kitchen."

"Your mother never taught you to cook?"

"We weren't on the best of terms." Alison smiled, although unlike her other smiles, this one seemed more forced than genuine. "Anyway, I'd love a piece of cake. Cranberries are one of my very favorite things in the whole world."

Again, I laughed. "I don't think I've ever met anyone who felt so passionately about cranberries. Could you hand me a knife?" I motioned toward a group of knives slid into the artfully arranged slots of a triangular chunk of wood that sat on the far end of the white tile countertop. Alison pulled out the top one, a foot-long monster with a tapered two-inch blade. "Whoa," I said. "Overkill, don't you think?"

She turned the knife over slowly in her hand, studying her reflection in the well-sharpened blade, gingerly running her finger along its side, temporarily lost in thought. Then she caught me looking at her and quickly replaced the knife with one of the smaller ones, watching intently as the knife sliced effortlessly through the large Bundt cake. Then it was my turn to watch as she wolfed it down, complimenting me all the while on its texture, its lightness, its taste. She finished it quickly, her entire focus on what she was doing, like a child.

Maybe I should have been more suspicious, or at the very least, more wary, especially after the experience with my last tenant. But likely it was precisely that experience that made me so susceptible to Alison's girlish charm. I wanted, really wanted, to believe she was exactly as she presented herself: a somewhat naive, lovely, sweet young woman.

Sweet, I think now.

Sweet is not exactly the word I would use.

How could anything that sweet be destructive? she'd asked.

Why wasn't I listening?

"You've obviously never had a problem with your weight," I observed as her fingers pressed down on several errant crumbs scattered across her plate before lifting them to her mouth.

"If anything, I have trouble keeping pounds on," she said. "I was always teased about it. Kids used to say things like, 'Skinny Minny, she grows like a weed.' And I was the last girl in my class to get boobs, such as they are, so I took a lot of flak for that. Now suddenly everybody wants to be thin, only I'm still catching flak. People accuse me of being anorexic. You should hear the things they say."

"People can be very insensitive," I agreed. "Where'd you go to school?"

"Nowhere special. I wasn't a very good student. I dropped out of college in my first year."

"To do what?"

"Let's see. I worked in a bank for a while, sold men's socks, was a hostess in a restaurant, a receptionist in a hair salon. Stuff like that. I never have any trouble finding a job. Do you think I could have some more coffee?"

I poured her a second cup, again adding cream and three heaping teaspoons of sugar. "Would you like to see the cottage?"

Instantly, she was on her feet, downing the coffee in one seamless gulp, wiping her lips with the back of her hand. "Can't wait. I just know it's going to be beautiful." She followed me to the back door, an eager puppy nipping at my heels. "Your notice said six hundred a month, right?"

"Will that be a problem? I require first and last month's rent up front."

"No problem. I intend to start looking for a job as soon as I get settled, and even if I don't find something right away, my grandmother left me some money when she died, so I'm actually in pretty good shape. Financially speaking," she added softly, strawberry-blond hair curling softly around the long oval of her face.

I had hair like that once, I thought, tucking several wayward waves of auburn hair behind one ear. "My last tenant was several months behind in her rent when she took off, that's why I have to ask . . ."

"Oh, I understand completely."

We crossed the small patch of lawn that separated the tiny cottage from the main house. I fished inside my jean pocket for the key to the front door, the heat of her gaze on my back rendering me unusually clumsy, so that the key fell from my hand and bounced on the grass. Alison immediately bent to pick it up, her fingers grazing mine as she returned it to the palm of my hand. I pushed open the cottage door and stood back to let her come inside.

A long sigh escaped her full lips. "It's even more beautiful than I thought it was going to be. It's like . . . magic." Alison danced around the tiny room in small, graceful circles, head arched back, arms outstretched, as if she could somehow capture the magic, draw it to her. She doesn't realize she *is* the magic, I thought, suddenly aware of how much I'd wanted her to like it, how much I wanted her to stay. "I'm so glad you kept the same colors as the main house," she was saying, briefly alighting, like a butterfly, on the small love seat, the large chair, the bentwood rocker in the corner. She admired the rug—mauve and white flowers woven into a pale pink background—and the framed prints on the wall—a group of Degas dancers preening backstage before a recital, Monet's cathedral at sunset, Mary Cassatt's loving portrait of a mother and her child.

"The other rooms are back here." I opened the double set of French doors to reveal a tidy arrangement of galley kitchen, bathroom, and bedroom.

"It's perfect. It's absolutely perfect." She bounced up and

down on the double bed, running eager palms across the antique white bedspread, before catching her reflection in the mirror above the white wicker dresser and instantly assuming a more ladylike demeanor. "I love everything. It's exactly the way I would have decorated it. Exactly."

"I used to live here," I told her, not sure why. I hadn't confided anything of the sort to my last tenant. "My mother lived in the main house. I lived back here."

A little half-smile played nervously with the corners of Alison's lips. "Does this mean we have a deal?"

"You can move in whenever you're ready."

She jumped to her feet. "I'm ready right now. All I have to do is go back to the motel and pack my suitcase. I can be back within the hour."

I nodded, only now becoming aware of the speed at which things had progressed. There was so much I didn't know about her. There were so many things we had yet to discuss. "We probably should talk about a few of the rules . . . ," I sidestepped.

"Rules?"

"No smoking, no loud parties, no roommates."

"No problem," she said eagerly. "I don't smoke, I don't party, I don't know anyone."

I dropped the key into her waiting palm, watched her fingers fold tightly over it.

"Thank you so much." Still clutching the key, she reached into her purse and counted out twelve crisp $100 bills, proudly handing them over. "Printed them fresh this morning," she said with a self-conscious smile.

I tried not to look shocked by the unexpected display of cash. "Would you like to come over for dinner after you get settled?" I heard myself ask, the invitation probably surprising me more than it did her.

"I'd like that very much."

After she was gone, I sat in the living room of the main house, marveling at my actions. I, Terry Painter, supposedly mature adult, who had spent my entire forty years being sensible and organized and anything but impulsive, had just rented out the small cottage behind my house to a virtual stranger, a young woman with no references beyond an ingratiating manner and a goofy smile, with no job and a purse full of cash. What, really, did I know about her? Nothing. Not where she came from. Not what had brought her to Delray. Not how long she was planning to stay. Not even what she'd been doing at the hospital when she saw my notice. Nothing really except her name.

She said her name was Alison Simms.

At the time, of course, I had no reason to doubt her.

TWO

She arrived for dinner at exactly seven o'clock, wearing a pair of black cotton pants and a sleeveless black sweater, with her hair pulled dramatically back and twisted into a long braid, so that she looked like an extended exclamation point. She was carrying a bouquet of freshly cut flowers in one hand and a bottle of red wine in the other. "It's an Italian Amarone, 1997," Alison announced proudly, then rolled her eyes. "Not that I know anything about wine, but the man in the liquor store assured me it was a very good year." She smiled, her lightly glossed lips overtaking the entire bottom half of her face, her mouth opening to reveal an acre of perfect teeth. My own lips immediately curled into a heartfelt smile of their own, although they stopped short of exposing the gentle overbite that not even years of expensive orthodontics had been able to correct completely. My mother had always claimed the overbite was the result of a stubborn childhood habit of sucking on the middle and fourth fingers of my left hand while simultaneously rubbing my nose with the tattered remains of a favorite baby blanket. But since my mother had virtually the same overbite, I'm inclined to believe this aesthetic deficiency is more genetic than willful.

Alison followed me through the living and dining rooms into the kitchen, where I unwrapped the flowers and filled a tall crystal vase with water. "Can I do anything to help?" Eager eyes ferreted into each corner of the room, as if memorizing each detail.

"Just pull up a chair, keep me company." I quickly deposited the flowers in the vase of lukewarm water, sniffing at the small pink roses, the delicate white daisies, the sprays of purple wildflowers. "They're beautiful. Thank you so much."

"My pleasure. Dinner smells wonderful."

"It's nothing fancy," I quickly demurred. "Just chicken. You eat chicken, don't you?"

"I eat everything. Put food in front of me and it's gone within seconds. I'm the world's fastest eater."

I smiled as I recalled the way she'd demolished the piece of cranberry-and-pumpkin cake I'd given her that afternoon. Had it only been a matter of hours ago that we'd met? For some reason, it seemed as if we'd known each other all our lives, that despite the difference in our ages, we'd been friends forever. I had to remind myself how little I actually knew about her. "So, tell me more about yourself," I said casually, searching through the kitchen drawers for a corkscrew.

"Not much to tell." She sank into one of the wicker chairs at the round glass kitchen table, although her posture remained erect, even alert, as if she were afraid of getting too comfortable.

"Where are you from?" I wasn't trying to pry. I was just curious, the way one is usually curious about a new acquaintance. I sensed a certain wariness on her part to talk about herself. Or maybe I didn't sense anything at all. Maybe the small talk we made in my kitchen that night before dinner was nothing more than it appeared to be, two people slowly and cautiously getting to know one another, asking normal questions, not overanalyzing the responses, moving from one topic to the next without any particular plan, no hidden agendas.

At least there were no hidden agendas on my part.

"Chicago," Alison answered.

"Really? I love Chicago. Where exactly?"

"Suburbs," she said vaguely. "How about you? Are you a native Floridian?"

I shook my head. "We moved here from Baltimore when I was fifteen. My father was in the waterproofing business. He thought Florida was the natural place to be, what with all the hurricanes and everything."

Alison's green eyes widened in alarm.

"Don't worry. Hurricane season is over." I laughed, finally locating the corkscrew at the back of the cutlery drawer. "That's the thing about Florida," I mused out loud. "On the surface, everything is so beautiful, so perfect. Paradise. But if you look a little closer, you'll see the deadly alligator lurking just below the water's smooth surface, you'll see the poisonous snake slithering through the emerald green grass, you'll hear the distant hurricane whispering through the leaves."

Alison smiled, the warmth of that smile filling the room, like steam from a kettle. "I could listen to you talk all night."

I waved the compliment aside, using my fingers as a fan, as if trying to protect myself from the heat. Knowing me, I probably blushed.

"Have you actually seen a hurricane?" Alison leaned forward in her chair.

"Several." I struggled to open the bottle of Amarone without breaking the cork in two. It had been a long time since I'd had to open a bottle of wine. I rarely entertained, and I'd never been much of a drinker. All it took was one glass of wine to start my head spinning. "Hurricane Andrew was the worst, of course. That one was something else. Makes you really respect Mother Nature when you witness something like that up close."

"What words would you use to describe it?" she asked, picking up the thread of our earlier game.

"Terrifying," I answered quickly. "Ferocious." I paused, twisting the corkscrew gently to the right, gradually feeling the cork surrender, begin its slow slide up the neck of the dark green bottle. I admit to being suffused with an almost childish sense of pride and accomplishment as I lifted the vanquished cork into the air. "Magnificent."

"I'll get the glasses." Alison was on her feet and in the dining room before I had time to tell her where the glasses were.

"They're in the cabinet," I called after her unnecessarily. It was almost as if she already knew where to look.

"Found them." She returned with two long-stemmed crystal goblets, holding out first one, then the other, as I filled each about a quarter of the way. "They're beautiful. Everything you have is so beautiful."

"Cheers," I said, clicking my glass gently against hers, marveling at the deep red of the wine.

"What are we drinking to?"

"Good health," the nurse in me responded immediately.

"And good friends," she added shyly.

"To new friends," I amended slightly, lifting my glass to my mouth, the rich aroma filling my head before I'd tasted a single drop.

"New beginnings," Alison whispered, her face disappearing into the roundness of the glass as she took a long, slow sip of the wine. "Mmm, this is yummy. What do you think?"

I quickly mulled over the adjectives experts generally employed when describing fine wine—*full-bodied, buttery, fruity,* occasionally even *whimsical.* Never *yummy.* What did they know? I thought, rolling the wine around in my mouth, the way I'd seen men do in fancy restaurants, feeling the flavor burst against my tongue. "*Yummy* is the perfect word," I agreed after swallowing. "Perfectly yummy."

Again the grin that transformed her face, engulfing her cheeks and swallowing her nose, so that it looked as if her eyes themselves were smiling. She took another long sip, then another. I followed her lead, and before long, it was time to refill our glasses. This time, I filled them almost halfway.

"So, what brought you from Chicago to Delray?" I asked.

"I was looking for a change." She might have stopped had it not been for the obvious questions on my face. "I don't know exactly." She stared absently at the rows of ladies' head vases on the shelves. "I guess I didn't particularly feel like going through another Chicago winter, and I had this friend who'd moved to Delray a few years back. I thought I could come down here and look her up."

"Did you?"

"Did I what?"

"Look her up."

Alison looked confused, as if unsure exactly what her answer should be.

That's the problem with lying.

A good liar is always one step ahead. She's always anticipating, answering one question with an ear to the next. She's on constant alert, always ready with a facile reply.

Of course, all a bad liar needs is an easy mark.

"I tried finding her," Alison said after a pause that lasted perhaps a beat too long. "That's what I was doing at the hospital when I saw your notice." The words flowed easier now. "She'd written that she was working at this private hospital called Mission Care in Delray, so I figured I'd surprise her, maybe take her to lunch, see if she was looking for a roommate. But personnel said she left a long time ago." Alison shrugged. Beautifully carved shoulders lifted up, then down. "Luckily I saw your notice."

"What's your friend's name? If she's a nurse, maybe I can find out where she went."

"She's not a nurse," Alison said quickly. "She was a secretary or something."

"What's her name?" I repeated. "I can ask around when I get to work tomorrow, see if anyone knows where she went."

"Don't bother." Alison ran a distracted finger along the rim of her wineglass. The glass made a slight purring sound, as if responding to a lover's gentle caress. "We weren't that close."

"And yet you left your home and traveled halfway across the country . . ."

Alison shrugged. "Her name is Rita Bishop. You know her?"

"Doesn't sound familiar."

She took a deep breath. Her shoulders relaxed. "I never liked the name Rita. Do you like it?"

"It's not one of my favorites," I admitted, allowing myself to be steered gently off-course.

"What *are* your favorites?"

"I don't think I ever really thought about it."

"I like Kelly," Alison said. "And Samantha. I think if I ever have a daughter, I'll name her one of those. And Joseph if I have a boy. Or maybe Max."

"You have it all planned out."

She stared thoughtfully into her goblet for several long seconds before taking another sip. "Do you have any children?" The question echoed against the side of the glass, barely escaped into the surrounding air.

"No. I'm afraid I never married."

"You don't have to get married to have babies."

"Maybe not today," I agreed. "But when I was growing up in Baltimore, trust me, it wasn't done." I opened the oven door, felt a warm rush of fragrant steam in my face. "Anyway, I hope you're hungry, because this chicken is ready to be devoured."

"Let's eat," Alison said with a wide smile.

Alison was right. She was the fastest eater I'd ever seen. Within minutes, everything on her plate—roast chicken, mashed potatoes, pureed carrots, multiple stalks of asparagus—had disappeared. I'd barely swallowed my first forkful of chicken and she was already helping herself to seconds.

"This is so delicious. You are the best cook ever," she pronounced, her mouth full.

"I'm glad you like everything."

"Too bad I didn't bring another bottle of wine." Alison gave one of her rare frowns, glancing past the tapered white candles in the middle of the dining room table toward the now empty bottle of Amarone.

"Good thing you didn't. My shift starts at six in the morning. I'm supposed to be able to stand up straight."

"What made you decide to be a nurse?" Alison finished off what little wine clung to the sides of her glass.

"I lost my father and a favorite aunt to cancer before either reached fifty," I explained, trying not to see their ravaged faces in the bottom of my glass. "I felt so helpless, and I didn't like that, so I decided to go into medicine. My mother didn't have the money to send me to medical school, and I didn't have the grades for a full scholarship, so being a doctor was out. I settled for the next best thing. And I love it."

"Even though it's exhausting, exacting, and infuriating?" Alison laughed as she gently tossed my earlier words back at me.

"Even though," I repeated. "And being a nurse meant I was able to care for my mother after her stroke, that I was able to keep her at home, that she died in her own bed, not in some sterile hospital room."

"Is that why you never got married?" Alison asked. "Because you were busy taking care of your mother?"

"No, I can't really blame her for that. Although I guess I can try," I said with a laugh. "I think I just assumed there was all this time, that eventually I'd meet someone, fall in love, get married, have a couple of beautiful babies, live happily ever after. Standard fantasy 101. It just didn't work out that way."

"There was never anyone special?"

"Not special enough, I guess."

"Well, time's not up yet. You never know . . ."

"I'm forty," I reminded her. "I know. So, what about you? No special someone in Chicago, waiting for you to come home?"

She shook her head. "No, not really." She volunteered nothing further.

"How did your parents feel about you moving so far away?"

Alison stopped eating, lay her fork neatly across her plate. "These dishes are really neat. I like the pattern. It's pretty, but it doesn't interfere with the food, you know what I mean?"

Strangely enough, I did. "Your parents don't know where you are, do they?" I asked tentatively, not wanting to trespass beyond invisible boundaries, but eager to know more.

"I'll call them after I find a job," she said, confirming my suspicions.

"Won't they be worried?"

"I doubt it." She paused, flipped her braid from one shoulder to the other. "As you've probably figured out, we weren't on the best of terms." She paused, her eyes darting back and forth, as if reading from an invisible text. "Unfortunately, I had this older brother who was absolutely perfect. Star forward of the basketball team in high school, champion swimmer in college, graduated summa cum laude from Brown. And here I was, this tall, skinny kid who was constantly tripping over her big, clumsy feet. No way I could ever measure up, so at some point, I stopped trying. I turned into this major brat, insisted on doing my own thing, positive I had all the answers. You know the type."

"Typical teenager, by the sound of it."

Large green eyes radiated gratitude. "Thank you, but I don't think *typical* is the word they would use."

"And what word would they use?"

Sad grin widened into a smile as her eyes scanned the ceiling for proper adjectives. "Impossible," she said after a brief pause. "Incorrigible. In trouble all the time," she continued with a laugh, the words running together as one. "They were always kicking me out of the house. I left for good the day I turned eighteen."

"And did what?"

"Got married."

"You got married when you were eighteen?"

"What can I say?" She shrugged. "Standard fantasy 101."

I nodded understanding and reached for the bread basket, accidentally knocking my fork into my lap, where it deposited a large gob of gravy on my white pants before bouncing to the floor. Alison immediately rescued the fork and ran to the kitchen for some soda water, while I scrambled to my feet, instantly feeling the effect of so many glasses of wine.

Slowly, cautiously, I walked into the living room, trying to remember the last time a few glasses of wine had left me so inebriated. I approached the window and leaned my forehead against the cool glass.

That's when I saw him.

He was standing across the street, as still as the majestic royal palm he was leaning against, and even though it was too dark to make out who it was, I knew from his posture that he was staring at the house. I squinted into the darkness, tried to gather the light from the streetlamps into a spotlight and shine it on his face. But the effect was something less than I bargained for, and the man almost disappeared in the resultant blur. "Not a good idea," I muttered, deciding to confront the man directly, ask him what he was doing standing there in the dark, staring at my house.

I stumbled toward the front door, pulled it open. "You there," I called out, pointing an accusing finger at the night.

There was no one there.

I craned my neck, peered into the stubborn darkness, twisted my head from left to right, followed the road to the corner and back. I strained my ears for the sound of footsteps in hasty retreat, heard nothing.

In the time it had taken for me to get from the window to the door, the man had vanished. If he'd been there at all, I thought, recalling the apparition I thought I'd seen earlier.

"What are you doing?" Alison asked, coming up behind me.

I felt her breath on the back of my neck. "Just needed some fresh air."

"Are you okay?"

"A bit too okay. Did you put something in my drink?" I joked as Alison closed the front door, then led me back into the living room, where she sat me down on one of the Queen Anne chairs and began dabbing at the gravy stain on my pant leg with a wet cloth until I felt the dampness clear to my skin.

I reached down, stilled her hand. It lingered on my thigh. "Stain's gone."

She was instantly on her feet. "Sorry. There I go again, everything in extremes, that's the only way I seem to operate. Sorry."

"Why are you apologizing?" I asked, genuinely curious. "You didn't do anything wrong."

"I didn't? That's a relief." She laughed, sank down into the other chair, her face flushed.

"What happened with your marriage?" I asked gently, fighting a gnawing unease in my gut, a sensation that was undoubtedly trying to warn me that Alison Simms might not be the charmingly uncomplicated young woman she'd first appeared to be when I'd handed over the keys to the cottage at the back of my house.

"What usually happens when you get married at eighteen," she said simply, lowering her gaze to mine, no trace of a smile. "It didn't work out."

"I'm sorry."

"Me too. We tried. We really did. We split up and got back together a whole bunch of times, even after our divorce was final." She impatiently pushed the stray hairs away from her forehead. "Sometimes it's hard to stay away from someone, even when you know they're all wrong for you."

"And that's why you came to Florida?"

"Maybe," she acknowledged, then flashed the glorious smile that obliterated all traces of sadness or self-doubt. "What's for dessert?"

THREE

I was fifteen when I lost my virginity," Alison was saying, pouring herself a second small glass of Baileys Irish Cream. We were sitting on the living room floor, our backs against the furniture, our legs splayed out carelessly in front of us, like two abandoned rag dolls. Alison had insisted on cleaning up after dinner, washing and drying the dishes by hand before returning everything to its proper place while I sat at the kitchen table and watched, marveling at the deftness of her touch, the speed with which she worked, the instinctive way she seemed to know where everything belonged, almost as if she'd been in the house before. She'd found the Baileys at the back of the dining room cabinet when she was returning the wineglasses to their shelf. I'd forgotten I even had it.

I don't know why we chose the floor over the sofa. Probably Alison simply plopped herself down and I followed suit. The same way with the Baileys. I'd certainly had no intention of having any more to drink, but suddenly the delicately sculpted liqueur glass was in my hand, and Alison was pouring and I was drinking, and there you have it. I suppose I could have said no, but the truth is I was having too good a time. You have to remember that my days were normally spent in the company of people who were old, ill, or in some form of acute distress. Alison was so young, so vibrant, so alive. She infused me with a sense of such profound well-being that whatever niggling doubts or petty reservations I may have had flew out the window, along with my common sense. Simply put, I was reluctant to see her leave, and if drinking a second glass of Baileys would prolong the evening, then a second glass of Baileys it would be. I eagerly proffered my glass for more. She promptly filled it. "I probably shouldn't have told you that," she said. "You'll think I'm a slut."

It took me a minute to realize that she was referring to her lost virginity. "Of course I don't think you're a slut," I said adamantly, as relief washed across Alison's face, like a paintbrush, almost as if she'd been waiting for me to exonerate her, to forgive her the sins of her sometimes errant past. "Besides, I've got you beat," I offered, trying to make her feel better, to prove I was hardly one to sit in judgment.

"What do you mean?" She leaned forward, lowered her glass to the carpet. It disappeared inside the pink petal of a woven flower.

"I was only fourteen when I lost mine," I whispered guiltily, as if my mother might still be listening from the upstairs bedroom.

"Get out. I don't believe you."

"It's true." I found myself eager to convince her, to show her that she wasn't the only one with a past, with skeletons in her closet, however small and insubstantial they might be. Maybe I even wanted to shock her, just a little, to prove to her—and to myself—that I was more than I appeared at first glance, that underneath my middle-aged exterior beat the heart of a wild child.

Or maybe I was just drunk.

"His name was Roger Stillman," I continued without prodding, conjuring up the image of the lanky young man with light brown hair and large hazel eyes who'd seduced me with ridiculous ease back when I was in the ninth grade. "He was two grades ahead of me at school, so of course I was monstrously flattered that he even talked to me. He asked me to the movies, and I lied to my parents about where I was going, because my mother had decreed I was too young to date. So I said I was going to a friend's house to study for a test, and instead I met Roger at the movie theater. I remember it was one of the James Bond movies—don't ask me which one—and I was very excited because I'd never seen a James Bond movie before. Not that I saw much of that one either," I recalled, remembering Roger's tobacco-scented breath on my neck as I'd tried to follow the movie's convoluted plot, his lips grazing the side of my ear as I'd strained to make sense of all the double entendres, his hand sliding down my shoulder to the tops of my breasts as James coaxed yet another willing female into his bed. "We left before the movie finished. Roger had a car." I shrugged, as if that said it all.

"Whatever happened to Roger?"

"He dumped me. No surprises there."

Alison's face registered her displeasure. "Were you heartbroken?"

"Devastated, as only a fourteen-year-old girl can be. Especially after he bragged about his conquest to the entire school."

"He didn't!"

I laughed at Alison's spontaneous outburst of indignation. "He did. Roger, I'm afraid, was a rat of the first order."

"And whatever happened to the rat?"

"I have no idea. We moved to Florida the next year, and I never saw him again." I shook my head, watched the room spin. "God, I haven't thought about any of that in so long. That's one of the amazing things about being young."

"What is?"

"You think you'll never get over something, and then, the next minute, you've forgotten all about it."

Alison smiled, twisted her head across the top of her spine, stretching her swanlike neck until the muscles groaned and released.

"Everything has such urgency. Everything is so important. And you think you have so much time," I said, almost forgetting I was speaking out loud as I watched her, mesmerized by the motion.

"Anyone interesting on the horizon?" Alison rolled her head from side to side.

"Not really. Well, there's this man," I confided, although I'd had no intention of doing so until I heard the words leave my mouth. "Josh Wylie. His mother is a patient at the hospital."

Alison's head returned to the middle of her shoulders. She said nothing, simply sat and waited for me to continue.

"That's it," I said. "He comes up once a week from Miami to see her. We've only spoken a few times. But he seems very nice, and . . ."

"And you wouldn't mind getting to know him," Alison said, finishing my sentence for me.

I nodded, deciding that was a mistake when the room continued bouncing around me like a rubber ball. Reluctantly, I struggled to my feet. "I think I'm going to have to call it a night."

Alison was immediately at my side, her hand warm on my arm. She seemed steady, as if the alcohol hadn't affected her at all. "Are you all right?"

"Fine," I said, though I wasn't. The floor kept shifting, and I had to balance against the side of the sofa to keep from falling over. I made an exaggerated show of checking my watch, but the numbers danced randomly across the dial, and I couldn't tell the small hand from the large. "It's late," I said anyway, "and I have to be up very early."

"I hope I didn't overstay my welcome."

"You didn't."

"You're sure?"

"Quite sure. I had a really nice evening." I suddenly had the strange sensation that she was about to kiss me goodnight. "We'll do it again soon," I said, lowering my head and leading Alison through the living and dining rooms to the kitchen, where I promptly walked into the table and all but fell into her arms.

"You're sure you're okay?" she asked as I struggled to recapture my balance, if not my dignity. "Maybe I should stay and make sure you get into bed all right."

"I'm fine. Really. I'm fine," I repeated before she could ask again.

Alison was half out the door when she stopped suddenly, reached into the left pocket of her black pants, and spun around. The motion left me reeling. "I just remembered—I found this." She held out her hand.

Even with my head spinning and my focus blurred, I recognized the tiny gold heart at the center of the slender golden thread in Alison's open hand. "Where did you get this?" I reached for it, watching it unravel. The delicate necklace hung from my fingers like a forgotten strand of tinsel on a discarded Christmas tree.

"I found it under my bed," Alison said, unconsciously assuming ownership of the contents of the cottage.

"Why were you looking under the bed?"

Surprisingly, Alison blushed bright red. She shuffled uneasily from one foot to the other, the first time I'd seen her look truly uncomfortable in her own skin. When she finally answered me, I thought I must have misunderstood.

"What did you say?"

"Looking for bogeymen," she repeated sheepishly, lifting her eyes to mine with obvious reluctance.

"Bogeymen?"

"I know it's ridiculous. But I can't help myself. I've been doing it ever since I was a little girl and my brother convinced me there was a monster hiding underneath my bed who was going to eat me as soon as I fell asleep."

"You check underneath the bed for bogeymen?" I repeated, thoroughly, if inexplicably, charmed by the notion.

"I check the closets too. Just in case."

"Do you ever find anyone?"

"Not so far." She laughed, held out the necklace for me to take. "Here. Before I forget and take it home with me."

"It's not mine." I took a step back, almost tripping over my own feet, and watching the room rotate ninety degrees.

Sixty-five ladies' head vases tilted on their shelves. "It belonged to Erica Hollander, my last tenant."

"The one who still owes you several months' rent?"

"The one and only."

"Then I'd say it belongs to you now." Again Alison tried to hand over the necklace.

"You keep it." I wanted nothing more to do with Erica Hollander.

"Oh, I couldn't," Alison said, but her fist was already closing around it.

"Finders, keepers. Come on, take it. It's very . . . you."

Alison required no further coaxing. "It is, isn't it?" She laughed, wrapping the thin chain around her neck in one fluid gesture, securing the tiny clasp with ease. "How does it look?"

"Like it belongs there."

Alison patted the heart at her throat, strained to see her reflection in the darkness of the kitchen window. "I love it."

"Wear it in good health."

"You don't think she'll come back for it, do you?"

It was my turn to laugh. "Just let her try. Anyway, it's late. I have to get some sleep."

"Good night." Alison leaned forward, kissed my cheek. Her hair smelled of strawberries, her skin of baby powder. Like a newborn baby, I thought with a smile. "Thanks again," she said. "For everything."

"My pleasure." I opened the back door and took a quick glance around.

There was no one waiting, no one watching.

I breathed a sigh of relief and waited until Alison was safely inside the cottage before closing the kitchen door.

My hand brushed against the spot on my cheek where Alison's lips had grazed, as I pictured her walking through the small living area to the bedroom at the back. In my mind's eye, I watched her kneel to look under the bed, then check the closet for any stray monsters who might be lurking. I thought absently of the man I'd seen standing in front of the house. Had there been anyone there? And had he been watching me—or Alison?

Such a sweet girl, I remember thinking. So childlike. So innocent.

Not so innocent, I reminded myself as I painstakingly made my way up the stairs to my bedroom. A teenage hellion. Married at eighteen. Divorced soon after. Not to mention she could hold her liquor with the best of them.

I vaguely remember getting undressed and into my nightgown. Actually, I remember this only because I put the nightgown on backward the first time and had to take it off and put it on again. I don't remember washing my face or brushing my teeth, although I'm sure I did. I *do* remember the way my bare toes sank into the ivory broadloom as I walked toward my bed, as if I were wading through thick clumps of mud. I remember the heaviness in my thighs, as if my legs had been anchored to the floor. The queen-size bed that sat in the middle of the room seemed miles away. It took forever to reach it. A colossal effort was required for my arms to pull down the bulky white comforter. I remember watching it billow around me like a collapsing parachute as I climbed underneath the covers. I remember the pillow reaching up to catch my head before it fell.

I expected to fall asleep immediately. That's the way it always is in the movies. People drink too much, they get dizzy and disoriented, they pass out. Sometimes they get sick first. But I didn't get sick and I didn't pass out. I just lay there, my head spinning in the darkness, knowing I had to get up in a matter of hours, desperate for a sleep that stubbornly refused to come. I flipped from my left side to my right, tried lying on my back, and even my stomach, before I gave up and returned to my original position. I brought my knees to my chest, threw one leg atop the other, twisted my body into shapes that would have made a contortionist proud. Nothing worked. I thought of taking a sleeping pill and was almost half out of bed before I remembered it was a mistake to mix pills and alcohol. In any event, it was too late for sedatives. By the time they took effect, my alarm clock would be shaking me awake, and I'd spend most of the next day in a dreary fog, like the worst kind of rainy day.

I thought of reading, but I'd been struggling with the book on my night table for weeks and still hadn't made it past the fourth chapter. Besides, my brain was as tired as my eyes, and trying to digest anything at this hour would be an exercise in frustration and futility. No, I decided, I had no choice but to lie there in bed and wait patiently for sleep to come.

It didn't.

Half an hour later, I was still waiting. I took several long, deep breaths and improvised a half dozen yoga exercises I'd seen illustrated in a magazine, although I had no idea if I was doing them correctly. The hospital offered yoga classes, but I'd never quite gotten around to signing up. Just as I'd never quite gotten around to trying Pilates or transcendental meditation, or sending away for the AB-DOer I saw regularly advertised on TV. I made a silent vow to do all those things first thing in the morning, if only I could fall asleep right now.

No deal.

I thought of turning on the television across from my bed—undoubtedly there was a rerun of *Law & Order* on somewhere, but decided against it, choosing to replay Alison's visit instead. What on earth had possessed me to tell her the things I had, information I'd never shared with anyone before? Roger Stillman, for God's sake! Where had that come from? I hadn't even thought of him since I'd left Baltimore.

And what had she really told me?

That she'd lost her virginity at fifteen.

What else?

Not much, I realized. Alison may have opened memory's floodgates, but she'd remained resolutely outside them. No, I was the one who'd rushed eagerly inside, throwing caution and good sense to the wind. That was one of the more interesting things about Alison, I decided, as a low buzz settled behind my ears. She only *seemed* to be confiding in you. What she was really doing was getting *you* to confide in *her*.

That's what I was thinking when I finally fell asleep. I don't remember drifting off. I *do* remember dreaming. Nothing substantial or particularly meaningful. Silly little vignettes: Roger Stillman imitating James Bond in the backseat of his car; Josh Wylie's mother smiling at me from her hospital bed, asking me to put the bouquet of yellow and orange roses her son had brought with him from Miami into a vase; my mother warning me I hadn't set my alarm clock.

It was this realization that I hadn't, in fact, remembered to set my alarm that woke me up at two minutes past four in the morning, sent me stretching toward the night table at the side of my bed. My hands reached out in the semidarkness, my eyes opening only with the greatest reluctance as my fingers searched for the clock radio.

It was at that moment that I saw the tall figure at the foot of my bed.

At first I thought it must be some sort of apparition, a trick my wine-saturated brain was playing on my senses, perhaps a dream that had failed to disperse upon waking, a haunting mixture of moonlight and shadows. It was only when the figure moved that I understood it was real.

And I screamed.

The scream sliced through the darkness like a blade through flesh, scraping at the surrounding air, leaving it tattered and bleeding. That this insane, inhuman sound could emanate from my body scared me almost as much as the figure moving slowly toward me, and I screamed again.

"I'm so sorry," a voice was whimpering. "I'm so sorry."

I'm not sure exactly when I realized the stranger in my room was Alison, whether it was the sound of her voice or the glint of the small gold heart at her throat. She was holding her head, as if she'd been struck, and swaying from side to side, as if she were a tree being buffeted by the wind. "I'm so sorry," she kept repeating. "I'm so sorry."

"What are you doing here?" I finally managed to get out, swallowing another scream that was rising in my throat, and stretching toward the lamp at the side of my bed.

"No!" she cried. "Please don't turn it on."

I froze, not sure what to do next. "What are you doing here?"

"I'm so sorry. I didn't mean to wake you up."

"What are you doing here?" I repeated over the loud pounding of my heart.

"My head . . ." She started pulling at her hair as if trying to pull it out by the roots. "I'm having a migraine."

I climbed out of bed, took several tentative steps toward her. "A migraine?"

"I guess all that red wine must have triggered something—" She stopped, as if unable to continue.

I reached her side, put my arm around her, lowered her to the side of my bed. She was wearing a long, white cotton nightgown not unlike my own, and her hair hung loose and free around a face wet with tears. "How did you get in the house?" I asked.

"The door wasn't locked."

"That's impossible. I always lock it." Although I'd been pretty woozy, I reminded myself. It was possible I'd forgotten to lock the door, just as I'd forgotten to set the alarm clock.

"It was open. I knocked first. You didn't answer. That's when I tried the door. I was hoping I could find something in your medicine cabinet without waking you up. I'm so sorry."

I glanced toward the bathroom. "The strongest thing I have is extra-strength Tylenol."

Alison nodded, as if to say anything was better than nothing.

I left her sitting on the edge of my bed while I ran into the bathroom and ferreted through the mostly useless items on the shelves of the medicine cabinet until I found the small bottle of pills. I shook four into the palm of my hand, filled a glass full of water, and returned with them to my bedroom.

"Take these," I instructed. "I'll try to get you something stronger in the morning."

"I'll be dead by morning," she said, and tried to laugh. But the laugh detoured into a moan as she swallowed the pills and buried her head against my shoulder, trying to block out what little light there was in the room.

"That'll teach both of us," I heard myself say in my mother's voice as I stroked her arm, rocked her gently back and forth, like a baby. "You'll sleep here tonight."

Alison offered no resistance as I led her around the side of the bed, pulled the covers around her. "What about you?" she asked, her eyes closed, the question an obvious afterthought.

"I'll sleep in the other room," I said.

But already Alison had pulled the comforter up over her head, and the only signs I had that she was there were a few strands of strawberry-blond hair that curled over the top of my pillow like a question mark.

FOUR

Alison was still sleeping when I left the house the next morning.

I thought of waking her up, ushering her back to her own bed, but she looked so peaceful lying there, so vulnerable, her soft blush of strawberry-blond hair in marked contrast to her skin's still ghostly pallor, that I hated to disturb her. My experience with migraine sufferers was that, like most drunks, they needed twenty-four hours to sleep it off. I did the math, decided there was a good chance Alison would still be sleeping when I arrived back home at four o'clock that afternoon. What was the point in waking her?

Looking back, this was undoubtedly a mistake, although not my first mistake where Alison was concerned, and certainly not my last. No, it was only one of many errors in judgment I made about the girl who called herself Alison Simms. But hindsight is easy. Of course it was stupid to allow a virtual stranger to stay unattended in my house. Of course I was asking for trouble. All I can say in my defense is that it didn't feel that way at the time. At barely 6 A.M., with maybe a total of four hours of sleep, leaving Alison alone in the house that morning felt natural and right. What was there to worry about after all? That she'd abscond with my ancient nineteen-inch TV? That she'd commandeer a wheelbarrow to cart away my mother's collection of china head vases, perhaps hold a garage sale on my front lawn? That I'd come back to find the house and cottage burned to the ground?

Maybe I should have been more careful, more circumspect, less trusting.

But I wasn't.

Besides, what is it they say about letting sleeping dogs lie?

Anyway, I left Alison sleeping in my bed, like Goldilocks, I remember thinking, chuckling as I tiptoed down the stairs in my clunky white nurse's shoes, opening and closing the front door as silently as possible. My car, a five-year-old, black Nissan, was parked in the driveway beside the house. I cast a desultory glance down the empty street, hearing the faint hum of traffic several blocks away. The city was waking up, I thought, wishing I could trade my polyester white uniform for my white cotton nightgown and crawl back into bed. Luckily, I wasn't as tired as I'd feared I might be. In fact, I was feeling surprisingly well.

I backed the car onto the street, opening the windows to let in the cool morning air. November is a lovely time of year in South Florida. The temperature usually stays on the comfortable side of eighty; the oppressive humidity of the summer months is pretty much gone; the threat of extreme weather is over. Instead, the sky provides a continually shifting combination of sun and clouds, along with the occasional burst of welcome rain. And we get more than our fair share of absolutely flawless afternoons, days when the sun sits high in a borderless panorama of shiny Kodacolor blue. Today looked as if it might be that kind of day. Maybe when I got home, I'd see if Alison was feeling well enough to go for a walk on the beach. There's nothing like the ocean to heal the spirit and calm the troubled soul. Maybe it could work its magic on a migraine headache, I thought, glancing up at my bedroom window.

For a minute, I thought I saw the curtains move, and I hit the brake, inched my face closer to the glass of the car's front window. But on closer inspection, it appeared I'd been mistaken, that it was only the outside shadows of nearby trees that were dancing against my bedroom window, creating the illusion of movement from inside the house. I sat watching the window for several seconds, listening to the whispering of the palm fronds in the breeze. The curtains at my bedroom window hung undisturbed.

My foot transferred from brake to gas pedal, and I proceeded slowly for several blocks along Seventh Avenue until I reached Atlantic, where I turned left. The normally congested main thoroughfare of Delray is largely empty at this hour of the morning, one of the few perks of having to be at work so early, and I had an unencumbered view of the many smart shops, galleries, and restaurants that had redefined the city in recent years. To the surprise of many, myself included, Delray had become something of a "hot spot," a destination as opposed to a drive-through. I loved the unexpected changes, the aura of excitement, even if I was rarely part of it. Alison, I knew instinctively, would love it here.

I passed the tennis center on the north side of Atlantic, where every spring they hold the Citrix Open, past the Old School Square on the northwest corner of Atlantic and Swinton, continued on past the South County Courthouse and the Delray Beach Fire Station on my left. I took the underpass at I-95 to Jog Road, then headed south. Five minutes later I was at the hospital.

Mission Care is a small, private health facility housed in a five-story building, painted bubblegum pink, that specializes in chronic care. The majority of patients are elderly and in considerable distress, and as a result, they're often angry and upset. Who can blame them? They know they aren't going to get better, that they're never going home, that this is, in fact, their final resting place. Some have been here for years, lying in their narrow beds, blank eyes staring at blank ceilings, waiting for the nurse to bathe them or adjust their position, longing for visitors who rarely come, silently praying for death while stubbornly clinging to life.

It must be so depressing, people are always saying to me, to be constantly surrounded by the sick and the dying. And sometimes, I admit, it is. It's never easy to watch people suffer, to comfort a young woman stricken by MS in the prime of her life, to tend to a comatose child who will never wake up, to try calming an old man with Alzheimer's as he shouts obscenities at the son he no longer remembers.

And yet, some moments make it all worthwhile. Moments when the most banal act of kindness is rewarded by a smile so blinding it brings tears to your eyes, or by a whispered thank-you so sincere it makes you go weak at the knees. This is why I became a nurse, I understand in moments like these, and if that makes me a hopeless romantic or a silly sentimentalist, so be it.

Probably it is this quality that makes me such an easy target. I suffer from Anne Frank's delusion that people are basically good at heart.

I parked my car in the staff parking lot at the front of the hospital and made my way through the lobby, past the gift shop and pharmacy that wouldn't be open for another few hours, to the coffee shop that was already busy. I waited in line for a cup of tasteless black coffee and a fat-free, cranberry-studded muffin. I thought of Alison, how much she loved cranberries. I had a recipe at the back of one of my drawers for banana-cranberry muffins. I decided to make a batch when I got home.

The administration offices were closed till nine, and I made a mental note to stop by later to inquire about Alison's friend, Rita Bishop. Even though Alison had told me not to bother, I thought it might be worth a try. Rita might have left a forwarding address. One of the secretaries might know where she'd gone.

I'd already finished my coffee and was halfway through my muffin when the doors of the excruciatingly slow-moving elevator finally opened onto the fourth floor. The nurses' station was already buzzing. "What's up?" I asked Margot King, a heavyset woman with copper-orange hair and blue contact lenses. Margot had been a nurse at Mission Care for more than ten years, and during that decade the color of her eyes had changed almost as often as the color of her hair. The only constant was the color of her uniform, which was a crisp Alpine white, and the color of her skin, which was a wondrous ebony black.

"Rape victim," Margot said, her voice a whisper.

"A rape victim? Why'd they bring her here?"

"The rape was three months ago. Guy beat her with a baseball bat, left her for dead. She's been in a coma ever since. Doesn't look like she's going home anytime soon. Her family decided to bring her here when Delray Medical Center needed the bed."

"How old?" I asked, bracing myself.

"Nineteen."

I sighed, my shoulders collapsing, as if someone had jumped on them from a great height. "Any more pleasant surprises?"

"Same old, same old. Mrs. Wylie's been asking for you."

"Already?"

"Since five o'clock. 'Where's my Terry? Where's my Terry?'" Margot repeated in Myra Wylie's frail voice.

"I'll look in on her." I started down the hall, stopped. "Is Caroline here yet?"

"Not till eleven."

"She gets migraines, doesn't she?"

"Oh, yeah. She suffers real bad from those damn things."

"When she gets in, will you tell her I need to see her?"

"Problems?"

"A friend," I said, continuing down the peach-colored hall toward Myra Wylie's room.

I slowly pushed open the door and peeked my head through, in case the frail, eighty-seven-year-old woman fighting both chronic leukemia and congenital heart disease might have drifted back to sleep.

"Terry!" Myra Wylie's voice wafted up from the center of her hospital bed, quivering into the air like smoke from a cigarette. "There's my Terry."

I approached the bed, patted the bony hand beneath the sterile white sheets, smiled at the graying face with the watery blue eyes. "How are you today, Myra?"

"Wonderful," she said, the same thing she said every time I asked, and I laughed. She laughed too, although the sound was weak and segued quickly into a cough.

Still, in those few seconds, I saw traces of the beautiful, vibrant woman Myra Wylie had been before her body began its slow, insidious betrayal. I could also make out the face of her son Josh in the sculpted lines of her cheekbones, the soft bow of her lips. Josh Wylie would be a very handsome old man, I couldn't help but think as I pulled up a chair and sat down beside his mother. "I understand you've been asking for me."

"I was thinking maybe we could do something different with my hair next time we wash it."

I smoothed the fine gray hair away from her face with my fingers. "What style do you think you'd like?"

"I don't know. Something more with it."

"With it?"

"Maybe a bob."

"A bob?" I fluffed out the fragile wisps of hair that framed Myra's face. Her skin was sinking, the heavy lines around her eyes and mouth becoming folds, caving in around her. Slowly, the living tissue was morphing into a death mask. How much longer did she have? "A bob," I repeated. "Sure. Why not?"

Myra smiled. "That cute little nurse with all the freckles was in last night. The young one, what's her name?"

"Sally?"

"Yes, Sally. She brought me my medicine and we got to

talking, and she asked me how old I was. You should have seen the look on her face when I told her I'm seventy-seven."

I searched Myra's eyes for signs she was teasing, saw none. "Myra," I told her gently. "You're not seventy-seven."

"I'm not?"

"You're *eighty*-seven."

"Eighty-seven?" There was a long pause as Myra's trembling hand reached for her heart. "That's a shock!"

I laughed, stroked her shoulder.

"Are you sure?"

"That's what it says on your chart. But we can check with your son next time he visits."

"I think that's a good idea." Myra's eyes fluttered to a close, her voice growing faint. "Because I think there has to be some mistake."

"We'll ask Josh on Friday." I eased out of my chair and walked to the door. When I turned back to check on her, she was sound asleep.

The rest of the morning was uneventful. I tended to patients, fed them their breakfast and lunch, changed soiled sheets, helped those who could still walk to the bathroom. I looked in on Sheena O'Connor, the nineteen-year-old rape victim who'd been transferred from Delray Medical Center, filling the room with idle chatter as I surveyed the scars and bruises that made a mockery of her once innocent face, but if she heard me, she gave no sign.

Normally, I eat lunch in the hospital cafeteria—the food is surprisingly good and you can't beat the price—but today I was anxious to check on Alison. I thought of phoning, but I didn't want to wake her in case she was still sleeping, and besides, I didn't think she'd answer my phone. So armed with two Imitrex tablets I'd bought from Caroline—"I'd give them to you, but they're so damned expensive!"—and the names of several doctors in the area I thought Alison should contact, I used my lunch hour to drive home and see how she was doing.

Pulling into my driveway, I saw a young man with a baseball cap pulled low on his forehead lurking behind a corner tree, in almost the same spot where I'd seen the man yesterday, but by the time I parked my car and came back to look, he was gone. I looked down the street in time to see him disappear around the corner and thought momentarily of going after him. Luckily I was distracted by the sound of barking dogs, and I turned back toward my house. Bettye McCoy was standing beside a neighbor's prized rosebush, pretending not to notice that one of her dogs was peeing all over it. I thought of asking her if she'd noticed any suspicious strangers in the area, but decided against it. Bettye McCoy had barely acknowledged my existence ever since I'd chased one of her precious Bichons out of my yard with a broomstick.

I slipped my shoes off at the front door, silently cursing the slight creaking noise the door made as I closed it, determining to oil it when I got home at the end of my shift. The house was eerily quiet except for the gentle hum of the air conditioner. A quick look around told me everything was in its correct place. Nothing had been disturbed.

I tiptoed up the stairs to my bedroom, coughed quietly so as not to scare Alison if she was awake, then opened the door.

The curtains were still pulled, so it took me a few seconds to determine that the room was empty and the bed neatly made. Goldilocks was no longer sleeping in my bed. "Alison?" I called out, checking the bathroom and the second bedroom before heading back downstairs. "Alison?" She was gone.

"Alison?" I called out again at the door to her cottage, knocking gently. No one answered. I tried peering in the windows, but I saw nothing. Nor could I hear anyone moving around inside. Was it possible Alison had felt well enough to go out? Or was she lying on her bathroom floor, her head pressed against the cold tiles for relief, too sick and weak to respond to my knock? Despite common sense telling me I was overreacting, I returned to the front door and knocked more forcefully. "Alison," I called loudly. "Alison, it's Terry. Are you all right?"

I waited only thirty more seconds before letting myself in. "Alison?" I called again once inside.

I knew the cottage was empty the minute I crossed the threshold, but still I persisted, repeatedly calling out Alison's name as I inched toward the bedroom. The clothes she'd worn last night lay in a careless diagonal across the bedroom floor, discarded and abandoned where they fell. The bed was unmade and redolent with her scent, a potent mix of strawberries and baby powder still clinging to the rumpled sheets and crumpled pillows, but Alison herself was nowhere to be seen. I'm embarrassed to say I actually checked underneath the bed. Did I think the dreaded bogeyman had surfaced, snatched Alison while she lay sleeping? I don't know what I thought. Nor do I know what possessed me to check the small, walk-in closet. Did I think she was hiding inside? Truth to tell, I don't know what I was thinking. Probably I wasn't thinking at all.

Alison had little in the way of clothes. A few dresses, including the blue sundress she'd worn at our first meeting. Several pairs of jeans. A white blouse. A black leather jacket. Perhaps half a dozen T-shirts were stacked in one corner of the long, built-in shelf, some lacy underwear crammed into the other. Well-worn, black-and-white sneakers sat beside a pair of obviously new, silver sling-back heels. I lifted one shoe into my hand, wondering how anyone managed to walk in those damn things. I hadn't worn a heel that high in—well, I'd *never* worn a heel that high, I realized, glancing toward my stockinged feet, reaching down before I was even aware of what I was doing and slipping on first one shoe, then the other.

It was at that moment—standing there in Alison's sexy shoes—that I heard movement in the next room and felt the vibration of footsteps as they drew near. I froze, not sure what to do. It was one thing to tell Alison that I'd been so concerned about her health I'd felt entitled to invade her privacy, but how was I going to explain being discovered in her closet, teetering precariously in her new, silver, sling-back, high-heeled shoes?

For one insane second, I actually thought of clicking those heels together and reciting, "There's no place like home; there's no place like home," in hopes that, like Dorothy in *The Wizard of Oz*, I would be transported miraculously back to my own living room. Or Kansas, for that matter. Anywhere but here, I thought, feeling Alison's presence in the doorway. "I'm so sorry," I said, waiting for her to appear. "Please forgive me."

Except no one was there. There was only me and my overactive imagination. Not to mention my guilt for being where I didn't belong. I stood in the closet, wobbling in those outrageous three-inch heels, waiting for my heartbeat to return to normal. Some criminal I'd make, I thought, kicking off the shoes and returning them to their place beside the tired-looking sneakers.

At that point, I should have gotten the hell out of there. Alison was obviously feeling better. There was no need to be concerned. Certainly no reason for me to be standing in the middle of what was now, after all, her place. And I was on my way out—I really was—when I saw it.

Her journal.

It was lying open on the top of the white wicker dresser, as if waiting to be read, almost as if Alison had left it that way deliberately, as if she'd been expecting me to drop by. I tried not to notice it, tried to walk by it without stopping to look, without *stooping* to look, I should probably say, but the damn thing drew me like a magnet. Almost against my will, I found my eyes dipping through the dramatic swirls and loops of Alison's elaborate scrawl, as if on some wild, visual roller-coaster ride.

Sunday, November 4: Well, I did it. I'm actually here.

I stopped, slammed the journal shut, then realized it had been open when I found it and quickly rifled through the pages looking for the last entry.

Thursday, October 11: Lance says I'm crazy. He says to remember what happened last time.

Friday, October 26: I'm getting nervous. Maybe this isn't such a good idea after all.

Sunday, October 28: Lance keeps warning me against getting too attached. Maybe he's right. Maybe this whole plan is just too crazy.

Back to the last entry without allowing my eyes to settle, the words to sink in.

Sunday, November 4: Well, I did it. I'm actually here. I'm living in the cottage behind her house, and she's even invited me over for dinner. She seems nice, if not exactly what I was expecting.

What did that mean?

What had she been expecting?

We'd spoken for less than a minute on the phone, scarcely enough time to form any impressions at all.

Lance says I'm crazy. He says to remember what happened last time.

Were these entries somehow related?

"I'm doing it again," I said out loud. Letting my imagination get the better of me. The snatches I'd read in Alison's journal could mean anything. Or nothing. The discomfort I was feeling had more to do with my own guilt for snooping through Alison's personal belongings than it did with her innocent scribblings. I pulled away from the diary as if it were a hissing snake.

And I did nothing. Not then, not later, not even after I returned home at the end of my shift and stopped by to see how Alison was doing, and she told me that, aside from a brief walk around the block, she'd spent pretty much the whole day in bed.

I left her with the Imitrex, a list of doctors in the area, and some homemade chicken soup, deciding to be pleasant, but to keep my distance—*not allow myself to get too attached,* as the mysterious Lance would undoubtedly advise—and somehow I managed to convince myself that as long as Alison paid her rent on time and followed my rules, everything would be fine.

FIVE

By Friday, I had all but forgotten the diary. One of the other nurses was sick with a nasty flu, so I'd volunteered to take her shift as well as my own on both Wednesday and Thursday, and as a result, I didn't see Alison at all. I *did* receive a lovely note from her, thanking me for dinner and apologizing profusely for being such a nuisance. She assured me she was feeling much better and suggested going to a movie on the weekend, if I had any free time. I didn't respond, deciding to plead exhaustion if and when we actually connected. If I turned down enough such overtures, I reasoned, Alison would get the message, and our relationship would revert to what it should have been in the first place, landlord and tenant. I'd been too hasty in allowing Alison into my life.

"What are you thinking about, dear?" the voice beside me asked with marked concern.

"Hmm? What? Sorry," I said, returning to the present, casting unwanted memories aside, returning my full attention to the withered old woman connected to life by a series of tubes that force-fed nutrients into her collapsing veins.

Myra Wylie's eyes radiated quiet curiosity. "You were a million miles away."

"Sorry. Did I hurt you?" My hands dropped from the IV I'd been adjusting.

"No, dear. You couldn't hurt me if you tried. Stop apologizing. Is everything all right?"

"Everything's fine." I secured the blanket at her toes. "You're doing remarkably well."

"I meant with you. Is everything all right with you?"

"Everything's fine," I repeated, as if trying to reassure myself as well.

"You can talk to me, you know. If you have a problem."

I smiled gratefully. "I appreciate that."

"I mean it."

"I know you do."

"You look like you have very deep thoughts," Myra Wylie remarked, and I laughed out loud. "Don't laugh. Josh thinks so too."

I felt my pulse quicken. "Your son thinks I have deep thoughts?"

"That's what he said last time he was here."

I felt almost ridiculously flattered, like a teenage girl who's just found out the silly boy she has a crush on feels the same way about her. I checked my watch, noted the trembling in my fingers. "Well, it's almost noon. He should be here any minute."

"He thinks you're very nice."

Was I mistaken, or was there a playful glint in Myra's watery eyes? "Oh, he does, does he?"

"Josh deserves someone nice," Myra was saying, almost to herself. "He's divorced, you know. I've told you about that, haven't I?"

I nodded, eager for more details, but careful to look only mildly curious.

"She left him for her aerobics instructor. Can you imagine? Stupid woman." Myra Wylie's frail shoulders stiffened with righteous indignation. "Destroys the family. Breaks my son's heart. And for what? So she can march off into the sunset with some muscle-bound bodybuilder ten years her junior, who dumps her less than six months later—what did she expect?—and of course, *now* she sees the error of her ways, *now* she wants him back. But Josh is too smart for that, thank God. He'll never let that woman back into his life." Myra's voice began breaking up, like a bad radio signal, then dissolved into a worrisome combination of coughs and wheezes.

"Take deep breaths," I cautioned, watching Myra's breathing gradually return to normal. "That's better. You shouldn't let yourself get so upset. It's not worth it. It's all over now. They're divorced."

"He will never let that woman back into his life."

"Never," I repeated.

"He deserves someone nice."

"Absolutely."

"Someone like you," Myra said. Then: "You like children, don't you?"

"I love children." I followed her eyes to the two silver-framed pictures of her smiling grandchildren that sat on the movable nightstand beside her bed.

"Of course they're older now than when these pictures were taken. Jillian is fifteen, and Trevor is almost twelve."

"I know. We've met," I reminded her. "They're lovely children."

"They went through hell after Jan left."

"I'm sure it wasn't easy." It's never easy to lose your mother, I remember thinking. No matter how old you are, no matter what the circumstances. A mother is a mother is a mother, I thought, and almost laughed. So much for the depth of my thoughts. "I should get going. Is there anything I can do for you before your son gets here?"

"Comb my hair a little, if you don't mind?"

"It will be my pleasure." I ran a gentle comb across Myra's scalp, watching the delicate strands of gray hair immediately fall back into place, as if untouched. "You were right about the bob. It's very becoming."

"You think so?" A smile, eager as a child's, spread across her face.

"Now all the nurses are asking me to cut their hair. They say I missed my calling."

"I don't think you miss a thing." Myra reached out to squeeze my hand.

"I'll be back to say hello to your son," I said with a wink.

"Terry?" she called as I was about to leave the room. I swiveled around as she brought her fingers to her lips. "Maybe a little lipstick?"

I started back toward the bed.

"No. Not me," she said quickly. "You."

I laughed, shaking my head as I returned to the door. I was still laughing as I stepped into the hall and saw Alison standing in front of the nurses' station.

"Terry!" Alison rushed forward to greet me, arms extended, face flushed with pride. She was wearing her blue sundress and her hair fell in lush tendrils around her shoulders. Erica Hollander's necklace hung around her neck, the tiny gold heart resting at her collarbone, as if it had been there all her life.

"Alison! What are you doing here?" I looked toward Margot and Caroline, both of whom were busy behind the long, curving desk of the nurses' station, Margot on the phone, Caroline entering notes in a patient's chart. They glanced in our direction, pretending not to be paying attention.

"I did it! I did it!" Alison was jumping up and down, like a small child.

I brought my finger to my lips in a silent signal for her to settle down and lower her voice. "Did what?"

"I got a job," she squealed, unable to contain herself. "At the Lorelli Gallery. On Atlantic Avenue. Four days a week, some Saturdays, some evenings. Shift work," she said, beaming. "Like you."

"That's great," I heard myself say, her enthusiasm catchy despite my effort to remain detached. "What exactly will you be doing?"

"Selling mostly. Of course, I don't know much about art, but Fern said she'd teach me everything I need to know. Fern's my boss. Fern Lorelli. She seems very nice. Do you know her?"

I started to shake my head, but Alison had already moved on.

"I told her I didn't know much about art, because I figured I should be honest, right? I didn't want her to give me the job under false pretenses. I mean, she'd find out soon enough anyway, right? But she said not to worry, she'd handle the art, that I should stick mostly to the jewelry and gift items they sell, although if I do manage to sell one of the paintings, I'd get a commission. Five percent. Isn't that great?"

"It's great," I agreed.

"Some of those paintings sell for thousands of dollars, so that'd be fantastic, if I sold one of them. But mostly I'll be behind the cash register. Me and this other girl who works there. Denise Nickson, I think her name is. She's Fern's niece. And what else? Oh—I get twelve dollars an hour, and I start on Monday. Isn't that great?"

"It's great," I said again.

"I couldn't wait to tell you, so I came right over."

"Congratulations."

"Can I take you to lunch?"

"Lunch?"

"To celebrate. My treat."

I shifted uneasily from one foot to the other. Technically, I was on my lunch break right now, and my stomach had been making hungry noises for the past hour. "I can't. Things are so busy here today. . . ."

"Dinner, then."

"I can't. I'm working a double shift."

"Tomorrow night," she persisted. "That's even better. It's a Saturday, so you can sleep in the next morning. You're not busy tomorrow night, are you?"

"No," I said, realizing that Alison wouldn't settle for less than a definite date, even if she had to go through every day from now till Christmas. "But really, it isn't necessary for you to take me out."

"Of course it is," Alison insisted. "Besides, I want to. To thank you for all you've done for me."

"I haven't done anything."

"Are you kidding? You gave me the best place in the whole wide world to live, you cooked me dinner, you made me feel welcome. You even took care of me when I got sick. I owe you big time, Terry Painter."

"You don't owe me anything but the rent," I said, struggling to keep my distance, feeling myself sway reluctantly back into her orbit, falling under her spell. *You gave me the best place in the whole wide world to live.* Who says things like that? How could you not be charmed?

Besides, what was I so worried about? What could I possibly have to fear, especially from someone like Alison? Even assuming the worst, that she was some sort of clever con artist, what could she possibly be after? I had little in the way of material goods—my small house, its tiny adjacent cottage, negligible savings, my mother's silly collection of ladies' head vases. So what? Small potatoes, all of it. This was Florida, for heaven's sake. Forty minutes north were the oceanside mansions of Palm Beach and Hobe Sound; forty minutes south were the palatial homes of Miami's infamous South Beach. Florida was synonymous with money, with wealthy old men just waiting to be taken advantage of by beautiful young girls. Hell, it's what was keeping them alive. It didn't make sense that Alison would waste her time with me.

I realize now that there are times when our brains will simply not allow us to accept the evidence our own eyes present, that the desire for self-delusion outweighs the instinct for self-preservation, that no matter how old we are or how wise we think we've become, we are never really convinced of our own mortality. Besides, since when do things have to make sense?

"So, are we on?" Alison's big, loopy grin widened with expectation.

"We're on," I heard myself reply.

"Great." She spun around in a full circle, the skirt of her sundress swirling around her knees. "Anywhere in particular you'd like to go?"

I shook my head. "Surprise me."

She rubbed the gold heart at her throat. "I love surprises."

As if on cue, the fire alarm sounded. It turned out to be a false alarm, but in the few minutes it took to make sure everything was okay, chaos reigned. When I returned to the nurses' station after reassuring several panicky patients that the hospital was not about to become a blazing inferno, Alison was gone.

"Everybody okay?" Margot asked.

"Mr. Austin said, fire or no fire, he wasn't going anywhere without his teeth." I laughed, picturing the feisty old man in room 411.

"Pretty girl you were talking to earlier," Margot remarked.

"My new tenant."

"Really? Well, I hope you have better luck this time around."

The next hour passed in relative calm. There were no more fire alarms, no unexpected visitors. After a brief lunch in the cafeteria, I kept busy checking pulses, delivering pain medication, helping patients to and from the bathroom, comforting them as they railed against their fate. At some point I found myself at the door to Sheena O'Connor's room. I hesitated briefly, then pushed the door open and stepped inside.

The teenager lay in the middle of her bed, staring at the ceiling with eyes wide with terror. Was she seeing the man who'd raped and beaten her senseless, then left her for dead? I approached the bed, reached out, and touched her hand, but if she felt my touch at all, she gave no sign. "It's okay," I whispered. "You're safe now."

I pulled up a chair, sat down beside her, the words to an old Irish lullaby suddenly dancing inside my head. It took a few seconds for me to find the tune, and next thing I knew I was singing—softly, gently, as one sings to a newborn baby—*"Too-ra-loo-ra-loo-ra . . . too-ra-loo-ra-lie . . ."*

I don't know what made me think of that particular song. I couldn't remember my mother ever singing it to me. Maybe it was the name O'Connor. Maybe I thought Sheena's mother might have sung it to her, that the song might stir something deep in the girl's subconscious, remind her of a time when she felt secure and protected, a time when no harm could befall her.

"Too-ra-loo-ra-loo-ra," I sang, my voice gaining strength with each repetition of the simple sounds. *"Too-ra-loo-ra-lie . . ."*

Sheena remained motionless.

"Too-ra-loo-ra-loo-ra . . . that's an Irish lullaby."

"And it's a very lovely one," a man's voice said from the doorway.

I recognized the voice without having to turn around. I swallowed the sounds in my throat and willed my face not to betray me as I turned toward the doorway. Josh Wylie, tall and almost carelessly handsome, with salt-and-pepper hair and his mother's blue eyes, stood watching me. "How long have you been standing there?"

"Long enough to realize you have a beautiful voice."

I gripped the railing at Sheena's bedside to steady myself as I rose to my feet. "Thank you." I walked across the room, my heart wobbling, although my feet were surprisingly steady. Josh Wylie backed into the hallway as I approached, and I shut the door to Sheena's room behind me.

"What's the matter with her?" Josh asked as we started down the corridor.

I related the gruesome details of the assault. "She's in a coma. Her eyes are open, but she doesn't see anything."

"Will she be that way forever?"

"Nobody knows."

"What a shame." Josh shook his head sadly. "So, how's my mother doing?" He smiled, a warm upturn of his lips that underlined the sparkle in his eyes. "I understand you cut her hair."

"Just a few snips here and there. She seems to like it."

"She's crazy about it. She's crazy about *you*," Josh emphasized. "Thinks you're the greatest thing since sliced bread."

"The feeling's mutual."

"Thinks I should take you out to lunch the next time I visit."

"What?"

"Lunch, next Friday. If you're free. If you're hungry . . ."

"I'm always hungry," I said, grateful when he laughed. "Lunch next Friday sounds great." I thought of Alison. Two surprising invitations in one day.

"Okay, then, next Friday it is." We reached the nurses' station. "Till then, I leave my mother in your capable and creative hands."

"Drive carefully," I called as Josh stepped inside the waiting elevator.

"And no uniform. This isn't a business lunch." He waved as the elevator door drew slowly closed.

This isn't a business lunch, I repeated silently, mentally raiding my closet, trying to decide what to wear, wondering whether to splurge on a new outfit. It was only then that I became aware of a slight commotion behind me. "Problems?" I asked, spinning around on my heels, seeing Margot and Caroline making exaggerated sweeps of the desk with their hands and eyes.

"Caroline's wallet is missing from her purse," Margot said.

I came around to the inside of the nurses' station, began my own head sweep. "You're sure? It's not in a pocket somewhere?"

"I've looked everywhere," Caroline moaned, brushing chin-length, brown hair away from her long face, emptying the contents of her purse onto the floor. At the best of times, Caroline looked vaguely depressed. Now she looked positively distraught.

"Maybe you left it in another purse. I did that once," I offered gamely, although I'd never done any such thing.

"No, I had it with me this morning. I know, because I bought a cup of coffee and a Danish downstairs."

"Maybe you left it on the counter after you paid."

Caroline shook her head. "I'm sure I put it back in my purse." She looked up and down the corridor, tears filling her dejected brown eyes. "Damn it. I had over a hundred dollars in there."

I thought of Alison. She'd been here when the fire alarm had sounded and the nursing station had been left temporarily unattended. And she'd been gone by the time everything had settled down. Was it possible she'd helped herself to Caroline's wallet?

Why would I think that?

Surely it was much more logical to assume that Caroline had left her wallet in the cafeteria. "I think you should call downstairs," I advised, opening and closing drawers, checking each small compartment behind the desk, then peeking into my own purse to make sure nothing was missing.

"I'll call the cafeteria," Caroline agreed grudgingly, "but I know it's not there. Somebody took it. Somebody took it."

SIX

Saturday night, the phone rang just as I was stepping out of the shower. I wrapped one large white towel around my body, threw another one across my shoulders, and padded across my bedroom floor toward the phone, wondering if Alison was calling to cancel our dinner. I lifted the phone to my ear and pushed my wet hair away from my cheek. "Hello?"

"I'd like to speak to Erica Hollander," the male voice announced without further preamble.

It took half a second for the name to register on my brain. "Erica Hollander is no longer my tenant," I said coolly, my eyes following several wayward trickles of water as they ran down my legs to the ivory carpet. Anxiety simultaneously trickled through my insides.

"Do you know where I can reach her?" The voice carried traces of a soft Southern twang. I didn't think I'd heard it before.

"I'm afraid I have no idea where she is."

"When did she leave?"

I thought back to the last time I'd seen Erica. "It was the end of August."

"She didn't leave a forwarding address?"

"She didn't leave a thing, and that includes the two months' rent she owed me. Who's calling?"

The answer to my question was a resounding click in my ear.

I dropped the receiver into its carriage, then plopped down on my bed, taking a series of long, deep breaths, trying to push unpleasant memories of Erica Hollander out of my head. But she was as stubborn in her absence as she'd been in her presence, and she refused to be so easily dismissed.

Erica Hollander was young, like Alison, and like Alison, willowy and tall, though not quite as tall, not quite as willowy. Her hair was a luxurious dark brown and hung straight to her shoulders, and she was continually tossing it from side to side, the way you see them do in those annoying television commercials that equate a good shampoo with a good orgasm. But her face, while pretty enough in a certain light, hovered perilously close to plain. Only her nose, a nose that was long and thin and veered suddenly to the left, gave her any character at all. It was her one distinguishing feature. Of course, she hated it. "I'm saving up to have it done," she'd told me on more than one occasion.

"Your nose is beautiful," I'd assured her, ever the mother hen.

"It's awful. I'm saving up to have it done."

I'd listened to her whine about her nose; I'd listened to her brag about her boyfriend—"Charlie's so handsome, Charlie's so smart"—who was spending a year working in Tokyo; I'd listened when she stopped bragging and started whining—"Charlie didn't call this week, Charlie better watch his step"—and I'd reserved judgment when she got involved with some guy she'd met at Elwood's, a well-known biker hangout on Atlantic Avenue. I'd even lent her money to buy a used portable computer. All because I thought we were friends. It never occurred to me that she'd skip out in the middle of the night, still owing me for the computer, not to mention several months in back rent.

Smart, handsome Charlie in Tokyo couldn't accept that his girlfriend had dumped him as unceremoniously as she'd dumped me and had plagued me with increasingly unpleasant phone calls from Japan, demanding to know her whereabouts. He'd even notified the police, who basically corroborated my story, but even that wasn't enough to satisfy him. He'd continued harassing me long-distance until I'd threatened to call his employer. And then suddenly, the phone calls stopped.

Until tonight.

I shook my head, amazed that though Erica Hollander had been gone for almost three months, she was still causing me grief. She'd been my first tenant and, I'd vowed after she'd taken off, my last.

What had happened to change my mind?

Truth be told, I missed having someone around. I don't have a lot of friends. There are my co-workers, women like Margot and Caroline, but we rarely socialize away from the hospital. Caroline has a demanding husband, and Margot has four kids to look after. And I've always been a little reserved. This shyness, coupled with my tendency to throw myself into my work, has made it hard for me to meet new people. Plus, my mother was sick for so long before she died, and between caring for my patients at the hospital and caring for her at home, well, there are only so many hours in a day.

Besides, something insidious happens to women in our society when they turn forty, especially if they're not married. We get lost in a heavy, free-floating haze. It becomes difficult to see us. People know we're there; it's just that we've become a little fuzzy, so blurred around the edges we've begun blending into the surrounding scenery. It's not that we're invisible exactly—people actually step around us to avoid confronting us—but the truth is we are no longer *seen*. And if you aren't seen, you aren't heard.

That's what happens to women over forty.

We lose our voice.

Maybe that's why we seem so angry. Maybe it's not hormones after all. Maybe we just want someone to pay attention.

Anyway, I started thinking about how nice it had been when Erica Hollander had first moved in, how much fun it had been having someone around, even if we didn't see each other all that much. I don't know. Somehow, just the fact that someone was sharing my space had made me feel less alone. So I decided to try it again. What is it they say about second marriages? That they're a triumph of hope over experience?

At any rate, I was determined not to make the same mistakes the second time around. That's why I'd decided against advertising for a tenant in the newspaper, choosing instead to post a number of discreet notices around the hospital. I reasoned that, this way, I was more likely to attract someone older, more responsible. Maybe a professional, perhaps even a woman like myself.

Instead I got Alison.

The phone rang, bringing me back to the present. I became aware of the air conditioner blowing against the back of my neck, like a lover's cool breath. I shuddered with the chill.

"Hi, it's me," Alison chirped as I lifted the receiver to my ear. "Didn't you hear me knock?"

The towel at my breast came loose and fell to the floor as I rose to my feet. "What? No. Where are you?"

"At your kitchen door. I'm on my cell. Is everything all right?"

"Fine. I'm just running a little late. Can I pick you up in ten minutes?"

"No problem."

Securing my towel around me, I walked to my bedroom window and watched from behind the white lace curtain as Alison ambled back toward the cottage. She was wearing a slinky, navy dress I didn't remember seeing in her closet, and her silver sling-back shoes, which she had no trouble walking in at all. I watched as she tucked her cell phone inside the silver purse dangling from her shoulder, only to withdraw it again almost immediately, several loose bills escaping their cramped confines and wafting toward the ground. Alison immediately scooped up the money and stuffed it back inside her small silver bag. I quickly recalled the handful of $100 bills Alison had given me for first and last month's rent, then found myself thinking about the $100 that had gone missing from Caroline's purse. Was it possible Alison had taken it?

"That's ridiculous," I said out loud, watching Alison punch a series of numbers into her cell phone. Alison had no need to steal money from strangers. I watched her whisper something into the receiver, then laugh. Suddenly she spun around, almost as if she'd known I was watching her. I flattened myself against the wall and didn't move again until I heard the cottage door open and close.

Fifteen minutes later, I was at her door, wearing a calf-length, pale yellow, sleeveless dress with a pronounced décolletage that I'd bought a year ago, but had never had the nerve to wear. "Sorry I took so long. I couldn't get my hair to sit right."

"You look fabulous." Alison regarded me with the practiced eye of women who are used to looking in mirrors. "You just need a little trim," she announced after a pause. "I could do it for you. Don't forget I worked for a few months in a hairdressing salon."

"You were a receptionist," I reminded her.

She laughed. "Yeah, but I watched and I learned, and I'm really pretty good. You want me to give it a try after dinner?"

I thought of the improvised bob I'd given Myra Wylie earlier in the week. Was I as brave as she was? "Where are you taking me?"

"It's this new place right across from the Lorelli Gallery. I already called them and said we'd be a bit late."

The restaurant was called Barrington's, and like many restaurants in South Florida, it was much bigger on the inside than it appeared from the street. The main room was decorated like a French bistro, lots of Tiffany lamps and leaded-glass windows, along with Toulouse-Lautrec posters of dancers from the Moulin Rouge suspended from pale yellow walls that were an exact—and unfortunate—match with my dress. Were it not for my ample cleavage, I might have vanished altogether.

The waiter brought over a basket of bread, the wine list, and two large menus, before reciting by heart the list of the night's specials. His eyes moved back and forth between Alison's face and my chest. Together, I remember thinking, we could rule the world.

"Dolphin!" Alison wailed in horror at one of the waiter's suggestions.

"Not Flipper," I explained quickly. "This dolphin's a fish, not a mammal. It's sometimes called mahi mahi."

"I like the sound of that much better."

"How's the salmon?" I asked.

"Tasty," the waiter said, looking at Alison. "But kind of boring," he said, looking at me.

"What about the swordfish?" Alison asked.

"Wonderful," the waiter enthused. "They grill it in a light Dijon mustard sauce. And it comes with sautéed vegetables and little red potatoes."

"Sounds great. I'll have that."

"I'll have the salmon," I offered, risking the young man's scorn, daring to be dull.

"Some wine?"

Alison motioned to me with her hand, as if giving me the floor. "Some wine?" she repeated.

"I think I'll skip the wine tonight."

"You can't skip the wine. This is a celebration. We have to have wine."

"Remember what happened last time," I cautioned.

She looked confused, as if she'd forgotten all about her recent migraine. "We'll have white wine, not red," she pronounced upon reflection. "That should be all right."

The waiter pointed out the choice of wines, and Alison followed his recommendation. Something from Chile, I believe. It was good, and it was cold, and it quickly gave me a pleasant buzz. Service was slow, and I'd already finished my glass by the time the food arrived. Alison poured me another, and I didn't object, although I noticed she'd only taken a few sips of her own drink. "Ooh, this is yummy delicious," she enthused, biting into the swordfish. "How's yours?"

"Yummy." I laughed at the sound.

"So, did you see your friend this week?" Alison asked suddenly.

"My friend?"

"Josh Wylie." Alison stole a look around the crowded restaurant, as if he might be there, as if she might recognize him if he were.

The salmon stuck in my throat. "How do you know about Josh Wylie?"

Alison swallowed one forkful of swordfish, then another. "You told me about him."

"I did?"

"Dinner at your house. I asked if you were interested in anyone, and you said there was this guy"—she lowered her voice, her eyes doing another slow spin around the room—"Josh Wylie, whose mother is one of your patients. Right?" She popped two small potatoes into her mouth, speared another forkful of fish.

"Right."

"So, did you see him?"

"Yes, I did. As a matter of fact, he's taking me to lunch next Friday."

Alison's eyes widened with delight. "Way to go, Terry!"

I laughed. "It's not a big deal," I cautioned, as much to myself as to Alison. "He probably just wants to talk about his mother."

"If he wanted to talk about his mother, he'd do it in the waiting room. Trust me, he's interested."

I shrugged, hoping she was right. "We'll see."

Alison waved my hesitation aside. "You'll have to tell me all about it." She clapped her hands together, as if congratulating me for a job well done, then finished off the last of her swordfish in three quick swallows. "This is so exciting. I can't wait till next Friday."

I don't remember much else about the meal, except that Alison insisted on ordering dessert, and that I ate more than I should have.

"Come on," I remember her saying as she pushed the large piece of banana-cream cake toward me. "You only live once."

After dinner, Alison was eager to show me the Lorelli Gallery. She grabbed my hand and all but pulled me across the busy street. I heard a car whiz by behind me, felt its exhaust on my bare calves. "Watch where you're going, lady," the driver yelled out.

"Be careful," Alison admonished as if I'd been crossing the street all by myself.

On weekends, the gallery stayed open till ten o'clock, hoping to attract tourists and passersby. I counted four people inside the well-lit store, including the spike-haired young woman behind the counter. The walls were covered with colorful paintings, mostly by artists I didn't recognize, although there was a typical Motherwell painting of a woman with large red lips and a prominent nipple, and three paintings of pears were stacked one on top of the other, by an artist whose name I could never remember no matter how many times I saw his work. I found my attention drawn to a small, rectangular painting of a woman, her face hidden behind a large hat, as she sunned herself on a pink, sandy beach.

"That's my favorite," Alison said, then lowered her voice. "It would go great in your living room, don't you think? On the wall behind the sofa?"

"It's beautiful."

Alison pulled me toward the center of the room, almost knocking over a sculpture of a large fiberglass frog. "Whoops." She giggled. "Isn't that the most hideous thing you've ever seen?"

I agreed it was.

"Fern says she can't keep the damn things in the store, they sell so fast. Can you believe it? Denise, hi," she continued in the same breath. "This is Terry Painter, my landlady. My friend," she added with a smile.

The girl behind the counter looked up from the fashion magazine she was perusing, extraordinary violet eyes overwhelming the rest of her small face. "Nice to meet you," she said, her voice surprisingly husky, the words emerging slowly from between small but full lips, as if she weren't quite sure whether meeting me was nice or not. She was dressed all in black, which made her look thinner than she already was, although her breasts were high and disproportionately large for her narrow frame.

"I don't think they're real," Alison would later say.

"I'm wondering how much that painting is," I said, glancing toward the painting of the girl on the pink, sandy beach, her face hidden by her wide-brimmed hat.

Denise raised bored violet eyes to the far wall. Then she reached under the counter and pulled out a plastic-covered sheet of paper to scan the typed list. "That one's fifteen hundred dollars."

"The wall behind the sofa in your living room," Alison said again. "What do you think?"

"I think you don't start work till Monday," I reminded her.

Alison's face broke into a wide smile. "I'm gonna be great at this, aren't I?"

I laughed, directing my attention to the display of jewelry in the glass counter that occupied the middle of the store. I found myself staring at a pair of long silver earrings in the shape of cupids.

"Aren't those great?" Alison knew exactly what pair I was looking at. "How much are these?" She poked at the glass above the earrings.

Denise opened the back of the case, lifted the earrings out, held them toward me. Deep purple nails protruded over the ends of long, tapered fingers. "Two hundred dollars."

I backed away, lifted my hands in the air. "Too rich for my blood."

Alison quickly scooped up the earrings. "Nonsense. She'll take them."

"No," I countered. "Two hundred dollars is way too much."

"My treat."

"What? No!"

"Yes." Alison gently removed the thin gold loops I was wearing and replaced them with the long silver cupids.

"You gave me a heart," she said, patting the tiny gold heart at her throat. "Now it's my turn."

"It's hardly the same thing."

"I won't take no for an answer. Besides, I get an employee discount. How much with my discount?" she asked Denise.

The young woman shrugged. "Take them. They're yours. Fern'll never miss them."

"What do you mean?" I asked, immediately preparing to take them off.

"She's just kidding," Alison said, already returning several loose $100 bills to her purse. She quickly ushered me to the front of the store. "Fern's her aunt," she reminded me, as if this should be explanation enough.

"Does she know her niece is a thief?"

"Don't worry. I'll settle with Fern on Monday."

"You promise?"

Alison smiled, tucked my hair behind my ears to better admire my new earrings. "I promise."

SEVEN

Don't you look lovely!" Myra Wylie lifted her head from the pillow, gnarled fingers, like turkey claws, beckoning me toward her bed.

I ran self-conscious hands across the front of my yellow dress as I approached. Myra had asked to see what I'd be wearing for lunch with her son, so I'd used her bathroom to change out of my nurse's uniform and into my street clothes. I'd decided on the same dress I'd worn to dinner with Alison the previous week.

"Thank you, dear." Myra lowered her head back to the pillow, although her eyes remained on me. "It was very sweet of you to show me your dress. I get a taste of what I missed by not having had a daughter. That former daughter-in-law of mine was for the birds. She was no fun at all. But you . . ."

"Me?" I prompted, eager to hear more.

"You're very good to me."

"Why wouldn't I be?"

"People aren't always kind," Myra said, her eyes on some distant memory.

"You make it very easy," I told her truthfully, pulling up a chair and sitting down beside her, stealing a glance at my watch. It was almost twelve-thirty.

"Don't worry," Myra said with a knowing smile. "He won't be late."

I leaned forward, pretended to be tucking in the blue cotton sheet that served as a bedspread.

"Those are lovely," Myra said. "Are they new?"

Her bony fingers were twisting toward the dangling cupids at my ears. "Yes, they are. A friend gave them to me." I wondered if Alison had settled with her boss, as she'd promised.

"A boyfriend?" Worry clouded Myra's eyes, like fresh cataracts.

"No. Actually, they were a gift from my new tenant." Again I pictured Alison. She'd started work on Monday, and except for one quick call to say she was loving every minute of her new job, I hadn't spoken to her all week. "Besides, I'm a little old for boyfriends, don't you think?"

"We're never too old for boyfriends."

"What's this about boyfriends?" the male voice boomed from the doorway.

"There he is," Myra said, all girlish flutter. "How are you, darling?" She held out her arms. I stepped out of the way and watched Josh fold inside them.

"Perfect," he said, looking right at me.

"Was the traffic bad?"

"It was miserable."

"You should take the turnpike."

"Yes, I should." He straightened up and smiled at me. "We have this same discussion every week."

"You should listen to your mother," I told him.

"Yes, I should."

"Doesn't Terry look beautiful?" Myra asked.

I looked to the floor to hide the blush I could feel spreading across my face. Not because I was embarrassed by the compliment, but because I'd been thinking exactly the same thing about her son. I don't think I'd realized before how deep were the dimples at his cheeks, how pronounced the muscles that bulged beneath his short-sleeved shirt. It was all I could do to keep from crossing my legs and screaming out loud. I hadn't felt this way in years.

"She looks very beautiful," Josh dutifully replied.

"Do you like her earrings?"

Josh lifted his fingers to my ear, his hand grazing the side of my cheek. "I like them very much."

I felt a rush of heat, as if he'd struck a match, held it against my flesh. "You're a troublemaker, you know that?" I told Myra, who looked inordinately pleased with herself.

"You ready?" Josh asked.

I nodded.

"I expect a full report after lunch," Myra called after us.

"I'll take notes," I called back as Josh ushered me into the hall.

"How would you like to have lunch by the ocean?" he asked.

"You read my mind."

We went to Luna Rosa, an upscale eatery located on South Ocean Boulevard, directly across from the beach.

The restaurant was one of my favorites, an easy walk from my house, although Josh had no way of knowing that. He'd reserved a table outside, and we sat along the narrow sidewalk, soaking in the ocean air, and watching the constant parade of people pass by our chairs.

"So, tell me, when did all this happen?" Josh's voice rose easily above the conflicting sounds of surf and automobiles.

"When did what happen?" I watched a young woman in a turquoise thong bikini as she ran barefoot across the road, then disappeared into a burst of sunlight.

Josh waved large, expressive hands into the air. "This. The Delray I remember was all pineapple fields and jungle."

I laughed. "You don't get out much, do you?"

"I guess not."

"Delray's changed a lot in the past ten years." I felt an unexpected surge of pride. "We've just been awarded our second All-American City designation by the National Civic League, and a few years back we were named 'the best-run town in Florida.'" I smiled. "How do you like them pineapples?"

He laughed, his eyes on mine. "Looks like I should visit more often."

"I'm sure your mother would like that."

"And you?"

I grabbed my ice water, took a long sip. "I'd like that too."

The waiter approached with our orders. Crab cakes for Josh, a seafood salad for me.

"Your mother's quite a character," I said, taking a mouthful of calamari, seeking safer ground. I'd never been a good flirt, and I was even worse when it came to playing games. I tended to blurt out whatever thought was on the tip of my tongue.

"Yes, she is. She's filled you in on the sordid family history, I take it."

"She told me you're divorced."

"I'm sure her description was considerably more colorful than that."

"Maybe just a little." I took another sip of ice water. Sensibly, I'd declined Josh's offer of a glass of wine. It was important to keep a clear head, to stay in control. Besides, I had barely an hour before I had to be back at work. I leaned back in the uncomfortable folding chair, listened to the sound of the waves somersaulting toward the shore, echoing the tumult taking place inside my body. God, what was the matter with me? I hadn't felt so overwhelmed, so smitten, so damn *girlish*, since I was fourteen years old.

I wanted to grab Josh Wylie by the collar of his white linen shirt and yank him across the table. *I haven't had sex in five years*, I wanted to shout. *Can we just skip all this verbal foreplay and get on with the real thing?*

But of course I didn't. I just sat there smiling at him. My mother would have been proud.

"She tells me you never married," Josh said, cutting into his crab cakes, unaware of the more interesting conversation taking place inside my head.

"She's right."

"Hard to believe."

"Really? Why?"

"Because you're a beautiful, intelligent woman, and I would have thought some guy would have snapped you up long ago."

"You would have thought," I agreed with a laugh.

"You have something against marriage?"

"Not a thing." I wondered why I always seemed to be explaining my single status. "As I told Alison, it wasn't any conscious decision on my part."

"Who's Alison?"

"What? Oh, my new tenant."

"Any regrets?"

"Regrets? About Alison?"

Josh smiled. "About life in general."

I released a long, deep breath. "A few. You?"

"A few."

We finished the rest of our meal, talking easily, laughing often, as the waves swept our unspoken regrets back and forth along the water's edge.

After lunch, Josh removed his socks and shoes and rolled his black linen trousers up around his knees, while I slipped off my sandals, and we walked along the beach. The ocean repeatedly rushed toward us, only to pull away upon contact. Like an eager lover tormented by second thoughts, it charged only to retreat. It seduced you with its monstrous beauty, then abandoned you, breathless and alone, on the shore. The eternal dance, I thought, the water cold as it licked at my toes.

"Aren't we just the luckiest people alive?" Josh said with an appreciative laugh.

"We are." I pushed my face toward the sky, squinting into the sun.

"I remember when I was a kid," he continued. "My father used to take me to the beach every Saturday afternoon while my mother was having her hair done."

"You're from Florida originally?" I wasn't sure why I asked that. I already knew everything there was to know about

Josh's background: that he'd been born in Boynton Beach, weighing a hefty nine pounds, two ounces; that his parents had lived at 212 Hibiscus Drive all their married life; that his mother had continued to live there after her husband's death a decade ago; that she'd refused her son's offer to move her down to Miami so that she could be closer to her grandchildren; that she'd continued to live in that little house she loved until she got too sick to look after it anymore; that she'd personally selected Mission Care over fancier facilities in Miami, insisting that she got nosebleeds south of Delray; that her son drove up at least once a week to see her; that he was still reeling from his divorce after seventeen years of marriage to his college sweetheart; that he was the single father of two lovely but confused children; that he was lonely; that he deserved a second chance at happiness; that I was more than prepared to provide him with that chance.

That I was completely out of my mind, I thought, realizing that I hadn't heard a single word he'd said in the last two minutes. What was the matter with me? Was I so starved for male companionship that a pleasant lunch instantly spawned fantasies of happily ever after? I needed to slow down, calm down, cool down. Before I ruined everything.

Deliberately, I allowed myself to be distracted by the sight of two boys, maybe five or six years old, in matching bright red bathing suits, tumbling over each other as they rolled, like runaway logs, into the water, before disappearing underneath a succession of increasingly large waves. I looked around the crowded beach. An elderly couple was relaxing under a red-and-white-striped umbrella; a young man was erecting a sand castle with his toddler son; two teenagers carelessly tossed a neon-pink Frisbee back and forth; a middle-aged woman, her large stomach protruding over a tiny bikini bottom, swung her arms with careless abandon as she marched along beside the ocean; a younger woman was soaking up the sun, breast implants proudly pointing toward the cloudless sky. No one was supervising the two boys, I realized, holding my breath as the boys' heads appeared above the water, only to disappear again under the next big wave.

"Do you see anyone watching those boys?" I asked Josh, hard pellets of sunshine bouncing off my eyes as I continued scanning the beach.

Josh's eyes joined in the search. "I'm sure there's someone," he said unconvincingly, as one of the youngsters began waving his arms in the air.

A fresh wave immediately slapped them down. This wave was immediately followed by a much larger one. A small voice rode the wave to shore. "Help!" the voice cried, wobbling like unsteady knees on a surfboard.

"Help!" I echoed loudly, motioning frantically to the lifeguard farther down the beach, but he was busy chatting up a teenage girl in a black-and-white string bikini, the girl's long, lean legs stretching all the way up to her baseball cap. I've had nightmares about drowning all my life, maybe because I never learned how to swim. I couldn't just stand there waiting for disaster to strike. I had to do something. "We have to do something," I shouted as Josh raced toward the lifeguard.

"Help! Help!" the small voice pleaded, now joined by a second voice, more plaintive than the first. Their cries skipped along the surface of the water like a stone, only to disappear beneath yet another rush of deadly white foam.

"Somebody do something!" I shouted at the people around me, but although a small crowd was starting to gather, nobody moved.

Without further thought, I dropped my purse and shoes to the sand and jumped into the surf after the boys, the cold water reaching between my thighs and whipping my dress around my legs. An unexpected undertow suddenly anchored my legs to the sand, and I struggled to maintain my balance, my hands circling my body like rusty propellers.

"Help!" the boys continued crying, their heads bobbing like apples in a bucket as I resolutely pushed myself forward, only to feel my legs collapse beneath me like the folding chair I'd been sitting on only moments before.

"I'm coming," I called out, the bitter taste of salt washing over my tongue as the ocean spilled into my mouth. "Hang on," I urged as the ground under my toes suddenly disappeared, as if I'd stepped off a steep cliff, and I fought to keep my head above water. My hands reached blindly for something to grab on to, accidentally smacking against what felt like a rock, but proved to be a small head. Hair curled between my fingers, like seaweed.

Whether through determination, good fortune, or just plain, dumb luck, I managed to get my hands around first one boy, then the other, and somehow catapulted their kicking frames toward the shore in time for anxious arms to reach them. I heard a series of excited, high-pitched exhortations—"Didn't I tell you to stay put until I got back? Look at you! You almost drowned!"—and then the water once again wrapped itself around my torso, like a hungry boa constrictor, and carried me back out to sea.

So this is what it feels like to drown, I remember thinking as the water covered my head like a heavy blanket, sneaking into all my private cavities, an impatient lover who would no longer be denied. "Terry," the water whispered seductively. Then louder, more insistent. "Terry . . . Terry."

"Terry!"

The voice exploded in my ear as determined hands reached under my arms to pull me toward the sky. My head burst through the surface of the water like a fist through glass.

"My God, are you all right?" Strong arms pushed me toward the shore where I collapsed onto my hands and knees.

Water clung to my eyes, like shards of glass, and I struggled to open them. Slivers of breath escaped my lungs in a series of short, painful spasms.

"Are you all right?" Josh's face formed around the edges of the words.

I nodded, coughed, sucked furiously at the air. "The boys . . . ?"

"They're fine."

"Thank God."

Josh's fingers pushed the hair out of my eyes, smoothed the water from my cheeks. "You're a hero, Terry Painter."

"I'm an idiot," I muttered. "I can't swim."

"So I noticed."

"You're not supposed to go in the water without a bathing suit," a little girl admonished from somewhere beside me.

I looked down at my once seductive dress, now wrapped around me like a bruised yellow tent. "Look at me," I wailed. "I look like an overripe banana."

Josh laughed. "Good enough to eat," I thought I heard him say, although in the ensuing commotion I couldn't be sure. A crowd was gathering. Unfamiliar voices were exclaiming their gratitude; strange hands were patting my back.

"Way to go!" someone enthused in passing.

"Are you okay?" a young woman asked, long legs approaching cautiously. I recognized the black-and-white string bikini and the baseball cap, knew she was the girl I'd seen earlier, talking to the lifeguard.

"I'm fine." I noted the lifeguard was standing directly behind her, and that he was suitably tall, blond, and muscular. The expression on his bland, bronzed face wavered between gratitude and resentment.

"I just wanted to thank you," the girl continued. "Those are my brothers. My mother would have killed me if anything had happened to them."

"You should keep a closer eye on them."

She nodded, glanced up the beach to where the boys were wrestling in the sand. "Yeah, well, I told them . . ." Her voice disappeared into a passing breeze. "Anyway, thanks again." She looked past me at Josh.

"You interested in a job?" the lifeguard joked uneasily.

"Just do yours," I told him, but he was already backing away, and he dismissed my admonishment with a wave of his hand, as if swatting at a pesky insect.

"My purse!" I said, suddenly remembering I'd dropped it on the shore. "My shoes . . ."

"Right here." Josh lifted them into the air, like a proud fisherman displaying his catch of the day.

"My God, look at you!" I exclaimed, realizing he was almost as wet as I was.

"We're quite a pair," he said, leaning his face toward mine.

I held my breath, didn't move. Was he going to kiss me?

A clump of hair promptly fell into my eyes, and I brushed it aside impatiently, feeling particles of sand attach themselves to my eyelashes, like globs of errant mascara. Great, I thought, trying to picture myself through his eyes. A regular beauty queen, I could almost hear my mother say.

"Terry?" a familiar voice asked from miles above my head.

I looked up, shielded my eyes. Alison loomed between me and the sun like a giant eclipse.

"Terry?" she said again, crouching down beside me. "My God, I can't believe it's you!"

"Alison! What are you doing here?"

"I have the day off. What's going on? Somebody said you saved two little boys from drowning."

"She was magnificent," Josh said proudly.

"Until I almost drowned myself."

"My God, are you all right?"

"She's magnificent," Josh repeated, extending his hand toward Alison. "I'm Josh Wylie, by the way."

Alison took his hand, shook it vigorously. "Alison Simms."

"Alison's my new tenant," I qualified.

"Pleasure to meet you, Alison."

"You too." Almost reluctantly, she relinquished his hand. "So, has Terry invited you over for Thanksgiving yet?"

"Alison!"

"Terry's only the best cook in the whole wide world. You're not busy, are you?"

"Well, no, but . . ."

"Good. Then it's settled. Don't worry, Terry," Alison cautioned, "I'll help."

I'm not sure exactly what happened after that. I remember wanting to wring Alison's lovely, swanlike neck. I also wanted to throw my arms around her and jump up and down with joy. At any rate, perhaps sensing my ambivalence, Alison muttered something about meeting with me later to discuss all the necessary details, then made a hasty retreat, disappearing into a swirl of pink sand. Josh drove me to my house, waiting in the car while I ran upstairs, towel-dried my hair, and changed out of my wet clothes. Then he drove me back to work. Neither one of us said anything until he pulled up in front of the hospital. Then we turned simultaneously toward one another.

"Josh . . ."

"Terry . . ."

"You don't have to come to dinner on Thanksgiving."

"You don't have to invite me."

"No, I'd love to invite you."

"Then I'd love to come."

"Really?"

"Jan's taking the kids that night, so I have no particular plans."

"Well, it wouldn't be anything fancy. . . ."

"I don't need fancy if I have the best cook in the whole wide world."

I laughed. "Well, that might be a slight exaggeration."

"She's quite a character, isn't she?"

"Yes, she is."

"A real whirling dervish. Slightly fey, very charming."

Charming, fey, I think now. Not the words I would use to describe her.

What words would you use? I hear Alison whisper slyly in my ear.

"You'll explain to my mother why I didn't come back to see her?" Josh asked, indicating his wet clothes.

"Can I leave out the part where I almost drowned?"

Josh laughed. "What time next Thursday?"

I quickly mulled over everything I had to do to prepare. It had been years since I'd cooked anyone Thanksgiving dinner. I couldn't remember the last time I'd bought a turkey. It's not something you normally buy when you're cooking for one. "Seven o'clock?"

"Seven o'clock," he repeated. "I'm thankful already."

I stepped out of the car and skipped up the hospital's front steps, turning back as I pulled open the door. My hero, I thought, watching Josh drive away, my head pleasantly dizzy with anticipation, the sound of the surf still ringing in my ears.

EIGHT

Okay, so are you ready for your whole new look?"

Alison, wearing blue shorts, a white halter top, and hot-pink nail polish on her bare toes, stood outside my kitchen door, her arms loaded with an interesting array of bottles and tubes. Her hair was pulled back into a ponytail. She looked about twelve.

My own hair was freshly washed, as per her instructions, and wrapped in a white towel that matched my white terry-cloth robe. "What's all this?" I stepped back to let her inside.

"Creams, oils, emulsions." She deposited the various items on my kitchen table and arranged them to her satisfaction. "What's an emulsion anyway?"

I thought back to my years at nursing school. "Any colloidal suspension of one liquid in another liquid," I said, almost by rote, startled by how easily such long-forgotten nuggets resurfaced.

"Colloidal?"

"A colloid is a gelatinous substance which when dissolved in a liquid will not diffuse readily through either vegetable or animal membranes."

Alison looked at me as if I were some new form of alien species. "Could you try that again?"

"It's a liquid preparation that's the color and consistency of milk," I said plainly.

She smiled, lifted a medium-sized glass bottle of white cream into her hands. "That would be this one."

"How can you buy products when you don't know what they are?"

"Nobody knows what they are. That's why they cost so much."

I laughed, thinking she was probably right. "What else have you got here?"

"Let's see. There's a pore-purifying microbead face wash, and an alpha hydroxy exfoliating peel-off masque—that's *masque* spelled with a *que,* which means it's *really* expensive. Then there's a botanical, gentle facial-buffing cream, another botanical cream with collagen and woodmallow. What's that? Never mind," she said in the same breath. "Then we have a soothing eye-contour mask—this one spelled with a *k,* so it's probably not as good—a milky refiner, not to be confused with the aforementioned milky emulsion, an oil-free moisturizing lotion, and a tube of concentrated apricot oil. Did you happen to catch my casual use of the word *aforementioned*?"

"I did."

"Were you impressed?"

"I was."

"Good." She dug into the right-side pocket of her blue shorts, pulled out several small bottles of nail polish. "Very Cherry and Luscious Lilac. Your choice." From her left-side pocket emerged cotton balls, emery boards, and assorted tiny implements of torture. Then she reached behind her and extricated a large pair of scissors from her back pocket, waving them before my eyes like a magic wand. "For Madame's new do."

"I'm not so sure about that," I wavered, pulling the towel off my head.

"Don't worry. I'm not going to do anything drastic. Just even it up a bit, maybe take an inch off the bottom. You said you have cucumbers?"

"In the fridge," I told her, trying to keep up with the conversation.

"Good. Then what say we get started?"

What could I do? Alison was so enthusiastic, so confident, so persuasive, I really didn't have a choice.

You want to be gorgeous for Thanksgiving, don't you? I can still hear her ask.

And the truth was, I *did* want to be gorgeous for Thanksgiving. I wanted to be drop-dead, knock-'em-down-and-drag-'em-out gorgeous for Thanksgiving. For Josh.

Not that you aren't gorgeous already, Alison had quickly amended.

All week I'd been walking around in a stupid haze, singing along with the radio, humming merrily off-key as I doled out medications, even waving a pleasant "Hello" to Bettye McCoy as she hurried those overgrown furballs past my house. And why? All because some guy I liked had been nice to me.

No, more than nice.

Interested.

Interested in me.

He's only using you, I could almost hear my mother say. *He'll break your heart.*

Yes, he probably will, I agreed.

But I didn't care. It didn't matter that Josh was still carrying a torch for his ex-wife, that he had two kids and a dying mother, that a serious involvement was probably the last thing he was looking for. It didn't matter that we'd had only one real date, a *lunch* date at that, and that I'd almost drowned during it. What mattered was that he was interested.

Good enough to eat, he'd said.

I felt an almost forgotten tingle between my legs.

What do you really know about this man? my mother asked.

Not much, I was forced to admit.

That didn't matter either. Josh Wylie could have been an ax murderer for all I cared. Sadistic killer or not, he made me feel things I hadn't felt in years. He resurrected emotions so long and deeply repressed I'd forgotten I had them. At forty, I felt like one of those silly teenage girls you see giggling in the mall with her friends: *And then he said; and then he said.* I was fourteen again, in love with Roger Stillman.

And look what happened there, my mother reminded me.

"We'll do your hair first," Alison was saying now, a comb appearing from out of nowhere to drag the wet tangles of my hair across my ears and forehead. Alison sat me down and knelt in front of me, her palm turning my chin from one side to the other as she studied my face. She smiled, as if privy to my innermost thoughts. Could she see Josh Wylie in the reflection of my eyes?

I heard the scissors, felt the blades snipping at the air

around my head, moving closer. "I'll clean up later," she announced as I felt first one tug, then another, and watched in horror as several wet clumps of hair fell to the white tile of the kitchen floor.

"Oh, God," I moaned.

"Close your eyes," Alison instructed. "Have faith."

With my eyes closed, the sound of cutting was even more intense. It was as if those scissors were slicing through all my protective outer layers, snipping away my secrets, sapping my strength. Samson and Delilah, I thought dramatically, taking a series of long, deep breaths, deciding to roll with the punches, go with the flow.

"I'll wait till after your facial to blow it dry properly. We can go into the living room now," she instructed as I stepped over the hair lying across the white tiles, like a small area rug. "Don't look," she said as a shudder shook my shoulders. "Have faith. Trust me."

I'd already laid a bedsheet across the living room sofa in preparation for my "night at the spa," as Alison had laughingly referred to it, and now I stood paralyzed in front of it, waiting for Alison to tell me what to do.

"Okay. Lie down, with your head at this end, and your feet . . . here. That's good. I want you to be really comfortable. You're going to enjoy this," Alison said as if she wasn't sure. "Now, you get cozy, and I'll bring all the stuff I need in here."

"The cucumber slices are in the fridge," I reminded her, closing my eyes, my fingers darting about my neck, feeling for hair.

"You didn't have to slice them," Alison called back from the kitchen. "I would have done that."

I heard her rifling around in the fridge, heard the tap running, listened to the sounds of cupboard doors opening and closing. What was she looking for?

In less than a minute, Alison was back. "We'll start with the exfoliating masque."

"Is that with a *que* or a *k*?"

She laughed. "The expensive one."

"Oh, good."

"Okay, so close your eyes, relax, think pleasant thoughts."

I felt something cold and slimy being spread across my face, like molasses on a slice of bread.

"This might feel a bit weird as it starts to harden."

"Feels weird now."

"You won't be able to talk," she warned, slathering the product around the outlines of my lips. "So it's best if you stay still."

Did I have a choice? Already it felt as if my face were encased in cement. A death mask, I remember thinking. Death *masque*, I amended, and might have laughed were it not for the stiffening of the muscles around my mouth. "For how long?" I asked through barely parted lips.

"Twenty minutes."

"Twenty minutes?" I opened my eyes, started to sit up.

Firm hands settled me back down. "Relax. The night is young, and we're just getting started. Close your eyes. I'm going to put the cucumbers on them."

"What are the cucumbers for?" I asked, although I was no longer able to pronounce the hard c's and the noun emerged as more of a verbal blur than an actual word.

"They reduce swelling. What kind of nurse are you that you don't know that?" she teased. Then: "Keep still. It was a rhetorical question." She fitted the cucumber slices gently into the empty circles around my eyes. Instantly, the room darkened, as if I were wearing sunglasses. "You like that word, *rhetorical*?"

"Good word," I managed to say without moving my mouth.

"I'm trying to learn three new words every day."

"Oh?" That was an easy one.

"Yeah, it's kind of fun. I just open up the dictionary and point to a word, and if I don't know what it means, I write it down and memorize the definition."

"Such as?"

"Well, let's see. Today I learned three very interesting words: *ineffable*, which means incapable of being expressed or described, like ineffable happiness, you know, so great you can't describe it. That's one. Then there's *epiphany*, which was a real shock because I thought I knew what that one meant, but I was wrong. I was *really* wrong. Do you know what it means?"

"A revelation of some sort," I managed to squeeze out, although the effort required all my concentration.

"An epiphany is 'the sudden, intuitive perception or insight into the reality or essential meaning of something,'" she recited, then paused. I could feel her shaking her head. "Do you want to know what I thought it meant?"

I nodded my chin, careful not to disturb the cucumbers at my eyes.

"Promise you won't laugh."

I grunted. I couldn't have laughed if I'd tried.

"Well, I saw this movie on TV when I was a kid. It was about a man who, for some unknown reason, turned into a chicken. And it was called *Epiphany*. So I assumed that an epiphany was when someone changed into a chicken. I actually grew up believing that. God, can you imagine if I'd tried to use it in a conversation?"

I shook my head, albeit gently. There was something so vulnerable about her, something so terribly raw, as if she were sitting there with all her nerve endings exposed. I wished I could take her in my arms and comfort her like the big overgrown child she was. "What's the third word?" I asked instead.

"*Meros*. It's a flat surface between two channels of a triglyph."

"What's a triglyph?"

"I have no idea." She laughed. "I only do three words, remember. Now that's enough talking. I want you to relax and just enjoy being pampered. Something tells me you don't pamper yourself nearly enough."

She was right. Being pampered was new to me. I'd worked hard all my life, first at school, then at my chosen profession, and even at home, looking after my mother. In some ways, I was grateful that I hadn't had an easy ride, that my mother hadn't spoiled me more. It made me that much more appreciative of the things I did have, more sensitive and caring toward others.

"Okay," Alison was saying. "So while this masque hardens, I'm going to start on your pedicure. I'll be right back. Take deep breaths. Let your whole body relax."

A sudden silence filled the room. I heard her moving about the kitchen. What was she doing? I wondered, taking one deep breath, then another, feeling the tension of the day seep slowly from my limbs.

"You have really strong toenails." Alison's fingers suddenly pulled on the big toe of my right foot.

I realized I hadn't heard her come back into the room. Was it possible I'd fallen asleep? For how long?

"I'm going to cut them now, so try not to move."

My feet squirmed under her touch.

"Don't move," she warned again.

I heard the rapid snipping of the nail clippers as her fingers flitted expertly from one toe to the next. *This little piggy went to market,* I recited silently, then stopped because I couldn't remember what had happened to the next little piggy.

"Now comes the best part," she announced, gently massaging my tired feet with lotion. The smell of apricots drifted toward my nostrils. "Feels good, huh?"

"Feels wonderful," I agreed, although I'm not sure I said the words out loud.

"Why, Terry Painter, I think you're actually beginning to enjoy this."

I nodded, tried to smile, felt tiny fissures at my cheeks, as if my flesh had turned to stone.

"My husband used to give the best foot massages," Alison said, although from the sudden faraway tone in her voice, I knew she was speaking more to herself than to me. "It's probably why I married him. Certainly it would explain why I kept going back to him. He had the best hands. Once he started massaging my feet, I was a goner."

I understood what she meant. Alison had obviously learned a great deal from her former spouse. Her hands were magic. In less than two minutes, I too was a goner.

"I still miss him," Alison continued. "I know I shouldn't, but I can't help myself. He's so cute. You should see him.

All the girls take one look at him and faint dead away. Which, of course, was part of the problem. He had no willpower whatsoever. 'Course, neither did I. He'd cheat on me, and I'd swear there was no way I was going to forgive him, no way I was ever going to take his sorry ass back, and then there he'd be one night, standing at my door, and he'd look so damn good, and of course I'd let him in. 'We're just gonna talk,' I'd say, and he'd agree, and we'd go sit on the sofa, and the next minute, he'd start rubbing my feet, and that was that. Back to square one."

I thought I should probably comment, assure her she wasn't the only woman in the world to fall for the wrong guy, or to forgive him too many times. But the truth was that, even had my face been free of its cosmetic constraints, I couldn't have found the strength to speak. Her little-girl voice was like a lullaby, singing me to sleep. I breathed deeply, the room growing ever darker as I drifted in and out of consciousness.

The next thing I remember was the sound of footsteps overhead. I opened my eyes, found myself staring at the white underside of two slices of cucumber. I removed them, my eyes adjusting quickly to the surrounding darkness. I felt my face, still hidden beneath a layer of hard alpha hydroxy. When had Alison turned off the light? How long had I been asleep?

Again I heard the sound of movement overhead, the opening and closing of drawers. Was she in my bedroom? I wondered, pushing myself to my feet and turning on the nearby lamp. What was she doing? Bright red toenails winked at me from beside the soft, white cotton balls wedged between each toe. Very Cherry, I remembered as I walked on my heels toward the stairs.

She was in the guest room, standing in front of the bookshelf that occupied most of the wall opposite the old burgundy velvet sofa bed. Her back was to me. Obviously, she hadn't heard me come up.

"What are you doing?" I asked, the masque around my mouth cracking like glass.

Alison spun around, the book in her hand dropping to the floor, landing on her toes. She gasped, although I'm not sure whether it was from pain or surprise. "Oh my God, you scared me."

"What are you doing?" I asked again, the cracks in my masque lengthening, reaching for my eyes.

Hesitation flickered briefly across her face, like a candle flame caught in an unexpected breeze. "Well, first I came up to look for these," she said, recovering quickly as she pulled a pair of tweezers from her pocket. "I realized I forgot mine, and you were snoring away, it was so cute, I didn't want to wake you up. I figured you must have a pair somewhere, but I had to go through practically every drawer in the bathroom till I found them. Why don't you keep them in the medicine cabinet like everyone else?"

"I thought I did," I answered lamely.

She shook her head. "They were next to your hot rollers, underneath the sink." She returned my tweezers to her pocket. "And then I was on my way back downstairs when I saw all the books, and I thought I'd take a second and look up word number four in the dictionary." She bent down to retrieve the large book with its glossy red-and-yellow cover, held it up for me to see. "A triglyph is a structural member of a Doric frieze," she announced triumphantly. "Please don't ask me what a Doric frieze is."

It was then that I caught sight of my reflection in the window and saw my newly shorn hair sticking out at weird angles from around my mummified face. “Oh, God, I look like the bogeyman.”

Alison winced. “Don’t even joke about that.” She replaced the book on the shelf, laced her arm through mine. “Let’s get that masque off your face. We still have lots more to do.”

“I think I’ve had about all the pampering I can take.”

“Nonsense. I’m just getting started.”

NINE

I took Thanksgiving off.

This was unusual because, since my mother's death five years ago, I'd worked every Thanksgiving. In fact I worked every holiday, and that included Christmas Day and New Year's Eve. Why not? I reasoned. Unlike Margot and Caroline, I had no family waiting for me at home, no one to bemoan my absence or complain they didn't see enough of me. And the residents of Mission Care still needed looking after, holiday or not. It was truly sad how few visitors some of them received, how perfunctory many of those visits were. If I could make the holidays less lonely for these people, many of whom I'd come to like and admire, then I was more than happy to do it. Besides, it was a trade-off: I was doing it as much for me as for them. I didn't want to spend the holidays alone any more than they did.

But this Thanksgiving was different. I wasn't going to be alone. I was having a dinner party, a slightly bigger dinner party than I'd first anticipated. Aside from Josh and Alison, the guest list now included Alison's co-worker, Denise Nickson. Alison had asked if we could include her, and although I was reluctant—I didn't really trust Denise after the incident with the earrings—Alison assured me that she was smart, funny, and basically good at heart. So, against my better judgment, I agreed to include her. Besides, with Denise around to talk to Alison, I reasoned I'd have more time to concentrate on Josh.

"Something smells absolutely fabulous." Alison swept into the kitchen from the dining room, where she'd been setting the table. She was wearing her blue sundress, and her hair, secured behind one ear by a delicate, blue dragonfly clip, hung in a wondrous rush around her shoulders. On her feet were her silver sling-back shoes. I still couldn't look at them without feeling a jolt of anxiety. "This turkey is going to be yummy delicious."

"I hope you're right."

"What else can I do to help?"

"The table's set?"

"Wait till you see it. It looks like something out of *Gourmet* magazine. I put the roses Josh sent in the middle, between the candles."

I blushed and turned back toward the stove, pretended to be watching the pot of small red potatoes that were boiling at a brisk and steady pace. Believe it or not, no one had ever sent me flowers before. "I think we're all set to go," I said, running through my mental checklist—turkey, stuffing, marshmallow-covered yams, small red potatoes, homemade cranberry sauce, a pear-and-walnut salad with Gorgonzola dressing.

"We have enough food for an army," Alison remarked,

throwing her hands into the air, as if she were tossing confetti. It was a gesture of pure joy, and it made me laugh out loud. "You're so pretty when you laugh," Alison said.

I smiled my appreciation, thinking that if I looked especially nice tonight, it was all because of her. Not only was the haircut she'd given me the best, most flattering haircut I'd ever had—it fell about my face in soft amber waves that stopped just below my chin—but my skin still glowed from the facial she'd administered, and the makeup she'd selected and meticulously applied several hours earlier had somehow managed to be both dramatic and natural. My fingernails matched my toenails, Very Cherry going very well with my navy slacks and newly purchased white silk shirt. My silver cupid earrings dangled from my ears. Tonight, I told myself, was going to be a very special night.

The doorbell rang.

"My God," I said. "What time is it?"

Alison checked her watch. "Only six-thirty. Somebody's very anxious to get here." Big eyes widened in anticipation.

"Do I really look okay?" I pulled my blue-and-white-checkered apron up over my head, careful not to disturb my hair, ran my tongue across the muted red of my lips.

"You look fantastic. Just relax. Take a deep breath."

I took one deep breath, then another for good luck, before proceeding out of the kitchen. Even before I reached the front door, I could hear giggling from outside. Clearly it was Denise, and not Josh, who'd been anxious to get here. Just as clearly, she wasn't alone. Had she and Josh arrived at the same time? I wondered, pulling open the door.

Denise, wearing a pink T-shirt with orange letters that said DUMP HIM, and a pair of tight black jeans, her dark hair spiking rudely around the pale triangle of her face, was standing on the outside landing, skinny arms wrapped around an equally scrawny young man with short brown hair, light brown eyes, and a strong, hawklike nose. The face was vaguely sinister, although it softened a bit when he smiled. Still, he filled me with unease.

"We're here," Denise announced gaily. "I know we're early, but . . ." She laughed, as if she'd said something funny. "This is K.C.," she said, and laughed again.

Was she drunk? I wondered. High? "Casey?"

"K.C.," the young man explained, biting off each letter. He was about the same age as Alison, I estimated. "Short for Kenneth Charles. But nobody ever calls me that."

I nodded, wondered who he was and what he was doing in my house.

"Denise?" Alison asked from behind me.

"Hi, you." Denise pushed past me into the living room of my home. "Wow. Nice house. Alison, meet K.C."

"Casey?"

"K.C.," the young man explained again. "Short for Kenneth Charles."

"But nobody ever calls him that," I added, thinking he must get awfully tired of having to explain himself.

"I didn't realize you were bringing a date," Alison said, nervous eyes flitting in my direction.

"Is it a problem? I just assumed it would be all right. Everybody always makes way too much food on Thanksgiving."

"If it's a problem," the young man interjected quickly, "I can go. I don't want to put anybody out."

"No," I heard myself say. "Denise is right. There's more than enough food. We can't very well toss you out on the street on Thanksgiving, can we?" I wasn't being especially magnanimous. It was more that I suddenly decided Josh might be more comfortable if another man was present.

"I'll set another place," Alison volunteered, disappearing into the dining room as I ushered Denise and K.C. toward the sofa and chairs.

"Can I get you something to drink?" I offered.

"Vodka?" Denise asked.

"Beer?" asked K.C.

I had neither, so they settled for white wine. We sat in my living room, sipping on our drinks—Alison and I were sticking to water for the time being—and making awkward conversation. Denise seemed neither particularly smart nor funny, and K.C., who said little, had a way of looking right through you, even in repose, that was quite unsettling. Tonight is going to be a disaster, I thought, almost praying Josh would call to cancel.

"So, where'd you two meet?" Alison asked.

"At the store." Denise shrugged, her eyes zeroing in on the large painting of lush pink and red peonies that hung on the wall across from the sofa. "That's a nice painting."

"Thank you."

"I don't usually like stuff like that. You know, flowers and fruit and stuff."

"Still life," I said.

"Yeah. I usually don't like it. I like art with more of an edge, you know? But this is kinda nice. Where'd you get it?"

"It was my mother's."

"Yeah? And what—you inherited it after she died?" Denise was seemingly oblivious to the fact this might be none of her business. "Along with the house and everything?"

I said nothing, not sure how to respond.

"I've been trying to talk Terry into buying that painting of the woman with the large sun hat on the beach," Alison chipped in, as if aware of my discomfort.

"You're an only child?" Denise pressed, ignoring her.

"Yes, I'm afraid so."

"No, you're lucky," Denise protested. "I have two sisters. We hate each other's guts. And Alison has a brother she never talks to. What about you, K.C.? You have any brothers or sisters you can't stand?"

"One of each," he said.

"And where are they tonight?" I asked.

"Back in Houston, I guess."

"I didn't know you were from Texas," Denise said. "I've always wanted to go to Texas."

"It doesn't sound like you've known each other very long," I remarked.

"We met last night." Denise giggled, the incongruously childish sound emerging from between deep-purple lips. "Actually, I'd seen him in the store a few times, but we didn't talk until last night."

"I thought you looked familiar," Alison suddenly exclaimed. "You were in on Monday. You asked about the frog sculpture."

K.C. looked vaguely embarrassed. "I was trying to pick you up," he admitted with a laugh.

"Oh, nice talk!" Denise said. "And what? It didn't work, so you came back last night and hit on me?"

"It doesn't mean I don't love you," K.C. said with a sly grin.

Denise laughed. "Isn't he cute? I think he's so cute." She reached over, scraped clawlike fingers across his skinny thigh. "The thing about art," she continued, as if this were the most logical of continua, her eyes back on the floral painting, "is that it's such a lie. Don't you think?"

"I'm not sure I follow," I answered.

"Take these flowers," Denise said. "Or the woman with the hat on the beach. I mean, when have you ever seen flowers this big and lush in real life, or sand that pink? It doesn't exist."

"It exists in the artist's imagination," I argued.

"My point exactly."

"Just because art is subjective doesn't make it a lie. Sometimes an artist's interpretation of something is ultimately more real than the thing itself. The artist is forcing you to view the subject in a new and different light, to arrive at a greater truth."

Denise waved my theories away with a careless hand. The wine sloshed around in her glass, veering dangerously toward the rim. "Artists distort, they enhance, they leave things out." She shrugged. "That makes them liars in my book."

"You got something against liars?" K.C. asked.

I heard a car pull into the driveway, listened to the sound of footsteps on the outside path, was already on my feet when the doorbell rang. I couldn't help but notice the look of anticipation on Alison's face as I walked to the door.

"You look great," she called after me, giving me two encouraging thumbs-up.

I laughed and opened the door, then had to lean against it in case my legs gave out and I fell over the large leafy plant to my right. Josh Wylie was wearing a blue silk shirt and carrying a bottle of Dom Pérignon. He looked absolutely gorgeous, and it was all I could do to keep from throwing myself into his arms. Calm down, I told myself. You're forty years old, not fourteen. Relax. Take deep breaths.

"Am I late?" Josh asked as I closed the door after him, then stood rooted to the floor, as if I'd been planted.

"No. You're perfect. Perfectly on time," I qualified quickly, letting go of the doorframe and accepting the bottle of Dom Pérignon. "You didn't have to bring champagne. Your flowers were more than enough."

"Ooh, champagne." Denise was suddenly at my side, lifting the bottle from my hands. "I'm Denise, and I love champagne." She extended her free hand.

"Denise Nickson, this is Josh Wylie," I said. "Denise works in the gallery with Alison."

Alison waved hello from the sofa.

"It's my aunt's gallery," Denise explained. "So I'm kind of a part-owner, I guess. This is my friend K.C."

"Nice to meet you, Casey."

"K.C.," we corrected in unison.

"Stands for Kenneth Charles," he said.

"But nobody calls him that," Alison said.

"You must get awfully tired of having to explain that to everyone," Josh said, and I smiled, hearing my own thoughts resonating through his words.

What can I say about that night?

My initial reservations were quickly dispelled in a wave of champagne and friendly banter. Despite the disparity in our ages and interests, the five of us made for a lively and interesting group. The food was delicious, the conversation effortless, the mood relaxed and happy.

"So what exactly does an investment counselor do?"

Denise asked Josh at one point, the cranberry sauce on her fork competing with the stubborn purple of her lips. "And don't say he counsels people on their investments."

"I'm afraid there's not much else I can say," Josh demurred.

"Are you counseling Terry on her investments?" K.C. asked.

I laughed. "First I'd have to have some money to invest."

"Oh, come on. You must have lots of money kicking around," Denise protested. "I mean, you work, you own your own house, you have a tenant. Plus I'm sure you have a nice pension."

"Which I don't collect till I retire," I told her, a slight twinge of discomfort worming its way into my gut. How had we come to be discussing my finances?

"What about you, K.C.?" Josh asked. "What is it you do?"

"Computer programmer." K.C. helped himself to another slice of turkey, another heaping spoonful of yams.

"Another job I'll never understand," Denise said. "Do you have a computer, Terry?"

"No," I answered. "I've never really needed one."

"How can you survive without E-mail?"

"You'd be surprised what you can survive without." I stared into my lap, trying not to picture Josh slamming me against the wall of my bedroom, eager fingers unbuttoning my blouse.

"You have no relatives across the country you need to keep in touch with?" Denise asked.

I shook my head, caught sight of K.C. as he leaned forward, cold eyes focused on me intently. Snake eyes, I thought with a shudder.

"Okay, so what are we all thankful for?" Alison suddenly asked. "Three things. Everybody."

"Oh, God," Denise groaned. "This is so *Oprah.*"

"You first, K.C.," Alison instructed. "Three things you're thankful for."

K.C. lifted his glass into the air. "Good food. Good champagne." He smiled, snake eyes slithering between Alison and Denise. "Bad women."

They laughed.

"Denise?"

Denise made a face that said this sort of game was beneath her, but that she'd indulge us anyway because she was such a good sport. "Let's see. I'm thankful the gallery was closed today and I didn't have to work. I'm thankful my aunt is visiting her daughter in New York and I didn't have to spend Thanksgiving with her. And"—she looked directly at me—"I'm thankful you're as good a cook as Alison said you were."

"Amen to that," Josh said, raising his glass in a toast.

"Okay, Josh," Alison directed, "your turn."

Josh paused, as if giving the matter careful thought. "I'm thankful for my children. I'm thankful for the wonderful care my mother gets each day. And for that, and for tonight, I'm especially thankful to—and for—our lovely hostess. Thank you, Terry Painter. You're a godsend."

"Thank *you,*" I whispered, dangerously close to tears.

"I'm thankful for Terry too," Alison said as I felt my cheeks grow warm. "Thankful that's she's given me a place to stay and welcomed me so warmly into her life. Secondly, I'm thankful for my instincts that told me to come here in the first place. And thirdly, I'm thankful for the chance I've been given to start over again."

"Aren't you a little young to be starting over?" Josh asked.

"Your turn." Alison blushed, swiveled toward me.

"I'm thankful for my health," I began.

Denise groaned. "That's like wishing for world peace."

"And I'm thankful for all your kind words," I continued, ignoring her. I looked from Alison to Josh, then back to Alison. "And I'm thankful for new friends and new opportunities. I consider myself very lucky."

"We're the lucky ones," Alison said.

"Does anyone here believe in God?" Denise asked suddenly.

And then everybody was speaking at once, as the conversation veered from philosophic to sophomoric to downright moronic and then back again. Not surprisingly, Alison was among the believers. Surprisingly, so was Denise. K.C. was an atheist, Josh an agnostic. As for me, I'd always wanted to believe, and on a good day, I did.

Today, I decided, perhaps prematurely, had been a good day.

TEN

At ten o'clock, Josh announced it was time for him to be heading back to Miami.

He was right. It was time to call it a night. We'd polished off the homemade pumpkin pie, drunk all the champagne, finished the last of the Baileys. Alison had cleared the table, hand-washed the dishes, and led us in an impromptu game of charades, which she'd handily won. "I'm very good at games," she'd said proudly.

"I'll walk you to your car," I told Josh, feeling a slight twinge in my stomach, like a poke in the ribs, as I rose from the living room sofa and followed him to the door.

"Nice meeting you, Josh," Denise called after him.

"See you again soon, I hope," Alison said.

K.C. said nothing, although I detected a slight nod of his head that meant either good-bye or that he was too drunk to do more.

No one else made a move to leave. Clearly, Josh and I

were the only two people in the room who understood the value of timing.

The warm air embraced us, like a lazy lover, as we stepped outside and gazed up at a sky heavy with stars. The smell of the ocean filtered through the night air like silver threads through a dark tapestry, lingering like an expensive perfume. "Beautiful night," I remarked, walking beside Josh to his car.

"Lovely evening all around."

"I'm so glad you could make it."

"So am I." He looked down the empty street. "Feel like taking a little walk? Just to the corner," he added when I hesitated.

I'm not sure why I hesitated. In truth, I wanted nothing more than to prolong my time with Josh for as long as humanly possible. Probably I was leery of leaving my other guests alone in the house for too long. "Sure," I heard myself say, ignoring my concerns, falling into step beside him. My arm brushed against his. I felt a jolt, like a small but potent electrical charge, shoot through my body.

"I was hoping for a few minutes alone with you," Josh said.

"Do you want to talk about your mother?"

He laughed, stopped walking. "You think I want to get you alone so I can talk about my mother?"

I looked toward the sidewalk, afraid I was so transparent my thoughts were visible on my forehead. I felt his hand at my chin, a succession of increasingly powerful shocks raising my eyes back to his, as I watched his face tilt toward mine. If he gets any closer, I thought, he's liable to be electrocuted.

"I'd really like to kiss you right now," he said.

A loud sigh escaped my lips as he moved closer. My heart was pounding right through my clothes, like a baby kicking in its mother's womb. Except it wasn't my heart, I realized with a sudden gasp. It was my stomach. And it wasn't passion. It was pain. My God, was I going to be sick? Was he going to kiss me and then shrink back in horror while I threw up all over him? Certainly that was one way of ensuring tonight would be a night to remember, I decided, as his lips settled gently on mine.

"Very nice," he whispered, kissing away my fears, his arms wrapping around me like a cloak.

Instantly I relaxed. *Come back into the house,* I wanted to say. *Come back and tell the others they have to leave. Stay and make love to me all night. You can drive back to Miami in the morning.*

Except, of course, I said no such thing. Instead I kissed him again and again, then stood there grinning like an idiot until it became obvious he wasn't going to kiss me anymore, and we turned back, walking hand in hand toward his car, my mind racing with my heart, my intestines doing a slow rope burn against the inside of my stomach. I was thinking that it doesn't matter how old we are, fourteen or forty, we're ageless when it comes to love.

"Thanks again for a wonderful evening," Josh said when we reached his car.

"Thank *you* for the champagne and the roses."

"I'm glad you liked them."

"They're beautiful."

"So are you."

He kissed me again, this time on the cheek, his eyelashes fluttering against my skin, like butterfly wings. "I'll see you next week," he said, climbing into his car.

I watched in silence as he backed his car onto the street, heading toward Atlantic Avenue. When he reached the stop sign at the corner, he waved without looking back, as if he knew I was still watching him. I waved back, but by then he was already halfway down the next block.

It took several minutes before I was able to move. Truthfully, it was as much the tingling on my lips and cheek as the renewed cramping in my gut that rendered me immobile. Too much rich food and excitement for an old lady, I decided when I was finally able to put one foot in front of the other. I returned to the house, prepared to tell the others that the party was officially over, but my living room was empty. Had everyone cleared out while I was gone?

It was then I heard the sound of careless laughter bouncing above my head like a rubber ball. What were they doing upstairs? I wondered, temporarily forgetting about the pains in my stomach. "Alison," I called from the foot of the stairs.

Immediately Alison's head popped into view at the top of the landing. "Josh leave?"

"What are you doing up there?" I asked, ignoring her question.

Denise suddenly appeared beside Alison. "My fault. I asked for a tour of the house."

"There's not much to see." I watched the two young women make their way down the stairs, K.C. nipping at their heels like a large, uncoordinated golden retriever.

"It's like a little dollhouse," Denise pronounced.

"I'm sorry," Alison whispered in my ear. "She was up the stairs before I could stop her."

Whatever annoyance I was feeling was replaced by a sharp jab to my solar plexus. I grimaced, grabbed my side.

"Something wrong?" Alison asked.

I shook my head. "I think I should have skipped that second helping of pie," I muttered, hoping I wouldn't have to say more.

"Okay, guys," Alison announced immediately. "Party's over. Time to pack it in."

We said our good-byes at the front door. Alison kissed me on the cheek. I think Denise hugged me. K.C. mumbled something about being slightly inebriated, then almost fell into the leafy branches of the large, white oleander that sat to the right of the front door. Then they were gone, and the house was quiet, save for the whispering of the leaves.

Surprisingly, I had no trouble falling asleep.

My stomach seemed to settle down the minute everyone left, so I attributed the discomfort to all the excitement: the elaborate dinner; a house full of new people; my first kiss in forever; Josh; Josh; Josh. "Yes!" I said in Alison's voice. Then again, watching her clap her hands together and jump up and down with glee. "Yes, yes, yes!"

And then I must have fallen asleep, because the next thing I knew I was dreaming. Wild dreams. Crazy dreams. Dreams where I was running around the house in helpless circles, trying to find Alison, to warn her of danger, although the danger was nonspecific, undefined. At one point, I was climbing up the stairs when K.C. jumped out at me from the shadows, long legs flying, karate-style, through the air toward my stomach.

I gasped, doubled forward in my bed, barely made it to the bathroom, where I threw up, copiously and repeatedly. But even a thorough purging of the night's dinner provided little relief. I sat on the tile floor, my head spinning, painful spasms shooting through my body like pinballs, wondering whether it was possible I was having an attack of appendicitis. Unlikely, I knew. It was much more likely to be a simple case of overindulgence, or perhaps even food poisoning. I wondered if any of my guests had gotten sick.

Oh, God, poor Josh, I thought, pushing myself to my feet and creeping slowly, my back hunched, like a doddering old woman, toward my bedroom window. I pulled back the lace curtains, stared at the cottage behind my house, surprised to see the lights still on. I glanced at the clock beside my bed. It was almost three in the morning, awfully late for Alison to be up. Was she sick as well? I pulled on my housecoat and gingerly made my way down the stairs.

I unlocked the kitchen door and tiptoed outside, the grass cool on my bare feet. A sudden rush of nausea almost overwhelmed me, and I gulped frantically at the fresh air until the feeling subsided. I took several long, deep breaths before continuing toward the cottage door. It was then I heard the sound of laughter from inside the cottage. Clearly, Alison wasn't sick. Nor was she alone.

I returned to the house, relieved that Alison was okay, that it appeared no one else had gotten sick. My reputation as a cook was safe, I thought, and might have laughed had it not been for the renewed spasms that catapulted me toward the kitchen sink. Dozens of ceramic eyes looked down disapprovingly from the shelves above my head, the pitiless, blank stares of the china ladies passing silent judgment on my condition. *Serves you right*, the women shouted through pouting, painted lips. *That'll teach you to have too good a time.*

I was halfway up the stairs when the phone rang.

Who would be calling me at this hour? I wondered, moving as quickly as my stomach would permit. Alison? Had she seen me outside the cottage door? I pushed my bent frame toward the phone beside my bed, answered it at the start of its fifth ring. "Hello?"

"Have a nice evening?" the voice asked.

Not Alison. A man. "Who is this?"

"I have a message for you from Erica Hollander."

"What!"

"She says you better watch your step."

"Who is this?" The phone went dead in my hands. "Hello? Hello?" I slammed down the receiver, too angry to speak, too weak to try. I fell back on the bed, hands shaking, heart pounding, my brain alternating between trying to place the voice and to put it out of my mind altogether. What did his strange message mean? Of course, sleep was no longer an option. I spent the balance of the night rolling from one side of the bed to the other, either too hot or too cold, my teeth chattering or my forehead bathed in sweat, my arms securing the blankets tightly under my chin, my feet kicking them angrily back to the foot of the bed. For hours I lay on my back observing the moonlight slither through the lace of my curtains, watching the darkness bleed from the sky until it grew light. Whenever it looked as if I might be granted a few minutes' respite, a not-quite-familiar voice would sneak up beside me and whisper in my ear: *I have a message for you from Erica Hollander. She says you better watch your step.*

At around eight o'clock, I pushed myself out of bed. I was still nauseous and weak, but at least my stomach was no longer threatening to burst from my body. My forehead felt a little warm to the touch, and my hands were still trembling. I decided to make some tea, maybe eat a piece of toast, although, at the thought of food, my stomach lurched. Maybe just tea, I decided, about to head downstairs when I heard voices outside my window.

I shuffled toward the sound and pulled back the curtains, careful to stay out of sight. Alison was standing in the open doorway of the cottage talking to Denise, both still dressed in last night's clothes. Denise was doing most of the talking, although I couldn't make out what she was saying. The look on Alison's face, however, told me she was paying close attention.

"Come on, sleepyhead," Denise suddenly shouted toward the inside of the cottage. "Time to get your bony ass out of there."

Seconds later, K.C. stood in the doorway. His shirt hung open and his blue jeans rode dangerously low on his skinny hips, emphasizing the line of dark hair that spiraled from the center of his bare chest down past his belly button, then disappeared beneath the buckle of his black leather belt. His short brown hair was matted and uncombed, and sleep clung to his eyes as carelessly as the half-smoked cigarette that dangled from his lips.

I watched him toss the cigarette into my bed of pink and white impatiens, then lean toward Alison and whisper something in her ear, his fingers playing with the gold necklace at her throat as his eyes glanced toward my bedroom window. Was he talking about me? I wondered, careful to keep out of sight. Did he know I was there?

Alison pushed him playfully aside, waving after them as he and Denise ambled along the side of the house to the street. My eyes followed after them until they disappeared into the shadow of a nearby tree. When I looked back, I saw Alison staring up at me, a strange look on her face. She waved, signaled that she was coming over. Seconds later, looking remarkably fresh and rested for someone who'd been up all night, she was at the kitchen door.

"Are you all right?" she asked as soon as she saw me.

"I was sick last night." I promptly collapsed into one of the kitchen chairs.

"Sick? You mean like throwing-up sick?"

"I mean like throwing-up sick."

"Oh, yuck! That's awful. I hate throwing up. It's my least favorite thing in the whole world."

"I can't say I'm overly fond of it myself."

"You know how some people tell you that throwing up will make you feel better? Not me. I'd rather feel sick as a dog for weeks on end than throw up. That's why it was always such a joke to me when people thought I was bulimic. As if I would ever do anything to make myself vomit. I mean, yuck!"

I could almost see the exclamation point.

"I remember when I was a little girl," she continued, "and I got sick one night after eating too much red licorice, and every night after that, when I'd climb into bed, I'd ask my mother if I was going to be all right. And she'd roll her eyes and say yes, but I wasn't convinced, so I'd make her promise. Even still, I'd grit my teeth until I fell asleep."

"You didn't believe your mother?"

Alison shrugged, her eyes circling the kitchen. "You want some tea?"

"I'd love some."

She busied herself with the mechanics of making tea. She filled the kettle with water, dropped a tea bag into a mug, got the milk out of the fridge. "You probably drank too much champagne," she ventured, eyes glued to the kettle.

"A watched pot never boils," I told her.

"What?"

"'A watched pot never boils.' One of my mother's little aphorisms."

"Aphorism? Good word. That's like, what, a saying?"

"More or less."

Alison obligingly looked away from the kettle and toward the window. "So I guess you saw me talking to Denise and K.C." It was more statement than question.

I nodded, said nothing.

"They wanted to see the cottage." She paused, studied her bare feet. "Anyway, we stayed up pretty late talking, and next thing I knew, Denise was curled up in my bed and K.C. was passed out on the floor." The teakettle whistled its readiness. Alison jumped at the sound, then laughed. "Looks like your mother was right. I just had to stop watching it."

"Mother knows best." I chose my next words carefully. "Did you call your family to wish them a happy Thanksgiving?"

"No." Alison poured my tea. "Not quite ready to do that yet. Here. Drink this. It'll make you feel better."

"I hope so." I took a tentative sip.

"So, did you enjoy last night? I mean, aside from the throwing-up part."

I laughed, understanding the subject of her family was closed, at least for now. "I had a wonderful time."

"I think Josh really likes you."

"You do?"

"I could tell by the way he looked at you. He thinks you're something special."

"He's a very nice man." I took another sip of my tea, felt it burn the tip of my tongue, pulled back.

"Careful," Alison warned too late. "It's hot."

"So, what are you up to today? Going to the beach with your friends?"

"Not a chance. I'm going to stay right here and make sure you're okay."

"Oh, no. I don't want you to do that."

Alison pulled up a chair, plunked down beside me. "You took care of me when I got sick, didn't you?"

"Yes, but . . ."

"No buts." She smiled. "It's settled. I'm not going anywhere."

Not long after I finished the tea, my nausea returned, and I suffered through an agonizing round of dry heaves. Surprisingly, Alison made a wonderful nurse, holding a cool compress to my head and not leaving my side until I was safely tucked back in bed. "Sleep," I can still hear her repeating as she stroked my hair. "Sleep . . . sleep."

Whether it was from exhaustion, the sound of her voice, or the touch of her hand, within minutes I was sound asleep. This time, no dreams plagued me. I slept soundly, deeply, for several hours. When I opened my eyes, it was almost noon.

I sat up in bed, twisting my neck from side to side to get rid of the stiffness that had settled in. Then I heard a voice talking quietly from the second bedroom and realized it was Alison. "I didn't call to fight," I heard her say as I climbed out of bed, steadying myself against the wall as I shuffled toward the door.

"Everything is going exactly as planned," she continued as I stepped into the hall, drew closer. "You're just going to have to trust that I know what I'm doing."

I must have made a sound because she suddenly spun around in her seat, went ghostly white.

"Terry! How long have you been standing there? Are you all right?" The words tumbled from her mouth in a frantic rush, like sand from a broken hourglass. "Look, I have to go," she said into the portable phone at her ear, before stuffing it unceremoniously into the pocket of her white shorts. She jumped to her feet and quickly ushered me toward the sofa, then sat so close to me, our knees were touching. "My brother," she explained, patting the phone in her pocket. "I decided you were right, that the least I could do was call my family and wish them a happy holiday, let them know I'm okay."

"It didn't go well?"

"About as well as expected. Anyway, how are you? You look a hundred percent better."

"I feel better," I said without much conviction. What had Alison been talking to her brother about? What, I wondered, was going exactly as planned? "What have you been doing all morning?" I asked instead.

"First I went home, took a shower, changed my clothes. Then"—a huge grin swept across Alison's face, temporarily obliterating my concerns—"I found this." She grabbed a large, leather-bound photo album from the pillow beside her, balanced it across her lap. "I hope you don't mind. I stumbled across it when I was looking for something to read." She flipped it open. "Are these your parents?"

I found myself staring at an old black-and-white photograph of a smiling young couple at a public swimming pool, my father's skinny legs sticking out from underneath a pair of dark, oversize swim trunks, loafers on his feet, a straw hat on his head, my mother sitting beside him in a modest gingham bathing suit, hands clasped primly in her lap, hair piled high on her head, large, white sunglasses swamping her small face. How long had it been since I'd looked at these pictures? The album had been tucked away at the back of the highest shelf. How had Alison simply stumbled across it? "That's them," I said, brushing an invisible hair away from my mother's face, feeling her swat my hand aside. "They weren't married yet."

As Alison steadily turned the pages, I watched my parents grow up before my eyes, from shy young lovers to self-conscious newlyweds to nervous parents. "This one's my favorite." Alison pointed to a picture of my mother pressing a sad-eyed baby to her cheek. "Look at how cute you were."

"Cute, my ass. Just look at those bags under my eyes." I shook my head in dismay. "My mother claimed I didn't sleep through the night until I was three years old. And I peed in my pants until I was seven. No wonder they decided not to have any more kids."

Alison laughed, studied each page in turn. "Which one's you?" she asked suddenly, indicating a large photograph of a bunch of small children arranged in neat little rows, like pansies in a garden—my senior kindergarten class.

I pointed to a little girl in a white dress, frowning from the back row.

"You don't look very happy."

"I never liked having my picture taken."

"No? I love it. Oh, look at this one. Is this you?" Alison's index finger landed on a little girl in a plaid jumper, scowling beside her third-grade teacher.

"That's me all right."

"Would you just look at that face." Alison laughed. "You have the same expression in every picture, even as a teenager. Which one's Roger Stillman?"

"What?"

"Roger Stillman. Is he in any of these pictures?"

"No. He was a few grades ahead of me," I reminded her.

"Too bad. I would have liked to see what he looked like. What do you think happened to him?"

"I have no idea."

"Do you ever think of just picking up the phone and calling him? Saying, 'Hi, Roger Stillman, this is Terry Painter. Remember me?'"

"Never," I said, louder than I'd intended.

"Do you think he still lives in Baltimore?"

I shrugged my lack of interest, flipped to another page, saw my parents, now in glorious color, posed together on the front lawn of their first house in Delray Beach. They looked a little stiff, as if aware there were difficult times ahead. "Would you mind making me another cup of tea?" I asked.

"It would be my supreme pleasure." Alison pushed herself off the sofa. "How about some toast and jam to go with it?"

"Why not?"

"That's the spirit."

I leaned my head against the burgundy velvet of the sofa, closed my eyes, the sound of Alison's voice soft against my ear. *Everything is going exactly as planned*, she purred. And then another voice: *I have a message for you from Erica Hollander*, the stranger whispered in my ear. *She says you better watch your step.*

But I was too tired, too weak, to listen.

ELEVEN

The weeks between Thanksgiving and Christmas were especially busy, both at the hospital and at home. In the five years since my mother's death, I hadn't bothered much with the festive trappings of the holiday season. Indeed, I'd gone out of my way to ignore the holidays, often working overtime and volunteering for the graveyard shift. But Alison was determined to change that.

"What do you mean you're working on Christmas?" she wailed.

"It's just another day."

"No, it's not. It's Christmas. Can't you switch with somebody else?"

I shook my head. It was late afternoon and I was working in my garden. Alison was pacing restlessly back and forth on the lawn behind me.

"But that really sucks!" she protested, looking and sounding at least a decade younger than her twenty-eight years. "I mean, I was kind of hoping we could have Christmas together."

"We could do Christmas Eve."

Immediately her face brightened. "That's right. Lots of families open their presents on Christmas Eve, don't they? I guess that would be okay. Can I go with you to pick out a tree?"

"A tree?" I couldn't remember the last time I'd had a Christmas tree.

"You have to have a tree! What's Christmas without a tree? And we'll get decorations and little white lights. My treat, of course. It's the least I can do. It'll be so great. Can we do that?"

How could I say no? In the weeks since I'd been sick, Alison had become a regular—and increasingly welcome—part of my day. We spoke often on the phone from our respective places of work, had dinner together two or three times a week, occasionally went to the movies or for a leisurely stroll along the beach. No matter how busy our schedules, Alison found time for us to be together. And despite my initial reservations about tenants in general, and Alison in particular, she simply ran roughshod over any misgivings I might have had. I was powerless where she was concerned, I realized as we drove along Military Trail some days later, a tall Scotch pine protruding from the half-open trunk of my car. Alison had managed, in the space of only several months, to become an integral part of my life, and despite the twelve-year difference in our ages, probably the closest friend I'd ever had.

"Is this not the most absolutely gorgeous tree in the whole wide world?" she asked after we'd finished attaching the last of the delicate, pink bows to its long, sharp branches. We stood back to admire our handiwork.

"It's absolutely the most gorgeous tree in the whole wide world," I concurred, and she hugged me.

"This is going to be the best Christmas ever," Alison declared as Christmas Eve drew closer, and she added yet another present to the growing pile under the tree that she'd stationed in the corner of my living room.

"I think she's homesick," I confided to Margot at work. "I mean, you should see what she's done to the house. There are decorations everywhere, mountains of holly sprigs, and I can't move without bumping into one of these weird little Santas she has everywhere."

"Sounds like she's taking over," Margot observed with a laugh. "How long before she moves in and you go back to living in the cottage?" She reached for a patient's file, answered the ringing phone beside her.

"I think she's just homesick," I repeated, vaguely annoyed with Margot, although I wasn't sure why.

Margot held out the phone. "For you."

"Terry Painter," I announced, expecting to hear Alison's voice. Had she somehow sensed we were talking about her?

"Terry, it's Josh Wylie."

My heart sank.

"I really hate to do this to you again," he was saying as I lowered my chin to my chest, silently mouthing the words along with him. "Something's come up, and I'm going to have to cancel our lunch. I'm really sorry."

"So am I," I said truthfully. This was the third lunch date Josh had canceled in as many weeks. Aside from a few quick exchanges when he'd dropped by to visit his mother, we hadn't seen each other since Thanksgiving.

"How about dinner?" he surprised me now by asking. "I have to be up your way later and I have a little something for you."

"You have something for me?"

"'Tis the season. It's just a little token of my appreciation. For being so nice to my mother," he added quickly. "How about I pick you up at seven o'clock?"

"Seven o'clock would be fine."

"Seven o'clock it is." He clicked off without saying good-bye.

"Somebody looks awfully pleased with herself," Margot said with a sly wink.

I said nothing, my mind already on the night ahead. So what if Josh had canceled three lunch dates in a row. One dinner equaled three lunches any day. Not only that, but he had a gift for me—a small token of his appreciation, he'd said. *For being so nice to my mother.* I tried to imagine what it could be. A bottle of perfume? Some fancy soaps? Maybe a silk scarf or even a small brooch? No, it was way too early for jewelry. Our relationship—if a few kisses and several canceled lunch dates could be called a relationship—was still in the beginning stages. It wouldn't be appropriate, as my mother might have said, for him to be showering me with extravagant gifts. It didn't matter. Whatever Josh gave me would be wonderful. I wondered what I could get him in return, deciding to ask Myra for her advice. Her condition had deteriorated in the last few weeks, and she was understandably depressed. Perhaps news of my upcoming dinner date with her son might cheer her up.

But Myra was asleep when I entered her room, so after checking her IV and adjusting her blankets, I left. "I'm having dinner with your son tonight," I said from the doorway. "Wish me luck."

But the only response I got was an involuntary whistle that escaped Myra's lips as she exhaled. I closed the door and stepped into the hall, where I was almost run over by one of the orderlies. "What's going on?" I called after him as he raced down the hall.

"Patient in 423 came out of her coma," he called back excitedly.

"Sheena O'Connor?" I asked, but the young man had already disappeared around a corner. "My God, I don't believe it."

I hurried to room 423, pushed open the door. The room was overflowing with doctors and assorted medical personnel, everyone moving about purposefully, their actions both condensed and exaggerated, as if the scene were being enacted in both slow motion and fast-forward simultaneously. I caught a glimpse of the pale young woman who was the calm at the center of the storm. She was sitting up in bed, still attached to a myriad of tubes, and our eyes connected for only the briefest of seconds as I was backing out of the room.

"Wait!" Her tiny voice pierced the air.

I froze as half a dozen bodies swiveled in my direction, half a dozen faces found my own.

"I know you," the girl said. "You're the one who's been singing to me, aren't you?"

"You heard me?" I approached the bed, the doctors and nurses who surrounded her clearing a path for me.

"I heard you," Sheena said softly, leaning back against her pillow, large, dark eyes fluttering to a close.

"It's a miracle," a hushed voice whispered from a corner of the room.

"Has anyone notified her family?" someone asked.

"Her parents are on their way."

"Should we call the police?"

"They've already been notified."

"It's a miracle," someone else said. "A true Christmas miracle."

I couldn't wait to share the news of Sheena's miraculous recovery with Alison, so I decided to stop off at the gallery where she worked. Maybe Alison could help me select a gift for Josh, something *appropriate*, I thought, feeling giddy and euphoric, as I pulled into a just vacated parking space right on Atlantic Avenue. Another miracle!

I didn't see Alison when I entered the store. Nor did I see Denise. Indeed, the gallery appeared to be deserted. How on earth did they stay in business? I wondered, looking around, noting that the painting of the woman with the wide-brimmed sun hat no longer occupied its usual place on the far wall. I felt a pang of regret. Alison had been right about it being the perfect painting for my living room. It was too bad I hadn't taken her advice and scooped it up when I had the chance. Obviously, someone much more decisive than I had done just that.

My life was a collection of missed opportunites, I thought glumly, deciding that was about to change.

Starting with tonight.

Starting with Josh.

"Hello?" I called out. "Alison?"

"Can I help you?"

I turned to see an attractive woman approximately my own age walking toward me, her high heels clicking against the hardwood floor.

"I'm sorry. I was in my office. Have you been waiting long?"

"Just got here."

The woman smiled, although the skin around her mouth was pulled so tight, it was hard to tell whether she was happy or in pain. Reflexively, I brought my hand to my cheek, pushed at the fine lines around my eyes. "Is there something in particular you're looking for?" she asked.

"Actually, I'm looking for someone who works here. Alison Simms."

The woman's smile became a tense, straight line. "Alison no longer works here," she said curtly.

"She doesn't?"

"She left last week."

"She left? Why?"

"I'm afraid I had to let her go."

"You had to let her go?" I repeated, feeling like a parrot. "Why?"

"Perhaps you should ask her."

Alison hadn't said a word about being let go. She *had* told me that her boss had requested she not receive any more calls at work. Dear God, was I the reason she'd lost her job? "And this happened last week?" I heard myself ask, my mind reeling.

"Is there anything *I* can help you with?" Fern Lorelli was clearly anxious to move on.

I muttered something about needing a Christmas gift for a friend and eventually purchased an attractively masculine ballpoint pen I thought Josh might like, but my heart wasn't in it. Why had Alison been fired? More importantly, why hadn't she told me? I made up my mind to ask her as soon as I got home.

My phone was ringing as I pulled into the driveway. I ran into the house, the bells Alison had hung on the front door jingling as I raced into the kitchen and grabbed for the phone. I dropped the small bag containing my new purchase on the counter beside three small plastic Santas, all of whom stared at the bag with bemused curiosity. "Hello?"

A soft male voice slithered through the phone wire like a snake. "Buy anything for me?"

My breath froze in my lungs, even as my eyes darted nervously toward the back window. Had someone been following me? Was I being watched? Why? I wondered, my arms folding protectively across my chest, as if I were standing in my kitchen completely naked. "Who is this? What do you want?"

My answer was a sly chuckle, followed by silence and the familiar drone of the dial tone.

"Damn it!" I hung up and immediately pressed *69. But whoever was calling had blocked the trace. I slammed the phone into its carriage.

It rang again almost immediately.

"Look, I don't know what your problem is," I said instead of hello. "But if you don't stop bothering me, I'm going to call the police."

"Terry?"

"Josh!"

"I know I broke our lunch date, but do you really think the police are necessary?"

"I'm so sorry. I've been getting these crank calls. . . . It's nothing." I sighed, shook thoughts of other voices out of my head.

"Rough day?"

"Actually, no," I said, regrouping, refocusing. "It was a great day." I wondered briefly why he was calling. Surely it wasn't to talk about my day. "You remember Sheena O'Connor? She came out of her coma this afternoon," I prattled on, almost afraid to let him speak. "It was incredible. Everyone's calling it a Christmas miracle."

"It must have been very exciting."

"It was amazing. And the best part was that she'd heard me singing to her while she was comatose. Isn't that incredible?" I asked, sounding just like Alison, aware I'd used superlatives three times in as many seconds. "Anyway, I'll tell you all about it tonight."

An awful silence followed. For the second time that day, my heart sank, my happiness crashing to the floor with such force I felt the room shake beneath my feet.

"I feel like such a jerk," Josh was saying.

"Is there a problem?" I opened the nearest drawer and stuffed the gift bag from Lorelli Gallery inside it. Clearly, I wasn't going to be seeing Josh Wylie anytime soon.

"It's Jillian," he said, referring to his daughter. "She came home from school and said she wasn't feeling very well."

"Does she have a fever?"

"I don't think so, but I just wouldn't feel comfortable about leaving her. I'm so sorry. I can't believe I'm doing this to you twice in one day. Maybe you *should* call the police."

"Some days are like that," I said gamely, slamming the cupboard drawer shut, watching the three Santas collapse against each other, like dominoes.

"I feel really terrible about this."

"You'll make it up to me," I ventured bravely.

"Absolutely. As soon as I get back from California."

"You're going away?"

"Just for a couple of weeks. The kids have cousins in San Francisco. We leave the day after tomorrow, get back January third."

So much for New Year's Eve, I thought.

"I hope you don't hate me."

"These things happen."

"I *will* make it up to you."

"Have a wonderful trip," I said. "And tell Jillian I hope she feels better soon."

"I will."

"See you next year," I said cheerily, then hung up the phone before I burst into tears. "Damn it!" I swore. "Damn it. Damn it. Damn it!"

There was a knock on the kitchen door. I gasped, budding tears coating my eyes, leaving a filmy residue.

"I'm sorry," Alison apologized over the sound of jingling bells as I opened the door to let her in. "I didn't mean to scare you."

I caught a glimpse of strawberry curls, white shorts, and long, tanned legs, before turning away.

"Terry, what's wrong?"

"Why didn't you tell me you lost your job?" I demanded, swiping at my eyes with the back of my hand, refusing to look at her.

I could almost feel the color drain from Alison's face. "What?"

"I dropped into the gallery this afternoon. I spoke to Fern Lorelli."

"Oh."

"She said she had to let you go."

Silence. Then: "What else did she say?"

"Not much."

"She didn't say why?"

Wiping the last errant tears from my eyes, I pivoted around to face her. Alison's gaze immediately dropped to the floor. "She said I should ask you."

Alison nodded, still unable to look me in the eye. "I was going to tell you."

"But you didn't."

"I thought I'd wait until I found another job. I didn't want you worrying about the rent. I didn't want to ruin Christmas."

"Why were you let go?"

Slowly Alison lifted her gaze to mine. "I didn't do anything wrong," her voice implored. "Apparently there was some money missing. Certain figures didn't add up. . . . I swear it wasn't me."

"It was just easier for her to fire you than confront her own niece," I offered after a pause, biting down on my tongue to keep from adding, *I told you so.*

"You don't have to worry about anything. Honestly. I have enough money."

"I'm not worried about the money."

"Then what is it? Are you worried about me? Don't be," she said before I could respond. "I'm sorry I didn't tell you.

I won't lie to you ever again. I promise. Please don't be angry with me."

"I'm not angry."

"You're sure?"

I nodded, realizing it was true, that if I was angry with anyone, it was with myself. For being such a damn fool.

"I have a great idea," Alison suddenly announced, running from the room.

Seconds later, I heard her foraging around under the Christmas tree, and seconds after that she was back, a brightly, if somewhat sloppily, wrapped gift in her hands. She extended it toward me. "Since we're opening the presents early anyway, it won't hurt to open this one now. Ignore the wrapping. I actually took a course in gift-wrapping once, would you believe? Go on. Open it. It'll make you feel better."

"What is it?"

"Open it."

I tore the wrapping off the brown cardboard box, opened it. Large dark eyes stared up at me from under a shroud of translucent bubble wrap. Slowly, carefully, I lifted the head vase into the air. The china lady sported an elaborate blond coif, a large blue bow at her throat, and mock diamond studs in her ears. "She's beautiful. Where did you find her?"

"At the flea market over by Woolbright. Isn't she great? I mean, I know you think they're junk and everything, but I couldn't resist. I saw her, and I thought it was kind of like a sign or something."

"A sign?"

"Like I was meant to find her, and you were meant to have her. Fate," she said with an embarrassed roll of her eyes. "I mean, the other heads were more your mother's. This one's, well . . . she's all yours. Your firstborn, so to speak. Do you like her?"

"I like her very much."

Alison squealed with delight. "She's in mint condition. Check the eyelashes."

"She's perfect." I turned the china head over in my hands. "Thank you."

"Feel better?"

"Much."

"Where are you going to put her?" Alison glanced toward the five shelves of ladies' heads.

"This one's pretty special. I think I'll keep her in my room."

Alison beamed, as if I'd just paid her the highest of compliments. "So, I guess I'll see you later?"

"Later," I agreed, hearing the bells jingle as the kitchen door closed behind her. I wandered into the dining area, smiling at the sprigs of holly and pine that lay across the top of the cabinet, at the apple-cheeked Santa Claus who stood in the middle of the dining room table, at the papier-mâché reindeer that leaned against the wall.

The living room was more of the same: more Santas, more reindeer, at least a dozen elves. If there was a space, something Christmassy was in it. And then there was the tree itself—tall and full and smelling of the forest, its branches swathed in pink bows and small white lights, presents swelling from beneath its base. Just looking at it buoyed my spirits. And it was all Alison's doing, I recognized, cradling the china head vase in my hands as if it were indeed my firstborn child.

Alison was the true Christmas miracle, I decided.

What was I doing moping around the house because some guy had stood me up? Just think of all the things I had to be grateful for.

Name three, I heard Alison urge.

"My health," I said reflexively, then groaned. "Sheena O'Connor's amazing recovery." My God, she'd actually heard me sing to her! "Alison," I whispered, then again, louder, more forcefully: "Alison."

I looked down at the china head in my hands, my heart full of remorse. I was no better than Fern Lorelli, I thought with disgust. I'd used Alison as a scapegoat, transferred my anger and disappointment with someone else to her.

How could I have let her leave without giving her something in return? I reached under the tree and selected a small parcel wrapped in silver foil. Then I carried it back into the kitchen, leaving the china head on the kitchen table, next to the Santa Claus salt-and-pepper shakers Alison had picked up at Target. The sound of jingle bells followed me across the small patch of yard to the cottage door.

I heard the voices as I was about to knock.

"I told you to let me handle this," Alison was saying, her voice an angry hiss, intense enough to be heard from outside.

"I'm just here to help."

"I don't need your help. I know what I'm doing."

"Since when?"

I turned to leave, my shoulder accidentally brushing against the bells hanging from the bronze knocker, setting them jangling. Almost immediately, the door opened, and Alison stood before me with questioning eyes. "Terry!"

Instinctively, I thrust the gift toward her. "I wanted you to have this."

"Oh, that's so sweet." She glanced toward the interior of the cottage. "You didn't have to."

"I know, but I thought . . ." What did I think? "Is someone here?" I ventured meekly.

There was a moment's strained silence as a handsome young man materialized behind Alison, as if waved there by a magic wand. He was several inches taller than Alison, with fair skin, curly, dark hair, and the disturbingly blue eyes of a Siamese cat. Well-defined biceps bulged from beneath the short sleeves of a black T-shirt that stretched tightly across his chest.

"That would be me," the young man said, smiling. He reached around Alison and extended his hand.

"Terry," Alison said, her gaze drifting toward the grass, the second time this afternoon she'd been too embarrassed to look me in the eyes, "I'd like you to meet Lance Palmay. My brother."

TWELVE

A pleasure to meet you," Lance said, his handshake surprisingly gentle.

"I called him after Thanksgiving. Remember?" Alison asked.

I nodded, recalling the one-sided conversation I'd overheard the morning I was so desperately sick.

Everything is going exactly as planned. You're just going to have to trust that I know what I'm doing.

"Lance decided he needed to fly down and see for himself how I'm making out."

"Looks like she's managing just fine," Lance pronounced.

"That's why I came over before, to tell you about Lance," Alison explained, inviting me inside the cottage with a sweep of her hand. "We got kind of sidetracked. . . ."

I'm not sure what I expected to see when I stepped inside—a tinsel-covered wonderland, a veritable army of toys, a re-creation of the North Pole? But surprisingly, the cottage bore only a few traces of Christmas—a large red candle, surrounded by a few careless sprigs of holly, on the glass coffee table in front of the deep purple love seat, a lonely Santa Claus doll lying facedown on the bentwood rocker. That was it.

"Do you want a cold drink?" Alison offered.

I shook my head, watched as Lance flopped down on the large floral-print chair. He looks way too comfortable, I thought, masking the unkind thought with a clearing of my throat. "When did you get in?"

"Plane got into Fort Lauderdale around twelve-thirty." He smiled at Alison. "I rented a car at the airport. White Lincoln Town Car, no less. It's parked across the street. You must have seen it. Surprised old sleepyhead here as she was getting out of bed."

Alison's eyes narrowed as her shoulders tensed.

"Where are you staying?" I asked.

The two exchanged wary glances.

"We were just talking about that," Alison began.

"I thought I could stay here for a few days," Lance said as if the decision had already been made.

"Here?" I repeated when I could think of nothing else to say.

"Of course if you have any objections . . ." Alison said quickly.

"Why would she object?" Lance asked, looking right at me.

"But where would you sleep?" The sofa was far too short for the elongated legs of a former high school basketball player, the double bed way too small to accommodate a brother and sister comfortably.

"This is a pretty neat chair." Lance pounded its oversize arms. "And I can always throw a pillow on the floor."

"Is it all right?" Alison asked me again. "Because honestly, if it isn't, Lance can find a motel."

"At this time of year? Without a reservation? I wouldn't count on it."

"I don't want you to be uncomfortable," Alison said.

"Absolutely not," Lance concurred. "If my staying here would make you feel uncomfortable in any way . . ."

"It's *your* comfort I'm concerned with."

"Don't worry about me."

"I'll pay you extra," Alison volunteered.

"Don't be silly. That's not the point."

"Terry had a bad experience with her last tenant," Alison told her brother.

"How so?"

"Too long a story." I shook my head. "Well, okay then, I guess it's okay. A few days, you said?"

"Absolutely," Alison agreed.

"Christmas . . . . New Year's, tops," Lance said, effortlessly stretching the few days to ten.

"Well . . ."

"Can I open my present now?" Alison asked eagerly. Without waiting for my reply, she tore off the silver wrapping paper, her eyes widening with delight when she saw what was inside. "A wallet! Oh, that's so great. I need a wallet. How'd you know that?"

I laughed, picturing the loose bills that were always tumbling around inside her purse.

"We are just so tuned in to each other, don't you think?" Alison stated more than asked, turning the honey-colored leather wallet over in her hands, caressing its smooth sides. "It's amazing. Don't you think?"

"I think it's a very nice wallet," Lance said. "Terry is obviously a woman of impeccable taste."

Was he being sarcastic? I couldn't tell.

"I should go." I turned toward the door.

"You'll come with us for dinner, won't you?" Alison asked.

"I don't think so. I'm not very hungry. You guys go, get reacquainted."

"Okay," Alison agreed reluctantly, "but only if you promise to spend the day with us tomorrow."

"Tomorrow?"

"I know you're not working tomorrow, and I want to show Lance all around Delray."

"You don't need me for that."

"Yeah, I do. Please. It won't be the same without you."

"You know it's pointless to argue," Lance said with a laugh.

He was right, and we all knew it.

"You have to come," Alison persisted. "Please. It'll be so fun. Please. Please. Say you'll at least think about it."

"I'll think about it," I said.

Of course, in the end I agreed to go. What other choice did I have? It's pointless to say that I was being dangerously naive, even reckless, that I was deluding myself into thinking that everything was going to be all right, that Alison and her brother were exactly the people they represented themselves to be. I've said all these things to myself, and much more besides. But I continued to rationalize my doubts away. I convinced myself Alison was sincere in her reasons for not telling me she'd been fired, and that, of course, she'd had nothing to do with any money that might be missing from the gallery.

And what of the conversation I'd overheard at the cottage door?

I told you to let me handle this.

Handle what?

I'm just here to help.

I don't need your help. I know what I'm doing.

What did it mean?

Nothing, I assured myself that night. Alison and her brother could have been talking about anything. What self-conscious paranoia made me think their conversation had anything to do with me? Not everything was about me, as my mother might have said. Whatever Alison and her brother had been arguing about probably didn't concern me at all.

Handle what?

I was too tired to try figuring it out. And the truth was, I didn't want to. I didn't want to believe that Alison was anything other than the beautiful free spirit who'd brought magic into my otherwise mundane existence. Why would I assume she had ulterior motives or that she might be planning anything sinister? Why couldn't her brother's visit be as unexpected and spontaneous as they claimed?

So I made a conscious decision to ignore the warning bells that were jingling like mad in my head, much like the bells Alison had hung from our doors. I rationalized away my instincts, reminded myself that Lance Palmay would be gone in a few days, scolded myself for being so suspicious, so uptight. Then I made a cup of tea and carried it into the living room, where I curled up on the sofa with a new book, the white lights of the Christmas tree winking behind me, the smell of pine needles competing with the aroma of white oleander. I took a sip of the soothingly hot liquid, read a few pages, read them again when they failed to register, then slowly drifted off to sleep, the book slipping from my hands to the floor, as old ghosts rushed toward me from the darkness and distant voices whispered in my ears.

In my dream I was kissing Roger Stillman in the backseat of his old red Thunderbird, his hands groping me under my sweater and skirt. A succession of increasingly loud moans escaped his lips as he triumphantly rolled my panties down over my hips and climbed on top of me. "Are you wearing a rubber?" I asked him, feeling my flesh tear as he pushed his way roughly inside me. I cried out, opening my eyes, eyes that had been tightly closed throughout most of our encounter, and that's when I saw the policeman staring at us through the car window, his flashlight illuminating the careless sprinkling of dark hairs across the top of Roger's bare buttocks. I screamed, but Roger continued humping away, like an unwelcome dog on a human leg. Any leg, any human, I realized, pushing him off me, watching him effortlessly morph into Alison's brother, Lance Palmay.

"Could you step out of the car, please?" the police officer directed, and Roger/Lance complied with an easy smile.

I struggled with my clothing, trying to push my skirt down over the panties twisted around my knees, but the policeman was already climbing into the backseat, assuming Roger's former position on top of me, his flashlight directed at my eyes so that I couldn't see his face, his large penis pushing its way toward my mouth. "You've been a bad girl," he was saying in Josh Wylie's soothing baritone. "I'm going to have to tell your mother."

"Please don't do that," I begged as his monstrous organ forced my lips apart. "Please don't tell my mother."

"Tell me what?" my mother asked, suddenly materializing on the seat beside me.

Which is when I woke up.

"Well, that was fun," I muttered, my heart pounding as I looked around the room, dark except for the flickering white lights of the tree behind me. I checked my watch, discovered I'd been sleeping for several hours, which meant I'd probably be up half the night. I rolled my head back, letting it drop lazily from one shoulder to the other, and waited for my heartbeat to return to normal. I realized, with equal amounts of shame and surprise, that the dream had excited me in spite of its peculiarities. In spite of my mother.

Or maybe because of her.

I marveled at the appearance of Roger Stillman in my dream. I didn't think I'd ever dreamed about him before, even during the heat of what might have been described, rather generously, as our relationship. And why the link to Alison's brother? Yes, they were both tall and good-looking, but so what? My subconscious had obviously intuited a deeper connection, even if my conscious mind had yet to determine what that connection might be.

I wiped a trickle of perspiration from the side of my neck, massaged the tenderness at my shoulders, my hand falling across my breast, the way Roger Stillman's hand had done, my nipples hardening at the memory of his fingers reaching underneath my blouse to unhook the clasp at the front of my bra. I felt my bare breasts rush into his waiting hands, recalled the way he fumbled with my pliant flesh, manipulating it like cookie dough, his eager mouth sucking on my nipples, as ferociously as a starving infant.

I remembered my mother's barely concealed disgust each time she looked at my maturing body, as if my breasts were a deliberate act of rebellion on my part, something for which I should be duly ashamed.

"Go away, Mother," I whispered now, lying back on the sofa, recalling how clumsily Roger had pulled on the zipper of my pants before pushing his hand down the front of my panties. I thought of Josh's hands, imagined his fingers in place of Roger's, felt them dancing around my most secret folds before disappearing inside me.

I cried out, my own fingers unable to follow my mind's lead, to provide my body the relief it craved. Instead I flipped onto my stomach and pressed myself against the hard edge of the sofa, its soft pillows muffling my embarrassed cries, my body shaking with a series of mild convulsions.

Instantly, my mother's shame swept over me.

I pushed myself to my feet and looked around, half-expecting my mother to be sitting in one of the Queen Anne chairs, watching me, as she had watched me in my dream. But the room was mercifully empty of ghosts.

I walked to the window, stared out at the street, watched large palm leaves dance in the shadows of the tall streetlight. I pressed my head against the glass, clasping my hands tightly behind my back. I caught a flicker of movement across the street, a shadow where before had been nothing. Was someone there? Dear God, had anyone seen me?

Someone's always watching, my mother admonished as I rushed to the front door, threw it open, and stared into the night.

Bettye McCoy and her two idiot dogs were rounding the corner and coming this way. I watched them approach, totally oblivious to my presence in the darkened doorway. She was wearing a pair of tight blue jeans and a cropped red sweater, with matching red heels. A red headband held her thick blond hair in place. Like an aging and surgically enhanced Alice in Wonderland, I thought cruelly, listening to her heels click against the pavement as she was pulled along by her two dogs. Of course the dogs stopped every few seconds to sniff at each and every bush, repeatedly lifting their legs to mark their territory. Just do your business and move on, I thought, watching in growing dismay as one of the dogs suddenly spun around and lifted his rump into the air, dropping several unwelcome deposits in the middle of the sidewalk at the end of my walkway. I waited for Bettye McCoy to scoop the droppings into her waiting plastic bag, but instead she only smirked, then tucked the empty bag back inside her jeans pocket before walking away.

I reacted without thinking. "Excuse me!" I ran down the front path, stopping just short of the neat pile of fresh excrement. "Excuse me," I called again when Bettye McCoy failed to take notice.

Her dogs began to bark and pull at their leashes. "I'm sorry," Bettye McCoy said, reluctantly turning around. "Were you addressing me?"

"Do you see anyone else?"

"Is there something I can do for you?" Bettye McCoy arched one disdainful eyebrow.

"You can clean up after your dogs."

"I always clean up after my dogs."

"Not tonight, you didn't." I pointed at the small pile of dog feces by my feet.

"My dogs didn't do that."

I could scarcely believe my ears. "What are you talking about? I watched him do it." I pointed at the smaller of the two white dogs, who looked as if he were in danger of strangling on his leash.

"It's not Corky's," Bettye McCoy insisted. "Corky didn't do it."

"I was standing right in the doorway. I saw the whole thing."

"Corky didn't do it."

"Look. Why don't you just admit your dog did it, clean it up, and be on your way. Don't treat me like an idiot."

"You *are* an idiot," Bettye McCoy muttered, not quite under her breath.

I couldn't believe my ears. "What did you say?"

"I said you're an idiot," Bettye McCoy repeated brazenly. "First you chase poor Cedric out of your yard with a broom, and now you accuse Corky of pooping on your precious sidewalk. You know what you need, don't you?"

"Suppose you tell me."

"Get a man, lady, and stop picking on my dogs!"

"Keep them off my property or I'll lay them flat," I countered, our voices bouncing off the trees, echoing through the leaves. From out of the corner of my eye, I saw Alison and her brother walking up the street.

"Terry!" Alison rushed to my side.

"What's going on here?" Lance asked, trying to keep the bemusement in his eyes from spreading to the rest of his face.

"The woman's a lunatic," Bettye McCoy shouted, already in retreat.

"She wouldn't clean up after her dog," I said, understanding how hopeless I must sound.

"Her dog did this?" Lance pointed to the dog feces he'd narrowly missed stepping in.

I nodded, then watched in shock as he scooped the offending dog poo into his hands, then hurled it, with stunning accuracy, at Bettye McCoy's head. It splattered against her blond hair, clinging to the back of her head, like mud.

Bettye McCoy stopped, her shoulders rising around her ears as she spun around to face us, her face mirroring the openmouthed amazement of my own.

"You better close your mouth," Lance warned. "There might be more."

"You're all crazy," Bettye McCoy stammered, backing up and getting entwined in the dogs' leashes, almost losing her balance, then bursting into tears. "All of you."

We watched as she extricated herself from the dogs' leashes, a small turd dropping from her hair to her right shoulder, then falling toward the ground, landing on the toe of one red shoe. A final outraged squeal escaped Bettye McCoy's lips as she kicked off her shoes, gathered one yapping dog under each arm, then ran to the end of the block and disappeared.

"Think she'll call the police?" Alison asked.

"Oh, I don't think she'd want to chance this story making the rounds." I looked at Lance, who was grinning like the proverbial Cheshire cat. Had he really picked up a dog turd with his bare hands and hurled it at my tormentor? My hero, I thought with a laugh. "Thank you."

"Anytime."

We returned to the house in silence. "How was dinner?" I asked before I went inside.

"Not nearly as exciting as what was going on here," Alison said. "God, I can't leave you alone for a minute. Speaking of which, have you decided about tomorrow?"

I smiled, then laughed out loud. "What time do you want me to be ready?"

THIRTEEN

Lance knocked on my kitchen door at ten minutes after noon the following day. He was all in black; I was all in white. We looked like opposing pawns on a chessboard. "I thought you said eleven o'clock," I said, trying to keep my mother out of my voice.

"Slept in," he said without apology. "You ready to go?"

"Where's Alison?"

"Still in bed. Migraine."

"Oh, no! Is she all right?"

"Should be fine in a few hours."

A verbal minimalist, I decided, watching his eyes swallow my kitchen whole. "I better go check."

"Not necessary." Lance grabbed my floppy straw bag from the kitchen table, slung it over my shoulder. "Alison instructed me to take you to lunch, said she'll join us as soon as she can stand up straight."

"I think I should check on her first," I protested,

remembering how sick Alison had been with her last migraine, but Lance was already ushering me out the door, guiding me away from the cottage and around the side of the house.

"She'll be fine," he said, giving my elbow an extra squeeze as we reached the street. "Stop worrying."

"I just don't feel right about going."

"Come on. It'll give us a chance to get better acquainted."

I looked up and down the sun-soaked street. Shadows, like puddles, spilled across the road from the high trees. Waves of heat, like ocean surf, rolled up from the pavement. Several houses down, a large snowy egret stood, straight and still as stone, on a manicured front lawn. "Anywhere in mind?"

"The Everglades?"

"What!"

"Just joking. Nature's not my thing. Thought we'd try Elwood's. We can walk, and we don't have to worry about snakes."

"Don't be too sure." Elwood's was a converted filling station turned biker hangout that specialized in barbecue and Elvis memorabilia. It was located on Atlantic Avenue several blocks west of the Lorelli Gallery. "How do you know about Elwood's?"

"Alison pointed it out last night. Thought it looked interesting."

I shrugged, recalling the last time I'd been to Elwood's had been with Erica Hollander. I was about to suggest an alternative, but I decided against it, instinctively understanding that to argue with Alison's brother would be as pointless as arguing with Alison herself. Taking no for an answer was clearly not a family trait.

"It's unusual to be this hot in December," I remarked idly as we fell into step beside one another, the heat wrapping itself around my shoulders like a scratchy shawl. But Lance wasn't paying attention, his eyes flitting restlessly from one side of the street to the other, as if half-expecting someone to jump out at us from behind a neatly trimmed hedge. "Looking for anything in particular?"

"What kind of tree is that?" he asked suddenly, his finger brushing against the tip of my nose as he pointed to the squat palm tree in the middle of my neighbor's front yard. "Looks like it has a bunch of penises hanging from it."

"I beg your pardon!"

Lance bounded across my neighbor's lawn, kneeling beside the tree in question, and pointed at the numerous protuberances of various lengths that hung from its trunk. "You don't think they look like a bunch of uncircumcised dicks? Take a good look."

"You're crazy." Reluctantly I rolled my eyes toward the tree. "Oh, my God. You're right."

Lance laughed so loud, he startled the nearby egret, who soared gracefully into the air, like a giant paper plane. "Ain't nature grand?"

"They're called screw palms," I whispered.

"What?"

"You heard me."

"You're kidding me, right?"

"Honestly. That's their name."

"Screw palms?"

"I couldn't possibly make up something like that."

Lance shook his head, grabbed my elbow, picked up the

pace of our walk. “Come on,” he said, laughing. “All this talk about screwing is making me hungry.”

“You should have seen this city twenty years ago,” I was saying between bites of my hamburger. “Half these storefronts were vacant, the school system was a disaster, race relations were a mess. About the only business that was doing well was the drug trade.”

“Really?” It was the first time since I’d started my verbal tour of Delray that Lance had shown any real interest. “And how’s the drug trade doing these days?” he asked, surveying the line of motorcycles parked outside the large front patio where we were sitting. “I mean, where would a person go if he were interested in such things?”

“Jail, most likely,” I said as Lance’s lips curled into a grudging smile.

“Cute. You’re very cute.”

My turn to smile. *Cute* had never been a word used to describe me.

We watched a middle-aged man whose ragged, gray ponytail extended halfway down the back of his black leather jacket as he wiggled his sagging gut between two chairs. Grandpas on wheels, I thought, taking another bite of my burger, wondering how anyone could wear leather in this heat. “Now, of course, the city’s completely changed.”

“And what changed it exactly?”

I paused, trying to choose between the short and long answers, deciding on the short. “Money.”

Lance laughed. “Ah, yes. Money makes the world go round.”

“I thought it was love.”

"That's because you're a hopeless romantic."

"I am?"

"You're not?"

"Maybe," I admitted, squirming under his sudden scrutiny. "Maybe I am a romantic."

"Don't forget hopeless." He reached across the table and peeled several sweat-dampened hairs away from my forehead with a gentle but confident hand, as if he were teasing a bra strap off my shoulder.

I lowered my gaze to the table, the tips of Lance's fingers lingering on my flesh even after he'd removed his hand. "What about you?"

He lifted a sauce-coated sparerib from his plate to his mouth, tearing the meat off with one neat tug. "Well," he said with a wink, "I love money. Does that qualify?"

I took a sip of my beer, held the ice-cold glass against my throat, trying to ignore the perspiration trickling into the deep vee of my white T-shirt.

"Wow! Would you look at those babies!" Lance exclaimed, and I saw that Lance's attention had been captured by the two shiny black motorcycles with chrome-plated monkey-hanger handlebars that had just pulled up in front of the restaurant. "Aren't they beauties?"

"Harley-Davidsons?" I asked, pulling out the only brand with which I was familiar, trying to sound interested.

Lance shook his head. "Yamaha 750cc Viragos." He punctuated his sentence with an appreciative whistle.

"You obviously know a lot about motorcycles."

"A bit." He raised another barbecued rib to his lips, then slowly and meticulously stripped it bare.

I thought of Alison. She would have polished off those

ribs in a heartbeat. "Maybe we should call Alison. See how she's doing."

Lance patted his cell phone, which lay on the table next to his plate. "She knows my number."

"It's been over an hour."

"She'll call."

I rubbed the back of my neck, the sweat coating my fingers like shellac. "Has your family been very worried about her?"

He shrugged. "Nah. They pretty much know what to expect by now."

"Which is?"

"Alison's gonna do what Alison's gonna do. No point arguing. No point getting in her face about it."

"But you obviously felt concerned enough to fly down here and see for yourself."

"Just checking to make sure she's okay. I mean, she comes to Florida, doesn't know a soul . . ."

"She knew Rita Bishop," I said, recalling the name of Alison's friend.

"Who?"

"Rita Bishop." I wondered if I had the name correct.

Lance looked confused, although he tried to hide it by tearing into another rib. "Oh, yeah, Rita. Whatever happened to her anyway?"

I realized I'd forgotten to ask personnel to find out where she'd gone. "I don't know. Alison couldn't locate her."

"Typical." Lance released a deep breath of air. "It's hot," he said, as if noticing the temperature for the first time.

"I think it's sweet that you were concerned about your sister. I didn't think you were that close."

"Close enough to worry." He shrugged, an increasingly familiar gesture. "What can I say? Maybe I'm a romantic after all."

I couldn't help but smile. I liked Lance for worrying about Alison's welfare. "It's nice you could take the time off work."

"No problem when you're self-employed."

"What is it you do?" I tried to remember if Alison had ever mentioned her brother's occupation.

Lance looked surprised by the question. He coughed, ran his hand through his hair. "Systems analyst," he said, so quietly I almost didn't hear him.

My turn to be surprised. "They teach that sort of thing at Brown?"

"Brown?"

"Alison said you graduated summa cum laude."

He laughed, coughed a second time. "Long time ago. A lot of beer under the bridge since then." He hoisted his mug into the space between us, finished what was left in his glass, and swiveled around in his chair, looking for the waiter. "You ready for another one?"

My own mug was still half-full. "I'm fine for the moment."

"Another draft," Lance called to a bald and heavily tattooed waiter resting against the far wall. FEAR was stamped in large blue letters along his right forearm; NO MAN was imprinted on the other. Charming, I thought, noticing a man nursing a beer at a small round table in the corner, a red bandanna wrapped around his forehead like a blood-soaked strip of gauze. Long, calloused fingers stroked a beard that was dark and scruffy. The man was staring at me, I realized, thinking there was something disturbingly familiar about him, trying to remember if and when I'd seen him before.

"How's your burger?" Lance asked, swatting a buzzing insect away from his head as he squinted into the sunlight.

"It's fine."

"Just fine? My ribs were fantastic. I'm thinking of ordering another pound."

I glanced at his empty plate. "Are you serious?"

"I'm always serious about what I put in my mouth." His tongue lapped some errant sauce from his upper lip.

Was he flirting with me? Or was the heat starting to affect my brain? *Should have worn a hat*, I could almost hear my mother say.

I looked away, my eyes pulled back toward the man with the red bandanna. He cocked his head to one side, then raised his beer mug in a silent toast, as if he'd been expecting me to look his way again. Where had I seen him before?

"So, tell me what you think of my baby sister," Lance instructed as the waiter approached with his beer. Lance gulped at its large head, chewed it as if it were solid food.

"I think she's great."

"She involved with anyone special these days?"

"Not to my knowledge."

"She tell you about her ex-husband?"

"Just that he was a mistake."

Lance laughed, shook his head.

"You don't agree?"

"Seemed like a nice enough guy to me. But, hey, what do I know? She's the one who lived with him. Although Alison doesn't always know what's good for her," he added, his face darkening as a cloud passed by overhead.

"I don't think I agree with that."

"I don't think you know Alison as well as I do."

"Maybe not," I conceded, deciding to shift the focus of the conversation away from Alison. "What about you? Any sweet young thing on the horizon?"

"Not really." Lance allowed a slow smile to creep across his lips. "Actually, I've always had a thing for older women."

I laughed. "You should drop by the hospital one day. I'll introduce you to some of my patients."

Lance stretched his neck back over the top of his spine and poured half his beer down his throat. "So, what's the story on this guy who sings here every Thursday night?" he asked, as if this were the most logical of follow-ups.

I glanced at the large cardboard cutout of a Las Vegas–styled Elvis impersonator—long sideburns, rhinestone-studded, white jumpsuit, flowing cape, classic karate pose—that greeted patrons at the door to the restaurant's interior. "He's a Delray policeman, believe it or not."

"Is he any good?"

"Very good." I'd heard him the time I was here with Erica. I gasped, suddenly realizing where I'd seen the man with the red bandanna before. I'd seen him with Erica Hollander. My eyes shot toward the corner of the patio, but the man was no longer there.

"Something wrong?" Lance asked, signaling the waiter for another half order of ribs and two more beers. Clearly we weren't going anywhere anytime soon.

"Will you excuse me a minute?" I was already out of my chair and heading for the washrooms at the back of the restaurant before he could answer. I needed to splash some cold water on my face. The heat was definitely getting to me.

The interior of the restaurant was soothingly dark and, while not exactly cold, considerably cooler than outside. I passed the large bar, its barstools constructed from the old hoists of the former gas station. Most people ate outside, but a few wooden tables hugged by leatherette furniture were scattered around the room for those who preferred not to see what they were eating. "The pig place," people called Elwood's, with affection. I wondered, as I brushed by another potbellied biker, if they were referring to the menu or the clientele.

I spent the next few minutes in the washroom, trying to convince myself that my mind was playing tricks on me, that the heat plus my overly active imagination had deceived me into thinking that the man with the red bandanna and scruffy goatee was anything but an overly familiar stereotype. Of course I didn't know him. Of course I'd never seen him with Erica.

Except even as I was trying to convince myself I was seeing bogeymen who didn't exist, I knew the truth—that I *had* seen the man before, seen him with Erica, and not just once, but several times. And not only here, I realized, as a series of suppressed images assaulted my already spinning brain, but much closer to home. Hadn't I seen him coming out of the cottage on several mornings with his arm around Erica's waist? Hadn't I heard the unmistakable sounds of a motorcycle disappearing down the middle of a darkened street on several evenings? And did the fact he was back mean Erica was back as well?

I sprinkled water on my neck, dabbed a few drops behind my ears, as if it were perfume, stared at myself in the grimy mirror over the sink. My mother stared back. "Dear God,"

I said out loud, realizing how much her features were starting to intrude upon my own.

Except for the eyes in the back of her head, I thought ruefully, remembering her terrifying admonition when I was a little girl. *There's no point in trying to fool me*, she'd warned. *I see everything. I have eyes in the back of my head.*

Too bad I hadn't inherited those, I thought, returning to the patio. My table was empty, and I looked around for Lance.

I saw the man with the red bandanna first. He was standing by the row of motorcycles parked along the curb, one hand resting on a pair of steel handlebars, and he and Lance were having an obviously serious conversation. I watched the man lean forward to whisper something in Lance's ear, before climbing on his bike and backing out into traffic, acknowledging me with a barely perceptible nod of his head. Lance remained where he was, as still as the cardboard-imitation Elvis, his fists clenched tightly at his sides.

"What was that about?" I asked when Lance returned to the table.

"What was what about?"

"That guy you were talking to."

"What about him?"

"How do you know him?"

"I don't know him." Lance's eyes squinted into the sunlight.

"You were talking to him."

"I'm a friendly guy."

"Don't play games with me, Lance."

"What kind of games?" Lance leaned back in his seat, ran his tongue along his lower lip.

"Look, that guy you were talking to is bad news. He was

involved with my previous tenant. I think he's been phoning me," I said, realizing this was true.

"You *think*? You don't know?" Lance looked amused.

"I'm not sure," I backpedaled, beginning to doubt my instincts.

"Sorry, sweetheart, I don't have a clue what you're talking about."

"Why were you talking to him?"

"Why is it so important?"

"What were you talking about?" I pressed, my voice rising in frustration.

"Hey," Lance said softly, his hand reaching across the table to stroke my arm. "No need to get upset. It was nothing. I was just telling him how much I liked his bike. That's all it was. You okay?"

I nodded, somewhat mollified. Already I was starting to feel foolish about my outburst.

Lance picked up his cell phone. "Time to give Alison a call."

FOURTEEN

Alison joined us at Elwood's within minutes of Lance's call, her migraine blissfully vanquished. "Those pills you gave me were a godsend," she told me repeatedly, looking radiant in her blue sundress, as she simultaneously wolfed down an order of spareribs and chewed on a mouthful of french fries. I marveled that she managed to do so with such grace. I also marveled that her headache had had no effect on her appetite. Indeed, she seemed in better shape than I did. "Are you okay?" she asked me as Lance was settling the bill.

"Me? I'm fine."

"You're so quiet."

"Terry thought she saw some guy who was involved with her last tenant," Lance interjected.

"Really? Who?"

I shook my head. "It probably wasn't him. Must be the heat," I demurred, now almost convinced I'd been mistaken.

"It's a scorcher all right." Alison looked around the

patio, still crowded at almost three o'clock. "Okay, so where should we go now?"

I suggested a visit to the Morikami Museum and Japanese Gardens, something I thought would be both soothing and interesting, but Alison said she wasn't in the mood for museums and Lance reiterated that nature wasn't his thing. So instead we went for a long walk along the Intracoastal Waterway and took a boat ride on the *Ramblin' Rose II*, then sat on the seawall at twilight and watched the bridge as it opened for a small parade of magnificent yachts on their way to the Bahamas.

"Did you know that alligators move really fast?" Alison asked later, apropos of nothing at all, as we strolled along Seventh Avenue, heading for home. "And that if you're ever being chased by one, you should run in a zigzag, because alligators can only move in a straight line?"

"I'll keep that in mind," I said.

"What's the difference between alligators and crocodiles?" Lance asked.

"Crocs are nastier," Alison said with the sweetest of smiles. She stretched her arms toward the sky, as if reaching for the full moon that dangled precariously overhead. "I'm starving."

"You just ate," I reminded her.

"That was hours ago. I'm famished. Come on, let's go to Boston's."

"I'm game," Lance said.

"You two go. I'm exhausted."

"Come on, Terry. You can't poop out on us now."

"Sorry, Alison. I have to be up really early in the morning. What I need now is a cup of herbal tea, a soothing bubble bath, and my nice comfortable bed."

"Let Terry go," Lance urged his sister softly.

"Did you have a good time?" Alison stared at me expectantly, the fat yellow moon reflected in eyes as eager as a child's. "Three words."

"Yes," I answered truthfully, dismissing any lingering concerns about the man in the red bandanna. I'd done my best to forget about him during the long afternoon, but like a bad penny, he kept popping up. "Yes. Yes. Yes," I said, banishing his image altogether.

Alison wrapped me in a tight embrace, several loose tendrils of her hair tickling my cheek, sneaking between my lips. "See you later, alligator," she said, kissing my forehead.

"In a while, crocodile," I answered back, watching them until they turned the corner and were swallowed by the night. I could hear Alison laughing in the dark, and I wondered briefly what she found so amusing. The echo of her laughter pursued me down the street, bouncing off my back like sharpened stones.

What's the difference between alligators and crocodiles? Lance had asked.

Crocs are nastier, Alison had replied.

My house was in total darkness. Normally I leave at least one light on, but Lance had ushered me out so quickly, I'd obviously forgotten. Proceeding cautiously, my eyes scanning the ground in case Bettye McCoy had returned with the dogs from hell, I zigzagged up my front path, mindful of hungry alligators that might have strayed dangerously off course.

Feeling both relieved and foolish—foolishly relieved?—I unlocked the front door and flicked on the light switch, my eyes sweeping across the sofa, the Queen Anne chairs, the painting of peonies on the wall beside the window, the

Christmas tree in the corner, the numerous presents beneath it, the daunting parade of Santas and reindeer and elves Alison had lovingly assembled.

"Merry Christmas, everybody," I said, locking the door behind me and heading for the kitchen. "And an especially merry Christmas to you, dear ladies," I greeted the sixty-five china heads regarding me with indifferent eyes. "I trust you were good little girls while I was away." I filled the kettle with water, made myself a cup of ginger-peach tea, and carried it up the stairs to the bathroom, where I stripped naked and poured myself a bath. I climbed inside and leaned my head against the cool enamel, jasmine-scented bubbles covering me like a blanket.

I remembered how once, when I was a little girl, my mother had found me in the tub, my legs akimbo, the water lapping against the insides of my thighs, as I giggled with childish abandon. The spanking I'd received that night was worse than any other she'd administered over the years, partly because I was soaking wet, and partly because I had no idea why I was being punished. I kept begging her to tell me what I'd done wrong, but my mother never said a word. To this day, I can feel the sting of her fingers on my bare buttocks, like the bite of thousands of tiny wasps, my wet skin a magnifying glass, reflecting and enlarging my pain and humiliation. More than anything, I remember the sound of those slaps as they resonated against my bare bottom, then ricocheted off the walls. Even now there are nights, when I close my eyes to sleep, that I hear it.

I shook my head free of such unpleasant thoughts and slid down in the tub, dragging my head under the water's surface, my hair floating around my head, like seaweed.

Immediately, another unpleasant memory attached itself to the insides of my closed eyelids: three little gray-and-white kittens, abandoned strays I'd found shivering in a corner of our garage, all mangy and mewing and "probably riddled with ringworm," as my mother had proclaimed before wresting them from my arms and drowning them in a pail of water in the backyard.

I tried unsuccessfully not to see the kittens as I lay in the tub, an inch of water covering my face, like a shroud. What was the matter with me? Why was my mother so much in my thoughts these days?

It seemed that ever since Alison's arrival, my mother had once again taken up residence in not only the house, but my brain. Probably it was all the questions Alison asked, the photographs we'd looked through together. They were responsible for my strange dreams, these unscheduled trips down memory lane. I hadn't thought of those damn kittens in years. Why now, for God's sake? Hadn't I made peace with my mother during those long, awful days of her illness? Hadn't she begged my forgiveness? Hadn't I gratefully bestowed it?

My mother was such a formidable presence, although I'm at a loss to say exactly why. At only five feet two inches tall, it was hardly her physical stature that made her so imposing. Indeed, her disproportionately large bosom gave her a pigeonlike shape that was almost comic, and her features were surprisingly small and nondescript.

I think what truly set her apart was the way she carried herself, proud shoulders rigid, stubborn head held high, so that her tiny, upturned nose always seemed to be looking down at you from a great height.

That posture infused all aspects of her life. She was

definite in her opinions, even on subjects she knew little about. Her temper was quick, her tongue sharp. I learned early that there was no point in trying to press my side of things, that only one side mattered.

Certainly my father was rarely consulted. If he had any opinions, he kept them to himself. I'd learned early to count on him for nothing, and in that way, he never disappointed me. If he had any regrets, they died with him.

My mother became even angrier after my father died, lashing out at me at the slightest provocation. *You're a stupid, stupid girl!* I can still hear her shout whenever I've done something particularly foolish.

Later, of course, when age rounded those stubborn shoulders and infirmity softened her more abrasive edges, she became gradually less formidable, less self-righteous, less prone to poisonous outbursts. Or maybe she just became less. After her stroke, my mother literally shrank to half her former size.

And a strange thing happened.

In becoming less, she became more, as the architect Mies van der Rohe might have said—more tolerant, more grateful, more vulnerable. Her shadow shrank to something approximating human size.

You know that everything I did, I did for your benefit, she said often in those last months of her life.

I know that, I told her. *Of course I know that.*

I didn't mean to be cruel.

I know.

It's the way I was raised. My mother was the same with me.

You were a good mother, I said.

I made a lot of mistakes.

We all make mistakes.

Can you forgive me?

Of course I forgive you. I kissed the flaky, dry skin of her forehead. *You're my mother. I love you.*

I love you too, she whispered.

Or maybe she didn't. Maybe I just wanted to hear her say the words so badly that I imagined she said them.

Why was she returning to haunt me now?

I pushed my head above the water's surface, felt the tiny soap bubbles evaporating on my skin. Was there something she was trying to tell me? Was she trying to warn me, to protect me, in death, the way she never had during her lifetime?

Protect me from what?

I pulled the plug with my toes, listening as the water gulped its way musically down the drain. It took a moment for me to become aware of other sounds, another moment for me to understand exactly what those sounds were. Bells, I realized, hearing a downstairs door open and close, as my heart slid down the drain with the last of the bubbles.

Someone was in the house.

I stepped softly from the tub, gathering my robe around me as I stretched over to lock the bathroom door. But the lock had been broken for the better part of a year, and the closest thing I had to a weapon was the blunt blade of a disposable razor. I might have laughed had I not been so terrified.

"Hello? Is someone there?" I called as I peeked out the bathroom door and stepped into the hall. "Alison? Is that you?" I waited for someone to respond, my wet feet leaving footprints on the hardwood floor as I ventured to the top of the stairs. "Alison? Lance? Is that you?"

Nothing.

Was it possible I'd been mistaken?

I did a quick check of the bedrooms before inching my way down the stairs toward the living room, half-expecting someone to lunge out of the shadows with each step I took. But no one lunged and nothing in the living room appeared to have been disturbed. Everything was in its proper place, exactly as it had been earlier.

I jiggled the front door handle and breathed a deep sigh of relief at finding the door securely locked. "Hello?" I called again as I headed toward the kitchen. "Is anybody here?" But the kitchen was as empty as the rest of the house. "So now I'm hearing things," I muttered, my shoulders relaxing as I reached for the back door.

It fell open at my touch.

"Oh, my God." I stepped back in mounting horror as the warm night air pushed its way rudely inside the kitchen. "Stay calm." Hadn't I just checked every room in the house and found nothing?

You didn't check the closets, I heard Alison say. *You didn't look under the bed.*

You're a stupid, stupid girl! my mother added for good measure.

"There are no such things as bogeymen," I told them loudly, deciding it was entirely possible I'd neglected to lock the back door when I'd left the house. I pictured Lance, unapologetic and an hour late, slipping my purse over my shoulder and ushering me outside, his hand on my elbow. I hadn't turned on any lights and I hadn't locked the kitchen door.

"I didn't lock the door!" I informed the rows of ladies' heads. "I didn't lock the door," I repeated, locking it now, laughing at my foolishness. “There are no such things as bogeymen.”

The phone rang.

“Don’t you know it’s dangerous to leave your door unlocked?” the voice asked before I had a chance to say hello. “You never know who might drop by.”

I spun around, my hand sweeping across the counter and knocking against the block of knives. I pulled the largest of the knives out of its slot, waved it in the air like a flag. “Who is this?”

“Sweet dreams, Terry. Take care of yourself.”

“Hello? Hello? Damn it! Who is this?” I slammed the phone back into its cradle, then immediately picked it up again, punched in 911.

“Emergency,” a woman’s voice stated after several minutes on hold.

“Well, it’s not exactly an emergency,” I qualified.

“This is 911, ma’am. If it’s not an emergency, you should call your local police station.”

“Well, I’m not sure exactly.”

“Ma’am, is this an emergency or isn’t it?”

“No,” I admitted, lowering the knife to my side.

“Please call your local police station if you have a problem.”

“Thank you. I’ll do that.”

Except I didn’t. What was I going to say, after all? That I suspected someone had broken into my house, except that I’d left the door unlocked and nothing had been taken? That I’d received a vaguely menacing call from an anonymous man whose words, on their surface, were decidedly more solicitous than threatening. *Don’t you know it’s dangerous to leave your door unlocked? You never know who might drop by. Sweet dreams. Take care of yourself.*

Sure. That would bring the police running.

I returned the phone to its cradle and sank into a kitchen chair, trying to decide my next move. Should I call the police anyway, risk their derision, or worse, their indifference? If only I had something more concrete to offer them, to prove I wasn't some lonely, middle-aged woman with a too active imagination and way too much time on her hands. If only I was sure about the voice on the other end of the phone.

I played the words back in my head, like a recording. *Sweet dreams, Terry. Take care of yourself.* But while there was something familiar about the speaker, I couldn't be sure it belonged to Erica's biker friend, the man I'd seen talking to Lance at Elwood's, the seriousness of their expressions indicative of more than a shared interest in motorcycles. Was there some connection between the two men? Between Lance and Erica? Between Erica and Alison?

Was it just a coincidence these phone calls had started around the time Alison had turned up on my doorstep?

What the hell was going on?

And then I saw him.

He was standing outside the kitchen window, his forehead pressed against the windowpane, the red of his bandanna bleeding into the glass.

"Oh, my God."

And then, as suddenly as his image had appeared, it vanished, absorbed by the night like a blotter.

Had I seen anyone at all?

I rushed to the window, peered out at the night.

I saw nothing.

No one.

I rifled through a kitchen drawer for the spare set of keys to the cottage. *You're a stupid, stupid girl*, my mother admonished, and for once, I had to agree with her. But I needed some answers, and those answers could very well be found in Alison's journal. I estimated I had at least half an hour before Alison and her brother returned home. More than enough time if I moved quickly.

Clutching the keys tightly, I threw open the door and stepped outside, my bare feet slipping into the night air, like a pair of slippers.

"Are you crazy? What are you doing?" I mumbled as I locked the door behind me and approached the cottage, hand extended, key pointing at the lock. I was almost at the door when I heard a twig snap behind me.

I gasped, spun around.

"Hi, there," a disembodied voice said from the darkness. Slowly, almost magically, a man materialized out of nothing to take shape in my backyard. With deliberate care, he stepped into the moon's spotlight. He was tall, skinny, clean-shaven. There was no scraggly beard, no red bandanna. "Remember me?"

"K.C.," I whispered.

"Short for Kenneth Charles, but nobody ever . . . hell, you know the rest."

"What are you doing here?"

"I came to see Alison."

"She's not home."

"Really? Then where are you going?"

I slipped the key to the cottage into the side pocket of

my robe, wondering if he'd noticed. "I thought I heard something. I was just checking to make sure everything was all right." I wondered why I was bothering to explain myself to someone I barely knew.

"It was probably just me."

"Did you just phone me?" I asked, my voice sharper than I'd intended.

K.C. produced a cell phone from his pocket, smiled lazily. "Was I supposed to?"

"You didn't answer my question."

"No, I didn't phone you." His eyes narrowed. "Are you okay?"

"I'm fine."

"You seem a little on edge."

"No," I said, forcing a yawn. "Just a little tired, I guess. Busy day." I looked down, realized my robe had fallen open. I quickly secured the two sides of the robe together, ignoring the growing smile on K.C.'s face. "I'll tell Alison you stopped by."

"If you don't mind, I think I'll wait till she gets back."

"Suit yourself." I turned back toward the house.

"Terry?" he called after me.

I stopped, turned around.

"I just wanted to thank you again for the lovely Thanksgiving dinner."

"I'm glad you enjoyed it."

"You don't find many people these days who are so willing to open their homes to strangers."

Or so stupid, I heard my mother say, the key to the cottage weighing heavily in my pocket. "I was happy to do it." Again I turned toward the house.

"Terry?" he called a second time.

Again I stopped, although this time I didn't turn around.

"Take care of yourself," he said, as I stepped inside the house and locked the door behind me.

FIFTEEN

"Merry Christmas!" Alison jumped into the air at precisely the stroke of midnight, clapping her hands with childish abandon.

"Merry Christmas," Lance echoed, clicking his glass of eggnog against Alison's, then mine.

"God bless us, everyone," I added, taking a tiny sip of the thick liquid, pungent fumes of nutmeg swirling through my nostrils.

The evening had been pleasant, filled with good food and happy chatter. Just the three of us. No uninvited guests. No apparitions in the glass. No unexpected phone calls. I'd asked Alison about K.C. She claimed not to have seen or heard from him since Thanksgiving. When I told her about my encounter with him, she'd shrugged and said, "That's odd. I wonder what he wanted." Ultimately I decided I'd probably blown the whole incident out of proportion and pushed it to the back of my mind.

"Where's that from?" Alison was asking now.

"Where's what from?"

"What you just said. 'God bless us, everyone.' That sounds so familiar."

"Charles Dickens," I told her. "*A Christmas Carol.*"

"That's right," Lance said. "We saw the movie. Remember? Bill Murray was in it."

"You should read the book."

Lance shrugged his indifference. "Don't read much."

"Why is that?"

"Not really interested."

"Lance had his fill of books at Brown," Alison was quick to explain.

"What *does* interest you?" I pressed.

Lance glanced across the table at his sister before returning his attention to me. "*You* interest me."

"*I* do?"

"Yes, lady, you certainly do."

I laughed. "Now you're mocking me."

"On the contrary. I find you fascinating."

It was my turn to glance at Alison. She seemed to be holding her breath. "And what exactly is it about me that fascinates you?"

He shook his head. "I'm not sure exactly. What is it they say about still waters running deep?"

Now I was the one holding my breath. "Just that they do."

"Guess I'd like to be around when they get all churned up." Lance took another sip of eggnog, the pale yellow cream creating a thin mustache across his upper lip. He ran a lazy tongue across it, his eyes fastened on mine.

"I don't read nearly as much as I should," Alison piped in.

"You don't read at all."

A flush of embarrassment stained Alison's cheeks, turning them almost the same color as her sweater. "Maybe you could recommend some good books for me, Terry. Something to get me started again."

"Sure. Although I probably don't read as much as I should either."

"We should all read more," Alison agreed.

"There's lots of things we should do," Lance said cryptically.

"Name three," I said, and Alison smiled, although the smile was tentative, as if she was afraid of what her brother might say.

"We should stop procrastinating," Lance said.

"Procrastinating," Alison repeated with a strained laugh. "Good word."

"Procrastinating over what?" I asked.

Lance ignored my question. "We should stop playing games."

"What kind of games?" I asked, watching the smile harden on Alison's face.

"We should shit or get off the pot." Lance finished the eggnog in his glass, then tossed his napkin onto the table, as if challenging his sister to a duel.

"Am I missing something here?"

Alison leaped to her feet. "Speaking of getting off the pot, can we open the presents now?" She was in the living room and at the tree before I could answer.

"Open this one first," she was saying, holding a small gift bag toward me as I approached. "It's from me. It's just little. I thought we could start with the small gifts first.

Save the best ones for last." I carefully withdrew a small crystal rock from its tissue. "It's a paperweight. I thought it was so pretty."

"I think it's lovely. Thank you." I sat down next to Alison on the floor, my mind still on our previous exchange—procrastinating over what? What kind of games?—as I ran my fingers along the jagged pink surface of the crystal. "I love it."

"Really?"

"It's beautiful." I motioned toward a small, square box wrapped in red and green. "Your turn."

Eager hands tore at the wrapping paper. "What is it?"

"Open it and find out."

"This is so exciting. Isn't this so exciting?" Alison discarded the last of the paper and ripped open the box. "Would you just look at this! Lance, look. Nail polish. Six bottles, all in fabulous colors."

"Be still my heart," Lance said from the sofa.

"Vanilla Milkshake, Mango Madness, Wildflower . . . These are so great."

"Use them well."

"We'll do another spa day."

"Now *that* sounds like fun," Lance said. "Can I come?"

"Only if you let us paint your toes with Mango Madness," I told him.

"Lady, you can paint whatever part of my anatomy your little heart desires." Lance flopped over the sofa and joined us on the floor. "Anything for me under there?"

Alison made a prolonged show of searching under the tree. "No, I'm afraid it doesn't look like there's anything for you. Oh, wait. Here's something." She extended an oblong box wrapped in gold. "It's a golf shirt," she announced before the package was half-unwrapped. "It's an extra-large because the salesman said they fit small. What do you think? Do you think it'll fit?"

Lance held the beige-and-black golf shirt against the navy one he was wearing. "Looks good. What do you think, Terry?"

"I think your sister has very good taste."

Lance laughed. "First time she's ever been accused of that."

"Very funny." Alison pointed at the design that criss-crossed the lightweight fabric. "Those are golf tees, in case you didn't know."

"Looks like I'll have to stick around," Lance said casually. "Take up golf."

Alison dropped her eyes to the floor. "Here's something for Terry." She read the sticker, glanced warily at her brother. "From Lance," she said with obvious surprise. "You didn't tell me you were buying Terry a present."

"What? You think I was raised in a barn?"

I opened the gift, my hands trembling with the knowledge I hadn't bought anything for him. Inside was a long, lilac-colored nightgown, its lace bodice scooped provocatively low.

"Oh, my," Alison said.

"It's silk."

"It's lovely. But I really can't accept something like this," I said in my mother's voice.

Totally inappropriate, I heard her agree.

"What are you talking about? Of course you can. Why don't you try it on right now, model it for us." Lance's fingers slipped under the long slit that ran up the side of the nightgown. I shivered, as if his hand were on my leg.

"I think you should save it for when Josh comes home," Alison said, eyes still on her brother.

"Josh?" Lance sat up straight, his interest clearly piqued. "First I'm hearing of any Josh."

"He's a friend of Terry's."

"Sounds like more than a friend."

"His mother is one of my patients," I qualified, not really wanting to discuss Josh with Alison's brother, wondering what Josh was doing at that moment. It was three hours earlier in California. Probably he was attending some big family dinner, or maybe he was out doing some last-minute shopping. Did he miss me? Had he thought about me at all?

"What's the matter with his mother?"

I pictured Myra Wylie asleep in her narrow hospital bed. "Everything," I said sadly.

Lance shrugged. "She exceeded her expiration date, did she?"

"What?"

"Lance thinks people should be stamped with a 'best before' date. You know, like dairy products."

I laughed in spite of myself.

"You ever consider pulling the plug on some of these people?"

"What!"

"I think you'd be doing most of them a favor. And yourself too, come to think of it."

"Now you've really lost me."

"Well, I'm just thinking out loud here, but I bet you get pretty close to some of these lonely old biddies. Am I right?"

I nodded, not sure where this conversation was going.

"And a few of them probably have a little something stashed away," Lance continued. "I bet it wouldn't be that difficult to get them to include you in their wills, have them sign over the bulk of their estates to you, their humble caregiver. Then after a suitable period of time, enough so as not to arouse undue suspicion, you just give nature a little push. You know, a stray air bubble in their IV; an extra dose of something to help them sleep. Hell, I don't have to tell you. You're the nurse. You'd know exactly how to do it. Wouldn't you?"

I looked for the familiar mischievous twinkle in his eyes, but he stared back at me with eyes as cold and humorless as a corpse's. Was he serious?

"What do you think, Terry?" he pressed. "Sounds like a plan to me."

"I think plans like that are the reason our jails are so overcrowded."

"Lance is just kidding," Alison said.

"Am I?"

"Is money really so important to you?"

"It's pretty important."

"So important you'd actually consider taking someone's life?"

"Guess that would depend."

"Lance is just joking," Alison interrupted again. "Enough, Lance. Terry doesn't understand your sense of humor."

"I think she understands me very well."

"It's my turn to open another present," Alison said, pulling a gift from under the tree with such force she almost knocked the whole thing over. "Look. It's from Denise."

"Where *is* Denise these days?" I asked, as eager as Alison to move on.

"She's spending Christmas with her folks up north. But she'll be back in time for New Year's. Speaking of which, I guess we should start making plans for New Year's Eve."

"I'm working New Year's Eve," I told her.

"You're not!"

"I'm afraid so."

"But it's the start of a whole new year. I can't believe you're working. It's not fair!"

I laughed. "Open your present."

Alison quietly unwrapped her gift and held out a pair of pink, heart-shaped earrings. I couldn't help but wonder if Denise had paid for them or simply helped herself to more of her aunt's inventory. Alison said nothing. She closed the small cardboard box and lowered it to the floor.

"Don't you like them?"

"They're very nice."

"Poor Alison's all upset because you won't be celebrating New Year's Eve with us."

"I'm just disappointed."

"Don't be. It's just another night," I said, although I didn't really believe it. Hadn't I been equally disappointed when Josh had announced he'd be out of town? "I just realized I forgot to put Lance's present under the tree." I scrambled to my feet, ran into the kitchen, retrieved the bag with the ballpoint pen I'd originally intended for Josh—what the hell? I'd buy him something better, something more personal—then headed back to the living room.

"What's the matter with you?" I heard Alison hiss as I approached.

"Lighten up," Lance said.

"What are you trying to pull?"

"I'm just having fun with her."

"I don't like it."

"Relax."

"I'm warning you . . ."

"Is that an ultimatum? Because we both know how much I love ultimatums."

"Here it is," I said, announcing my presence before I walked back into the room.

Lance reached across the top of the sofa to take the small bag dangling from my fingers. "Just what I wanted," he said without a trace of irony as he extricated the thick, black pen from its layers of tissue. "Thank you, Terry. I'm touched." He stood up, walked around the sofa, and extended his hand.

I took it, expecting a small handshake of gratitude, but instead he pulled me toward him, bringing his face so close to mine I tasted his breath in my mouth. I turned my cheek, but it was almost as if he'd anticipated my reaction, and he turned with me, catching me fully on the lips. "What are you doing?" I asked, attempting a smile but breaking away, the taste of him lingering.

He looked surprised, as if he had no idea what I was talking about. Had he thought I wouldn't notice? "It's a great pen," he said.

"Okay, you guys," Alison called. "There's still lots to go here. My turn."

"It's always your turn." Lance resumed his place on the sofa.

Alison pulled a baseball cap with a logo from the Houston Astros out of a bag without examining the card. "Look. It's from K.C. Isn't that sweet?" She put the hat on her head. "He dropped by this afternoon," she explained before I had time to ask. "He told me he came over the other night to give it to me, but I wasn't home," she continued unprompted. "That's why he was here."

I nodded, although I couldn't recall any gift in K.C.'s hands. "What do you know about him?" I asked, straining to sound casual.

"Not much. Why?"

"Just curious."

"He thinks you don't like him."

"He's right."

"Why is that?"

"I don't trust him, I guess."

"Seemed like a nice enough guy to me," Lance interjected.

"I think he's nice too," Alison agreed.

"Name three things you like about him," I challenged.

Alison smiled. "Let's see. I like his accent."

K.C.'s gentle Texas twang slammed against my ears.

"I like his eyes."

I hated K.C.'s eyes, I thought, seeing them laughing at me through the darkness of the other night.

"I like that he bought me a present."

"What three things do you like about *me*?" Lance asked suddenly, turning to me.

"I'm not sure I like anything about you at all."

He laughed, although it was the truth, and I think he knew that. "Sure you do," he insisted anyway. "Think."

"I can't."

"No more presents till you come up with something."

"Okay," I said, giving up. "I like that you threw dog poop at Bettye McCoy."

He laughed. "Are you saying you like my spunk?"

"I think she's saying you're full of you know what," Alison corrected.

"What else do you like?" Lance asked, ignoring his sister.

"I like your taste in nightgowns," I admitted, watching my mother shake her head in the reflection from the front window.

"You like the way I taste," Lance translated, blue eyes dancing.

I shook my head, declined comment. "I like your belt," I said finally.

"You like my belt?"

"It's a very nice belt."

Lance Palmay glanced down at the black leather belt that was secured around his slender waist by a large silver buckle. "You like my belt," he repeated wondrously. "Anyone ever tell you that you're a very strange woman, Terry Painter?"

We opened the remainder of the gifts in relative silence. A T-shirt from me to Alison, a photograph album from Alison to me. Some movie tickets, a box of shortbread cookies, a travel alarm clock, a pair of fluffy pink slippers. "Last one," I said, reaching under the tree and extricating a small package with a large white bow.

"What is it?" Alison looked almost afraid to open it.

"I hope you like it." I watched as she gently lifted off the bow and discarded the paper, removing the lid from the top of the box. "I thought it was time for you to have a necklace of your own," I said as she held up the thin gold necklace that spelled out her name.

Tears formed in Alison's eyes, fell freely down her face. Silently, she reached up and removed the heart necklace, replacing it with the new one. "It's beautiful. I'll never take it off."

I laughed, but tears were in my own eyes as well.

Alison suddenly got up and reached to the very back of the tree, pulling out a long, thin, rectangular present wrapped in dark green paper. "It's for you," she said, laying it across my lap.

Even before I unwrapped it, I knew what it was. "This is too much," I whispered, staring at the painting of a woman in a large-brimmed hat relaxing on a beach of pink sand. "This is way too much."

"You like it, don't you?"

"Of course I like it. I *love* it. But it's way too expensive."

"I got my employee discount. This was before I got canned, of course."

We both laughed, although we were crying too.

"Even so . . ."

"Even so, nothing. It belongs here. Right here." Alison pointed to the blank space on the wall behind the sofa. "Lance'll help you hang it. He's good at hanging stuff."

"Are you suggesting I'm well hung?" Lance asked as he pushed himself to his feet.

"Lance!"

But I barely heard them. "Nobody's ever done anything like this for me before," I whispered. Whatever reservations I harbored, whatever questions remained unanswered, whatever doubts still lingered, they vanished in that instant.

"Me neither," Alison said, stroking the gold at her neck, then extending her arms toward me.

"Careful, you two," Lance said. "I might get jealous."

Alison ignored him, wrapping me in an almost suffocating embrace. I felt the wetness of her tears on my cheeks, the pounding of her heart against my own. At that moment it was impossible to tell where I left off and she began.

"Merry Christmas, Terry," she cried softly.

"Merry Christmas, Alison."

SIXTEEN

Merry Christmas," I called as I pushed open the door to Myra Wylie's hospital room.

It was just past eight o'clock in the morning, and Myra Wylie was lying in her bed, her head turned toward the window. She made no move to turn around, even as I closed the door behind me and cautiously approached, holding my breath. I'd been through this routine already twice this morning, and both times had found Myra Wylie sleeping soundly. I hadn't disturbed her. How often did the poor woman get a good night's sleep anymore?

I remembered that my mother's last months had been marked by extreme restlessness. She'd tossed and turned in her bed all night, hardly closing her eyes at all. If Christmas had managed to bring a measure of peace to Myra Wylie's tortured existence, then who was I to disturb her?

Except that there was something different about her posture this morning, something worrisome about the way her shoulders slumped against their covers, something unsettling in the angle of her head. "Myra?" I reached for the skeletal hand beneath the sheet, praying for a pulse.

"It's all right," she said, her voice clear but dull, as if it had been stripped of its natural shine by a harsh abrasive. "I'm not dead yet."

Lance thinks people should be stamped with a "best before" date, I heard Alison say.

Immediately I rushed around to the other side of the bed, positioned myself directly in front of her, and realized instantly that she'd been crying. "Myra, what's the matter? Has something happened? Are you in pain? What's wrong?"

"Nothing's wrong."

"Something's obviously upset you."

She shrugged, the tiny gesture upsetting her delicate equilibrium, throwing her frail body into a series of exaggerated spasms. I grabbed a glass of water from the night table, extended the straw to her lips, watched as she coaxed the tepid liquid into her mouth.

"Do you want me to call a doctor?"

Myra shook her head, said nothing.

"What is it? You can tell me."

"I'm just a silly old woman," Myra said, really looking at me for the first time since I'd walked into the room. She tried to smile, but the attempt disappeared into a prolonged set of twitches that made her jaw quiver like a ventriloquist's dummy.

"No, you're not." I smoothed several fine wisps of hair—more like threads really—away from her forehead. "I think you're just feeling a little sorry for yourself, that's all."

"I'm a silly old woman."

"I brought you a present." I watched her eyes fill instantly with a child's delight. We're never too old for presents, I thought, pulling a small package out of the pocket of my uniform.

She struggled with the wrapping for several seconds, then gave up and handed the present back to me. "You open it," she instructed eagerly, and I discarded the paper to reveal a pair of bright, red-and-green Christmas socks.

"So your feet will stay nice and warm."

She brought her hand to her heart, as pleased as if I'd brought her diamonds. "Will you put them on for me?"

"It will be my pleasure." I lifted up the bottom of the sheets, felt her toes ice-cold against the palms of my hands. "How's that?" I asked, slipping on first one sock, then the other.

"Wonderful. Just wonderful."

"Merry Christmas, Myra."

A shadow, like a large palm frond, passed across her face. "I don't have anything for you."

"I wasn't expecting anything."

The shadow disappeared as quickly as it had come, her eyes noticeably brightening. "I might have some money in my purse." She nodded toward the end table. "You could take as much as you want, buy yourself something nice from me."

I bet you get pretty close to some of these lonely old biddies, I heard Lance say. *I bet it wouldn't be too difficult to get them to include you in their wills, have them sign over the bulk of their estates to you.*

He was right, I realized in that instant. It wouldn't be difficult at all.

And once I had their money, then what? Was I expected to sign over my own estate to Alison? Was that the plan?

Was I the lonely old biddy to whom he'd been referring? Was I the real target here?

Why not? I had a home, a cottage, a retirement savings plan.

Sounds like a plan to me, I heard Lance say.

Everything is going exactly as planned, I recalled Alison telling her brother over the phone after Thanksgiving.

What was the matter with me? I wondered impatiently. Where were these thoughts coming from? Hadn't I made a conscious decision to banish such silliness from my mind?

"Terry," Myra was saying. "Terry, dear, what's the matter?"

Instantly, I snapped back into the here and now. "I'm sorry. Did you say something?"

"I asked if you could get my purse from the drawer."

"Myra, Josh took your purse home with him months ago. Don't you remember?"

She shook her head, dislodged several fresh tears.

"You miss Josh, don't you? That's why you're so depressed."

Myra buried her cheek into the side of her pillow.

"I miss him too," I said, trying to sound upbeat and cheerful. "But he'll be back real soon."

She nodded.

I checked my watch. "It's only five o'clock in the morning in California. I'm sure he's planning to phone you as soon as he wakes up."

"He called last night."

"He did? That's great. How is he?"

"Fine. He's fine." Myra's voice was curiously flat, as if someone had rolled over it with a tire.

"Myra, are you sure you're okay? Does something hurt you?"

"Nothing hurts. You're here. My feet are warm. What more could I want?"

"How about a piece of marzipan?" I pulled a miniature marzipan banana out of my pocket.

"Oh—I love marzipan. How did you know?"

"One marzipan lover can always spot another." I unwrapped the marzipan candy, placed it between her lips, felt her nibble at it like a squirrel.

"It's delicious." Her hand reached toward my face. I leaned forward, felt her fingers trembling against my cheek. "Thank you, dear."

"Anytime."

"Terry . . ."

"Yes?"

She lifted her mouth to my ear. "You've been so kind. The daughter I never had."

You've been so kind, I repeated silently back at her. *The mother I never had.*

"I want you to know how grateful I am for everything you've done for me."

"I know."

"I love you."

"I love you too," I whispered, burying my tears in the soft threads of her silver hair.

There was a knock on the door, and I turned, half-expecting to find Josh standing there. If this were the movies, I thought, then Josh Wylie would have flown in as a surprise gift for his mother on Christmas morning. He would have seen me standing beside her bed, recognized me as the great love of his life, and instantly dropped to his knees, begging me to be his wife. But as this wasn't the movies, when I turned toward the knock I saw, not a love-struck suitor, but an indifferent, gum-chewing orderly. "Yes?"

"Phone call for you at the nurses' station."

"For me? Are you sure?"

"Beverley said to tell you it was important."

Who would be calling me at work on Christmas morning? It had to be Alison. Had something happened? Was anything wrong?

"You go, dear," Myra said. "I'll see you later."

"You're sure you're all right?"

"I'm always all right when you're around."

"Then I'll be back before you know it."

I left the room and headed for the nurses' station. "Line two," Beverley said as soon as she saw me. "He said it couldn't wait."

"He?" Josh? I wondered. Calling from San Francisco to wish me a merry Christmas, to say he missed me, to tell me he was coming home early? Or maybe Lance, I second-guessed, calling to tell me there'd been an accident, that Alison had been critically injured. "Hello?"

"Merry Christmas."

"Merry Christmas to you," I repeated, disappointed it wasn't Josh, relieved it wasn't Lance.

"Erica sends her love, says she's sorry she couldn't be with you for the holidays."

"Who are you?" I shouted, unmindful of the people walking by. "Enough is enough! I don't know what your game is but—"

"Terry!" Beverley cautioned from somewhere beside me, lifting a silencing finger to her mouth.

I dropped the receiver angrily into its cradle. "Sorry. I didn't mean to raise my voice."

"Who was that?"

"I don't know."

"You don't know?"

"I've been getting these nuisance calls."

Beverley nodded. "You don't have to tell me about those," she said, chubby fingers carelessly tapping the desk as she leafed through a small stack of patients' files. She was thrice-divorced and at least twice her fighting weight. Her hair was too short, too permed, and too many shades of blond. Clearly, this was a woman only comfortable with extremes, possibly the reason for the three divorces, I thought, but then, who was I to judge? I'd always felt vaguely sorry for her. Now I wondered if she felt the same about me. "After my last divorce," Beverley was saying, "my ex-husband called me fifty times a day. Fifty! I changed my number four times, didn't do any good. I finally had to sic the police on him."

"I guess I might have to do that."

"Kind of hard when you don't know who it is. You have no idea . . . ?"

A smiling trio appeared before my eyes—Lance and K.C. flanking the man with the red bandanna. "No," I said.

"Too bad. He sounded so sexy, the way he said your name. Real slow. Kind of like he was purring. I thought it might be, you know, someone special." She shrugged, returning her attention to the stack of papers in front of her. "Probably just some stupid kid getting his jollies."

"Well, if anybody else calls, just tell him . . . I don't know. Use your imagination."

"Don't worry. I'll think of something."

I heard her laughing as I walked down the hall, no clear idea where I was headed until I found myself in front of Sheena O'Connor's door. I peeked inside, saw her sitting up and talking animatedly on the phone. I was about to withdraw when her voice stopped me.

"No, wait." She waved me inside the room. "Come in. I'll just be another minute."

While she finished her conversation, I checked on the many flower arrangements and poinsettias that filled the room, watering several that were in dire need, and silently counting the others, stopping at fifteen. *We love you, Mom and Dad. Merry Christmas, Munchkin, from Aunt Kathy and Uncle Steve. Way to go, Love Annie.* I paused the longest at the two dozen long-stemmed yellow roses, recalling the roses Josh had sent me for Thanksgiving, wondering if there'd be a surprise bouquet waiting for me when I got home.

"Smells like a funeral parlor in here." Sheena laughed as she replaced the receiver.

She looks beautiful, I thought, brown eyes as soft as sable against the whiteness of her skin. Her face was still swollen from the beating she'd received and her subsequent corrective surgery, but the deep scratches around her mouth had faded into fine lines, and the only sign her nose had been broken was a slight curvature to the left, an imperfection I rather liked, but one she probably wouldn't.

"I think it smells nice," I said truthfully.

"I guess." She nodded toward the phone. "That was my parents. They're on their way over with a truckful of presents."

"I bet they are."

"I just wish I could go home."

"I would think you'll be going home very soon. You've made remarkable progress."

"Why don't you sit down," Sheena suggested. "Talk to me for a while. Unless you're busy . . ."

I pulled up a nearby chair, plopped down into it. "I'm not busy."

"How come you're working today? Doesn't your family mind?"

"They don't mind," I said, deciding Sheena wasn't really interested in the details of my life story. She was just making pleasant conversation as a way of passing the time before her own family arrived.

"Are you married?" she asked unexpectedly, glancing at my bare ring finger.

I pictured Josh, his warm eyes and warmer lips. I felt his mouth graze mine as his eyelids fluttered against my cheek. "Yes," I told her. "I am."

"Do you have any kids? I bet you have lots of kids."

"I have a daughter," I heard myself say, and almost gasped at my audacity. What was I doing? I tried picturing Alison as she must have looked as a little girl. "She's older than you are."

"Just the one child?"

"Just the one."

"I'm surprised. I would have thought you'd have at least three."

"Really? Why?"

"Just 'cause I think you'd be a really good mother." She smiled shyly. "I remember the way you sang to me. How did that song go?"

"*Too-ra-loo-ra-loo-ra,*" I sang softly. "*Too-ra-loo-ra-lie . . .*"

"That's it. It was so beautiful. It was calling to me."

I stopped singing. "What was it like?"

"Being in a coma?"

I nodded.

She shook her head. "I guess it was like being asleep. I don't really remember anything specific. Mostly voices off in the distance, like if I was dreaming, except there were no pictures. And then the sound of someone singing. You," she said, and smiled. "You brought me back."

"Do you remember anything about the attack?"

A shiver swept the smile from Sheena's face.

"I'm sorry," I apologized immediately. "I shouldn't have asked."

"No, that's all right," Sheena said quickly. "The police have asked me about it a hundred times. I wish I had something to tell them. But the truth is, I don't remember a thing about the attack itself. I just remember that I was lying in my backyard, working on my tan. My parents were out and my sister was at the beach. I was waiting for a phone call—this guy I liked at school—so I didn't want to leave the house. I stretched a blanket across the grass and lay down on my stomach. I remember undoing the back of my bikini top. It's pretty secluded in my backyard. I didn't think anyone could see me. I was almost dozing off when I heard it." She stopped, her eyes coming to rest on a large red poinsettia behind my head.

"Heard what?"

"There was this sound. The leaves were rustling. No," she corrected immediately. "It wasn't as strong as that. It was quieter."

"They were whispering," I said, my own voice hushed.

"Yes! That's exactly what it was." Her eyes fastened on mine. "I remember thinking it was so strange that the leaves would be moving when there was no wind at all. And then I felt someone standing over me, and it was too late."

"I'm so sorry."

"My instincts were trying to warn me, but I didn't listen."

I nodded. How often we ignore our instincts, I was thinking. How often we ignore the whispering of the leaves.

"Will you sing to me again?" Sheena asked, lying back against her pillow and closing her eyes.

"Too-ra-loo-ra-loo-ra," I began softly.

"Too-ra-loo-ra-lie," Sheena sang with me.

"Too-ra-loo-ra-loo-ra," we sang together, our voices steadily gaining strength. And I was able, for a few fleeting minutes, to pretend that the leaves had stopped whispering, and all was right with the world.

SEVENTEEN

He called again," Beverley said as I returned to the nurses' station at the end of my shift.

I didn't have to ask whom she meant. "When?"

Beverley glanced at the large, round clock on the wall. "About forty minutes ago. I told him you were dead."

I laughed in spite of myself. "What did he say?"

"Said he'd catch you later." She shrugged, as if to ask, What can you do? "Holiday season brings out all the crazies, I guess."

"I guess," I repeated, moving like an automaton toward the elevators, pressing the button repeatedly until the doors opened. Was that all it was?

My instincts were trying to warn me, I heard Sheena O'Connor repeat, *but I didn't listen.*

The elevator was already pretty full, and I had to squeeze in between two middle-aged men, one of whom smelled of liquor, the other of poor personal hygiene. I watched the doors drag to a close and steadied my feet as the elevator lurched into its slow, almost painful descent. "Merry Christmas," one of the men said, the smell of whiskey overwhelming the small space, like fumes of poisonous gas.

I held my breath, nodded, and prayed the elevator wouldn't stop at every floor. Of course it did, and even more people crowded inside. "Merry Christmas," the man beside me greeted each new occupant, at one point even attempting a courtly bow. He promptly lost his balance and fell against me, his hand brushing against my breast as he tried to right himself. "Sorry about that," he said with a stupid grin as I fought back the urge to throw up all over him. Unlike Alison, I had no phobias in that department.

The elevator finally reached the lobby, bouncing several times on its arrival, as if it were surprised it had landed in one piece, and its doors yawned open. Everyone folded together as one, pouring from the elevator like water from a glass. I felt a hand on my rear end and initially dismissed the intrusion as an unavoidable consequence of so many people being squished together like sardines, until I felt stray fingers trying to worm their way between my legs. I angrily swatted the hand away and glared at the drunk beside me, whose stupid grin had now settled across his entire face. "Jerk," I muttered. I stepped into the lobby, releasing the trapped air from my lungs and brushing another phantom hand from my backside, feeling its illusion linger, invisible fingers continuing to probe.

"Terry," a voice said from somewhere behind me, and I found myself staring at an attractive, olive-skinned woman about five years younger than I, whose name stubbornly refused to materialize. "Luisa," she said, as if sensing my predicament. "From Admitting. I thought I recognized you when you got in the elevator, but it was so crowded . . ."

"And smelly."

She laughed. "Wasn't that awful? Were you working today?"

I nodded. "You?"

She shook her head. Several black curls fell across her wide forehead. "No. I was visiting my grandmother. She tripped on a tiny crack in the sidewalk last week and broke her hip. Can you believe it?"

"I'm sorry."

"This getting older is for the birds."

I thought of my mother, of Myra Wylie, of all the sick and helpless men and women who'd exceeded their "best before" dates.

"Well, have a merry Christmas," Luisa said. "And if I don't see you before, have a healthy and happy New Year."

"The same to you." I watched her turn and walk away. "Luisa," I called out suddenly, the unexpected urgency in my voice stopping us both dead in our tracks. Luisa eyed me quizzically as I ran to catch up to her. "Sorry, I just remembered something I need to ask you about."

Luisa said nothing, waited for me to continue.

"A friend of mine is trying to locate a woman who used to work here. Rita Bishop." Why was I bringing this up now? I wondered. Hadn't Alison herself told me not to bother?

Luisa raised thick, black eyebrows, furrowed her wide brow. "Name doesn't ring a bell."

"She left about six, seven months ago."

"Do you know what department she worked in?"

"I think she was a secretary or something."

"Well, I've been here for three years and I've never heard of any Rita Bishop, but that doesn't necessarily mean anything. Would you like me to check the files?"

"I don't want to put you to any trouble."

"It'll only take a minute."

I followed Luisa to the main office, waited while she unlocked the door. This is silly, I told myself, watching while she flipped on the lights and quickly activated the computer on her desk.

But my conversation with Sheena O'Connor had left me a little unsettled. *My instincts were trying to warn me*, she'd said, and I'd nodded understanding, realizing how successfully I'd buried my own instincts, feeling them stubbornly reasserting themselves now, refusing to be ignored any longer.

"I'm pulling up the personnel files," Luisa explained, her eyes on the screen. "I don't see anyone by that name. You said she left about six or seven months ago?"

"Maybe eight," I qualified.

"Well, I can't find anyone by that name at all." Luisa paused, typed in some further information. "You said Rita Bishop, right?"

"Right."

"I show a Sally Pope."

I laughed. "Close, but no cigar."

"Let me check something else." She pressed a few more keys. "I'll enter her name, let the computer run a search."

I nodded, although I already knew what the outcome of that search would be. Mission Care would have no record of Rita Bishop ever having worked here. In fact, it was highly doubtful that anyone named Rita Bishop worked anywhere, that she existed at all. Alison hadn't shown up at

Mission Care looking for an old friend named Rita Bishop. She'd shown up at Mission Care looking for me.

There was no other plausible explanation.

The only remaining question was why.

"No." Luisa shook her head. "There's nothing. I'm not sure where else to look."

"That's okay. Don't bother."

"Sorry." Luisa shut off the computer. "There's an assisted-living community not far from here called Manor Care. Maybe your friend got the name confused."

"Maybe," I said hopefully, grasping at proverbial straws, still trying to ignore my instincts, to silence the whispering of the leaves by convincing myself that Alison was exactly whom she claimed to be, that she hadn't lied to me, that she wasn't lying to me still. "Thanks for trying," I told Luisa, offering her a lift home. But she had her own car, and we wished each other a final merry Christmas in the parking lot. Ten minutes later, I was still sitting in my car, trying to figure out what it all meant, and more importantly, what I was going to do next.

It was already dark when I pulled my car into my driveway. Lance's white Lincoln Town Car was parked on the street, and I debated whether to knock on the cottage door and confront Alison and her brother with my latest discovery. Except that I was confused and exhausted and vulnerable, and Alison always had a plausible explanation for everything. Besides, what exactly was I so upset about? That I was being played for a fool? Or that I still hadn't figured out what the game was?

One thing was clear: I wasn't some random victim. I'd obviously been researched carefully, chosen for a specific purpose, although the reason I'd been selected continued to elude me. A lot of time and money—I thought of the expensive painting Alison had presented me with at midnight—had gone into whatever plan she and her brother had concocted. But why? What could they possibly want with me? What could they possibly expect *from* me? And what, if anything, did Erica Hollander have to do with any of it?

I got out of the car, fished in my purse for my keys, reconsidered calling the police. And saying what exactly? That I'd rented out the small cottage behind my house to a young woman I now suspected of being a con artist? Or worse.

And what has this young woman done to arouse your suspicions? I could hear them ask. *Has she asked you for money? Is she behind in her rent?*

Well, no. She pays her rent exactly on time, and she's never asked me for a thing. In fact, she's bought me expensive presents and gone out of her way to be nice to me.

Well, that's certainly suspicious. No wonder you called us.

You don't understand. I'm afraid.

Afraid of what exactly?

I don't know.

Listen, lady, it's your house. If you don't like her, ask her to leave.

Exactly. So simple. Ask her to leave. That's all I had to do. So, why didn't I? What was stopping me? Was I trying to persuade myself that, despite mounting evidence to the contrary, there was a simple and perfectly reasonable answer for each and every deception, that nothing had happened that couldn't be neatly explained away? Was I still trying to convince myself that there were no ulterior motives, no grand conspiracy, no risk to my safety and well-being?

I can't ask her to leave.

Why not?

Because I don't want her to go, I acknowledged silently.

It was her brother I wanted gone, and in another week, he would be. Happy New Year indeed! Then we could go back to the way it had been in the beginning. We could go back to pretending that Alison wasn't pretending, that she was everything she had initially represented herself to be.

At that moment, I tripped across the image of Sheena O'Connor, who appeared before me, stretched out on a blanket across my front lawn. I watched her reach behind her back to untie the top of her bikini, then turn her profile lazily toward the indifferent moon overhead. I heard the cool breeze rustling through the trees, listened to the subtle whispers warning her of danger, saw her wave them away with a careless toss of her hand, as if brushing off a pesky mosquito.

Could I really afford to be so cavalier?

The only solution was to talk to Alison. If she could provide me with a plausible explanation for what was going on, I would consider the matter settled. If not, I'd have to insist she leave.

Before I could change my mind, I marched around the side of the house and stepped up to the cottage door, knocking forcefully. Immediately, I thought better of it. I was being too hasty, too foolhardy, too naive. At the very least, I should tell someone of my concerns. If not the police, then maybe Josh or someone at work. Except that Josh was out of town and my coworkers had their own problems to deal with. Besides, it was Christmas. I thought of all the lovely gifts Alison had given me, the beautiful painting, the china head vase. Christmas Day was hardly the time to question her sincerity, to accuse her of sinister plans and nefarious motives.

Nefarious, I could hear her say. *Good word.*

There was plenty of time to confront her, I decided, turning to leave.

"Door's open," Lance called from inside the cottage.

Reluctantly, I pushed open the door. What other choice did I have? I stepped over the threshold and shut the door behind me, glancing past the empty living room toward the rumpled bed in the next room. *You made your bed*, I heard my mother say.

"What's the matter? You forget your key?" Lance asked, emerging from the bathroom, wearing nothing but a towel around his slender waist. His hair was wet. Beads of water glistened from his sculpted chest.

"Oh."

"Oh yourself," he said with a mischievous smile.

"I'm sorry. I didn't realize . . ."

"Didn't realize what? That I was naked?" He took two steps toward me.

I took two steps back. "I've obviously interrupted you."

"Shower's all finished." Lance lifted muscular arms into the air. "See? Clean all over." He turned, the towel lifting slightly as he spun around, exposing a flash of inner thigh.

I pretended not to notice. "Is Alison here?" Silly question, I thought, biting down on my tongue. Obviously, she wasn't.

"She went for a walk."

"A walk?"

"Said she needed some air."

"Is she feeling all right?"

"Sure. Why wouldn't she be?"

"No migraine?"

He laughed. "She's fine." He took another step toward me. "Is there anything *I* can do for you? Keep you entertained until Alison gets back?"

I backed up until I felt the door handle press against the small of my back. "No. I just wanted to thank her again for the beautiful painting."

"I can come over," he offered, his right thumb hooking into the top of his towel. "Hang it for you right now."

"It can wait till morning."

"Some things are better hung at night." His tongue darted between newly parted lips.

"Some things are better left to the imagination," I countered.

"And I bet you have quite the imagination."

"What makes you say that?"

His eyes traveled down my white sweater and black pants, lingering on my breasts, stopping on my crotch. "I've been watching you."

"You've been watching me," I repeated, afraid to say more. I felt an unwanted tingle between my legs.

"Just trying to figure you out."

I lifted my hands into the air. Two can play this game, I thought, curiously emboldened. "What you see is what you get."

"Is that so?"

I nodded as he edged closer, so close now I felt the dampness of his recent shower on my skin.

"No secrets?" he asked provocatively.

I shook my head, his breath brushing against the side of my cheek like a furtive kiss. "I'm very boring, I'm afraid."

"What exactly is it you're afraid of?"

I almost laughed, would have had he not been standing so close. "What *exactly*," I repeated in a voice not quite my own, "do you want from me?"

"What do *you* want from *me*?"

This time I did laugh, immediately tasting his breath on mine. "I've never been very good at games."

"I love games," Lance countered. "You ever see a cat playing with a mouse? Cat gets the poor mouse cornered, no question the mouse is gonna bite the dust, but the cat isn't satisfied with just the kill. The kill's the least interesting part, as far as the cat's concerned. No, the cat likes to play awhile first."

"Is that what you're doing? Playing with me?"

"Is that what *you're* doing?" he repeated slowly. "Playing with *me*?"

I heard footsteps behind me, felt the doorknob turn against the small of my back, and suddenly the door opened, and I was propelled into Lance's waiting arms. Immediately, he grabbed my hand, slid it beneath the towel at his waist. I felt the wet curls of his pubic hair as his organ stiffened against my unwilling fingers. Without pausing to consider my actions, I reached up with my free hand and slapped him hard across the face. "Okay, that's it. I want you out of here right now."

"Terry!" Alison exclaimed, stepping inside as I struggled to compose myself. "What's the matter?" She looked at her brother. "What's going on here? What did you say to Terry? What have you done?"

"Just a slight misunderstanding," Lance said, flopping down on the large chair and extending one leg across its overstuffed arm, so that his entire expanse of inner thigh was clearly visible. His cheek was red where I'd slapped him. "Isn't that right, Terry?"

"I was just telling your brother that I think it's time he found another place to stay."

Alison's expression vacillated between confusion and anger as her eyes traveled back and forth between us. "Whatever he's done, please let me apologize—"

"Hey," Lance interrupted, bringing both legs to the floor. "You don't have to apologize for me. I was walking out of the shower when she came waltzing in."

"I knocked," I offered quickly. "Lance said to come in, the door was open."

"You don't have to explain," Alison said, staring at her brother. "Whatever you said or did, I want you to apologize right now."

"I didn't do anything."

"Apologize anyway."

Lance glared at his sister, although by the time he turned to me, his face had softened, and he managed to look suitably contrite. "I'm sorry, Terry," he said quietly and with conviction. "I thought we were just having some fun. I guess sometimes I get carried away. I really *am* sorry."

I nodded, silently accepting his apology. "I should go."

"I'll be out of your hair in a few days. How's that?" Lance asked as I opened the cottage door.

Again I nodded, stepping outside and closing the door behind me, hoping to overhear snatches of their conversation, but there was nothing. In the ensuing silence, I stumbled toward my back door, the night air cool against my skin, still damp from contact with Lance's body, my fingers tingling with unwanted echoes of the feel of his flesh. *You ever see a cat playing with a mouse?* I heard him whisper in my ear.

"The cat isn't satisfied with just the kill," I acknowledged out loud as, moments later, I stepped into my own shower, tried washing the smell of him from my fingertips.

The cat likes to play awhile first.

EIGHTEEN

The last time I made love was on New Year's Eve," Myra Wylie said, her voice heavy with age and infirmity, although a youthful glint was in her eyes. I pulled my chair closer to her bedside and leaned forward, eager to catch each word. "It was ten years ago. Steve and I—Steve was my husband—had been invited to this ghastly party, you know, one of those overblown affairs where there are too many people, most of them strangers, and everybody drinks too much, and laughs too loud, and makes a great show of having a good time, but they're really pretty miserable. You know the kind of party I mean."

I nodded, although I had no real idea what she was talking about. I'd never been to one of those parties. I'd never had a date for New Year's Eve.

"Well, I wasn't in a great mood because I didn't want to go to the damn party, and Steve knew that, but it was at the home of one of his former business partners, and he didn't think we could say no. You know how it is."

I didn't, but I agreed anyway.

"So, I got all dolled up in my fancy new dress, and Steve put on his tuxedo. He always looked so handsome in his tuxedo. Not that I told him how handsome he looked." Myra's eyes grew wistful, filled with tears. "I should have told him."

I grabbed a tissue from the night table beside Myra's bed and dabbed gently at the rolling waves of flesh beneath her eyes. "I'm sure he knew how you felt about him."

"Oh, he knew. But I should have told him anyway. It never hurts to tell someone he's loved."

"So you went to the party," I encouraged when she failed to continue.

"We went to the party," Myra repeated, picking up the thread of her earlier musings, "and it was every bit as awful as I knew it was going to be, so I guess there was a certain satisfaction in that. And we drank too much champagne, and laughed too loud at jokes that were only mildly funny, and pretended to be having the best time of our lives, just like everybody else, and at midnight, we yelled, 'Happy New Year,' like a bunch of drunken old idiots, and kissed everyone in sight. Pretty soon after that, we left for home. I was very nervous. I was always on the lookout for drunk drivers—I had an uncle who'd been killed by one when I was a little girl—and this being New Year's Eve, well . . ." She coughed, gasped for air. I lifted the nearby glass of water to her lips.

"All out of champagne, I'm afraid," I said, watching her gulp it down.

"Tastes even better." She finished the last of the water, lay back against her pillows. "Shouldn't get so excited. It's all this talk about sex, I guess."

"I must have missed something," I said, and she laughed.

"I haven't gotten to the good part yet." She cleared her throat. "Not that there was much of a good part."

"No?"

"Not that it was bad," she qualified. "What is it they say about sex? When it's good, it's really good, and when it's bad, it's still good? It was that kind of bad. Do you follow?"

Again I nodded, although my own experiences with sex had been decidedly more bad than good.

"Well, we got home around twelve-thirty, maybe later. I guess it doesn't matter. The point is that it was later than we were used to staying up, and we were exhausted. I don't know why we felt we had to have sex that night just because it was New Year's Eve. I mean, we weren't kids anymore. We were in our late seventies, for heaven's sake. It wasn't like we weren't going to see each other the next morning. It wasn't like we hadn't been having sex for almost half a century." She stopped. "Am I making you uncomfortable?"

I shook my head.

"I'm glad. Because I'm rather enjoying talking about this. I never have before, you know. Out loud, that is. You're sure you don't mind?"

"I'm sure."

"It's been my experience that young people don't like to hear about old people having sex. They think it's, I don't know . . . yicky," she settled on finally.

I laughed. "Yicky?"

Good word, I heard Alison say.

I quickly pushed thoughts of Alison from my mind. I'd seen almost nothing of either her or her brother since the episode in the cottage. Alison had come over early the next morning to apologize again for her brother's inappropriate behavior, and to assure me he'd be leaving in a matter of days. But Lance's rented white Lincoln was still parked in my driveway when I'd left for work this evening, and the painting Alison had bought me for Christmas remained on my living room floor, waiting to be hung.

"Children, especially, don't like to think of their parents having sex, even when they're older and should know better. They prefer to think of their conception as some sort of miracle birth, or that their parents only did it that once or maybe twice and stopped altogether once they'd completed their families. But, God, Steve and I did it all the time. Sorry, I can see by the look on your face that was rather indelicate."

"No, of course not," I stammered, pushing some nonexistent hairs away from my forehead, trying to arrange my features into a placid mask. I was thinking of my own parents, how certain I'd always been that my birth had been a freak of nature, or that sex had been something they'd tried once, disliked intensely, and had never attempted again, that that was the reason I was an only child. Now Myra was telling me this wasn't necessarily the case.

"Too much information," Myra joked. "That's what Josh always says."

"He'll be home soon."

"Yes." She looked toward the window. "Where was I?"

"You were having sex all the time."

Myra all but hooted with glee. It was the most animated I'd

ever seen her. "Oh, I was such a bad girl." She laughed even harder. "Can I tell you something I've never told anyone?"

"Of course." I held my breath, almost afraid of what she was about to say.

"Steve wasn't the only man I ever had sex with."

I said nothing, although truthfully, I was almost relieved. Myra Wylie was so full of surprises tonight, I hadn't been sure what she was about to confide.

"No, there were several others before him. And this was in the days before birth control, when girls who had sex before marriage were considered loose women, although, of course, that never stopped anyone from doing it. Well, you know . . ."

I nodded. This time I *did* know.

"Anyway, there were several young men before I met Steve, although I told him he was the first, and he believed me."

"Were you *his* first?"

She leaned forward, cupped withered hands around her mouth, lowered her voice, as if afraid her late husband might be eavesdropping at the door. "I think I was." A smile pulled at her powdery skin. "Steve was such a natural lover. Much better than the other boys I'd been with."

"And were there others after you got married?" I ventured.

"Heavens, no! Once I'd made that commitment, that was it. Not that there weren't opportunities. But after I got married, I never really looked at other men in that way. I had my Stevie, and he kept me plenty busy." Her voice trailed off. She stared at the ceiling. For a minute, I thought she might have fallen asleep. "So on New Year's Eve," she started up again, her eyes flickering across the ceiling as if her past were being projected on it, "we got home and went to bed, and we kissed each other and wished each other a happy New Year, and Steve said, 'What do you think? Are you too tired?' And I was, but I didn't want to say so, so instead I said, 'No. I'm okay. How about you?' So, of course, he said he was okay too, and we made love, although neither of us really felt like it, and it was a bit of an effort, if you know what I mean."

Again I nodded, hoping she wouldn't go into details.

"But we managed. I think we felt we should, it being the New Year and everything. Sort of like on your anniversary or your birthday. You just feel you *should*. Anyway, we made love and then we fell asleep. Sex always puts me right to sleep." She laughed. "And later, I was so glad we'd made love that night because it turned out to be the last time we ever did. Steve had a heart attack the following week and died a month after that."

"You must miss him a great deal."

"There isn't a day goes by that I don't think about him. But I guess I'll be seeing him again pretty soon," she said brightly.

"Well, let's hope not too soon." I patted her arm and stood up, straightening her covers, although there was no need. I checked my watch. Another twenty minutes and it would be a brand-new year.

"Will you sit with me until midnight?" she asked. "Then I promise to go to sleep like a good little girl."

I sat back down, watched Myra's eyes flutter to a close.

"I'm not asleep," she warned. "Just resting my eyes."

"I'm not going anywhere," I assured her, watching the steady rise and fall of her chest beneath the covers, noting the satisfied smile that lingered in the folds of her ancient face.

At seventy-seven, she'd still been sexually active. At eighty-seven, the thought of sex still made her smile. I was envious, I realized. When had sex ever made me smile? When had it brought me anything but embarrassment and shame?

My first time had been fast and uncomfortable and not particularly pleasant. I remember Roger Stillman trying to pry my legs apart, the few hurried grabs at my breasts that served as foreplay. And then the sudden jolt of pain as his body pushed into mine, the unexpected weight of his torso as he collapsed on top of me when it was over.

The last time I'd had sex hadn't been much of an improvement, I thought with a shudder, again envying the dying old woman lying in bed before me. She'd been so open, so honest with me. What would she think if I were to be equally open and honest with her?

Could I tell her that the last time I'd had sex—real sex, not just the hint of it with Josh or the threat of it with Lance—had been the night my mother died? I shook my head in disbelief. Dear God, how could I have done anything so vile? What on earth had possessed me?

In truth, I'd all but pushed the details of that night out of my mind altogether. But Myra's memories had unleashed a flood of my own. I sat back in my chair, stared at the window, saw the ghosts of my past etched in the dark mirror of glass.

I watched myself as I sat stiffly by my mother's bedside, her death obvious in the grayness of her pallor, and the stillness that had settled over her body like a fine coating of wax. Her eyes and mouth were open, and I reached out to close them, her skin already cool against my fingers. Even in death, there remained a hint of the anger that had fueled her life. Even with her eyes closed and her breath stopped, a certain ferocity clung to her features. She was still a force to be reckoned with, I remember thinking as I bent down to kiss her lips, surprised to find them so soft and pliant. When had I ever experienced softness from those lips? Had she ever kissed me as a baby, a toddler, a child? Had those lips ever brushed across my forehead to check if I was feverish? Had they ever whispered "I love you" while I slept?

The sad fact was that I'd hated my mother almost as much as I'd loved her, that I'd spent my entire life trying to please her, to make up for whatever wrongs, both real and imaginary, I'd committed. After she'd suffered her stroke, I'd tried everything in my power to nurse her back to health, and when it became obvious to both of us she wouldn't get better, I'd continued to do my best to make sure she was as comfortable as possible. I'd sacrificed so much of my life for her, and suddenly she was gone, and I had nothing. No one. I was left with an emptiness so overwhelming I didn't know what to do.

I remember pacing back and forth at the foot of her bed. Back and forth. Back and forth. I could feel her watching me through closed, dead eyes, casting her continuing disapproval across my shoulders like a heavy cloak. *What kind of nurse are you that you couldn't keep your own mother alive?* I could hear her demand through cold, dead lips. And it was true, I conceded. I'd failed her. Again. As I'd always failed her.

"I'm so sorry," I cried out loud. "So sorry."

Sorry, sorry, sorry.

A sorry excuse for a nurse. A sorrier excuse for a daughter.

I don't remember leaving the house, although at some point I obviously did. I must have showered and changed my clothes, although I have no memory of having done so. I *do* remember being in a bar on Atlantic Avenue, throwing back several glasses of tequila, and flirting with the handsomely nondescript bartender until he abandoned me for a girl who kept tossing her long blond hair from one shoulder to the other at the far end of the bar. I then turned my attention to another generically handsome man, this one wearing a bright Hawaiian shirt, who casually slipped his wedding band into the pocket of his tight jeans as he sidled up beside me.

"I don't think I've seen you in here before," he said.

Yes, he actually said that. Maybe because it was true, maybe because he was too lazy to think of anything more original, maybe because he sensed I was such an easy mark that nothing was to be gained by being more creative.

"It's my first time," I told him, trying—and failing—to toss my hair over my shoulder like the blonde at the end of the bar.

"First time, huh?" He signaled the bartender to refill our drinks. "I like first times. Don't you?"

I gave him what I hoped would pass as a mysterious smile and said nothing. Instead I pushed my shoulders back and crossed my legs, his eyes tracing each move. I was wearing a striped jersey that accentuated the swell of my bosom, and strappy sandals that dangled provocatively from my bare toes. He was tall and slender, with hair as black as coal and eyes the color of cool mint. He did most of the talking—about what I don't remember. I'm sure he told me his name, but I've successfully blocked it out. Jack, John, Jerrod. Something with a *J*. I don't think I told him mine. I'm not sure he asked.

We had a few more drinks, and he suggested going somewhere more private. Without another word, I slid from my barstool and walked to the door. Surprisingly, I had no trouble walking, despite all the liquor in my system. In fact, I didn't feel the least bit drunk, although afterward, I convinced myself I'd been very drunk indeed. But as much as I'd like to blame what happened that night on a combination of grief and alcohol, I'm no longer sure I can do that. The truth is that I wasn't drunk that night, at least not so drunk I wasn't responsible for my actions. The truth is that I knew *exactly* what I was doing when I agreed to leave that bar for somewhere more private, when I let Jack or John or Jerrod feel me up as we stumbled toward his car, when I whispered that I lived just around the corner.

He parked on the street in front of my house, and I led him around the side to the cottage at the back. "Who lives in the main house?" he asked as I opened the cottage door and began turning on the lights.

"My mother," I told him, glancing toward her bedroom window.

"Aren't you afraid she'll see us with all these lights on?"

"She's a very sound sleeper," I said, pulling off my jersey in front of the window, hearing my mother's silent gasp.

After that, we said little. But if I'd been expecting great sex, I was sorely disappointed. If I'd been looking for some kind of release, I got nothing of the sort. Instead I got a lot of grunting and thrashing about to no particular purpose, and when it was over—too fast, yet not nearly fast enough—I couldn't wait for Jack or John or Jerrod to put on his tight jeans and Hawaiian shirt and leave.

"I'll call you," he said on his way out the door.

I nodded, looking up at my mother's room, feeling the crushing weight of her disapproval, as heavy as the weight of the man who'd just left my bed. I took a shower and got dressed, then I called for an ambulance and returned to the main house, where I sat dutifully by my mother's side until it arrived. Then I wiped that night from my mind as if it had never happened and refused to think of it again.

Until now.

I glanced at my watch. It was midnight. "Happy New Year," I whispered, kissing Myra's warm cheek.

"Happy New Year," she repeated, opening her eyes briefly, her thin lashes brushing against my skin.

Seconds later, she was asleep, and once again, I was alone.

NINETEEN

I thought I heard something when I stepped into the hallway. I stopped, looked around, saw nothing but an empty corridor. I stood there, my hand still on the door to Myra's room, my head cocked to one side, like an attentive puppy, my ears on full alert for any errant sounds—a stray step, a heavy breath—anything at all out of the ordinary.

But there was nothing.

I shook my head and started down the hall, looking in on my patients as I passed each joyless room. Most were asleep, or pretending to be. Only Eliot Winchell, a middle-aged man saddled with the brain of a toddler as the result of a seemingly harmless spill from a bicycle, was awake. He waved when he saw me.

"Happy New Year, Mr. Winchell," I said, automatically checking his pulse. "Is there anything I can get for you?"

He smiled his eerie child's smile and said nothing.

"Do you need to go to the bathroom?"

He shook his head, smiled wider, the white of his teeth flashing in the semidarkness of the room.

"Then try to get some sleep now, Mr. Winchell. You have a very busy day ahead of you." I doubted this was true, but what difference did it make? One day would be pretty much the same as the next for Eliot Winchell for the rest of his life. "Why weren't you wearing your helmet, Eliot?" I scolded in my mother's voice, watching the child's smile vanish abruptly from his face. "Get some sleep," I said, softening, patting his arm, and making sure his covers were secure. "I'll see you tomorrow."

I heard the noise as soon as I stepped back into the hall.

I spun around, my eyes darting back and forth, up and down the brightly lit corridor. But again, there was nothing. I held my breath, waited, tried unsuccessfully to figure out exactly what it was I thought I'd heard. But there was nothing I could put my finger on, nothing but a vague sense of disquiet.

"It's nothing," I said out loud as I walked past Sheena O'Connor's former room. Sheena O'Connor was no longer a patient at Mission Care. Her doctors felt she'd recovered sufficiently to release her, and her parents had arrived to take her home the day before yesterday.

"Isn't it great? I'll be home for New Year's," she'd exclaimed.

"You take good care of yourself," I urged.

"You'll keep in touch, won't you? You'll come visit me?"

"Of course I will," I said, but I think we both knew that once she left the hospital, I'd never see her again.

She hugged me. "I'm gonna call you every time I can't sleep," she warned. "Have you sing to me."

"You won't have any trouble sleeping."

What was she doing now? I wondered, returning to the nurses' station, realizing I missed having someone to sing to.

On holidays, the hospital retained only a skeletal staff. Beverley and I were the only nurses on the floor. Truthfully, I would have preferred total solitude. Then I wouldn't have to spend the first moments of the New Year mired in boring small talk or pretend to be interested in Beverley's mind-numbingly stupid problems. I wouldn't be expected to offer advice I knew would never be followed. I could simply enjoy this time alone. Chances were slight there'd be an emergency, and doctors were on call if I needed them. *A glorified babysitter, that's all you are,* I heard my mother whisper.

"Did you hear something?" I asked Beverley, drowning out the sound of my mother's voice.

"Like what?" Beverley looked up from the double issue of *People* she was perusing and listened. "I don't hear anything."

I shrugged, unconvinced. The silence of the night pounded against my head like a hammer.

"Just your imagination working overtime," Beverley pronounced.

God knows I have plenty of imagination, I thought. Yes, sir—lots of imagination.

And no life.

The people dying in their beds just down the hall had more life than I did. Myra Wylie, for God's sake, at eighty-seven and sick with leukemia and heart disease, still grew wistful at the very thought of sex. Ten years ago, *ten years ago*, she'd still been sexually active! And here was I, almost half her age, with only a tiny fraction of her life experience. What was I waiting for? How much of my life was I going to waste?

I'd never made New Year's resolutions before, but I made

one now. Come hell or high water, this year was going to be different. Josh would be back from California in a few days, and I was going to be ready for him.

"Who would you sleep with if you had the chance?" Beverley startled me by asking, as if privy to my thoughts. "Tom Cruise or Russell Crowe?" She held up the magazine, tapped fake, orange nails against the appropriate pictures.

"Is George Clooney an option?"

She laughed, and I listened in mounting fear as the laugh spun circles around us. "Don't tell me you didn't hear that."

"I heard it." Beverley dropped the magazine to the counter and rose to her feet. "Probably Larry Foster in 415. He has that weird little laugh. I'll go check on him."

"Maybe we should call security."

Fake, orange nails waved my concerns aside as Beverley headed down the hall.

I picked up the *People* magazine and flipped through its pages, trying to pretend there was no cause for alarm by concentrating on which stars had undergone plastic surgery in the last year. "You, definitely," I said, pointing to the picture of an aging starlet who, except for an exaggerated mane of curly blond hair, barely resembled her former self. In fact, it was only after I read the name beneath the photograph that I realized who she was.

That's when I heard the sound again.

The magazine dropped from my hands and slid off my lap as I jumped to my feet. "Who's there?" I demanded, eyes straying toward the alarm button on the wall.

A figure emerged from behind a nearby pillar and sauntered slowly toward me, his fingers hooked into the pockets of his black jeans, a cruel smile tugging at his lips. Tall, skinny, dressed all in black, his brown eyes laughed at me from atop his hawklike nose. I didn't need a name beneath a photograph to identify him.

"K.C.!"

"Happy New Year, Terry."

I fought to get air into my lungs. "What are you doing here? How did you get past security?"

"You mean my friend Sylvester?"

"What did you do to him?"

The smile disappeared from his mouth. "You mean after I slit his throat?"

My voice fell to my knees. "Oh, my God!"

K.C. laughed, slapped his thigh in disbelief. "What—you think I'm serious? You think I'd hurt my friend Sylvester? What kind of people have you been hanging out with, lady? Of course I didn't hurt him. I just explained how unfair I thought it was you had to miss out on all the festivities and said I wanted to surprise you with a party of your own. Sylvester was very understanding, especially when I presented him with a nice bottle of ten-year-old Scotch. What's the matter, Terry? You don't look very happy to see me."

"Are you alone?"

"What do you think?" He lifted his right hand, aimed it at my heart. It was only then I saw the gun.

There was a loud bang, and in a blinding flash, the world exploded. I fell back, cried out, glanced toward my chest, waiting for the sight of my blood to seep through the whiteness of my uniform.

"My God, what's going on here?" Beverley exclaimed as my vision began to blur. "Who are you?" she demanded of K.C. as the taste of blood filled my mouth.

"Friends of Terry's," K.C. answered easily, and I was too weak to object.

And then Alison suddenly jumped into view. "Happy New Year!" she shouted.

"Happy New Year!" echoed Denise, popping up beside her.

"Welcome to the first day of the rest of your life," Lance announced from another corner, laughing as champagne gushed from the large bottle in his hand to spill across the floor. "That was one noisy cork. Anybody see where it went?"

"What's going on here?" Beverley asked again, although a smile was already creeping into her voice.

"New Year's celebration," Lance told her. "We didn't think you angels of mercy should miss out on all the fun."

"Well, aren't you sweet. I'm Beverley, by the way."

"Pleasure to meet you, Beverley. I'm Lance. This is Alison, Denise, and K.C."

"Any friends of Terry's"—Beverley began, then stopped when she saw the look on my face.

"You scared me half to death," I said, realizing I hadn't been shot after all.

Lance laughed. "A little scare's good for you. Gets the adrenaline pumping."

"We didn't mean to scare you," Alison apologized. "We just wanted to surprise you."

"Don't you like surprises, Terry?" Denise asked, approaching the nurses' station. Her black hair had outgrown its trendy cut, and as a result, its spikes had lost some of their sharp edges, collapsing around her pale face like ash from a cigarette. Her eyes were rimmed with black, making her look more ghoulish than sophisticated, an effect I don't think was intentional, although knowing Denise, perhaps it was.

"Please don't touch anything," I admonished, still trying to catch my breath.

"We brought glasses," Alison said, producing them from the large shopping bag in her hands.

"We thought of everything," K.C. added.

"Where do you keep the drugs?" Denise asked.

"What!"

"Just joking."

"What happened to your lip?" Alison asked.

I touched the side of my mouth where I must have bitten down. Immediately, Lance was beside me, licking the drop of blood from my finger with the exaggerated gusto of a movie vampire. "Hmm. Two thousand two. A very good year."

I pulled my hand away. "Save it, Bela Lugosi," I told him, struggling to keep everyone in my line of sight. Beverley already had a glass in her hand.

"Don't be upset with us, Terry," Alison pleaded. She was dressed all in white, her strawberry-blond curls falling loosely around her face, Botticelli's Venus removed from her shell.

"I'm just not sure this is such a good idea."

"It's a great idea," Beverley countered with a slap on my arm, as Lance began carefully measuring out equal amounts of champagne. I noticed that he too was dressed all in white.

"We couldn't let you spend New Year's Eve alone," K.C. said.

"That wouldn't have been very nice of us." Denise began rifling through a nearby stack of patients' charts.

I quickly moved them out of her reach. "You shouldn't be back here."

"Why not?"

"Denise," Alison said.

Denise promptly left the nurses' station, grabbing a glass of champagne from the counter as she brushed by. "Cheers, everybody."

"Wait. We have to make a toast." Alison waited to make sure we each had a glass.

"What are we drinking to?" Lance asked his sister.

"To the best year ever." Alison raised her glass into the air.

"The best year ever," we all agreed.

I didn't want to be considered a wet blanket, so I took one sip, then another. The champagne tasted surprisingly refreshing, so I took several more, the bubbles stinging the insides of my nose. "Good health," I said under my breath.

"And wealth," Denise added quickly.

"May we all get exactly what we want in the coming year," Lance continued.

"Everything that's coming to us," K.C. added, smiling at me from over the rim of his glass as everyone took another sip of champagne.

"Everything we deserve," Denise said.

"Everything we need," said Alison.

"And what exactly is that?" her brother challenged.

Alison buried her nose inside her glass of champagne and said nothing. I finished the last of my champagne in two quick gulps.

"Well, I know what I need," Denise said, laughing. "I need a change of scenery."

"Weren't you just in New York?"

"New York doesn't count. I was with my mother."

"What's wrong with your mother?"

"Nothing—if you like uptight, anal-retentive, old farts." Denise immediately doubled over with laughter.

"Alison likes uptight, anal-retentive, old farts," Lance said, looking directly at me. "Don't you, Alison?"

"I like everyone." Alison finished the contents of her glass and poured herself another. I could tell by the way she was swaying, by the way they were *all* swaying, that this wasn't the evening's first bottle of booze. "Terry, your glass is empty." Alison filled it to the top before I had time to object. "Drink up," she urged, watching as I lifted the glass to my mouth.

"I'm serious," Denise was saying. "I've had it with the East Coast. It's time for a change."

"Could this have anything to do with getting fired by your aunt?" K.C. asked.

"My aunt's an uptight, anal-retentive, old fart."

"Why'd she fire you?" Beverley asked, holding out her glass for a refill.

Denise shrugged. "Because she's jealous of me. She's always been jealous of me."

"I thought it was because she caught you stealing from the till."

Denise waved away K.C.'s unwanted explanation. "Wouldn't have happened if she wasn't such a damn tightwad. She was paying me next to nothing, for God's sake. And she has all this money. Plus, I'm family. You'd think she could afford to be more generous. I hate people like that. Don't you hate people like that, Terry?"

"I think people have a right to decide what to do with their own money." I took another long sip of champagne, struggled to stay focused.

"Yeah, well, I think she's—"

"—an uptight, anal-retentive, old fart?" Lance asked slyly.

"Exactly." Denise wobbled toward him, pushed her breasts against his chest. "I was thinking of trying New Mexico. Want to come with me?"

"Sounds like a plan." Lance put his arms around Denise's waist, stared over her wilting dark spikes at Alison. "I'm getting a little tired of South Florida myself."

Alison looked away, smiled in my direction, though her smile was tight, as if it were holding back a torrent of angry words.

A buzzer sounded.

"What's that?" Denise raised her head from Lance's chest.

I glanced at the wall behind the nurses' station. The button indicating Eliot Winchell's room was lit up. "It's one of my patients. I have to go."

"We'll come with you," Lance said.

I shook my head in an effort to clear it, watched the room spin instead. "No. You have to leave now."

The buzzer sounded again.

"Come on, guys. We should get going," Alison said. "We don't want to get Terry in trouble."

Denise shook her head. "Oh, come on. Don't be such an uptight—"

"—anal retentive—" K.C. continued.

"—old fart," Lance concluded, and they all laughed. Except for Alison, who had the decency to look both embarrassed and ashamed.

The buzzer sounded again.

"Persistent little bugger, isn't he?" Beverley said, making no move to respond to his call.

"Okay, guys, I appreciate your coming here, and bringing the champagne, and celebrating New Year's Eve with us, but I really have to go now. And so do you."

"We understand," K.C. said.

"We can show ourselves out," Lance offered, guiding the others to the elevator as the buzzer sounded yet again.

"Thanks for dropping by," I heard Beverley say as I headed down the hall. The floor was sliding under my feet, like a moving sidewalk, and I grabbed the wall for support, trying to control the spinning of my head. Was I drunk already, on only two glasses of champagne? The only other time I'd gotten this drunk this fast, I realized, I'd also been with Alison.

I pushed open the door to Eliot Winchell's room. He was sitting up in bed, his covers bunched up around his ankles, the front of his pajamas wet with his urine. "Oh, Eliot. Have you had an accident?"

"I'm sorry," he said sheepishly.

"No. Don't be sorry. It's not your fault."

"Really?" Lance asked, pushing past me into the room, followed by Denise and K.C. Alison hung back in the doorway as the others approached the bed. "Then whose fault is it? Hello, I'm Dr. Palmay," Lance continued before I had time to react. "And these are my colleagues, Dr. Austin and Dr. Powers."

Denise laughed, and Eliot laughed with her, although I doubt he got the joke.

"He's so cute," Denise said. "What's his problem?"

"Obviously, he's wet his pants," Lance answered. "What kind of doctor are you anyway?"

"Oh, gross," Denise said.

"You have to leave now," I said when I could find my voice. My mouth was dry. Thoughts swirled helplessly around my brain, as if trapped in an unexpected eddy. I steadied myself against Eliot Winchell's bed.

"Yes, we do," Alison agreed from the doorway. "Come on, Doctors. We have to go now and let Terry do her job."

"Looks like Terry could use a bit of help," K.C. said. "She's looking a little green around the gills."

"I'm sorry, Terry," Alison said. "I didn't know they were going to do this."

"What are you talking about?" Lance shot back angrily. "This whole thing was your idea."

And then they were gone. In the merciful silence that followed, I changed Eliot into another pair of pajamas and settled him back in his bed. I did all this by rote, my head spinning, my vision impaired by a cluster of bright neon bubbles exploding before my eyes. Had my glass contained something more potent than champagne?

I clung to the walls as I navigated the moving hallway back to the nurses' station, my concerns swept away in an unexpected fit of adolescent giggles that burst from my throat like kernels of corn from a popper. Seconds later, I collapsed into my chair, wondering at what precise moment I'd lost control of my life, knowing it was exactly the moment Alison had shown up at my door.

TWENTY

They were waiting for me in the parking lot at the end of my shift.

I saw Denise first. She was sitting on the trunk of a car, drinking wine directly from a bottle and kicking her feet into the air, as if she were lounging at the end of a dock on the Intracoastal. A small gold loop flashed at me from the side of her right nostril. I didn't remember seeing it earlier.

K.C. was standing beside her, his hands crammed into the pockets of his tight jeans, his eyes on the ground. He looked as if he'd just been sick or was about to be, although when he raised his head in my direction, I saw he was smiling. Surprisingly, I smiled back, as if I were no longer in charge of my own reflexes, as if I'd been reduced to a puppetlike state, and I went wherever my strings pulled me. I'd expected the champagne to have worn off by now, but if anything, I was feeling even more discombobulated than before. Strange images were dancing around my head, refusing to settle long enough for me to identify them. Bright colors continued to float, like loose balloons, across my line of vision. It required all my concentration just to put one foot in front of the other.

Alison and Lance were sitting, half-in, half-out of the white Lincoln that was parked several empty spaces away, its doors open to the early-morning air. Lance was in the front seat, Alison the back, and when she leaned forward, balancing her elbows on her knees, I saw that her eyes were puffy and wet, as if she'd been crying. Or maybe she was just stoned, I realized, as the unmistakable odor of marijuana wafted toward my nose, and I saw the rich orange glow of a hand-rolled cigarette dangling casually from Lance's fingers.

"Well, look who's here," Denise said.

"About time." K.C. straightened up, lifted his arms above his head in a prolonged, catlike stretch, as if he were getting ready to pounce.

"What are you still doing here?" I looked around, the scenery blurring as I strained to see whether anyone else was in the parking lot, but there was no one. Great security, I thought, wondering who would hear me if I screamed.

Alison climbed out of the rented Lincoln, swiped at her eyes with the back of her hand. "I didn't want you driving home alone on New Year's Eve."

Lance took a long drag of his cigarette. "Party's just beginning."

"Party's over," I told them, trying to remember where I'd parked my car. "I'm exhausted. I just want to go home and crawl into bed."

"Now that's a plan," Lance said, as he had said earlier. He extended the marijuana cigarette in my direction. Smoke filled my nostrils, like a too sweet perfume.

I shook my head no, although I had to admit the sensation was not altogether unpleasant.

"For strictly medicinal purposes, of course." Denise slid off the trunk of the car and inhaled deeply from the smoldering joint in Lance's fingers.

"K.C., you and Denise take my car," Lance instructed. "Alison and I'll go with Terry." Without asking, he lifted my purse from my hands and extricated the keys to my car. "I'll drive," he said, the words crawling around the joint now pressed between his lips.

"I'm not sure this is such a good idea."

"You shouldn't be driving in your condition." Lance laughed, as if he knew something I didn't, and I felt my legs buckle beneath me. They *had* put something in my champagne. Probably a hallucinogen, I decided, trying to hang on to reality, like a child clinging to the handlebars of a runaway bicycle. *Let go*, a little voice urged inside my head. Give in and let go.

I felt a wave of euphoria wash over me as I released my grip on the here and now. I pictured myself flying backward through the air without a helmet, the wind whipping at my hair. Instead I found myself squashed beside Alison in the passenger seat of my car, her arm around me in a protective, almost smothering embrace. The oppressive smell of marijuana circled my head like an errant halo, forcing its way up my sinuses, like wads of cotton batten. "What exactly did you put in my drink?" I heard someone ask, understanding it was me only by the echo bouncing between my ears.

"You mean aside from the rufies and the LSD?" Lance laughed as we sped out of the parking lot and turned onto Jog Road, the white Lincoln following close behind.

"Shut up, Lance," Alison said. "She'll think you're serious."

"I *am* serious. I'm a very serious fellow. Come on, Terry." He waved what was left of the marijauna cigarette in front of my face. "In for a penny, in for a pound. Isn't that what they say?"

"She said she doesn't want any," Alison said.

"No, that's all right," I surprised us all by saying. What the hell, I remember thinking. My life was no longer my own. Whatever was going to happen was no longer up to me. I'd been excluded from the decision-making process, and instead of feeling threatened and afraid, I felt relieved, even excited. I was walking a tightrope without a safety net. I was free.

So I laughed as I accepted the joint from Lance's waiting fingers, then raised it to my lips and inhaled deeply, holding it in my lungs the way I'd seen Denise do in the parking lot, until my throat burned and my chest threatened to explode.

"Look at that." Lance laughed. "She's an old pro."

I took another drag, this one longer than the first, watching dispassionately as the thin paper burned its way down to the tips of my fingers. Unfamiliar stirrings of well-being whooshed through my body, like a fresh transfusion of blood. I'd never smoked marijuana before, although I'd been tempted as a teenager. This had less to do with any great moral integrity on my part than it did with my greater fear of my mother finding out.

I drew another long drag into my lungs, then sank into a deep well of complete and utter calm, realizing I never wanted to resurface. I clung to the sensation, as a drowning woman clings to a life buoy, pressing the smoke against my lungs like a branding iron, exhaling only the faintest puff, and only when I could no longer hold my breath.

"Easy does it," Lance warned as I inhaled again, a small tower of ash replacing the paper in my hand.

I gasped as the cigarette burned into my fingers.

"Are you all right?" Alison asked. "Did you burn yourself?"

"Let me see that." Lance grabbed my right hand, forced my index and middle fingers into his mouth, sucked greedily on their tips.

"Oh, for God's sake." Alison slapped her brother's hand with such force, his teeth scraped my knuckles. "Terry, are you okay?"

I stared at my tingling fingers.

"That's first-rate weed, isn't it?" Lance asked proudly.

"Where'd you get it?" I asked in return.

"Trust me. The drug trade still thrives in Delray Beach."

I looked around, trying to make sense of what was once familiar territory. "Where are we?" I asked as we turned onto Linton Boulevard.

"Lakeview Golf Course," Lance announced, reading the large sign on our left. "You ever play golf, Terry?"

I shook my head, not sure whether I'd answered him out loud.

"I tried it once," Lance said, "but it was a disaster. Balls splaying all over the damn place. It's not as easy as it looks on TV, I'll tell you that."

"I think it's the sort of thing you need lessons for," I heard myself say, remarkably self-assured for someone who had no idea what she was talking about.

"I have no patience for lessons."

"Lance has no patience for anything." Alison turned toward the window. Were there tears in her eyes?

"Are you okay?" I wondered if Lance had another of his

magic cigarettes to give to his sister, get her to relax. Why was she so uptight?

Alison nodded without looking back. "You?"

"Fine." I lay my head against her shoulder, snuggled into the crook of her arm, closed my eyes.

"Terry?" Lance said. "Terry, are you asleep? Is she asleep?" he asked Alison before I could formulate a response.

I felt Alison swivel toward me, her breath warm on my face as she spoke. "I hope you're proud of yourself," she said in my mother's voice, and I jumped up, startled, sure she was speaking to me.

"So, you're not asleep," Lance said. "Trying to trick us, were you?"

"Where are we?" I asked again. How many times had I asked that already? "Where are we going?"

"Thought we'd go for a little New Year's dip in the ocean," Lance answered.

"Are you crazy?" Alison asked. "It's the middle of the night. It's pitch-black out there."

A sudden disquiet gnawed at my newfound serenity, like a mouse on a piece of rope. I pushed myself up in my seat and rubbed my forehead, as if trying to clear it. Maybe a dip in the ocean was exactly what I needed. Just what the doctor ordered, I thought, then laughed.

"What's so funny?" Lance asked, laughing with me.

Alison was the only one who didn't laugh. Worry clung to her eyes like wraparound shades. What's *her* problem? I thought with growing irritation.

I looked out the car window at the largely deserted thoroughfare. Where was everybody? It was New Year's Eve, for God's sake. Where were all the drunken revelers, not to mention all the extra police cars supposedly trolling the streets? Here we were, three plastered partiers crowded into the front seat of a car heading for the Atlantic Ocean. Surely we deserved a citation for that, I thought, giggling at the convoluted absurdity of my reasoning.

"Maybe we should just go home," Alison said. "I think Terry's had enough excitement for one night."

"Every party needs a pooper," Lance began singing. "That's why we invited you."

"Party pooper," I joined in, laughing so hard now I could barely catch my breath. Whatever twinge of trepidation I might have felt earlier had vanished as quickly as it had appeared, carried away by wave after wave of intense euphoria. I would ride those waves right into the middle of the sea, I thought as the ocean miraculously appeared before us, and Lance pulled to a stop at the side of the road, the white Lincoln stopping right behind.

In the next instant, four doors opened as one and both cars emptied. We raced each other toward the deserted beach, so dark it was almost impossible to see where the sand ended and the water began. In the distance, several lonely firecrackers exploded, and I looked up to see a spray of brilliant pink and green burst briefly across the sky. Aside from that, and the low growl of a passing motorcycle, it was quiet. I suppressed a shudder as the cool night air blew through my hair, then wrapped itself tightly around my neck, like a tourniquet.

"This is so great," Denise exclaimed, throwing her arm over my shoulder and dragging me across the sand. "Isn't this so great, Terry?"

"Let's get naked." Lance was already kicking off his shoes and pulling his shirt over his head.

"Let's not," Alison quickly countered. "What are you trying to do, Lance?" she asked above the roar of the ocean. "Draw as much attention to us as possible?"

"Not a good idea," Lance agreed quickly. "Okay, everybody. Clothes back on." He tried dragging his shirt back over his head, but his head got caught in one of the sleeves, and he gave up, throwing the shirt to the ground in frustration, then laughing as he stomped it into the sand with his bare feet. "Never did like that stupid shirt," he said, and we all laughed, as if he'd just told the funniest joke in the world.

Except Alison. She wasn't laughing.

I pulled off my clumsy nurse's shoes and surveyed the ocean stretched out before me—cold, dark, hypnotic. It beckoned me forward, pulling me like a giant magnet, and I rushed toward its angry waves as if possessed, the sand cold against my stockinged feet, the icy water rushing over my toes.

"Way to go, Terry!" Lance yelled from the darkness.

"Wait for us," Denise called out as a wave, like an oversize boxer's glove, pummeled my back.

I looked toward the shore, saw several vague shapes lumbering toward me, hands waving in the air, like delicate tree branches swaying in the wind. I waved back, lost my balance, and stumbled over a rock. Struggling to maintain my footing, I saw the darkness swirling around me and wondered briefly what in God's name I was doing. Hadn't I pulled this stunt once before? Hadn't I almost drowned?

"Terry, be careful," Alison cried out, fighting her way through the surf. "You're out too deep. Come back."

"Happy New Year," I shouted, splashing at the water with my hands.

"Somebody's stoned," Lance said, drawing closer, his voice a singsong.

I pushed myself to my feet, only to be slapped down on all fours by another wave. The taste of salt filled my mouth and I laughed, remembering the time I'd mistakenly sprinkled salt, instead of sugar, on my breakfast cereal, and my mother had insisted I eat it anyway. A lesson, she'd said, so I wouldn't make the same mistake again. But I was always making the same mistakes again, I realized, laughing even louder.

Once again, I tried to stand up, but my feet could no longer find the ocean floor, and I was drifting farther and farther away from the others. "Help!" I cried as the water crept above my head, and unseen hands reached for me in the dark.

Strong hands pulled at my clothing. "Stop struggling," Lance ordered, his voice as cold as the ocean. "You only make things worse by struggling."

I lunged into Lance's arms, the wet hairs of his bare chest rough against my cheek, his heartbeat resonating against my ears. I gasped for breath, my hands flailing wildly in the air as another wave tore us apart, then crashed over my head like a collapsing tent. I screamed, my mouth filling with water, as my fingers reached across the darkness for something solid to grab on to. I felt a large fish slap against my calves and I kicked it away.

"What are you doing?" Lance yelled above the sound of the angry surf. "Stay still."

"Help me!" The cold water swirled around my legs, tugging at my feet like heavy weights, pulling me under. I felt Lance close beside me and struggled through the darkness toward him.

It was then that I felt a weight on the top of my head, pushing me back under, holding me down. "No," I cried, although no sound emerged. I opened my eyes underwater, saw Lance beside me, his hands somewhere above my head.

Was he trying to save me or kill me?

"Stop fighting me," Lance ordered gruffly.

I reached frantically for the water's surface, but my body was growing weak, and my legs were constrained by the tightness of my uniform. My lungs felt as if they were about to burst, the sensation eerily similar to the one I'd enjoyed earlier with my first marijuana cigarette. So this is what it feels like to drown, I thought, remembering the fate of those unfortunate kittens at my mother's cruel hands. Had they been scared? I wondered. Had they fought back, clawed at her murderous fingers? Or had they quietly accepted their fate, as Lance was urging me to do now. "Damn it! Stop struggling," he bellowed as my head finally shattered the surface of the water, like a fist through glass.

And suddenly a bright light was shining toward me, and for one insane second, I wondered if I was already dead, if this was the white light patients who'd suffered near-death experiences sometimes talked about. And then I heard the distant voice—"Police," the voice announced. "What's going on out there?"

"Goddamn it," Lance said, pulling me up and securing me underneath his arm, pushing me roughly toward the shore.

"What's going on here?" the police officer asked again as I collapsed on the sand by his feet, gulping wildly at the air, unable to speak. Alison was immediately on her hands and knees, hugging me to her side. K.C. and Denise hovered silently nearby.

"Sorry, Officer," Lance said, shaking the water from his hair, like a dog. "Our friend forgot she doesn't know how to swim."

"You all right?" the officer asked me. I could tell by the timbre of his voice that he was young and more amused than concerned.

"She's fine," Lance said with another shake of his head. "I'm the one you should be worrying about. She almost killed me out there. Last time I play hero, I'll tell you that."

"Pretty stupid stunt, lady," a second officer admonished, looking directly at me, and I understood by his tone that it was the end of a long shift, and the last thing he wanted was unnecessary overtime. I noted that he was about the same height and weight as his partner, with the same thick neck and square chest. "You better get this lady home," he advised. "I think she's done enough celebrating for one night."

I opened my mouth and tried to speak, but no sound emerged. What could I tell them after all? That I was drunk on champagne and high on marijuana? That I suspected I'd been slipped some LSD? Did I really think that? Truthfully, at that moment, I didn't know what to think. I wasn't certain of anything, not what had happened earlier, not what was happening now.

"Thank you, Officers," Lance was calling after the already retreating policemen. "Happy New Year." When they were out of sight, he turned back to me as Alison's arm tightened around my waist. "You heard what the man said. Time to get you home."

TWENTY-ONE

The rest of the night is a blur.

I remember images—Lance's knuckles, white against the black of the steering wheel; Alison's wet hair clinging to the gaunt crevices of her face as tears continued spilling from her eyes; my uniform, wet and cold, riding high on my thighs, my sheer stockings ripped and speckled with sand.

I remember sounds—the wetness of our clothes against the leather of the seats; a horn blasting as a car sped past us on the inside lane; the nervous tapping of Lance's foot on the brake as we waited for a light to change from red to green.

I remember the silence.

And then we were home, and everyone was talking at once.

"What a night!"

"How is she?"

"What happens now?"

I remember being half-carried, half-dragged toward my front door.

"What are you going to do to me?" I recall whispering.

"What did she say?"

"What do you think we're going to do to you?"

"What's she babbling about?"

Alison's voice, as clear as the proverbial bell: "You guys should go now. We can handle it from here."

I remember stumbling up the steps, Alison's hand loosely on my elbow, Lance's arm tight now around my waist. My bedroom swirled around me, as if I were on an ocean liner during stormy seas. I fought to stay upright as Alison slipped from my side, ended up on her knees beside my bed.

"What the hell are you doing?" Lance demanded, gripping me tighter, as if afraid I might bolt, his fingernails carving small niches into my flesh.

"You know what I'm doing," Alison answered defensively, pushing herself back to her feet.

Checking for bogeymen, I told him silently, then laughed out loud.

"Jeez, two lunatics," Lance said, his fingers at the front of my uniform, struggling with the top button, as Alison left the room.

"Don't," I protested weakly.

"You want to go to bed soaking wet?"

"I can get undressed by myself."

Lance took a step back. "Suit yourself. I'm happy to watch."

"I think you should leave."

"Now, that's not very hospitable," Lance said, managing to sound hurt. "Especially after I saved your life."

Had he? I wondered again. Or had he tried to end it?

Alison reentered the room, several large white towels in

her hands. She threw one at Lance. Were they going to tie me up, gag me, then smother me with my own pillow?

I felt the towels in my hair, at my breasts, between my legs. My wet uniform was scraped from my body, a dry nightgown lowered over my head, like a shroud.

"Hold still," Lance said.

"I'll do it," Alison instructed.

Strong hands guided me toward the bed, pushed me down on top of it, covered me with a blanket.

"Think she has any clue what's going on?" Lance asked as I buried my head in the pillow and curled into a fetal ball.

"No. She's really out of it," Alison said.

"So, what do we do now?"

I felt them watching me from the foot of the bed, as if considering my fate, weighing the alternatives. I feigned sleep, hinted at a snore.

"I should probably stay with her overnight," Alison said.

"What for? She's not going anywhere."

"I know. But I'd still like to keep an eye on her."

"Fine. I'll keep you company."

"No. You go. Get some sleep."

"You know I don't sleep well when you're not beside me."

I felt him move to her side.

"Lance, don't."

"Come on, Sis. Don't be like that."

I tilted my chin, opened my eyes just enough to peek through the layers of lashes, see two forms merging at the foot of my bed.

"Don't," Alison said again, this time with less conviction, as Lance, standing behind her, reached around to caress her breasts.

I felt a gasp building in my throat, held my breath to keep it from escaping my lips.

"I saw you, you know," Alison continued as Lance began nuzzling her neck. "Flirting with Denise. Don't think I didn't see you."

"What's the matter, Sis? You jealous?"

"This isn't right," Alison said as he twisted her around, kissed her right on the lips.

"We're gonna burn in hell," he agreed, kissing her again.

I buried my face in the pillow, smothered the fresh scream building in the pit of my stomach.

"Not here," Alison said huskily, taking her brother's hand, leading him from the room.

I waited until I knew they were gone before opening my eyes. Were they still in the house, making love on the downstairs sofa? In the next room? I listened for sounds of their voices, fearful of what other noises I might hear. I lay there in the semidarkness for what felt like an eternity, afraid to move, the first moon of the new year filtering through the ivory curtains. I was trapped inside my own house, tied to my bed by invisible wires. There was no escape.

I closed my eyes, opened them again, found myself staring into the blank eyes of the ladies' head vase that sat on my night table, the vase Alison had bought me for Christmas. Keeping an eye on me, I thought, and might have laughed had I not been so sickened by everything I'd seen. I pushed myself into a sitting position, determined to make a run for it.

But even as I watched myself in my mind's eye, climbing out of bed and getting dressed, phoning for a taxi, getting the hell out of my own house, I knew I didn't have the strength to go anywhere. My arms and legs were useless. They hung from my sides like anchors. My head felt as if some insane dentist had pumped it full of Novocain. Already I was losing consciousness, drifting in and out of reality. I knew I had only seconds left before I fell into whatever void was waiting.

I threw myself off the bed, my arms flailing about madly, as if I were still in the ocean and unseen hands were pressing into the top of my head, holding me down. My hand smacked against the lamp on the night table, and I heard something shatter. The sound bounced off the walls, whizzed by my ear like a bullet. I looked toward the door, expecting Alison and her brother to come bursting through, restrain me. But no one came, and I collapsed back into bed, my strength gone. I closed my eyes, abandoned myself to whatever fate had in store.

I awoke to bright sunshine and the sound of Alison's voice. "Good morning, sleepyhead. Happy New Year!"

She advanced toward me, wearing a pink sweater over matching pink jeans, looking like a long stick of cotton candy. I pushed myself up in bed, trying to clear my head, the events of the night before coming to me in fits and starts, like a videotape skipping in midreel.

What had happened last night?

"What time is it?"

"It's after twelve. I guess I should have said, 'Good afternoon.'" Alison deposited a tray of freshly squeezed orange juice, hot coffee, and croissants across my lap. "Breakfast in bed," she said, then laughed. "Or lunch. Whatever. The croissants are nice and fresh. Lance went to Publix."

Lance poked his head around Alison's shoulder. "How you feeling?"

I stared at him, unable to speak. Had he tried to drown me in the ocean last night or had he saved my life? Had I really seen him and Alison embracing at the foot of my bed? Had I dreamed the whole damn thing? Was that possible?

"Oh, no!" Alison cried suddenly. "What happened here?" Alison knelt beside the bed and began picking up the broken pieces of the china head vase she'd bought me for Christmas. "What happened?" she repeated, trying to fit the pieces back together.

I fought to remember, the back of my hand tingling with the memory of having smacked against something the previous night.

"Maybe we can fix it."

"Don't bother," Lance said, removing the shards from Alison's hands. "Couldn't have happened to a nicer girl, if you ask me." He shuddered visibly. "These ladies give me the creeps." Then he carried the pieces out of the room.

"Terry, are you all right?" Alison asked. "Terry? Is something wrong?"

"I know," I said to her under my breath.

"Know what?"

"I saw you," I continued boldly. "Last night. With your brother."

"Oh, God," Alison said as Lance returned to the room, smiling broadly, one broken lady easily disposed of.

Was I next?

"So, has Terry recovered from her excellent adventure?"

"She saw us," Alison said, her voice a monotone.

"Saw us?" The smile slowly faded from his face as his eyes moved rapidly between us.

"I saw you kissing," I said flatly.

"You saw us kissing?" The smile returned to Lance's eyes, played with the corners of his lips. "What else did you see?"

"Enough." I pushed the breakfast tray aside, climbed out of bed, not sure whether my legs would hold me. Immediately, something stabbed at the bottom of my foot. I cried out, fell back against the bed, hugged my knee to my chest, saw a small sliver of china sticking out from between my toes.

"Looks like the lady bites," Lance said, taking my injured foot in his hands.

"Don't," I said, as Alison had said last night, weakly, without much conviction. Alison ran from the room, returned seconds later with a wet towel.

"Be still," Lance said. "Relax."

I watched as he gently plucked the piece of china from my foot, drawing only a drop of blood, then patting it away with the towel.

"Seems like I'm always coming to your rescue," he said without a trace of irony.

I tried to remove my foot from his grasp, but he held on tight. "I'd like you to leave."

"Please, Terry," Alison said from somewhere beside me. "I can explain."

"I don't need any explanations."

"Please. It's not what you think."

"And what do I think?" Again I tried to remove my leg from Lance's sturdy hands, but his fingers had begun expertly massaging the sole of my foot, and I realized with no small degree of shock that I didn't want him to stop.

"You think he's my brother," Alison said.

Lance's knuckles moved to the base of my toes, kneading my calloused flesh, manipulating my muscles as easily as Alison manipulated my emotions.

"He's not my brother."

My husband used to give the best foot massages. It's probably why I married him. Certainly it would explain why I kept going back to him. He had the best hands. Once he started massaging my feet, I was a goner.

"He's your husband," I said, my voice free of inflection. Why hadn't I realized it earlier? Why had it taken me so long to figure out what should have been obvious all along?

"Ex-husband," Alison qualified.

"Lance Palmay," he said, extending his right hand. "Pleasure to meet you."

I ignored him, concentrated on Alison. "You lied to me," I said, stating the obvious. "Why?"

"I'm so sorry. I didn't know what else to do."

"Have you ever heard of the truth?" I reclaimed my foot from Lance's grasp, pushed past him toward my closet, where I threw a robe over my nightgown, drew it tight around me. Never had I felt more vulnerable, more exposed.

"I wanted to tell you the truth," Alison protested, "but I was afraid."

"Afraid of what exactly?"

"Afraid you'd think I was some stupid, weak-willed bimbo who falls to pieces every time her no-good ex-husband shows up."

"Hey—" Lance interrupted.

"I wanted you to think well of me. I wanted you to like me."

"By lying to me?"

"It was stupid. I can see that now. But—"

"It seemed like a good idea at the time?" Lance interjected.

"Shut up, Lance."

"You're sure that's his real name?" I said.

Alison looked stricken, as if I'd slapped her across the face. "I phoned him after Thanksgiving. You were after me to call my family. . . ."

"You're saying this is my fault?"

"No, of course not. I'm just saying that in a moment of weakness, I called Lance and told him where I was. I didn't know he'd come to Florida. Or maybe I did. I don't know. I only know that when he showed up at my door, I couldn't help myself. He promised he'd only stay a few days. And I didn't want to upset you. I knew your rules about no roommates. I knew how skittish you were. Skittish," she repeated softly, smiling hopefully at me. "Good word."

I felt a familiar tug, the unwanted urge to take her in my arms and reassure her everything was going to be all right. God, I was as bad where she was concerned as she was with regard to her former husband. If he *was* her former husband, I thought, wondering why I should believe anything she said. Alison changed stories as easily as she changed clothes. What made me think she wasn't lying to me now?

"So I lied to you," Alison continued, as if reading my thoughts, "told you Lance was my brother. It just seemed easier that way."

"You don't have a brother," I stated more than asked.

"No, I do," Alison said quickly. "I do," she repeated unnecessarily, looking toward the floor, as if afraid to let me see her face.

"There's something you're not telling me."

"No. Nothing. I've told you everything."

She was lying. I knew it, and she knew I did. It was the reason she couldn't look me in the eye.

"I thought we were friends," I said weakly, not sure what else to say.

"We *are* friends," she pleaded.

"Friends don't lie to each other. They don't keep secrets. They don't have hidden agendas."

Alison's eyes shot to mine. For a second it looked as if she were about to break down and tell me everything, reveal the whole ugly truth of what she was really up to, confess her part in last night's mayhem, unravel the entire charade. But she said nothing, and the moment passed.

"I think you should leave now," I told her.

She nodded, turned to go. "I'll call you later."

"No, you don't understand. I want you to leave—for good."

"What?"

"I want you out of here."

"You can't mean that."

"Hey, Terry," Lance interjected. "Don't you think you're overreacting?"

"Was I overreacting last night when you tried to kill me?" I shot back.

"What!" Lance said.

"What!" Alison echoed.

"What the hell are you talking about?" The look Lance gave me was equal parts amusement and fury. "You're out of your fucking mind. You know that, lady?"

"I want you out of my cottage," I insisted. "Out of my life."

"No, please," Alison cried.

"I'll give you till the end of the day," I said.

"But that's so unfair."

"I think the law says you've got to give us at least a month's notice," Lance said lazily. "And I don't know about you, Terry, but I don't react too well to ultimatums."

"If you don't leave, I'll call the police. How's that for an ultimatum?"

"Pretty lame," Lance said. "Think you better call your lawyer too."

"Lance will be gone within the hour," Alison said forcefully.

"What!" Lance exclaimed. "You can't be serious."

"Just go," Alison told him, her eyes never leaving mine. "Now."

Lance shifted uneasily from one foot to the other, his hands slapping his sides in frustration. Then he stormed from the room.

"If you could just give me a few days to find another place," Alison said softly, "I promise I'll be out of your hair, if that's what you still want."

In truth, I didn't know what I wanted. Part of me wanted Alison gone immediately; part of me wanted her to stay. I said nothing for several seconds, waiting for her to fill in the empty spaces, the way she usually did, to offer even a semiplausible explanation I could latch onto. Even after everything that had happened, I was still looking for a reason to believe her.

"Fine." I spit out the word as if it were a piece of rotten meat. "You have till the weekend. If you're not gone by then, I'll call the authorities."

"Thank you." Alison breathed a deep sigh of relief. Then she spun around, her face disappearing inside a blur of strawberry curls. I heard her footsteps retreating down the stairs, the kitchen door opening and slamming shut. I watched her from the bedroom window as she ran toward the cottage, then stopped, turned back toward the house. I thought I saw her smile.

TWENTY-TWO

I didn't see Alison at all during the next several days. Nor did I see Lance, although I doubted he was really gone. I knew the matter was far from resolved, that they weren't likely to leave empty-handed, not with all the time and effort invested in me so far. I lay in bed that first night trying to figure out how much of what Alison had told me was true, wondering where the lies ended and the truth began, if indeed there'd been any truth to anything she'd said. Ever.

What difference did the truth make anyway?

Looking back, I see that Alison's great gift was her uncanny ability to make me doubt myself, to make me question what was beyond question, to make me see things that weren't really there.

To not see things that were.

In spite of everything, I had to keep reminding myself that Alison was not the sweet young woman I'd welcomed into my life, but a liar, a con artist, and quite possibly, a cold-blooded killer. I wasn't her friend—I was her target, a carefully selected one at that. And judging by what I'd read in her journal, I wasn't the first unsuspecting woman she'd duped. What had happened to the others?

And why?

That was the part I couldn't get past, the part that kept me awake at night, tossing restlessly back and forth in my bed. Not *when* Alison and her cohorts might strike again, but why?

Why?

What was she after?

What do you want from me? I should have demanded of her. *Why did you seek me out, work so hard to make me your friend? What is it you think I have that's of any value?*

What was the point?

What do you mean? would have come her inevitable response, green eyes wide with confusion, expressive hands aflutter. *I don't know what you're talking about.*

In my lighter moments, I told myself I was out of danger, that by confronting Alison and ordering her to vacate the premises, by threatening to call the police if she wasn't gone by the end of the week, I'd effectively put the kibosh to her little scheme. But in my darker moments, I recognized that the only thing I'd accomplished was a slight delay, a modest retooling of her plans, that Alison was simply biding her time, waiting for just the right moment to come at me again.

At any rate, several days passed without further incident. Alison made no further attempts to talk to me; the white Lincoln disappeared from my street. I went to work, tended to my patients, and almost managed to convince myself that the worst was over.

On the morning of January 4, I was getting ready for work when the phone rang. I knew that Josh had returned from California the night before, and I'd been eagerly anticipating his call all morning. I glanced in the mirror over my dresser, trying to see myself through Josh's eyes, noting the cut Alison had given me was growing out and I was in need of a trim. Impatiently pushing my hair behind my ears, I pinched my cheeks to give them needed color, then walked to the phone and, not wanting to appear too anxious, waited one more ring before answering it. "Hello," I said huskily, as if freshly roused from sleep, although I'd been up for hours.

"Erica says to wish you a happy New Year," the voice announced.

"Go to hell!" I shot back, about to hang up the phone.

"I believe you have something that belongs to her," the voice continued, undeterred.

"I don't know what you're talking about."

"I think you do."

"You're wrong. I have no idea what you want."

"She'd like it back."

"Like what back?" I felt the line go dead in my hands. "Wait! What do you mean, I have something of Erica's? Wait!" I continued shouting long after I knew the caller had hung up.

What could I possibly have of Erica's?

The necklace, I realized with a start. The heart-shaped pendant Alison had found beneath her bed and worn proudly around her neck, until I'd bought her one all her own. But it couldn't be worth more than a few hundred dollars, and Erica owed me far more than that in back rent. Erica had never struck me as the sentimental type. But then

I was a lousy judge of character, I reminded myself. Look how easily I'd allowed myself to be duped by Alison.

My mind was racing, thoughts crashing into one another, like ocean waves. What was Erica's connection to Alison? Had Erica left behind more than the necklace, something valuable she'd hidden inside the cottage? And was that something the reason Alison had shown up on my doorstep, gone out of her way to befriend me? What did she think I had?

"Good God," I said, my head swimming as I grabbed my purse and ran down the stairs and out the front door. Did I really think Alison had any intention of vacating my cottage by the end of the week? That she and Lance would depart empty-handed?

I stood paralyzed by the side of my car, not knowing what to do, knowing only that time was running out, that I couldn't continue to stay in my house, that I had to talk to someone.

I had to talk to Josh.

I returned to the house, full of fresh resolve, locking the door behind me and marching purposefully to the phone in the kitchen. I punched in the familiar numbers, then waited while the phone rang once, twice, three times, before someone picked it up.

"Fourth-floor nurses' station. Margot speaking."

"Margot, it's Terry." There was desperation in my voice, as if someone had pushed it from a high ledge.

"What's the matter? You sound awful."

"I don't think I can come in today."

"Don't tell me you've got that horrible flu bug that's making the rounds."

"I don't know. Maybe. Can you manage without me?"

"Guess we'll have to. Don't want you coming in sick."

"I'm so sorry. It just hit all of a sudden."

"That's how these things work."

"I felt fine last night," I embellished, knowing I should stop while I was ahead, that the more lies I told, the more likely I was to trip myself up. Wasn't that what had happened to Alison?

"Well, get back into bed, take two Tylenol, and drink plenty of fluids. You know the routine."

"I feel really bad about this."

"Just feel better," Margot instructed.

I raced up the stairs to my bedroom, where I swapped my nurse's uniform for a pair of navy pants and matching jersey. I packed the uniform, along with another change of clothes and some underwear, into the large overnight bag I kept at the back of my closet. I wasn't sure how long I'd be gone, or where I'd be staying, but one thing was now crystal clear—I couldn't stay here.

Would Josh insist I stay at his place? I wondered, throwing in my yellow dress with the plunging neckline, in case he suggested somewhere nice for dinner. Or maybe I'd stay in one of those funky little art deco hotels in South Beach. Maybe Josh would stay with me, I projected giddily, opening the bottom drawer of my dresser and removing the slinky, lavender nightgown Lance had given me for Christmas. I tossed it into the bag, thinking how ironic it would be to wear a gift from my would-be killer to a tryst with my would-be lover, recognizing I was beyond giddy and was now verging on outright hysteria.

I took a series of long, deep breaths, trying to calm myself down. I knew I was behaving foolishly, even irrationally.

But it was as if, in finally deciding to take action, I'd unleashed a part of me I'd repressed for far too long—the part that was determined to enjoy life, take risks, have fun. The part that was tired of being surrounded by death. The part that wanted to live.

I finished packing, debated whether to call Josh, tell him I was coming, then decided to surprise him instead. I told myself I didn't have time for unnecessary phone calls, but maybe I was just afraid he'd tell me not to come, that he was too busy to see me. And I couldn't risk that. I needed Josh to be there for me.

I was at the car when I realized I'd left my nurse's shoes on the floor by the bed. I knew I'd need them if I chose to return to work the next day. So I tossed my overnight bag into the backseat and reluctantly returned to the house, taking the stairs two at a time. I was doubled over and gasping for air when I reached my bedroom and saw my shoes standing by the foot of the bed, as if waiting for me. I was leaving the room when a cursory glance out the bedroom window revealed Alison emerging from the cottage.

I raced downstairs, coming to an abrupt halt at my front door, fighting to catch my breath. I couldn't appear panicky. It was imperative everything appear normal. Alison couldn't suspect I was poised to take flight.

"Going somewhere?" she asked, waiting by the side of my car, her head tilting toward the overnight bag on the backseat.

"I joined a gym. Thought I'd work out before going to the hospital." I held up my nurse's shoes for added credibility.

She seemed to accept my explanation. "Terry—"

"I'm going to be late." I opened the car door, threw my shoes inside, walked around to the driver's side of the car.

"Please, I need to talk to you."

"Really, Alison, I don't see the point."

"Just hear me out. Then, if you still want me to leave, I will. I promise."

"I've already rented out the cottage," I told her, watching her eyes widen in alarm. "A nurse at the hospital. She's moving in on Saturday."

Alison's head snapped toward the cottage. A gasp caught in her throat.

"Look," I backtracked, suddenly afraid she might try to restrain me if she thought she'd run out of time. "If you really want to talk, we'll do it when I get home from work."

Relief flooded Alison's face. "That'd be great."

"It might be quite late."

"That's fine. I'll wait up."

"Okay." I climbed into the car and started the engine. "I'll see you later."

"Later," she agreed, tapping on the hood of the car as I backed out of the driveway.

Later, I thought.

I'm not sure why I chose I-95 over the turnpike. *Always take the turnpike,* I recalled Myra Wylie's advice to her son. *You get in an accident on 95 and you can be stuck all day.*

Which was exactly what was happening, I realized, opening my window and craning my neck to see what was causing the prolonged delay. But all I saw were long lines of cars, like brightly colored snakes, stalled and going nowhere. "God, get me out of here," I whispered, flicking the dials of the car radio, trying to find a traffic report. "I don't have time for this."

I heard Alan Jackson singing about lost love on one station, and Janet Jackson singing about finding it on another. Maybe it was the same love, I thought, a laugh catching in my throat. Maybe Alan and Janet Jackson were brother and sister. Or husband and wife. Just like Alison and Lance. I laughed out loud, catching the worried glance of the driver in the car beside me.

"I am not going to think about Alison," I whispered through barely parted lips, then flipped to another station, listening as a male announcer swapped inane banter with his female counterpart.

"So, Cathy, how many New Year's resolutions have you broken so far?"

"I never make New Year's resolutions, Dave."

"Why, Cathy?"

"Because I always break them."

I flipped to another station. "A four-car collision just south of the exit to Broward Boulevard is holding up traffic on I-95," the newscaster announced with the practiced calm of someone used to detailing disasters. "Ambulances are on the scene—"

"Great." I turned off the radio, not wanting to hear more. A four-car collision, complete with ambulances and police cars, meant I wasn't going anywhere for some time. There was nothing I could do about it, so there was no point in getting upset about it. Too bad I hadn't packed a book, I thought, swiveling around to check the backseat. Maybe there was a magazine on the floor. . . .

That's when I saw him.

"Oh, God."

He was several cars behind me, in the row to my right, and after the initial shock, I told myself I must be mistaken, that my eyes were playing tricks on me again, that the sunlight and my overactive imagination had combined to produce an image that couldn't possibly be real, that when I looked again, the image would be gone.

Except that when I looked again, he was still there.

Tall, even sitting down, his skinny frame was hunched over the wheel of his car, small brown eyes peering over the top of his strong, hawklike nose. He was staring straight ahead, as if unaware of my existence. Was it possible he didn't know I was there? That our being on the same stretch of highway at the same time was nothing but a strange coincidence?

And then he leaned forward, rested his chin on the top of his steering wheel, and turned his gaze purposefully to mine, his narrow lips creasing into a slow smile. *Why, Terry Painter*, I could almost hear him say. *As I live and breathe.*

"Shit!" I cursed out loud, watching as K.C. emerged from his car and sauntered lazily between the intervening cars toward me, his fingers hooked into the pockets of his tight jeans. What was I going to do? What *could* I do? Make a run for it? Where would I go? Damn it! Why didn't I have a cell phone? I was probably the only person left on the planet who didn't own one, who hated their mounting proliferation, their intrusion into every facet of our lives. Was I the only person who bristled at the sight of teenagers walking down the street, phones dangling from their ears like earrings, the person on the other end of the line more important than the person right beside them? I loathed the selfishness, the weird antisocialness of it all. Besides, it wasn't as if I got that many calls, I thought, as a shadow fell across the side window of my car.

I heard a tapping at my head and turned to see K.C. staring at me through the tinted glass. He signaled for me to roll down my window, and I complied. It was unlikely he'd try to harm me here, I reasoned, in the middle of a traffic jam, with so many witnesses.

"Well, well, well," he said. That was all. *Well, well, well.*

"Do you think it's a good idea to get out of your car?"

He shrugged. "Doesn't look like we're going anywhere."

I nodded, turned away. "Where are you headed?" I asked, not looking at him, pretending to be concentrating on the traffic ahead.

"Nowhere in particular. You?"

"Nowhere in particular," I repeated.

"Thought you might be going to see Josh," he said, catching me by surprise. I'd forgotten they'd met at my house over Thanksgiving.

I noticed him looking at my overnight bag on the backseat, ignored the snide grin that crept into his eyes, as if he could see the silk lavender nightgown inside.

"So, I take it you're all recovered from your little New Year's Eve swim?"

A shiver traveled the length of my spine. What exactly was K.C.'s role in all this? "Yes, I'm fine now. Thank you."

"You had us pretty worried."

"I'm fine."

"Yeah, well, you should be more careful. Wouldn't want anything to happen to you, would we?"

"I don't know. Would you?"

His grin spread from his eyes to his lips. He said nothing.

"Are you following me?" I demanded suddenly.

The grin overtook his entire face. "Why would I be following you?"

"You tell me."

He shook his head. "You're imagining things, Terry." Then he straightened up, slapped his open palm on the side of my car and took a step back, as all around me, cars began inching forward.

I heard the approaching roar of a motorcycle, held my breath as first one, then two more motorbikes whizzed by. My eyes followed them as they weaved in and out of the stalled traffic, shiny black helmets hiding their riders' faces. Was the man in the red bandanna among them?

"Be sure to give Josh my regards," K.C. called as he returned to his car. Minutes later, when I finally worked up the nerve to check in my rearview mirror, I could still see him, sitting behind the wheel of his car, watching me.

TWENTY-THREE

We crawled along I-95 for the better part of an hour. By the time we reached Broward Boulevard, the four cars involved in the accident had been moved to the side of the road and the ambulances had already gone. Judging by the mangled remains of two of the automobiles, one a bright red Porsche that now resembled nothing so much as a squashed tomato, and a puddle of what appeared to be blood beside one of the tires, I suspected serious injuries, possibly even fatalities. I wondered briefly whether any of the victims would eventually find their way to my ward at Mission Care, prayed we'd all be spared. Several police cars remained on the scene, their officers trying to persuade motorists not to waste time gawking, but, of course, everyone did. We couldn't help ourselves.

"Keep moving," one of the officers directed as I again checked my rearview mirror. Immediately, K.C. waved his fingers at me in greeting, as if he knew I was looking at him, as if he'd been watching all along, waiting for our eyes to meet.

On impulse, I lowered my window, beckoned the policeman forward.

"Keep moving," he repeated, louder this time, his large hands waving the traffic forward.

"Please, can you help me? I'm being followed," I ventured timidly, trying to make out the features beneath the officer's protective helmet, seeing only his dark glasses and the impatient set of his jaw.

"Sorry, ma'am," the policeman said, his eyes darting back and forth among the cars, clearly oblivious to what I'd said. "I'm afraid I have to ask you to move along."

I nodded, raised the window, glanced into the rearview mirror in time to see K.C. shaking his head and laughing, as if he understood what I'd tried to do and was amused by my audacity. Or my stupidity.

What had I hoped to accomplish? Under the circumstances, had I really expected the officer to listen to me, let alone take my concerns seriously? And even if he had, what could he have done? Questioned K.C. on the spot, thereby causing further traffic jams and longer delays? Then what? Would he have arrested him? Highly doubtful. At best, he would have hauled both of us off to the station. A lot of good that would have done me.

Excuse me, sir, but this woman claims you were following her.

Following her? Terry, did you tell the officer I was following you?

Do you two know each other?

We're friends, Officer. She had me over to her house for Thanksgiving dinner.

Is this true, ma'am?

Yes, but . . .

To tell you the truth, Officer, she's been acting very strangely lately. All her friends are worried about her.

I felt the officer's judgmental nod. Still, I reminded myself, no matter how strong K.C.'s denials, my complaint would be a matter of record. At the very least, it might buy me some time. Again I lowered my window, waved the officer over. "Please, Officer, can you help me?"

"Is there a problem, ma'am?" He leaned in toward me, removing his dark glasses with an impatient hand.

I saw that he was young, younger than I, maybe even younger than K.C. I also heard by his tone, by the way he said "ma'am," that he would have a hard time believing a young man like K.C. would waste his time following a middle-aged woman like me. The thought now occurred to me that I would be dismissed as a troublemaker, that by mouthing off prematurely, I would effectively destroy any credibility I might need in the future. No, I decided, I would accomplish nothing by crying wolf. And I would miss seeing Josh, who was my only real hope. "Was anybody hurt?" I asked.

"'Fraid so," the officer said, pushing his sunglasses back across the bridge of his nose, backing away.

"I'm a nurse. If there's anything I can do . . ."

But the policeman wasn't interested in my offer of help. "It's been taken care of" came his curt reply. "Keep moving, please."

The traffic thinned out after that, and by the time we reached Hollywood Boulevard, it was back to its normal pace. I picked up my speed, zigzagging between lanes whenever possible, trying to escape K.C., but he remained stubbornly on my tail. In an effort to shake him, I almost took the exit at Miami Shores, then decided against it. I didn't know the area, and if I was going to try to lose K.C., it was probably better to do it somewhere I wouldn't get lost myself.

He was still behind me when I transferred onto U.S. 1, heading south. Somewhere between Coconut Grove and Coral Gables, where Josh lived, K.C. vanished. This wasn't due to any clever maneuvering on my part. On the contrary—one minute he was behind me; the next minute he was gone.

I checked my rearview mirror at each stoplight. I saw a woman in a black Accord talking animatedly on her cell phone, a woman in a cream-colored minivan trying to subdue a backseat of unruly children, and a man picking his nose in a green BMW.

K.C. and his maroon-colored Impala were nowhere to be seen. Which didn't mean he wasn't lurking about, I realized, repeatedly swiveling around in my seat, scanning my surroundings for anyone remotely suspicious. Both the make and color of K.C.'s car told me it was likely a rental. Again, I wondered how he fit into Alison's plan.

The sound of a car horn brought me back to the here and now. The light had turned green and I was being urged forward. I continued driving north along U.S. 1, repeatedly checking my rearview mirror, twisting around in my seat at each subsequent red light, but it appeared my efforts had been successful. "I lost him," I announced triumphantly, turning to the car next to me in time to see a well-dressed, middle-aged man jam his index finger high inside his left nostril. "Wonderful," I said, entering the town of Coral Gables and continuing past the grand, geometrically designed entertainment and shopping complex known as

Paseos, in the heart of the tidy Miami suburb. I deliberately avoided the famous Miracle Mile District, turning left, then right, then right again, looking for Sunset Place. I took several wrong turns, found myself back where I started, and almost had a heart attack when I saw a maroon-colored Impala pull up behind me. But one peek at the wizened, gray-haired man stooped over the steering wheel quickly brought my heart rate back to normal. I laughed at my paranoia and shook my head, continuing on.

Eventually I found myself on the right street, albeit at the wrong end. Sunset Place was typical of many streets in the area, a palm-lined avenue full of small Spanish-style bungalows in all the colors of the rainbow. Josh lived with his children at number 1044, a neat, white house with a sloping brown-tile roof, and a beautiful front garden filled with coral and white impatiens, as well as a variety of other flowers whose blooms I recognized, but whose names always eluded me.

I parked on the street directly across from Josh's house, then sat for several minutes trying to decide my next move. How had I come this far without a plan? What was I doing, showing up at his door, uninvited and unannounced, at just after one o'clock on a Friday afternoon?

My stomach was rumbling as I opened the car door and climbed out. Black rain clouds hovered ominously overhead, like bruises on an otherwise blue sky, and I debated whether I should go somewhere for lunch before seeing Josh, then decided to wait. Maybe Josh would suggest lunch at his favorite neighborhood café.

Unless he wasn't alone, I thought, stopping in the middle of the road. School didn't start till Monday. It was entirely possible his children would be at home. What was I going to say to them? *Hi, it's your aunt Terry, come for an extended stay?*

And what if Josh wasn't there? I asked myself, returning to the sidewalk. His car wasn't in the driveway, so it was entirely possible that, despite his having just returned from his vacation, he was already off visiting clients. Or maybe he was in Delray seeing his mother, I realized with a start. It was Friday, after all. Didn't he always visit his mother on Fridays? Of course he was in Delray! What a fool I was, coming all this way when all I'd had to do was go to work as usual. What was the matter with me? What in the world had I been thinking?

And then the wood-paneled front door to Josh's house opened, and suddenly Josh was standing in the doorway, looking tanned and unbearably handsome in a dark, short-sleeved shirt and faded denim jeans. He looked up and down the street, glanced at the increasingly menacing clouds, and was about to go back inside when his gaze drifted across the street toward me. "Terry?" he mouthed in obvious surprise, crossing the street in several long, quick strides. "It *is* you!"

"Josh, hello."

"Has something happened to my mother? Is she all right? What is it?" The questions toppled from his mouth like a line of dominoes.

"Nothing's happened to your mother. She's fine."

"I talked to her less than an hour ago," he said as if I hadn't spoken.

"Josh, your mother's fine."

His shoulders relaxed, although tension still narrowed his eyes. "Then I don't understand. What are you doing here?"

"I need to talk to you."

"About my mother?"

What was the matter with him? Hadn't I already explained my visit had nothing to do with his mother? "No, Josh. Your mother is doing remarkably well for a woman with both cancer and heart disease. She's been a little depressed lately, yes, but that's pretty normal during the holiday season. She'll bounce back. In fact, I'm beginning to think she'll outlive us all."

He smiled, the lines on his forehead releasing slowly, like an elastic band. "Well, that's a relief anyway. I've been feeling so guilty these last weeks."

"Nonsense," I said in my mother's voice, before biting down on my tongue, allowing a softer voice to emerge. "You weren't gone long enough to feel guilty." I lay my hand on his arm, trying to reassure him.

He flinched, as if I'd burned him with a match, and pulled away, coughing into his hand. He stared in the direction of his open front door. Was he thinking of inviting me inside or making a run for the house? "Feel like a cup of coffee?" he asked, surprising me with the sudden warmth of his smile.

"Coffee sounds good."

Actually lunch sounded even better, but he didn't suggest it, and since he already seemed spooked by my showing up on his doorstep without prior notice, I didn't want to appear too presumptuous. Maybe we'd go for an early dinner, I thought hopefully, as he led me into the rose marble foyer.

The interior of the house was surprisingly spacious, consisting of one large common area that encompassed living, dining, and family rooms. The kitchen was at the back, as were two small bedrooms. I caught only a brief glimpse of the master bedroom suite at the front, noticed the bed was unmade, and felt a slight weakening of my knees. "Your home is lovely," I remarked, leaning against the tan ultrasuede of the living room sofa for support, eyeing the clean lines of the modern, minimalist furniture throughout the house.

"How do you take your coffee?"

"Black," I reminded him, a smile masking my disappointment that he hadn't remembered.

"Be right back. Make yourself at home." He disappeared into the kitchen.

I crossed the white-tiled floor, punctuated at irregular intervals by a series of muted needlepoint rugs. The room surprised me. It didn't seem to reflect the Josh Wylie I knew at all. Not that I knew him that well, but I'd always assumed that Josh's tastes would be closer to my own, that they leaned more toward comfort than style, more toward tradition than trends. I reminded myself that this was the house Josh had shared with his former wife, decided that the decor was probably more to her taste than his. He just hadn't gotten around to changing it, I concluded. Perhaps out of respect for his children's feelings.

The walls were white and largely bare. A few unimpressive lithographs hung at either side of the dining room table, and a large abstract painting of what looked to be a bowl of fruit occupied the far wall of the family room. I thought how nicely my own paintings would go in these rooms, the lush flowers replacing the anemic bowl of fruit, the unimaginative mirror by the front door usurped by the girl with the large hat on the beach.

Why had Alison given me such an expensive gift? I wondered suddenly, feeling my stomach cramp, as if I'd been sucker punched. I'd let my guard down for only a fraction of a second, and Alison had used it to sneak inside my head. Go away, I warned her. You're not welcome in this house. I'm safe here.

Still, experience had shown me that once Alison had her foot in the door, she was remarkably difficult to dislodge. Thoughts of her now swirled about my head: the first image of her in my doorway; the magic way she'd twirled about the cottage; her wondrous hair on my pillow as she slept; Erica's necklace around her neck; the necklace I'd given her at Christmas to replace it. And all the gifts she'd given me—the earrings, the head vase, the painting. So extravagant! Had she paid for it at all, or had Denise simply removed it from her aunt's inventory? And what exactly was Denise's part in all this? Was it possible the women had known each other all along, that Denise Nickson and Erica Hollander were two pieces of the puzzle that was Alison Simms?

You're a stupid, stupid girl, I heard my mother say.

"I hope the coffee's still good. It's been brewing all morning," Josh announced, returning to the room with two steaming mugs, coming to an abrupt stop when he saw me. "Terry, what's wrong? You look like you've just seen a ghost."

I raised my hands in the air, felt them shake. I opened my mouth, but no words came. Tears filled my eyes. Until this moment, I hadn't realized how scared I really was, how long I'd been denying my anxieties, suppressing my fears, and how desperately lonely I'd been and for how long. I was tired of being brave, rational, and independent. I was none of those things, and I couldn't survive this on my own. I needed someone to stand beside me, someone to protect me from harm. I needed Josh.

It took all my resolve to keep from throwing myself into his arms, to refrain from telling him what was in my heart—how much I needed him, wanted him, loved him. Yes, loved him, I realized, catching my breath in my lungs, holding the words tight against my chest, like smoke from a marijuana cigarette. "Hold me," I whispered, my voice a plea.

Immediately, I felt Josh's arms around me, his lips in my hair. "I'm sorry I haven't called you," he was saying.

"You've been away." I wiped the tears from my eyes, raised my lips to his. "You're here now."

"I'm here now," he repeated, pressing his lips to mine, lifting me into his arms and into the air, carrying me toward the master bedroom, like Clark Gable carrying Vivien Leigh, grappling with my clothes as he fell on top of me across the unmade bed.

Except he did none of those things, said nothing of the sort.

While my imagination was busy sweeping me into his arms and into his bed, he was already pulling out of my arms and out of my reach.

"Please," I heard myself say in a desperate bid to hold on to him.

"Terry, listen . . ."

"I'm so glad you're back. I've missed you so much."

"Oh, God. Terry, I owe you an apology."

"An apology? No. There's nothing to apologize for." Please tell me there's nothing to apologize for.

"So much has happened," Josh said, retreating to the other side of the glass table that held our coffee. The steam from the mugs wafted into the still air, like delicate streamers, creating a scrim between us.

"What do you mean? What's happened?"

"I'm so sorry if I've misled you in any way."

"I don't understand. How have you misled me?"

"I should have told you earlier. Actually, I assumed my mother already had."

"Told me what?"

He lowered his head as if he were ashamed. "Jan and I are back together."

His words slammed against my ears. "What?"

"Jan and I," he began, as if he actually thought I hadn't heard him the first time.

"When?" I interrupted, feeling sick to my stomach.

"Just before Christmas."

"Before Christmas?" I echoed, as if only the repetition of the words would make them sink in.

"I wanted to tell you."

"But you didn't."

"I'm a coward. It was easier to just keep canceling our dates. And, to be honest, I wasn't sure if things would work out with Jan."

"So, what are you saying? That you were using me as backup, in case your reconciliation didn't take?"

"I didn't mean it that way."

"How exactly did you mean it?"

"The kids are so happy," he said after a pause, as if this explained everything.

A numbness was creeping steadily into my arms and legs, buzzing about my head, like a pesky mosquito. "So, Thanksgiving meant nothing to you."

"That's not true. Thanksgiving was wonderful."

"The kiss . . . kisses . . . they were meaningless."

"They were beautiful."

"But meaningless."

Another pause, longer than the first. "Terry, let's not do this."

"Let's not do what?"

"I'd like us to stay friends."

"Friends don't lie to each other." Hadn't I just said the same thing to Alison?

"It was never my intention to lie." Then: "Listen, I have a little something for you." He walked quickly to the bedroom at the front of the house, returned seconds later with a package wrapped in bright blue foil. "I meant to give it to you earlier." He dropped the package into my hands.

"What's this?"

"I wanted to thank you again for taking such good care of my mother."

"Your mother." I felt a stab of humiliation so deep I almost doubled over. "I take it she knew you and Jan were back together?"

"Why do you think she's been so depressed?"

"She didn't tell me."

"She's not too happy about it."

"She's your mother. She'll come around."

"Aren't you going to open your present?"

I tore at the paper without enthusiasm. "A journal," I said, turning it over in my hands, thinking of Alison.

"I wasn't sure if you kept one or not."

"Guess I'll have to start."

"I'm really sorry, Terry. I never meant to hurt you." He broke off, looked toward the front door.

"Expecting company?" I asked coldly.

"Jan and the kids are at the mall. They should be home pretty soon." He looked anxiously at his watch.

"I guess your wife wouldn't be too happy to find me here."

"It would probably just confuse things."

"Well, we certainly wouldn't want anyone to be confused," I said, walking to the door. Had I really expected him to protect me from anyone?

"Terry," he called after me.

I stopped, turned around.

Don't go. I need you. I'll find a way out of this mess. I love you.

"Do you think you might talk to my mother, try to get her to understand? She loves you like a daughter. I know she'd listen to you."

Again I nodded, thinking this whole scene might be funny if it weren't so mind-numbingly awful. "I'll see what I can do."

"Thank you."

"Good-bye, Josh."

"Take care of yourself."

"I'll try," I said, closing the door behind me.

TWENTY-FOUR

Goddamn you, you stupid, stupid girl!" I railed at myself in my mother's voice. "How could you be so dumb? Have you no pride? No self-respect? You're forty years old, for God's sake. Have you learned nothing in all that time? Do you know so little about men? Ha!" I laughed, ignoring the not-so-furtive glances of other drivers as I banged down on the steering wheel, inadvertently blasting the horn. "Why stop with men? You know nothing about anyone. There isn't a worse judge of character in the entire world. All someone has to do is show you a little kindness, the tiniest bit of interest, and you can't do enough for them. You open your house, you open your heart." You open your legs, I continued silently, too ashamed to say the words out loud, even in the closed confines of my car. "A man takes you out for one measly little lunch and already you have him marching down the aisle. You're a stupid, stupid girl! You deserve to be taken advantage of. You deserve to lose everything. You're too damn stupid to live!"

You're a stupid, stupid girl, I heard my mother say.

I thought of the unmade bed in Josh's bedroom. Had he and Jan had sex this morning before she'd left for the mall? Were the crumpled sheets still redolent with the scent of their lovemaking?

"You're an idiot!" I shouted, my words bouncing off the car windows to slap me in the face. "People as stupid as you are don't deserve to live."

I looked into the rearview mirror, saw my mother's eyes. I didn't need the sound of her voice to know what she was thinking: *How could you do this?* Her eyes burned into mine, until my own eyes clouded over with so many tears she was no longer visible. Who needed my mother's harsh pronouncements when I was doing such a good job on my own?

"You're a stupid, stupid girl," I was still repeating as I pulled into my driveway and fumbled in my purse for my house keys. "You deserve whatever happens to you." I checked the street for Lance's white Lincoln. "Come and get me," I cried at the quiet street, the threat of rain still hovering overhead. "Game over. I give up."

But a quick glance told me Lance's car was nowhere in sight. Probably had it parked somewhere around the block, I decided, pushing the tears away from my swollen eyes with the palms of my hands, and running toward my front door, repeatedly jabbing the key into the lock until I heard the familiar click. The door fell open.

I marched into the living room, roughly pushing the Christmas tree out of my way, then watched it teeter precariously on its stand before falling against the wall. Its ornaments dropped from its branches and burst into delicate slivers of silver and pink on the hard floor. "Should have taken this stupid thing down days ago." Should never have put it up in the first place. "Stupid, stupid, stupid!" I ripped a handful of festive bows from the tree's drying limbs, then stomped on them. To imagine that Alison had ever really liked me. To think Josh had ever really cared. "Why would anyone want you? Why would anyone want to be your friend, your lover?"

My mother was right. She was always right. I was nothing but a stupid, *stupid* girl. I deserved everything that happened to me.

How could you do this? my mother demanded, sneaking up behind me as I entered the kitchen.

"Go away," I cried. "Please, go away. Leave me alone. You did your job well. I don't need you anymore."

From their lofty position, my mother's collection of ladies' head vases sneered at my naïveté, my mother's words continuing to assault me through their empty eyes and forced smiles. I watched in horror as my arm suddenly shot out and swept across the bottom shelf. Instantly the line of china heads went flying in all directions, like a swarm of angry bees. And then the next row, and the next. I grabbed the head that Alison had admired her first time in this room, the one that resembled my mother, with her judgmental, imperious gaze, *like some snooty society matron, looking down her nose at the rest of us*, Alison had said. I held the china head high into the air, then flung it with all my might across the room.

It exploded upon contact with the wall, bursting into the air like a firecracker. I laughed as colorful shards of porcelain flew about the room, covering the floor like confetti.

"Terry!" a voice cried out from outside the kitchen door. "Terry, what's happening? Let me in. Please, let me in!"

The doorknob twisted frantically from side to side. I took a second to catch my breath, then pulled open the kitchen door.

"My God, Terry!" Alison exclaimed, a look of horror overwhelming her sweet face. "What's going on here? What are you doing? Look at you. You're bleeding."

I raised a hand to my forehead, felt blood on my fingers.

"Terry, what's wrong? Did something happen?"

A wail, like an ancient chant, began building in my gut, filling my mouth like water, until it poured from my lips, spilled onto the floor, and eventually flooded the room. I fell to my knees, the sound of bottomless grief bouncing off the walls, pieces of broken china piercing my clothing, attaching themselves to my skin like burrs.

Instantly Alison was at my side, rocking me in her arms, kissing my bloodied forehead, begging me to tell her what was wrong. Almost immediately, I felt myself being sucked back into her orbit, falling under her spell. Even now, after all the lies and deceit, after everything I knew to be true, and everything I knew to be false, I wanted nothing more than to believe she was truly concerned about me, that no matter what was about to happen, she wouldn't let any harm come my way.

"I'm such a fool," I whispered.

"No. No, you're not a fool."

"I am."

"Tell me what happened. Please, Terry. Tell me."

I looked into her eyes. Through the thick veil of my tears, I was almost able to convince myself of her sincerity.

Might as well tell her what happened, I decided, wincing at the sight of my blood on her lips. She and her friends could have a good laugh about it later.

"Josh is back with his wife," I said simply, then almost laughed myself.

"Oh, Terry, I'm so sorry."

This time I actually did manage a strangulated chuckle. "That's what he said."

"You saw him?"

I told her the whole pathetic story of my visit with Josh, knowing K.C. had probably already phoned her, informed her of my plans. Had she been sitting by the window, anxiously awaiting my return?

"Bastard," she uttered now, giving my shoulder a gentle squeeze.

"No. It's my fault."

"How is it your fault?"

Because it always is, I thought but didn't say. "Because I'm such a fool," I said instead.

"If you're a fool, that must make me a full-out moron."

I laughed, as I did so often when I was with her.

"I mean, look at me and Lance, for heaven's sake," Alison continued without prompting. "After everything I've been through with him, after all my resolutions about not letting him back into my life, what do I do the first time he shows up at my door? I invite him in. Hell, I practically drag him inside the house. It doesn't matter that I know he's no good for me, that I know, sooner or later, he's going to break my heart, screw things up, the way he always does."

"What things?" I interrupted.

She shrugged sadly. "Things. Like he did with you."

I waited, feeling the tension in her arms, wondering if she was about to open up, tell me everything. But she didn't, and the moment passed.

"Where *is* Lance?" I looked toward the back door, half-expecting him to be standing there.

"Gone."

"Gone where?"

Alison shook her head, her hair tickling the side of my face. "Don't know. Don't care."

"You mean he's gone back to Chicago?"

"Don't know," Alison said again. "I guess he'll go wherever Denise tells him to."

"He's with Denise?"

"Should have seen that one coming, I guess." She hit her forehead with her hand, as if trying to knock some sense into it. "What the hell—it was over anyway. Finally. About time," she added for emphasis.

I nodded, although I doubted Lance was really gone.

"Men," she said, as if the word were a curse. "Can't live with 'em—"

"Can't shoot 'em," I said, recalling the words to an old country song.

"I'm so sorry about everything. If I could just go back to the beginning, start over again . . ."

"What would you do?"

"I wouldn't give Lance the time of day, that's for sure. I'd run for the hills the minute I saw him. Before it was too late."

"It's never too late," I said, as if pleading my case.

"Do you really believe that?"

I shrugged. Who knew what I believed anymore? "I've been such a fool."

Alison's eyes probed mine, as if she were reaching into my soul. "He's the fool. How could anyone not want you?"

I studied her face for signs of ridicule, but all I saw were fresh tears welling up in those enormous green eyes. Her lips quivered as I rubbed her tears away, the blood from my finger staining her skin, like an errant brushstroke, as I took her cheeks in my hands and drew her face gently toward mine.

I don't know what it was—fear, disillusion, longing—maybe a combination of all those things—that brought my lips so close to hers. I wondered only briefly what I was doing, then closed my mind to further thought as I shut my eyes, grazed her lips with my own.

Instantly, Alison pulled back, as Josh had earlier. Out of my arms. Out of my reach. "No! That's not what I meant. You don't understand."

"My God," I said, scrambling to my feet, my hand covering my mouth. "My God, oh my God."

Alison was on her feet beside me. "It's all right, Terry. Please, it was a misunderstanding. It's all my fault."

"What have I done?" I stared down at all the shattered women at my feet, at their lost earrings and broken strands of pearls, pieces of their smiles mixed with stiff strands of their hair. All the king's horses, and all the king's men, I thought, seeing my reflection in Alison's horrified eyes, knowing we were all broken beyond repair, that nothing could be done to put any of us back together again. "I have to get out of here," I cried, fleeing the carnage, racing for the front door.

Alison was right behind me. "Terry, wait! Let me come with you."

"No, please. Just leave me alone. Leave me alone." I was in my car before she could stop me, the doors locked, the engine running, the car in reverse, my foot on the gas.

"Terry, please, come back."

I backed out of the driveway and onto the street, mowing over the grass of the corner lot and almost colliding with Bettye McCoy and her stupid dogs two blocks away. In response, she gave me the finger and called me a name, although it was my mother's voice I heard.

I drove through the streets of Delray for the better part of an hour, drawing comfort from the little seaside town that had somehow managed to retain its quaint, thriving downtown without falling prey to the towering office buildings and ugly strip malls of most of Florida's older cities. I drove past the small, old homes of the historic marina district, past the newer oceanfront condominiums and luxury estates along the coast, then doubled back, headed for the gated communities, retirement enclaves, and country clubs that existed west of the city limits. I drove until my legs were stiff and my hands felt welded to the steering wheel. I drove until the dark black clouds spreading above my head exploded in a thunderous rage, flooding the thoroughfares with sheets of angry rain. Then I pulled the car over to the side of the road and quietly watched the rain as it pounded against my windshield, an eerie calm settling over me, like a warm blanket. My tears stopped. My head cleared. And I was no longer afraid.

I knew exactly what I had to do.

Twenty minutes later, I pulled my car into the parking lot of Mission Care and ran through the continuing downpour into the lobby, shaking the water from my hair as I headed for the stairwell. I kept my head down, not wanting anyone to see me. I was supposed to be in bed with the flu after all, not gallivanting around in the rain. Besides, my visit was personal, not professional. There was no reason for anyone to know I was there.

I climbed the steps to the fourth floor, stopping at the landing to catch my breath before cracking open the door and peeking my head around. No one was there, so I proceeded cautiously down the corridor. I was halfway down the hall when one of the staff doctors emerged from a patient's room, heading right for me. I thought of lowering my head, stooping to pick up an invisible penny from the floor, maybe even ducking into a nearby room, but I did none of those things. Instead I gave the young doctor a shy smile, preparing to tell him how much better I was feeling, thank him so much for asking. But the vacant smile he offered in return announced he had no idea who I was, that I was as faceless to him in my street clothes as I was in my nurse's uniform. I could have been anyone, I realized.

In fact, I was no one.

Myra Wylie was lying in bed staring at the ceiling when I pushed open the door to her room and stepped inside. "Please go away," she said without looking to see who it was.

"Myra, it's me, Terry."

"Terry?" She turned her cheek to me, smiled with her eyes.

"How are you today?" I walked to her side, grasped the bruised hand she extended toward me.

"They told me you were sick."

"I was. I'm feeling much better now."

"Me too. Now that you're here."

"Has the doctor been in to see you yet?"

"He was here a little while ago. He poked and prodded, lectured me about eating more if I want to keep up my strength."

"He's right."

"I know. I just don't seem to have much of an appetite these days."

"Not even for a piece of marzipan?" I produced a small candied apple from the pocket of my navy pants. "I stopped at the bakery on my way over."

"In this rain?"

"It's not so bad."

"You're a darling girl."

I opened the wrapping, broke the small piece of candy into two pieces, placed one on the tip of her tongue, enjoyed the pleasure that filled her eyes. "I saw Josh today," I said.

Immediately her eyes darkened, like the sky. "Josh was here?"

"No. I drove to Coral Gables."

"You went to Coral Gables?"

"To his house." I deposited the remaining piece of marzipan on her tongue.

"To his house? Why?"

"I wanted to see him."

"Is there something wrong? Something the doctors haven't told me?"

"No," I reassured her quickly, as I'd reassured her son only hours ago. "This wasn't about you. It was about me."

Concern swam through the milkiness of her eyes. "Are you all right?"

"I'm fine. I just needed to talk to Josh."

Myra looked puzzled. She waited for me to continue.

"He told me he's back with his wife."

"Yes."

"He says you're not very happy about it."

"I'm his mother. If that's what he wants, then I'm happy."

"It seems it is."

"I'm just an old worrywart, I guess. I don't want to see him get hurt again."

"He's a big boy."

"Do they ever really grow up?" she asked.

"How long have you known?"

"I think I've always known they'd get back together. He never stopped loving her, even after the divorce. The minute she started making reconciliation noises, I knew it was only a matter of time." Myra twisted her head from side to side, no longer able to find a comfortable position.

"Here, let me fluff that up for you."

"Thank you, darling." She smiled, lifted her head, allowed me to extricate one of the meager pillows from behind her head.

"I wish you'd told me," I said, kneading it with my fingers.

"I wanted to. But I felt a bit foolish after the things I'd said about her. I hope you understand."

"It would have saved me a lot of embarrassment."

"I'm sorry, dear. I didn't think it would be a big deal."

"I drove all the way down there, made a complete fool of myself." A sound, halfway between a laugh and a cry, escaped my lips. "How could you let me do that?"

"I'm so sorry, dear. I had no idea. Please forgive me."

I smiled, smoothed several fine strands of hair away from her forehead. "I forgive you."

Then I lowered the pillow I was holding to her face and held it over her nose and mouth until she stopped breathing.

TWENTY-FIVE

It's such a strange sensation, killing another person.

Myra Wylie was surprisingly strong for someone so frail. She fought me with a determination that was stunning in its ferocity, her long, skeletal arms flailing blindly toward me, gnarled and brittle fingers clawing helplessly toward my throat, the muscles in her neck warring with the pillow in my hands as her desperate lungs screamed silently for air. Such stubborn tenacity, the instinct to survive in the face of certain, even longed-for, death, caught me temporarily off-guard, and I almost lost my grip. Myra seized that split second's hesitation with all the strength left in her, twisting her head wildly from side to side and kicking frantically at her sheets.

I quickly refocused, pressing down harder on the pillow, patiently watching as her feet twitched to an almost graceful stop beneath the tightly tucked hospital corners of her narrow bed. I listened to her last desperate intake of breath and smelled the pungent odor of urine as it leaked from her body. Then I counted slowly to one hundred and waited for the unmistakable stillness of death to overwhelm her. Only then did I remove the pillow from her face, fluffing it out before returning it to behind her head, careful to arrange her hair the way she liked it. It was damp with the sweat of her exertion, and I blew gently on the matted strands at her forehead in an effort to dry them, watching as Myra's thin eyelashes fluttered girlishly in my warm breath, as if she were flirting with me.

Watery blue eyes stared up at me in frozen disbelief, and I closed them with my lips, my hands trembling toward the exaggerated, open oval of her mouth, contorted in a way to suggest that, even now, she was still trying to suck air into her withered, broken frame. My fingers quickly molded her lips into a more pleasing shape, as if I were an artist working with fast-drying clay. Then I stood back and observed my handiwork. She reminded me of one of those floats people buy for their pool, stretched out and waiting to be inflated. Still, I was satisfied that Myra looked peaceful, even happy, as if she'd simply slipped away from life in the middle of a pleasant dream.

"Good-bye, Myra," I told her from the door. "Sleep well."

I proceeded briskly down the hall toward the exit, confident no one would notice me. I even smiled at a young man on his way to visit his father, the blank look I received in return reassuring me I was still invisible—a ghost haunting the hallowed hospital halls, as insubstantial and fleeting as a whisper in the wind.

How did I feel?

Energized, relieved, possibly a little sad. I'd always liked and admired Myra Wylie, considered her a friend. Until she'd betrayed me, abused the many kindnesses I'd shown her. Until I realized she was no better than any of the others who'd abused and betrayed me over the years, and that, like those others, she was the author of her own misfortune, responsible for, and deserving of, her fate.

Not that I enjoyed being the minister of that fate. The truth is that I've never liked watching people die, never really gotten used to it, no matter how many times I've borne witness. Maybe that's what makes me such a good nurse, the fact that I genuinely care about people, that I want nothing but the best for everyone. The idea of taking a life is genuinely abhorrent to me. As a nurse, I've been trained to do everything in my power to sustain life. Although, some might argue, why sustain a life void of purpose, a life that is increasingly more parasitic than human?

Besides, whom am I kidding? Nurses have no power. Even doctors, whose exalted egos we stroke daily and whose daily mistakes we're constantly covering up, have no real power when it comes to matters of life and death. We're not the caregivers we claim to be. We're care*takers*. Janitors, really—that's all we are—looking after the leftover detritus of all the people who've exceeded their "best before" dates.

Lance was right.

I pictured Alison's ex-husband, if that's who he truly was, tall, slim-hipped, irredeemably handsome, and wondered if he was really gone. Or was he still in Delray, squatting among the obscene appendages of an overgrown screw palm, biding his time, waiting for just the right moment to leap out at me from the darkness?

Time's up, I thought with a smile.

I walked calmly down the four flights of stairs to the exit, grateful to see the rain had stopped, and that the storm clouds that had carpeted the sky all day had given way to the cautiously optimistic sun of twilight. Happy hour, I thought, checking my watch as I climbed into my car, debating whether to stop on my way home for a celebratory drink, deciding that it was still too early to celebrate, that much still required my attention. It was important that I be fully alert for the night ahead, that I not let down my guard in any way.

A siren was wailing as I turned my car into the rush-hour traffic along Jog Road, and I watched an ambulance speed by on the outside shoulder, probably on its way to the Delray Medical Center. I wondered how long it would be before one of the nurses looked in on Myra, checked her vital signs, and realized she was dead. I wondered if anyone would call me to relay the sad news. She was my patient after all. *Where's my Terry?* she would say, the first words out of her mouth every morning, as if I weren't entitled to a few hours away from her side, as if I weren't entitled to a life of my own.

Where's my Terry? Where's my Terry?

Everyone always thought it was so cute.

"Here's your Terry," I said now, gripping the steering wheel as if it were a pillow, pushing on it with all my strength, hearing the loud blast of the horn as it spun out into the traffic, then crashed into the dying afternoon. Instantly, half a dozen other horns began polluting the air with their mindless bleating. Like lambs to the slaughter, I thought, smiling at the motorist in the car ahead of mine as he extended the middle finger of his right hand into the air without even bothering to turn around.

Why should he turn around? What was there to see? I was invisible.

There would be no autopsy. There was no need. Myra's death had been expected, even anticipated. It was long overdue. There was nothing remotely surprising or suspicious about it. An eighty-seven-year-old woman with both cancer and heart disease—her death would be considered a blessing. The nurses would acknowledge her passing with a collective nod of their heads and a brief notation in their charts. The doctors would record the time of death and move on to the next cadaver-in-waiting. Josh Wylie would quietly arrange for his mother's burial. A few weeks from now, he might even send the staff an arrangement of flowers in appreciation of the excellent care his mother had received during her stay at Mission Care. Soon a new patient would occupy Myra's bed. After eighty-seven years, it would be as if she'd never existed.

An old song by the Beatles—*She loves you, yeah, yeah, yeah!*—came on the radio, and I sang along loudly with it, surprised to discover I knew all the words. This made me feel strangely exhilarated, even elated. The Beatles were followed by Neil Diamond, then Elton John. "Sweet Caroline," "Goodbye Yellow Brick Road." Long a devotee of golden oldies, I knew every word, every beat, every pause. *"Soldier boy!"* I belted out along with the Shirelles. *"Oh, my little soldier boy! Bum bum bum bum bum. I'll—be—true—to—you."*

I'm not sure why I decided not to park in my driveway, why I chose to drive past my house, circle back around the block instead, and park around the corner. Was I looking for Lance's car? If so, I didn't see it. Was it possible he was really gone? That I was truly safe?

I scoffed at my own naïveté, rechecking the street before getting out of my car and continuing briskly on foot,

way, her face full of worry. Wondering where I am, I realized. Wondering when I'm coming home.

She lingered at the window for several long seconds, then backed away, the curtains hiding her continuing vigil. I had to be careful, keep to the corners, not let her know I was home until I had everything in place. There was still so much to be done.

I pushed myself toward the kitchen counter, reached for the shelves, began gathering together the ingredients I would need: Duncan Hines yellow cake mix, a small box of instant chocolate pudding, a cup of Crisco oil, a package of chopped walnuts, a quarter cup of chocolate chippets, four eggs and a cup of sour cream from the fridge. Terry's magic chocolate cake. My mother's favorite. I hadn't made it in years.

Not since the night she died.

Terry! I could still hear her yelling at me from upstairs, her voice strong despite the stroke that had rendered her body useless.

I'll be up in a minute, Mother.

Now!

I'm coming.

What's taking you so long?

I'll be right up.

I stirred the ingredients together in a large bowl, dropping the eggs onto the top of the cake mix, instant pudding, Crisco, and sour cream, then mixing them in by hand so that I wouldn't make any noise. There was always the chance that Alison might sneak out of the cottage without my noticing, hear the whir of an electric mixer, interrupt me before I was ready. I couldn't take that chance. I watched the yolks of the eggs separate from the whites and spill across the light brown of the pudding. Then I wove my spatula through the mix, producing vibrant yellow swirls, like paint on a canvas. Creating my own masterpiece.

Still life.

Terry, for God's sake, what are you doing down there?

I'm almost done.

I need the bedpan. I can't hold it any longer.

I'll be right there.

I folded the chopped nuts and the chocolate chippets into the rest of the mix, then ran my index finger along the top of the bowl, lifting a large gob of batter to my mouth and greedily sucking it from my fingertip. Then I did it again, this time using two fingers. A loud groan inadvertently escaped my throat as I slowly manipulated my fingers in and out of my mouth.

What are you doing down there? my mother cried.

When I was a little girl, I used to watch my mother in the kitchen. She was always baking something, and I often pleaded with her to let me help. Of course, she always refused, told me I'd only make a mess. But one afternoon when she was out, I decided to surprise her by making a cake of my own. I gathered up the necessary ingredients and mixed them together, careful to beat out all the lumps, just as I'd watched her do week after week. Then I baked the whole thing for an hour at 350 degrees.

When my mother came home, I presented her with my beautiful chocolate cake. She surveyed the neat countertop, checked the floor for spillage, then silently sat down at the table and waited to be served. With great pride, I cut into the cake and produced a perfect slice, then watched eagerly as my mother raised her fork to her lips. I waited for her words of praise, the tap on the top of my head that told me she was pleased. Instead, I recoiled in horror as her face began collapsing in on itself, her cheeks hollowing, disappearing into the sides of her mouth as she spit the cake into the air, shouting, *What have you done, you stupid girl? What have you done?*

What I'd done was use bitter chocolate instead of sweet. A careless mistake no doubt, but I was only nine or ten, and surely the look on my mother's face, the knowledge that she'd been right about me all along, was punishment enough.

Except that it wasn't. And I knew it. It was never enough.

Even now I can feel my body tense as I waited for the blow to strike the side of my face, the blow that would send my head spinning and my ears ringing. But the blow never came. Instead came an eerie calm, a misplaced smile. My mother simply pointed to the chair beside her and instructed me to sit down. Then she took the knife and cut into my cake, producing a perfect piece similar to the one I'd cut for her, pushed it toward me, and waited for me to take a bite.

I can still feel my hands shaking as I pushed the cake into my mouth. Instantly, the bitter taste settled on my tongue, combining with the bitter salt of my tears as they fell down my cheeks and ran between my lips.

She made me eat the entire cake.

Only when I was sick and vomiting on the floor did she stop, and only then to make me clean it up.

Terry, for God's sake, what are you doing down there?

Coming, Mother.

I glanced back at the cottage, then preset the oven to 350 degrees and lightly greased a large Bundt pan. I poured the batter inside it, then added my secret ingredient.

What on earth took you so long? I need the bedpan.

It's right beside you. No need to get so upset.

I've been calling you for forty-five minutes.

I'm sorry. I was baking you a cake.

What kind of cake?

It's chocolate. Your favorite.

When the oven reached 350 degrees, I put the cake inside, then licked the bowl free of whatever batter remained. "You never let me lick the bowl, did you, Mother?" The best part, I've always thought. "I always missed out on the best part."

I know you blame me.

I don't blame you.

Yes, you do. You blame me for the way your life has turned out, for the fact you never married or had children. That whole episode with Roger Stillman. . . .

That was a long time ago, Mother. I've let it go.

Have you? Have you really?

I nodded, cut her a large slice of cake, pressed a forkful to her lips.

You know that everything I did, I did for your benefit.

I know that. Of course I know that.

I didn't mean to be cruel.

I know.

It's the way I was raised. My mother was the same with me.

You were a good mother.

I made a lot of mistakes.

We all make mistakes.

Can you forgive me?

Of course I forgive you. I kissed the flaky, dry skin of her forehead. *You're my mother. I love you.*

She whispered something unintelligible, maybe "I love you," maybe not. Whatever it was, I knew it was a lie. Everything she said was a goddamn lie. She didn't love me. She wasn't sorry about anything except that she was the one in that bed, and not me. I pushed another forkful of cake into her stupid, eager mouth.

My reveries were interrupted by a loud knocking and I raced to the kitchen door. A man was standing outside the cottage, his back to me. Suddenly Alison opened her door, the light from inside the cottage throwing a spotlight on the now familiar figure.

"K.C.!" Alison exclaimed as his profile came clearly into view. "Come in." She cast a furtive glance around the cottage before ushering him inside and closing the door.

Look at the lowlife you've allowed into my home, I heard my mother hiss.

"*My* home," I corrected her now. "You died, remember?"

With the help of Terry's magic chocolate cake and a favorite pillow.

"Taste buds failed you that time, didn't they, Mother?" Whoever said that Percodan and chocolate pudding didn't mix?

I smelled the aroma of freshly baking cake, glanced at the oven, then back to the cottage in time to see the door reopen, and Alison step outside behind K.C. "Terry should be home soon," she was saying. "I can't be gone long."

I ran through the kitchen to the front of the house, watched through the living room window as Alison and K.C. marched purposefully down the front path to the street, then turned the corner, their arms brushing up against one another as they walked. Were they going to meet Lance and Denise? How long before they'd be back? And would Erica's biker friend be with them?

I wasted no more time. Clutching the spare key to the cottage between my fingers, and carefully sliding the foot-long butcher knife with its tapered two-inch blade from its wooden slot, I opened the back door and stepped into a night redolent with whispers and lies.

TWENTY-SIX

I'm not sure what I was looking for, or what exactly I thought I'd find.

Maybe I was checking to make sure Lance was really gone. Or maybe I was looking for Alison's journal, something I could take to the police, point to as proof positive that my life was at risk. I don't know. As I stood in the middle of the brightly lit living room, my hands trembling, my knees all but knocking together, I had absolutely no thought in my head as to what to do next.

I had no idea how long Alison and K.C. would be gone. And how did I know Lance wasn't hiding in the bedroom, watching and waiting for my next stupid move? Hadn't I parked my car around the block to avoid discovery? Couldn't he have done exactly the same thing?

Except there was no sign of him anywhere: no rumpled clothing strewn carelessly on the floor; no wayward creases in the furniture where he might have sat; no stray masculine smells permeating the air, disturbing the scent of baby powder and strawberries. I tiptoed toward the bedroom, the handle of the large butcher knife clutched tightly in the palm of my hand, the blade protruding from my body like the thorn of a giant rose.

But nothing in the bedroom indicated Lance might still be in residence. No shirts in the drawers, no suitcase in the closet, no shaving kit in the medicine cabinet. I even checked under the bed. "Nothing," I said to the reflection that flickered at me from the long, sharp blade of the knife. Was it possible he was really gone, that he'd taken off with Denise, just as Alison had claimed?

If so, then why was K.C. still around? What was his connection to Alison?

I laid the knife across the top of the white wicker dresser, watched it wobble against the uneven surface as I rifled through each drawer. But the drawers were mostly empty—a few push-up bras from Victoria's Secret, half a dozen pairs of panties, several uncomfortable-looking thongs, and a pair of yellow cotton pajamas decorated with images from *I Love Lucy*.

Where was her journal? Surely that would tell me something.

Only after searching through every drawer several times did I spot the damn thing sitting on the night table beside the bed. "Stupid," I said in my mother's voice. "It was right there the whole time. Open your eyes." I marched to the nightstand, grabbed the journal, turned swiftly to its final entry.

Everything's falling apart, I read.

As if on cue, a series of loud bangs, like small explosions, erupted from the street, followed by an even louder voice, then more banging. "Terry!" the voice shouted. "Terry, I know you're in there. Terry, please! Open the door!"

I dropped the journal onto the bed, raced to the side window, watched as Alison came running around the side of my house from the front to the back door, K.C. at her heels.

"Terry!" she persisted, banging repeatedly on my back door with her open palm. "Terry, please. Open up. We have to talk."

"She's not there," K.C. said.

"She *is* there. Terry, please. Open the door."

Suddenly Alison was vaulting toward the cottage. Had she seen me watching from the window? I spun around in helpless circles, knowing there was nowhere for me to go.

I was trapped.

I ran toward the closet, noting only at the last second the journal I'd carelessly dropped on Alison's bed. I hurried back, scooped it up, and returned it to its rightful place on the nightstand, then scrambled across the bed toward the closet, bringing the door closed after me just as Alison's key turned in the front lock.

It was then, my fingers tightly curled around the doorknob, that I realized I'd left the knife—the foot-long behemoth with its tapered two-inch blade—lying on top of the dresser. *Stupid, stupid girl!* my mother whispered in my ear. *She's not likely to miss that, is she?*

"Maybe it wasn't her car," K.C. was saying from the next room. "There are lots of black Nissans."

"It *was* her car," Alison insisted, confusion bracketing her words. "Why would she park it around the block and not in the driveway?"

"Maybe she's visiting a friend."

"She doesn't have any friends. I'm the only friend she's got."

"Doesn't that strike you as strange?"

There followed a long pause in which we all seemed to be holding our breath.

"What are you talking about?" Alison asked.

I heard the shuffling sounds of two wary people walking around in circles. How long before one of them stepped into the bedroom, saw the knife? How long before Alison checked the closet for bogeymen?

"Look, Alison, there are some things I have to tell you."

"What kind of things?"

Another pause, this one even longer than the first. "I haven't been very honest with you."

"Welcome to the club," Alison muttered. "Listen, on second thought, I don't think I'm up for this discussion right now."

"No—you need to hear me out."

"I need to pee."

Dear God, I thought, as I shot from the closet like a yo-yo on a string. I grabbed the knife, the blade slicing across my palm as my fingers closed around it. Then I leaped back inside the closet, the door closing after me just as Alison entered the room.

I stuffed my wounded hand inside my mouth, sucked at the steady stream of blood issuing from my palm, and tried not to cry out. From the bathroom, I heard Alison grumbling as she relieved herself. "What in the world is going on here?" she kept repeating over and over. "What in the world is going on?"

Alison flushed the toilet, washed her hands, and reentered the bedroom, then stopped, as if not sure of her next move. Or had something suspicious caught her eye?

A drop of blood on the dresser? A suspicious footprint in the carpet? Was her journal lying wrong-side up? I raised my knife, steeled my body for her approach.

"Alison?" K.C. called from the living room. "Are you all right?"

"That depends." A pronounced sigh of resignation. "What is it you want to tell me?"

K.C.'s voice drew closer. I felt him standing in the doorway. "Maybe you should sit down."

Alison obediently plopped down on her bed. "I'm liking this less and less."

"For starters, my name isn't K.C."

"It isn't," Alison said, more statement than question.

"It's Charlie. Charlie Kentish."

Charlie Kentish? Where had I heard that name before?

"Charlie Kentish," Alison repeated, as if thinking the same thing. "Not K.C., short for Kenneth Charles."

"No."

"No wonder nobody ever calls you that," she observed wryly, and I almost laughed. "I don't understand," she continued in almost the same breath. "Why would you lie about your name?"

"Because I didn't know if I could trust you."

"Why wouldn't you trust me?"

I felt him shrug. "I'm not sure where to start." Another shrug, perhaps a shake of his head.

"Then maybe you shouldn't bother." Alison jumped to her feet. I felt her moving around, pacing back and forth in front of the bed. "Maybe it's not important who you really are or what you have to tell me. Maybe you should just leave, so that you can get on with your life, whose ever it is, and I'll get on with mine, and we can all live happily ever after. Don't you think that's a good idea?"

"Only if you come with me."

"Come with you?"

"You're in danger if you stay here."

"I'm in danger?" Alison laughed. "Are you completely nuts?"

"Please listen to me—"

"No," Alison said resolutely. "You're starting to scare me, and I want you to leave."

"It's not me you have to worry about."

"Listen, K.C., or Charlie, or whoever the hell you really are—"

"I'm Charlie Kentish."

Charlie Kentish, I repeated. Why was that name so damn familiar?

"I don't want to have this conversation. If you don't leave, I'm going to call the police."

"Erica Hollander is my fiancée."

"What?"

"The woman who used to live here."

"I know who Erica Hollander is."

So that's where I knew the name. Of course. Charlie Kentish. Erica's fiancé, the one she was always going on about. *Charlie this. Charlie that. Charlie's so handsome. Charlie's so smart. Charlie's got this great job in Japan for a year. Charlie and I are getting married as soon as he comes home.*

"Your precious fiancée ran out on Terry in the middle of the night, owing several months' rent," Alison said.

"She didn't go anywhere."

"What do you mean?"

"I mean, she didn't go anywhere," he repeated, as if that explained everything.

"I don't understand. What are you saying?"

"I was hoping you could tell me."

"Tell you what? I don't have a clue what you're talking about."

"Maybe if you'd stop pacing for two minutes and sit down . . ."

"I don't want to sit down."

"Please. Just hear me out."

"And then you'll leave?"

"If that's what you want."

I heard the bed squeak as Alison resumed her former position. "I'm listening," she said in a tone that indicated she'd rather not be.

"Erica and I had been living together for about six months when I got this great job offer to work in Japan for a year. We decided I should go, and she'd stay here, move into a cheaper apartment, and we'd save our money so we could get married as soon as I got home."

"I thought you were from Texas."

"Originally, yes. I moved here after college."

"Okay, so off you went to Japan," Alison said, getting back on track.

"And Erica E-mailed me about finding this great little place, a small cottage behind a house belonging to a nurse. She was thrilled."

"I'm sure she was."

"Everything seemed perfect. I'd get these glowing E-mails telling me how wonderful Terry was, how she was always inviting Erica over for dinner, doing little things for her.

Erica's mother died a couple of years ago, and her father had remarried and moved to Arizona, so I guess she was just really grateful to have someone like Terry in her life."

"So she could take advantage of her."

"Erica wasn't like that. She was the sweetest—" His voice cracked, threatened to break. "Then things started to change."

"What do you mean? What things?"

"The letters stopped being so positive. Erica wrote that Terry was starting to behave strangely, that she seemed fixated on some biker Erica once said hello to in a restaurant, that she was getting paranoid."

"Paranoid? In what way?"

"She never went into detail. She just said that Terry was starting to make her feel uncomfortable, that she was afraid she might have to start looking for another place."

"So she skipped out in the middle of the night."

"No. I was due back in a few months. We decided she might as well stay put until I got back to Delray and we could look for a place together. But then, the E-mails suddenly stopped. I tried calling her cell phone, but no one ever answered. That's when I started calling Terry. She told me Erica had moved out."

"You didn't believe her?"

"It seemed odd that Erica would move out without telling me, let alone go anywhere without leaving a forwarding address."

"Terry told me she was hanging out with a bad crowd."

"No."

"That she met someone else."

"I don't believe it."

"Things like that happen every day."

"I'm sure they do. But that's not what happened here."

"Did you check with her employer?"

"Erica didn't have a regular employer. She worked for Kelly Services. They hadn't heard from her in weeks."

"Did you go to the police?"

"I called them from Japan. There wasn't much they could do long-distance. They contacted Terry. She gave them the same story she gave me."

"Which you can't accept."

"Because it isn't true."

"Did you go to the police when you got back home?"

"As soon as I got off the plane. They reacted pretty much the same way you are now. 'She found somebody else, buddy. Move on.'"

"But you can't."

"Not till I find out what happened to her."

"And you think Terry is somehow involved? That *I'm* involved?"

"I thought that in the beginning."

"The beginning?"

"When you first moved in."

I could almost feel the quizzical look on Alison's face.

"I'd been watching the house for about a month at that point," K.C. explained. "After you moved in, I started following you. You got a job at that gallery, and I started hanging around. I almost had a heart attack when I saw you wearing Erica's necklace. I gave her that necklace."

"I found it under the bed," Alison protested.

"I believe you. But in the beginning, I didn't know what to think. I had to find out the extent of your involvement, how much you knew. I tried flirting with you, but you weren't interested, so I hit on Denise, convinced her to let me tag along for Thanksgiving dinner. I realized pretty quickly that you had nothing to do with Erica's disappearance. But the more I got to know Terry, the more convinced I became she did."

"And why is that?"

"Because there's something very weird about that lady."

"Don't be ridiculous."

"I've been watching her for months, phoning her, following her in my car, trying to spook her, anything to get her to slip up. And she's starting to crack. I can feel it."

So it hadn't been my imagination. Someone *had* been watching me. And not just today. K.C. was the shifting shadow outside my window, the anonymous, yet strangely familiar, voice on my telephone. That subtle Texas twang he couldn't quite disguise—how had I failed to recognize it before now?

"You've been harassing her for months," Alison stated, "and you're surprised she's acting strangely?"

"Terry knows what happened to Erica. Damn it, she's responsible."

"Are you finished? Because if you're finished, then it's time for you to leave."

"Haven't you heard anything I've said?"

"You haven't said anything," Alison shot back. "Your girlfriend pulled a disappearing act. I'm sorry. I know being dumped is a hard thing to accept. But what you're suggesting is outrageous. And I've heard quite enough, thank you. I want you to go now."

There was a second's silence, then the sound of feet shuffling reluctantly toward the front door.

"Wait!" Alison called out, and I held my breath, inched forward, leaned my head against the closet door. "You should have this." She walked around the side of the bed, pulled open the drawer of the nightstand. "You said you gave it to her. You should have it back."

I pictured Alison walking toward him, Erica's thin gold necklace dangling from her fingertips.

"Come with me," he urged. "It's not safe for you to stay here."

"Don't worry about me," she told him flatly. "I'll be fine."

I heard the front door open as I crept out of the closet and inched along the side of the dresser, my palm leaving a bloody trail on the white wicker as I balanced against it.

"Be careful," the man calling himself K.C. warned the young woman who called herself Alison Simms.

And then he was gone.

TWENTY-SEVEN

I don't know how long I stood there, my breath caught somewhere between my lungs and my mouth, my hand pulsating with pain as I pressed the handle of the knife against my torn flesh, like a branding iron. Could I really use this knife against Alison, even in self-defense?

"What the hell is going on here?" Alison demanded suddenly, and I lunged forward in response, my arm instinctively arcing into the air, while blood from my palm streaked down my arm, as if someone had outlined the path of one of my veins in red ink.

But Alison hadn't been speaking to me, and she was already out the door and on her way to the main house when I emerged from the shadows, her anguished, unanswered question vibrating against the still air, like smoke from a discarded cigarette. "Terry!" I heard her shouting, as once more she pounded on my kitchen door. "Terry, open the door. I know you're in there."

I watched as she backed away from the door, her head tilted toward my bedroom. "Terry!" she shouted, her voice targeting my window like a well-aimed stone, before she gave up in defeat. What now? I wondered, swallowing what little air I could find, holding it hostage against my lungs.

Alison stood very still for what seemed an excruciatingly long time. Weighing her options, I thought. Just like me. Ultimately she decided to give it one last try, turning on her heels and running around the side of the house to the front. Only then did I push open the cottage door and creep into the night, a sudden breeze scratching at my neck, like the tongue of a cat. As Alison banged on the front door, I was opening the back.

In the next instant, I was inside my kitchen, the aroma of freshly baked chocolate cake settling about my head, like a bridal veil. I slid the bloody knife back into its triangular wooden holder, then wrapped my bleeding palm inside a dishcloth as Alison returned to the back door, her eyes widening with shock as I flipped on the light and opened the door to let her in.

"Terry! What's going on? Where have you been? I've been so worried."

"I was taking a nap," I answered sleepily, in a voice not quite my own. Hell, K.C. wasn't the only one capable of disguising his voice.

"Are you all right?"

"I'm fine." I waved my hand into the air, as if to dismiss her concerns.

"My God, what happened to your hand?"

I glanced at my injured arm, as if seeing it for the first time. Blood had already soaked through the thin, cotton towel. "I cut it. It's nothing."

"It's not nothing. Let me have a look at it." She unwrapped the towel before I could protest further. "Oh, my God! This is awful. Maybe we should go to the hospital."

"Alison, it's just a little cut."

"It's not just a little cut. You might need stitches." She pulled me toward the sink, ran the cold water, guided my hand under the steady stream. "How long has it been bleeding like this?"

"Not long." I winced as the water hit my palm, pushing the blood aside, and exposing the fragile white line of my wound. My wounded lifeline, I thought, as blood continued to wash across the inside of my hand.

"What's that smell?" Alison looked toward the stove.

"Terry's magic chocolate cake," I said with a shrug.

Confusion brought her eyebrows together at the bridge of her nose. "I don't understand. When did you have time to bake? I've been waiting for you for hours. When did you get back? And what's your car doing parked around the corner?" The questions were coming faster now, out of her mouth as soon as they entered her head, one piled on top of the other, like pancakes. Alison shut off the water, grabbed a handful of paper towels from the roll on the wall, and pressed the absorbent white towels into my cupped hand. "Tell me what's going on, Terry."

I shook my head, trying to gather my thoughts together, to give order to my lies. "There's not that much to tell."

"Start with when you left here. Where did you go?" Alison prompted. She didn't have to say any more. She didn't have to mention the aborted kiss.

I noted a small red circle metastasizing in the middle of the white paper towels, like menstrual blood, I thought, watching it grow wider and darker, reach toward the edges. "I'm so embarrassed about what happened," I whispered as she led me to a chair. "I don't know what came over me."

"It was all my fault," Alison interjected immediately, sitting down beside me. "I obviously gave you the wrong impression."

"I've never done anything like that before in my life."

"I know. You were just upset about Josh."

"Yes," I agreed, thinking this was probably true. "Anyway, I'm not sure where I went after I left here. I was pretty confused, so I just drove around for a while, tried to clear my head."

"And you parked around the corner because you didn't want me to know you were back," Alison stated quietly, traces of guilt bracketing her words.

"I was feeling pretty shaky. I thought it was best if we didn't see each other right away."

"I was so worried about you."

"I'm sorry."

"Don't be."

I looked around the room. It felt so bare, so empty, without the women watching. "Baking's always been a kind of therapy for me," I continued, glancing from the shelves to the oven. "So, I decided, why not bake a cake? I don't know. It seemed like a good idea at the time. Isn't that what they say?"

She nodded. "Seems like they're always saying something."

I smiled. "You like chocolate cake, don't you?"

Her turn to smile. "Is that a rhetorical question?"

I patted her hand. It felt ice-cold. "It should be ready in a few minutes."

"Is that how you cut your hand? Baking?"

"It was stupid," I began, the lie wiggling around the tip of my tongue, like a worm on a fisherman's hook. "I was reaching for something in a drawer, and I sliced it on a small paring knife."

Alison clutched her own hand in sympathy. "Ooh, that hurts."

"It's a bit better now." I glanced back at the oven, smiled. "Cake should be ready. Feel like a piece?"

"Don't you have to let it cool off for a while?"

"No. It's best fresh out of the oven." I rose from my seat, walked to the stove, opened the oven door with my left hand. A gust of heat rolled toward me like an ocean wave as I bent forward and inhaled the rich chocolate perfume. I reached for my oven mitts on the counter.

"I'll do it," Alison offered immediately, sliding her hands inside the waiting pink mitts, then gingerly transferring the cake to a nearby trivet. "This looks as good as it smells. Should I make some coffee?"

"Coffee sounds wonderful."

"You sit. Keep that hand still. Raise it above your heart." She rolled her eyes. "Listen to me—you're the nurse, and I'm telling you what to do." She shook her head, laughed with what I recognized was relief—relief that I seemed to have a reasonable explanation for everything, relief that I seemed no longer angry with her, relief that things seemed back to normal.

Seemed, I thought, sitting back in my chair. Good word.

I smiled as I watched Alison prepare the coffee. It was amazing how comfortable she was in my kitchen, among my things. She knew without asking that I kept the coffee in the freezer and the sugar in the cupboard to the left of the sink. "There's whipped cream in the fridge," I told her as she measured out the coffee and poured the water into the back of the coffeemaker.

"You're amazing," she said. "You're always prepared for everything."

"Sometimes it pays to be prepared."

"I wish I was more like that." Alison leaned against the counter. "I've always acted more on impulse."

"That can be pretty dangerous."

"Tell me about it." There was a moment's silence. Alison glanced at the floor, then at the empty shelves, an impish grin spreading across her face. "Smashing all those heads was a pretty impulsive thing to do."

I laughed. "I guess it was."

"Maybe we're more alike than you think."

"Maybe." Our eyes locked, and for a moment, neither of us moved, as if we were daring each other to be the first to look away. Of course I was the one to blink first. "What say we have some of that cake?"

"You stay right where you are. Keep that hand up. I'll do everything." Alison removed two small plates from the cupboard, along with two sets of cups and saucers, and set them on the table beside several paper napkins, the sugar, and the bowl of whipped cream. Then she returned to the counter and reached for a knife. "Remember the first day I was here, and I grabbed the wrong knife," she said, pulling the giant butcher knife from its wooden block as my breath froze in my throat, "and you said, 'Whoa! Overkill, don't you think?' Whoa!" she repeated now, staring with openmouthed wonder at the blood-encrusted blade. "What's this? Is this blood?" Her focus shifted to the shaft of the knife. "And it looks like there's blood on the handle too." She stared at her palm.

"More like blood on the brain," I said, rising quickly from my chair and removing the knife from her hands, then dropping it into the sink and running hot water over it. "It's not blood," I told her.

"What is it?"

"Just a stubborn case of strawberry jam."

"Jam? On the handle?"

"Are you going to cut me a piece of cake, or what?" I asked impatiently.

Alison grabbed another knife and proceeded to slice into the warm cake. "Oh, no, it's starting to crumble. You're sure it's not too soon to do this?"

"The timing is perfect," I said as she slid a large piece of cake onto a plate. "Give me one half that size."

"You're sure?"

"I can always come back for more."

"Don't count on it." Alison returned to her seat and eagerly stuffed a heaping forkful of cake into her mouth.

I watched the crumbs form a dark outline around her lips. Like a clown's mouth, I thought, as she licked the errant crumbs into her mouth with the flick of her tongue. A snake's tongue, I thought, watching her swallow.

"This is absolutely the best cake you have ever made. The best." She swallowed another forkful. "Will you teach me how to bake one day?"

"It's really very easy."

"Don't worry. I'll find a way to make it difficult." Alison laughed self-consciously, quickly finishing what was left on her plate. "This is so yummy delicious. Why aren't you eating?"

"Thought I'd wait for the coffee."

Alison glanced at the coffeemaker. "Looks like it'll be a few more minutes. 'A watched kettle never boils,'" she reminded me, looking away. "You told me that."

"Do you remember everything I say?"

"I try to."

"Why?" I asked, genuinely curious.

"Because I think you're smart. Because I admire you." Alison hesitated, as if there was more she wanted to say, then obviously thought better of it. "Can I have another piece? I can't wait for the coffee."

"Be my guest. Try it with some whipped cream."

Alison cut herself another, even larger slice of cake, then spooned a large dollop of the whipped cream on top of it. "This is heaven," she enthused, filling her mouth. "Absolute heaven. You have to taste this." She extended her fork toward me.

I shook my head, pointed toward the coffee.

"You have such willpower."

"It won't be long now." I watched as she wolfed down the second piece of cake. A human Garburetor, I thought, with something approaching awe. "Ready for thirds?"

"Are you kidding? One more piece and it won't be just the china heads exploding around here." She hesitated. "Although maybe I have room for one more very tiny piece. With my coffee." She laughed. She lowered her gaze to her lap, closed her eyes. "I'll miss this," she whispered, her body swaying.

I leaned forward, wondering if she was about to fall, thinking that even a strong sedative like Percodan needs more than a few minutes to work its magic.

Instead of falling over, Alison bolted upright in her chair, her eyes popping open, as if she'd just awakened from a bad dream. "Please don't make me leave."

"What?"

"I know you said you've already rented out the cottage to someone at work, but I'm really praying you'll change your mind and give me another chance. I promise I won't mess up this time. I'll do everything you say. I'll follow all your rules. I won't screw up again. Honest."

She sounded so sincere that I almost found myself believing her. In spite of everything, I realized I *wanted* to believe her. "What about Lance?"

"Lance? That's over. Lance is gone."

"How do I know he won't come back?"

"Because I give you my solemn vow."

"You lied to me before."

"I know. And I'm so sorry. It was stupid. *I* was stupid. Stupid to think Lance would ever change, that things would be any different this time."

"What about the next time?"

"There won't be a next time. Lance knows he went too far, that he crossed the line when he came on to you."

"Why am I any different than anyone else?"

She paused, looked up, then down, as if searching for just the right words. "Because he knew how important you are to me."

"And what makes me so important?"

Another pause. "You just are." Alison jumped to her feet, then grabbed for the table.

"Alison? Are you all right?"

"Yeah. I just got a little dizzy there for a minute. I guess I must have moved too fast."

"Are you still dizzy?"

She shook her head slowly, as if she wasn't sure. "I think I'm okay now. Kind of scary though."

"Have some coffee. Coffee's a good antidote to dizziness."

"It is?"

"I'm the nurse, remember?"

She smiled. "Two cups of coffee coming right up." She poured the freshly brewed coffee into each cup, then added three heaping spoonfuls of sugar and a large dollop of whipped cream to hers.

"Cheers." I clicked my cup against hers.

"To us."

"To us," I agreed, watching as she took a long sip.

She made a face, lowered the cup to its saucer. "Kind of bitter."

I took a sip from my own cup. "Tastes fine to me."

"I think I made it too strong."

"Maybe you need more sugar," I teased.

Alison added a fourth spoonful, took another sip. "No. Still not quite right." She brought her hand to her head.

"Alison, are you okay?"

"I don't know. I feel a little strange."

"Drink some more coffee. It'll help."

Alison did as she was told, throwing back the coffee as if it were a glass of tequila, then taking a long, deep breath. "Is it warm in here?"

"Not really."

"Oh, God. I hope I'm not getting a migraine."

"Is this how they usually start?"

"No. Usually I get this kind of tunnel-vision thing going, and then this horrible headache takes over."

"I have some more of those pills." I got up from my chair and pretended to fish around in a drawer. "Why don't you take a couple? Strike a preemptive blow." I handed her two little white pills, returned the bottle of Percodan to the drawer.

She took the pills without even bothering to examine them. "So, what do you think?" she asked, pushing her hair away from her forehead.

I noticed she was beginning to perspire. "I think you'll start to feel better soon."

"No. I mean about me staying."

"You can stay as long as you like."

Tears immediately appeared in the corners of each eye. "Really? You mean that?"

"Absolutely."

"You're not kicking me out?"

"How could I? This is your home."

Alison brought her hands to her mouth, muffled a gasp of pure joy. "Oh, thank you. Thank you so much. You won't be sorry. I promise you."

"But no more lies."

"I promise I'll never lie to you again."

"Good. Because lies destroy trust, and without trust . . ."

"You're right. Of course you're right." She ran her hand through her hair, rolled her neck from side to side, wet her lips with her tongue.

"Are you all right, Alison? Would you like to lie down?"

"No. I'll be okay."

"What was K.C. doing here before?" I asked, slipping the question in casually as her eyes struggled to stay focused.

"What?"

"No more lies, Alison. You promised."

"No more lies," she whispered.

"What was K.C. doing here?"

She shook her head, then raised her hands to her temples, as if to steady her head, prevent it from rolling off altogether. "His name isn't K.C."

"It isn't?"

"No. It's Charlie. Charlie something-or-other. I don't remember. He was Erica Hollander's fiancé."

"Erica's fiancé? What was he doing here?"

"I don't know." Alison's eyes struggled to find my face. "He was talking crazy."

"What did he say?"

"Nothing that made any sense." She laughed, but the weak sound wobbled, then died in her throat. "He says that she didn't run off, that she never went anywhere. He has this ridiculous idea that you know where she is."

"Maybe it's not such a ridiculous idea."

"What? What are you saying?"

"Maybe I *do* know where she is."

"Do you?" Alison tried to stand up, stumbled, collapsed back in the chair.

"I really think you'd be much more comfortable lying down. Why don't we go into the living room?" I helped Alison to her feet, lifting one long, slender arm over my shoulder, and guiding her from the kitchen, her feet shuffling along the floor, like whispers from a crowd.

"What happened to the Christmas tree?" she asked as we entered the living room.

"It had a little accident." I directed her to the sofa and sat down beside her, lifting her feet into my lap.

"Are you going to give me a pedicure?" she asked with a smile that refused to settle.

"Maybe later."

"I feel so strange. Maybe it's the pills."

"And the cake," I said, removing her sandals, massaging her bare feet the way I knew she liked. "And the coffee."

She regarded me quizzically.

"I believe you had four spoonfuls of sugar this time. Not a good idea, Alison. They say sugar's poison for your system."

"I don't understand." For the first time, a look of fear flashed through Alison's beautiful green eyes. "What are you talking about?"

"You thought you had me, didn't you, Alison? You thought all you had to do was smile and pay me a few stupid compliments, and I'd fall under your magic spell all over again. Except it didn't work. This time I'm the one with all the magic: Terry's magic chocolate cake; Terry's magic sugar; Terry's magic pills."

"What are you talking about? What have you done to me?"

"Who are you?" I demanded.

"What!"

"Who are you?"

"You know who I am. I'm Alison."

"Alison Simms?" I didn't give her a chance to answer. "I doubt that. There is no Alison Simms." I watched her flinch, as if I'd raised my hand to strike her. "Just like there's no K.C."

"But I didn't know about K.C. I didn't know—"

"Just like there's no Rita Bishop."

She rubbed her mouth, her neck, her hair. "Who?"

"Your friend from Chicago. The one you were looking

for at Mission Care when you just happened to stumble across my notice."

"Oh, God."

"Let's play our little game. Three words to describe Alison."

"Terry, please. You don't understand."

"Let's see. Oh, I know: liar, liar, liar."

"But I haven't lied. Please, I haven't lied."

"You've done nothing *but* lie since the moment I met you. I read your journal, Alison."

"You read my journal? But then you know—"

"I know your coming here was no accident. I know you and Lance have been plotting for months to get rid of me."

"Get rid of you? No!" Alison swung her legs off my lap, tried to get up, only half-succeeded before her knees gave out and she teetered to the floor. "Oh, God. What's happening to me?"

"Who are you, Alison? Who are you *really*?"

"Please help me."

"The Lord helps those who help themselves," I said coldly, in my mother's voice.

"It's all a huge misunderstanding. Please. Take me to the hospital. I promise I'll tell you everything as soon as I feel better."

"Tell me now." I pushed her back on the sofa, watching her disappear into the deep, down-filled cushions, their pretty pink and mauve flowers threatening to swallow her whole. I settled into the striped Queen Anne chair directly across from her and waited. "The truth," I warned her. "Don't leave anything out."

TWENTY-EIGHT

"Can I have a glass of water?" Alison asked.

"Later. After you tell me."

Tears fell the length of Alison's face. Her color was ashen, a once vibrant photograph fading before my eyes. "I don't know where to start."

"Start with who you really are. Start with your name."

"It's Alison."

"Not Simms," I said matter-of-factly.

"Not Simms," she repeated dully. "Sinukoff." A sudden spark of interest. "Does that name mean anything to you?"

"Should it?"

She shrugged. "I wasn't sure if it would or not."

"It doesn't."

"I didn't know if it would. I had to be sure."

"Sure of what?"

"I didn't want to make another mistake."

"What are you talking about? What kind of mistake?"

Alison's head rolled back across her shoulders, swayed precariously, as if it might fall off. "I'm so tired."

"Why did you come to Florida, Alison?" I demanded. "What were you after?"

"I came to find you."

"I know that. What I don't know is why. I'm not rich. I'm not famous. I have nothing that could possibly interest you."

She steadied her head, concentrated all her attention on my face. "You have everything," she said simply.

"I'm afraid you'll have to explain that one."

Her eyes fluttered to a close, and for a moment I thought she might have succumbed to all the sedatives in her system, but then she started to speak, slowly at first, and with obvious effort, as if trying to keep track of her words, as one thought merged with another, and one word slurred into the next. "I'd been looking for you for a while without any luck. I decided to hire a private detective. The first one didn't work out, so I hired someone else. He said you were working in a hospital in Delray. So I went there to see for myself. That's when I saw your notice at the nurses' station. I couldn't believe my luck. I made up the story about Rita Bishop. I thought it would give us a chance to get to know one another before . . ."

"Before what?"

"Before I told you."

"Told me what, for God's sake?"

"Don't you know?"

"Know what?"

"I don't understand. You said you read my journal."

"Know what?" I repeated, my voice a low roar, like the sound of an approaching wave.

Her eyes locked on mine, snapped into focus, as if seeing me for the first time. "That you're my mother."

For an instant I didn't know whether to laugh or cry, so I did both, the strangled sound emerging from my mouth foreign even to my own ears. I jumped to my feet, began pacing back and forth in front of her. "What are you talking about? That's impossible. What are you talking about?"

"I'm your daughter," she said, fresh tears forming in her eyes.

"You're crazy! Your mother lives in Chicago."

"I'm not from Chicago. I'm from Baltimore, like you."

"You're lying!"

"I was adopted as an infant by John and Carole Sinukoff. Did you know them?"

I shook my head vigorously, distant images flashing through my mind like a strobe light. I shielded my eyes, struggled to keep unwanted memories at bay.

"They already had a son, but they couldn't have any more children, and they wanted a daughter, so they picked me. A mistake," she acknowledged, licking at her lips. "I was this awful kid. Pretty much like I told you. I never felt I belonged. I was so different from everyone else. And it didn't help that my perfect older brother kept reminding me I wasn't really part of the family. One Christmas when he came home from Brown, he told me that my real mother was a fourteen-year-old slut who couldn't keep her legs together."

"Oh, God."

"I kicked him where it counts. He certainly didn't have any trouble keeping *his* legs together after that." She attempted a laugh, wheezed instead.

"But what you're saying is impossible," I told her, my head spinning as much as hers. Images of the past snuck through decades-old defenses to assault my brain: Roger Stillman clumsily pushing his way inside me in the backseat of his car; my frantic eyes checking my underwear every day after that for signs of a period that stubbornly refused to come; my child's belly growing more distended every day, no matter how baggy the clothes I wore. "It's impossible," I repeated, more forcefully this time, trying in vain to frighten the images away. "Do the math. I'm forty. You're twenty-eight. That would have made me twelve—"

"I'm not twenty-eight. I'm twenty-five. I'll be twenty-six . . ."

On February 9, I mouthed silently as she spoke the words out loud. I covered my ears with my hands in an effort to block out her voice. When had it gotten so loud, so strong?

"I was afraid if I told you my real age, you might figure everything out before you had the chance to get to know me. And I didn't know how you'd feel about having me back in your life. I wanted so much for you to like me. No, that's a lie," she said, correcting herself. "I wanted more than that. I wanted you to *love* me. So you wouldn't be able to give me up again."

I sank back into the Queen Anne chair. She was crazy, of course. Even if some of what she said was true, it was impossible for her to be my daughter. She was so tall, so beautiful. Just like Roger Stillman, I thought. "It's not true," I insisted. "I'm sorry. You've made a mistake."

"No. Not this time. The first detective I hired found some woman in Hagerstown he thought was you. I got so excited, I went to see her, but it turned out he was wrong. Then I found you. Lance said I was crazy to come all the way down here, that I was only going to get hurt again, but I had to see you. And the minute I did, the minute I talked to you, I knew I was right. Even before you told me about Roger Stillman, I knew you were my mother."

"Well, I'm sorry, but you're wrong."

"I'm not wrong. You know I'm not."

"The only thing I know is that you're a stupid, stupid girl!" I heard myself shout.

My mother's voice bounced off the walls.

You're a stupid, stupid girl!

"No, please don't say that."

How could you do this? How could you let some ridiculous boy stick his awful thing inside you?

I'll take care of the baby, Mommy. I promise I'll take good care of it.

Don't think for one minute that I'm going to allow a bastard child into this house. I'll drown it in a basin, just like I drowned those damn kittens!

"'Terry," Alison was whispering. "Terry, I'm not feeling very well."

I moved swiftly to her side, wrapped her in my arms. "It's all right, Alison. Don't worry. You won't throw up. I know how much you hate throwing up."

"Please take me to the hospital."

"Later, sweetheart. After you've had a little nap."

"I don't want to fall asleep."

"Ssh. Don't fight it, darling. It'll all be over soon."

"No! Oh, God, no! Please. You have to help me."

We heard the noise at the same moment, our heads twisting in unison toward the kitchen door. Pounding, yelling, ringing. "Alison!" a voice bellowed over the cacophony of sounds. "Alison, are you in there?"

"K.C.!" Alison exclaimed, her voice scarcely audible. "I'm here. Oh, God, help me! I'm in here."

"Terry!" K.C. hollered. "Terry, open this door right now or I'm calling the police."

"Just a minute," I called back calmly, gently extricating myself from Alison's side, hearing her groan as she toppled over, too drugged to move. I walked quickly to the back door. "I'm coming. Hold your horses."

"Where is she?" K.C. pushed roughly past me into the house. "What have you done with her?"

"Who are we talking about?" I asked him pleasantly. "Erica? Or Alison?"

But K.C. was already in the living room. "Alison! My God! What has that lunatic done to you?"

I reached into the sink and carefully removed the butcher knife from the white enamel basin. It fit comfortably into the center of my hand, as if it belonged there. I squeezed it, felt it damp against my tender skin as the cut reopened in my palm. Then I returned to the living room, watching from behind the dying branches of the Christmas tree as K.C. struggled to lift Alison to her feet.

"Can you walk?"

"I don't think so."

"Put your arms around my neck. I'll carry you."

How can I describe what happened next?

It was as if I'd been handed the starring role in a play. No, not a play. More like a ballet, full of grand gestures and exaggerated mime, each move carefully planned and choreographed. As Alison raised her arms, so did I. As K.C. was bending to scoop her up, I was swooping down. As he took the first of several awkward steps, I was flying across the room with savage grace. As Alison was resting her head against K.C.'s shoulder, I was plunging the foot-long blade into his back with such force the handle snapped off in my hands.

K.C. staggered forward, Alison dropping from his arms and landing with a dull thud on the floor. K.C. spun around in a sloppy pirouette, his hands losing their graceful rhythm and flailing about for the blade that was buried deep in his back. The growing swell of Alison's screams filled the air, like a third-rate orchestra, as K.C. balanced on his toes, his arms extended toward me, as if asking me to join him for one final twirl around the room. I declined his silent invitation, taking a step back as he fell forward, his disbelieving eyes glazing over with the approach of imminent death. He hit the floor, the top of his head just missing the base of the overturned tree.

It took a few seconds for me to realize that Alison had stopped screaming, that she was no longer sprawled carelessly across the floor, that she had somehow managed to gather whatever strength she still possessed and was making a desperate scramble for the front door. That she actually succeeded in getting it open and was halfway down the front steps before I caught up to her is a great tribute to her strength and determination.

The instinct for survival, the will to live, is an amazing thing.

I remembered having had similar thoughts about Myra Wylie. Only Erica Hollander had gone quietly, dozing off within minutes of finishing the late-night snack I'd prepared. The pillow I'd subsequently held over her nose and mouth had brought only token resistance.

"No!" Alison was screaming as I reached for her arm.

"Alison, please. Don't make a scene."

"No! Don't touch me! Leave me alone!"

"Come back inside, Alison." I grabbed her elbow, dug my fingers into her flesh.

"No!" she screamed again, wresting her arm away from me with such force I almost lost my balance. She made it halfway to the street before her legs simply gave out, and she collapsed like the proverbial rag doll. Even then, she refused to give up, crawling on her hands and knees toward the sidewalk.

It was then we heard the barking, followed immediately by the click of high heels on pavement. Bettye McCoy and her two lunatic dogs, I realized, trying to drag Alison to her feet.

"Help me!" Alison cried as the third Mrs. McCoy wiggled around the corner in a pair of leopard-print capri pants. "Help me!"

But Alison's cries were drowned out by the angry yapping of the dogs.

"It's okay," I called to the aging Alice in Wonderland. "She's just had a bit too much to drink."

Bettye McCoy tossed her overly teased blond mane disdainfully over her shoulder and gathered the two dogs into her arms before crossing the street and walking briskly in the opposite direction.

"No, please!" Alison called after her. "You have to help me! Help me!"

"You really need to sleep this off," I said loudly, in case anyone was listening.

"Please," Alison begged the now empty street. "Please, don't go."

"I'm right here, baby," I told her, gathering her into my arms, guiding her toward the house. "I'm not going anywhere."

When we reached the door, she stopped fighting. Whether it was the drugs or the realization that such struggles were useless, I don't know. She simply sighed and went limp in my arms. I carried her across the threshold, as a new husband lovingly transports his bride.

Do they even do that anymore? I don't know. I doubt I'll ever have the opportunity to find out. It's too late for me, just as it was too late for Alison. And it's too bad, because I think I would have made a fine wife. That's all I ever really wanted. To love someone, to be loved in return, to make a home, have a family. A child on whom I could lavish all the tenderness I'd been denied. A daughter.

I've always wanted a daughter.

I carried Alison to the sofa, cradled her in my arms. *"Too-ra-loo-ra-loo-ra,"* I sang tenderly. *"Too-ra-loo-ra-lie . . ."*

Alison raised her eyes slowly to mine. Her mouth opened. Whispers filled the air. I think I heard the word *Mommy.*

TWENTY-NINE

Of course, I don't believe for a minute that Alison was my child.

She probably heard about how I'd disgraced my family from the Sinukoffs. The name sounds vaguely familiar. Perhaps they were neighbors. Perhaps not. Baltimore's a big city. You can't know everyone, despite my mother's assertion that the whole town knew about my condition, that she was a laughingstock, too ashamed ever to show her face in public again.

That's why we moved to Florida. Not because my father's job demanded it. Because of me.

I stayed in school until my condition became too obvious to ignore, then I was asked to leave. Nothing happened to Roger Stillman. My shame was his badge of honor, and he was allowed to remain in school and graduate with his classmates.

I endured almost twenty hours of labor before my mother let my father drive me to the hospital. It was another ten hours before the baby—weighing in at an impressive eight pounds, seven ounces—was born. I never got the chance to hold her. Never even got the chance to see her. My mother made sure of that.

Of course she was right. What else could she have done? I was only fourteen years old, after all, a baby myself. What did I know of life, of looking after another human being? It was a ridiculous notion, one I'm sure I would have lived to regret.

And yet, maybe not. Would I have been such a bad mother? I've often wondered. I'd secretly loved that little baby growing inside me from the first minute I felt her moving around. I talked to her when no one was home, sang to her when we were alone in my room, assuring her that I would never lose my temper with her, never hit her or disparage her in any way, that I would shower her with kisses, assure her each and every day how very much she was loved. "I'll take care of you," I promised her when no one was listening. Instead, she was pulled from my body and banished from my side before her sweet little face had time to register, and I spent my whole life taking care of other people instead.

Of course Alison wasn't my child.

She'd undoubtedly heard about "the fourteen-year-old slut who couldn't keep her legs together" from someone back in Baltimore, possibly even her older brother, as she'd claimed. Then she and her friends had concocted this elaborate scenario, determined to insinuate themselves into my life. *I wanted you to like me. No. I wanted you to* love *me,* Alison herself had admitted shortly before she died.

I miss her terribly, of course, think of her often, and

always with great affection, even love. So maybe Alison got what she came for after all.

She didn't suffer. She simply fell asleep in my arms. The rest was easy. There were so many drugs in her system, I doubt she was even aware of the pillow I held against her face for the better part of two minutes. Later, I dressed her in her pretty blue sundress—the one she had been wearing the first day we met—and then buried her in the garden beside Erica. The flowers are especially lush in that corner of the yard, and I think she would have approved.

K.C. was a different story. I'd never killed a man before, never used a knife, never had to resort to such brutality. It took days for the vibrations to stop echoing through my hand, weeks till I was finally able to scrub all the blood from my living room floor. Of course, I had to get rid of the rug. It was ruined. Alison was right—a white rug in the living room hadn't proved very practical. At any rate, it was time for a change.

I didn't want K.C. polluting my garden, so I waited until the middle of the night, then bundled him into the trunk of my car and drove all the way to the Everglades, where I tossed him into a slime-covered swamp. It seemed fitting, and I'm sure the alligators appreciated my efforts.

It's been three months since Alison died. The season is almost over. Every day there are fewer cars on the roads, fewer tourists prowling the streets. It's easier to get into restaurants now. There are shorter lines at the movies. Bettye McCoy still walks her two lunatic dogs down the street several times a day, and occasionally one breaks away from her, makes a beeline for my backyard. I've erected a small fence to keep them out. Hopefully, that will suffice. Should one of those mangy mutts manage to get into my yard again, I won't be chasing it out with anything as gentle as a broom.

Occasionally, I wonder what would happen if Lance and Denise came back, looking for Alison. But so far, there's been no sign of either of them, so maybe Alison was telling the truth about their taking off together, about her relationship with her ex-husband being over once and for all. I hope so. Still, I can't let down my guard.

My job at the hospital continues much as it always has. Myra's bed has been filled by an elderly gentleman with advanced Parkinson's. I take very good care of him. His family think I'm the greatest thing since sliced bread.

Incidentally, I was right about Josh. He did send flowers to the staff several weeks after his mother's funeral. Actually, the flowers were from both him *and* his wife. The note thanked everyone on the ward. No one was singled out for special mention.

The journal he gave me has proved useful, however. It's nice to have somewhere to record my thoughts, as I'm doing now. A place to set the record straight.

And who knows? Maybe one day I'll find true love. Just because Josh proved both weak and unworthy doesn't mean there isn't someone out there who's right for me. It's not too late. I'm only forty. I'm still reasonably attractive. I could meet someone tomorrow, get married, have the family I've always craved. Many women over forty are having babies. It could happen. I'm praying it does.

And that's about it. Life goes on, as they say.

Who are they *anyway?* I can hear Alison ask, her voice never very far from my ear.

I turn around, look the other way. She's right beside me.

Describe your life since I went away, she whispers playfully. *Three words.*

"Uneventful," I reply obediently. "Unexciting." I survey the empty shelves that line the kitchen walls, thinking that perhaps the time has come to start rebuilding my collection. "Lonely," I admit, choking back tears.

I stare out my back window at the small, empty cottage behind my house. It has been unoccupied for three months now and is starting to look a little neglected. It needs someone as much as I do. Someone who will love it and take care of it, who will show it the love and respect it deserves. After the debacles with Erica and Alison, I'm not sure such a person even exists. But maybe it's time to find out. Maybe it's time to bury the whispers and lies of the past, time to start afresh.

"Afresh," I repeat out loud in Alison's voice, deciding to place an ad in the weekend paper. "Good word."